The Life of Marie Antoinette, Queen of France

Charles Duke Yonge

Contents

THE LIFE OF MARIE ANTOINETTE, QUEEN OF FRANCE

BY

Charles Duke Yonge

PREFACE.

The principal authorities for the following work are the four volumes of Correspondence published by M. Arneth, and the six volumes published by M. Feuillet de Conches. M. Arneth's two collections[1] contain not only a number of letters which passed between the queen, her mother the Empress- queen (Maria Teresa), and her brothers Joseph and Leopold, who successively became emperors after the death of their father; but also a regular series of letters from the imperial embassador at Paris, the Count Mercy d'Argenteau, which may almost be said to form a complete history of the court of France, especially in all the transactions in which Marie Antoinette, whether as dauphiness or queen, was concerned, till the death of Maria Teresa, at Christmas, 1780. The correspondence with her two brothers, the emperors Joseph and Leopold, only ceases with the death of the latter in March, 1792.

The collection published by M. Feuillet de Conches[2] has been vehemently attacked, as containing a series of clever forgeries rather than of genuine letters. And there does seem reason to believe that in a few instances, chiefly in the earlier portion of the correspondence, the critical acuteness of the editor was imposed upon, and that some of the letters inserted were not written by the persons alleged to be the authors. But of the majority of the letters there seems no solid ground for questioning the authenticity. Indeed, in the later and more important portion of the correspondence, that which belongs to the period after the death of the Empress-queen, the genuineness of the Queen's letters is continually supported by the collection of M. Arneth, who has himself published many of them, having found them in the archives at Vienna, where M.F. de Conches had previously copied them,[3] and who refers to others, the publication of which did not come within his own plan. M. Feuillet de Conches' work also contains narratives of some of the most important transactions after the commencement of the Revolution, which are of great value, as having been compiled from authentic sources.

Besides these collections, the author has consulted the lives of Marie Antoinette by Montjoye, Lafont d'Aussonne, Chambrier, and the MM. Goncourt; "La Vraie Marie Antoinette" of M. Lescure; the Memoirs of Mme. Campan, Clery, Hue, the Duchesse d'Angouleme, Bertrand de Moleville ("Memoires Particuliers"), the Comte de Tilly, the Baron de Besenval, the Marquis de la Fayette, the Marquise de Crequy, the Princess Lamballe; the "Souvenirs de Quarante Ans," by Mlle. de Tourzel; the "Diary" of M. de Viel Castel; the correspondence of Mme. du Deffand; the account of the affair of the necklace by M. de Campardon; the very valuable correspondence between the Count de la Marck and Mirabeau, which also contains a narrative by the Count de la Marck of many very important incidents; Dumont's "Souvenirs sur Mirabeau;" "Beaumarchais et son Temps," by M. de Lomenie; "Gustavus III. et la Cour de Paris," by M. Geoffroy; the first seven volumes of the Histoire de la Terreur, by M. Mortimer Ternaux; Dr. Moore's journal of his visit to France, and view of the French Revolution; and a great number of other works in which there is cursory mention of different incidents, especially in the earlier part of the Revolution; such as the journals of Arthur Young, Madame de Stael's elaborate treatise on the Revolution; several articles in the last series of the "Causeries de Lundi," by Sainte-Beuve, and others in the **Revue des Deux Mondes**, etc., etc., and to those may of course be added the regular histories of Lacretelle, Sismondi, Martin, and Lamartine's "History of the Girondins."

LIFE OF MARIE ANTOINETTE.
CHAPTER I.

Importance of Marie Antoinette in the Revolution.--Value of her Correspondence as a Means of estimating her Character.--Her Birth, November 2d, 1755.--Epigram of Metastasio.--Habits of the Imperial Family.--Schoenbrunn.--Death of the Emperor.--Projects for the Marriage of the Archduchess.--Her Education.--The Abbe de Vermond.--Metastasio.--Gluck.

The most striking event in the annals of modern Europe is unquestionably the French Revolution of 1789--a Revolution which, in one sense, may be said to be still in progress, but which, is a more limited view, may be regarded as having been, consummated by the deposition and murder of the sovereign of the country. It is equally undeniable that, during its first period, the person who most attracts and rivets attention is the queen. One of the moat brilliant of modern French writers[1] has recently remarked that, in spite of the number of years which have elapsed since the grave closed over the sorrows of Marie Antoinette, and of the almost unbroken series of exciting events which have marked the annals of France in the interval, the interest excited by her story is as fresh and engrossing as ever; that such as Hecuba and Andromache were to the ancients, objects never named to inattentive ears, never contemplated without lively sympathy, such still is their hapless queen to all honest and intelligent Frenchmen. It may even be said that that interest has increased of late years. The respectful and remorseful pity which her fate could not fail to awaken has been quickened by the publication of her correspondence with her family and intimate friends, which has laid bare, without disguise, all her inmost thoughts and feelings, her errors as well as her good deeds, her weaknesses equally with her virtues. Few, indeed, even of those whom the world regards with its highest favor and esteem, could endure such an ordeal without some diminution of their fame. Yet it is but recording the general verdict of all whose judgment is of value, to affirm that Marie Antoinette has triumphantly surmounted it; and that the result of a scrutiny as minute and severe as any to which a human being has ever been subjected, has been greatly to raise her reputation.

Not that she was one of those paragons whom painters of model heroines have delighted to imagine to themselves; one who from childhood gave manifest indications of excellence and greatness, and whose whole life was but a steady progressive development of its early promise. She was rather one in whom adversity brought forth great qualities, her possession of which, had her life been one of that unbroken sunshine which is regarded by many as the natural and inseparable attendant of royalty, might never have been even suspected. We meet with her first, at an age scarcely advanced beyond childhood, transported from her school-room to a foreign court, as wife to the heir of one of the noblest kingdoms of Europe. And in that situation we see her for a while a light-hearted, merry girl, annoyed rather than elated by her new magnificence; thoughtless, if not frivolous, in her pursuits; fond of dress; eager in her appetite for amusement, tempered only by an innate purity of feeling which never deserted her; the brightest features of her character being apparently a frank affability, and a genuine and active kindness and humanity which were displayed to all classes and on all occasions. We see her presently as queen, hardly yet arrived at womanhood, little changed in disposition or in outward demeanor, though profiting to the utmost by the opportunities which her increased power afforded her of proving the genuine tenderness of her heart, by munificent and judicious works of charity and benevolence; and exerting her authority, if possible, still more beneficially by protecting virtue, discountenancing vice, and purifying a court whose shameless profligacy had for many generations been the scandal of Christendom. It is probable, indeed, that much of her early levity was prompted by a desire to drive from her mind disappointments and mortifications of which few suspected the existence, but which were only the more keenly felt because she was compelled to keep them to herself; but it is certain that during the first eight or ten years of her residence in France there was little in her habits and conduct, however amiable and attractive, which could have led her warmest friends to discern in her the high qualities which she was destined to exhibit before its close.

Presently, however, she becomes a mother; and in this new relation we begin to perceive glimpses of a loftier nature. From the moment of the birth of her first child, she performed those new duties which, perhaps more than any others, call forth all the best and most peculiar virtues of the female heart in such a manner as to add esteem and respect to the good-will which her affability and courtesy had already inspired; recognizing to the full the claims which the nation had upon her, that she should, in person, superintend the education of her children, and especially of her son as its future ruler; and discharging that sacred duty, not only with the most affectionate solicitude, but also with the most admirable judgment.

But years so spent were years of happiness; and, though such may suffice to display the amiable virtues, it is by adversity that the grander qualities of the head and heart are more strikingly drawn forth. To the trials of that stern inquisitress, Marie Antoinette was fully exposed in her later years; and not only did she rise above them, but the more terrible and unexampled they were, the more conspicuous was the superiority of her mind to fortune. It is no exaggeration to say that the history of the whole world has preserved no record of greater heroism, in either sex, than was shown by Marie Antoinette during the closing years of her life. No courage was ever put to the proof by such a variety and such an accumulation of dangers and miseries; and no one ever came out of an encounter with even far inferior calamities with greater glory. Her moral courage and her physical courage were equally tried. It was not only that her own life, and lives far dearer to her than her own, were exposed to daily and hourly peril, or that to this danger were added repeated vexations of hopes baffled and trusts betrayed; but these griefs were largely aggravated by the character and conduct of those nearest to her. Instead of meeting with counsel and support from her husband and his brothers, she had to guide and support Louis himself, and even to find him so incurably weak as to be incapable of being kept in the path of wisdom by her sagacity, or of deriving vigor from her fortitude; while the princes were acting in selfish and disloyal opposition to him, and so, in a great degree, sacrificing him and her to their perverse conceit, if we may not say to their faithless ambition. She had to think for all, to act for all, to struggle for all; and to beat up against the conviction that her thoughts, and actions, and struggles were being balked of their effect by the very persona for whom she was exerting herself; that she was but laboring to save those who would not be saved. Yet, throughout that protracted agony of more than four years she bore herself with an unswerving righteousness of purpose and an unfaltering fearlessness of resolution which could not have been exceeded had she been encouraged by the most constant success. And in the last terrible hours, when the monsters who had already murdered her husband were preparing the same fate for herself, she met their hatred and ferocity with a loftiness of spirit which even hopelessness could not subdue. Long before, she had declared that she had learned, from the example of her mother, not to fear death; and she showed that this was no empty boast when she rose in the last scenes of her life as much even above her earlier displays of courage and magnanimity as she also rose above the utmost malice of her vile enemies.

*   *   *   *   *

Marie Antoinette Josephe Jeanne was the youngest daughter of Francis, originally Duke of Lorraine, afterward Grand Duke of Tuscany, and eventually Emperor of Germany, and of Maria Teresa, Archduchess of Austria, Queen of Hungary and Bohemia, more generally known, after the attainment of the imperial dignity by her husband in 1745, as the Empress- queen. Of her brothers, two, Joseph and Leopold, succeeded in turn to the imperial dignity; and one of her sisters, Caroline, became the wife of the King of Naples. She was born on the 2d of November, 1755, a day which, when her later years were darkened by misfortune, was often referred to as having foreshadowed it by its evil omens, since it was that on which the terrible earthquake which laid Lisbon in ruins reached its height. But, at the time, the Viennese rejoiced too sincerely at every event which could contribute to their sovereign's happiness to pay any regard to the calamities of another capital, and the courtly poet was but giving utterance to the unanimous feeling of her subjects when he spoke of the princess's birth as calculated to diffuse universal joy. Daughters had been by far the larger part of Maria Teresa's family, so that she was, consequently, anxious for another son; and, knowing her wishes, the Duke of Tarouka, one of the nobles whom she admitted to her intimacy, laid her a small wager that they would be realized by the sex of the expected infant. He lost his bet, but felt some embarrassment, in devising a graceful mode of paying it. In his perplexity, he sought the advice of the celebrated Metastasio, who had been for some time established at Vienna as the favorite poet of the court, and the Italian, with the ready wit of his country, at once supplied him with a quatrain, which, in her disappointment itself, could mid ground for compliment:

"Io perdei; l' augusta figlia   A pagar m' ha condannato;   Ma s'e ver che a voi somiglia,   Tutto il mondo ha guadagnato."

The customs of the imperial court had undergone a great change since the death of Charles VI. It had been pre-eminent for pompous ceremony, which was thought to become the dignity of the sovereign who boasted of being the representative of the Roman Caesars. But the Lorraine princes had been bred up in a simpler fashion; and Francis had an innate dislike to all ostentation, while Maria Teresa had her attention too constantly fixed on matters of solid importance to have much leisure to spare for the consideration of trifles. Both husband and wife greatly preferred to their gorgeous palace at Vienna a smaller house which they possessed in the neighborhood, called Schoenbrunn, where they could lay aside their state, and enjoy the unpretending pleasures of domestic and rural life, cultivating their garden, and, as far as the imperious calls of public affairs would allow them time, watching over the education of their children, to whom the example of their own tastes and habits was imperceptibly affording the best of all lessons, a preference for simple and innocent pleasures.

In this tranquil retreat, the childhood of Marie Antoinette was happily passed; her bright looks, which already gave promise of future loveliness, her quick intelligence, and her affectionate disposition combining to make her the special favorite of her parents. It was she whom Francis, when quitting his family in the summer of 1764 for that journey to Innspruck which proved his last, specially ordered to be brought to him, saying, as if he felt some foreboding of his approaching illness, that he must embrace her once more before he departed; and his death, which took place before she was nine years old, was the first sorrow which ever brought a tear into her eyes.

The superintendence of her vast empire occupied a greater share of Maria Teresa's attention than the management of her family. But as Marie Antoinette grew up, the Empress-queen's ambition, ever on the watch to maintain and augment the prosperity of her country, perceived in her child's increasing attractions a prospect of cementing more closely an alliance which she had contracted some years before, and on which she prided herself the more because it had terminated an enmity of two centuries and a half. From the day on which Charles V, prevailed over Francis I. in the competition for the imperial crown, the attitude of the Emperor of Germany and of the King of France to each other had been one of mutual hostility, which, with but rare exceptions, had been greatly in favor of the latter country. The very first years of Maria Teresa's own reign had been imbittered by the union of France with Prussia in a war which had deprived her of an extensive province; and she regarded it as one of the great triumphs of Austrian diplomacy to have subsequently won over the French ministry to exchange the friendship of Frederick of Prussia for her own, and to engage as her ally in a war which had for its object the recovery of the lost Silesia. Silesia was not recovered. But she still clung to the French alliance as fondly as if the objects which she had originally hoped to gain by it had been fully accomplished; and, as the heir to the French monarchy was very nearly of the same age as the young archduchess, she began to entertain hopes of uniting the two royal families by a marriage which should render the union between the two nations indissoluble. She mentioned the project to some of the French visitors at her court, whom she thought likely to repeat her conversation on their return to their own country. She took care that reports of her daughter's beauty should from time to time reach the ears of Louis XV. She had her picture painted by French artists. She made a proficiency in the French language the principal object of her education; bringing over some French actors to Vienna to instruct her in the graces of elocution, and subsequently establishing as her chief tutor a French ecclesiastic, the Abbe de Vermond, a man of extensive learning, of excellent judgment, and of most conscientious integrity. The appointment would have been in every respect a most fortunate one, had it not been suggested by Lomenie de Brienne, Archbishop of Toulouse, who thus laid the abbe under an obligation which was requited, to the great injury of France, nearly twenty years afterward, when M. de Vermond, who still remained about the person of his royal mistress, had an opportunity of exerting his influence to make the archbishop prime minister.

Not that her studies were confined to French. Metastasio taught her Italian; Gluck, whose recently published opera of "Orfeo" had, established for him a reputation as one of the greatest musicians of the age, gave her lessons on the harpsichord. But we fear it can not be said that she obtained any high degree of excellence in these or in any other accomplishments. She was not inclined to study; and, with the exception of the abbe, her masters and mistresses were too courtly to be peremptory with an archduchess. Their favorable reports to the Empress-queen were indeed neutralized by the frankness with which their pupil herself confessed her idleness and failure to improve. But Maria Teresa was too much absorbed in politics to give much heed to the confession, or to insist on greater diligence; though at a later day Marie Antoinette herself repented of her neglect, and did her best to repair it, taking lessons in more than one accomplishment with great perseverance during the first years of her residence at Versailles, because, as she expressed herself, the dauphiness was bound to take care of the character of the archduchess.

There are, however, lessons of greater importance to a child than any which are given by even the most accomplished masters--those which flow from the example of a virtuous and sensible mother; and those the young archduchess showed a greater aptitude for learning. Maria Teresa had set an example not only to her own family, but to all sovereigns, among whom principles and practices such as hers had hitherto been little recognized, of regarding an attention to the personal welfare of all her subjects, even of those of the lowest class, as among the most imperative of her duties. She had been accessible to all. She had accustomed the peasantry to accost her in her walks; she had visited their cottages to inquire into and relieve their wants. And the little Antoinette, who, more than any other of her children, seems to have taken her for an especial model, had thus, from her very earliest childhood, learned to feel a friendly interest in the well-doing of the people in general; to think no one too lowly for her notice, to sympathize with sorrow, to be indignant at injustice and ingratitude, to succor misfortune and distress. And these were habits which, as being implanted in her heart, she was not likely to forget; but which might be expected rather to gain strength by indulgence, and to make her both welcome and useful to any people among whom her lot might be cast.

CHAPTER II.

Proposal for the Marriage of Marie Antoinette to the Dauphin.--Early Education of the Dauphin.--The Archduchess leaves Vienna in April, 1770.--Her Reception at Strasburg.--She meets the King at Compiegne.--The Marriage takes place May 16th, 1770.

Royal marriages had been so constantly regarded as affairs of state, to be arranged for political reasons, that it had become usual on the Continent to betroth princes and princesses to each other at a very early age; and it was therefore not considered as denoting any premature impatience on the part of either the Empress-queen or the King of France, Louis XV., when, at the beginning of 1769, when Marie Antoinette had but just completed her thirteenth year, the Duc de Choiseul, the French Minister for Foreign Affairs, who was himself a native of Lorraine, instructed the Marquis de Durfort, the French embassador at Vienna, to negotiate with the celebrated Austrian prime minister, the Prince de Kaunitz, for her marriage to the heir of the French throne, who was not quite fifteen months older. Louis XV. had had several daughters, but only one son. That son, born in 1729, had been married at the age of fifteen to a Spanish infanta, who, within a year of her marriage, died in her confinement, and whom he replaced in a few months by a daughter of Augustus III., King of Saxony. His second wife bore him four sons and two daughters. The eldest son, the Duc de Bourgogne, who was born in 1750, and was generally regarded as a child of great promise, died in his eleventh year; and when he himself died in 1765, his second son, previously known as the Duc de Berri, succeeded him in his title of dauphin. This prince, now the suitor of the archduchess, had been born on the 23d of August, 1754, and was therefore not quite fifteen. As yet but little was known of him. Very little pains had been taken with his education; his governor, the Duc de la Vauguyon, was a man who had been appointed to that most important post by the cabals of the infamous mistress and parasites who formed the court of Louis XV., without one qualification for the discharge of its duties. A servile, intriguing spirit had alone recommended him to his patrons, while his frivolous indolence was in harmony with the inclinations of the king himself, who, worn out with a long course of profligacy, had no longer sufficient energy even for vice. Under such a governor, the young prince had but little chance of receiving a wholesome education, even if there was not a settled design to enfeeble his mind by neglect.

His father had been a man of a character very different from that of the king. By a sort of natural reaction or silent protest against the infamies which he saw around him, he had cherished a serious and devout disposition, and had observed a conduct of the most rigorous virtue. He was even suspected of regarding the Jesuits with especial favor, and was believed to have formed plans for the reformation of morals, and perhaps of the State. It was not strange that, on the first news of the illness which proved fatal to him, the people flocked to the churches with prayers for his recovery, and that his death was regarded by all the right- thinking portion of the community as a national calamity. But the courtiers, who had regarded his approaching reign with not unnatural alarm, hailed his removal with joy, and were, above all things, anxious to prevent his son, who had now become the heir to the crown, from following such a path as the father had marked out for himself. The negligence of some, thus combining with the deliberate malice of others, and aided by peculiarities in the constitution and disposition of the young prince himself, which became more and more marked as he grew up, exercised a pernicious influence on his boyhood. Not only was his education in the ordinary branches of youthful knowledge neglected, but no care was even taken to cultivate his taste or to polish his manners, though a certain delicacy of taste and refinement of manners were regarded by the courtiers, and by Louis XV. himself, as the pre-eminent distinction of his reign. He was kept studiously in the background, discountenanced and depressed, till he contracted an awkward timidity and reserve which throughout his life he could never shake off; while a still more unfortunate defect, which was another result of this system, was an inability to think or decide for himself, or even to act steadily on the advice of others after he had professed to adopt it.

But these deficiencies in his character had as yet hardly had time to display themselves; and, had they been ever so notorious, they were not of a nature to divert Maria Teresa from her purpose. For her political objects, it would not, perhaps, have seemed to her altogether undesirable that the future sovereign of France should be likely to rely on the judgment and to submit to the influence of another, so long as the person who should have the best opportunity of influencing him was her own daughter. A negotiation for the success of which both parties were equally anxious did not require a long time for its conclusion; and by the beginning of July, 1769, all the preliminaries were arranged; the French newspapers were authorized to allude to the marriage, and to speak of the diligence with which preparations for it were being made in both countries; those in which the French king took the greatest interest being the building of some carriages of extraordinary magnificence, to receive the archduchess as soon as she should have arrived on French ground; while those which were being made in Germany indicated a more elementary state of civilization, as the first requisite appeared to be to put the roads between Vienna and the frontier in a state of repair, to prevent the journey from being too fatiguing.

By the spring of the next year all the necessary preparations had been completed; and on the evening of the 10th of April, 1770, a grand court was held in the Palace of Vienna. Through a double row of guards of the palace, of body-guards, and of a still more select guard, composed wholly of nobles, M. de Durfort was conducted into the presence of the Emperor Joseph II., and of his widowed mother, the Empress-queen, still, though only dowager-empress, the independent sovereign of her own hereditary dominions; and to both he proffered, on the part of the King of France, a formal request for the hand of the Archduchess Marie Antoinette for the dauphin. When the Emperor and Empress had given their gracious consent to the demand, the archduchess herself was summoned to the hall and informed of the proposal which had been made, and of the approval which her mother and her brother had announced; while, to incline her also to regard it with equal favor, the embassador presented her with a letter from her intended husband, and with his miniature, which she at once hung round her neck. After which, the whole party adjourned to the private theatre of the palace to witness the performance of a French play, "The Confident Mother" of Marivaux, the title of which, so emblematic of the feelings of Maria Teresa, may probably have procured it the honor of selection.

The next day the young princess executed a formal renunciation of all right of succession to any part of her mother's dominions which might at any time devolve on her; though the number of her brothers and elder sisters rendered any such occurrence in the highest degree improbable, and though one conspicuous precedent in the history of both countries had, within the memory of persons still living, proved the worthlessness of such renunciations.[1] A few days were then devoted to appropriate festivities. That which is most especially mentioned by the chroniclers of the court being, in accordance with the prevailing taste of the time, a grand masked ball,[2] for which a saloon four hundred feet long had been expressly constructed. And on the 26th of April the young bride quit her home, the mother from whom she had never been separated, and the friends and playmates among whom her whole life had been hitherto passed, for a country which was wholly strange to her, and in which she had not as yet a single acquaintance. Her very husband, to whom she was to be confided, she had never seen.

Though both mother and daughter felt the most entire confidence that the new position, on which she was about to enter, would be full of nothing but glory and happiness, it was inevitable that they should be, as they were, deeply agitated at so complete a separation. And, if we may believe the testimony of witnesses who were at Vienna at the time,[3] the grief of the mother, who was never to see her child again, was shared not only by the members of the imperial household, whom constant intercourse had enabled to know and appreciate her amiable qualities, but by the population of the capital and the surrounding districts, all of whom had heard of her numerous acts of kindness and benevolence, which, young as she was, many of them had also experienced, and who thronged the streets along which she passed on her departure, mingling tears of genuine sorrow with their acclamations, and following her carriage to the outermost gate of the city that they might gaze their last on the darling of many hearts.

Kehl was the last German town through which she was to pass, Strasburg was the first French city which was to receive her, and, as the islands which dot the Rhine at that portion of the noble boundary river were regarded as a kind of neutral ground, the French monarch had selected the principal one to be occupied by a pavilion built for the purpose and decorated with great magnificence, that it might serve for another stage of the wedding ceremony. In this pavilion she was to cease to be German, and was to become French; she was to bid farewell to her Austrian attendants, and to receive into her service the French officers of her household, male and female, who were to replace them. She was even to divest herself of every article of her German attire, and to apparel herself anew in garments of French manufacture sent from Paris. The pavilion was divided into two compartments. In the chief apartment of the German division, the Austrian officials who had escorted her so far formally resigned their charge, and surrendered her to the Comte de Noailles, who had been appointed embassador extraordinary to receive her; and, when all the deeds necessary to release from their responsibly the German nobles whose duties were now terminated had been duly signed, the doors were thrown open, and Marie Antoinette passed into the French division, as a French princess, to receive the homage of a splendid train of French courtiers, who were waiting in loyal eagerness to offer their first salutations to their new mistress. Yet, as if at every period of her life she was to be beset with omens, the celebrated German writer, Goethe, who was at that time pursuing his studies at Strasburg, perceived one which he regarded as of most inauspicious significance in the tapestry which decorated the walls of the chief saloon. It represented the history of Jason and Medea. On one side was portrayed the king's bride in the agonies of death; on the other, the royal father was bewailing his murdered children. Above them both, Medea was fleeing away in a car drawn by fire-breathing dragons, and driven by the Furies; and the youthful poet could not avoid reflecting that a record of the most miserable union that even the ancient mythology had recorded was a singularly inappropriate and ill-omened ornament for nuptial festivities.[4]

A bridge reached from the island to the left bank of the river; and, on quitting the pavilion, the archduchess found the carriages, which had been built for her in Paris, ready to receive her, that she might make her state entry into Strasburg. They were marvels of the coach-maker's art. The prime minister himself had furnished the designs, and they had attracted the curiosity of the fashionable world in Paris throughout the winter. One was covered with crimson velvet, having pictures, emblematical of the four seasons, embroidered in gold on the principal panels; on the other the velvet was blue, and the elements took the place of the seasons; while the roof of each was surmounted by nosegays of flowers, carved in gold, enameled in appropriate colors, and wrought with such exquisite delicacy that every movement of the carriage, or even the lightest breeze, caused them to wave as if they were the natural produce of the garden.[5]

In this superb conveyance Marie Antoinette passed on under a succession of triumphal arches to the gates of Strasburg, which, on this auspicious occasion, seemed as if it desired to put itself forward as the representative of the joy of the whole nation by the splendid cordiality of its welcome. Whole regiments of cavalry, drawn up in line of battle, received her with a grand salute as she advanced. Battery after battery pealed forth along the whole extent of the vast ramparts; the bells of every church rang out a festive peal; fountains ran with wine in the Grand Square. She proceeded to the episcopal palace, where the archbishop, the Cardinal de Rohan, with his coadjutor, the Prince Louis de Rohan (a man afterward rendered unhappily notorious by his complicity in a vile conspiracy against her) received her at the head of the most august chapter that the whole land could produce, the counts of the cathedral, as they were styled; the Prince of Lorraine being the grand dean, the Archbishop of Bordeaux the grand provost, and not one post in the chapter being filled by any one below the rank of count. She held a court for the reception of all the female nobility of the province. She dined publicly in state; a procession of the municipal magistrates presented her a sample of the wines of the district; and, as she tasted the luscious offering, the coopers celebrated what they called a feast of Bacchus, waving their hoops as they danced round the room in grotesque figures.

It was a busy day for her, that first day of her arrival on French soil. From the dinner-table she went to the theatre; on quitting the theatre, she was driven through the streets to see the illuminations, which made every part of the city as bright as at midday, the great square in front of the episcopal palace being converted into a complete garden of fire-works; and at midnight she attended a ball which the governor of the province, the Marechal de Contades, gave in her honor to all the principal inhabitants of the city and district. Quitting Strasburg the next day, after a grand reception of the clergy, the nobles, and the magistrates of the province, she proceeded by easy stages through Nancy, Chalons, Rheims, and Soissons, the whole population of every town through which she passed collecting on the road to gaze on her beauty, the renown of which had readied the least curious ears; and to receive marks of her affability, reports of which were at least as widely spread, in the cheerful eagerness with which she threw down the windows of her carriage, and the frank, smiling recognition and genuine pleasure with which she replied to their enthusiastic acclamations. It was long remembered that, when the students of the college at Soissons presented her with a Latin address, she replied to them in a sentence or two in the same language.

Soissons was her last resting-place before she was introduced to her new family. On the afternoon of Monday, the 14th of May, she quit it for Compiegne, which the king and all the court had reached in the course of the morning. As she approached the town she was met by the minister, the Duc de Choiseul, and he was the precursor of Louis himself, who, accompanied by the dauphin and his daughters, and escorted by his gorgeous company of the guards of the household,[6] had driven out to receive her. She and all her train dismounted from their carriages. Her master of the horse and her "knight of honor[7]" took her by the hand and conducted her to the royal coach. She sunk on her knee in the performance of her respectful homage; but Louis promptly raised her up, and, having embraced her with a tenderness which gracefully combined royal dignity with paternal affection, and having addressed her in a brief speech,[8] which was specially acceptable to her, as containing a well-timed compliment to her mother, introduced her to the dauphin; and, when they reached the palace, he also presented to her his more distant relatives, the princes and princesses of the blood,[9] the Duc d'Orleans and his son, the Duc de Chartres, destined hereafter to prove one of the foulest and most mischievous of her enemies; the Duc de Bourbon, the Princes of Conde and Conti, and one lady whose connection with royalty was Italian rather than French, but to whom the acquaintance, commenced on this day, proved the cause of a miserable and horrible death, the beautiful Princesse de Lamballe.

Compiegne, however, was not to be honored by the marriage ceremony. The next morning the whole party started for Versailles, turning out of the road, at the express request of the archduchess herself, to pay a brief visit to the king's youngest daughter, the Princess Louise, who had taken on herself the Carmelite vows, and resided in the Convent of St. Denis. The request had been suggested by Choiseul, who was well aware that the princess shared the dislike entertained by her more worldly sisters to the house of Austria; but it was accepted as a personal compliment by the king himself, who was already fascinated by her charms, which, as he affirmed, surpassed those of her portrait, and was predisposed to view all her words and actions in the most favorable light. Avoiding Paris, which Louis, ever since the riots of 1750, had constantly refused to enter, they reached the hunting-lodge of La Muette, in the Bois de Boulogne, for supper. Here she made the acquaintance of the brothers and sisters of her future husband, the Counts of Provence and Artois, both destined, in their turn, to succeed him on the throne; of the Princess Clotilde, who may be regarded as the most fortunate of her race, in being saved by a foreign marriage and an early death from witnessing the worst calamities of her family and her native land; of the Princess Elizabeth, who was fated to share them in all their bitterness and horror; and (a strangely incongruous sequel to the morning visit to the Carmelite convent), the Countess du Barri also came into her presence, and was admitted to sup at the royal table; as if, even at the very moment when he might have been expected to conduct himself with some degree of respectful decency to the pure-minded young girl whom he was receiving into his family, Louis XV. was bent on exhibiting to the whole world his incurable shamelessness in its most offensive form.

At midnight he, with the dauphin, proceeded to Versailles, whither, the next morning, the archduchess followed them. And at one o'clock on the 16th, in the chapel of the palace, the Primate of France, the Archbishop of Rheims, performed the marriage ceremony. A canopy of cloth of silver was held over the heads of the youthful pair by the bishops of Senlis and Chartres. The dauphin, after he had placed the wedding-ring on his bride's finger, added, as a token that he endowed her with his worldly wealth, a gift of thirteen pieces of gold, which, as well as the ring, had received the episcopal benediction, and Marie Antoinette was dauphiness of France.

CHAPTER III.

The marriage which was thus accomplished was regarded with unmodified pleasure by the family of the bride, and with almost equal satisfaction by the French king. In spite of the public rejoicings in both countries with which it was accompanied, it can not be said to have been equally acceptable to the majority of the people of either nation. There was still a strong anti-French party at Vienna,[1] and (a circumstance of far greater influence on the fortunes of the young couple) there was a strong anti-Austrian party in France, which was not without its supporters even in the king's palace. That the marriage should have been so earnestly desired at the imperial court is a strange instance of the extent to which political motives overpowered every other consideration in the mind of the great Empress-queen, for she was not ignorant of the real character of the French court, of the degree in which it was divided by factions, of the base and unworthy intrigues which were its sole business, and of the sagacity and address which were requisite for any one who would steer his way with safety and honor through its complicated mazes.

Judgment and prudence were not the qualities most naturally to be expected in a young princess not yet fifteen years old. The best prospect which Marie Antoinette had of surmounting the numerous and varied difficulties which beset her lay in the affection which she speedily conceived for her husband, and in the sincerity, we can hardly say warmth, with which he returned her love. Maria Teresa had bespoken his tenderness for her in a letter which she wrote to him on the day on which her daughter left Vienna, and which has often been quoted as a composition worthy of her alike as a mother and as a Christian sovereign; and as admirably calculated to impress the heart of her new son-in-law by claiming his attachment for his bride, on the ground of the pains which she had taken to make her worthy of her fortune.

"Your bride, my dear dauphin, has just left me. I do hope that she will cause your happiness. I have brought her up with the design that she should do so, because I have for some time forseen that she would share your destiny.

"I have inspired her with an eager desire to do her duty to you, with a tender attachment to your person, with a resolution to be attentive to think and do every thing which may please you. I have also been most careful to enjoin her a tender devotion toward the Master of all Sovereigns, being thoroughly persuaded that we are but badly providing for the welfare of the nations which are intrusted to us when we fail in our duty to Him who breaks sceptres and overthrows thrones according to his pleasure.

"I say, then, to you, my dear dauphin, as I say to my daughter: 'Cultivate your duties toward God. Seek to cause the happiness of the people over whom you will reign (it will be too soon, come when it may). Love the king, your grandfather; be humane like him; be always accessible to the unfortunate. If you behave in this manner, it is impossible that happiness can fail to be your lot.' My daughter will love you, I am certain, because I know her. But the more that I answer to you for her affection, and for her anxiety to please you, the more earnestly do I entreat you to vow to her the most sincere attachment.

"Farewell, my dear dauphin. May you be happy. I am bathed in tears.[2]"

The dauphin did not falsify the hopes thus expressed by the Empress-queen. But his was not the character to afford his wife either the advice or support which she needed, while, strange to say, he was the only member of the royal family to whom she could look for either. The king was not only utterly worthless and shameless, but weak and irresolute in the most ordinary matters. Even when in the flower and vigor of his age, he had never been able to summon courage to give verbal orders or reproofs to his own children,[3] but had intimated his pleasure or displeasure by letters. He had been gradually falling lower and lower, both in his own vices and in the estimation of the world; and was now, still more than when Lord Chesterfield first drew his picture,[4] both hated and despised. The dauphin's brothers, for such mere boys, were singularly selfish and unamiable; and the only female relations of her husband, his aunts, to whom, as such, it would have been natural that a young foreigner should look for friendship and advice, were not only narrow-minded, intriguing, and malicious, but were predisposed to regard her with jealousy as likely to interfere with the influence which they had hoped to exert over their nephew when he should become their sovereign.

Marie Antoinette had, therefore, difficulties and enemies to contend with from the very first commencement of her residence in France. And many even of her own virtues were unfavorable to her chances of happiness, calculated as they were to lay her at the mercy of her ill-wishers, and to deprive her of some of the defenses which might have been found in a different temperament. Full of health and spirits, she was naturally eager in the pursuit of enjoyment, and anxious to please every one, from feeling nothing but kindness toward every one; she was frank, open, and sincere; and, being perfectly guileless herself, she was, as through her whole life she continued to be, entirely unsuspicious of unfriendliness, much more of treachery in others. Her affability and condescension combined with this trustful disposition to make her too often the tool of designing and grasping courtiers, who sought to gain their own ends at her expense, and who presumed on her good-nature and inexperience to make requests which, as they well knew, should never have been made, but which they also reckoned that she would be unwilling to refuse.

But lest this general amiability and desire to give pleasure to those around her might seem to impart a prevailing tinge of weakness to her character, it is fair to add that she united to these softer feelings, robuster virtues calculated to deserve and to win universal admiration; though some of them, never having yet been called forth by circumstances, were for a long time unsuspected by the world at large. She had pride-- pride of birth, pride of rank--though never did that feeling show itself more nobly or more beneficially. It never led her to think herself above the very meanest of her subjects. It never made her indifferent to the interests, to the joys or sorrows, of a single individual. The idea with which it inspired her was, that a princess of her race was never to commit an unworthy act, was never to fail in purity of virtue, in truth, in courage; that she was to be careful to set an example of these virtues to those who would naturally look up to her; and that she herself was to keep constantly in her mind the example of her illustrious mother, and never, by act, or word, or thought, to discredit her mother's name. And as she thus regarded courage as her birthright, so she possessed it in abundance and in variety. She had courage to plan, and courage to act; courage to resolve, and courage to adhere to the resolution once deliberately formed; and, above all, courage to endure and to suffer, and, in the very extremity of misery, to animate and support others less royally endowed.

Such, then, as she was, with both her manifest and her latent excellencies, as well as with those more mixed qualities which had some defects mingled with their sweetness, Marie Antoinette, at the age of fourteen years and a half, was thrown into a world wholly new to her, to guide herself so far by her own discretion that there was no one who had both judgment and authority to control her in her line of conduct or in any single action. She had, indeed, an adviser whom her mother had provided for her, though without allowing her to suspect the nature or full extent of the duties which she had imposed upon him. Maria Teresa had been in some respects a strict mother, one whom her children in general feared almost as much as they loved her; and the rigorous superintendence on some points of conduct which she had exercised over Marie Antoinette while at home, she was not inclined wholly to resign, even after she had made her apparently independent. At the moment of her departure from Vienna, she gave her a letter of advice which she entreated her to read over every month, and in which the most affectionate and judicious counsel is more than once couched in a tone of very authoritative command; the whole letter showing not only the most experienced wisdom and the most affectionate interest in her daughter's happiness, but likewise a thorough insight into her character, so precisely are some of the errors against which the letter most emphatically warns her those into which she most frequently fell. And she appointed a statesman in whom she deservedly placed great confidence, the Count de Mercy-Argenteau, her embassador to the court at Versailles, with the express design that he should always be at hand to afford the dauphiness his advice in all the difficulties which she could not avoid foreseeing for her; and who should also keep the Empress-queen herself fully informed of every particular of her conduct, and of every transaction by which she was in any way affected. This part of his commission was wholly unsuspected by the young princess; but the count discharged such portions of the delicate duty thus imposed upon him with rare discretion, contriving in its performance to combine the strictest fidelity to his imperial mistress with the most entire devotion to the interests of his pupil, and to preserve the unqualified regard and esteem of both mother and daughter to the end of their lives. Toward the latter, as dauphiness, and even as queen, he stood for some years in a position very similar to that which Baron Stockmar fills in the history of the late Prince Consort of England, being, however, more frequent in his admonitions, and occasionally more severe in his reproofs, as the youth and inexperience of Marie Antoinette not unnaturally led her into greater mistakes than the scrupulous conscientiousness and almost premature prudence of the prince consort ever suffered him to commit; and his diligent reports to the Empress-queen, amounting at times to a diary of the proceedings of the French court, have a lasting and inestimable value, since they furnish us with so trustworthy a record of the whole life of Marie Antoinette for the first ten years of her residence in France,[5] of her actions, her language, and her very thoughts (for she ever scorned to give a reason or to make an excuse which was not absolutely and strictly true), that there is perhaps no person of historical importance whose conduct in every transaction of gravity or interest is more minutely known, or whose character there are fuller materials for appreciating.

The very day of her marriage did not pass without her receiving a strange specimen of the factious spirit which prevailed at the court, and of the hollowness of the welcome with which the chief nobles had greeted her arrival. A state ball was given at the palace to celebrate the wedding, and as the Princess of Lorraine, a cousin of the Emperor Francis, was the only blood-relation of Marie Antoinette who was at Versailles at the time, the king assigned her a place in the first quadrille, giving her precedence for that occasion, next to the princes of the blood. It did not seem a great stretch of courtesy to show to a foreigner, even had she not been related to the princess in whose honor the ball was given; but the dukes and peers fired up at the arrangement, as if an insult had been offered them. They held a meeting at which they resolved that no member of their families should attend, and carried out their resolution so obstinately that at five o'clock, when the dancing was to commence, except the royal princesses there were only three ladies in the room. The king, who, following the example of Louis XIV., acted on these occasions as his own master of ceremonies, was forced to send special and personal orders to some of those who had absented themselves to attend without delay. And so by seven o'clock twelve or fourteen couples were collected[6] (the number of persons admitted to such entertainments was always extremely small), and the rude disloyalty of the protest was to outward appearance effaced by the submission of the recusants.

But all the troubles which arose out of the wedding festivities were not so easily terminated. Little as was the good-will which subsisted between Louis XV. and the Parisians, the civic authorities thought their own credit at stake in doing appropriate honor to an occasion so important as the marriage of the heir of the monarchy, and on the 30th of May they closed a succession of balls and banquets by a display of fire-works, in which the ingenuity of the most celebrated artists had been exhausted to outshine all previous displays of the sort. Three sides of the Place Louis XV. were filled up with pyramids and colonnades. Here dolphins darted out many-colored flames from their ever-open mouths. There, rivers of fire poured forth cascades spangled with all the variegated brilliancy with which the chemist's art can embellish the work of the pyrotechnist. The centre was occupied with a gorgeous Temple of Hymen, which seemed to lean for support on the well-known statue of the king, in front of which it was constructed; and which was, as it were, to be carried up to the skies by above three thousand rockets and fire-balls into which it was intended to dissolve. The whole square was packed with spectators, the pedestrians in front, the carriages in the rear, when one of the explosions set fire to a portion of the platforms on which the different figures had been constructed. At first the increase of the blaze was regarded only as an ingenious surprise on the part of the artist. But soon it became clear that the conflagration was undesigned and real; panic-succeeded to delight, and the terror-stricken crowd, seeing themselves surrounded with flames, began to make frantic efforts to escape from the danger; but there was only one side of the square uninclosed, and that was blocked up by carriages. The uproar and the glare made the horses unmanageable, and in a few moments the whole mass, human beings and animals, was mingled in helpless confusion, making flight impossible by their very eagerness to fly, and trampling one another underfoot in bewildered misery. Of those who did succeed in extricating themselves from the square, half made their way to the road which runs along the bank of the river, and found that they had only exchanged one danger for another, which, though of an opposite character, was equally destructive. Still overwhelmed with terror, though the first peril was over, the fugitives pushed one another into the stream, in which great numbers were drowned. The number of the killed could never be accurately ascertained: but no calculation estimated the number of those who perished at less than six hundred, while those who were grievously injured were at least as many more.

The dauphin and dauphiness were deeply shocked by a disaster so painfully at variance with their own happiness, which, in one sense, had caused it. Their first thought was, as far as they might be able, to mitigate it. Most of the victims were of the poorer class, the grief of whose surviving relatives was, in many instances, aggravated by the loss of the means of livelihood which the labors of those who had been cut off had hitherto supplied; and, to give temporary succor to this distress, the dauphin and dauphiness at once drew out from the royal treasury the sums allowed to them for their private expenses for the month, and sent the money to the municipal authorities to be applied to the relief of the sufferers. But Marie Antoinette did more. She felt that to give money only was but cold benevolence; and she made personal visits to many of those families which had been most grievously afflicted, showing the sincerity of her sympathy by the touching kindness of her language, and by the tears which she mingled with those of the widow and the orphan.[7] Such unmerited kindness made a deep impression on the citizens. Since the time of Henry IV. no prince had ever shown the slightest interest in the happiness or misery of the lower classes; and the feeling of affectionate gratitude which this unprecedented recognition of their claims to be sympathized with as fellow-creatures awakened was fixed still more deeply in their hearts a short time afterward, when, at one of the hunting-parties which took place at Fontainebleau, the stag charged a crowd of the spectators and severely wounded a peasant with his horns. Marie Antoinette sprung to the ground at the sight, helped to bind up the wound, and had the man driven in her own carriage to his cabin, whither she followed him herself to see that every proper attention was paid to him.[8] And the affection which she thus inspired among the poor was fully shared by the chief personage in the kingdom, the sovereign himself. A life of profligacy had not rendered Louis wholly insensible to the superior attractions of innocence and virtue. Perhaps a secret sense of shame at the slavery in which his vices held him, and which, as he well knew, excited the contempt of even his most dissolute courtiers, though he had not sufficient energy to shake it off, may have for a moment quickened his better feelings; and the fresh beauty of the young princess, who, from the first moment of her arrival at the court, treated him with the most affectionate and caressing respect, awakened in him a genuine admiration and good-will. He praised her beauty and her grace to all his nobles with a warmth that excited the jealousy of his infamous mistress, the Countess du Barri. He made allowance for some childishness of manner as natural at her age,[9] showed an anxiety for every thing which could amuse or gratify her, which afforded a marked contrast to his ordinary apathy. And, though in so young a girl it was rather the promise of future beauty than its developed perfection that her feat-* as yet presented, they already exhibited sufficient charms to exempt those who extolled them from the suspicion of flattery. A clear and open forehead, a delicately cut nose, a complexion of dazzling brilliancy, with bright blue eyes, whose ever-varying lustre seemed equally calculated to show every feeling which could move her heart; which could, at times seem almost fierce with anger, indignation, or contempt, but whose prevailing expression was that of kindly benevolence or light-hearted mirth were united with a figure of exquisite proportions, sufficiently tall for dignity, though as yet, of course, slight and unformed, and every movement of which was directed by a grace that could neither be taught nor imitated. If any defect could be discovered in her face, it consisted in a somewhat undue thickness of the lips, especially of the lower lip, which had for some generations been the prevailing characteristic of her family.

Accordingly, a month after her marriage, Mercy could report to Maria Teresa that she had had complete success, and was a universal favorite; that, besides the king, who openly expressed his satisfaction, she had won the heart of the dauphin, who had been very unqualified in the language in which he had praised both her beauty and her agreeable qualities to his aunts; and that even those princesses were "enchanted" with her. The whole court, and the people in general, extolled her affability, and the graciousness with which she said kind things to all who approached

her. Though the well-informed embassador had already discovered signs of the cabals which the mistress and her partisans were forming against her, and had been
rendered a little uneasy by the handle which she had more than once afforded to
her secret enemies, when, "in gayety of heart and without the slightest ill-will," she
had allowed herself to jest on some persons and circumstances which struck her as
ridiculous, her jests being seasoned with a wit and piquancy which rendered them
keener to those who were their objects, and more so mischievous to herself. He
especially praised the unaffected dignity with which she had received the mistress
who had attended in her apartments to pay her court, though in no respect deceived
as to the lady's disposition, her penetration into the characters of all with whom she
had been brought into contact, denoting, as it struck him, "a sagacity" which, at her
age, was "truly astonishing.[10]"

CHAPTER IV.

Marie Antoinette gives her Mother her First Impressions of the Court and of her own Position and Prospects.--Court Life at Versailles.--Marie Antoinette shows her Dislike of Etiquette.--Character of the Duc d'Aiguillon.--Cabals against the Dauphiness.--Jealousy of Mme. du Barri.-- The Aunts, too, are Jealous of Her.--She becomes more and more Popular.-- Parties for Donkey-riding.--Scantiness of the Dauphiness's Income.--Her Influence over the King.--The Duc de Choiseul is dismissed.--She begins to have Great Influence over the Dauphin.

Marie Antoinette herself was inclined to be delighted with all that befell her, and to make light of what she could hardly regard as pleasant or becoming; and two of her first letters to her mother, written in the early part of July,[1] give us an insight into the feelings with which she regarded her new family and her own position, as well as a picture of her daily occupations and of the singular customs of the French court, strangely inconsistent in what it permitted and in what it disallowed, and, in the publicity in which its princes lived, curiously incompatible with ordinary ideas of comfort and even delicacy.

"The king," she says, "is full of kindnesses toward me, and I love him tenderly. But it is pitiable to see his weakness for Madame du Barri, who is the silliest and most impertinent creature that it is possible to conceive. She has played with us every evening at Marly,[2] and she has twice been seated next to me; but she has not spoken to me, and I have not attempted to engage in conversation with her; but, when it was necessary, I have said a word or two to her.

"As for my dear husband, he is greatly changed, and in a most advantageous manner. He shows a great deal of affection for me, and is even beginning to treat me with great confidence. He certainly does not like M. de la, Vauguyon; but he is afraid of him. A curious thing happened about the duke the other day. I was alone with my husband, when M. de la Vauguyon stole hurriedly up to the doors to listen. A servant, who was either a fool or a very honest man, opened the door, and there stood his grace the duke planted like a sentinel, without being able to retreat. I pointed out to my husband the inconvenience that there was in having people listening at the doors, and he took my remark very well."

She did not tell the empress the whole of this occurrence; she had been too indignant at the duke's meanness to suppress her feelings, and she reproved the duke himself with a severity which can hardly be said to have been misplaced.

"Duke de la Vauguyon," she said, "my lord the dauphin is now of an age to dispense with a governor; and I have no need of a spy. I beg you not to appear again in my presence.[3]"

Between the writing of her first and second letters she had heard from Maria Teresa; and she "can not describe how the affection her mother expresses for her has gone to her heart. Every letter which she has received has filled her eyes with tears of regret at being separated from so tender and loving a mother, and, happy as she is in France, she would give the world to see her family again, if it were but for a moment. As her mother wishes to know how the days are passed; she gets up between nine and ten, and, having dressed herself and said her morning prayers, she breakfasts, and then she goes to the apartments of her aunts, whose she usually finds the king. That lasts till half-past ten; then at eleven she has her hair dressed.

"At twelve," she proceeds to say, "what is called the Chamber is held, and there every one who does not belong to the common people may enter. I put on my rouge and wash my hands before all the world; the men go out, and the women remain; and then I dress myself in their presence. Then comes mass. If the king is at Versailles, I go to mass with him, my husband, and my aunts; if he is not there, I go alone with the dauphin, but always at the same hour. After mass we two dine by ourselves in the presence of all the world; but dinner is over by half-past one, as we both eat very fast. From the dinner-table I go to the dauphin's apartments, and if he has business, I return to my own rooms, where I read, write, or work; for I am making a waistcoat for the king, which gets on but slowly, though, I trust, with God's grace, it will be finished before many years are over. At three o'clock I go again to visit my aunts, and the king comes to them at the same hour. At four the abbe[4] comes to me, and at five I have every day either my harpsichord-master or my singing-master till six. At half-past six I go almost every day to my aunts, except when I go out walking. And you must understand that when I go to visit my aunts, my husband almost always goes with me. At seven we play cards till nine o'clock; but when the weather is fine I go out walking, and then there is no play in my apartments, but it is held at my aunts'. At nine we sup; and when the king is not there, my aunts come to sup with us; but when the king is there, we go after supper to their rooms, waiting there for the king, who usually comes about a quarter to eleven; and I lie down on a grand sofa and go to sleep till he comes. But when he is not there, we go to bed at eleven o'clock."

The play-table which is alluded to in these letters was one of the most curious and mischievous institutions of the court. Gambling had been one of its established vices ever since the time of Henry IV., whose enormous losses at play had formed the subject of Sully's most incessant remonstrances. And from the beginning of the reign of Louis XIV., a gaming-table had formed a regular part of the evening's amusement. It was the one thing which was allowed to break down the barrier of etiquette. On all other occasions, the rules which regulated who might and who might not be admitted to the royal presence were as precise and strict as in many cases they were unreasonable and unintelligible. But at the gaming-table every one who could make the slightest pretensions to gentle birth was allowed to present himself and stake his money; [5] and the leveling influence of play was almost as fully exemplified in the king's palace as in the ordinary gaming-houses, since, though the presence of royalty so far acted as a restraint on the gamblers as to prevent any open explosion, accusations of foul play and dishonest tricks were as rife as in the most vulgar company.

Marie Antoinette was winning many hearts by her loveliness and affability; but she could not scatter her kind speeches and friendly smiles among all with whom she came into contact without running counter to the prejudices of some of the old courtiers who had been formed on a different system; to whom the maintenance of a rigid etiquette was as the very breath of their nostrils, and in whose eyes its very first rule and principle was that princes should keep all the world at a distance. Foremost among these sticklers for old ideas was the Countess de Noailles, her principal "lady of honor," whose uneasiness on the subject speedily became so notorious as to give rise to numerous court squibs and satirical odes, the authors of which seemed glad to compliment the dauphin and to vex her ladyship at the same time, but who could not be deterred by these effusions from lecturing Marie Antoinette on her disregard of her rank, and on the danger of making herself too familiar, till she provoked the young princess into giving her the nickname of Madame Etiquette; and, no doubt, in her childish playfulness, to utter many a speech and do many an act whose principle object was to excite the astonishment or provoke the frowns of the too prim lady of honor.

There can be no doubt that, though she often pushed her strictness too far, Madame de Noailles to some extent had reason on her side; and that a certain degree of ceremony and stately reserve is indispensable in court life. It is a penalty which those born in the purple must pay for their dignity, that they can have no friend on a perfect equality with themselves; and those who in different ages and countries have tried to emancipate themselves from this law of their rank have not generally won even the respect of those to whom they have condescended, and still less the approbation of the outer world, whose members have perhaps a secret dislike to see those whom they regard as their own equals lifted above them by the familiarity of princes.

This, however, was a matter of comparatively slight importance. An excess of condescension is at the worst a venial and an amiable error; but even at the early period plots were being contrived against the young princess, which, if successful, would have been wholly destructive of her happiness, and which, though she was fully aware of them, she had not means by herself to disconcert or defeat. They were the more formidable because they were partly political, embracing a scheme for the removal of a minister, and consequently conciliated more supporters and insured greater perseverance than if they had merely aimed at securing a preponderance of court favor for the plotters. Like all the other mistresses who had successfully reigned in the French courts, Madame du Barri had a party of adherents who hoped to rise by her patronage. The Duc de Choiseul himself had owed his promotion to her predecessor, Madame de Pompadour, and those who hoped to supplant him saw in a similar influence the best prospect of attaining their end. One of the least respectable of the French nobles was the Duc d'Aiguillon. As Governor of Brittany, he had behaved with notorious cowardice in the Seven Years' War. He had since been, if possible, still more dishonored by charges of oppression, peculation, and subornation, on which the authorities of the province had prosecuted him, and which the Parisian Parliament had pronounced to be established. But no kind of infamy was a barrier to the favor of Louis XV. He cancelled the resolution of the Parliament, and showed such countenance to the culprit that d'Aiguillon, who was both ambitious and covetous, conceived the idea of supplanting Choiseul in the Government. As one of Choiseul's principal measures had been the negotiation of the dauphin's marriage, Marie Antoinette was known to regard him with a good-will which was founded on gratitude. But, unfortunately, her feelings on this point were not shared by her husband; for Choiseul had had notorious differences with his father, the late dauphin, and, though it was perfectly certain that that prince had died of natural disease, people had been found to whisper in his son's ear suspicions that he had been poisoned, and that the minister to whom he was unfriendly had been concerned in his death.

The two plots, therefore, to overthrow the minister and to weaken the influence of the dauphiness, went hand-in-hand, and, as might have been expected from the character of the patroness of both, no means were too vile or wicked for the intriguers who had set them on foot. Madame du Barri was, indeed, seriously alarmed for the maintenance of her own ascendency. The king took such undisguised pleasure in his new granddaughter's company, that some of the most experienced courtiers began to anticipate that she would soon gain entire influence over him[6]. The mistress began, therefore, to disparage her personal charms, never speaking of her to Louis ("France," as she generally called him), except as "the little blowsy,[7]" while her ally, De la Vauguyon, endeavored to further her views by exerting the influence which he mistakenly flattered himself that he still retained over the dauphin, to surround her with his own creatures. He tried to procure the dismissal of the Abbe de Vermond, who, having been, as we have seen, the tutor of Marie Antoinette at Vienna, still remained attached to her person as her reader; and whose complete knowledge of all the ways of the court, joined to a thorough honesty and devoted fidelity to her best interests, rendered his services most valuable to his mistress in her new sphere. He sought to recommend a creature of his own as her confessor; to obtain for his own daughter the appointment of one of her chief ladies; and, with a wickedness peculiar to the French court, he even endeavored to imitate the vile arts by which the Duc de Richelieu had deprived Marie Leczinska of the affections of the king, to alienate the dauphin from his young wife, and to induce him to commit himself to the guidance of Madame du Barri. But this part of the scheme failed. The dauphin was strangely insensible to the personal charms of Marie Antoinette herself, and was wholly inaccessible to any inferior temptations; and, as far as the arrangements of the court were concerned, the success of the mistress's cabal was limited to procuring the dismissal of the mistress of the robes, the Countess de Grammont, for refusing to cede to Madame du Barri and some of her friends the place which belonged to her office at some private theatricals which were held in the palace.

Louis XIV. had taught his nobles the pernicious notion that an order to withdraw from the court was a penal banishment, and his successor now banished Madame de Grammont fourteen leagues from Versailles, and for some time refused to recall his sentence, though Marie Antoinette herself wrote to him to complain of one of her servants being so treated for such a cause. She had not, as she reported to her mother, been very willing to write, knowing that Madame du Barri read all the king's letters; but Mercy had urged her to take the step, thinking it very important that she should establish the practice of communicating directly with Louis on all matters relating to her own household, and that she should avoid the blunder of his daughters, her aunts, whose conduct toward their father had, in his opinion, been mischievously timid, and to follow whose example would be prejudicial both to her dignity and to her comfort.

The aunts too, and especially the eldest, Madame Adelaide, had schemes of their own, which, they also sought to carry out by underhand methods. The more conscious they were that they themselves had no influence over their father, the less could they endure the chance of their niece acquiring any, though it could not have been said to have been established at their expense. On the other hand, they had before his marriage had considerable power with the dauphin, which they had now but little hope of retaining. They saw also that Marie Antoinette had in a few weeks gained a general popularity such as they had never won in their whole lives, and on all these accounts they were painfully jealous of her. They put ideas and plans into her head which they expected to grate upon their father's taste or indolence, and then contrived to have them represented or misrepresented to him, though he disappointed their malice by regarding such things as childish ebullitions natural to a girl of her age, and was far more inclined to humor than to reprove her. With the same object, they tried to induce her to interfere in appointments in which she had no concern; but she remembered her mother's advice, and on this point kept steadily in the path which that affectionate adviser had marked out for her. They even ventured to make disparaging observations on her manners, as inexperienced and unformed, to the dauphin himself, till he silenced them by the warmth of his praises alike of her beauty and of her disposition; and they were so afraid of any addition to her popularity with the nation at large, that, when the city of Paris and the states of Languedoc presented her with an address, they recommended her to make no reply, assuring her that on similar occasions they themselves had never given any answers. Luckily, she had a better adviser, who on this occasion was the Abbe de Vermond. He told her truly that in this matter the conduct which the older princesses had pursued was a warning, not a pattern: that they had made all France discontented; and at his suggestion Marie Antoinette gave to each address "an answer full of graciousness, with which the public was enchanted."

Thus in the first year of her marriage, by her kindness of heart, guided by the advice of Mercy and the abbe, to which she listened with the greatest docility, she had won general affection, and had made no enemies but those whose enmity was an honor. She was, as she wrote to her mother, perfectly happy, though, had she not wished to make the best of matters, she was not, in fact, wholly free from disappointments and vexations, some of which continued for years to cause her uneasiness and anxiety, though others were comparatively trivial or temporary, while one was of an almost comical nature.

She had conceived a great desire to learn to ride. Her mother had been a great horsewoman; and, as the dauphin, like the king, was passionately addicted to hunting, which hitherto she had only witnessed from a carriage, Marie Antoinette not unnaturally desired to be mistress of an accomplishment which would enable her to give him more of her companionship. Unluckily Mercy disapproved of the idea. It is impossible to read his correspondence with the empress, and in subsequent years with Marie Antoinette herself, without being forcibly impressed with respect for his consummate prudence, his sound judgment in matters of public policy, and his unswerving fidelity to the interests of both mother and daughter. But at the same time it is difficult to avoid seeing that he was too little inclined to make allowance for the youthful eagerness for amusements which was natural to her age, and that at times he carried his supervision into matters on which his statesman-like experience and sagacity had hardly qualified him to form an opinion. He was proud of his princess's beauty; and, considering himself in charge of her figure as well as of her conduct, he had made himself very uneasy by the fancied discovery that she was becoming crooked. He was sure that one shoulder was growing higher than the other; he earnestly recommended stays, and was very much displeased with her aunts for setting her against them, because they were not fashionable in Paris. And when the horse exercise was proposed, he set his face against it; he wrote to Maria Teresa, who agreed with him in thinking it ruinous to the complexion, injurious to the shape, and not to be safely indulged in under thirty years of age[8]; and, lest distance should weaken the authority of the empress, he enlisted Madame de Noailles and Choiseul on his side, and Choiseul persuaded the king that it was a very objectionable pastime for a young bride.

There was not as yet the slightest prospect of the dauphiness becoming a mother (a circumstance which was, in fact, the most serious of her vexations, and that which lasted longest): but the king on this point agreed with his minister, and after some discussion a compromise was hit upon, and it was decided that she might ride a donkey. The whole country was immediately ransacked for a stud of quiet donkeys.[9] In September the court moved to Compiegne, and day after day, while the king and the dauphin were shooting in one part of the woods, on the other side a cavalcade of donkey-riders, the aunts and the king's brothers all swelling Marie Antoinette's train, trotted up and down the glades, and sought out shady spots for rural luncheons out-of-doors; and, though even this pastime was occasionally found liable to as much danger as an expedition on nobler steeds, the merry dauphiness contrived to extract amusement for herself and her followers from her very disasters. It was long a standing joke that on one occasion, when her donkey and herself came down in a soft place, her royal highness, before she would allow her attendants to extricate her from the mud, bid them go to Madame de Noailles, and ask her what the rules of etiquette prescribed when a dauphiness of France failed to keep her seat upon a donkey.

She had also another annoyance which was even of a less royal character than being doomed to ride on a donkey. She had absolutely no pocket-money. For many generations the princes of the country had been accustomed to dip their hands so unrestrainedly into the national treasury, that their legitimate appointments had been fixed on a very moderate, if not scanty, scale; so that any one who, like the dauphin and dauphiness, might be scrupulous not to exceed their income (though that scruple had probably affected no one before) could not fail to be greatly straitened. The allowance of Marie Antoinette was fixed at no higher amount than six thousand francs a month; and of this small sum, according to a report which, in the course of the autumn, Mercy made to the empress, not a single crown really reached the princess for her private use.[10] Nearly half of the money was stopped to pay some pensions granted Marie Leczinska, with which the dauphiness could by no possibility have the slightest concern. Almost as much more was intrusted to the gentlemen of her chamber for the expenses of the play table, at which she was expected to preside, since there was no queen to discharge that duty; and whether her royal highness's cards won or lost, the money equally disappeared,[11] and the remainder was distributed in presents to her ladies, at the discretion of Madame de Noailles. Had not Maria Teresa, when she first quit Vienna, intrusted Mercy with a thousand pounds for her use, and had she not herself been singularly economical in her ideas, she would have been in the humiliating position of being unable to provide for her own most ordinary wants, and, a matter about which she was even more anxious, for her constant charities. Yet so inveterate was the mismanagement in both the court and the government, that it was some time before Mercy could succeed, by the strongest remonstrances supported by clear proofs of the real situation of her royal highness, in getting her affairs and her resources placed upon a proper footing.

In spite of all the efforts of the cabal, the king's regard for her increased daily. He had not for many years been used to being treated with respect, and she, not from any artfulness, but from her native propriety of feeling, which forbade her ever to forget that he was her husband's grandfather and her king, united a tone of the most loyal respect with her filial caresses. She called him papa, and even paid him the tacit compliment of grounding occasional requests on considerations of humanity and justice, little as such motives had ever influenced Louis, and rarely as their names had of late been heard in the precincts of the palace. She even induced him to pardon Madame de Grammont; insisting on such a concession as due to herself, when she demanded it for one of her own retinue, till he laughed, and replied, "Madame, your orders shall be executed." And the steadiness she thus showed in protecting her own servants won her many hearts among the courtiers, at the same time that it filled her aunts with astonishment, who, while commending her firmness, could not avoid adding that "it was easy to see that she did not belong to their race.[12]" And how strong as well as how general was of respect and good-will which she had thus diffused was seen in a remarkable manner at some of the private theatricals, which were a frequent diversion of the king, when the actor, at the end of one of his songs, introduced some verses which he had composed in her honor, and the whole body of courtiers who were present showed their approbation by a vehement clapping of their hands, in defiance of a standing order of the court, which prohibited any such demonstrations being made in the sovereign's presence.[13]

It, however, more than counterbalanced these triumphs that, before the end of the year, the cabal of the mistress succeeded in procuring the dismissal of the Choiseul, and the appointment of the Duc d'Aiguillon as minister. For Choiseul had been not only a faithful, but a most judicious, friend to her. If others showed too often that they regarded her as a foreigner, he only remembered it as a reason for giving her hints as to the feelings of the nation or of individuals which a native would not have required. And she thankfully acknowledged that his suggestions had always been both kind and useful, and expressed her sense of her obligations to him, and her concern at his dismissal to her mother, who fully shared her feelings on the subject.

And, encouraged by this victory over her most powerful adherent, the cabal began to venture to attack Marie Antoinette herself. They surrounded her with spies; they even spread a report that Louis had begun to see through and to distrust her, in the hope that, when it should reach the king's own ears, it might perhaps lay the foundation of the alienation which it pretended to assert; and they grew the bolder because the king's next brother was about to be married to a Savoyard princess, of whose favor De la Vauguyon flattered himself that he was already assured. Under these circumstances Marie Antoinette behaved with consummate prudence, as far at least as her enemies were concerned. She despised the efforts made to lower her in the general estimation so completely that she seemed wholly unconscious of them. She did not even allow herself to be provoked into treating the authors of the calumnies with additional coldness; but gave no handle to any of them to complain of her, so that the critical and anxious eyes of Mercy himself found nothing to wish altered in her conduct toward them.[14] And throughout the winter she pursued the even tenor of her way, making herself chiefly remarkable by almost countless acts of charity, which she dispensed with such judgment as showed that they proceeded, not from a heedless disregard of money, but from a thoughtful and vigilant kindness, which did not think the feelings any more than the necessities of the poor beneath her notice.

Circumstances to which she contributed only indirectly enhanced her popularity and weakened the effects of the mistress's hostility. Versailles had not been so gay for many winters, and the votaries of mere amusement, always a strong party at every court, rejoiced at the addition to the royal family to whom the gayety was owing. Louis roused himself to gratify the young princess, who enlivened his place with the first respectable pleasures which it or he had known for years. When he saw that she liked dramatic performances, he opened the private theatre of the palace twice a week. Because she was fond of dancing, he encouraged her to have a weekly ball in her own apartments, at which she herself was the principal attraction, not solely by the elegance of her every movement, but still more by the graciousness with which she received and treated her guests, having a kind smile and an affable word for all, apparently forgetting her rank in the frankness of her condescension, yet at the same time bearing herself with an innate dignity which prevented the most forward from presuming on her kindness or venturing on any undue familiarity.[15]

The winter of 1770 was one of unusual severity; and she found resources for a further enlivenment of the court in the frost itself. Sledging on the snow was an habitual pastime at Vienna, where the cold is more severe than at Paris; nor in former years had sledges been wholly unknown in the Bois de Boulogne. And now Marie Antoinette, whose hardy habits made exercise in the fresh air almost a necessity for her, had sledges built for herself and her attendants; and the inhabitants of Versailles and the neighborhood, as fond of novelty as all their countrymen, were delighted at the merry sledging-parties which, as long as the snow lasted, explored the surrounding country, while the woods rang with the horses' bells, and, almost as loudly and still more cheerfully, with the laughter of the company.

Her liveliness had, as it were, given a new tone to the whole court; and though the dauphin held out longer against the genial influence of his wife's disposition than most people, it at last in some degree thawed even his frigidity. She ascribed his apathy and apparent dislike to female society rather to the neglect or malice of his early tutors than to any natural defect of capacity or perversity of disposition; and often lectured him on his deficiencies, and even on some of his favorite pursuits, which she looked upon as contributing to strengthen his shyness with ladies. She was not unacquainted with English literature, in which the rusticity and coarseness of the fox-hunting squires formed a piquant subject for the mirth of dramatists and novelists; and if Squire Western had been the type of sportsmen in all countries, she could not have inveighed more vigorously than she did against her husband's addiction to hunting. One evening, when he did not return from the field till the play in the theatre was half over, she not only frowned upon him all the rest of the entertainment, but when, after the company had retired, he began to enter into an explanation of the cause of his delay, a scene ensued which it will be best to give in the very words of Mercy's report to the empress.

"The dauphiness made him a short but very energetic sermon, in which she represented to him with vivacity all the evils of the uncivilized kind of life he was leading. She showed him that no one of his attendants could stand that kind of life, and that they would like it the less that his own air and rude manners made no amends to those who were attached to his train; and that, by following this plan of life, he would end by ruining his health and making himself detested. The dauphin received this lecture with gentleness and submission, confessed that he was wrong, promised to amend, and formally begged her pardon. This circumstance is certainly very remarkable, and the more so because the next day people observed that he paid the dauphiness much more attention, and behaved toward her with a much more lively affection than usual.[16]"

We do not, however, find in reality that the severity of her admonitions produced any permanent diminution of his fondness for hunting and shooting; but the gentleness of her general manners, and the delight which he saw that all around her took in her graciousness, so far excited his admiration that he began to follow her example. He said that "she had such native grace that every thing which she did succeeded to perfection; that it must be admitted that she was charming." And before the end of the winter he had come to take an active part both in her Monday balls, and in those which her ladies occasionally gave in her honor; "dancing himself the whole of the evening, and conversing with all the company with an air of cheerfulness and good-nature of which no one before had ever thought him capable.[17]" The happy change in his demeanor was universally attributed to the dauphiness; and, as the character of their future king was naturally watched with anxiety as a matter of the highest importance, it greatly increased the attachment of all who had the welfare of the nation at heart to the princess, whose general example had produced so beneficial an effect.

CHAPTER V.

Marie Antoinette was not a very zealous or copious letter-writer. Her only correspondent In her earlier years was her mother, and even to her her letters are less effusive and less full of details than might have been expected, one reason for their brevity arising out of the intrigues of the court, since she had cause to believe herself so watched and spied upon that her very desk was not safe; and, consequently, she never ventured to begin a letter to the empress before the morning on which it was to be sent, lest it should be read by those for whose eyes it was not intended. For our knowledge, therefore, of her acts and feelings at this period of her life, we still have to rely principally on Mercy's correspondence, which is, however, a sufficiently trustworthy guide, so accurate was his information, and so entire the frankness with which she opened herself to him on all occasions and on all subjects.

The spring of 1771 opened very unfavorably for the new administration; omens of impending dangers were to be seen on all sides. Ten or twelve years before, Goldsmith, whose occasional silliness of manner prevented him from always obtaining the attention to which his sagacity entitled him, had named the growing audacity of the French parliaments as not only an indication of the approach of great changes in that country, but as likely also to be their moving cause.[1] And they had recently shown such determined resistance to the royal authority, that, though in the most conspicuous instance of it, their assertion of their right to pronounce an independent judgment on the charges brought against the Duc d'Aiguillon, they were unquestionably in the right; and though their pretensions were supported by almost the whole body of the princes of the blood, some of whom were immediately banished for their contumacy, Louis had been persuaded to abolish them altogether. And Marie Antoinette, though she carefully avoided mixing herself up with politics, was, as she reported to her mother,[2] astonished beyond measure at their conduct, which she looked upon as arising out of the grossest disloyalty, and which certainly indicated the existence of a feeling very dangerous to the maintenance of the royal authority on the part of those very men who were most bound to uphold it. There was also great and general distress. For a moment in the autumn it had been relieved by a fall in the price of bread, which the unreasoning gratitude of the populace had attributed to the benevolence of the dauphiness; but the severity of the winter had brought it back with aggravated intensity till it reached even to the palace, and compelled a curtailment of some of the festivities with which it had been intended to celebrate the marriage of the Count de Provence, which was fixed for the approaching May.

Distress is the sure parent of discontent, unless the people have a very complete confidence in their government. And this was so far from being the case in France at this time, that the distrust of and contempt for those in the highest places increased daily more and more. The influence which Madame du Barri exerted over the king became more rooted as he became more used to submit to it, and more notorious as he grew more shameless in his avowal of it. She felt her power, and her intrigues became in the same proportion more busy and more diversified in their objects. In the vigorous description of Mercy, Versailles was wholly occupied by treachery, hatred, and vengeance; not one feeling of honesty or decency remained; while the people, ever quick-witted to perceive the vices of their rulers, especially when they are indulged at their expense, revenged themselves by bitter and seditious language, and by satires and pasquinades in which neither respect nor mercy was shown even to the sacred person of the sovereign himself. He was callous to all marks of contempt displayed for himself; but was, or was induced to profess himself, deeply annoyed at the conduct of the dauphin, who showed a fixed aversion for the mistress, which, however, his grandfather did not regard as dictated by his own feelings. Louis rather believed that it was fostered by Marie Antoinette, and that she, in encouraging her husband, was but following the advice of her aunts; and he threatened to remonstrate with the dauphiness on the subject, though, as Mercy correctly divined, he could not nerve himself to the necessary resolution.

It was true that Marie Antoinette did often allow herself to be far too much influenced by those princesses. She confessed to Mercy that she was afraid to displease or thwart them; a feeling which he regarded as the more unfortunate because, when she was not actuated by that consideration, her own judgment and her own impulses would always guide her aright; and because, too, the elder princesses were the most unsafe of all advisers. They were notoriously jealous of one another, and each at times tried to inspire her niece with her feelings toward the other two; and they often, without meaning it, played into the hands of the mistress's cabal, intriguing for selfish objects of their own with as much malice and meanness as could be practiced by Madame du Barri herself.

Still, in spite of these drawbacks, it was almost inevitable that they should have great influence over their niece. Their experience might well be presumed by her to have given them a correct insight into the ways of the court, and the best mode of behaving to their own father; and she, a foreigner and almost a child, was not only in need of counsel and guidance, but had no one else of her own sex to whom she could so naturally look for information or advice. They were, as she explained to Mercy, her only society; and, though she was too clear-sighted not to see their faults, and not at times to be aware that she was suffering from their perverseness, she, like other people, was often compelled to tolerate what she could not mend, and to shut her eyes to disagreeable qualities when forced to live on terms of intimacy with the possessors.

On this point Maria Teresa was, perhaps, hardly inclined to make sufficient allowance for her difficulties, and insisted over and over again on the mischief which would arise to her from the habit of surrendering her judgment to these princesses. She told her that, though far from being devoid of virtues and real merit, "they had never succeeded in making themselves loved or esteemed by either their father or the public;[3]" and she added other admonitions which, as they were avowedly suggested by reports that had reached her, may be taken as indicating some errors into which her daughter's lightness of heart had occasionally betrayed her. She entreated her not to show an exclusive preference for the more youthful portion of her society, to the neglect of those who were older, and commonly of higher consideration; never to laugh at people or turn them into ridicule--no habit could be more injurious to herself, and indulgence in it would give reason to doubt her good-nature; it might gain her the applause of a few young people, but it would alienate a much greater number, and those the people of the most real weight and respectability. "This is not," said the experienced and wise empress, "a trivial matter in a princess. We live on the stage of the great world, and it is above all things essential that people should entertain a high idea of us. If you will only not allow others to lead you astray, you are sure of success; a kind Providence has endowed you so liberally with beauty, and with so many charms, that all hearts are yours if you are but prudent.[4]"

The empress would have had her exhibit this prudence in her conduct also to Madame du Barri. She pressed upon her that she was justified in appearing ignorant of that lady's real position and character; that she need only be aware that she was received at court, and that respect for the king should prevent her from suspecting him of countenancing undeserving people.

One other detail in the accounts of Marie Antoinette's conduct, which from time to time reached Vienna, had also vexed the empress, and it should be kept in mind by any one who would fairly estimate the truth of the charge brought against her, and urged with such rancor after she had become queen--of postponing the interests of France to those of her native land, of being Austrian at heart. Maria Teresa had heard, on the contrary, that she had given those Austrians who had presented themselves at Versailles but a cold reception, and she did not attempt to conceal her discontent. With a natural and becoming pride in and jealousy for her own loyal and devoted subjects, she entreated her daughter never to feel ashamed of them, or ashamed of being German herself, even if, comparatively speaking, the name should imply some deficiency in polish. "The French themselves would esteem her more if they saw in her something of German solidity and frankness.[5]"

The daughter answered the mother with some adroitness. She took no notice of the advice about her behavior to Madame du Barri. It was the one topic on which her own feelings of propriety, as well as those of the dauphin, coincided with the suggestions of the aunts, and she did not desire to vex or provoke the empress by a prolonged discussion of the question; but the charge of coldness to her own countrymen she denied earnestly. "She should always glory in being a German. Some of those nobles whom the empress had expressly named she had treated with careful distinction, and had even danced with them, though they were not men of the very highest character. She well knew that the Germans had many good qualities which she could wish that the French shared with them;" and she promised that, whenever any of her mother's subjects of such standing and merit as to be worthy of her attention came to the court, they should have no cause to complain of her reception of them. Her language on the subject is so measured and careful as to lead us almost inevitably to the inference that the reports which had excited such dissatisfaction at Vienna were not without foundation, but that the French gayety, even if often descending to frivolity, was more to her taste than the German solidity which her mother so highly esteemed, and that she had been at no great pains to hide a preference which must naturally he acceptable to those among whom her future life was to be spent.

In the middle of May, the Count de Provence was married to the Princess Josephine Louise of Savoy, and the court went to Fontainebleau to receive the bride. The necessity for leaving Madame du Barri behind threw the king more into the company of the dauphiness than he had been on any previous occasion, and her unaffected graces seemed for the moment to have made a complete conquest of him. He came in his dressing-gown to her apartments for breakfast, and spent a great portion of the day there. The courtiers again began to speculate on her breaking down the ascendency of the favorite, remarking that, though Louis was careful to pay his new relative the honors which, were her due as a stranger and a bride, he returned as speedily as he could with decency to the dauphiness as if for relief; and that, though she herself took care to put her new sister-in-law forward on all occasions, and treated her with the most marked cordiality and affection, every one else made the dauphiness the principal object of homage even in the festivities which were celebrated in honor of the countess. Indeed, it was evident from the very first that any attempt of the mistress's cabal to establish a rivalry between the two princesses must be out of the question. The Countess de Provence had no beauty, nor accomplishments, nor graciousness. Horace Walpole, who was meditating a visit to Paris, where he had some diligent correspondents, was told that he would lose his senses when he saw the dauphiness, but would be disenchanted by her sister; and the saying, though that of a blind old lady, expressed the opinion of all Frenchmen who could see.[6]

Indeed, so obvious was the king's partiality for her that even Madame du Barri more than once sought to propitiate her by speaking in praise of her to Mercy, and professing an eager desire to aid in procuring the gratification of any of her wishes. But he was too shrewd and too well-informed to place the least confidence in her sincerity, though he did not fear half as much harm to his pupil from her enmity as from the pretended affection of the aunts, who, from a mixture of folly and treachery, were unwearied in their attempts to keep her at a distance from the king, by inspiring her with a fear of him, for which his disposition, which had as much good-nature in it as was compatible with weakness, gave no ground whatever. Indeed, the mischief they did was not confined to their influence over her, if Mercy was correct in his belief that it was their disagreeable tempers and manners which at this time, and for the remainder of the reign, prevented Louis from associating more with his family, which, had all been like the dauphiness, he would have preferred to do.

It would probably have been in vain that Mercy remonstrated against her submitting as she did to the aunts, had he not been at all times able to secure the co-operation of the empress, who placed the most implicit confidence in his judgment in all matters relating to the French court, and remonstrated with her daughter energetically on the want of proper self-respect which was implied in her surrendering her own judgment to that of the aunts, as if she were a slave or a child. And Marie Antoinette replied to her mother in a tone of such mingled submissiveness and affection as showed how sincere was her desire to remove every shade of annoyance from the empress's mind; and which may, perhaps, lead to a suspicion that even her subservience to the aunts proceeded in a great degree from her anxiety to win the good-will of every one, and from the kindness which could not endure to thwart those with whom she was much associated; though at the same time she complained to the ambassador that her mother wrote without sufficient knowledge of the difficulties with which she was surrounded. But she had too deep an affection and reverence for her mother to allow her words to fall to the ground; and gradually Mercy began to see a difference in her conduct, and a greater inclination to assert her own independence, which was the feeling that above all others he thought most desirable to foster in her.

Another topic which we find constantly urged in the empress's letters would seem strangely inconsistent with Marie Antoinette's position, if we did not remember how very young she still was. For her mother writes to her in many respects as if she were still at school, and continually inculcates on her the necessity of profiting by De Vermond's instructions, and applying herself to a course of solid reading in theology and history. And here, though her natural appetite for amusement interfered with her studies somewhat more than the empress, prompted by Mercy, was willing to make allowance for, she profited much more willingly by her mother's advice, having indeed a natural inclination for the works of history and biography, and a decided distaste for novels and romances. She could not have had a better guide in such matters than De Vermond, who was a man of extensive information and of a very correct taste; and under his guidance and with his assistance she studied Sully's memoirs, Madame de Sevigne's letters, and any other books which he recommended to her, and which gave her an idea of the past history of the country as well as the masterpieces of the great French dramatists.[7]

The latter part of the year 1771 was marked by no very striking occurrences. Marie Antoinette had carried her point, and had begun to ride on horseback without either her figure or her complexion suffering from the exercise. On the contrary, she was admitted to have improved in beauty. She sent her measure to Vienna, to show Maria Teresa how much she had grown, adding that her husband had grown as much, and had become stronger and more healthy-looking, and that she had made use of her saddle-horses to accompany him in his hunting and shooting excursions. Like a true wife, she boasted to her mother of his skill as a shot: the very day that she wrote he had killed forty head of game. (She did not mention that a French sportsman's bag was not confined to the larger game, but that thrushes, blackbirds, and even, red-breasts, were admitted to swell the list.) And the increased facilities for companionship with him that her riding afforded increased his tenderness for her, so that she was happier than ever. Except that as yet she saw no prospect of presenting the empress with a grandchild, she had hardly a wish ungratified.

Her taste for open-air exercise of this kind added also to the attachment felt for her by the lower classes, from the opportunities which arose out of it for showing her unvarying and considerate kindness. The contrast which her conduct afforded to that of previous princes, and indeed to that of all the present race except her husband, caused her actions of this sort to be estimated rather above their real importance. But how great was the impression which they did make on those who witnessed them may be seen in the unanimity with which the chroniclers of the time record her forbidding her postilions to drive over a field of corn which lay between her and the stag, because she would rather miss the sight of the chase than injure the farmer; and relate how, on one occasion, she gave up riding for a week or two, and sent her horses back from Compiegne to Versailles, because the wife of her head-groom was on the point of her confinement, and she wished her to have her husband near her at such a moment; and on another, when the horse of one of her attendants kicked her, and inflicted a severe bruise on her foot, she abstained from mentioning the hurt, lest it should bring the rider into disgrace by being attributed to his awkward management.

Not that the intrigues of the mistress and her adherents were at all diminished. They were even more active than ever since the marriage of the Count de Provence, who, in an underhanded way, instigated his wife to show countenance to Madame du Barri, and who allowed, if he did not encourage, the mistress and her friends to speak slightingly of the dauphiness in his presence. But, as Marie Antoinette felt firmer in her own position, she could afford to disregard the malice of these caballers more than she had felt that she could do at first, and even to defy them. On one occasion that the Count de Provence was imprudent enough to discuss some of his schemes with the door open while she was in the next room, she told him frankly that she had heard all that he said, and reproached him for his duplicity; and the dauphin coming in at the moment, she flew to him, throwing her arms round his neck, and telling him how she appreciated his honesty and candor, and how the more she compared him with the others, the more she saw his superiority. Indeed, she soon began to find that the Countess de Provence was as little to be trusted as her husband; and the only member of the family whom she really liked, or of whom she had at all a favorable opinion, was the Count d'Artois, who, though not yet out of the school-room, "showed," as she told her mother, "sentiments of honesty which he could never have learned of his governor.[8]"

Her indefatigable guardian, Mercy, reported to the empress that she improved every day. He had learned to conceive a very high idea of her abilities; and he dilated with especial satisfaction on the powers of conversation which she was developing; on her wit and readiness in repartee; on her originality, as well as facility of expression; and on her perfect possession of the royal art of speaking to a whole company with such notice of each member of it, that each thought himself the person to whom her remarks were principally addressed. She possessed another accomplishment, also, of great value to princes--a tenacious recollection of faces and names. And she had made herself acquainted with the history of all the chief nobles, so as to be able to make graceful allusions to facts in their family annals of which they were proud, and, what was perhaps even more important, to avoid unpleasant or dangerous topics. The king himself was not insensible to the increase of attraction which her charms, both of person and manner, conferred on the royal palace. He was perfectly satisfied with the civility of her behavior to Madame du Barri, who admitted that she had nothing to complain of. And the only point in which even Mercy, the most critical of judges, saw any room for alteration in her conduct was a certain remissness in bestowing her notice on men of real eminence, and on foreign visitors if they were not of the very highest rank; the remark as to the latter class being perhaps dictated by a somewhat excessive natural susceptibility, and by a laudable desire that any Germans who returned from France to their own country should sing her praises in her native land.

Perhaps one of the strongest proofs of the regard in which, at this time, she was held by all parties in the court is found in the circumstance that the Count de Provence himself very soon found it impossible to continue his countenance to the intrigues against her which he had previously favored. He preferred ingratiating himself and the countess with her. Marie Antoinette was always placable, and from the first had been eager, as the head of the family, to place her sister-in-law at her ease; so that when the count evinced his desire to stand on a friendly footing with her, she showed every disposition to meet his wishes, and the spring and summer of 1772 exhibited to the courtiers, who were little accustomed to such scenes, a happy example of an intimate family union. Marie Antoinette had always been fond of music, and, as we have seen before, ever since her arrival in France, had devoted fixed hours to her music-master. And now, on almost every evening which was not otherwise preoccupied, she gave little concerts in her apartments to the royal family, their principal attendants, and a few of the chief nobles of the court; being herself occasionally one of the performers, and maintaining her character as a hostess by a combined affability and dignity which made all her guests pleased with themselves as with her, and set all imitation and all detraction alike at defiance.

CHAPTER VI.

It was a curious proof of the mischievousness as well as of the extent of the
influence which Madame Adelaide and her sister were able to exert over the
indolence and apathy of their father, that when Marie Antoinette had for
more than two years been married and living within twelve miles of Paris, she
had never yet seen it by daylight, although the universal and natural expectation of
the citizens had been that the royal pair would pay the city a state visit immediately
after their marriage. Her own wishes had not been consulted in the matter; for she
was naturally anxious to see the beautiful city of which she had heard so much;
and the delay which had taken place was equally at variance with Madame de Noailles' notions of propriety. But when the countess suggested a plan for visiting the
capital *incognito*, proposing that the dauphiness should drive as far as the entrance
to the suburbs, and then, having sent on her saddle-horses, should ride along the
boulevards, Madame Adelaide, professing a desire to join the party, raised so many
difficulties on the subject of the retinue which was to follow, and was so successful in creating jealousies between her own ladies and those in attendance on Marie
Antoinette, that Madame de Noailles was forced to recommend the abandonment

of the project. Mercy was far more annoyed than his young mistress; he saw that the secret object of Madame Adelaide was to throw as many hindrance as possible in the way of the dauphiness winning popularity by appearing in public, while he also correctly judged hat it would be consistent both with propriety and with her interest, as the future queen of the country, rather to seek and even make opportunities for enabling the people to become acquainted with her. But to Marie Antoinette any disappointment of that kind was a very trifling matter. She had vexations which, as she told the embassador, she could not explain even to him; and they kept alive in her a feeling of homesickness which, in all persons of amiable and affectionate disposition, must require some, time to subdue. Even when her brother, the Archduke Ferdinand, had quit Vienna in the preceding autumn to enter on the honorable post of Governor of Lombardy, she had not congratulated, but condoled with him, "feeling by her own experience how much it costs to be separated from one's family." And what she had found in her own home did not as yet make up to her for all she had left behind. Even her husband, though uniformly kind in language and behavior, was of a singularly cold and undemonstrative disposition; and it almost seemed as if the gayety which he exhibited at her balls were an effort so foreign to his nature that he indemnified himself by unpardonable boorishness on other occasions. The Count de Provence had but little more polish, and a far worse temper. Squabbles often took place between the two brothers. Though both married men, they were still in age only boys; and on more than one occasion they proceeded to acts of personal violence to each other in her presence. Luckily no one else was by, and she was able to pacify and reconcile them; but she could hardly avoid feeling ashamed of having been called on to exert herself in such a cause, or contrasting the undignified boisterousness (to give it no worse name) of such scenes with the decorous self-respect which, with all their simplicity of character, had always governed the conduct of her own relations.

Not but that, in the opinion of Mercy,[1] the dauphin was endowed by nature with a more than ordinary share of good qualities. His faults were only such as proceeded from an excessively bad education. He had many most essential virtues. He was a young man of perfect integrity and straightforwardness; he was desirous to hear the truth; and it was never necessary to beat about the bush, or to have recourse to roundabout ways of bringing it before him. On the contrary, to speak to him with perfect frankness was the surest way both to win his esteem and to convince his reason. On one or two occasions in which he had consulted the embassador, Mercy had expressed his opinions without the least reserve, and had perceived that the young prince had liked him better for his candor.

The king still kept up the habit of spending the greater part of the autumn at Compiegne and Fontainebleau, visits which Marie Antoinette welcomed as a holiday from the etiquette of Versailles. She wrote word to her mother that she was growing very fast, and taking asses' milk to keep up her strength; that that regimen, with constant exercise, was doing her great good; and that she had gained great praise for the excellence of her riding. On one occasion, when they were at Fontainebleau, she especially delighted the officers of her husband's regiment of cuirassiers, when the king reviewed it in person. The dauphin himself took the command of his men, and put them through their evolutions while she rode by his side; he then presented each of the officers to her separately, and she distributed cockades to the whole body. The first she gave to the dauphin himself,[2] who placed it in his hat. Each officer, as he received his, did the same. And after the king had taken his departure, she, with her husband, remained on the field for an hour, conversing freely with the soldiers, and showing the greatest interest in all that concerned the regiment. Throughout the day the young prince had exhibited a knowledge of the profession, and a readiness as well as an ease of manner, which had surprised all the spectators, and Mercy had the satisfaction of hearing every one attribute the admirable appearance which he had made on so important an occasion (for it was the first time of his appearing in such a position) to the example and hints of the dauphiness.

It was scarcely less of a public appearance, while it was one in which the king himself probably took more interest, when, a few days afterward, on the occasion of a grand stag-hunt in the forest, she joined in the chase in a hunting uniform of her own devising. The king was so delighted that he scarcely left her side, and extolled her taste in dress, as well as her skill in horsemanship, to all whom he honored with his conversation. But the empress was not quite so well pleased. Her disapproval of horse exercise for young married women was as strong as ever. She had also interpreted some of her daughter's submissive replies to her admonitions on the subject as a promise that she would not ride, and she scolded her severely (no weaker word can express the asperity of her language) for neglect of her engagement, as well as for the risk of accidents which are incurred by those who follow the hounds, and some of which, as she heard, had befallen the dauphiness herself. Her daughter's explanation was as frank as it deserved to be accounted sufficient, while her letter is interesting also, as showing her constant eagerness to exculpate herself from the charge of indifference to her German countrymen, an eagerness which proves how firmly she believed the notion to be fixed in the empress's mind.

"I expect, my dear mamma, that people must have told you more about my rides than there really was to be told. I will tell you the exact truth. The king and the dauphin both like to see me on horseback. I only say this because all the world perceives it, and especially while we were absent from Versailles they were delighted to see me in my riding-habit. But, though I own it was no great effort for me to conform myself to their desires, I can assure you that I never once let myself he carried away by too much eagerness to keep close to the hounds; and I hope that, in spite of all my giddiness, I shall always allow myself to be restrained by the experienced hunters who constantly accompany me, and I shall never thrust myself into the crowd. I should never have supposed any one could have reported to you as an accident what happened to me in Fontainebleau. Every now and then one finds in the forest large stepping stones; and as we were going on very gently my horse stumbled on one covered with sand, which he did not see; but I easily held him up, and we went on…. Esterhazy was at our ball yesterday. Every one was greatly pleased with his dignified manner and with his style of dancing. I ought to have spoken to him when he was presented to me, and my silence only proceeded from embarrassment, as I did not know him. It would be doing me great injustice to think that I have any feeling of indifference to my country; I have more reason than any one to feel, every day of my life, the value of the blood which flows in my veins, and it is only from prudence that at times I abstain from showing how proud I am of it…. I never neglect any mode of paying attention to the king, and of anticipating his wishes as far as I can. I hope that he is pleased with me. It is my duty to please him, my duty and also my glory, if by such means I can contribute to maintain the alliance of the two houses….[3]"

The empress was but half pacified about the riding and hunting. She owned that, if both the king and the dauphin approved of it, she had nothing more to say, though she still blamed the dauphiness for forgetting a promise which she understood to have been made to herself. At the same time, no language could be kinder than that in which she asked "whether her daughter could believe that she would wish to deprive her of so innocent a pleasure, she who would give her very life to procure her one, if she were not apprehensive of mischievous consequences;" her apprehensions being solely dictated by her anxiety to see her daughter bear an heir to the throne. But she would by no means admit her excuses for giving the Hungarian prince a cold reception. "How," she said, "could she forget that her little Antoinette, when not above twelve or thirteen years old, knew how to receive people publicly, and say something polite and gracious to every one, and how could she suppose that the same daughter, now that she was dauphiness, could feel embarrassment? Embarrassment was a mere chimera."

But the truth was that it was not a mere chimera. Mercy had more than once deplored, as one among the mischievous effects of Madame Adelaide's constant interference and domineering influence, that it had bred in Marie Antoinette a timidity which was wholly foreign to her nature. And indeed it was hardly possible for one still so young to be aware that she was surrounded by unfriendly intriguers and spies, and to preserve that uniform presence of mind which her rank and position made so desirable for her, and which was in truth so natural to her that she at once recovered it the moment that her circumstances changed.

And a probability of an early change was already apparent. During the last months of 1772 there was a general idea that the king's health and mental faculties were both giving away; and all the different parties about Versailles began to show their sense of her approaching authority. It was remarked that both the ministers and the mistress had become very guarded in their language, and in their behavior to her and her husband. The Count de Provence took a curious way of showing his expectation of a change, by delivering her a long paper of counsels for her guidance, the chief object of which was to warn her against holding such frequent conversations with Mercy. She apparently thought that the writer's desire was to remove the embassador from her confidence that he himself might occupy the vacant place, and she showed her opinion of the value of the advice by reading it to Mercy and then putting it into the fire.

Some extracts from the first letter which she wrote to her mother in 1773 will serve to give us a fair idea of her feelings at this time, both from what it does and from what it does not mention. The intelligence which has reached her about her sister recalls to her mind her own anxiety to become a mother, her disappointment in this matter being, indeed, one of the most constant topics of lamentation in the letters of both daughter and mother, till it was removed by the birth of the princess royal. But that is her only vexation. In every other respect she seems perfectly contented with the course which affairs are taking; while we see how thoroughly unspoiled she is both in the warmth of the affection with which she speaks of her family and greets the little memorials of home which have been sent her; and still more in the continuance of her acts of charity, and in her design that her benevolence should be unknown.

"I hear that the queen[4] is expecting to be confined. I hope her child will be a son. When shall I be able to say the same of myself? They tell me, too, that the grand duke[5] and his wife are going into Spain. I greatly wish that they would conceive a dread of the sea-voyage, and take this place in their way. The journey would be a little longer; but they would be well received here, for my brother is very highly thought of; and, besides, I am somewhat jealous at being the only one of my family unacquainted with my sister-in-law.

"The pictures of my little brothers which you have sent me have given me great pleasure. I have had them set in a ring, and wear it every day. Those who have seen my brothers at Vienna pronounce the pictures very like, and every one thinks them very good-looking. New-year's-day here is a day of a great crowd and grand ceremony. There was nothing either to blame or to praise in the degree in which I adopted my dear mamma's advice. The Favorite came to pay her respects to me at a moment when my apartment was very full It was impossible for me to address myself to every one separately, so I spoke to the whole company in a body; and I have reason to believe that both the Favorite and her sister, who is her principal adviser, were pleased; though I have also reason to believe that, two days afterward, M. d'Aiguillon tried to persuade them that they had been ill-treated. As for the minister himself, he has never complained of me, and, indeed, I have always been careful to treat him equally well with the rest of his colleagues.

"You will have learned, my dear mamma, that the Duc d'Orleans and the Duc de Chartres are returned from banishment. I am glad of it for the sake of peace, and for that of the tranquillity and comfort of the king. But, if she had been in the king's place, I do not think my dear mamma would have accepted the letter which they have dared to write, and which they have got printed in foreign newspapers.[6]

"I was glad to see M. de Stormont.[7] I asked him all the news about my dear family, and it was a pleasure to him to inform me. He seems to me to have overcome his prejudices, and every one here thinks him a man of thorough high-breeding. I have desired M. de Mercy to invite him to one of my Monday balls. We are going to have one at, Madame de Noailles'. They will last till Ash-Wednesday. They will begin an hour or two later than they used to, that we may not be so tired as we were last year when we came to Lent In spite of the amusements of the carnival, I am always faithful to my poor harp, and they say that I make great progress with it. I sing, too, every week at the concert given by my sister of Provence. Although there are very few people there, they are very well amused; and my singing gives great pleasure to my two sisters.[8] I also find time to read a little. I have begun the 'History of England' by Mr. Hume. It seems to me very interesting, though it is necessary to recollect that it is a Protestant who has written it.

"All the newspapers have spoken of the terrible fire at the Hotel-Dieu.[9] They were obliged to remove the patients into the cathedral and the archbishop's palace. There are generally from five to six thousand patients in the hospital. In spite of all the exertions that were made, it was impossible to prevent the destruction of a great part of the building; and, though it is now a fortnight since the accident happened, the tire is still smoldering in the cellars. The archbishop has enjoined a collection to be made for the sufferers, and I have sent him a thousand crowns. I said nothing of my having done so to any one, and the compliments which they have paid me on it have been embarrassing to me; but they have said it was right to let it be known that I had sent this money, for the sake of the example."

She was on this, as on many other occasions, one of those who

"Do good by stealth, and blush to find it fame."

One of her sayings, with which she more than once repressed the panegyrics of those who, as it seemed to her, extolled her benevolence too loudly, was that it was not worth while to say a great deal about giving a little assistance; and, on this occasion, so secret had she intended to keep her benevolence that she had not mentioned it to De Vermond, or even to Mercy. But she judged rightly that the empress would enter into the feelings which had prompted both the act and also the silence; and she was amply rewarded by her mother's praise.

"I have been enchanted," the empress wrote, in instant reply, "with the thousand crowns that you have sent to the Hotel-Dieu, and you speak very properly in saying that you have been vexed at people speaking to you about it. Such actions ought to be known to God alone, and I am certain that you acted in that spirit. Still, those who published your act had good reasons for what they did, as you say yourself, thinking of the influence of your example. My dear little girl, we owe this example to the world, and to set such is one of the most essential and most delicate duties of our condition. The more frequently you can perform acts of benevolence and generosity without crippling your means too much, the better; and what would be ostentation and prodigality in another is becoming and necessary for those of our rank. We have no other resources but those of conferring benefits and showing kindness; and this is even more the case with a dauphiness or a queen consort, which I myself have not been."

There could hardly be a better specimen of the principles on which the empress herself had governed her extensive dominions, or of the value of her example and instructions to her daughter, than that which is contained in these few lines; but it is not always that such lessons are so closely followed as they were by the virtuous and beneficent dauphiness. The winter passed on cheerfully; the ordinary amusements of the palace being varied by her going with the dauphin and the Count and Countess of Provence to one of the public masked balls of the opera-house, a diversion which, considering the unavoidably mixed character of the company, it is hard to avoid thinking somewhat unsuited to so august a party, but one which had been too frequently countenanced by different members of the royal family for several years for such a visit to cause remarks, though the masks of the princes and princesses could not long preserve their secret Another favorite amusement of the court at this time was the representation of proverbs, in which Marie Antoinette acted with the little Elizabeth; and we have a special account of one such performance, which was given in her honor by one of her ladies, having been originally devised for the Day of Saint Anthony, as her saint's day,[10] though it was postponed on account of her being confined to her room with a cold. The proverb was, "Better late than never;" and, as the most acceptable compliment to the dauphiness, the managers introduced a number of characters attired in a diversity of costumes, intended to represent the natives of all the countries ruled over by the Empress-queen, each of whom made a speech, in which the praises of Maria Teresa and Marie Antoinette were happily combined.

The king got better, and intrigues of all kinds were revived; but, aided by Mercy's counsels, and supported by the dauphin's unalterable affection, Marie Antoinette disconcerted all that were aimed at her by the uniform prudence of her conduct. Happily for her, with all his defects, her husband was still one in whom she could feel perfect confidence. As she told Mercy, under any conceivable circumstances she was sure of his views and intentions being always right; the only difficulty was to engage him in a sufficiently decided course of action, which his timid and sluggish disposition rendered almost painful to him. And just at this moment she was more anxious than usual to inspire him with her own feelings and spirit, because she could not avoid fearing that the discontent with which the few people in France who deserved the name of statesmen regarded the recent partition of Poland might create a coolness between France and Austria, calculated to endanger the alliance, the continuance of which was so indispensable to her happiness, and, as she was firmly convinced, to the welfare of both countries. She conversed more than once with Mercy on the subject, and her reflections, both on the partition, and on the degree in which the mutual interest of the two nations was concerned in their remaining united, gave him a very good idea of her political capacity. He also reported to his imperial mistress that he had found out that King Louis had conceived the same opinion of her, and had begun to discuss affairs of importance with her. He trusted that his majesty would get a habit of doing so; since, if his life should be spared, she would thus in time become able to exert a very useful influence over him; and as, at all events, "it was absolutely certain that some day or other she would govern the kingdom, it was of the very greatest consequence to the success of the great and brilliant career which she had before her that she should previously accustom herself to regard affairs with such principles and views as were suitable to the position which she must occupy."

CHAPTER VII.

Marie Antoinette is anxious for the Maintenance of the Alliance between France and Austria.--She, with the Dauphin, makes a State Entry into Paris.--The "Dames de la Halle."--She praises the Courtesy of the Dauphin.--Her Delight at the Enthusiasm of the Citizens.--She, with the Dauphin, goes to the Theatre, and to the Fair of St. Ovide, and to St. Cloud.--Is enthusiastically received everywhere.--She learns to drive.-- She makes some Relaxations in Etiquette.--Marriage of the Comte d'Artois. --The King's Health grows Bad.--Visit of Marshal Lacy to Versailles.--The King catches the Small-pox.--Madame du Barri quits Versailles.--The King dies.

Politics were, indeed, taking such a hold over Marie Antoinette that they begin to furnish some topics for her letters to her mother, one of which shows that she had already formed that opinion of French fickleness which she had afterward too abundant cause to maintain. "I do hope," she says, "that the good intelligence between our two nations will last. One good thing in this country is, that if ill-natured feelings are quick to arise, they disappear with equal rapidity. The King of Prussia is innately a bad neighbor, but the English will also always be bad neighbors to France, and the sea has never prevented them from doing her great mischief." We might, firstly, demur to any actions of our statesmen being classed with the treacherous aggressions of Frederick of Prussia, nor did many years of her husband's reign pass over before the greatest of English ministers proposed and concluded a treaty between the two countries, which he fondly and wisely hoped would lay the foundations of a better understanding, if not of a lasting peace, between the two countries. But even before that treaty was framed, and before Pitt's voice had become predominant in the State, Marie Antoinette's complaint that the sea had never disarmed us of power to injure France had received the strongest exemplification that as yet the history of the two nations afforded in Rodney's great victory. However, she soon turns to more agreeable subject, and proceeds to speak of a pleasure to which she was looking forward, and which, as we have already seen, had been unaccountably deferred till this time, in defiance of all propriety and of all precedent. "I hope that the dauphin and I shall make our entry into Paris next month, which will be a great delight to me. I do not venture to speak of it yet, though I have the king's promise: it would not be the first time that they had made him change his mind."

The most elaborate exposure of the cabals and intrigues which ever since her marriage had been persistently directed against Marie Antoinette could not paint them so forcibly as the simple fact that three years had now elapsed since her marriage; and that, though the state entrance of the heir of the crown and his bride into the metropolis of the kingdom ought to have been a prominent part of the marriage festivities, it had never yet taken place. Nor, though Louis had at last given his formal promise that it should be no longer delayed, did the young pair even yet feel sure that an influence superior to theirs might not induce him to recall it. However, at last the intrigues were baffled, and, on the 8th of June, the visit, which had been expected by the Parisians with an eagerness exceeding that of the dauphiness herself, was made. It was in every respect successful; and it is due to Marie Antoinette to let the outline of the proceeding be described by herself.

"Versailles, June 14th.

"MY DEAREST MOTHER,--I absolutely blush for your kindness to me. The day before yesterday Mercy sent me your precious letter, and yesterday I received a second. That is indeed passing one's fete day happily. On Tuesday I had a fete which I shall never forget all my life. We made our entrance into Paris. As for honors, we received all that we could possibly imagine; but they, though very well in their way, were not what touched me most. What was really affecting was the tenderness and earnestness of the poor people, who, in spite of the taxes with which they are overwhelmed, were transported with joy at seeing us. When we went to walk in the Tuileries, there was so vast a crowd that we were three-quarters of an hour without being able to move either forward or backward. The dauphin and I gave repeated orders to the Guards not to beat any one, which had a very good effect. Such excellent order was kept the whole day that, in spite of the enormous crowd which followed us everywhere, not a person was hurt. When we returned from our walk we went up to an open terrace, and staid there half an hour. I can not describe to you, my dear mamma, the transports of joy and affection which every one exhibited toward us. Before we withdrew we kissed our hands to the people, which gave them great pleasure. What a happy, thing it is for persons in our rank to gain the love of a whole nation so cheaply! Yet there is nothing so precious; I felt it thoroughly, and shall never forget it.

"Another circumstance which gave great pleasure on that glorious day was the behavior of the dauphin. He made admirable replies to every address, and remarked every thing that was done in his honor, and especially the earnestness and delight of the people, to whom he showed great kindness. Of all the copies of verses which were given me on this occasion, these are the prettiest which I inclose to you.[1] Tomorrow we are going to Paris to the opera, There is great anxiety for us to do so; and I believe that we shall go on two other days also to visit the French and the Italian comedy. I feel more and more, every day of my life, how much my dear mamma has done for my establishment. I was the youngest of all her daughters, and she has treated me as if I were the eldest; so that my whole soul is filled with the most tender gratitude.

"The king has had the kindness to procure the release of three hundred and twenty prisoners, for debts due to nurses who have brought up their children. Their release took place two days after our entrance. I wished to attend Divine service on my fete day; but the evening before, my sister, the Countess of Provence, had a party for me, a proverb with songs and fire-works, and this distraction forced me to put off going to church till the next day.

"I am very glad to hear that you have such good hope of the continuance of peace. While the intriguers of this country are devouring one another, they will not harass their neighbors nor their allies."

She does not enter into details; the pomp and ceremony of their reception by nobles and magistrates had been in her eyes as nothing in comparison with the cordial welcome given to them by the poorer citizens. While they, on their part, must have been equally gratified at perceiving the sincere pleasure with which she and the dauphin accepted their salutations; a feeling how different from that which had animated any of their princes for many years, we may judge from the order given to the guards to forbear beating the crowd which gathered round them, as no doubt, without such an order, the soldiers would have thought it usual and natural to do.

Not that the proceedings of the day had not been magnificent and imposing enough to attract the admiration of any who thought less of the hearts of the citizens than of pomp and splendor. The royal train, conveyed from Versailles in six state carriages, was received at the city gate by the governor, the Marshal Duc de Brissac, accompanied by the head of the police, the provost of the merchants, and all the other municipal authorities. The marshal himself was the heir of the Comte de Brissac who, nearly two centuries before, being also Governor of Paris, had tendered to the victorious Henry IV. the submission of the city. But Henry was as yet only the chief of a party, not the accepted sovereign of the whole nation; and the enthusiasm with which half the citizens rained their shouts of exultation in his honor had its drawback in the sullen silence of the other half, who regarded the great Bourbon as their conqueror rather than their king, and his triumphant entrance as their defeat and humiliation.

To-day all the citizens were but one party. As but one voice was heard, so but one heart gave utterance to it. The joy was as unanimous as it was loud. From the city gates the royal party passed on to the great national cathedral of Notre Dame, and from thence to the church dedicated by Clovis, the first Christian king, to St. Genevieve, whose recent restoration was the most creditable work of the present reign, and which subsequently, under the new name of the Pantheon, was destined to become the resting-place of many of the worthies whose memory the nation cherishes with enduring pride. At last they reached the Tuileries, their progress having been arrested at different points by deputations of all kinds with loyal and congratulatory addresses; at the Hotel-Dieu by the prioress with a company of nuns; on the Quai Conti by the Provost of the Mint with his officers; before the college bearing the name of its founder, Louis le Grand, the Rector of the University, at the head of his students, greeted them in a Latin speech, at the close of which he secured the re-doubling of the acclamations of the pupils by promising them a holiday. Not that the cheers required any increase. The citizens in their ecstasy did not even think their voices sufficient. As the royal couple moved slowly through the gardens of the Tuileries arm-in-arm, every hand was employed in clapping, hats were thrown up, and every token of joy which enthusiasm ever devised was displayed to the equally delighted visitors. "Good heavens, what a crowd!" said Marie Antoinette to De Brissac, who had some difficulty in keeping his place at her side. "Madame," said the old warrior, as courtly as he was valiant, "if I may say so without offending my lord the dauphin, they are all so many lovers." When they had made the circuit of the garden and returned to the palace, the most curious part of the day's ceremonies awaited them. A banqueting-table was arranged for six hundred guests, and those guests were not the nobles of the nation, nor the clergy, nor the must renowned warriors, nor the municipal officers, but the fish-women of the city market. A custom so old that its origin can not be traced had established the right of these dames to bear an especial part in such festivities. In the course of the morning they had made their future queen free of their market, with an offering of fruits and flowers. And now, as, according to a singular usage of the court, no male subject was ever allowed to sit at table with a queen or dauphiness of France, the dinner party over which the youthful pair, sitting side by side, presided, consisted wholly of these dames whose profession is not generally considered as imparting any great refinement to the manners, and who, before the close of the entertainment, showed, in more cases than one, that they had imported some of the notions and fashions of their more ordinary places of resort into the royal palace.

It was characteristic of Marie Antoinette that, in her description of the day to her mother, she had dwelt with special emphasis on the gracious deportment of her husband. It was equally natural for Mercy to assure the empress[2] that it had been the grace and elegance of the dauphiness herself which had attracted general admiration, and that it was to her example and instruction that every one attributed the courteous demeanor which, as he did not deny, the young prince had unquestionably exhibited. It was she whom the king, as he affirmed, had complimented on the result of the day; a success which she had gracefully attributed to himself, saying that he must be greatly beloved by the Parisians to induce them to give his children so splendid a reception[3]. To whomsoever it was owing, the embassador certainly did not exaggerate the opinion of the world around him when he affirmed that, in the memory of man, no one recollected any ceremony which had made so great a sensation, and had been attended by so complete a success.

And it was followed up, as she expected, by several visits to the different Parisian theatres, which, in compliance with the king's express direction, were made in all the state which would have been observed had he himself been present. Salutes were fired from the Bastile and the Hotel des Invalides; companies of Royal Guards lined the vestibule and the passage of the theatre; sentinels stood even on the stage; but, fond as the French are of martial finery and parade, the spectators paid little attention to the soldiers, or even to the actors. All eyes were fixed on the dauphiness alone. At Mercy's suggestion, the dauphin and she had previously obtained the king's permission to allow the violation of the rule which forbade any clapping of hands in the presence of royalty. This relaxation of etiquette was hailed as a great condescension by the play-goers, and throughout the evening of their appearance at the Italian comedy the spectators had already made abundant use of their new privilege, when the enthusiasm was brought to a height by a chorus which ended with the loyal burden of "Vive le roi!" Clerval, the performer of the principal part, added, "Et ses chers enfants;" and the compliment was re-echoed from every part of the house with continued clapping and cheering, till it reminded Marie Antoinette of a somewhat similar scene which, as a child, she had witnessed in the theatre of Vienna,[4] when the empress, from her box, had announced to the audience that a son (the heir to the empire) had just been born to the Archduke Leopold.

The ice being, thus, as it were, once broken, the dauphin and dauphiness took many opportunities of appearing in public during the following months, visiting the great Paris fair of St. Ovide, as it was called, walking up and down the alleys, and making purchases at the stalls the whole Place Louis XV., to which the fair had recently been removed, being illuminated, and the crowd greeting them with repeated and enthusiastic cheers. They also went in state to the exhibition of pictures at the Louvre, and drove to St. Cloud to walk about the park attached to that palace, which was one of the most favorite places of resort for the Parisians on the fine summer evenings; so that, while the court was at Versailles, scarcely a week elapsed without her giving them an opportunity of seeing her, in which it was evident that she fully shared their pleasure. To be loved was with her a necessity of her very nature; and, as she was constantly referring with pride to the attachment felt by the Austrians for her mother, she fixed her own chief wishes on inspiring with a similar feeling those who were to become her and her husband's subjects. She was, at least for the time, rewarded as she desired. This is, indeed, said they, the best of innovations, the best of revolutions,[5] to see the princes mingling with the people, and interesting themselves in their amusements. This was really to unite all classes; to attach the country to the palace and the palace to the country; and it was to the dauphiness that the credit of this new state of things was universally attributed.

She was looking forward to a greater pleasure in a visit from her. brother, the emperor, which the empress hoped might be attended with consequences more important than those of passing pleasure; since she trusted to his influence, and, if opportunity should occur, to his remonstrances, to induce the dauphin to break through the unaccountable coldness with which, in some respects, he still treated his beautiful wife. But Joseph was forced to postpone his visit, and the fulfillment of the empress's anticipations was also postponed for some years.

However, Marie Antoinette never allowed disappointments to dwell in her mind longer than she could help. She rather strove to dispel the recollection of them by such amusements as were within her reach. She learned to drive, and found great diversion in being her own charioteer through the glades of the forest. She began to make further inroads in the court etiquette, giving balls in which she broke through the custom which prescribed that special places should be marked out for the royal family, and directed that the princes and princesses should sit with the rest of the company during the intervals between the dances; an arrangement which enabled her to talk to every one, and which gained her general good-will from the graciousness of her manner. She did not greatly trouble herself at the jealousy of her popularity openly displayed by her aunts and her sister-in-law, who could not bear to hear her called "La bellissima.[6]" Nor was her influence weakened when, in November, a fresh princess, the sister of Madame de Provence, arrived from Italy, to be married to the Comte d'Artois, for the bride was even less attractive than her sister. According to Mercy, she was pale and thin, had a long nose and a wide mouth, danced badly, and was very awkward in manner. So that Louis himself, though usually very punctilious in his courtesies to those in her position, could not forbear showing how little he admired her.

An incident occurred on the evening of the marriage which is worth remarking, from the change which subsequently took place in the taste of the dauphiness, who a few years afterward provoked unfavorable comments by the ardor with which she surrendered herself to the excitement of the gaming-table. As a matter of course, a grand party was invited to the palace to celebrate the event of the morning; and, as an invariable part of such entertainments, a table was set out for the then fashionable game of lansquenet, at which the king himself played, with the royal family and all the principal persons of the court. In the course of the evening Marie Antoinette won more than seven hundred pounds; but she was rather embarrassed than gratified by her good fortune. She had tried to lose the money back; but, as she had been unable to succeed, the next morning she sent the greater part of it to the curates of Versailles to be distributed among the poor, and gave the rest to some of her own attendants who seemed to her to need it, being determined, as she said, to keep none of it for herself.

The winter revived the apprehensions concerning the king's health; he was manifestly sinking into the grave, while

"That which should accompany old age,   As love, obedience, honor, troops of friends,   He might not look to have."

His very mistress began with great zeal than ever, though with no better taste, to seek to conciliate the dauphiness. She tried to purchase her good-will by a bribe. She was aware that the princess greatly admired diamonds, and, learning that a jeweler of Paris had a pair of ear-rings of a size and brilliancy so extraordinary that the price which he asked for them was 700,000 francs, she persuaded the Comte de Noailles to carry them to Marie Antoinette to show them, with a message from herself that if the dauphiness liked to keep them, she would induce the king to make her a present of them.[7] Whether Marie Antoinette admired them or not, she had far too proper a sense of dignity to allow herself to be entrapped into the acceptance of an obligation by one whom she so deservedly despised. She replied coldly that she had jewels enough, and did not desire to increase the number. But the overture thus made by Madame du Barri could not be kept secret, and more than one of her partisans followed the hint afforded by her example, and showed a desire to make their peace with their future queen. The Duc d'Aiguillon himself was among the foremost of her courtiers, and entreated the mediation of Mercy in his favor, making the ambassador his messenger to assure her that "he should impose it upon himself as a law to comply with her wishes in every thing;" and only desired that he might be allowed to know which of the requests that she might make were dictated by her own judgment, and which merely proceeded from her indulgent favor to the importunities of others. For Marie Antoinette had of late often broken through the rule which, in compliance with her mother's advice, she had at first laid down for herself, to abstain from recommending persons for preferment; and had pressed many a petition on the minister's notice as to which it was self-evident that she could know nothing of their merits, nor feel any personal interest in their success.

In the spring of 1774 she had an opportunity of convincing her mother that any imputation of neglect of her countrymen when visiting the court was unfounded, by the marked honors which she paid to Marshal Lacy, one of the most honored veterans of the Seven Years' War. Knowing how highly he was esteemed by her mother, she took care to be informed beforehand of the day of his arrival. She gave orders that he should find invitations to her parties awaiting him. She made arrangements to give him a private audience even before he saw the king, where her reception of him showed how deep and ineffaceable was her love for her family and her old home, even while fairly recognizing the fact that her first duties and her first affections now belonged to France. The old warrior avowed that he had been greatly moved by the touching affection with which she spoke to him of her love and veneration for her mother; and by the tears which he saw in her eyes when she said that the one thing wanting to her happiness was the hope of being allowed one day to see that dear mother once more. She showed him some of the last presents which the empress had sent her, and dwelt with fond minuteness of observation on some views of Schoenbrunn and other spots in the neighborhood of Vienna which were endeared to her by her early recollections.

The return of mild weather seemed to be bringing with it same return of strength to the king, when, on the 28th of April, he was suddenly seized with illness, which was presently pronounced by the physicians to be the small-pox. All was consternation at Versailles, for it was soon perceived to be a severe if not a malignant attack; and at the same time all was perplexity. Thirty years before, when Louis had been supposed to be on his deathbed at Metz, bishops, peers, and ministers had found in the loss of royal favor reason to repent the precipitation with which they had insisted on the withdrawal of Madame de Chateauroux; and now, should he again recover, it was likely that Madame du Barri would he equally resentful, and that the confessor who should make her removal a necessary condition of his administering the sacraments of the Church to the king, and the courtiers who should support or act upon their requisition, would surely find reason to repent it. Accordingly, for the first few days of Louis's illness, she remained at Versailles; but he grew visibly worse. His daughters, who, though they had not had the disease themselves, tended his sick-bed with the most devoted and fearless affection, consulted the physicians, who declared it dangerous to admit of any further delay in the ministration of the rites of the Church. He himself gave his sanction to the ladies' departure, and then the royal confessor administered the sacraments, and drew up a declaration to be published in the royal name, that, "though he owed no account of his conduct to any but God alone, he nevertheless declared that he repented having given rise to scandal among his subjects, and only desired to live for the support of religion and the welfare of his people."

Even this avowal the Cardinal de Roche-Aymer promised Madame du Barri to suppress; but the royal confessor, the Abbe Mandoux, overruled him, and compelled its publication, in spite of the Duc de Richelieu, the chief confidant of the mistress, and long the chief minister and promoter of the king's debaucheries, who insulted the cardinal with the grossest abuse for his breach of promise.[8] It may be doubted whether such a compromise with profligacy, and such a profanation of the most solemn rites of the Church by its ministers, were not the greatest scandal of all; but it was in too complete harmony with their conduct throughout the whole of the reign. And, as it was impossible but that religion itself should suffer in the estimation of worldly men from such an open disregard of all but its mere outward forms, it can hardly be denied that the French cardinals and prelates about the court had almost as great a share in bringing about that general feeling of contempt for all religion which led to that formal disavowal of God himself which was witnessed twenty years later, as the scoffers who were now uniting against it, or the professed infidels who then, renounced it. Such as it was, the king's act of penitence was not performed too soon. At the end of the first week of May all prospect of his recovery vanished. Mortification set in, and on the 10th of May he died.

CHAPTER VIII.

The Court leaves Versailles for La Muette.--Feelings of the New Sovereigns.--Madame du Barri is sent to a Convent.--Marie Antoinette writes to Maria Teresa.--The Good Intentions of the New Sovereigns.-- Madame Adelaide has the Small-pox.--Anxieties of Maria Teresa.-- Mischievous Influence of the Aunts.--Position and Influence of the Count de Mercy.--Louis consults the Queen on Matters of Policy.--Her Prudence.-- She begins to Purify the Court, and to relax the Rules of Etiquette.--Her Care of her Pages.--The King and the renounce the Gifts of Le Joyeux Avenement and La Ceinture de la Reine.---She procures the Pardon of the Due de Choiseul.

Throughout the morning of the 10th of May there was great confusion and agitation at Versailles. The physicians declared that the king could not live out the day; and the dauphin had decided on removing his household to the smaller palace of La Muette at Choisy, to spend in that comparative retirement the first week or two after his grandfather's death, during which it would hardly be decorous for the royal family to be seen in public. But, as it was not thought seemly to appear to anticipate the event by quitting Versailles while Louis was still alive, a lighted candle was placed in the window of the sick-room, which, the moment that the king had expired, was to be extinguished, as a signal to the equerries to prepare the carriages. The dauphin and dauphiness were in an adjoining room awaiting the intelligence, when, at about three o'clock in the afternoon, a sudden trampling of feet was heard, and Madame de Noailles entered the apartment to entreat them to advance into the saloon to receive the homage of the princes and principal officers of the court, who were waiting to pay their respects to their new sovereigns. They came forward arm-in-arm; and in tears, in which sincere sorrow was mingled with not unnatural nervousness, received the salutations of the courtiers, and immediately afterward left Versailles with all the family.

Louis XVI. and Marie Antoinette had now reached the pinnacle of human greatness, as sovereigns of one of the noblest empires in the world. Yet the first feelings which their elevation had excited in both, and especially in the queen, were rather those of dismay and perplexity than of exultation. In the preceding autumn, Mercy[1] had remarked to the empress, with surprise and vexation, that, though the dauphiness exhibited singular readiness and acuteness in comprehending political questions, she was very unwilling, and, as it seemed to him, afraid of dealing with them, and that she shrunk from the thought that the day would come when she must possess power and authority. And the continuance of this feeling is visible in her first letter to her mother, some passages of which show a sobriety of mind under such a change of circumstances, which, almost as much as the benevolence which the letter also displays, augured well for the happiness of the people over whom she was to reign, so far at least as that happiness depended on the virtues of the sovereign.

"Choisy, May 14th.

"My Dearest Mother,--Mercy will have informed you of the circumstances of our misfortune. Happily his cruel disease left the king in possession of his senses till the last moment, and his end was very edifying. The new king seems to have the affection of his people. Two days before the death of his grandfather, he sent two hundred thousand[2] francs to the poor, which has produced a great effect. Since he has been here, he has been working unceasingly, answering with his own hand the letters of the ministers, whom as yet he can not see, and many others likewise. One thing is certain, and that is that he has a taste for economy, and the greatest desire possible to make his people happy. In every thing he has as great a desire to be rightly instructed as he has need to be. I trust that God will bless his good intentions.

"The public expected great changes in a moment. The king has limited himself to sending away the creature[3] to a convent, and to driving from the court every thing which is connected with that scandal. The king even owed this example to the people of Versailles, who, at the very moment of his grandfather's death, insulted Madame do Mazarin,[4] one of the humblest servants of the favorite. I am earnestly entreated to exhort the king to mercy toward a number of corrupt souls who had done much mischief for many years; and I am strongly inclined to comply with the request.

*   *   *   *   *

"A messenger has just arrived to forbid my going to see my Aunt Adelaide, who has a great deal of fever. They are afraid of the small-pox for her. I am horrified, and can not bring myself to think of the consequences. It is a terrible thing for her to pay so immediately for the sacrifice which she made.

"I am very glad that Marshal Lacy was pleased with me. I confess, my dear mamma, that I was greatly affected when he took leave of me, at thinking how rarely it happens to me to see any of my countrymen, and especially of those who have the happiness to approach you. A little time back I saw Madame de Marmier, which was a great pleasure to me, since I know how highly you value her.

"The king has allowed me myself to name the ladies who are to have places in my household, now that I am queen; and I have had the satisfaction of giving the Lorrainers[5] a proof of my regard, in taking for my chief almoner the Abbe de Sabran, a man of excellent character, of noble birth, and already named for the bishopric about to be established at Nancy.

"Although it pleased God that I should be born in the rank which I this day occupy, still I can not forbear admiring the bounty of Providence in choosing me, the youngest of your daughters, for the noblest kingdom in Europe. I feel more than ever what I owe to the tenderness of my august mother, who expended such pains and labor in procuring for me this splendid establishment. I have never so greatly longed to throw myself at her feet, to embrace her, to lay open my whole soul to her, and to show her how entirely it is filled with respect and tenderness and gratitude."

It is impossible to read these glowing words, so full of the joy and hope of youth, and breathing a confidence of happiness apparently so well-founded, since it was built on a resolution to use the power placed in the writer's hands for the welfare of the people over whom it was to be exerted, without reflecting how painful a contrast to the hopes now expressed is presented by the reality of the destiny in store for her and her husband. At the moment he was as little disturbed by fore-bodings of evil as his queen, and willingly yielded to her request to add a few lines with his own hand to the empress, that, on so momentous an occasion as his acces-sion she might not be left to gather his feelings solely from her report of them. The postscript of the letter is accordingly their joint performance, he evidently desiring to gratify Maria Teresa by praise of her daughter; and she, while pleased at his ac-quiescence, not concealing her amusement at the clumsiness, or, to say the least, the rusticity, of some of his expressions.

P.S. in the king's hand: "I am very glad, my dear mamma, to find an occasion to prove to you my tenderness and my attachment. I should be very glad to have your advice at this time, which is so embarrassing. I should be enchanted to be able to please you, and to show by my conduct all my attachment and the gratitude which I feel for your kindness in giving me your daughter, with whom I am as well satis-fied as possible."

P.S. by the queen: "The king would not let my letter go without adding a word from himself. I am quite aware that it would not have been too much for him to do to write an entire letter. But I must beg my dear mamma to excuse him, in consider-ation of the mass of business with which he is occupied, and also a little on account of his timidity and the embarrassed manner which is natural to him. You see, my dear mamma, by his compliment at the end, that, though he has great affection for me, he does not spoil me by insipid flatteries."

It is almost equally remarkable that the empress herself, though thus to see her favorite daughter on the throne of France had been her most ardent wish, was far from regarding the consummation of her desires with unalloyed pleasure. She was so completely a politician above all things, that, though she was well aware that Louis XV. had been one of the most infamous kings that ever dishonored a throne, she looked upon him solely as an ally; described him to her daughter as "that good and tender prince;" declared that she should never cease to regret him, and that she would wear mourning for him all the rest of her life. At the same time, she did not conceal from herself that he had left his kingdom in a most deplorable condi-tion. She had, as she declared, herself experienced how heavy is the burden of an empire; she reflected how young her daughter was; and expressed a sad fear that "her days of happiness were over." "She was now in a position in which there was no half-way between complete greatness and great misery.[6]" The best hopes for her future the empress saw in the character for purity and kindness which Marie Antoinette had already established and in the esteem and affection of the people which those qualities had won for her; and she entreated her, taking it for granted that in advising her she was advising the king also, to be prudent and cautious, to avoid making any sudden changes, and above all things to maintain the alliance between the two countries, and to listen to the experienced and faithful advice of her embassador.

Maria Teresa was mistaken when she thought that her daughter would at all times be able to lead her husband. Though slow in action, Louis was not deficient in perception. On many subjects he had views of his own, which, in some cases, were clear and sound enough, and to which, even when they were not so, he adhered with considerable tenacity. At the same time, though he had but little affection for his aunts, and still less respect for their judgment, he had been so long accustomed to listen to their advice while he had no authority, that he could not as yet wholly shake off all feeling of deference for it, and their influence was exerted with most mischievous effect in the first week of his reign. Indeed, it had been exhibited even before the reign began, though the form which it took greatly interfered with the personal comfort of the young sovereigns. It had been settled that the king and queen should go by themselves to La Muette, and that the rest of the royal family should remove to the Trianon. But Madame Adelaide had no inclination for a plan which would separate her from her nephew at a moment when so many matters of importance would come before her for decision. At the last moment she prevailed upon him to consent that the whole family should go to Choisy together; and the very next day she induced him to dismiss his ministers, and to place the Comte de Maurepas at the head of the Government, though Louis himself had selected anoth-er-statesman for the office, M. Machault, who, as finance minister twenty-five years before, had shown both ability and integrity, and who had enjoyed the confidence of the king's father, and though Maurepas had never been supposed to be either able or honest, and might well have been regarded as superannuated, since he had begun his official life under Louis XIV.

With the change in the position of Marie Antoinette, Mercy's position had also been changed, and likewise his view of the line of conduct which it was desirable for her to adopt. Hitherto he had been the counselor of a princess who, without wary walking, was liable every moment to be overwhelmed by the intrigues with which she was surrounded; and his chief object had been to enable his royal pupil to escape the snares and dangers which encompassed her. Now, as far as his duties could be determined by the wish of the empress, in which her daughter fully acquiesced, he was elevated to the post of confidential adviser to a great queen, who, in his opinion, was inevitably destined to be the real ruler of the kingdom. It was a strange position for so experienced a politician as the empress to desire for him, and for so prudent a statesman to accept. Yet, anomalous as it was, and dangerous as it would usually be for a foreign embassador to interfere in the internal politics of the kingdom to which he is sent, his correspondence bears ample testimony to both his sagacity and his disinterestedness. And it would have been well for both his royal pupil and her adopted country had his advice more frequently and more steadily guided the course of both.

On one point of primary importance his advice to the queen differed from that which he had been wont to give to the dauphiness. While dauphiness, he had urged her to abstain from any interference in public affairs. He now, on the contrary, desired to see her take an active part in them, explaining to the empress that the reason which actuated him was the character of the new king, who, as he regarded him, was never likely to exert the authority which belonged to him with independence or steadiness, but was certain to be led by some one or other, while it would in the highest degree endanger the maintenance of the alliance between France and Austria (which, coinciding with the judgment of his imperial mistress, he regarded as the most important of all political objects), and be most injurious to the welfare of France and to her own personal comfort, if that leader should be any one but the queen.[7]

But, as we have seen, he could not prevent Louis from yielding at times to other influences. Taking the same view of the situation as the empress, if indeed Maria Teresa had not adopted it from him, he had urged Marie Antoinette to prevent any change in the ministry being made at first, in which it is highly probable that she did not coincide with him, though equally likely that Maurepas was not the minister whom she would have preferred. Another piece of advice which he gave was, however, taken, and with the happiest effect The poorer classes in Paris and its neighborhood were suffering from a scarcity which almost amounted to a famine; and, before the death of Louis XV., Mercy had recommended that the first measure of the new reign should be one which should lower the price of bread. That counsel was too entirely in harmony with the active benevolence of the new monarch to be neglected. The necessary edicts were issued. In twenty-four hours the price of the loaf was reduced by two-fifths, and Mercy had the satisfaction of hearing the relief generally attributed to the influence of the new queen.

It can not he supposed that the king knew either the opinion which the empress and the embassador had formed of his capacity and disposition, or the advice which they had consequently given to the queen. But he very early began to show that he himself also appreciated his wife's quickness of intelligence and correctness of judgment. Maria Teresa, in pressing on her daughter her opinion of the general character of the policy which the interest of France required, explained her view of her daughter's position to be that she was "the friend and confidante of the king.[8]" And June had hardly arrived before he began to discuss all his plans and difficulties with her; while she spared his pride and won his further confidence by avoiding all appearances of pressing for it, as if her advice were necessary to him, but at the same time showing with what satisfaction she received it. To those who solicited her intervention, her language was most carefully guarded. "She did not," she said, "interfere in any affair of state; she only coincided in all the wishes and intentions of the king."

There were, however, matters which were strictly and exclusively within her own province; and in them she at once began to exert her authority most beneficially. Her first desire was to purify the court where licentiousness in either sex had long been the surest road to royal favor. She began by making a regulation, that she would receive no lady who was separated from her husband; and she abolished a senseless and inexplicable rule of etiquette which had hitherto prohibited the queen and princesses from dining or supping in company with their husbands.[9] Such an exclusion from the king's table of those who were its most natural and becoming ornaments had notoriously facilitated and augmented the disorders of the last reign; and it was obvious that its maintenance must at least have a tendency to lead to a repetition of the old irregularities. Fortunately, the king was as little inclined to approve of it as the queen. All his tastes were domestic, and he gladly assented to her proposal to abolish the custom. Throughout the reign, at all ordinary meals, at his suppers when he came in late from hunting, when he had perhaps invited some of his fellow-sportsmen to share his repast, and at State banquets, Marie Antoinette took her seat at his side, not only adding grace and liveliness to the entertainment, but effectually preventing license, and even the suspicion of scandal; and, as she desired that her household as well as her family should set an example of regularity and propriety to the nation, she exercised a careful superintendence over the behavior of those who had hitherto been among the least-considered members of the royal establishment. Even the king's confessor had thought the morals of the royal pages either beneath his notice or beyond his control; but Marie Antoinette took a higher view of her duties. She considered her pages[10] as placed under her charge, and herself as bound to extend what one of themselves calls a maternal care and kindness to them, restraining as far as she could, and when she could not restrain, reproving their boyish excesses, softening their hearts and winning their affections by the gentle dignity of her admonitions, and by the condescending and hopeful indulgence with which she accepted their expressions of contrition and their promises of amendment. In one matter, too, which, if not exactly political, was at all events of public interest, she acted in a manner of which none of her predecessors had set an example. By a custom of immemorial antiquity, at the accession of a new sovereign, a tax had been levied on the whole kingdom as an offering to the king, known as "the gift of the happy accession;[11]" when there was a queen, a similar tax was imposed upon the Parisians, to provide what was called "the girdle of the queen.[12]" It has already been mentioned that the distress which existed in Paris at this time was so severe that, just before the death of the late king, Louis and Marie Antoinette had relieved it by a munificent gift from their private purse; and to lay additional burdens on the people at such a time was not only repugnant to their feelings, but seemed especially inconsistent with their recent generosity. Accordingly, the very first edict of the new reign announced that neither tax would be imposed. The people felt the kindness which dictated such a relief more than even the relief itself, and repaid it with expressions of gratitude such as no French sovereign had heard for above a century; but Marie Antoinette, with the humility natural to her on such subjects, made light of her own share in the act of benevolence, turning off the compliments which were paid to her with a playful jest, that it was impossible for a queen to affix a purse to her girdle, now that girdles had gone out of fashion.[13]

On another subject, also, not wholly unconnected with politics, Since the nobleman concerned had once been the chief minister, but in which Marie Antoinette's interest was personal, she broke through her usual rule of not beginning the discussion with the king, and requested the recall from banishment of the Due de Choiseul. An unfounded prejudice based upon calumnies set on foot by the cabal of Madame du Barri, had envenomed Louis's mind against the duke. He bad been led to suspect that his own father, the late dauphin, had been poisoned, and that Choiseul had been accessory to the crime. There was nothing more certain than that the dauphin's death had been natural; but a dislike of the accused duke lingered in the king's mind, and he eluded compliance with his wife's request till she put it on entirely personal grounds, by declaring it to be humiliating to herself that one to whom she was under the deepest obligations as the negotiator of her own happy marriage should be under the king's displeasure without her being able to procure his pardon. Louis felt the force of the appeal thus made to him. "If she used that argument, he could deny her nothing," and the duke's sentence was remitted, though his royal patroness was unable to procure his re-admission to office. Nor did Maria Teresa regret that she failed in that object; since she feared his restless character, and felt the alliance between the two countries safer in the hands of the new foreign secretary, the Count de Vergennes.

CHAPTER IX.

Her accession to the throne, however, had not entirely delivered Marie Antoinette from intrigues. It had only changed their direction and object, and also the persona of the intriguers. Her chief enemy now was the prince who ought to have been her best friend, the next brother of her husband, the Comte de Provence. Among the papers of Louis XV. the king had found proofs, in letters from both count and countess, that they had both been actively employed in trying to make mischief, and to poison the mind of their grandfather against the dauphiness. They became still more busy now, since each day seemed to diminish the probability of Marie Antoinette becoming a mother; while, if she should leave no children, the Comte de Provence would be heir to the throne. He scarcely made any secret that he was already contemplating the probability of his succession; and, as there were not wanting courtiers to speculate also on the chance, it soon became known that there was no such sure road to the favor of monsieur[1] as that of disparaging and vilifying the queen. There might have been some safety for her in being put on her guard against her enemy; and the king himself, who called his brother Tartuffe, did, in consequence of his discovery, use great caution and circumspection in his behavior toward him; but Marie Antoinette was of a temper as singularly forgiving as it was open: she could not bear to regard with suspicion even those of whose unfriendliness and treachery she had had proofs; and after a few days she resumed her old familiarity with the pair, as if she had no reason to distrust them, slighting on this subject the remonstrances of Mercy, who pointed out to her in vain that she was putting weapons into their hands which they would be sure to turn against herself.

At this moment she was especially happy with a new pastime. Amidst the stately halls of Versailles she had often longed for a villa on a smaller scale, which she might call her own; and the wish was now gratified. On one side of the park of Versailles, and about a mile from the palace, the late king had built an exquisite little pavilion for his mistress, which was known as the Little Trianon. There had been a building of one kind or another on the same spot for above a century. Louis XIV. had erected there a cottage of porcelain for his imperious favorite, Madame de Montespan; and it was the more sumptuous palace with which, after her death, he replaced it, that gave rise to the strange quarrel between the haughty monarch and his equally haughty minister, Louvois, of which St. Simon has left us so curious an account.[2] This had been allowed to fall into a state of decay; and a few years before his death, Louis XV. had pulled down what remained of it, and had built a third on its foundations, which had been the most favorite abode of Madame du Barri during his life, but which was now rendered vacant by her dismissal. The house was decorated with an exquisite delicacy of taste, in which Louis XV. had far surpassed his predecessor; but the chief charm of the place was generally accounted to be the garden, which had been laid out by Le Notre, an artist, whose original genius as a landscape gardener was regarded by many of his contemporaries as greatly superior to his more technical skill as an architect.[3]

A few hundred yards off was another palace, the Great Trianon; but it was the Little Trianon which caught the queen's fancy; and, on her expression of a wish to have it for her own, the king at once made it over to her; and, pleased with her new toy, Marie Antoinette, still a girl in her impulsive eagerness for a fresh pleasure (she was not yet nineteen), began to busy herself with remodeling the pleasure-grounds with which it was surrounded. Before the time of Le Notre, the finest gardens in the country had been laid out on what was called the Italian plan. He was too good a patriot to copy the foreigners: he drove out the Italians, and introduced a new arrangement, known as the French style, which was, in fact, but an imitation of the stiff, formal Dutch mode. But of late the English gardeners had established that supremacy in the art which they have ever since maintained; and the present aim of every fashionable horticulturist in France was to copy the effects produced on the banks of the Thames by Wise and Browne.

Marie Antoinette fell in with the prevailing taste. She imported English drawings and hired English, gardeners. She visited in person the Count de Caraman, and one or two other nobles, who had already done something by their example to inoculate the Parisians with the new fashion. And presently lawns and shrubberies, widening invariably simple flower-beds, supplanted the stately uniformity of terraces, alleys converging on central fountains, or on alcoves as solid and stiff as the palace itself, and trees cut into all kinds of fantastic shapes, which had previously been regarded as the masterpieces of the gardeners' invention. Her happiness was at its height when, at the end of a few months, all was completed to her liking, and she could invite her husband to an entertainment in a retreat which was wholly her own, and the chief beauties of which were her own work.

As yet, therefore, all was happiness, and prospect of happiness. Even Maria Teresa, whose unceasing anxiety for her daughter often induced her to see the worst side of things, was rendered for a moment almost playful by the reports which reached Vienna of the universal popularity of "Louis XVI. and his little queen!" "She blushed," she said, "to think that in thirty-three years of her reign she had not done as much as Louis had done in thirty-three days.[4]" But she still warned her daughter that every thing depended on keeping up the happy impression already made; that much still remained to be done. And the queen's answer showed that her new authority had brought with it some cares. "It is true," she writes, "that the praises of the king resound everywhere. He deserves it well by the uprightness of his heart, and the desire which he has to act rightly; but this French enthusiasm disquiets me for the future. The little that I understand of business shows me that some matters are full of difficulty and embarrassment. All agree that the late king has left his affairs in a very bad state. Men's minds are divided; and it will be impossible to please all the world in a country where the vivacity of the people wants every thing to be done in a moment. My dear mamma is quite right when she says we must lay down principles, and not depart from them. The king will not have the same weakness as his grandfather. I hope that he will have no favorites; but I am afraid that he is too mild and too easy. You may depend upon it that I will not draw the king into any great expenses." (The empress had expressed a fear lest the Trianon might prove a cause of extravagance.) "On the contrary, I, of my own accord, have refused to make demands on him for money which some have recommended me to make."

Some relaxations, too, of the formality which had previously been maintained between the sovereign and the subordinate members of the royal family, and especially an order of the king that his brothers and sisters were not in private intercourse to address him as his majesty, had grated on the empress's sense of the distance always to be preserved between a monarch and the very highest of his subjects. And she had complained that reports had reached her that "there was no distinction between the queen and the other princesses; and that the familiarity subsisting in the court was extreme." But Marie Antoinette replied, in defense of the king and herself, that there was "great exaggeration in these reports, as indeed there was about every thing that went on at the court; that the familiarity spoken of was seen but by very few. It is not for me," she said, "to judge; but it seems to me that what exists among us is only the air of kindly affection and gayety which is suitable to our age. It is true that the Count d'Artois" (who had been the special subject of some of the empress's unfavorable comments) "is very lively and very giddy, but I can always keep him in order. As for my aunts, no one can any longer say that they lead me; and as for monsieur and madame, I am very far from placing entire confidence in them.

"I must confess that I am fond of amusement, and am not very greatly inclined to grave subjects. I hope, however, to improve by degrees; and, without ever mixing myself up in intrigues, to qualify myself gradually to be of service to the king when he makes me his confidante, since he treats me at all times with the most perfect affection."

Her reflections on the impulsiveness and impatience of the French character, and of the difficulties which those qualities placed in the path of their rulers, justify the praises which Mercy had lavished on her sagacity, for it is evident that to them the chief troubles of her later years may be clearly traced. And it is difficult to avoid agreeing with her rather than with her mother, and thinking the most entire freedom of intercourse between the king and his nearest relations as desirable as it was natural. Royalty is, as the empress herself described it, a burden sufficiently heavy, without its weight being augmented by observances and restrictions which would leave the rulers without a single friend even among the members of their own family. And probably the empress herself might have seen less reason for her admonitions on the subject, had it not been for the circumstance, which was no doubt unfortunate, that the royal family at this time contained no member of a graver age and a settled respectability of character who might, by his example, have tempered the exuberance natural to the extreme youth of the sovereigns and their brothers.

Not that Marie Antoinette was content to limit the number of those whom she admitted to familiarity to her husband's kinsmen and kinswomen. Still fretting in secret over the want of any object on whom to lavish a mother's tenderness, she sought for friendship as a substitute, shutting her eyes to the fact that persons in her rank, as having no equals, can have no friends, in the true sense of the word. Nor, had such a thing been possible anywhere, was France the country in which to find it. There disinterestedness and integrity had long been banished from her own sex almost as completely as from the other; and most of those whom she took into favor made it their first object to render that favor profitable to themselves. If she professed in their society to forget for a few hours that she was queen, they never forgot it; they never lost sight of the fact that she could confer places and pensions, and they often discarded moderation and decency in the extravagance of their solicitations; while she frequently, with an overamiable facility, surrendering her own judgment to their importunities, not only granted their requests, but at times even adopted their prejudices, and yielded herself as an instrument to gratify their antipathies or resentments.

And the same feeling of vacancy in her heart, of which she was ever painfully conscious, produced in her also a constant restlessness, and a craving for excitement which exhibited itself in an insatiable appetite for amusement (as she confessed to her mother), and led her to seek distraction even in pastimes for which naturally she had but little inclination. In these respects it can not be said that, during the first year of her reign, she was as uniformly prudent as she had been while dauphiness. The restraint in which she had lived for those four years had not been unwholesome for one so young; but it had no doubt been irksome to her. And the feeling of complete liberty and independence which had succeeded it had, by a sort of natural reaction, sharpened the energy with which she now pursued her various diversions. It is possible, too, that the zest with which she indulged herself may have derived additional keenness from the knowledge that her ill-wishers found in it pretext for misconstruction and calumny; and that, being conscious of entire purity in thought, word, and deed, she looked on it as due to her own character to show that she set all such detraction and detractors at defiance. To all cavilers, as also to her mother, whose uneasiness was frequently aroused by gossip which reached Vienna from Paris, her invariable reply was that her way of life had the king her husband's entire approbation. And while he felt a conjugal satisfaction in the contemplation of his queen's attractions and graces, the qualities in which, as he was well aware, he himself was most deficient, Louis might well also cherish the most absolute reliance on her unswerving rectitude, knowing the pride with which she was wont to refer to her mother's example, and to boast that the lesson which, above all others, she had learned from it was that to princes of her birth and rank wickedness and baseness were unpardonable.

Indeed, many of the amusements Louis not only approved, but shared with her, while she associated herself with those in which he delighted, as far as she could, joining his hunting parties twice a week, either on horseback or in her carriage, and at all times exhibiting a pattern of domestic union of which the whole previous history of the nation afforded no similar example. The citizens of Paris could hardly believe their eyes when they saw their king and queen walk arm-in-arm along the boulevards; and the courtiers received a lesson, if they had been disposed to profit by it, when on each Sunday morning they saw the royal pair repair to the parish church for divine service, the day being closed by their public supper in the queen's apartment.

And this appearance of domestic felicity was augmented by the introduction of what may be called private parties, with which, at the queen's instigation, Louis consented to vary the cold formality of the ordinary entertainments of the court. In the autumn they followed the example of Louis XV. by exchanging for a few weeks the grandeur of Versailles for the comparative quiet of some of their smaller palaces; and, while they were at Choisy, they issued invitations once or twice a week to several of the Parisian ladies to come out and spend the day at the palace, when, as the principal officers of the household were not on duty, they themselves did the honors to their guests, the queen conversing with every one with her habitual graciousness, while the king also threw off his ordinary reserve, and seemed to enter into the pleasures of the day with a gayety and cordiality which surprised the party, and which, from the contrast that it presented to his manner when he was by himself, was very generally attributed to the influence of the queen's example.

And these quiet festivities were so much to his taste that afterward, when the court moved to Fontainebleau, and when they settled at Versailles for the winter, he cheerfully agreed to a proposal of Marie Antoinette to have a weekly supper party; adopting also another suggestion of hers which was indispensable to render such reunions agreeable, or even, it may be said, practicable. At her request he abolished the ridiculous rule which, under the last two kings, had forbidden gentlemen to be admitted to sit at table with any princess of the royal family. But natural as the idea seemed, it was not carried out without opposition on the part of Madame Adelaide and her sisters, who remonstrated against it as an infraction of all the old observances of the court, till it became a contest for superiority between the queen and themselves. Marie Antoinette took counsel with Mercy, and, by his advice, pointed out to her husband that to abandon the plan after it had been announced, in submission to an opposition which the princesses had no right to make, would be to humiliate her in the eyes of the whole court. Louis had not yet shaken off all fear of his aunts; but they were luckily absent, so he yielded to the influence which was nearest. The suppers took place. He and the queen themselves made out the lists of the guests to be invited, the men being named by him, and the ladies being selected by the queen. They were a great success; and, as the history of the affair became known, the court and the Parisians generally rejoiced in the queen's triumph, and were grateful to her for this as for every other innovation which had a tendency to break down the haughty barrier which, during the last two reigns, had been established between the sovereign and his subjects. Nor were these pleasant informal parties the only instances in which, great inroads were made on the old etiquette. The Comte de Mirabeau, a man fatally connected in subsequent years with some of the most terrible of the insults which were offered to the royal family, about this time described etiquette as a system invented for the express purpose of blunting the capacity of the French princes, and fixing them in position of complete dependence. And Marie Antoinette seems to have regarded it with similar eyes; her dislike of it being quickened by the expectations which its partisans and champions entertained that her every movement was to be regulated by it. And its requirements were sufficiently burdensome to tax a far better-trained patience that was natural to one who though a queen, was not yet nineteen. Not only was no guest of the male sex, except the king, allowed to sit at table with her, but no man-servant, no male officer of her household, might be present when the king and she dined together, as indeed usually happened; even his presence could not sanction the introduction of any other man. The lady of honor, on her knees, though in full dress, presented him the napkin to wipe his fingers and filled his glass; ladies in waiting in the same grand attire changed the plates of the royal pair; and after dinner, as indeed throughout the day, the queen could not quit one room in the palace for another, unless some of her ladies were at hand in complete court dress to attend upon her.[5] These usages, which were in reality so many chains to restrain all freedom, and to render comfort impossible, were abolished in the first few months of the new reign; but, little as was the foundation which they had in common sense, and equally little as was the addition which they made to the royal dignity, it is certain that many of the courtiers, besides Madame de Noailles, were greatly disconcerted at their extinction. They regarded the queen's orders on the subject as a proof of a settled preference for Austrian over French fashions. They began to speak of her as "the Austrian," a name which, though Madame Adelaide had more than once chosen it to describe her during the first year of her marriage, had since that time been almost forgotten, but which was now revived, and was continually reproduced by a certain party to cast odium on many of her most simple tastes and most innocent actions. Her enemies oven affirmed that in private she was wont to call the Trianon her "little Vienna,[6]" as if the garden, which she was laying out with a taste that long made it the admiration of all the visitors to Versailles, were dear to her, not as affording a healthful and becoming occupation, nor for the sale of the giver, but only because it recalled to her memory the gardens of Schoenbrunn, to which, as their malice suggested, she never ceased to look back with unpatriotic regret.

In one point of view they were unquestionably correct. The queen did undoubtedly desire to establish in the French court the customs and the feelings which, during her childhood, had prevailed at Vienna; but they were wholly wrong in thinking them Austrian usages. They were Lorrainese in their origin; they had been imported to Vienna for the first time by her own father, the Emperor Francis; when she referred to them, it was as "the patriarchal manners of the House of Lorraine[7]" that she spoke of them; and her preference for them was founded on the conviction that it was to them that her mother and her mother's family were indebted for the love and reverence of the people which all the trials and distresses of the struggle against Frederic had never been able to impair.

Nor was it only the old stiffness and formality, which had been compatible with the grossest license, that was now discountenanced. A wholly new spirit was introduced to animate the conversation with which those royal entertainments were enlivened. Under Louis XV., and indeed before his reign, intrigue and faction had been the real rulers of the court, spiteful detraction and scandal had been its sole language. But, to the dispositions, as benevolent as they were pure, of the young queen and her husband, malice and calumny were almost as hateful as profligacy itself. She held, with the great English dramatist, her contemporary, that true wit was nearly allied to good-nature;[8] and she showed herself more decided in nothing than in discouraging and checking every tendency to disparagement of the absent, and diffusing a tone of friendly kindness over society. On one occasion, when she heard some of her ladies laughing over a spiteful story, she reproved them plainly for their mirth as "bad taste." On another she asked some who were thus amusing themselves, "How they would like any one to speak thus of themselves in their absence, and before her?" and her precept, fortified by example (for no unkind comment on any one was ever heard to pass her lips), so effectually extinguished the habit of detraction that in a very short time it was remarked that no courtier ventured on an ill-natured word in her presence, and that even the Comte de Provence, who especially aimed at the reputation of a sayer of good things, and affected a character for cynical sharpness, learned at last to restrain his sarcastic tongue, and at least to pretend a disposition to look at people's characters and actions with as much indulgence as herself.

CHAPTER X.

Settlement of the Queen's Allowance.--Character and Views of Turgot.--She induces Gluck to visit Paris.--Performance of his Opera of "Iphigenie en Aulide."--The First Encore.--Marie Antoinette advocates the Re-establishment of the Parliaments, and receives an Address from them.-- English Visitors at the Court.--The King is compared to Louis XII. and Henri IV.--The Archduke Maximilian visits his Sister.--Factious Conduct of the Princes of the Blood.--Anti-Austrian Feeling in Paris.--The War of Grains.--The King is crowned at Rheims.--Feelings of Marie Antoinette.-- Her Improvements at the Trianon.--Her Garden Parties there.--Description of her Beauty by Burke, and by Horace Walpole.

Maria Teresa had warned her daughter against extravagance, a warning which would have been regarded as wholly misplaced by any other of the French princes, who were accustomed to treat the national treasury as a fund intended to supply the means for their utmost profusion, but which certainly coincided with the views of Marie Antoinette herself, who, as we have seen, vindicated herself from the charge of prodigality, and declared that she took great care that her improvements at the Trianon should not be beyond her means. Yet it would not have been surprising if they had been found to be so, since, even after she became queen, her income continued to be far too narrow for her rank. The nominal allowance of all former kings and queens had been fixed at an unreasonably low rate, from the pernicious custom of drawing on the treasury for all deficiencies; but this mode of proceeding was inconsistent with the notions of propriety entertained by the new sovereigns, and with those of the new finance minister.

Maurepas himself had never been distinguished for ability, but he was sufficiently clear-sighted to be aware that the principal difficulties of the State arose from the disorder into which the profligacy and prodigality of the late reign, ever since the death of the wise Fleury, had thrown its finances; and he had made a most happy choice for the office of comptroller-general of finance, appointing to it a man named Turgot, who, as Intendant of the Limousin, had brought that province into a condition of prosperity which had made it a model for the rest of the kingdom. In his new and more enlarged sphere of action, Turgot's abilities expanded; or, perhaps it should rather be said, had a fairer field for their display. He showed himself equally capable in every department of his duties; as a financial reformer, as an administrator, and as a legislator. No minister in the history of the nation had ever so united large-minded genius with disinterested integrity. He had not accepted office without a full perception of its difficulties. He saw all that had to be done, and applied himself to putting the finances of the nation on a healthy footing, as an indispensable preface to other reforms equally necessary. He easily secured the co-operation of the king and queen, Louis cheerfully adopting the retrenchments which he recommended, though some of them, such as the reduction in the hunting establishment, touched his personal tastes. But at the same time, as there was no illiberality in his economy, or, rather, as he saw that real economy could only be practiced if the sovereigns had a fixed income really adequate to the call upon it, he placed their allowances on a more satisfactory footing than had ever been fixed for them before, the queen's privy purse being settled at a sum which Mercy agreed with him would prove sufficient for all her expenses, though it was but 200,000 francs a year.

And so it was generally found to be; for, with the exception of an occasional fancy for some splendid jewel, Marie Antoinette had no expensive tastes. Her economy was even far greater than her attendants approved, extending to details which they would have wished her to regard as beneath the dignity of a sovereign;[1] and so judiciously did she manage her resources that she was able to defray out of her privy purse the pensions which she occasionally conferred on men eminent in arts or literature, whom she rightly judged it a royal duty to encourage.

One of her first acts of liberality of this kind was exercised in favor of a countryman of her own, the celebrated Gluck. Music was one of her most favorite accomplishments. She still devoted a portion of almost every day in taking lessons on the harp; but the French music was not to her taste; while, since the death of Handel, Gluck's superiority to all his other musical contemporaries had been generally acknowledged in all countries. She now, by the gift of a pension of 6000 francs, induced him to visit Paris. It was at the French opera that many of his most celebrated works were first given to the world; and an incident which took place at the performance of one of them showed that, if the frequenters of Versailles were dissatisfied at the inroads lately made on the old etiquette, the queen had a compensation in the warm attachment with which she had inspired the Parisians. Instead of conveying the performers to Versailles, as had been the extravagant practice of the late reign, Louis and Marie Antoinette went into Paris when they desired to visit the theatre. The citizens, delighted at the contrast which their frequent visits to the capital afforded to the marked dislike of it shown by the late king, crowded the theatre on every night on which they were expected; and on one of these occasions Gluck's "Iphigenie" was the opera selected for performance. It contains a chorus in which, according to the design of the dramatist, Achilles was directed to turn to his followers with the words

"Chantez, celebrez votre reine."

But the French opera-singers were a courtly race. The French opera had been established a century before as a Royal Academy of Music by Louis XIV., who had issued letters patent which declared the profession of an opera-singer one that might be followed even by a nobleman; and it seemed, therefore, quite consistent with the rank thus conferred on them that they should take the lead in paying loyal compliments to their princes. Accordingly, when the performer who represented the invincible son of Thetis, the popular tenor singer, Le Gros, came to the chorus in question, he was found to have prepared a slight change in his part. He did not address himself to the myrmidons behind him, but he came forward, and, with a bow to the boxes and pit, substituted the following,

"Chantons, celebrons notre reine,   L'hymen, que sous ses lois l'enchaine,   Va nous rendre a jamais heureux."

The audience was taken by surprise, but it was a surprise of delight. The whole house rose to its feet, cheering and clapping their hands. For the first time in theatrical history, the repetition of a song was demanded. The now familiar term of "Encore!" was heard and obeyed. The queen herself was affected to tears by the enthusiastic affection displayed toward her, nor at such a moment did she suffer her feeling of the evanescent character of popularity among so light-minded a people to dwell in her mind, or to mar the pleasure which such a reception was well calculated to impart.

Popularity at this moment seemed doubly valuable to her, because she was not ignorant that the feeling of disappointment at the unproductiveness of her marriage had recently been increased by the knowledge that the young Countess d'Artois was about to become a mother. And the attachment which she inspired was not confined to the play-goers; it was shared by a body so little inclined to exhibitions of impulsive loyalty as the Parliament. It has been seen that Louis XV. had abolished that body; but one of the first proposals made by Maurepas to the new king had had its re-establishment for its object. The question had been discussed in the king's council, and also in the royal family, with great eagerness. The ablest of the ministers protested against the restoration of an assembly which had invariably shown itself turbulent and usurping, and the king himself was generally understood to share their views. But Marie Antoinette, led by the advice of Choiseul, was eager in her support of Maurepas, and it was believed that her influence decided Louis. If it was so, it was an exertion of her power that she had ample cause to repent at a subsequent period; but at the time she thought of nothing but showing her sense of the general superiority of Choiseul, and so requiting some of the obligations under which she considered that she lay to him for arranging her marriage; and she received a deputation from the re-established Parliament with marked pleasure, and replied to their address with a graciousness which seemed intended to show that she sincerely rejoiced at the event which had given cause for it.

It was not till Christmas that the royal family went out of mourning; but, as soon as it was left off, the court returned to its accustomed gayety-- balls, concerts, and private theatricals occupying the evenings; though the people remarked with undisguised satisfaction that the expenses of former years had been greatly retrenched. It was also noticed that many foreigners of distinction, and especially some English ladies of high rank, gladly accepted invitations to the balls, which they certainly would not have done while their presence was likely to bring them into contact with Madame du Barri. Lady Ailesbury is especially mentioned as having been received with marked distinction by the queen, and also by the king, who was careful to show his approval of her entertainments by the share which he took in them; and, as he paraded the saloons arm-in-arm with her, to distinguish those whom she noticed, so that, to quote the words of one of the most lively chroniclers of the day, their example seemed to be fast bringing conjugal love and fidelity into fashion. She even persuaded him to depart still further from his usual reserve, so as to appear in costume at more than one fancy ball; the dress which he chose being that of the only predecessor of his own house whom he could in any point have desired to resemble, Henry IV. He had already been indirectly compared to that monarch, the first Bourbon king, by the ingenious flattery of a print- *seller. In the long list of sovereigns who had reigned over France in the five hundred years which had passed by since the warrior-saint of the Crusades had laid down his life on the sands of Tunis, there had been but two to whom their countrymen could look back with affection or respect-- Louis XII., to whom his subjects had given the title of The Good, and Henry, to whom more than one memorial still preserved the sur-name of The Great. And the courtly picture-dealer, eager to make his market of the gratitude with which his fellow-citizens greeted the reforms with which the reign-ing sovereign had already inaugurated his reign, contrived to extract a compliment to him even out of the severe prose of the multiplication-table; publishing a joint portrait of the three kings, Louis XII., Henry IV., and Louis XVI., with an inscrip-tion beneath to testify that 12 and 4 made 16.

In the spring of 1775, Marie Antoinette received a great pleasure in a visit from her younger brother, Maximilian. He was the only member of her family whom she had seen in the five years that had elapsed since she left Vienna. But, eagerly as she had looked forward to his visit, it did not bring her unmixed satisfaction, being marred by the ill-breeding of the princes of the blood, and still more by the approval of their conduct displayed by the citizens of Paris, which seemed to afford a convincing evidence of the small effect which even the queen's virtues and graces had produced in softening the old national feeling of enmity to the house of Austria. The archduke, who was still but a youth, did not assert his royal rank while on his travels, but preserved such an ***incognito*** as princes on such occasions are wont to as-sume, and took the title of Count de Burgau. The king's brothers, however, like the king himself, paid no regard to his disguise, but visited him at the first instant of his arrival; but the princes of the blood stood on their dignity, refused to acknowledge a rank which was not publicly avowed, or to recollect that the visitor was a foreigner and brother to their queen, and insisted on receiving the attention of the first visit from him. The excitement which the question caused in the palace, and the queen's indignation at the slight thus offered, as she conceived, to her brother, were great. High words passed between her and the Duc d'Orleans, the chief of the recusants, on the subject; and one part of her remonstrance throws a curious additional light on the strange distance which, as has been already pointed out, the etiquette of the French court had established between the sovereigns and the very highest of their subjects, even the nearest of their relations. The duke had insisted on the *incognito* as debarring Maximilian from all claim to attention from a prince like himself whose rank was not concealed. She urged that the king and his brothers had not regarded it in that light. "The duke knew," she said, "that the king had treated Maximilian as a brother; that he even invited him to sup in private with himself and her, an honor to which no prince of the blood had ever pretended." And, finally, warming with her subject, she told him that, though her brother would be sorry not to make the acquaintance of the princes of the blood, he had many other things in Paris to see, and would manage to do without it.[2] Her expostulation was fruitless. The princes adhered to their resolution, and she to hers. They were not admitted to any of the festivities of the palace during the archduke's stay, and were even excluded from all the private entertainments which were given in his honor, since she made it known that the king and she would refuse to attend any to which they were invited. But, though their conduct was surely both discourteous to a foreigner and disrespectful to their sovereign, the Parisian populace took their part; and some of them who showed themselves ostentatiously in the streets of the city on days on which there were parties at Versailles were loudly applauded by a crowd which was not entirely drawn from the lower classes. It was noticed that the Duc de Chartres, the son of the Duc d'Orleans, was one of the foremost in exciting this anti-Austrian feeling, the outbreak of which was especially remarkable as the first instance in which the enthusiasm of the citizens for Marie Antoinette seemed to have cooled, or at least to have been interrupted. And this change in their feelings produced so painful an impression on her mind, that, after her brother's departure, she abandoned her intention of going to the opera, though Gluck's "Orfeo" was to be performed, lest she should meet with a reception less cordial than that to which she had hitherto been accustomed.

This ebullition against the house of Austria, however, was at the moment dictated rather by discontent with the Home Government than by any settled feeling on the subject of foreign politics. Corn had been at a rather high price in Paris and its neighborhood throughout the winter; and the dearness was taken advantage of by the enemies of Turgot, and employed by them as an argument to prove the impolicy of his measures to introduce freedom of trade. They even organized[3] formidable riots at Paris and Versailles, which, however, Turgot, whose resolution was equal to his capacity, prevailed on the king to repress by acts of vigor very unusual to him, and very foreign to his disposition. The troops were called out; the Parliament was summoned to a Bed of Justice, and enjoined to put the law in force against the guilty; two of the most violent revolters were executed; order was restored, and the wholly factitious character of the outbreak was proved by the tranquillity which ensued, though the price of bread remained unaltered till the commencement of the harvest, the citizens themselves presently making a jest of their sedition, and nicknaming it The War of the Grains.[4]

In France, one excitement soon drives out another, and the whole attention of the nation was now fixed on the coronation, which had been appointed to take place in June. After some discussion, it had been settled that Louis should be crowned alone. There had not been many precedents for the coronation of a queen in France; and the last instance, that of Marie de Medicis, as having been followed by the assassination of her husband, was regarded by many as a bad omen. If Marie Antoinette had herself expressed any wish to be her husband's partner in the solemnity, it would certainly have been complied with, and their subsequent fate would have been regarded as a confirmation of the evil augury. But she was indifferent on the subject, and quite contented to behold it as a spectator. It took place on Sunday, the 11th of June, in the grand Cathedral at Rheims. The progress of the royal family, which had quit Versailles for that city on the preceding Monday, had resembled a triumphant procession, so enthusiastic had been the acclamations which had greeted the king and queen at each town through which they had passed; and all the previous displays of joy were outdone by the demonstrations afforded by the citizens of Rheims itself. It was midnight, on the 8th of June, when the queen reached the gates; but the road outside and the streets inside were thronged with a crowd as dense as midday could have produced, which followed her to the archbishop's palace, making the whole city resound with their loyal cheers; and which, the next morning, awaited her coming-forth after holding a grand reception of all the nobles of the province, to meet the king when he made his solemn entry in the afternoon. The ceremony in the cathedral was one of great magnificence; but, in the account of the day which, after her return to Versailles, she wrote to her mother, she does not enter into details, as being necessarily known to the empress in their general character; confining herself rather to a description of the impression which the manifest cordiality with which the whole people had entered into the spirit of the solemnity had made upon her own mind and heart.[5]

"The coronation was perfect in every respect. It was made plain that every one was highly delighted with the king, and so he deserves that all his subjects should be. Great and small, all displayed the greatest interest in him; and at the moment of placing the crown on his head the ceremonies of the church were interrupted by the most touching acclamations. I could not restrain myself; my tears flowed in spite of all my efforts, and the people were pleased to see them. During the whole time of our journey I did my best to correspond to the earnestness of the people; and although the heat was great, and the crowd immense, I do not regret my fatigue, which, moreover, has not injured my health. It is a very astonishing circumstance, but at the same time a very pleasant one, to be so well received only two months after the revolt, and in spite of the high price of bread, which unhappily still continues. It is a strange peculiarity in the French character to allow themselves to be so easily led away by mischievous suggestions, and then immediately to return to good behavior. It is very certain that when we see people, even in times of distress, treating us so well, we are the more bound to labor for their happiness. The king seems to me penetrated with this truth. As for me, I feel that all my life, even if I were to live a hundred years, I shall never forget the coronation day."

But all the tumultuous pomp and exultation only made her return with renewed pleasure to her quiet retreat of the Trianon, which, with the assistance of the illustrious Buffon, then superintendent of the king's gardens, and of Bernard de Jussieu, Director of the Jardin des Plantes, and celebrated as one of the first botanists of Europe, she was laying out with a delicate taste that long rendered it one of the chief attractions to all the inhabitants of the district. For the sentiment which she expressed in the letter to the empress, which has just been quoted, was not the mere formal utterance of a barren philanthropy, but was dictated and carried out by an active benevolence. She felt in her inmost heart the duty which she there professed, of exerting herself to promote the happiness of the people, and was far too unselfish to desire to keep to herself the whole of the delight her gardens were calculated to afford. The Trianon was a possession exactly calculated to gratify her taste for inno-cent rural pleasure. As she said herself, at Versailles she was a queen; here she was a plain country lady, superintending not only her flowers, but her farm-yard and her dairy, taking pride in her stock and her produce. She would invite the king and the rest of the royal family to garden parties, where, at a table set out under a bower of honeysuckle, she would pour out their coffee with her own hands, boasting of the thickness of her cream, the freshness of her eggs, the ruddiness and flavor of her strawberries, as so many proofs of her skill in managing her establishment; and would not fear to shock her aunts by tempting one of her sisters-in-law to a game at ball, or battledoor and shuttlecock. But she probably enjoyed still more the power of gratifying the inhabitants of Versailles and the neighborhood. The moment that her improvements were completed, she opened the gardens to the public to walk in, and gave out-of-door parties and children's dances, to which all the inhabit-ants of Versailles who presented themselves in decent apparel were admitted. She would even open the dance herself with some well-conducted boy, and afterward stroll among the crowd, talking affably to all the company, even to the governesses and nurses, and delighting the parents with the interest which she exhibited in the characters, the growth, and even the names of the children.

There were some who, startled at the unwonted sight of a sovereign so treat-ing her subjects as fellow-creatures, confessed a fear that such familiarity was not without its dangers;[6] but the objects of her condescension worshiped her for it; and for a time at least the great majority of the nation forgot that she was Austrian. She was now nearly twenty years of age. Her form had developed into a rare per-fection of elegance. Her features had added to the original brilliancy of her girlish loveliness something of that higher beauty which judgment and sagacity inspire, and which dignity renders only the more imposing; while the same benevolence and purity beamed in every look which were remarked as her most sterling char-acteristics on her first arrival in the country. And it is not to her French or German admirers alone that we are reduced to trust for the impression which at this time she made on all beholders. We have seen that English gentlemen and ladies of rank were frequent visitors to the French court; and from two of these, men of widely different characters, talents, and turns of mind, we have a striking concurrence of testimony as to the power of the fascination which she exerted on all who came within the sphere of her influence. Burke was the earlier visitor. Indeed, it was in the last months of the preceding reign, while she was still dauphiness, that she had excited in his enthusiastic imagination those emotions which he afterward described in words which will live as long as the English language. It was in the spring of 1774 that it seemed to him that "surely never lighted on this orb, which she hardly seemed to touch, a more delightful vision. I saw her just above the horizon, decorating and cheering the elevated sphere she just began to move in-- glittering like the morning-star, full of life, and splendor, and joy." No one could be less like Burke than Horace Walpole, a cynical observer, who piqued himself on indifference, and especially on a superiority to the vulgar belief in the merits and attractions of kings and princes. Yet his report of the charms of Marie Antoinette, as he saw them in the autumn of this year, 1775, reveals an admiration of them as vivid as that of the warm-hearted and more poetical Irishman. He saw her, as he reports to Lady Ossory, first at a state court hall,[7] given on the occasion of the marriage of the Princess Clotilde, in the theatre of the palace; and he would have desired to give his correspondent some description of the beauty of the building; "the bravest in the universe, and yet one in which taste predominates over expense;" but he was absorbed by the still more powerful attractions of the princess whom he had seen in it: "What I have to say I can tell your ladyship in a word, for it was impossible to see any thing but the queen. Hebes, and Floras, and Helens, and Graces are street-walkers to her. She is a statue and beauty when standing or sitting; grace itself when she moves." As he is writing to a lady, he proceeds to describe her dress, which to ladies of the present day may still have its interest: "She was dressed in silver, scattered over with *laurier* roses; few diamonds; and feathers, much lower than the monument." He proceeds to describe the ball itself, and some of the company, which was, however, very select; but at every sentence or two he comes back to the queen, so deep and so real was the impression which she had made on him. "Monsieur is very handsome. The Comte d'Artois is a better figure and a better dancer. Their characters approach to those of two other royal dukes.[8] There were but eight minuets, and, except the queen and princesses, only eight lady dancers; I was not so much struck with the dancing as I expected. For beauty I saw none, or the queen effaced all the rest. After the minuets were French country-dances, much incumbered by the long trains, longer tresses, and hoops. In the intervals of dancing, baskets of peaches, china oranges (a little out of season), biscuits, ices, and wine-and-water were presented to the royal family and dancers. The ball lasted just two hours. The monarch did not dance, but for the first two rounds of the minuet even the queen does not turn her back to him. Yet her behavior is as easy as divine."

Such was a French court ball on days of most special ceremony, a somewhat solemn affair, which required graciousness such as that of Marie Antoinette to make admission to every one a very enviable privilege; even though its stiffness had been in some degree relieved by a new regulation of the queen, that the invitations, which had hitherto been confined to matrons, should be extended to unmarried girls. Scarcely any change produced greater consternation among the admirers of old customs. The dowagers searched all the registers of those who had been admitted to the court balls since the beginning of the century to fortify their objections. But, to their dismay, some of the early festivities in the time of Marie Leczinska proved to have been shared by one or two noble maidens. The discovery was of little importance, since Marie Antoinette had shown that she was not afraid of making precedents. But still it in some degree silenced the grumblers, and for the rest of the reign no one contested the queen's right to decide who should, and who should not, be admitted to her society.

CHAPTER XI.

Tea is introduced.--Horse-racing of Count d'Artois.--Marie Antoinette goes to see it--The Queen's Submissiveness to the Reproofs of the Empress.-- Birth of the Duc d'Angouleme.--She at times speaks lightly of the King.-- The Emperor remonstrates with her.--Character of some of the Queen's Friends.--The Princess de Lamballe.--The Countess Jules de Polignac.-- They set the Queen against Turgot.--She procures his Dismissal.--She grati- fies Madame Polignac's Friends.--Her Regard for the French People.-- Wa- ter Parties on the Seine.--Her Health is Delicate.--Gambling at the Palace.

Nor were these the only innovations which marked the age. A rage for adopting English fashions--*Anglomanie*, as it was called--began to pre- vail; and, among the different modes in which it exhibited itself, it is especially noticed that tea[1] was now introduced, and began to share with coffee the privileges of affording sober refreshment to those who aspired in their different ways to give the tone to French society.

A less innocent novelty was a passion for horse-racing, in which the Comte d'Artois and the Duc de Chartres set the example of indulging, establishing a race- course in the Bois de Boulogne. The count had but little difficulty in persuading the queen to attend it, and she soon showed so decided a fancy for the sport, and became so regular a visitor of it, that a small stand was built for her, which in sub- sequent years provoked some unfavorable comments, when the princess obtained her leave to give luncheon in it to some of their racing friends, who were not in all instances of a character deserving to be brought into a royal presence.

She pursued this, as she pursued every other amusement which she took up, with great keenness for a while, so much so as to provoke earnest remonstrances from her mother, whose letters were commonly dictated by Mercy's reports and suggestions. Nor, if she felt uneasiness, did Maria Teresa spare her daughter, or take any great care to moderate her language of reproof. At times her tone is so severe as to excite a feeling of wonder at the submissiveness with which her letters were received. No express eulogy of her admirers could give so great an idea of Marie Antoinette's amiability, good-nature, genuine modesty, and sincere affection for her mother, as the ingenuousness with which she admits errors, or the temper with which she urges excuses. To that venerated parent she is just as patient of admonition, now that she is seated on a throne, as she could have been in her schoolroom at Schoenbrunn; and, in reply to the scoldings (no milder word can do justice to the earnest vehemence of the letters which at this time she received from Vienna), she pleads not only that an appetite for amusement is natural to her age, but that she enters into none of which the king does not fully approve, and none which are ever allowed to interfere with her giving him full enjoyment of her society whenever he has leisure or inclination for it.

But her replies to her mother hint also at the continuance of the old causes for her restlessness, and for her eager pursuit of new diversions to distract her thoughts. Her natural desire for children of her own was greatly increased when, on the 12th of August, her sister-in-law, the Countess d'Artois, presented her husband with a son.[2] She treated the young mother with a sisterly kindness suited to the occasion, which extorted the unqualified praise of Mercy himself; but she could not restrain her feelings on the subject to her mother, and she expressed to her frankly the extreme pain "which she suffered at thus seeing an heir to the throne who was not her own child." Nor is it strange that at such moments she should feel hurt at the coldness with which her husband continued to behave toward her, or that she should ran eagerly after any excitement which might aid in diverting her mind from a comparison of her own position with that of her happier sister-in-law.[3]

It would have been well if she had confined her expressions of disappointment to her mother. But since we may not disguise her occasional acts of imprudence, it must be confessed that at times her mortification led her to speak of her husband to strangers in a tone of disparagement which was highly unbecoming. Maximilian had been accompanied by the Count de Rosenburg, who had in consequence been admitted to the intimate society of the court during the archduke's visit, and who had inspired Marie Antoinette with so favorable an opinion of his character and judgment that after his return to Vienna she more than once sent him an account of the proceedings at the palace since her brother's departure. She describes to him a series of concerts, at which she had sung herself with some of her ladies. She gives him a list of the guests, remarking, with a particularity which seems to show that she expects her words to be reported to the empress, that the gentlemen, though amiable and well bred, were not young. But she also complains that the king's tastes do not resemble hers, that he cares for nothing but hunting and mechanical employments; and, indulging in an unwonted bit of sarcasm, she proceeds: "You will allow that I should not look well beside a forge. I could never become a Vulcan; and the part of Venus would displease him more than my real tastes, which he does not disapprove." In another letter she mentions him in a tone of contemptuous pity, almost equally unbecoming, speaking of him as "the poor man" whom she had made a tool of to further some views of her own, though Mercy assured the empress that her assertion of having so treated him was a mere fiction of her imagination, to impart a sort of lively tone to her letter; that, in spite of occasional outbursts of levity, she had in reality the firmest affection and esteem for Louis; and that nothing could be more irreproachable than her conduct toward him in every respect. He added that the people in general did her full justice on this head; that if her popularity with the Parisians had for a moment suffered any diminution through the artifices of faction, the cloud had been blown away; and that she had been recently received at the different theatres with as fervent a loyalty as had greeted even her first appearance.

The empress, however, was so uneasy that she induced her son, the Emperor Joseph, to add his expostulations to hers; and he, who was a prince of considerable shrewdness, as well as of a high idea of the proprieties of his rank, wrote her a long letter of remonstrance; imputing with great truth the failings, which he pointed out with sufficient plainness, to a facility of disposition which made her indulgent to the manoeuvres of those whom she admitted to her friendship, but who did not deserve such an honor. He even spoke of the society which she had gathered round her, as calculated to prevent him from performing his promise of paying her a visit; "for what should he do in a court of frivolous intriguers?" And he concluded by urging her to prevent these false friends from making a tool of her for the gratification of their own selfishness and rapacity; and to be solicitous for no friendship or confidence but that of her husband; the study of whose wishes was to her not only a state duty, but the only one which would make her permanently happy, and secure to her the lasting affection of the people.

There was, however, no subject on which Marie Antoinette was so little amenable to advice as the choice of her friends, and none on which she more required it. Above all the frequenters of the court, two ladies were distinguished by her especial favor--the Princess de Lamballe and the Countess de Polignac. The princess, a daughter of the Prince de Carignan in Savoy, having been married to the son of the Duc de Penthievre, was left a widow before she was twenty years of age. She had been originally recommended to Mario Antoinette in the first year of her residence in France, partly by her royal birth, and partly by her misfortunes; and the attachment which the dauphiness at once conceived for her was cemented by the ardor with which it was returned. In many respects the princess well deserved the favor with which she was regarded. Her temper was sweet and amiable; her character singularly truthful and sincere; and, that she might never be separated from her friend, the place of superintendent of the queen's household was revived for her. Some cavilers were disposed to grumble at the re-establishment of an office which had been suppressed as useless and costly; but no one could allege that Madame de Lamballe abused the royal favor, and her share in the calamities of later days justified the queen's choice by the proof it afforded of the princess's unalterable fidelity and devotion.

But the countess was a very different character. She had, indeed, a well-bred air of good humor, but that, with her youth (she was but twenty years of age), was her only qualification; for her capacity was narrow, her disposition selfish and grasping, and she was so inveterate a manoeuvrer, that, when she had no intrigues of her own on foot, she was always ready to lend herself to the plots of others. What was worse, she did not enjoy an untainted character. The name of the Comte de Vaudreuil was often coupled with hers in the scandals of the court. And the queen, since she could hardly be ignorant of the reports which were circulated, incurred, by the marked favor which she showed to the countess, the imputation of shutting her eyes to the frailties of her friends, and thus showing that dissoluteness was not an insuperable barrier to her partiality. It was only the earnest remonstrance of Mercy which prevented her from conferring the place of lady of honor on the countess; but she allowed her to exert a pernicious influence over her in many ways, for the countess was unwearied in soliciting appointments and pensions for her relatives; at times making demands in such numbers, and of so exorbitant a character, that the queen herself was forced to admit the impossibility of granting them all, though she still sought to gratify her to far too great an extent, and would not allow the proved insatiability of her and her family to open her eyes to her real character.

It was, however, a far more mischievous submission to the influence of the countess and her coterie, when she permitted them to prejudice her against Turgot, whom she had more than once described to her mother as an upright statesman, and who had constantly shown, so far as he could make compliance consistent with his duty to the State, a sincere desire to consult her wishes. But as the Polignac party saw in his prudence, integrity, and firmness the most formidable obstacle to their project of using the queen's favor to enrich themselves, she now yielded up her judgment to their calumnies. Forgetting her former praises of the minister's integrity, she began to disparage him as one whose measures caused general dissatisfaction, and at last she pushed her hostility to him so far that she actually tried to induce Louis not to be content with dismissing him from office, but to send him as a prisoner to the Bastille.[4] That she could not avoid feeling some shame at the part which she had acted may be inferred from the pains which she took to conceal it from her mother, whom she assured that, though she was not sorry for his dismissal, she had in no degree interfered in the matter; but "her conduct and even her intentions were well known, and known to be far removed from all manoeuvres and intrigues.[5]"

Unfortunately the ambassador's letters tell a different story. As a sincere friend as well as a loyal servant of Marie Antoinette, he expresses to the empress his deep feeling that, "as the comptroller- general enjoyed a great reputation for integrity, and was beloved by the people, it was a melancholy thing that his dismissal should be in part the queen's work,[6]" and his fear that her conduct in the affair may "hereafter bring upon her the reproaches of the king her husband, and even of the entire nation." The foreboding thus uttered was but too sadly realized. She had driven from her husband's councils the only man who combined with the penetration to perceive the absolute necessity of a large reform and the character of the changes required, the genius to devise them and the firmness to carry them out.

Thirteen years later, a variety of causes, some of which will be unfolded in the course of this narrative, had contributed to irritate the impatience of the nation, while the unskillfulness of the existing minister had disarmed the royal authority. And the very same reforms which would now have been accepted with general thankfulness were then only used by demagogues as a pretext for further inflaming the minds of the multitude against every thing which bore the slightest appearance of authority, even against the very sovereign who had granted them. France and all Europe to this day feel the sad effects of Marie Antoinette's interference.

She had given fatal proof of the truth of the words wrung from her by nervous excitement at the moment of the late king's death, when she declared that Louis and she were too young to reign; and the best excuse that can be found for her is that she was not yet one-and-twenty. It was not, however, wholly from submission to the interested malevolence of others that she had shown herself the enemy of the great financier and statesman. She had a spontaneous dislike to the retrenchments which necessarily formed a great portion of his economical measures; not as interfering with the indulgence of any extravagant tastes of her own, but as restraining her power of gratifying her friends. For she was entirely impressed with the idea that no person or body could have any right to call in question the king's disposal of the national revenue; and that there was no prerogative of the crown of which the exercise was more becoming to the royal dignity than that of granting pensions or creating sinecures with no limitations but such as might be imposed by his own will or discretion. And on this point her husband fully shared her feelings. "What," said he, on one occasion to Turgot, who was urging him to refuse an utterly unwarrantable application for a pension. "What are a thousand crowns a year?" "Sire," replied the minister, "they are the taxation of a village." The king acquiesced for the moment, but probably not without some secret wincing at the control to which he seemed to be subjected; and we may, perhaps, suppose that even the queen's disapproval of the minister would have been less effectual had it not been re-enforced by the king's own feelings.

In fact, that the part which she took against the great minister was the fruit of mere inconsiderateness and ignorance of the feelings and necessities of the nation, and that, if she had known the depth of the people's distress, and the degree in which it was caused by the viciousness of the whole existing system of government, she would gladly have promoted every measure which could tend to their relief, we may find abundant proof in a letter which she had written to her mother, a few weeks earlier. Maria Teresa had spoken with some harshness of the French fickleness. Marie Antoinette replies:[7]

"You are quite right in all you say about French levity, but I am truly grieved that on that account you should conceive an aversion for the nation. The disposition of the people is very inconsistent, but it is not bad. Pens and tongues utter a great many things which are not in their heart. The proof that they do not cherish hatred is that on the very slightest occasion they speak well of one, and even praise one much more than one deserves. I have just this moment myself had experience of this. There had been a terrible fire in Paris in the Palace of Justice, and the same day I was to have gone to the opera, so I did not go, but sent two hundred louis to relieve the most pressing cases of distress;[8] and ever since the fire, the very same people who had been circulating libels and songs against me[9] have been extolling me to the skies."

These revelations of her inmost thoughts to her mother show how real and warm was her affection for the French as a nation, as well as how little she claimed any merit for her endeavors to benefit them; though a subsequent passage in the same letter also shows that she had been so much annoyed by some pasquinades and libels, of which she had been the subject, that she had become careful not to furnish fresh opportunities to her enemies: "We have had here such a quantity of snow as has not been seen for many years, so that people are going about in sledges, as they do at Vienna. We were out in them yesterday about this place; and to-day there is to be a grand procession of them through Paris. I should greatly have liked to be able to go; but, as a queen has never been seen at such things, people might have made up stories if I had gone, and I preferred giving up the pleasure to being worried by fresh libels."

She was still as eager as ever in the pursuit of amusement, and especially of novelties in that way, when not restrained by considerations such as those which she here mentions. When at Choisy, she gave water parties on the river in boats with awnings, which she called gondolas, rowing down as far as the very entrance to the city. It was not quite a prudent diversion for her, for at this time her health was not very strong. She easily caught cold, and the reports of such attacks often caused great uneasiness at Vienna; but the watermen were highly delighted, looking on her act in putting herself under their care as a compliment to their craft; and some of them, to increase her pleasure, jumped overboard and swam about. Their well-meant gallantry, however, was nearly having an unfavorable effect; unaware that it was not an accident, she thought that their lives were in danger, and the fear for them turned her sick, while Madame de Lamballe fainted away. But when she perceived the truth, the qualm passed away, and she rewarded them handsomely for their ducking; begging, however, that it might not be repeated, and assuring them that she needed no such proof to convince her of their dutiful and faithful loyalty.

But the craving for excitement which was bred and nourished by the continuance of her unnatural position with respect to her husband in some parts of his treatment of her, was threatening to produce a very pernicious effect by leading her to become a gambler. Some of those ladies whom she admitted to her intimacy were deeply infected with this fatal passion; and one of the most mischievous and intriguing of the whole company, the Princess de Guimenee, introduced a play-table at some of her balls, which she induced Marie Antoinette to attend. At first the queen took no share in the play; as she had hitherto borne none, or only a formal part, in the gaming which, as we have seen, had long been a recognized feature in court entertainments; but gradually the hope of banishing vexation, if only by the substitution of a heavier care, got dominion over her, and in the autumn of 1776 we find Mercy commenting on her losses at lansquenet and faro, at that time the two most fashionable round games, the stakes at which often rose to a very considerable amount. Though she continued to indulge in this unhealthy pastime for some time, in Mercy's opinion she never took any real interest in it. She practiced it only because she wished to pass the time, and to drive away thought; and because the one accomplishment she wanted was the art of refusing. She even carried her complaisance so far as to allow professed gaming-table keepers to be brought from Paris to manage a faro-bank in her apartments, where the play was often continued long after midnight. It was not the least evil of this habit that it unavoidably left the king, who never quit his own apartments in the evening, to pass a great deal of time by himself; but, as if to make up for his coldness in one way, he was most indulgent in every other, and seemed to have made it a rule never to discountenance any thing which could amuse her. His behavior to her, in Mercy's eyes, seemed to resemble servility; "it was that of the most attentive courtier," and was carried so far as to treat with marked distinction persons whose character he was known to disapprove, solely because she regarded them with favor.[10]

In cases such as these the defects in the king's character contributed very injuriously to aggravate those in hers. She required control, and he was too young to exercise it. He had too little liveliness to enter into her amusements; too little penetration to see that, though many of them-- it may be said all, except the gaming-table--were innocent if he partook of them, indulgence in them, when he did not share them, could hardly fail to lead to unfriendly comments and misconstruction; though even his presence could hardly have saved his queen's dignity from some humiliation when wrangles took place, and accusations of cheating were made in her presence. The gaming-table is a notorious leveler of distinctions, and the worst-behaved of the guests were too frequently the king's own brothers; they were rude, overbearing, and ill-tempered. The Count de Provence on one occasion so wholly forgot the respect due to her, that he assaulted a gentleman in her presence; and the Count d'Artois, who played for very high stakes, invariably lost his temper when he lost his money. Indeed, the queen seems to have felt the discredit of such scenes; and it is probable that it was their frequent occurrence which led to a temporary suspension of the faro-bank; as a violent quarrel on the race-course between d'Artois and his cousin, the Duke de Chartres, whom he openly accused of cheating him, for a while disgusted her with horse-races, and led her to propose a substitution of some of the old exercises of chivalry, such as running at the ring; a proposal which had a great element of popularity in it, as being calculated to lead to a renewal of the old French pastimes, which seemed greatly preferable to the existing rage for copying, and copying badly, the fashions and pursuits of England.

CHAPTER XII.

Marie Antoinette finds herself in Debt.--Forgeries of her Name are committed.--The Queen devotes herself too much to Madame de Polignac and others.--Versailles is less frequented.--Remonstrances of the Empress.--Volatile Character of the Queen.--She goes to the Bals d'Opera at Paris.--She receives the Duke of Dorset and other English Nobles with Favor.--Grand Entertainment given her by the Count de Provence.--Character of the Emperor Joseph.--He visits Paris and Versailles.--His Feelings toward and Conversations with the King and Queen.--He goes to the Opera.--His Opinion of the Queen's Friends.--Marie Antoinette's Letter to the Empress on his Departure.--The Emperor leaves her a Letter of Advice.

But this addiction to play, though it was that consequence of the influence of the society to which Marie Antoinette was at this time so devoted, which would have seemed the most objectionable in the eyes of rigid moralists, was not that which excited the greatest dissatisfaction in the neighborhood of the court. Excessive gambling had so long been a notorious vice of the French princes, that her letting herself down to join the gaming-table was not regarded as indicating any peculiar laxity of principle; while the stakes which she permitted herself, and the losses she incurred, though they seemed heavy to her anxious German friends, were as nothing when compared with those of the king's brothers. Even when it became known that she was involved in debt, that again was regarded as an ordinary occurrence, apparently even by the king himself, who paid the amount (about L20,000) without a word of remonstrance, merely remarking that he did not wonder at her funds being exhausted since she had such a passion for diamonds. For a great portion of the debts had been incurred for some diamond ear-rings which the queen herself did not wish for, and had only bought to gratify Madame de Polignac, who had promised her custom to the jeweler who had them for sale. Marie Antoinette had evidently become less careful in regulating her expenses, till she was awakened by the discovery of a crime which she herself imputed to her own carelessness in such matters. The wife of the king's treasurer had borrowed money in her name, and had forged her handwriting to letters of acknowledgment of the loans. The fraud was only discovered through Mercy's vigilance, and the criminal was at seized and punished, but it proved a wholesome lesson to the queen, who never forgot it, though, as we shall see hereafter, if others remembered it, the recollection only served to induce them to try and enrich themselves by similar knaveries.

And this devotion of the queen to the society of the Polignacs and Guimenees, "her society," as she sometimes called it,[1] had also a mischievous effect in diminishing her popularity with the great body of the nobles. The custom of former sovereigns had been to hold receptions several evenings in each week, to which the men and women of the highest rank were proud to repair to pay their court. But now the royal apartments were generally empty, the king being alone in his private cabinet, while the queen was passing her time at some small private party of young people, by her presence often seeming to countenance intrigues of which she did not in her heart approve, and giddy conversation which was hardly consistent with her royal position; though Mercy, in reporting these habits to the empress, adds that the queen's own demeanor, even in the moments of apparently unrestrained familiarity, was marked by such uniform self-possession and dignity, that no one ever ventured to take liberties with her, or to approach her without the most entire respect.[2]

It was hardly strange, then, that those who were not members of this society should feel offended at finding the court, as it were, closed against them, and should cease to frequent the palace when they had no certainty of meeting any thing but empty rooms. They even absented themselves from the queen's balls, which in consequence were so thinly attended that sometimes there were scarcely a dozen dancers of each sex, so that it was universally remarked that never within the memory of the oldest courtiers had Versailles been so deserted as it was this winter; the difference between the scene which the palace presented now from what had been witnessed in previous seasons striking the queen herself, and inclining her to listen more readily to the remonstrances which, at Mercy's instigation, the empress addressed to her. Her mother pointed out to her, with all the weight of her own long experience, the incompatibility of a private mode of life, such as is suitable for subjects, with the state befitting a great sovereign; and urged her to recollect that all the king's subjects, so long as their rank and characters were such as to entitle them to admission at court, had an equal right to her attention; and that the system of exclusiveness which she had adopted was a dereliction of her duty, not only to those who were thus deprived of the honors of the reception to which they were entitled, but also to the king, her husband, who was injured by any line of conduct which tended to discourage the nobles of the land from paying their respects to him.

In the midst of all her giddiness, Marie Antoinette always listened with good humor, it may even be said with docility, to honest advice. No one ever in her rank was so unspoiled by authority; and more than one conversation which she held with the ambassador on the subject showed that these remonstrances, re-enforced as they were by the undeniable fact of the thinness of the company at the palace, had made an impression on her mind; though such impressions were as yet too apt to be fleeting, and too liable to be overborne by fresh temptations; for in volatile impulsiveness she resembled the French themselves, and the good resolutions she made one day were always liable to be forgotten the next. Nothing as yet was steady and unalterable in her character but her kindness of heart and graciousness of manner; they never changed; and it was on her genuine goodness of disposition and righteousness of intention that her German friends relied for producing an amendment as she grew older, far more than on any regrets for the past, or intentions of improvement for the future, which might be wrung from her by any momentary reflection or vexation.

If Versailles was less lively than usual, Paris, on the other hand, had never been so gay as during the carnival of 1777. The queen went to several of the masked balls at the opera with one or other of her brothers-in-law and their wives; the king expressing his perfect willingness that she should so amuse herself, but never being able to overcome his own indolence and shyness so far as to accompany her. It could not have been a very lively amusement. She did not dance, but sat in an arm-chair surveying the dancers, or walked down the saloon attended by an officer of the bodyguard and one lady in waiting, both masked like herself. Occasionally she would grant to some noble of high rank the honor of walking at her side; but it was remarked that those whom she thus distinguished were often foreigners; some English noblemen, such as the Duke of Dorset and Lord Strathavon being especially favored, for a reason which, as given by Mercy, shows that that insular stiffness which, with national self-complacency, Britons sometimes confess as a not unbecoming characteristic, was not at that time attributed to them by others; since the ambassador explains the queen's preference by the self-evident fact that the English gentlemen were the best dancers, and made the best figure in the ball-room.

But all the other festivities of this winter were thrown into the shade by an entertainment of extraordinary magnificence, which was given in the queen's honor by the Count de Provence at his villa at Brunoy.[3] The count was an admirer of Spenser, and appeared to desire to embody the spirit of that poet of the ancient chivalry in the scene which he presented to the view of his illustrious guest when she entered his grounds. Every one seemed asleep. Groups of cavaliers, armed *cap-a-pie*, and surrounded by a splendid retinue of squires and pages, were seen slumbering on the ground; their lances lying by their sides, their shields hanging on the trees which overshadowed them; their very horses reposing idly on the grass on which they cared not to browse. All seemed under the influence of a spell as powerful as that under which Merlin had bound the pitiless daughter of Arthur; but the moment that Marie Antoinette passed within the gates the enchantment was dissolved; the pages sprung to their feet, and brought the easily roused steeds to their awakened masters. Twenty-five challengers, with scarfs of green, the queen's favorite color, on snow-white chargers, overthrew an equal number of antagonists; but no deadly wounds were given. The victory of her champions having been decided, both parties of combatants mingled as spectators at a play, and afterward as dancers at a grand ball which was wound up by a display of fire-works and a superb illumination, of which the principal ornament was a gorgeous bouquet of flowers, in many-colored fire, lighting up the inscription "Vive Louis! Vive Marie Antoinette!"

At last, however, the carnival came to an end. Not too soon for the queen's good, since hunts and long rides by day, and balls kept up till a late hour by night, had been too much for her strength,[4] so that even indifferent observers remarked that she looked ill and had grown thin. But even had Lent not interrupted her amusements, she would have ceased for a while to regard them, her whole mind being now devoted to preparing for the reception of her brother, the Emperor Joseph, whose visit, which had been promised in the previous year, was at last fixed for the month of April. It was anticipated with anxiety by the Empress and Mercy, as well as by Marie Antoinette. He was a prince of a peculiar disposition and habits. Before his accession to the imperial throne, he had been kept, apparently not greatly against his will, in the background. Nor, while his father lived, did he give any indications of a desire for power, or of any capacity for exercising it; but since he had been placed on the throne he had displayed great activity and energy, though he was still, in the opinion of many, more of a philosopher--a detractor might said more of a pedant--than of a statesman. He studied theories of government, and was extremely fond of giving advice; and as both Louis and Marie Antoinette were persons who in many respects stood in need of friendly counsel, Mercy and Maria Teresa had both looked forward to his visit to the French court as an event likely to be of material service to both, while his sister regarded it with a mixed feeling of hope and fear, in which, however, the pleasurable emotions predominated.

She was not insensible to the probability that he would disapprove of some of her habits; indeed, we have already seen that he had expressed his disapproval of them, and of some of her friends, in the preceding year; and she dreaded his lectures; but, on the other hand, she felt confident that a personal acquaintance with the court would prove to him that many of the tales to her prejudice which had readied him had been mischievous exaggerations, and that thus he would be able to disabuse their mother, and to tranquilize her mind on many points. She hoped, too, that a personal knowledge of each other by him and her own husband would tend to cement a real friendship between them; and that his stronger mind would obtain an influence over Louis, which might induce him to rouse himself from his ordinary apathy and reserve, and make him more of a man of the world and more of a companion for her. Lastly, but probably above all, she thirsted with sisterly affection for the sight of her brother, and anticipated with pride the opportunity of presenting to her new countrymen a relation of whom she was proud on account of his personal endowments and character, and whose imperial rank made his visit wear the appearance of a marked compliment to the whole French nation.

High-strung expectations often insure their own disappointment, but it was not so in this instance; though the august visitor's first act displayed an eccentricity of disposition which must have led more people than one to entertain secret misgivings as to the consequences which might flow from a visit which had such a commencement. Like his brother Maximilian, he too traveled incognito, under the title of the Count Falkenstein; and he persisted in maintaining his disguise so absolutely that he refused to occupy the apartments which the queen had prepared for him in the palace, and insisted on taking up his quarters with Mercy in Paris, and at a hotel, for the few days which he passed at Versailles.

However, though by his conduct in this matter he to some extent disappointed the hope which his sister had conceived of an uninterrupted intercourse with him during his stay in France, in every other respect the visit passed off to the satisfaction of all the parties principally concerned. Fortunately, at their first interview Marie Antoinette herself made a most favorable impression on him. She had been but a child when he had last seen her. She was now a woman, and he was wholly unprepared for the matured and queenly beauty at which she had arrived. He was not a man to flatter any one, but almost his first words to her were that, had she not been his sister, he could not have refrained from seeking her hand that he might secure to himself so lovely a partner; and each succeeding meeting strengthened his admiration of her personal graces. She, always eager to please, was gratified at the feeling she had inspired; and thus an affectionate tone was from the first established between them, and all reserve was banished from their conversation. It was not diminished by the admonitions which, as he conceived, his age and greater experience entitled him to address to her, though sometimes they took the form of banter and ridicule, sometimes that of serious reproof;[5] but she bore all his lectures with unvarying good humor, promising him that the time should come when she would make the amendment which he desired; never attempting to conceal from him, and scarcely to excuse, the faults of which she was not unconscious, nor the vexations which in some particulars continually disquieted her.

It was, at least, equally fortunate that the king also conceived a great liking for his brother-in-law at first sight. His character disposed him to receive with eagerness advice from one who had himself occupied a throne for several years, and whose relationship seemed a sufficient warrant that his counsels would be honest and disinterested. Accordingly those about him soon remarked that Louis treated the emperor with a cordiality that he had never shown to any one else. They had many long and interesting conversations, sometimes with Marie Antoinette as a third party, sometimes by themselves. Louis discussed with the emperor his anxiety to have a family, and his hopes of such a result; and Joseph expressed his opinion freely on all subjects, even volunteering suggestions of a change in the king's habits; as when he recommended him, as a part of his kingly duty, to visit the different provinces, sea-ports, cities, and manufacturing towns of his kingdom, so as to acquaint himself generally with the feelings and resources of the people. Louis listened with attention. If there was any case in which the emperor's advice was thrown away, it was, if the queen's suspicions were correct, when he recommended to the king a line of conduct adverse to her influence.

Mercy had told the emperor that Louis was devotedly attached to the queen, but that he feared her at least as much as he loved her; and Joseph would have desired to see some of this fear transferred to and felt by her; and showed his wish that the king should exert his legitimate authority as a husband to check those habits of his wife of which they both disapproved, and which she herself did not defend. But, even if Louis did for a moment make up his mind to adopt a tone of authority, his resolution faded away in his wife's presence before her superior resolution; and to the end of their days she continued to be the leader, and he to follow her guidance.

It need hardly be told that so august a visitor had entertainments given in his honor. The king gave banquets at Versailles, the queen less formal parties at her Little Trianon, though gayeties were not much to Joseph's taste; and, at a visit which his sister compelled him to pay to the opera, he remained ensconced at the back of her box till she dragged him forward, and, as if by main force, presented him to the audience. The whole theatre resounded with applause, expressed in such a way as to mark that it was to the queen's brother, fully as much as to the emperor, that the homage was paid. The opera was "Iphigenie," the chorus in which, "***Chantons, celebrons notre reine***," had by this time been almost as fully adopted, as the expression of the national loyalty, as "God save the Queen" is in England. But even on its first performance it had not been hailed with more rapturous cheering than shook the whole house on this occasion; and Joseph had the satisfaction of believing that his sister's hold on the affection and on the respect of the Parisians was securely established.

He was less pleased at the races in the Bois de Boulogne, which he visited the next day. No inconsiderable part of Mercy's disapproval of such gatherings had been founded on the impropriety of gentlemen appearing in the queen's presence in top-boots and leather breeches, instead of in court dress; and the emperor's displeasure appears to have been chiefly excited by the hurry and want of stately order which were inseparable from the excitement of a race-course, and which, indifferent as he was to many points of etiquette, seemed even to him derogatory to the majesty of a queen to witness so closely. But he was far more dissatisfied with the company at the Princess de Guimenee's, to which the queen, with not quite her usual judgment, persuaded him one evening to accompany her. He saw not only gambling for much higher stakes than could be right for any lady to venture (the queen did not play herself), but he saw those who took part in the play lose their tempers over their cards and quarrel with one another; while he heard the hostess herself accused of cheating, the gamesters forgetting the respect due to their queen in their excitement and intemperance. He spoke strongly on the subject to Marie Antoinette, declaring that the apartment was no better than a common gaming-house; but was greatly mortified to see that his reproofs on this subject were received with less than the usual attention, and that she allowed her partiality for those whom she called her friends to outweigh her feeling of the impropriety of disorders of which she could not deny the existence.

But entertainments and amusements were not permitted to engross much of his time. If he visited the king and queen as a brother, he was visiting France and Paris as a sovereign and a statesman, and as such he made a careful inspection of all that Paris had most worthy of his attention--of the barracks, the arsenals, the hospitals, the manufactories. And he acquired a very high idea of the capabilities and resources of the country, though, at the same time, a very low opinion of the talents and integrity of the existing ministers. Of the king himself he conceived a favorable estimate. Of his desire to do his duty to his people he had always been convinced, but, in a long conversation which he had held with him on the character of the French people,[6] and of the best mode of governing them, in which Louis entered into many details, he found his correctness of judgment and general knowledge of sound principles of policy far superior to his anticipations, though at the same time he felt convinced that his want of readiness and decision, and his timidity in action, would always render and keep him very inferior to the queen, especially whenever it should be necessary to come to a prompt decision on matters of moment.

After a visit of six weeks, he quit Paris for his dominions in the Netherlands at the end of May, and a letter of the queen to her mother is very expressive of the pleasure which she had received from his visit, and of the lasting benefits which she hoped to derive from it.

"Versailles, June 14th.

"MY DEAREST MOTHER,--It is plain truth that the departure of the emperor has left a void in my heart from which I can not recover. I was so happy during the short time of his visit that at this moment it all seems like a dream. But one thing will never be a dream to me, and that is, the good advice and counsel which he gave me, and which is forever engraven in my heart.

"I must tell my dear mamma that he gave me one thing which I earnestly begged of him, and which causes me the greatest pleasure: it is a packet of advice, which he has left me in writing. At this moment it constitutes my chief reading; and, if ever I could forget what he said to me, which I do not believe I ever could, I should still have this paper always before me, which would soon recall me to my duty. My dear mamma will have learned by the courier, who started yesterday, how well the king behaved during the last moments of my brother's visit. I can assure you that I thoroughly understand him, and that he was really affected at the emperor's departure. As he does not always recollect to pay attention to forms, he does not at all times show his feelings to the outer world, but all that I see proves to me that he is truly attached to my brother, and that he has the greatest regard for him; and at the moment of my brother's departure, when I was in the deepest distress, he showed an attention to, and a tenderness for, me which all my life I shall never forget, and which would attach me to him, if I had not been attached to him already.

"It is impossible that my brother should not have been pleased with this nation. For one who, like him, knows how to estimate men, must have seen that, in spite of the exceeding levity which is inveterate in the people, there is a manliness and cleverness in them, and, speaking generally, an excellent heart, and a desire to do right. The only thing is to manage them properly.... I have this moment received your dear letter by the post. What goodness yours is, at a moment when you have so much business to think of, to recollect my name day! It overwhelms me. You offer up prayers for my happiness. The greatest happiness that I can have is to know that you are pleased with me, to deserve your kindness, and to convince you that no one in the world feels greater affection or greater respect for you than I."

It is a letter very characteristic of the writer, as showing that neither time nor distance could chill her affection for her family; and that the attainment of royal authority had in no degree extinguished her habitual feeling of duty: that it had even strengthened it by making its performance of importance not only to herself, but to others. Nor is the jealousy for the reputation of the French people, and the desire so warmly professed that they should have won her brother's favorable opinion, less becoming in a queen of France; while, to descend to minor points, the neatness and felicity of the language may be admitted to prove, if her education had been incomplete when she left Austria, with how much pains, since her progress had depended on herself, she had labored to make up for its deficiencies. That she should have asked her brother, as she here mentions, to leave her his advice in writing, is a practical proof that her expression of an earnest desire to do her duty was not a mere form of words; while the resolution which she avows never to forget his admonitions shows a genuine humility and candor, a sincere desire to be told of and to amend her faults, which one is hardly prepared to meet with in a queen of one-and-twenty. For Joseph did not spare her, nor forbear to set before her in the plainest light those parts of her conduct which he disapproved. He told her plainly that if in France people paid her respect and observance, it was only as the wife of their king that they honored her; and that the tone of superiority in which she sometimes allowed herself to speak of him was as ill-judged as it was unbecoming. He hinted his dissatisfaction at her conduct toward him as her husband in a series of questions which, unless she could answer as he wished, must, even in her own judgment, convict her of some failure in her duties to him. Did she show him that she was wholly occupied with him, that her study was to make him shine in the opinion of his subjects without any thought of herself? Did she stifle every wish to shine at his expense, to be affable when he was not so, to seem to attend to matters which he neglected? Did she preserve a discreet silence as to his faults and weaknesses, and make others keep silence about them also? Did she make excuses for him, and keep secret the fact of her acting as his adviser? Did, she study his character, his wishes? Did she take care never to seem cold or weary when with him, never indifferent to his conversation or his caresses?

The other matters on which the emperor chiefly dwells were those on which Mercy, and, by Mercy's advice, Maria Teresa also, had repeatedly pressed her. But those questions of Joseph's set plainly before us some of his young sister's difficulties and temptations, and, it must be confessed, some points in which her conduct was not wholly unimpeachable in discretion, even though her solid affection for her husband never wavered for a moment. In some respects they were an ill-assorted couple. He was slow, reserved, and awkward. She was clever, graceful, lively, and looking for liveliness. Both were thoroughly upright and conscientious; but he was indifferent to the opinions formed of him, while she was eager to please, to be ap-plauded, to be loved. The temptation was great, to one so young, at times to put her graces in contrast to his uncouthness; to be seen to lead him who had a right to lead her; and, though we may regret, we can not greatly wonder, that she had not always steadiness to resist it. One tie was still wanting to bind her to him more closely; and happily the day was not far distant when that was added to complete and rivet their union.

CHAPTER XIII.

Impressions made on the Queen by the Emperor's Visit.--Mutual Jealousies of her Favorites.--The Story of the Chevalier d'Assas.--The Terrace Concerts at Versailles--More Inroads on Etiquette.--Insolence and Unpopularity of the Count d'Artois.--Marie Antoinette takes Interest in Politics.--France concludes an Alliance with the United States.--Affairs of Bavaria.--Character of the Queen's Letters on Politics.--The Queen expects to become a Mother.--Voltaire returns to Paris.--The Queen declines to receive him.--Misconduct of the Duke of Orleans in the Action off Ushant.--The Queen uses her Influence in his Favor.

The emperor's admonitions and counsels had not been altogether unfruitful. If they had not at once entirely extinguished his sister's taste for the practices which he condemned, they had evidently weakened it; even though, as the first impression wore off, and her fear of being overwhelmed with *ennui*[1] resumed its empire, she relapsed for a while into her old habits, it was no longer with the same eagerness as before, and not without frequent avowals that they had lost their attraction. She visibly drew off from the entanglements of the coterie with which she had surrounded herself. The members had grown jealous of one another. Madame de Polignac feared the influence of the superior disinterestedness of the Princess de Lamballe; Madame de Guimenee, who was suspected of a want of even common honesty, grudged every favor that was bestowed on Madame de Polignac; and their rivalry, which was not always suppressed even in the queen's presence, was not only felt by her to be degrading to herself, but was also wearisome.

Throughout the autumn her occupations and amusements were of a simpler kind. She read more, and agreeably surprised De Vermond by the soundness of her reflections on many incidents and characters in history. Accounts of chivalrous deeds had an especial charm for her. Hume was still her favorite author. And it happened that, while the gallantry of the loyal champions of Charles I. was fresh in her memory, a casual conversation threw in her way an opportunity of doing honor to the self-devoted heroism of a French soldier whom the proudest of the British cavaliers might have welcomed as a brother, but whose valiant and self-sacrificing fidelity had been left unnoticed by the worthless sovereign in whose service he had perished, and by his ministers, who thought only of securing the favor of the reigning mistress--favor to be won by actions of a very different complexion.

In the Seven Years' War, when the French army, under the Marshal De Broglie, and the Prussians, under Prince Ferdinand of Brunswick, were watching one another in the neighborhood of Wesel, the Chevalier d'Assas, a captain in the regiment of Auvergne, was in command of an outpost on a dark night of October. He had strolled a little in advance of his sentries into the wood which fronted his position, when suddenly he found himself surrounded and seized by a body of armed enemies. They were the advanced guard of the prince's army, who was marching to surprise De Broglie by a night attack, and they threatened him with instant death if he made the slightest noise. If he were but silent, he was safe as a prisoner of war; but his safety would have been the ruin of the whole French army, which had no suspicion of its danger. He did not for even a moment hesitate. With all the strength of his voice he shouted to his men, who were within hearing, that the enemy were upon them, and fell, bayoneted to death, almost before the words had passed his lips. He had saved his comrades and his commander, and had influenced the issue of the whole campaign. The enemy, whose well-planned enterprise his self-devotion had baffled, paid a cordial tribute of praise to his heroism, Ferdinand himself publicly expressing his regret at the fate of one whose valor had shed honor on every brother-soldier; but not the slightest notice had been taken of him by those in authority in France till his exploit was accidentally mentioned in the queen's apartments. It filled her with admiration. She asked what had been done to commemorate so noble a deed. She was told "nothing;" the man and his gallantry had been alike forgotten. "Had he left descendants or kinsmen?" "He had a brother and two nephews; the brother a retired veteran of the same regiment, the nephews officers in different corps of the army." The dead hero was forgotten no longer. Marie

Antoinette never rested till she had procured an adequate pension for the brother, which was settled in perpetuity on the family; and promotion for both the nephews; and, as a further compliment, Clostercamp, the name of the village which was the scene of the brave deed, was added forever to their family name. The pension is paid to this day. For a time, indeed, it was suspended while France was under the sway of the rapacious and insensible murderers of the king who had granted it; but Napoleon restored it; and, amidst all the changes that have since taken place in the government of the country, every succeeding ruler has felt it equally honorable and politic to recognize the eternal claims which patriotic virtue has on the gratitude of the country.

Marie Antoinette had thus the honor of setting an example to the Government and the nation. Her heart was getting lighter as the vexations under which she had so long fretted began to disappear. The late card-parties were often superseded, throughout the autumn, by concerts on the terrace at Versailles, where the regimental bands were the performers, and to which all the well-dressed towns-people were admitted, while the queen, attended by the princesses and her ladies, and occasionally escorted by Louis himself, strolled up and down and among the crowd, diffusing even greater pleasure than they themselves enjoyed; Marie Antoinette, as usual, being the central object of attraction, and greeting all with a teaming brightness of expression, and an affability as cordial as it was dignified, which deserved to win all hearts. One of the entertainments which she gave to the king at the Little Trianon may he recorded, not for any unusual sumptuousness of the spectacle, but as having been the occasion on which she made one more inroad on the established etiquette of the court in one of its most unaccountable restrictions: to such royal parties the king's ministers had never been regarded as admissible, but on this night Marie Antoinette commanded the company of the Count and Countess de Maurepas. And the innovation was regarded not only by them as a singular favor, but by all their colleagues as a marked compliment to the whole body of ministers, and served to increase their desire to consult her inclinations in every matter in which she took an interest.

And the esteem which she thus conciliated was at this time not destitute of real importance, since the conduct of the other members of the royal family excited very different feelings. The Count de Provence was generally distrusted as intriguing and insincere. And the Count d'Artois, whose bad qualities were of a more conspicuous character, was becoming an object of general dislike, not so much from his dissipated mode of life as from the overbearing arrogance which he imparted into his pleasures. No rank was high enough to protect the objects of his displeasure from his insolence; even ladies were not safe from it;[2] while his extravagance was beyond all bounds since he considered himself entitled to claim from, the national treasury whatever he might require in addition to his stated income. He was at the same time repairing one castle, that of St. Germain, which the king had given him; rebuilding another large house which he had purchased in the same neighborhood; and pulling down and rebuilding a third, named Bagatelle, in the Bois de Boulogne, which he had just bought, and as to which he had laid an enormous wager that it should be completed and furnished in sixty days. To win his bet nearly a thousand workmen were employed day and night, and, as the requisite materials could not be provided at so short a notice, he sent patrols of his regiment to scour the roads, and seize every cart loaded with stones or timber for other employers, which he thus appropriated to his own use. He did, indeed, pay for the goods thus seized, and he won his bet, but when the princes of the land made so open a parade of their disregard of all law and all decency, one can hardly wonder that men in secret began, to talk of a revolution, or that all the graces and gentleness of the queen should be needed to outweigh such grave causes of discontent and indignation.

As the new year opened, affairs of a very different kind began to occupy the queen's attention. On political questions, the advice which the empress gave her differed in some degree from that of her embassador. Maria Teresa was an earnest politician, but she was also a mother; and, as being eager above all things for her daughter's happiness, while she entreated Marie Antoinette to study politics, history, and such other subjects as might qualify her to be an intelligent companion of the king, and so far as or whenever he might require it, his chief confidante, she warned her also against ever wishing to rule him. But Mercy was a statesman above every thing, and, feeling secure of being able to guide the queen, he desired to instill into her mind an ambition to govern the king. On one most important question she proved wholly unable to do so, since the decision taken was not even in accordance with the judgment or inclination of Louis himself; but he allowed himself to be persuaded by two of his ministers to adopt a course against which Joseph had earnestly warned him in the preceding year, and which, as he had been then convinced, was inconsistent alike with his position as a king and with his interests as King of France.

England had been for some years engaged in a civil war with her colonies in North America, and from the commencement of the contest a strong sympathy for the colonists had been evinced by a considerable party in France. Louis, who, for several reasons disliked England and English ideas, was at first inclined to coincide in this feeling as a development of anti-English principles: he was far from suspecting that its source was rather a revolutionary and republican sentiment. But he had conversed with his brother-in-law on the possibility of advantages which might accrue to France from the weakening of her old foe, if French aid should enable the Americans to establish their independence. Joseph's opinion was clear and unhesitating: "I am a king; it is my business to be royalist." And he easily convinced Louis that for one sovereign to assist the subjects of another monarch who were in open revolt, was to set a mischievous example which might in time be turned against himself. But since his return to Vienna, unprecedented disasters had befallen England; a whole army had laid down its arms; the ultimate success of the Americans seemed to every statesman in Europe to be assured, and the prospect gave such encouragement to the war party in the French cabinet that Louis could resist it no longer. In February, 1778, a treaty was concluded with the United States, as the insurgents called themselves; and France plunged into a war from which she had nothing to gain, which involved her in enormous expenses, which brought on her overwhelming defeats, and which, from its effects upon the troops sent to serve with the American army, who thus became infected with republican principles, had no slight influence in bringing about the calamities which, a few years later, overwhelmed both king and people.

All Marie Antoinette's language on the subject shows that she viewed the quarrel with England with even greater repugnance than her husband; but it is curious to see that her chief fear was lest the war should be waged by land, and that she felt much greater confidence in the French navy than in the army;[3] though it was just at this time that Voltaire was pointing out to his countrymen that England had always enjoyed and always would possess a maritime superiority which different inquirers might attribute to various causes, but which none could deny.[4]

Even before the conclusion of this treaty, however, the Americans had found sympathizers in France, to one of whom some of the circumstances of the war which they were now waging gave a subsequent importance to which no talents or virtues of his own entitled him. The Marquis de La Fayette was a young man of ancient family, and of fair but not excessive fortune. He was awkward in appearance and manner, gawky, red-haired, and singularly deficient in the accomplishments which were cultivated by other youths of his age and rank.[5] But he was deeply imbued with the doctrines of the new philosophy which saw virtue in the mere fact of resistance to authority; and when the colonists took up arms, he became eager to afford them such aid as he could give. He made the acquaintance of Silas Deane, one of the most unscrupulous of the American agents, who promised him, though he was only twenty years of age, the rank of major-general. As he was at all times the slave of a most overweening conceit, he was tempted by that bait; and, though he could not leave France without incurring the forfeiture of his military rank in the army of his own country, in April, 1777, he crossed over to America to serve as a volunteer under Washington, who naturally received with special distinction a recruit of such political importance. He was present at more than one battle, and was wounded at Brandywine; but the exploit which made him most conspicuous was a ridiculous act of bravado in sending a challenge to Lord Carlisle, the chief of the English Commissioners who in 1778 were dispatched to America to endeavor to re-establish peace. However, the close of the war, which ended, as is well known, in the humiliation of Great Britain and the establishment of the independence of the colonies, made him seem a hero to his countrymen on his return. The queen, always eager to encourage and reward feats of warlike enterprise, treated him with marked distinction, and procured him from her husband not only the restoration of his commission, but promotion to the command of a regiment;[6] kindness which, as will be seen, he afterward requited with the foulest ingratitude.

Nor was this most imprudent war with England the only question of foreign politics which at this time interested Marie Antoinette. Her native land, her mother's hereditary dominions, were also threatened with war. On the death of the Elector of Bavaria at the end of 1777, Joseph, who had been married to his sister, claimed a portion of his territories; and Frederick of Prussia, that "bad neighbor," as Marie Antoinette was wont to call him, announced his resolution to resist that claim, by force of arms if necessary. If he should carry out the resolution which he had announced, and if war should in consequence break out, much would depend on the attitude which France would assume on her fidelity to or disregard of the alliance which had now subsisted more than twenty years. So all-important to Austria was her decision, that Maria Teresa forgot the line which, as a general rule of conduct, she had recommended to her daughter, and wrote to her with the most extreme earnestness to entreat her to lose no opportunity of influencing the King's council. If it depended upon Maria Teresa, the claim would probably not have been advanced; but Joseph had made it on the part of the empire, and, when it was once made, the empress could not withhold her support from her son. She therefore threw herself into the quarrel with as much earnestness as if it had been her own. Indeed, since Joseph had as yet no authority over her hereditary possessions, it was only by her armies that it could be maintained; and in her letters to her daughter she declared that Marie Antoinette had her happiness, the welfare of her house, and of the whole Austrian nation in her hands; that all depended on her activity and affection. She knew that the French ministers were inclined to favor the views of Frederick, but if the alliance should be dissolved it would kill her.[7] Marie Antoinette grew pale at reading so ominous a denunciation. It required no art to inflame her against Frederick. The Seven Years' War had begun when she was but a year old; and all her life she had heard of nothing more frequently than of the rapacity and dishonesty of that unprincipled aggressor. She now entered with eagerness into her mother's views, and pressed them on Louis with unremitting diligence and considerable fertility of argument, though she was greatly dismayed at finding that not only his ministers, but he himself, regarded Austria as actuated by an aggressive ambition, and compared her claim to a portion of Bavaria to the partition of Poland, which, six years before, had drawn forth unwonted expressions of honorable indignation from even his unworthy grandfather. The idea that the alliance between France and the empire was itself at stake on the question, made her so anxious that she sent for the ministers themselves, pressing her views on both Maurepas and Vergennes with great earnestness. But they, though still faithful to the maintenance of the alliance, sympathized with the king rather than with her in his view of the character of the claim which the emperor had put forward; and they also urged another argument for abstaining from any active intervention, that the finances of the country were in so deplorable a state that France could not afford to go to war. It was plain, as she told them, that this consideration should at least equally have prevented their quarreling with England. But, in spite of all her persistence, they were not to be moved from this view of the true interest of France in the conjuncture that had arisen; and, accordingly, in the brief war which ensued between the empire and Prussia, France took no part, though it is more than probable that her mediation between the belligerents, which had no little share in bringing about the peace of Teschen,[8] was in a great degree owing to the queen's influence.

For she was not discouraged by her first failure, but renewed her importunities from time to time; and at last did succeed in wringing a promise from her husband that if Prussia should invade the Flemish provinces of Austria, France would arm on the empress's side. So fully did the affair absorb her attention that it made her indifferent to the gayeties which the carnival always brought round. She did, indeed, as a matter of duty, give one or two grand state balls, one of which, in which the dancers of the quadrilles were masked, and in which their dresses represented the male and female costumes of India, was long talked of for both the magnificence and the novelty of the spectacle; and she attended one or two of the opera-balls, under the escort of her brothers-in-law and their countesses; but they had begun to pall upon her, and she made repeated offers to the king to give them up and to spend her evenings in quiet with him. But he was more inclined to prompt her to seek amusement than to allow her to sacrifice any,[9] even such as he did not care to partake of; nevertheless, he was pleased with the offer, and it was observed by the courtiers that the mutual confidence of the husband and wife in each other was more marked and more firmly established than ever. He showed her all the dispatches, consulted her on all points, and explained his reasons when he could not adopt all her views. As Marie Antoinette wrote to her brother, "If it were possible to reckon wholly on any man, the king was the one on whom she could thoroughly rely.[10]"

So greatly, indeed, did the quarrel between Austria and Prussia engross her, that it even occupied the greater part of letters whose ostensible object is to announce prospects of personal happiness which might have been expected to extinguished every other consideration. In one, after touching briefly on her health and hopes, she proceeds:

"How kind my dear mamma is, to express her approval of the way in which I have conducted myself in these affairs up to the present time! Alas! there is no need for you to feel obliged to me; it was my heart that acted in the whole matter. I am only vexed at not being able to enter myself into the feelings of all these ministers, so as to be able to make them comprehend how every thing which has been done and demanded by the authorities at Vienna is just and reasonable. But unluckily none are more deaf than those who will not hear; and, besides, they have such a number of terms and phrases which mean nothing, that they bewilder themselves before they come to say a single reasonable thing. I will try one plan, and that is to speak to them both in the king's presence, to induce them, at least, to hold language suitable to the occasion to the King of Prussia; and in good truth it is for the interest and glory of the king[11] himself that I am anxious to see this done; for he can not but gain by supporting allies who on every account ought to be so dear to him.

"In other respects, and especially in my present conditions, he behaves most admirably, and is most attentive to me. I protest to you, my dear mamma, that my heart would be torn by the idea that you could for a moment suspect his good-will in what has been done. No; it is the terrible weakness of his ministers, and tis own great want of self-reliance, which does all the mischief; and I am sure that if he would never act but on his own judgment, every one would see his honesty, his correctness of feeling, and his tact, which at present they are far from appreciating. [12]"

And at the end of the month she writes again:

"I saw Mercy a day or two ago: he showed me the articles which the King of Prussia sent to my brother. I think it is impossible to see any thing more absurd than his proposals. In fact, they are so ridiculous that they must strike every one here; I can answer for their appearing so to the king. I have not been able to see the ministers. M. de Vergennes has not been here [she is writing from Marly]; he is not well, so that I must wait till we return to Versailles.

"I had seen before the correspondence of the King of Prussia with my brother. It is most abominable of the former to have sent it here, and the more so since, in truth, he has not much to boast of. His imprudence, his bad faith, and his malignant temper are visible in every line. I have been enchanted with my brother's answers. It is impossible to put into letters more grace, more moderation, and at the same time more force. I am going to say something which is very vain; but I do believe that there is not in the whole world any one but the emperor, the son of my dearest mother, who has the happiness of seeing her every day, who could write in such a manner."

There is no trace in these letters of the levity and giddiness of which Mercy so often complains, and which she at times did not deny. On the contrary, they display an earnestness as well as a good sense and an energy which are gracefully set off by the affection for her mother, and the pride in her brother's firmness and address which they also express. With respect to the conduct of Louis at this crisis we may perhaps differ from her; and may think that he rarely showed so much self-reliance, the general want of which was in truth his greatest defect, as when he preferred the arguments of Vergennes to her entreaties. But if her praises of the emperor are, as she herself terms them, vanity, it is the vanity of sisterly and patriotic affection, which can not but be regarded with approval; and we may see in it an additional proof of the correctness of an assertion, repeated over and over again in Mercy's correspondence, that, whenever Marie Antoinette gave the rein to her own natural impulses, she invariably both thought and acted rightly.

In one of the extracts which have just been quoted, the queen alludes to her own condition; and that, in any one less unselfish, might well have driven all other thoughts from her head. For the event to which she had so long looked forward as that which was wanted to crown her happiness, and which had been so long deferred that at times she had ceased to hope for it at all, was at last about to take place--she was about to become a mother. Her own joy at the prospect was shared to its full extent by both the king and the empress. Louis, roused out of his usual reserve, wrote with his own hand to both the empress and the emperor, to give the intelligence; and Maria Teresa declared that she had nothing left to wish for, and that she could now close her eyes in peace. And the news was received with almost equal pleasure by the citizens of Paris, who had long desired to see an heir born to the crown; and by those of Vienna, who had not yet forgotten the fair young princess, the flower of her mother's flock, as they had fondly called her, whom they had sent to fill a foreign throne. Her own happiness exhibited itself, as usual, in acts of benevolence, in the distribution of liberal gifts to the poor of Paris and Versailles, and a foundation of a hospital for those in a similar condition with herself.[13]

In the course of the spring, Paris was for a moment excited even more than by the declaration of war against England, or than by the expectation of the queen's confinement, by the return of Voltaire, who had long been in disgrace with the court, and had been for many years living in a sort of tacit exile on the borders of the Lake of Geneva. He was now in extreme old age, and, believing himself to have but a short time to live, he wished to see Paris once more, putting forward as his principal motive his desire to superintend the performance of his tragedy of "Irene." His admirers could easily secure him a brilliant reception at the theatre; but they were anxious above all things to obtain for him admission to the court, or at least a private interview with the queen. She felt in a dilemma. Joseph, a year before, had warned her against giving encouragement to a man whose principles deserved the reprobation of all sovereigns. He himself, though on his return to Vienna he had passed through Geneva, had avoided an interview with him, while the empress had been far more explicit in her condemnation of his character. On the other hand, Marie Antoinette had not yet learned the art of refusing, when those who solicited a favor had personal access to her; and she had also some curiosity to see a man whose literary fame was accounted one of the chief glories of the nation and the age. She consulted the king, but found Louis, on this subject, in entire agreement with her mother and her brother. He had no literary curiosity, and he disapproved equally the lessons which Voltaire had throughout his life sought to inculcate upon others, and the licentious habits with which he had exemplified his own principles in action. She yielded to his objections, and Voltaire, deeply mortified at the refusal,[14] was left to console himself as best he could with the enthusiastic acclamations of the play-goers of the capital, who crowned his bust on the stage, while he sat exultingly in his box, and escorted him back in triumph to his house; those who could approach near enough even kissing his garments as he passed, till he asked them whether they designed to kill him with delight; as, indeed, in some sense, they may be said to have done, for the excitement of the homage thus paid to him day after day, whenever he was seen in public, proved too much for his feeble frame. He was seized with illness, which, however, was but a natural decay, and in a few weeks after his arrival in Paris he died.

As the year wore on, Marie Antoinette was fully occupied in making arrangements for the child whose coming was expected with such impatience. Her mother is of course her chief confidante. She is to be the child's godmother; her name shall be the first its tongue is to learn to pronounce; while for its early management the advice of so experienced a parent is naturally sought with unhesitating deference. Still, Marie Antoinette is far from being always joyful. Russia has made an alliance with Prussia; Frederick has invaded Bohemia, and she is so overwhelmed with anxiety that she cancels invitations for parties which she was about to give at the Trianon, and would absent herself from the theatre and from all public places, did not Mercy persuade her that such a withdrawal would seem to be the effect, not of a natural anxiety, but of a despondency which would be both unroyal and unworthy of the reliance which she ought to feel on the proved valor of the Austrian armies.

The war with England, also, was an additional cause of solicitude and vexation. The sailors in whom she had expressed such confidence were not better able than before to contend with British antagonists. In an undecisive skirmish which took place in July between two fleets of the first magnitude, the French admiral, D'Orvilliers, had made a practical acknowledgment of his inferiority by retreating in the night, and eluding all the exertions of the English admiral, Keppel, to renew the action. The discontent in Paris was great; the populace was severe on one or two of the captains, who were thought to have taken undue care of their ships and of themselves, and especially bitter against the Duke de Chartres, who had had a rear-admiral's command in the fleet, and who, after having made himself conspicuous before D'Orvilliers sailed, by his boasts of the prowess which he intended to exhibit, had made himself equally notorious in the action itself by the pains he took to keep himself out of danger. On his return to Paris, shameless as he was, he scarcely dared show his face, till the Comte d'Artois persuaded the queen to throw her shield over him. It was impossible for him to remain in the navy; but, to soften his fall, the count proposed that the king should create a new appointment for him, as colonel-general of the light cavalry. Louis saw the impropriety of such a step: truly it was but a questionable compliment to pay to his hussars, to place in authority over them a man under whom no sailor would willingly serve. Marie Antoinette in her heart was as indignant as any one. Constitutionally an admirer of bravery, she had taken especial interest in the affairs of the fleet and in the details of this action. She had honored with the most marked eulogy the gallantry of Admiral du Chaffault, who had been severely wounded; but now she allowed herself to be persuaded that the duke's public disgrace would reflect on the whole royal family, and pressed the request so earnestly on the king that at last he yielded. In outward appearance the duke's honor was saved; but the public, whose judgment on such matter is generally sound, and who had revived against him some of the jests with which the comrades of Luxemburg had shown their scorn of the Duke de Maine, blamed her interference; and the duke himself, by the vile ingratitude with which he subsequently repaid her protection, gave but too sad proof that of all offenders against honor the most unworthy of royal indulgence is a coward.

CHAPTER XIV.

Birth of Madame Royale.--Festivities of Thanksgiving.--The Dames de la Halle at the Theatre.--Thanksgiving at Notre Dame.--The King goes to a Bal d'Opera.--The Queen's Carriage breaks down.--Marie Antoinette has the Measles.--Her Anxiety about the War.--Retrenchments of Expense.

Mercy, while deploring the occasional levity of the queen's conduct, and her immoderate thirst for amusement, had constantly looked forward to the birth of a child as the event which, by the fresh and engrossing occupation it would afford to her mind, would be the surest remedy for her juvenile heedlessness. And, as we have seen, the absence of any prospect of becoming a mother had, till recently, been a constant source of anxiety and vexation to the queen herself--the one drop of bitterness in her cup, which, but for that, would have been filled with delights. But this disappointment was now to pass away. From the moment that it was publicly announced that the queen was in the way to become a mother, one general desire seemed to prevail to show how deep an interest the whole nation felt in the event. In cathedrals, monasteries, abbeys, universities, and parish churches, masses were celebrated and prayers offered for her safe delivery. In many instances, private individuals even gave extraordinary alms to bring down the blessing of Heaven on the nation, so interested in the expected event. And on the 19th of December, 1778, the prayers were answered, and the hopes of the country in great measure realized by the birth of a princess, who was instantly christened Maria Therese Charlotte, in compliment to the empress, her godmother.

The labor was long, and had nearly proved fatal to the mother, from the strange and senseless custom which made the queen's bed-chamber on such an occasion a reception-room for every one, of whatever rank or station, who could force his way in.[1] In most countries, perhaps in all, the genuineness of a royal infant is assured by the presence of a few great officers of state; but on this occasion not only all the ministers, with all the members of the king's or of the queen's household, were present in the chamber, but a promiscuous rabble filled the adjacent saloon and gallery, and, the moment that it was announced that the birth was about to take place, rushed in disorderly tumult into the apartment, some climbing on the chairs and sofas, and even on the tables and wardrobes, to obtain a better sight of the patient. The uproar was great. The heat became intense; the queen fainted. The king himself dashed at the windows, which were firmly closed, and by an unusual effort of strength tore down the fastenings and admitted air into the room. The crowd was driven out, but Marie Antoinette continued insensible; and the moment was so critical that the physician had recourse to his lancet, and opened a vein in her foot. As the blood came she revived. The king himself came to her side, and announced to her that she was the mother of a daughter.

It can hardly be said that the hopes of the nation, or of the king himself, had been fully realized, since an heir to the throne, a dauphin, that had been universally hoped for. But in the general joy that was felt at the queen's safety the disappointment of this hope was disregarded, and the little princess, Madame Royale, as she was called from her birth, was received by the still loyal people in the same spirit as that in which Anne Boleyn's lady in waiting had announced to Henry VIII. the birth of her "fair young maid:"

"***King Henry***. Now by thy looks   I guess thy message. Is the queen delivered? Say ay; and of a boy.

"***Lady***. Ay, ay, my liege,   And of a lovely boy. The God of Heaven   Both now and ever bless her. 'Tis a girl,   Promises boys hereafter."

And a month before the empress had expressed a similar sentiment: "I trust," she wrote to her daughter in November, "that God will grant me the comfort of knowing that you are safely delivered. Every thing else is a matter of indifference. Boys will come after girls.[2]" And the same feeling was shared by the Parisians in general, and embodied by M. Imbert, a courtly poet, whose odes were greatly in vogue in the fashionable circles, in an epigram which was set to music and sung in the theatres.

"Pour toi, France, un dauphin doit naitre,   Une Princesse vient pour en etre

temoin,   Sitot qu'on voit une grace paraitre,   Croyez que l'amour n'est pas loin.
[3]"

Marie Antoinette herself was scarcely disappointed at all. When the attendants brought her her babe, she pressed it to her bosom. "Poor little thing," said she, "you are not what was desired, but you shall not be the less dear to me. A son would have belonged to the State; you will be my own: you shall have all my care, you shall share my happiness and sweeten my vexations.[4]"

The Count de Provence made no secret of his joy. He was still heir presumptive to the throne. And, though no one shared his feelings on the subject, for the next few weeks the whole kingdom, and especially the capital, was absorbed in public rejoicings. Her own thankfullness was displayed by Marie Antoinette in her usual way, by acts of benevolence. She sent large sums of money to the prisons to release poor debtors; she gave dowries to a hundred poor maidens; she applied to the chief officers of both army and navy to recommend her veterans worthy of especial reward; and to the curates of the metropolitan parishes to point out to her any deserving objects of charity; and she also settled pensions on a number of poor children who were born on the same day as the princess; one of whom, who owed her education to this grateful and royal liberality, became afterward known to every visitor of Paris as Madame Mars, the most accomplished of comic actresses.[5]

One portion of the rejoicings was marked by a curious incident, in which the same body whose right to a special place of honor at ceremonies connected with the personal happiness of the royal family we have already seen admitted--the ladies of the fish-market--again asserted their pretensions with triumphant success. On Christmas-eve the theatres were opened gratuitously, but these ladies, who, with their friends, the coal-heavers, selected the most aristocratic theatre, La Comedie Francaise, for the honor of their visit, arrived with aristocratic unpunctuality, so late that the guards stopped them at the doors, declaring that the house was full, and that there was not a seat vacant. They declared that in any event room must be made for them. "Who were in the boxes of the king and queen? for on such occasions those places were theirs of right." Even they, however, were full, and the guards demurred to the ladies' claim to be considered, though for this night only, as the representatives of royalty, and to have the existing occupants of the seats demanded turned out to make room for them. The box-keeper and the manager were sent for. The registers of the house confirmed the validity of the claim by former precedents, and a compromise was at last effected. Rows of benches were placed on each side of the stage itself. Those on the right were allotted to the coal-heavers as representatives of Louis; the ladies of the fish-market sat on the left as the deputies of Marie Antoinette. Before the play was allowed to begin, his majesty the king of the coal-heavers read the bulletin of the day announcing the rapid progress of the queen toward recovery; and then, giving his hand to the queen of the fish-wives, the august pair, followed by their respective suites, executed a dance expressive of their delight at the good news, and then resumed their seats, and listened to Voltaire's "Zaire" with the most edifying gravity.[6] It was evident that in some things there was already enough, and rather more than enough, of that equality the unreasonable and unpractical passion for which proved, a few years later, the most pregnant cause of immeasurable misery to the whole nation.

But the demonstration most in accordance with the queen's own taste was that which took place a few weeks later, when she went in a state procession to the great national cathedral of Notre Dame to return thanks; one most interesting part of the ceremony being the weddings of the hundred young couples to whom she had given dowries, who also received a silver medal to commemorate the day. The gay-ety of the spectacle, since they, with the formal witnesses of their marriage, filled a great part of the antechapel; and the blessings invoked on the queen's head as she left the cathedral by the prisoners whom she had released, and by the poor whose destitution she had relieved, made so great an impression on the spectators, that even the highest dignitaries of the court added their cheers and applause to those of the populace who escorted her coach to the gates on its return to Versailles.

She was now, for the first time since her arrival in France, really and entirely happy, without one vexation or one foreboding of evil. The king's attachment to her was rendered, if not deeper than before, at least far more lively and demonstra-tive by the birth of his daughter; his delight carrying him at times to most unaccus-tomed ebullitions of gayety. On the last Sunday of the carnival, he even went alone with the queen to the masked opera ball, and was highly amused at finding that not one of the company recognized either him or her. He even proposed to repeat his visit on Shrove-Tuesday; but when the evening came he changed his mind, and in-sisted on the queen's going by herself with one of her ladies, and the change of plan led to an incident which at the time afforded great amusement to Marie Antoinette, though it afterward proved a great annoyance, as furnishing a pretext for malicious stories and scandal. To preserve her *incognito*, a private carriage was hired for her, which broke down in the street close by a silk-mercer's shop. As the queen was already masked, the shop-men did not know her, and, at the request of the lady who attended her, stopped for her the first hackney-coach which passed, and in that unroyal vehicle, such as certainly no sovereign of France had ever set foot in before, she at last reached the theatre. As before, no one recognized her, and she might have enjoyed the scene and returned to Versailles in the most absolute secrecy, had not her sense of the fun of a queen using such a conveyance overpowered her wish for concealment, so that when, in the course of the evening, she met one or two persons of distinction whom she knew, she could not forbear telling them who she was, and that she had come in a hackney-coach.

Her health seemed less delicate than it had been before her confinement. But in the spring she was attacked by the measles, and her illness, slight as it was, gave occasion to a curious passage in court history. The fear of infection was always great at Versailles, and, as the king himself and some of the ladies had never had the complaint, they were excluded from her room. But that she might not be left without attendants, four nobles of the court, the Duke de Coigny, the Duke de Guines, the Count Esterhazy, and the Baron de Besenval, in something of the old spirit of chivalry, devoted themselves to her service, and solicited permission to watch by her bedside till she recovered. As has been already seen, the bed-chamber and dressing-room of a queen of France had never been guarded from intrusion with the jealousy which protects the apartments of ladies in other countries, so that the proposal was less startling than it would have been considered elsewhere, while the number of nurses removed all pretext for scandal. Louis willingly gave the required permission, being apparently flattered by the solicitude exhibited for his queen's health. And each morning at seven the sick-watchers[7] took their seats in the queen's chamber, sharing with the Countess of Provence, the Princesse de Lamballe, and the Count d'Artois the task of keeping order and quiet in the sick-room till eleven at night. Though there was no scandal, there was plenty of jesting at so novel an arrangement. Wags proposed that in the case of the king being taken ill, a list should be prepared of the ladies who should tend his sick-bed. However, the champions were not long on duty: at the end of little more than a week their pa-tient was convalescent. She herself took off the sentence of banishment which she had pronounced against the king in a brief and affectionate note, which said "that she had suffered a great deal, but what she had felt most was to be for so many days deprived of the pleasure of embracing him." And the temporary separation seemed to have but increased their mutual affection for each other.

The Trianon was now more than ever delightful to her. The new plantations, which contained no fewer than eight hundred different kinds of trees, rich with every variety of foliage, were beginning, by their effectiveness, to give evidence of the taste with which they had been laid out; while with a charity which could not bear to keep her blessings wholly to herself, she had set apart one corner of the grounds for a row of picturesque cottages, in which she had established a number of pensioners whom age or infirmity had rendered destitute, and whom she constantly visited with presents from her dairy or her fruit-trees. Roaming about the lawns and walks, which she had made herself, in a muslin gown and a plain straw hat, she could forget that she was a queen. She did not suspect that the intriguers, who from time to time maligned her most innocent actions, were misrepresenting even these simple and natural pleasures, and whispering in their secret cabals that her very dress was a proof that she still clung as resolutely as ever to her Austrian pref-erences; that she discarded her silk gowns because they were the work of French manufacturers, while they were her brother's Flemish subjects who supplied her with muslins.

But, far beyond her plantations and her flowers, her child was to her a source of unceasing delight. She could be carried by her side about the garden a great part of the day. For, as in her anticipations and preparations she had told her mother long before, French parents kept their children as much as possible in the open air,[8] a fashion which fully accorded with her own notions of what was best calculated to give an infant health and strength. And before the babe was five months old,[9] she flattered herself that it already distinguished her from its nurses. That nothing might be wanting to her comfort, peace was re-established between Austria and Prussia; and if at this time the war with England did make her in some degree uneasy, she yet felt a sanguine anticipation of triumph for the French arms, in the event of a battle between the hostile fleets; a result of which, when the antagonists did come within sight of each other, it appeared that the French and Spanish admirals felt far less confident. Her anxieties and hopes are vividly set forth in a letter which, in the course of the summer, she wrote to her mother, which is also singularly interesting from its self-examination, and from the substantial proof it supplies of the correctness of those anticipations which were based on the salutary effect which her novel position as a mother might be expected to have upon her character.

"Versailles, August 16th.

"My Dearest Mother,--I can not find language to express to my dear mamma my thanks for her two letters, and for the kindness with which she expresses her willingness to exert herself to the utmost to procure us peace.[10] It is true that that would be a great happiness, and my heart desires it more than any thing in the world; but, unhappily, I do not see any appearance of it at present. Every thing depends on the moment. Our fleets, the French and Spanish, being now united, we have a considerable superiority.[11]

"They are now in the Channel; and I can not without great agitation reflect that at any instant the whole fate of the war may be decided. I am also terrified at the approach of September, when the sea is no longer practicable. In short, it is only on the bosom of my dearest mamma that I lay aside all my disquiet God grant that it may be groundless, but her kindness encourages me to speak to her as I think. The king is touched, quite as he should be, with all the service you so kindly propose to render him; and I do not doubt that he will be always eager to profit by it, rather than to deliver himself up to the intrigues of those who have so frequently deceived France, and whom we must regard as our natural enemies.

"My health is completely re-established. I am going to resume my ordinary way of life, and consequently I hope soon to be able to announce to my dearest mother fresh news such as that of last year. She may feel quite re-assured now as to my behavior. I feel too strongly the necessity of having more children to be careless in that. If I have formerly done amiss, it was my youth and my levity; but now my head is thoroughly steadied, and you may reckon confidently on my properly feeling all my duties. Besides that, I owe such conduct to the king as a reward for his tenderness, and, I will venture to say it, his confidence in me, for which I can only praise him more find more.

"... I venture to send my dear mamma the picture of my daughter: it is very like her. The dear little thing begins to walk very well in her leading-strings. She has been able to say "papa" for some days. Her teeth have not yet come through, but we can feel them all. I am very glad that her first word has been her father's name. It is one more tie for him. He behaves to me most admirably, and nothing could be wanting to make me love him more. My dear mamma will forgive my twaddling about the little one; but she is so kind that sometimes I abuse her kindness."

It was well for Marie Antoinette's happiness that her husband was one in whom, as we have seen that she told her mother, she could feel entire confidence, for during her seclusion in the measles the intriguers of the court had ventured to try and work upon him. Mercy had reason to suspect that some were even wicked enough to desire to influence him against his wife by the same means by which the Duke de Richelieu had formerly alienated his grandfather from Marie Leczinska; and the queen herself received proof positive that Maurepas, in spite of her civilities to him and his countess, had become jealous of her political influence, and had endeavored to prevent his consulting her on public affairs. But all manoeuvres intended to disturb the conjugal felicity of the royal pair were harmless against the honest fidelity of the king, the graceful affection of the queen, and the firm confidence of each in the other. The people generally felt that the influence which it was now notorious that the queen did exert on public affairs was a salutary one; and great satisfaction was expressed when it became known in the autumn that the usual visit to Fontainebleau was given up, partly as being costly, and therefore undesirable while the nation had need to concentrate all its resources on the effective prosecution of the war, and partly that the king might be always within reach of his ministers in the event of any intelligence of importance arriving which required prompt decision.

Her letters to her mother at this time show how entirely her whole attention was engrossed by the war; and, at the same time, with what wise earnestness she desired the re-establishment of peace. Even some gleams of success which had attended the French arms in the West Indies, where the Marquis de Bouille, the most skillful soldier of whom France at that time could boast, took one or two of the British islands, and the Count d'Estaing, whose fleet of thirty-six sail was for a short time far superior to the English force in that quarter, captured one or two more, did not diminish her eagerness for a cessation of the war. Though it is curious to see that she had become so deeply imbued with the principles of statesmanship with which

M. Necker, the present financial minister, was seeking to inspire the nation, that her objections to the continuance of the war turned chiefly on the degree in which it affected the revenue and expenditure of the kingdom. She evidently sympathizes in the disappointment which, as she reports to the empress, is generally felt by the public at the mismanagement of the admiral, M. d'Orvilliers, who, with forces so superior to those of the English, has neither been able to fall in with them so as to give them battle, nor to hinder any of their merchantmen from reaching their harbors in safety. As it is, he will have spent a great deal of money in doing nothing. [12] And a month later she repeats the complaints.[13] The king and she have renounced the journey to Fontainebleau because of the expenses of the war; and also that they may be in the way to receive earlier intelligence from the army. But the fleet has not been able to fall in with the English, and has done nothing at all. It is a campaign lost, and which has cost a great deal of money. What is still more afflicting is, that disease has broken out on board the ships, and has caused great havoc; and the dysentery, which is raging as an epidemic in Brittany and Normandy, has attacked the land force also, which was intended to embark for England ... "I greatly fear," she proceeds, "that these misfortunes of ours will render the English difficult to treat with, and may prevent proposals of peace, of which I see no immediate prospect. I am constantly persuaded that if the king should require a mediation, the intrigues of the King of Prussia will fail, and will not prevent the king from availing himself of the offers of my dear mamma. I shall take care never to lose sight of this object, which is of such interest to the whole happiness of my life." So full is her mind of the war, that four or five words in each letter to report that "her daughter is in perfect health," or that "she has cut four teeth," are all that she can spare for that subject, generally of such engrossing interest to herself and the empress; while, before the end of the year, we find her taking even the domestic troubles of England into her calculations,[14] and speculating on the degree in which the aspect of affairs in Ireland may affect the great preparations which the English ministers are making for the next campaign.

The mere habit of devoting so much consideration to affairs of this kind was beneficial as tending to mature and develop her capacity. She was rapidly learning to take large views of political questions, even if they were not always correct. And the acuteness and earnestness of her comments on them daily increased her influence over both the king and the ministers, so that in the course of the autumn Mercy could assure the empress[15] that "the king's complaisance toward her increased every day," that "he made it his study to anticipate all her wishes, and that this attention showed itself in every kind of detail," while Maurepas also was unable to conceal from himself that her voice always prevailed "in every case in which she chose to exert a decisive will," and accordingly "bent himself very prudently" before a power which he had no means of resisting. So solicitous indeed did the whole council show itself to please her, that when the king, who was aware that her allowance, in spite of its recent increase was insufficient to defray the charges to which she was liable, proposed to double it, Necker himself, with all his zeal for economy and retrenchment, eagerly embraced the suggestion; and its adoption gave the queen a fresh opportunity of strengthening the esteem and affection of the nation, by declaring that while the war lasted she would only accept half the sum thus placed at her disposal.

The continuance of the war was not without its effect on the gayety of the court, from the number of officers whom their military duties detained with their regiments; but the quiet was beneficial to Marie Antoinette, whose health was again becoming delicate, so much so, that after a grand drawing-room which she held on New-year's-eve, and which was attended by nearly two hundred of the chief ladies of the city, she was completely knocked up, and forced to put herself under the care of her physician.

Meanwhile the war became more formidable. The English admiral, Rodney, the greatest sailor who, as yet, had ever commanded a British fleet, in the middle of January utterly destroyed a strong Spanish squadron off Cape St. Vincent; and as from the coast of Spain he proceeded to the West Indies, the French ministry had ample reason to be alarmed for the safety of the force which they had in those regions. It was evident that it would require every effort that could be made to enable their sailors to maintain the contest against an antagonist so brave and so skillful And, as one of the first steps toward such a result, Necker obtained the king's consent to a great reform in the expenditure of the court and in the civil service; and to the abolition of a great number of costly sinecures. We may be able to form some idea of the prodigality which had hitherto wasted the revenues of the country, from the circumstance that a single edict suppressed above four hundred offices; and

Marie Antoinette was so sincere in her desire to promote such measures, that she speaks warmly in their praise to her mother, even though they greatly curtailed her power of gratifying her own favorites.

"The king," she says, "has just issued an edict which is as yet only the forerunner of a reform which he designs, to make both in his own household and in mine. If it be carried out, it will be a great benefit, not only for the economy which it will introduce, but still more for its agreement with public opinion, and for the satisfaction it will give the nation." It is impossible for any language to show more completely how, above all things, she made the good of the country her first object. And she was the more inclined to approve of all that was being done in this way from her conviction that Necker was both honest and able; an opinion which she shared with, if she had not learned it from, her mother and her brother, and which was to some extent justified by the comparative order which he had re-established in the finance of the country, and by the degree in which he had revived public credit. She was not aware that the real dangers of the situation had a source deeper than any financial difficulty, a fact which Necker himself was unable to comprehend. And she could not foresee, when it became necessary to grapple with those dangers, how unequal to the struggle the great banker would be found.

It may, perhaps, be inferred that she did suspect Necker of some deficiency in the higher qualities of statesmanship when, in the spring of 1780, she told her mother that "she would give every thing in the world to have a Prince Kaunitz in the ministry;[16] but that such men were rare, and were only to be found by those who, like the empress herself, had the sagacity to discover and the judgment to appreciate such merit." She was, however, shutting her eyes to the fact that her husband had had a minister far superior to Kaunitz; and that she herself had lent her aid to drive him from his service.

CHAPTER XV.

Anglomania in Paris.--The Winter at Versailles.--Hunting.--Private Theatricals.--Death of Prince Charles of Lorraine.--Successes of the English in America.--Education of the Duc d'Angouleme.--Libelous Attacks on the Queen.--Death of the Empress.--Favor shown to some of the Swedish Nobles.--The Count de Fersen.--Necker retires from Office.--His Character.

It is curious, while the resources of the kingdom were so severely taxed to maintain the war against England, of which every succeeding dispatch from the seat of war showed more and more the imprudence, to read in Mercy's correspondence accounts of the Anglomania, which still subsisted in Paris; surpassing that which the letters of the empress describe as reigning in Vienna, though it did not show itself now in quite the same manner as a year or two before, in the aping of English vices, gambling at races, and hard drinking, but rather in a copying of the fashions of men's dress; in the introduction of top-boots; and, very wholesomely, in the adoption of a country life by many of the great nobles, in imitation of the English gentry; so that, for the first time since the coronation of Louis XIV., the great territorial lords began to spend a considerable part of the year on their estates, and no longer to think the interests and requirements of their tenants and dependents beneath their notice.

The winter of 1779 and the spring of 1780 passed very happily. If Versailles, from the reasons mentioned above, was not as crowded as in former years, it was very lively. The season was unusually mild; the hunting was scarcely ever interrupted, and Marie Antoinette, who now made it a rule to accompany her husband on every possible occasion, sometimes did not return from the hunt till the night was far advanced, and found her health much benefited by the habit of spending the greater part of even a winter's day in the open air. Her garden, too, which daily occupied more and more of her attention, as it increased in beauty, had the same tendency; and her anxiety to profit by the experience of others on one occasion inflicted a whimsical disappointment of the free-thinkers of the court. The profligate and sentimental infidel Rousseau had died a couple of years before, and had been buried at Ermenonville, in the park of the Count de Girardin. In the course of the summer the queen drove over to Ermenonville, and the admirers of the versatile writer flattered themselves that her object was to pay a visit of homage to the shrine of their idol; but they wore greatly mortified to find that, though his tomb was pointed out to her, she took no further notice of it than such as consisted of a passing remark that it was very neat, and very prettily placed; and that what had attracted her curiosity was the English garden which the count had recently laid out at a great expense, and from which she had been led to expect that she might derive some hints for the further improvement of her own Little Trianon.

She had not yet entirely given up her desire for novelty in her amusements; and she began now to establish private theatricals at Versailles, choosing light comedies interspersed with song, and with but few characters, the male parts being filled by the Count d'Artois and some of the most distinguished officers of the household, while she herself took one of the female parts; the spectators being confined to the royal family and those nobles whose posts entitled them to immediate attendance on the king and queen. She was so anxious to perform her own part well, though she did not take any of the principal characters, but preferred to act the waiting-woman rather than the mistress, that she placed herself under the tuition of Michu, a professional actor of reputation from one of the Parisian theatres; but, though the audience was far too courtly to greet her appearance on the stage without vociferous applause, the preponderance of evidence must lead us to believe that her majesty was not a good actress.[1] And perhaps we may think that as the parts which she selected required rather an arch pertness than the grace and majesty which were more natural to her, so, also, they were not altogether in keeping with the stately dignity which queens should never wholly lay aside.

It was well, however, that she should have amusements to cheer her, for the year was destined to bring her heavy troubles before its close: losses in her own family, which would be felt with terrible heaviness by her affectionate disposition, were impending over her; while the news from America, where the English army at this time was achieving triumphs which seemed likely to have a decisive influence on the result of the war, caused her great anxiety. How great, a letter which she wrote to her mother in July affords a striking proof. In June, when she heard of the dangerous illness of her uncle, Prince Charles of Lorraine, now Governor of the Low Countries, formerly the gallant antagonist of Frederick of Prussia, she declared that "the intelligence overwhelmed her with an agitation and grief such as she had never before experienced," and she lamented with evidently deep and genuine distress the threatened extinction of the male line of the house of Lorraine. But before she wrote again, the news of Sir Henry Clinton's exploits in Carolina had arrived, and, though almost the same post informed her of the prince's death, the sorrow which that bereavement awakened in her mind was scarcely allowed, even in its first freshness, an equal share of her lamentations with the more absorbing importance of the events of the campaign beyond the Atlantic.

"MY DEAREST MOTHER,--I wrote to you the moment that I received the sad intelligence of my uncle's death; though, as the Brussels courier had already started, I fear my letter may have arrived rather late. I will not venture to say more on the subject, lest I should be reopening a sorrow for which you have so much cause to grieve.... The capture of Charleston[2] is a most disastrous event, both for the facilities it will afford the English and for the encouragement which it will give to their pride. It is perhaps still more serious because of the miserable defense made by the Americans. One can hope nothing from such bad troops."

It is curious to contrast the angry jealousy which she here betrays of our disposition and policy as a nation, with the partiality which, as we have seen, she showed for the agreeable qualities of individual Englishmen. But her uneasiness on this subject led to practical results, by inducing her to add her influence to that of a party which was discontented with the ministry; and was especially laboring to persuade the king to make a change in the War Department, and to dismiss the Prince de Montbarey, whose sole recommendation for the office of secretary of state seemed to be that he was a friend of the prime minister, and to give his place to the Count de Segur. The change was made, as any change was sure to be made in favor of which she personally exerted herself; even the partisans of M. de Maurepas himself were forced to allow that the new minister was in every respect far superior to his predecessor; and Mercy was desirous that she should procure the dismissal of Maurepas also, thinking it of great importance to her own comfort that the prime minister should be bound to her interests.

But she was far more anxious on other subjects. Nearly two years had now elapsed since the birth of the princess royal; and there was as yet no prospect of a companion to her, so that the Count d'Artois began to make arrangements for the education of his infant son, the Duc d'Angouleme, with a premature solicitude, which was evidently designed to point the child out to the nation as its future sovereign.[3] The queen was greatly annoyed; and, to add to her vexation, one of the teething illnesses to which children are subject at this time threw the little princess into convulsions, which, to a mother's anxiety, seemed even dangerous to her life; though in a day or two that apprehension passed away.

But these hopes of D'Artois and his flatterers again filled the court with intrigues. In the course of the summer she was made highly indignant by finding that news from the court, with malicious comments, were sent from Paris across the frontier to be printed at Deux-Ponts or Duesseldorf, and then circulated in Paris and in Vienna; and it was difficult to avoid connecting these libels with those who in the palace itself were manifestly building hopes on the diminution of her influence and the disparagement of her character.

But this and all other vexations were presently thrown into the shade by a great grief, the more difficult to bear because it was wholly unexpected by her--the death of her mother. In reality, Maria Teresa had been unwell for some time; but the suspicions of the serious character of her complaint, which she secretly entertained, she had never revealed to Marie Antoinette; and at last the end followed too quickly on the first appearance of danger to allow time for any preparatory warnings to be received at Versailles before the fatal intelligence arrived. On the 24th of November she was taken ill in a manner which excited the alarm of her physicians, but her family felt no apprehensions. Even on the 27th, the emperor felt so sanguine that the cough which seemed her most distressing symptom was but temporary, that it was with the greatest unwillingness that he consented to her receiving the communion, as the physicians recommended; but the next day even he was forced to acquiesce in the hopeless view which they took of their patient; and on the 29th she died, after having borne sufferings, which for the last three days had been of the most painful character, with the same heroism with which, in her earlier life, she had struggled against griefs of a different kind.

The dispatch announcing her death was brought to the king; and it is characteristic of his timid disposition that he could not nerve himself to communicate it to his wife, but suppressed all mention of it during the evening; and in the morning summoned the Abbe de Vermond, and employed him to break the news to her, reserving for himself the less painful task of approaching her with words of affectionate consolation after the first shock was over. For a time, however, she was almost overwhelmed with sorrow. She attempted to write to her brother, but after a few lines she closed the letter, declaring that her tears prevented her from seeing the paper; and those about her found that for some time she could bear no other topic of conversation than the courage, the wisdom, the greatness of her mother, and, above all, her warm affection for herself and for all her other children.[4]

With the death of the empress we lose the aid of Mercy's correspondence, which has afforded such invaluable service in the light it has thrown on the peculiarities of Marie Antoinette's position, and the gradual development of her character during the earlier years of her residence in France. We shall again obtain light from the same source of almost greater importance, when the still more terrible dangers of the Revolution rendered the queen more dependent than ever on his counsels. But for the next few years we shall be compelled to content ourselves with scantier materials than have been furnished by the empress's unceasing interest in her daughter's welfare, and the embassador's faithful and candid reports.

The death of Maria Teresa naturally closed the court of her daughter against all gayeties during the spring of 1781. Still, one of the taxes which princes pay for their grandeur is the force which, at times, they are compelled to put upon their inclinations, when they dispense with that retirement which their own feelings would render acceptable; and, after a few weeks of seclusion, a few guests began to be admitted to the royal supper-table, among whom, as a very extraordinary favor, were some Swedish nobles;[5] one of whom, the Count de Stedingk, had established a claim to the royal favor by serving, with several of his countrymen, as a volunteer in the Count d'Estaing's fleet in the West Indies. Such service was highly esteemed by both king and queen, since Louis, though he had been unwillingly dragged into the war by the ambition of the Count de Vergennes and the popular enthusiasm, naturally, when once engaged in it, took as vivid an interest in the prowess of his forces as if he had never been troubled with any misgivings as to the policy which had set them in motion; and Marie Antoinette was at all times excited to enthusiasm by any deed of valor, and, as we have seen, took an especial interest in the achievements of the navy.

The King of Sweden, the chivalrous Gustavus III., had already made the acquaintance of Louis and Marie Antoinette in a short visit which he had paid to France the year after their marriage; and the queen now wrote to him in warm praise of M. de Stedingk, and all his countrymen who had come under her notice, while the king rewarded the count's valor and the wounds which had been incurred in its exhibition by an order of knighthood,[6] and the more substantial gift of a pension. But the Swede who soon outran all his compatriots in the race for the royal favor of both king and queen was the Count Axel de Fersen, a descendant, it was believed, of one of the Scotch officers of the great Macpherson clan, who, in the stormy times of the Thirty Years' War, had sought fame and fortune under the banner of Gustavus Adolphus. The beauty of his countess was celebrated throughout both Sweden and France, and his own was but little inferior to it. If she was known as "The Rose of the North," his name was rarely mentioned without the addition of "The handsome." He was a perfect master of all noble and knightly accomplishments, and was also distinguished for a certain high-souled and romantic[7] enthusiasm, which lent a tinge to all his conversation and demeanor; and this combination won for him the marked favor of Marie Antoinette. The calumniators, whom the condition and prospects of the royal family made more busy than ever at this time, insinuated that he had touched her heart; but those who knew best the manners of life and characters of both denounced it as the vilest of libels. The count's was a loyal attachment, doing nothing but honor to him who felt it, and to the queen who inspired it; and it was marked by a permanence which distinguishes no devotion but that which is pure and noble, as he showed ten years later by the well-planned and courageous, though unsuccessful, efforts which he made for the deliverance of the queen and all her family.

That Marie Antoinette, who from early youth had shown an intuitive accuracy of judgment in her estimate of character, should, from the very first, honorably distinguish a man capable of such devotion to her service was not unnatural;

but there was another circumstance in his favor, which he shared with the other foreign nobles, English and German, who in these years were well received by the queen. Their disinterestedness presented a striking contrast to the rapacity of the French. Every French noble valued the court only for what he could obtain from it. Even Madame de Polignac, whom the queen specially honored with the title of her friend, exhibited an all-grasping covetousness, of which, with all her efforts to shut her eyes to it, Marie Antoinette could not be unconscious; and her perception of the difference between her French and her foreign courtiers was marked by herself in a few words, when the Comte de la Marck, who was himself of foreign extraction, ventured once to recommend to her greater caution in her display of liking for the foreign nobles, as what might excite the jealousy of the French;[8] and she replied that "he might be right, but the foreigners were the only people who asked her for nothing."

Meanwhile, the war went on in America; the colonists themselves were making but little, if any, progress, and the French contingent were certainly reaping no honor, M. de La Fayette, the only officer who came in contact with a British force, showing no military skill or capacity, and not even much courage. But in the course of the spring France sustained a far heavier loss than even the defeat of an army could have inflicted on her, in the retirement of Necker from the ministry. As a statesman, he was certainly not entitled to any very high rank. He had neither extensive knowledge, nor large views, nor firmness; the only project of constitutional reform which he had brought forward had been but a mutilated and imperfect copy of the system devised by the original and statesman-like daring of Turgot. At a subsequent period he proved himself incapable of discerning the true character of the circumstances which surrounded him, and wholly ignorant of the feelings of the nation, and of the principles and objects of those who aspired to take a lead in its councils. But as yet his financial policy had undoubtedly been successful. He had greatly relieved the general distress, he had maintained the public credit, and he had inspired the nation with confidence in itself, and other countries also with confidence in its resources; but he had made many and powerful enemies by the retrenchments which had been a necessary part of his system. As early as the spring of 1780, Mercy had reported to the empress that both the king's brothers and the Duc d'Orleans complained that some of his measures infringed upon their established rights; that the Count d'Artois had had a very stormy discussion with Necker himself, and, when he could neither convince nor overbear him, had tried, though unsuccessfully, to enlist the queen against him. The count had since employed the controller of his own household, M. Boutourlin, to write pamphlets against him, and, in point of fact, many of the most elaborate details of a financial statement which Necker had recently published were very ill-calculated to endure a strict scrutiny; but M. Boutourlin did his work so badly that Necker had no difficulty in repelling him, and for a moment seemed the stronger for the attack that had been made upon him.

He had been so far right in his estimate of his position that he could rely on the support of the queen, who was aware that both her mother and her brother had a high opinion of his integrity; but though the king also had from time to time given his cordial sanction to his different measures, it was not in the nature of Louis to withstand repeated pressure and solicitation. Necker, too, himself unintentionally played into the hands of his enemies. He had nominally only a subordinate position in the ministry. As he was a Protestant, Louis had feared to offend the clergy by giving him a seat in the council, or the title of comptroller-general; but had conferred that post on M. Taboureau des Reaux, making Necker director of the treasury under him. The real management of the exchequer was, however, placed wholly in his hands; and, as he was one of the vainest of men, he had gradually assumed a tone of importance as if his were the paramount influence in the Government; going so far as even to open negotiations with foreign statesmen to which none of his colleagues were privy.[9] It was not strange that he was not very well satisfied with a position which seemed as if it had been contrived in order to keep him out of sight, and to deprive him of the credit belonging to his financial successes; but hitherto he had been satisfied to bide his time. Now, however, his triumph over M. Boutourlin seemed to him so to have established his supremacy as to entitle him to insist on a promotion which should be a public recognition of his position as the real minister of finance, and as entitled to a preponderating voice in all matters of general policy. He accordingly demanded admission to the council, and, on its being refused, at once resigned his office.

The consternation was universal; the general public had gradually learned to place such confidence in him that they looked on his loss as irreparable. Some even of the princes who had originally striven to prepossess the king against him either changed their minds or feared to show their disagreement with the common feeling. And Marie Antoinette, who fully shared his views as to the primary importance of finance in all questions of government, condescended to admit him to an interview; requested him, as a personal favor to herself, to recall his resignation, urging upon him that patience would surely in time procure him all that he asked; and, in her honest earnestness for the welfare of the nation, wept when he withdrew without having yielded to her solicitations. It was late in the evening and dark when he took his leave, and afterward, when he was told that he had drawn tears from her eyes by his refusal, he said that, had he seen them, he should have submitted to a wish so enforced, even at the sacrifice of his own comfort and reputation.

CHAPTER XVI.

The Queen expects to be confined again.--Increasing Unpopularity of the King's Brothers.--Birth of the Dauphin.--Festivities.--Deputations from the Different Trades.--Songs of the Dames de la Halle.--Ball given by the Body-guard.--Unwavering Fidelity of the Regiment.--The Queen offers up her Thanksgiving at Notre Dame.--Banquet at the Hotel de Ville.--Rejoicing in Paris.

How irreparable his loss was, was shown by the rapid succession of finance ministers who, in the course of the next seven years, successively held the office of comptroller-general. All were equally incompetent, and under their administration, sometimes merely incapable, sometimes combining recklessness and corruption with incapacity, the treasury again became exhausted, the resources of the nation dwindled away, and the distress of all but the wealthiest classes became more and more insupportable. But for a time the attention of Marie Antoinette was drawn off from political embarrassments by the event which alone seemed wanting to complete her personal happiness, and to place her position and popularity on an impregnable foundation.

In the spring she discovered that she was again about to become a mother. The whole nation expected the result with an intense anxiety. The king's brothers were daily becoming more and more deservedly unpopular. The Count d'Artois, who as the father of a son, occupied more of the general attention than his elder brother, seemed to take pains to parade his contempt for the commercial class, and still more for the lower orders, and his disapproval of every proposal which had for its object to conciliate the traders or to relieve the sufferings of the poor; while the Count de Provence openly established a mistress, the Countess de Balbi, at the Luxembourg Palace, his residence in the capital, where she presided over the receptions which he took upon himself to hold, to the exclusion of his lawful princess. The Countess de Provence was not well calculated to excite admiration or sympathy, since she was plain and ungracious. But Madame de Balbi, whose character had been disgracefully notorious even before her connection with the count, was not more attractive in appearance or manner than the Savoy princess; and the citizens of Paris, who in this instance faithfully represented the feelings of the entire nation, did not disguise their anxiety that the child about to be born should be a prince, who might extinguish the hopes and projects of both his uncles.

Their wishes were gratified. On the morning of the 22d of October the king was starting from the palace on a hunting expedition with his brothers, when it was announced to him that the queen was taken ill.[1] He at once returned to her room, and, mindful of the danger which she had incurred on the occasion of the birth of Madame Royale from the greatness and disorder of the crowd, he broke through the ancient custom, and ordered that the doors should be closed, and that no one should be admitted beyond a very small number of the great officers, male and female, of the household. His cares were rewarded by a comparatively easy birth; and his anxiety to protect his wife from agitation was further shown by a second arrangement, which was perhaps hardly so easy to carry out, but which was also perfectly successful. As was most natural, the queen and himself fully shared the ardent wishes of the nation that the expected child should prove an heir to the throne; and he consequently feared that, should it not be so, the disappointment might produce an injurious effect on the mother's health; or, should their hopes be realized, that the excessive joy might be equally dangerous. With a desire, therefore, to avoid exposing her to either shock in the first moments of weakness, he forbade any announcement of the sex of the child being made to any one but himself. The instant that the child was born, he hastened to the bedside to judge for himself whether she could bear the news. Presently she came to herself; and it seemed to her that the general silence indicated that she had become the mother of a second daughter. But she desired to be assured of the fact. "See," said she to Louis, "how reasonable I am. I ask no questions.[2]" And Louis, who from joy was scarcely able to contain himself, seeing her freedom from agitation, thought he might safely reveal to her the whole extent of their happiness. He called out, so as to be heard by the Princess de Guimenee, who still held the post of governess to the royal children, and who had already exhibited the child to the witnesses in the antechamber, and was now awaiting his summons at the open door, "My lord the dauphin begs to be admitted." The Princess de Guimenee brought "my lord the dauphin" to his mother's arms, and for a few minutes the small company in the room gazed in respectful silence while the father and mother mingled tears of joy with broken words of thanksgiving.

Yet even in this moment of exultation Marie Antoinette could not forget her first-born, nor the feelings which had made her rejoice at the birth of a daughter, who still had, as it were, no rival in her eyes, because no rival claim to her own could be set up with respect to a princess. She kissed the long-wished-for infant over and over again; pressed him fondly to her heart; and then, after she had perused each feature with anxious scrutiny, and pointed out some resemblances, such as mothers see, to his father, "Take him," said she, to Madame de Guimenee; "he belongs to the State; but my daughter is still mine.[3]"

Presently the chamber was cleared; and in a few minutes the glad tidings were carried to every corner of the palace and town of Versailles, and, as speedily as expresses could gallop, to the anxious city of Paris. By a somewhat whimsical coincidence, the Count de Stedingk, who, from having been one of the intended hunting-party, had been admitted into the antechamber, rushing down-stairs in his haste to spread the intelligence, met the Countess de Provence on the staircase. "It is a dauphin, madame," he cried; "what a happy event!" The countess made him no reply. Nor did she or her husband pretend to disguise their mortification. The Count d'Artois was a little less open in the display of his discontent, which was, however, sufficiently notorious. But, with these exceptions, all France, or at least all France sufficiently near the court to feel any personal interest in its concerns, was unanimous in its exultation.

As soon as the new-born child was dressed, his father took him in his arms, and, carrying him to the window, showed him to the crowd[4] which, on the first news of the queen's illness, had thronged the court-yard, and was waiting in breathless expectation the result. A rumor had already begun to penetrate the throng that the child was a son, and the moment that the happy tidings were confirmed, and the infant--their future king, as they undoubtingly hailed him--was presented to their view, their joy broke forth in such vociferous acclamations that it became necessary to silence them by an appeal to them to show consideration for the mother's weakness.

For the next three months all was joy and festivity. When the little Duc d'Angouleme, now a sprightly boy of six years old, was taken into the nursery to see, or, in the court language, to pay his homage to, the heir to the throne, he said to his father, as he left the room, "Papa, how little my cousin is!" "The day will come, my boy," replied the count, "when you will find him quite great enough." And it seemed as if the whole nation, and especially the city of Paris, thought no celebration of the birth of its future king could be too sumptuous for his greatness. It was a real heart-felt joy that was awakened in the people. On the day following the birth, chroniclers of the time remarked that no other subject was spoken of; that even strangers stopped one another in the streets to exchange congratulations.[5]

The different trades and guilds led the way in the expression of these loyal felicitations. When his royal highness was a week old, he held a grand reception. Deputations from different bodies of artisans, each with a band of music at its head, and each carrying some emblem of its occupation, marched in a long procession to Versailles. The chimney-sweeps bore aloft a chimney entwined with garlands, on the top of which was perched one of the smallest of their boys; the chairmen carried a chair superbly gilt, on which sat in state a representative of the royal nurse, with a child in her arms in royal robes; the butchers drove a fat ox; the pastry-cooks bore on a splendid tray a variety of pastry and sweetmeats such as might tempt children of a larger growth than the little prince they had come to honor; the blacksmiths beat an anvil in time to their cheers; the shoe-makers brought a pair of miniature boots; the tailors had devoted elaborate and minute pains to the embroidering of a uniform of the dauphin's regiment, such as might even now fit its young colonel, if his parents would permit him to be attired in it. The crowd was too great to be received in even the largest saloon of the palace; but it filled the court-yard beneath; and, as the weather was luckily favorable, the dauphin was brought to the balcony and displayed to the people, while they greeted him with cheers, which were renewed from time to time, even after he had been withdrawn, till the shouting seemed as if it would have no end.

One deputation, consisting of members of the fairer sex, received even higher honors. Fifty ladies of the fish-market vindicated the long-acknowledged claims of their body by forming a separate procession. Each dame was dressed in a gown of rich black silk, their established court-dress, and nearly every one had diamond ornaments. To them, the celebrated antechamber, from the oval window at the end known as the Bull's Eye, was opened;[6] and three of their body were admitted even into the queen's room, and to the side of the bed. The popular poet La Harpe, whom the partiality of Voltaire had designated as the heir of his genius, had composed an address, which the spokeswoman of the party had written out on the back of her fan, and now read with a sweet voice, which had procured her the honor of being so selected,[7] and with very appropriate delivery. The queen made a brief but most gracious answer, and then, on their retirement, the whole company, with a train of fish-women of the lower class, was entertained at a grand banquet, which they enlivened with songs composed for the occasion. One of them so hit the fancy of the king and queen that they quoted it more than once in their letters to their correspondents, and Marie Antoinette even sung it occasionally to her harp:

"Ne craignez pas,   Cher papa,   D' voir augmenter vot' famille,   Le Bon Dieu z'y pourvoira: Fait's en tant qu' Versailles en fourmille   Y eut-il cent Bourbons chez nous,   Y a du pain, du laurier pour tous."

The body-guard celebrated the auspicious event by giving a grand ball in the concert-room of the palace to the queen on her recovery; it was attended by the whole court, and Marie Antoinette opened it herself, dancing a minuet with one of the troop, whom his comrades had selected for the honor, and whom the king promoted, as a memorial of the occasion and as a testimony of his approval of the loyalty of that gallant regiment.

Amidst all the troubles of later years, the fidelity of those noble troops never wavered. They had even in one hour of terrible danger the honor, in the same palace, of saving the life of their queen. But it is a melancholy proof of the fleeting character and instability of popular favor which is supplied by the recollection that these very artisans who were now so vociferous, and undoubtedly at this moment so sincere in their profession of loyalty, were afterward her foul and ferocious enemies. And yet between 1781 and 1789 there had been no change in the character or conduct of the king and queen, or rather, it may be said, the intervening years had been a period during which a countless series of acts of beneficence had displayed their unceasing affection for their subjects.

The festivities were crowned in the most appropriate manner by a public thanksgiving, offered by the queen herself to Heaven for the gift of a son, and for her own recovery. But that celebration was necessarily postponed till her strength was entirely re-established; and it was not till the 21st of January that the physicians would allow her to encounter the excitement of so interesting but fatiguing a day. The court had quit Versailles for La Muette the day before, to be nearer the city; and on the appointed morning, which the watchers for omens delightedly remarked as one of midsummer brilliancy,[8] the most superb procession that even Paris had ever witnessed issued from the gates of the old hunting-lodge, whose earlier occupants had been animated by a very different spirit.[9]

That the honors of the day might be wholly the queen's, Louis himself did not accompany her, but followed her three hours later, to meet her at the Hotel de Ville. Nineteen coaches, glittering with burnished gold, and every panel of which was embellished with crowns, wreaths, or allegorical pictures, marching on at a stately walk toward the city gate, conveyed the queen, radiant with beauty and happiness, the sisters and aunts of the king, the long train of her and their ladies, and all the great officers of her household. Squadrons of the body-guard furnished the escort, riding in front of the queen's carriage and behind it, but not on either side, she herself having forbidden any arrangement which might intercept the full sight of herself from a single citizen. Companies of other regiments awaited the procession at different points, and closed up behind it as it passed, swelling the vast train which thus grew at every step. An additional escort, almost an army in itself, in double rank, lined the whole road from the barrier of the Champs Elysees of the great cathedral; and, as the royal coach passed through the city gate, a herald proclaimed that "The king wishing to consecrate by fresh acts of kindness the happy moment when God showered his mercies on him by the birth of a dauphin, and at the same time to give to the inhabitants of his good city of Paris some special mark of his beneficence, granted an exemption from the poll-tax to all the burgesses, traders, and artisans who were not in such circumstances as made the payment easy."

The proclamation was received with all the thankfulness of surprise; the cheers, which had never censed from the moment that the procession first came in sight, were redoubled, and it was amidst shouts of congratulation both to themselves and to her that the queen proceeded onward to Notre Dame. Having paid her vows and made her offerings in the cathedral of the nation, she passed on to the Church of

Ste. Genevieve, the especial patroness of the city, and repeated her thanksgiving before the tomb of Clovis, the founder of the monarchy. At the Hotel de Ville she was met by the king, with the princess, his brothers, the great officers of his household, and the ministers; and there (after having first come forward on the balcony to afford the multitude, who completely filled the vast square in front of the building, a sight of their sovereigns), the royal pair, sitting side by side, presided at a banquet of unsurpassed magnificence and luxury. In compliance with the strictest laws of the old etiquette, none but ladies were admitted to the king's table, but other tables were provided for the male guests. The most renowned musicians performed the sweetest airs, but the melodies of Gluck and Gretry were drowned in the cheers of the multitude outside, who thus relieved their impatience for the re-appearance of their queen.

The banquet was succeeded by a grand reception, with its singular but invariable accompaniment of a gaming-table,[10] and the whole was concluded by a grand illumination and display of fireworks, in which the pyrotechnists had exhausted their allegorical ingenuity. A Temple of Hymen occupied the centre, and the God of Marriage--never, so far as present appearances indicated, more auspiciously employed--presented to France the precious infant who was the most recent fruit of his favor; while the flame upon his altar, which never had burned with a brighter light, was fed by the thank-offerings of the whole French people. As each new feature of the display burst upon their eyes, the acclamations of the populace redoubled, and their enthusiasm was kindled to the utmost pitch when Louis and Marie Antoinette descended the stairs, and, arm-in-arm, walked out among the crowd, ostensibly to see the illuminations from the different points which presented the most imposing spectacle; but really, as the citizens perceived, to show their sympathy with the joy of the people by mingling with the multitude, and thus allowing all to approach and even to accost them; while they, and especially the queen, replied to every loyal cheer or homely word of congratulation by a cordial smile or expression of approval or thanks, which long dwelt in the memory of those to whom they were addressed.

CHAPTER XVII.

Madame de Guimenee resigns the Office of Governess of the Royal Children. --Madame de Polignac succeeds her.--Marie Antoinette's Views of Education.--Character of Madame Royale.--The Grand Duke Paul and his Grand Duchess visit the French Court.--Their Characters.--Entertainments given in their Honor.--Insolence of the Cardinal de Rohan.--His Character and previous Life.--Grand Festivities at Chantilly.--Events of the War.--Rodney defeats de Grasse.--The Siege of Gilbralter fails.--M. de Suffrein fights five Drawn Battles with Sir E. Hughes in the Indian Seas.--The Queen receives him with great Honor on his Return.

The post of governess to the royal children was one which was conferred for life, and did not even cease on the accession of a new sovereign, and the birth of a new royal family. Madame de Guimenee, therefore, having been appointed to that office on the birth of the first child of the late dauphin, the father of Louis XVI., still retained it, and on the birth of Madame Royale transferred her services to that princess. The arrangement had been far from acceptable to Marie Antoinette, who had no great liking for the lady, though, with her habitual kindness of disposition, she had accepted her attentions, and had often condescended to appear as a guest at her evening parties, taking only the precaution of ascertaining beforehand whom she was likely to meet there.[1] But, in the spring of 1782, the Prince de Guimenee became involved in pecuniary difficulties that compelled him to retire from the court, and his princess to resign her appointment, which Marie Antoinette at once bestowed on Madame de Polignac. Her attachment to that lady affords a striking exemplification of one feature in her character, a steady adherence to friendships once formed, which can never be otherwise than amiable, even when, as it may be thought was the case in this and one or two other instances, she carried it to excess; for she could hardly fail to be aware that Madame de Polignac was most unpopular with all classes, and that her unpopularity was not undeserved. She was covetous for herself, and she had a number of relations, equally rapacious, who regarded her court favor solely as a means of enriching the whole family. She had procured a valuable reversion for her husband; and subsequently the rare favor of an hereditary dukedom; and it was characteristic of her disposition that she might have attained the rank of duchess for herself at an earlier date, but that she preferred to it the chance of other favors of a more practically useful nature; nor was it till she had received such sums of money that nothing more could well be asked, that she turned her ambition to titles, and to the much-coveted dignity of a stool to sit upon in the presence of royalty.[2]

But the more people spoke ill of her, the more the queen protected her; and if she received the resignation of Madame de Guimenee with pleasure, much of her joy seemed to be owing to the opportunity which it afforded her of promoting the new duchess to the vacant place, while Madame de Polignac had even the address to persuade her that she accepted the post unwillingly, and, in undertaking it, was making a sacrifice to loyalty and friendship. But if the queen was duped on that point, she was not deceived on others. She knew that the duchess had no qualifications for the office; that she was neither clever nor accomplished. But her absence of any special qualifications was, in fact, her best recommendation in the eyes of her patroness; for Marie Antoinette had high ideas of the duty which a mother owes to her children. She thought herself bound to take upon herself the real superintendence of their education, and, having this view, she preferred a governess who would be content that her children's minds should receive their color from herself. Her own idea of education, as we shall see it hereafter described by herself,[3] was that example was more powerful than precept, and that love was a better teacher than fear; and, acting on this principle, from the moment that her little daughter was old enough to comprehend her intentions and wishes, she began to make her her companion; abandoning, or at least relaxing, her pursuit of other pleasures for that which was now her chief delight, as well as in her eyes her chief duty--the task of watching over the early promise, the opening talents and virtues of those who were destined, as she hoped, to have a predominant influence on the future welfare of the nation. Especially she made a rule of taking the little princess with her on the different errands of humanity and benevolence, which, wherever she might be, and more particularly while she was at Versailles, formed an almost habitual part of her occupations. She saw that much of the distress which now seemed to be the normal condition of the humbler classes, and much of the discontent, which was felt by all classes but the highest, were caused by the pride of the princes and nobles, who, in France, drew a far more rigorous and unbending line of demarkation between themselves and their inferiors than prevailed in other countries; and she desired from their earliest infancy to imbue her children with a different principle, and to teach them by her own example that none could be so lowly as to be beneath the notice even of a sovereign; and that, on the contrary, the greater the depression of the poor, the greater claim did it give them on the solicitude and protection of their princes and rulers.

Nor were these lessons, which even worldly policy might have dictated, the only ones which she sought to inculcate on the little princess before the more exciting pursuits of society should have rendered her less susceptible to good impressions. Unfriendly as her husband's aunts had always been to herself, and little as there was that was really amiable in their characters, there was yet one, the Princess Louise, the Nun of St. Denis, whose renunciation of the world seemed to point her out to her family as a model of holiness and devotion; and as, above all things, Marie Antoinette desired to inspire her little daughter with a deep sense of religious obligation, she soon began to take her with her in all her visits to the convent, and to encourage her to converse with the other Sisters of the house. Nor did she abandon the practice even when it was suggested to her that such an intercourse with those who were notoriously always on the watch to attract recruits of rank or consideration, might have the result of inclining the child to follow her great-aunt's example; and perhaps, by renouncing the world, to counteract plans which her parents might have preferred for her establishment in life. Marie Antoinette declared that should the princess express such a desire, far from being annoyed, "she should feel flattered by it;[4]" she would, it may be presumed, have regarded it as a convincing testimony of the soundness of her own system of education, and of the purity of the instruction which she had given.

But such was not to be the destiny of her whose life at this moment seemed to beam with prospects of happiness which it would have been cruel to allow her to exchange for the gloom of a convent, though, even before she arrived at woman-hood, the most austere seclusion of such an abode would have seemed a welcome asylum from dangers yet undreamed of. Her destiny was indeed to be one of trials and afflictions even to the end; trials very different in their kind from those which the gates of the Carmelite sisterhood would have opened to her. But her mother's early lessons of humility and piety, and still more her mother's virtuous and heroic example, never ceased to bear their fruit in their influence on her character, amidst all the vicissitudes of fortune. The unhappy daughter,[5] as she was styled by the faithful and eloquent champion of her race, lived to win the respect even of its enemies,[6] supplying, at more than one critical moment, a courage and decision of which her male relatives were destitute; and, in the second and final ruin of her house, her fortitude and resignation still commanded the loyal adherence of a large party among her countrymen, and the esteem of foreign statesmen, who gladly recognized in her no small portion of the nobility of her female ancestors.

In the spring of 1782 the attention of the Parisians was occupied for a while by the arrival of two visitors from a nation which as yet had sent forth but few of its sons to mingle in society with those of other countries. The Grand Duke of Russia, who had indeed been its rightful emperor ever since the murder of his father twenty years before, but who had been compelled to postpone his claims to those of his ambitious and unscrupulous mother, Catherine II., had conceived a desire so far to imitate the example of his great ancestor, the founder of the Russian empire, Peter the Great, as to make a personal investigation of the manners of other people besides his own. To use the language in which the empress communicated to Louis XVI. her son's wish to pay him a visit, he sought, in the first instance, "to take lessons in courtesy and nobility from the most elegant court in the world." And as Louis had responded with a cordial invitation to Versailles, at the end of May he, with his grand duchess, a princess of Wuertemberg, arrived at the palace.

Paul had not as yet given any indications of the brutal and ferocious disposition which distinguished him in his later years, till it gradually developed into a savage insanity which neither his nobles nor even his sons could endure. He appeared rather a young man of frank and open temper, somewhat more unguarded in his language, especially concerning his own affairs and position, than was quite prudent or becoming; but kind in intention, sometimes even courteous in manner, shrewd in discerning what things and what persons were most worthy of his notice, and showing no deficiency of judgment in the observations which he made upon them. The grand duchess, however, was generally regarded as greatly superior to her husband in every respect. He was almost repulsive in his ugliness. She was extremely handsome in feature, though disfigured by a stoutness extraordinary in one so young. She had also a high reputation for accomplishments and general ability, though that too was disguised by a coldness or ungraciousness of manner that gave strangers a disagreeable impression of her; which, however, a more intimate acquaintance greatly removed.

Their characters had preceded them, and Marie Antoinette, for perhaps the first time in her life, felt very uneasy as to her own power of receiving them with the dignity which became both her and them. As she afterward explained her feelings to Madame de Campan, "she found the part of a queen much move difficult to play in the presence of other sovereigns, or of princes who were born to become sovereigns, than before ordinary courtiers.[7]" She even fortified her courage before dinner with a glass of water, and the medicine proved effectual. Even if it cost her an effort to preserve her habitual gayety, her difficulty was unperceived, and indeed, after the few first moments, ceased to be a difficulty. Paul himself cared but little for female attractions or graces; but the archduchess was charmed with her union of liveliness and dignity, which surpassed all her previous experiences of courts; and one of her ladies, Madame d'Oberkirch, who has left behind her some memoirs, to which all succeeding writers have been indebted for many particulars of this visit, could scarcely find words to describe the impression the queen's beauty had made upon her and all her fellow-travelers. "The queen was marvelously beautiful; she fascinated every eye. It was absolutely impossible for any one to display a greater grace and nobility of demeanor.[8]" Madame d'Oberkirch, like herself, was German by birth; and Marie Antoinette begged her to speak German to her, that she might refresh her recollection of her native language; but she found that she had almost forgotten it. "Ah," said she, "German is a fine language; but French, in the mouths of my children, seems to me the finest language in the world." And in the same spirit of entire adoption of French feelings, and even of French prejudices, she declared to the baroness that though the Rhine and the Danube were both noble rivers, the Seine was so much more beautiful that it had made her forget them both.

But her preference for every thing French did not make her neglect the duties of hospitality to her foreign visitors; she wished rather that they should carry with them as fixed an idea as she herself entertained of the superiority of France to their own country, in this as in every other particular. And she gave two magnificent entertainments in their honor at the Little Trianon, displaying the beauties of her garden by day, and also by night, by an illumination of extraordinary splendor. They were highly delighted with the beauty and the novelty of a scene such as they had never before witnessed; but her pleasure was in a great degree marred by the indecent boldness of one whose sacred profession, as well as his ancient lineage, ought to have restrained him from such misconduct, though it was but too completely in harmony with his previous life. Prince Louis de Rohan was a descendant of the great Duke de Sully, and a member of a family which, during the last reign, had possessed an influence at court which was surpassed by that of no other house among the French nobles.[9] He himself had reaped the full advantage of its interest. As we have already seen, he had been coadjutor of Strasburg when Marie Antoinette passed through that city on her way to France in 1770. He had subsequently been promoted to the rank of cardinal; and, though he was notoriously devoid of capacity, yet through the influence of his relations, and that of Madame du Barri, with whom they maintained an intimate connection, he had obtained the post of embassador to the court of Vienna, where he had made himself conspicuous for every species of disorder. His whole life in the Austrian capital had been a round of shameless profligacy and extravagance. The conduct of the inferior members of the embassy, stimulated by his example, and protected by his official character, had been equally scandalous, till at last Maria Teresa had felt herself bound, in justice to her subjects, to insist on his recall. The moment that he became aware that his position was in danger, he began to write abusive letters against the Empress-queen, and to circulate libels at Vienna against both her and Marie Antoinette, on whom he openly threatened to avenge himself, if his pleasures or his prospects should in any way be interfered with.[10]

Since his return to France he had had the address to conciliate Maurepas, who, adding the authority of his ministerial office to the solicitations of the cardinal's sister, Madame de Marsan, had succeeded in wringing from the unwilling king his appointment to the honorable and lucrative preferment of grand almoner. But even that post, though it made him one of the great officers of the court, did not weaken his desire to annoy the queen, for having, as he believed, used her influence to deprive him of his embassy, and for having by her marked coldness since his return from Vienna, showed her disapproval of his profligate character, and of his insolence to her mother.

And, unhappily, there were not wanting persons base enough to co-operate with him, generally discredited as he was, as instruments of their own secret malice. The birth of the dauphin had been a fatal blow to the hopes which had been founded on the possible succession of the king's brothers; and from this time forth the whisperers of detraction and calumny were more than ever busy, sometimes venturing to forge her handwriting, and sometimes daring, with still fouler audacity, to invent stories designed to tarnish her reputation by throwing doubts on her conjugal fidelity. At such a moment the presence of such a man as the cardinal on the stage was an evil omen. His audacity, it seemed, could hardly be purposeless, and his purpose could not be innocent.

He had been most anxious to obtain admission to one of the entertainments which the queen gave to the Russian princes; and, when he was disappointed, he had the silly audacity to bribe the porter of the Trianon to admit him into the garden, where, as the royal party passed down the different walks, he thrust himself ostentatiously at different points into their sight, professing to disguise himself by throwing a mantle over his shoulders, but taking care that his scarlet stockings should prevent any uncertainty from being felt as to his identity. That he should have presumed to intrude into the queen's presence in her own palace without permission was in itself an insult; but those behind the scenes believed that he had a deeper design, and that he wished to diffuse a belief that Marie Antoinette secretly regarded him with a favor which she was unwilling to show openly, and that he had not obtained admission to her garden without her connivance.

The princes of the blood, too, the Prince de Conde and the Duke de Bourbon, invited Paul and his archduchess to an entertainment at Chantilly, which far surpassed in splendor the display at Trianon. But the queen was willing, on such an occasion, to be eclipsed by her subjects. "The princes," she said, "might well give festivities of vast cost, because they defrayed the charges out of their private revenues; but the expenses of entertainments given by the king or by herself fell on the national treasury, of which they were bound to be the guardians in the interest of the poor tax-payers."

Not that, in all probability, Paul and his archduchess noticed the inferiority. Court festivities at St. Petersburg were as yet neither numerous nor magnificent, and they soon showed themselves so wearied with the round of gayety which had been forced upon them, that some of the diversions which had been projected at other royal palaces besides Versailles were given up to avoid distressing them.[11] The sight which pleased them most was the play, to which, at their own special request, the queen accompanied them, and where they were greatly struck by the magnificence of the theatre and every thing connected with the performance, as well as with the reception which the audience gave the queen. Much as they had admired what they had seen, it was her grace and kind solicitude for their gratification which made the greatest impression on them; and the archduchess kept up a correspondence with her during the rest of their travels, especially dwelling on the scenes which pleased her most in Germany, and on the persons she met who were known to and regarded by the queen.

Political affairs were at this time causing Marie Antoinette great anxiety. One of her most frequently expressed wishes had been that the French fleet should have an opportunity of engaging that of England in a pitched battle, when the judicious care which M. de Sartines had bestowed on the marine would be seen to bear its fruit. But when the battle did take place, the result was such as to confound instead of justifying her patriotic expectations. In April, the English Admiral Rodney inflicted on the Count de Grasse a crushing defeat off the coast of Jamaica. In September, the combined forces of France and Spain were beaten off with still heavier loss from the impregnable fortress of Gibraltar; and the only region in which a French admiral escaped disaster was the Indian Sea, where the Bailli de Suffrein, an officer of rare energy and ability, encountered the British admiral, Sir Edward Hughes, in a series of severe actions, and, except on one occasion in which he lost a few transports, never permitted his antagonist to claim any advantage over him; the single loss which he sustained in his first combat being more than counterbalanced by his success on land, where, by the aid of Hyder Ali's son, the celebrated Tippoo, be made himself master of Cuddalore; and then, dropping down to the Cingalese coast, recaptured Trincomalee, the conquest of which had been one of Hughes's most recent achievements.[12] The queen felt the reverses keenly. She even curtailed some of her own expenses in order to contribute to the building of new ships to replace those which had been lost; and she received M. de Suffrein, on his return from India at the conclusion of the war, with the most sincere and marked congratulations. She invited him to the palace, and, when he arrived, she caused Madame de Polignac to bring both her children into the room. "My children," said she, "and especially you, my son, know that this M. de Suffrein. We are all under the greatest obligations to him. Look well at him, and ever remember his name. It is one of the first that all my children must learn to pronounce, and one which they must never forgot.[13]"

She was acting up to her mother's example, than whom no sovereign had better known how to give their due honor to bravery and loyalty. Such a queen deserved to have faithful friends; and Suffrein was a man who, had his life been spared, might, like the Marquis de Bouille, have shown that even in France the feelings of chivalry and devotion to kings and ladies were not yet extinguished. But he died before either his country or his queen had again need of his services, or before he had any opportunity of proving by fresh achievements his gratitude to a sovereign who knew so well how to appreciate and to honor merit.

CHAPTER XVIII.

The conclusion of peace between France and England was one of the earliest events of the year 1783, but it brought no strength to the ministry; or, rather, it placed its weakness in a more conspicuous light. Maurepas had died at the end of 1781, and, since his death, the Count de Vergennes had been the chief adviser of the king; but his attention was almost exclusively directed to the conduct of the diplomacy of the kingdom, and to its foreign affairs, and he made no pretensions to financial knowledge. Unluckily the professed ministers of finance, Joly de Fleury and his successor, D'Ormesson, were as ignorant of that great subject as himself, and, within two years after Necker's retirement, their mismanagement had brought the kingdom to the very verge of bankruptcy. D'Ormesson was dismissed, and for many days it was anxiously deliberated in the palace by whom he should be replaced. Some proposed that Necker should he recalled, but the king had felt himself personally offended by some circumstances which had attended the resignation of that minister two years before. The queen inclined to favor the pretensions of Lomenie de Brienne, Archbishop of Toulouse; not because he had any official experience, but because fifteen years before he had recommended the Abbe de Vermond to Maria Teresa; and the abbe, seeing in the present embarrassment an opportunity of repaying the obligation, now spoke highly to her of the archbishop's talents. But Madame de Polignac and her party persuaded her majesty to acquiesce in the appointment of M. de Calonne, a man who, like Turgot, had already distinguished himself as intendant of a province, though he had not inspired those who watched his career with as high an opinion of his uprightness as of his talents. He had also secured the support of the Count d'Artois by promising to pay his debts; and Louis himself was won to think well of him by the confidence which he expressed in his own capacity to grapple with the existing, or even with still greater difficulties.

Nor, indeed, had he been possessed of steadiness, prudence, and principle, was he very unfit for such a post at such a time. For he was very fertile in resources, and well-endowed with both physical and moral courage; but these faculties were combined with, were indeed the parents of, a mischievous defect. He had such reliance on his own ingenuity and ability to deal with each difficulty or danger as it should arise, that he was indifferent to precautions which might prevent it from arising. The spirit in which he took office was exemplified in one of his first speeches to the queen. Knowing that he was not the minister whom she would have preferred, he made it his especial business to win her confidence; and he had not been long installed in office when she expressed to him her wish that he would find means of accomplishing some object which she desired to promote. "Madame," was his courtly reply, "if it is possible, it is done already. If it is impossible, I will take care and manage it." But being very unscrupulous himself, he overshot his mark when he sought to propitiate her further by offering to represent as hers acts of charity which she had not performed. The winter of 1783 was one of unusual severity. The thermometer at Paris was, for some weeks, scarcely above zero; scarcity, with its inevitable companion, clearness of price, reduced the poor of the northern provinces, and especially of the capital and its neighborhood, to the verge of starvation. The king, queen, and princesses gave large sums from their privy purses for their relief; but as such supplies were manifestly inadequate, Louis ordered the minister to draw three millions of francs from the treasury, and to apply them for the alleviation of the universal distress. Calonne cheerfully received and executed the beneficent command. He was perhaps not sorry, at his first entrance on his duties, to show how easy it was for him to meet even an unforeseen demand of so heavy an amount; and he fancied he saw in it a means of ingratiating himself with Marie Antoinette. He proposed to her that he should pay one of the millions to her treasurer, that that officer might distribute it, in her name, as a gift from her own allowance; but Marie Antoinette disdained such unworthy artifice. She would have felt ashamed to receive praise or gratitude to which she was not entitled. She rejected the proposal, insisting that the king's gift should be attributed to himself alone, and expressing her intention to add to it by curtailing her personal expenditure, by abridging her entertainments so long as the distress should last, and by dedicating the sums usually appropriated to pleasure and festivity to the relief of those whose very existence seemed to depend on the aid which it was her duty and that of the king to furnish. For there was this especial characteristic in Marie Antoinette's charity, that it did not proceed solely from kindness of heart and tenderness of disposition, though these were never wanting, but also from a settled principle of duty, which, in her opinion, imposed upon sovereigns, as a primary obligation, the task of watching over the welfare of their subjects as persons intrusted by Providence to their care; and such a feeling was obviously more to be depended upon as a constant motive for action than the most vivid emotion of the moment, which, if easily excited, is not unfrequently as easily overpowered by some fresh object.

Meanwhile events were gradually compelling her to take a more active part in politics. Maurepas had been jealous of her influence, and, while that old minister lived, Louis, who from his childhood had been accustomed to see him in office, committed almost every thing to his guidance. But, as he always required some one of stronger mind than himself to lean upon, as soon as Maurepas was gone he turned to the queen. It was to her that he now chiefly confided his anxieties and perplexities; from her that he sought counsel and strength; and the ministers naturally came to regard her as the real ruler of the State. Accordingly, we find from her correspondence of this period that even such matters as the appointment of the embassadors to foreign states were often referred to her decision; and how greatly the habit of considering affairs of importance expanded her capacity we may learn from the opinion which her brother, the emperor, who was never disposed to flatter, or even to spare her, had evidently come to entertain of her judgment. In one long letter, written in September of the year 1783, he discussed with her the attitude which France had assumed toward Austria ever since the dismissal of Choiseul; the willingness of her ministers to listen to Prussian calumnies; the encouragement which they had given to the opposition in the empire; and their obsequiousness to

Prussia; while Austria had not retaliated, as she had had many opportunities of doing, by any complaisance toward England, though the English statesmen had made many advances toward her. It is a curious instance of fears being realized in a sense very different from that which troubled the writer at the moment, that among the acts of France of which, had he been inclined to be captious, he might justly have complained, he enumerates her recent acquisition of Corsica, as one which, "for a number of reasons, might be very prejudicial to the possessions of the house of Austria and its branches in Italy." It did indeed prove an acquisition which largely influenced the future history, not only of Austria, but of the whole world, when the little island, which hitherto had been but a hot-bed of disorder, and a battle-field of faction burdensome to its Genoese masters, gave a general to the armies of France whose most brilliant exploits were a succession of triumphs over the Austrian commanders in every part of the emperor's dominion. His letter concludes with warnings drawn from the present condition and views of the different states of Europe, and especially of France, whose "finances and resources, to speak with moderation, have been greatly strained" in the recent war; embracing in their scope even the designs of Russia on the independence of Turkey; and with a request that his sister would inform him frankly what he is to believe as to the opinions of the king; and in what light he is to regard the recent letters of Vergennes, which, to his apprehension, show an indifference to the maintenance of the alliance between the two countries.[1]

It is altogether a letter such as might pass between statesmen, and proves clearly that Joseph regarded his sister now as one fully capable of taking large views of the situation of both countries. And her answer shows that she fully enters into all the different questions which he has raised, though it also shows that she is guided by her heart as well as by her judgment; still looks on the continuance of the friendship between her native and her adopted country as essential not only to her comfort, but even in some degree to her honor, and also that on that account she is desirous at times of exerting a greater influence than is always allowed her.

"Versailles, September 29th, 1783.

"Shall I tell you, my dear brother, that your letter has delighted me by its energy and nobleness of thought and why should I not tell you so? I am sure that you will never confound your sister and your friend with the tricks and manoeuvres of politicians.

"I have read your letter to the king. You may be sure that it, like all your other letters, shall never go out of my hands. The king was struck with many of your reflections, and has even corroborated them himself.

"He has said to me that he both desired and hoped always to maintain a friendship and a good understanding with the empire; but yet that it was impossible to answer for it that the difference of interests might not at times lead to a difference in the way of looking at and judging of affairs. This idea appeared to me to come from himself alone, and from the distrust with which people have been inspiring him for a long time. For, when I spoke to him, I believe it to be certain that he had not seen M. de Vergennes since the arrival of your courier. M. de Mercy will have reported to you the quietness and gentleness with which this minister has spoken to him. I have had occasion to see that the heads of the other ministers, which were a little heated, have since cooled again. I trust, that this quiet spirit will last, and in that case the firmness of your reply ought to lead to the rudeness of style which the people here adopted being forgotten. You know the ground and the characters, so you can not be surprised if the king sometimes allows answers to pass which he would not have given of his own accord.

"My health, considering my present condition,[2] is perfect. I had a slight accident after my last letter; but it produced no bad consequences: it only made a little more care necessary. Accordingly I shall go from Choisy to Fontainebleau by water. My children are quite well. My boy will spend his time at La Muette while we are absent. It is just a piece of stupidity of the doctors, who do not like him to take so long a journey at his age, though he has two teeth and is very strong. I should be perfectly happy if I were but assured of the general tranquillity, and, above all, of the happiness of my much-loved brother, whom I love with all my heart.[3]"

Another letter, written three months later, explains to the emperor the object of some of the new arrangements which Calonne had introduced, having for one object, among others, the facilitation of a commercial intercourse, especially in tobacco, with the United States. She hopes that another consequence of them will be the abolition of the whole system of farmers-general of the revenue; and she explains to him both the advantages of such a measure, and at the same time the difficulties of carrying it out immediately after so costly a war, since it would involve the instant repayment of large sums to the farmers, with all the clearness of a practiced financier. She mentions also the appointment of the Baron de Breteuil as the new minister of the king's household,[4] and her estimate of his character is rendered important by his promotion, six years later, to the post of prime minister. The emperor also had ample means of judging of it himself, since the baron had succeeded the Cardinal de Rohan as embassador at Vienna. "I think, with you, that he requires to be kept within bounds; and he will be so more than other ministers by the nature of his office, which is very limited, and entirely under the eyes of the king and of his colleagues, who will be glad of any opportunities of mortifying his vanity. However, his activity will be very useful in a thousand details of a department which has been neglected and badly managed for the last sixty years." And though it is a slight anticipation of the order of our narrative, it will not be inconvenient to give here some extracts from a third letter to the same brother, written in the autumn of the following year, in which she describes the king's character, and points out the difficulties which it often interposes to her desire of influencing his views and measures.

It may perhaps be thought that she unconsciously underrates her influence over her husband, though there can be no doubt that he was one of those men whom it is hardest to manage; wholly without self-reliance, yet with a scrupulous wish to do right that made him distrustful of others, even, of those whose advice he sought, or whose judgment he most highly valued.

"September 22d, 1784.

"I will not contradict you, my dear brother, on what you say about the short-sightedness of our ministry. I have long ago made some of the reflections which you express in your letter. I have spoken on the subject more than once to the king; but one must know him thoroughly to be able to judge of the extent to which, his character and prejudices cripple my resources and means of influencing him. He is by nature very taciturn; and it often happens that he does not speak to me about matters of importance even when he has not the least wish to conceal them from me. He answers me when I speak to him about them, but he scarcely ever opens the subject; and when I have learned a quarter of the business, I am then forced to use some address to make the ministers tell me the rest, by letting them think that the king has told me every thing. When I reproach him for not having spoken to me of such and such matters, he is not annoyed, but only seems a little embarrassed, and sometimes answers, in an off-hand way, that he had never thought of it. This distrust, which is natural to him, was at first strengthened by his govern--or before my marriage. M. de Vauguyon had alarmed him about the authority which his wife would desire to assume over him, and the duke's black disposition delighted in terrifying his pupil with all the phantom stories invented against the house of Austria. M. de Maurepas, though less obstinate and less malicious, still thought it advantageous to his own credit to keep up the same notions in the king's mind. M. de Vergennes follows the same plan, and perhaps avails himself of his correspondence on foreign affairs to propagate falsehoods. I have spoken plainly about this to the king more than once. He has sometimes answered me rather peevishly, and, as he is never fond of discussion, I have not been able to persuade him that his minister was deceived, or was deceiving him. I do not blind myself as to the extent of my own influence. I know that I have no great ascendency over the king's mind, especially in politics; and would it be prudent in me to have scenes with his ministers on such subjects, on which it is almost certain that the king would not support me? Without ever boasting or saying a word that is not true, I, however, let the public believe that I have more influence than I really have, because, if they did not think so, I should have still less. The avowals which I am making to you, my dear brother, are not very flattering to my self-love; but I do not like to hide any thing from you, in order that you may be able to judge of my conduct as correctly as is possible at this terrible distance from you, at which my destiny has placed me.[5]"

A melancholy interest attunes to sentences such as these, from the influence which the defects in her husband's character, when joined to those of his minister, had on the future destinies of both, and of the nation over which he ruled. It was natural that she should explain them to a brother; and though, as a general rule, it is clearly undesirable for queens consort to interfere in politics, it is clear that with such a husband, and with the nation and court in such a condition as then existed in France, it was indispensable that Marie Antoinette should covet, and, so far as she was able, exert, influence over the king, if she were not prepared to see him the victim or the tool of caballers and intriguers who cared far more for their own interests than for those of either king or kingdom. But as yet, though, as we see, these deficiencies of Louis occasionally caused her annoyance, she had no foreboding of evil. Her general feeling was one of entire happiness; her children were growing and thriving, her own health was far stronger than it had been, and she entered with as keen a relish as ever into the excitements and amusements becoming her position, and what we may still call her youth, since she was even now only eight-and-twenty.

CHAPTER XIX.

In the spring of 1784, the court and capital wore wrought up to a high pitch
of excitement by an incident which was in reality of so ordinary and trivial
a character, that it would be hard to find a more striking proof how thoroughly unhealthy the whole condition and feeling of the nation must have
been, when such a matter could have been regarded as important. It was simply
a question whether a play, which had been recently accepted by the manager of
the principal theatre in Paris, should receive the license from the theatrical censor
which was necessary to its being performed.

The play was entitled "The Marriage of Figaro." The history of the author, M.
Beaumarchais, is curious, as that of a rare specimen of the literary adventurer of his
time. He was born in the year 1732. His father was a watch-maker named Caron,
and he himself followed that trade till he was three or four and twenty, and attained
considerable skill in it. But he was ambitious. He was conscious of a handsome
face and figure, and knew their value in such a court as that of Louis XV. He gave
up his trade as a watch-maker, and bought successively different places about the
court, the last of which was sold at a price sufficient to entitle him to claim gentil-
ity; so that, in one of his subsequent railings against the nobles, he declared that
his nobility was more incontestable than that of most of the body, since he could
produce the stamped receipt for it. Following the example of Moliere and Voltaire,
he changed his name, and called himself Beaumarchais. He married two rich wid-
ows. He formed a connection with the celebrated financier, Paris Duverney, who

initiated him in the mysteries of stock-jobbing. Being a good musician, he obtained the protection of the king's daughters, taught them the harp, and conducted the weekly concerts which, during the life of Marie Leczinska, they gave to the king and the royal family. He wrote two or three plays, none of which had any great success, while one was a decided failure. He became involved in lawsuits, one of which he conducted himself against the best ability of the Parisian bar, and displayed such wit and readiness that he not only gained his cause, but established a notoriety which throughout life was apparently his dearest object. He crossed over to England, where he made the acquaintance of Wilkes, and one or two agents of the American colonies, then just commencing their insurrection; and, partly from political sympathy with their views of freedom, partly, as he declared, to retaliate on England for the injuries which France had suffered at her hands in the Seven Years' War, he became a political agent himself, procuring arms and ships to be sent across the Atlantic, and also a great quantity of stores of a more peaceful character, out of which he had hoped to make a handsome profit. But the Americans gave him credit for greater disinterestedness; the President of Congress wrote him a letter thanking him for his zeal, but refused to pay for his stores, for which he demanded nearly a hundred and fifty thousand francs. He commenced an action for the money in the American courts, but, as he could not conduct it himself, he did not obtain an early decision; indeed, the matter imbittered all his closing days, and was not settled when he died.

But while he was in the full flush of self-congratulation at the degree in which, as he flattered himself, he had contributed to the downfall of England, the exuberance of his spirits prompted him to try his hand at a fourth play, a sort of sequel to one of his earlier performances--"The Barber of Seville." He finished it about the end of the year 1781, and, as the manager of the theatre was willing to act it, he at once applied for the necessary license. But it had already been talked about: if one party had pronounced it lively, witty, and the cleverest play that had been seen since the death of Moliere, another set of readers declared it full of immoral and dangerous satire on the institutions of the country. It is almost inseparable from the very nature of comedy that it should be to some extent satirical. The offense which those who complained of "The Marriage of Figaro" on that account really found in it was, that it satirized classes and institutions which could not bear such attacks, and had not been used to them. Moliere had ridiculed the lower middle class; the newly rich; the tradesman who, because he had made a fortune, thought himself a gentleman; but, as one whose father was in the employ of royalty, he laid no hand on any pillar of the throne. But Beaumarchais, in "The Marriage of Figaro," singled out especially what were called the privileged classes; he attacked the licentiousness of the nobles; the pretentious imbecility of ministers and diplomatists; the cruel injustice of wanton arrests and imprisonments of protracted severity against which there was no appeal nor remedy; and the privileged classes in consequence denounced his work, and their complaints of its character and tendency made such an impression that the court resolved that the license should not he granted.

The refusal, however, was not at first pronounced in a straightforward way; but was deferred, as if those who had resolved on it feared to pronounce it. For a long time the censor gave no reply at all, till Beaumarchais complained of the delay as more injurious to him than a direct denial. When at last his application was formally rejected, he induced his friends to raise such a clamor in his favor, that Louis determined to judge for himself, and caused Madame de Campan to read it to himself and the queen. He fully agreed with the censor. Many passages he pronounced to be in extremely bad taste. When the reader came to the allusions to secret arrests, protracted imprisonments, and the tedious formalities of the law and lawyers, he declared that it would be necessary to pull down the Bastile before it could be acted with safety, as Beaumarchais was ridiculing every thing which ought to be respected. "It is not to be performed, then?" said the queen. "No," replied the king, "you may depend upon that."

Similar refusals of a license had been common enough, so that there was no reason in the world why this decision should have attracted any notice whatever. But Beaumarchais was the fashion. He had influential patrons even in the palace: the Count d'Artois and Madame de Polignac, with the coterie which met in her apartments, being among them; and the mere idea that the court or the Government was afraid to let the play be acted caused thousands to desire to see it, who, without such a temptation, would have been wholly indifferent to its fate. The censor could not prevent its being read at private parties, and such readings became so popular that, in 1782, one was got up for the amusement of the Russian prince, who was greatly pleased by the liveliness of the dramatic situations, and, probably, not sufficiently aware of the prevalence of discontent in many circles of French society to sympathize with those who saw danger in its satire.

The praises lavished on it gave the author greater boldness, which was quite unnecessary. He even meditated an evasion of the law by getting it acted in a place which was not a theatre, and tickets were actually issued for the performance in a saloon which was often used for rehearsals, when a royal warrant[1] peremptorily forbidding such a proceeding was sent down from the palace. A clamor was at once raised by the friends of Beaumarchais, as if "sealed letters" had never been issued before. They talked in a loud voice of "oppression" and "tyranny;" and any one who knew the king's disposition might have divined that such an act of vigor was sure to be followed by one of weakness. Presently Beaumarchais changed his tone. He gave out that he had retrenched the passages which had excited the royal disapproval, and requested that the play might be re-examined. A new censor of high literary reputation reported to the head of the police[2] that if one or two passages were corrected, and one or two expressions, which were liable to be misinterpreted, were suppressed, he foresaw no danger in allowing the representation. Beaumarchais at once promised to make the required corrections, and one of Madame de Polignac's friends, the Count de Vaudreuil, the very nobleman with whom that lady's name was by many discreditably connected, obtained the king's leave to perform it at his country house, that thus an opportunity might be afforded for judging whether or not the alterations which had been made were sufficient to render its performance innocent.

The king was assured that the passages which he had regarded as mischievous were suppressed or divested of their sting. Marie Antoinette apparently had her suspicions; but Louis could never long withstand repeated solicitations, and, as he had not, when Madame de Campan read it, formed any very high opinion of its literary merits, he thought that, now that it was deprived of its venom, it would be looked upon as heavy, and would fail accordingly. Some good judges, such as the Marquis de Montesquieu, were of the same opinion. The actors thought differently. "It is my belief," said a man of fashion to the witty Mademoiselle Arnould, using the technical language of the theatre, "that your play will be 'damned.'" "Yes," she replied, "it will, fifty nights running." But, even if Louis had heard of her prophecy, he would have disregarded it. He gave his permission for the performance to take place, and on the 27th April, 1784, "The Marriage of Figaro" was accordingly acted to an audience which filled the house to the very ceiling; and which the long uncertainty as to whether it would ever be seen or not had disposed to applaud every scene and every repartee, and even to see wit where none existed. To an impartial critic, removed both by time and country from the agitation which had taken place, it will probably seem that the play thus obtained a reception far beyond its merits. It was undoubtedly what managers would call a good acting play. Its plot was complicated without being confused. It contained many striking situations; the dialogue was lively, but there was more humor in the surprises and discoveries than verbal wit in the repartees. Some strokes of satire were leveled at the grasping disposition of the existing race of courtiers, whose whole trade was represented as consisting of getting all they could, and asking for more; and others at the tricks of modern politicians, feigning to be ignorant of what they knew; to know what they were ignorant of; to keep secrets which had no existence; to lock the door to mend a pen; to appear deep when they were shallow; to set spies in motion, and to intercept letters; to try to ennoble the poverty of their means by the grandeur of their objects. The censorship, of course, did not escape. The scene being laid in Spain, Figaro affirmed that at Madrid the liberty of the press meant that, so long as an author spoke neither of authority, nor of public worship, nor of politics, nor of morality, nor of men in power, nor of the opera, nor of any other exhibition, nor of any one who was concerned in any thing, he might print what be pleased. The lawyers were reproached with a scrupulous adherence to forms, and a connivance at needless delays, which put money into their pockets; and the nobles, with thinking that, as long as they gave themselves the trouble to be born, society had no right to expect from them any further useful action. But such satire was too general, it might have been thought, to cause uneasiness, much more to do specific injury to any particular individual, or to any company or profession. Figaro himself is represented as saying that none but little men feared little writings.[3] And one of the advisers whom King Louis consulted as to the possibility of any mischief arising from the performance of the play, is said to have expressed his opinion in the form of an apothegm, that "none but dead men were killed by jests." The author might even have argued that his keenest satire had been poured upon those national enemies, the English, when he declared what has been sometimes regarded as the national oath to be the pith and marrow of the English language, the open sesame to English society, the key to unlock the English heart, and to obtain the judicious swearer all that he could desire.[4]

And an English writer, with English notions of the liberty of the press, would hardly have thought it worth while to notice such an affair at all, did he not feel bound to submit his judgment to that of the French themselves. And if their view be correct, almost every institution in France must have been a dead man past all hopes of recovery, since the French historical writers, to whatever party they belong, are unanimous in declaring that it was from this play that many of the oldest institutions in the country received their death-blow, and that Beaumarchais was at once the herald and the pioneer of the approaching Revolution.

Paris had scarcely cooled down after this excitement, when its attention was more agreeably attracted by the arrival of a king, Gustavus III. of Sweden. He had paid a visit to France in 1771, which had been cut short by the sudden death of his father, necessitating his immediate return to his own country to take possession of his throne; but the brief acquaintance which Marie Antoinette had then made with him had inspired her with a great admiration of his chivalrous character; and in the preceding year, hearing that he was contemplating a tour in Southern Europe, she had written to him to express a hope that he would repeat his visit to Versailles, promising him "such a reception as was due to an ancient ally of France;[5]" and adding that "she should personally have great pleasure in testifying to him how greatly she valued his friendship."

Her mention of the ancient alliance between the two countries, which, indeed, had subsisted ever since the days of Francis I., was very welcome to Gustavus, since the object of his journey was purely political, and he desired to negotiate a fresh treaty. But those matters he, of course, arranged with the ministers. The queen was only concerned in the entertainments due from royal hosts to so distinguished a guest. Most of them were of the ordinary character, there being a sort of established routine of festivity for such occasions. And it may be taken as a proof that the court had abated somewhat of its alarm at Beaumarchais's play that "The Marriage of Figaro" was allowed to be acted on one of the king's visits to the theatre. She also gave him an entertainment of more than usual splendor at the Trianon, at which all the ladies present, and the invitations were very numerous, were required to be dressed in white, while all the walks and shrubberies of the garden were illuminated, so that the whole scene presented a spectacle which he described in one of his letters as "a complete fairy-land; a sight worthy of the Elysian Fields themselves.[6]" But, as usual, the queen herself was the chief ornament of the whole, as she moved graciously among her guests, laying aside the character of queen to assume that of the cordial hostess; and not even taking her place at the banquet, but devoting herself wholly to the pleasurable duty of doing honor to her guests.

One of the displays was of a novel character, from which its inventors and patrons expected scientific results of importance, which, though nearly a century has since elapsed, have not yet been realized. In the preceding year, Montgolfier had for the first time sent up a balloon, and the new invention was now exhibited in the Court of Versailles: the queen allowed the balloon to be called by her name; and, to the great admiration of Gustavus, who had a decided taste for matters which were in any way connected with practical science, the "Marie Antoinette" made a successful voyage to Chantilly. The date of another invention, if, indeed, it deserves so respectable a title, is also fixed by this royal visit. Mesmer had recently begun to astonish or bewilder the Parisians with his theory of animal magnetism; and Gustavus spent some time in discussing the question with him, and seems for a moment to have flattered himself that he comprehended his principles. But the only durable result which arose from his stay in France was the sincere regard and esteem which he and the queen mutually conceived for each other. They established a correspondence, in which Marie Antoinette repeatedly showed her eagerness to gratify his wishes and to attend to his recommendations; and when, at a later period, unexpected troubles fell on her and her husband, there was no one whom their troubles inspired with greater eagerness to serve them than Gustavus, whose last projects, before he fell by the hand of an assassin, were directed to their deliverance from the dangers which, though neither he nor they were as yet fully alive to their magnitude, were on the point of overwhelming them.

CHAPTER XX.

M arie Antoinette had long since completed her gardens at the Trianon, but the gradual change in the arrangements of the court had made a number of alterations requisite at Versailles, with which the difficulty of finding money rendered it desirable to proceed slowly. It was reckoned that it would be necessary to give up the greater part of the palace to workmen for ten years; and as the other palaces which the king possessed in the neighborhood of Paris were hardly suited for the permanent residence of the court, the queen proposed to her husband to obtain St. Cloud from the Duc d'Orleans, giving him in exchange La Muette, the Castle of Choisy, and a small adjacent forest. Such an arrangement would have produced a considerable saving by the reduction of the establishments kept up at those places, at which the court only spent a few days in each year. And as the duke was disposed to think that he should be a gainer by the exchange, it is not very easy to explain how it was that the original project was given up, and that St. Cloud was eventually sold to the crown for a sum of money, Choisy and La Muette being also retained.

St. Cloud was bought; and Marie Antoinette, still eager to prevent her own acquisition from being too costly, proposed to the king that it should he bought in her name, and called her property; since an establishment for her would naturally lie framed on a more moderate scale than that of any palace belonging to the king, which was held always to require the appointment of a governor and deputy-governors, with a corresponding staff of underlings, while she should only require a porter at the outer gate. The advantage of such a plan was so obvious that it was at once adopted. The porters and servants wore the queen's livery; and all notices of the regulations to be observed were signed "In the queen's name.[1]" Yet so busy were her enemies at this time, that even this simple arrangement, devised solely for the benefit of the people who were intimately concerned in every thing that tended to diminish the royal expenditure, gave rise to numberless cavils. Some affirmed that the issue of such notices in the name of the queen instead of in that of the king was an infringement on his authority. One most able and influential counselor of the Parliament, Duval d'Espremesnil, who in more than one discussion in subsequent years showed that in general he fully appreciated the principles of constitutional government, but who at this time seems to have been animated by no other feeling than that of hatred for the existing ministers, even went the length of affirming that there was "something not only impolitic but immoral in the idea of any palace belonging to a queen of France.[2]" But when the arrangements had once been made, Marie Antoinette not unnaturally thought her honor concerned in not abandoning it in deference to clamor so absurd, as well as so disrespectful to herself; and St. Cloud, to which she had always been partial, continued hers, and for the next five years divided her attention with the Trianon.

But though she herself disregarded all such attacks with the calm dignity which belonged to her character, her friends were not free from serious apprehensions as to the power of persistent detraction and calumny. It was one of the penalties which the nation had to pay for the infamies which had stained the crown during the last three centuries, that the people had learned to think that nothing was too bad to say and to believe of their kings; and Marie Antoinette seemed as yet a fairer mark than usual for slanderous attack, because her position was weaker than that of a King.[3] It depended on the life of her husband and of a single son, who was already beginning to show signs of weakness of constitution. It was therefore with exceeding satisfaction that in the autumn of 1784 her friends learned that she was again about to become a mother. They prayed with inexpressible anxiety that the expected child should prove a son; and on the 27th of March, 1785, their prayers were granted. A son was born, whom his delighted father at once took in his arms, calling him "his little Norman," and, saying "that the name alone would bring him happiness," created Duke of Normandy. No prophecy was ever so sadly falsified; no king's son had ever so miserable a lot; but no forebodings of evil as yet disturbed his parents. Their delight was fully shared by the body of the people; for the cabals against the queen were as yet confined to the immediate precincts of the court, and had not descended to infect the middle classes. It was with difficulty when, after her confinement, she paid her visit to Paris to return thanks at Notre Dame and St. Genevieve, that the citizens could he prevented from unharnessing her horses and dragging her coach in triumph through the streets.[4] And their exultation was fully shared by the better-intentioned class of courtiers, and by all Marie Antoinette's real friends, who felt assured that the birth of this second son had given her the security which had hitherto been wanting to her position.

Meanwhile, she was again led to interest herself greatly in foreign politics, though in truth she hardly regarded any thing in which her brother's empire was interested as foreign, so deep was her conviction that the interests of France and Austria were identical and inseparable, and so unwearied were her endeavors to make her husband's ministers see all questions that concerned her brother's dominions with her eyes. Throughout the latter part of 1784, and the earlier months of 1785, Joseph, who was always restless in his ambition, was full of schemes of aggrandizement which he desired to carry out through the favor and co-operation of France. At one moment he projected obtaining Bavaria in exchange for the Netherlands, at another he aimed at procuring the opening of the Scheldt by threatening the Dutch with instant war if they resisted. But, as all these schemes were eventually abandoned, they would hardly require to be mentioned here, were it not for the proofs which his correspondence with his sister affords of his increasing esteem for her capacity, and his evident conviction of her growing influence in the French Government, and for the light which some of her answers to his letters throw on her relations with the ministers, which had perhaps some share in increasing the annoyance that the affair of "the necklace," as will be presently mentioned, caused her before the end of the year. Her difficulties with Louis himself were the same as she had already described to her brother on former occasions. "It was impossible to induce him to take a strong line, so as to speak resolutely to M. de Vergennes in her presence, and equally so to prevent his changing his mind afterward;[5]" while she distrusted the good faith of the minister so much that, though she resolved to speak to him strongly on the subject, she would not do so till she could discuss the question with him "in the presence of the king, that he might not be able to disfigure or to exaggerate what she said." Yet she did not always find her precautions effectual. Louis's judgment was always at the mercy of the last speaker. She assured her brother that "he had abundant reason to be contented with the king's personal feelings on the subject. When he received the emperor's letter, he spoke to her about it in a way that delighted her. He regarded Joseph's demands as just, and his motives as most reasonable. Yet--she blushed to own it even to her brother--after he had seen his minister, his tone was no longer the same; he was embarrassed; he shunned the subject with her, and often found some new objection to weaken the effect of his previous admissions."

At one time she even feared a rupture between the two countries. Vergennes was urging the king to send an army of observation to the frontier; and, if it were sent, the proximity of such a force to the Austrian troops in the Netherlands would, to her apprehension, be full of danger. There was sound political acuteness in her remark that the dispatch of an army of observation was not "in itself a declaration of war, but that when two armies are so near to one another an order to advance is very soon executed;" and, with a shrewd perception of the argument which was most likely to influence the humane disposition of her husband, she pressed upon him that "the delays and shuffling of his ministers might very probably involve him in war, in spite of his own intentions." However, eventually the clouds which had caused her anxiety were dissipated; the mediation of France had even some share in leading to a conclusion of these disputes in a manner in which Joseph himself acquiesced; and the good understanding between the two crowns, on which, as Marie Antoinette often declared, her happiness greatly depended, was preserved, or, as she hoped, even strengthened, by the result of these negotiations.

But on one occasion of real moment to the personal comfort and credit of the queen, Louis behaved with a clear good sense, and, what was equally important, with a firmness which she gratefully acknowledged,[6] and contrasted remarkably with the pusillanimous advice that had been given by more than one of the ministers. That the affair in which he exhibited these qualities should for a moment have been regarded as one of political importance, is another testimony to the diseased state of the public mind at the time; and that it should have been possible so to use it as to attach the slightest degree of discredit to the queen, is a proof as strange as melancholy how greatly the secret intrigues of the basest cabal that ever disgraced a court had succeeded in undermining her reputation, and poisoning the very hearts of the people against her.[7]

Boehmer, the court jeweler, had collected a large number of diamonds of unusual size and brilliancy, which he had formed into a necklace, in the hope of selling it to the queen, whose fancy for such jewels had some years before been very great. She had at one time spent sums on diamond ornaments, large enough to provoke warm remonstrances from her mother, though certainly not excessive for her rank; and Louis, knowing her partiality for them, had more than once made her costly gifts of the kind. But her taste for them had cooled; her children now engrossed far more of her attention than her dress, and she was keenly alive to the distress which still prevailed in many parts of the kingdom, and to the embarrassments of the revenue, which the ingenuity of Calonne did not relieve half so rapidly as his rashness encumbered it. Accordingly, her reply to Boehmer's application that she would purchase his necklace was that her jewel-case was sufficiently full, and that she had almost given up wearing diamonds; and that if such a sum as he asked, which was nearly seventy thousand pounds, were available, she should greatly prefer its being spent on a ship for the nation, to replace the *Ville de Paris*, whose loss still rankled in her breast.

The king, who thought that she must secretly wish for a jewel of such unequalled splendor, offered to make her a present of the necklace, but she adhered to her refusal. Boehmer was greatly disappointed; he had exhausted his resources and his credit in collecting the stones in the hope of making a grand profit, and declared loudly to his patrons that he should be ruined if the queen could not be induced to change her mind. His complaints were so unrestrained that they reached the ears of those who saw in his despair a possibility of enriching themselves at his expense. There was in Paris at the time a Countess de la Mothe, who, as claiming descent from a natural son of Henri II., had added Valois to her name, and had her claim to royal birth so far allowed that, as she was in very destitute circumstances, she had obtained a small pension from the crown. Her pension and her pretensions had perhaps united to procure her the hand of the Count de la Mothe, who had for some time been discreditably known as one of the most worthless and dangerous adventurers who infested the capital. But her marriage had been no restraint on a life of unconcealed profligacy, and among her lovers she reckoned the Cardinal de Rohan, who, as we have already seen, was as little scrupulous or decent as herself.

As, however, the cardinal's extravagance had left him with little means of supplying her necessities, Madame La Mothe conceived the idea of swindling Boehmer out of his necklace, and of making de Rohan an accomplice in the fraud. The one thing which in the transaction is difficult to determine is whether the cardinal was her willing and conscious assistant, or her dupe. That his capacity was of the very lowest order was notorious, but he was a man who had been bred in courts; he knew the manner in which princes transacted their business, and in which queens signed their names. He had long been acquainted with Marie Antoinette's figure and gestures and voice; while, unhappily, there was nothing in his character which was incompatible with his becoming an accomplice in any act of baseness.

What followed was a drama of surprises. It was with as much astonishment as indignation that Marie Antoinette learned that Boehmer believed that she had secretly bought the necklace, which openly and formally she had refused, and that he was looking to her for the payment of its price. And about a fortnight later it was like a thunder-clap that a summons came upon the Cardinal de Rohan, who had just been performing mass before the king and queen, to appear before them in Louis's private cabinet, and that he found himself subjected to an examination by Louis himself, who demanded of him with great indignation an explanation of the circumstances that had led him to represent himself to Boehmer as authorized to buy a necklace for the queen. Terrified and confused, he gave an explanation which was half a confession; but which was too complicated to be thoroughly intelligible. He was ordered to retire into the next room and write out his statement. His written narrative proved more obscure than his spoken words. In spite of his prayers that he might be spared the degradation of being arrested while still clad in his pontifical habits, he was at once sent to the Bastile. A day or two afterward Madame La Mothe was apprehended in the provinces, and Louis directed that a prosecution should be instantly commenced against all who had been concerned in the transaction.

For the queen's name had been forged. The cardinal did not deny that he had represented himself to Boehmer as employed by her for the purchase of the jewel which, as he said, she secretly coveted, and for the payment of its price by installments. But, as his justification, he produced a letter desiring him to undertake the business, and signed "Marie Antoinette de France." He declared that he had never suspected the genuineness of this letter, though it was notorious that such an addition to their Christian names was used by none but the sons and daughters of the reigning sovereign, and never by a queen. And eventually his whole story was found to be that Madame La Mothe had induced him to believe that she was in the queen's confidence, and also that the queen coveted the necklace and was resolved to obtain it; but that she was unable at once to pay for it; and that, being desirous to make amends to the cardinal for the neglect with which she had hitherto treated him, she had resolved on employing him to make arrangements with Boehmer for the instant delivery of the ornament, and for her payment of the price by installments.

This was strange enough to have excited the suspicions of most men. What followed was stranger still. Not content with forging the queen's handwriting, Madame La Mothe had even, if one may say so, forged the queen herself. She had assured the cardinal that Marie Antoinette had consented to grant him a secret interview; and at midnight, in the gardens of Versailles, had introduced him to a woman of notoriously bad character named Oliva, who in height resembled the queen, and who, in a conference of half a minute, gave him a letter and a rose with the words, "You know what this means." She had hardly uttered the words when Madame La Mothe interrupted the pair with the warning the Countesses of Provence and Artois were approaching. The mock queen retired in haste. The cardinal pressed the rose to his heart; acted on the letter; and protested that he had never doubted that he had seen the queen, and had been acting on her commands in obtaining the necklace from Boehmer and delivering it to Madame La Mothe, though he now acknowledged that he had been imposed upon, and offered to pay the jeweler for his property.

There were not wanting those who advised that this offer should be accepted, and that the matter should be hushed up, rather than that a prince of the Church should be publicly disgraced by a prosecution for fraud. But Louis and Marie Antoinette both rightly judged that their duty as sovereigns of the kingdom forbade them to compromise justice by screening dishonesty. It was but two years before that a great noble, the most eloquent of all French orators, had singled out Marie Antoinette's love of justice as one of her most conspicuous, as it was one of her most noble, qualities; and the words deserve especially to be remembered from the melancholy contrast which his subsequent conduct presents to the voluntary tribute which he now paid to her excellence. In 1783, the young Count de Mirabeau, pleading for the restitution of his conjugal rights, put the question to the judges at Aix before whom he was arguing, "Which of you, if he desired to consecrate a living personification of justice, and to embellish it with all the charms of beauty, would not set up the august image of our queen?"

She and her husband might well have felt they were bound to act up to such a eulogy. Some of their advisers also, and especially the Baron de Breteuil and the Abbe de Yermond, fortified their decision with their advice; being, in truth, greatly influenced by a reason which they forbore to mention, namely, by their suspicion that the untiring malice of the queen's enemies would not have failed to represent that the suppression of the slightest particle of the truth could only have been dictated by a guilty consciousness which felt that it could not bear the light; and that the queen had forborne to bring the cardinal into court solely because she knew that he was in a situation to prove facts which would deservedly damage her reputation.

It is impossible to doubt that the resolution which was adopted was the only one consistent with either propriety or common sense. However plausible may be the arguments which in this or that case may be adduced for concealment, the common instinct of mankind, which rarely errs in such matters, always conceives a suspicion that it is dictated by secret and discreditable motives; and that he who screens manifest guilt from exposure and punishment makes himself an accomplice in the wrong-doing, if he was not so before. But, though Louis judged rightly for his own and his queen's character in bringing those who were guilty of forgery and robbery to a public trial, the result inflicted an irremediable wound on one great institution, furnishing an additional proof how incurably rotten the whole system of the Government must have been, when corruption without shame or disguise was allowed to sway the highest judicial tribunal in the country.

The Parliament of Paris, constantly endeavoring throughout its whole history to encroach upon the royal prerogative, had always founded its pretensions on its purity and disinterestedness. Since its re-establishment at the beginning of the present reign, it had advanced its claim to the possession of those virtues more loudly than ever; yet now, in the very first case which came before it in which a noble of the highest rank was concerned, it was made apparent not only that it was wholly destitute of every quality which ought to belong to a judicial bench, of a regard for truth and justice, and even of a knowledge of the law; but that no one gave it credit for them, and that every one regarded the decision to be given as one which would depend, not on the merits of the case, but on the interest which the culprits might be able to make with the judges.[8]

The trial took place in May of the following year. We need not enter into its details; the denials, the admissions, the mutual recriminations of the persons accused. In the fate of the La Mothes and Mademoiselle Oliva no one professed to be concerned; but the friends of the cardinal were numerous, rich, and powerful; and for months had been and still were indefatigable in his cause. Some days before the trial, the attorney- general had become aware that nearly the whole of the Parliament had been gained by them; he even furnished the queen with a list of the names of those judges who had promised their verdict beforehand, and of the means by which they had been won over. And on the decisive morning the cardinal and his friends made a theatrical display which was evidently intended to overawe those members of the Parliament who were yet unconvinced, and to enlist the sympathies of the public in general. He himself appeared at the bar in a long violet cloak, the mourning robe of cardinals; and all the passages leading to the hall of justice were lined by his partisans, also in deep mourning; and they were not solely his own relations, the nobles of the different branches of his family, the Soubises, the Rohans, the Guimenees; but though, as princes of the blood, the Condes were nearly allied to the king and queen, they also were not ashamed to swell the company assembled, and to solicit the judges as they passed into the court to disregard alike justice and their own oaths, and to acquit the cardinal, whatever the evidence might be which had been, or was to be, produced against him. They were only asking what they had already assured themselves of obtaining. The queen's signature was indeed declared to be a forgery, and the La Mothes, Mademoiselle Oliva, and a man named Retaux de Villette, who had been the actual writer of the forged letters, were convicted and sentenced to the punishment which the counsel for the crown had demanded. But the cardinal was acquitted, as well as a notorious juggler and impostor of the day, called Cagliostro, who had apparently been so entirely unconnected with the transaction that it is not easy to see how he became included in the prosecution; and permission was given to the cardinal to make his acquittal public in any manner and to any extent which he might desire.[9]

The subsequent history of the La Mothes was singular and characteristic. The countess, who had been sentenced to be flogged, branded, and imprisoned for life, after a time contrived, it is believed by the aid of some of the Rohan family, to escape from prison. She fled to London, where for some time she and her husband lived on the proceeds of the necklace, which they had broken up and sold piecemeal to jewelers in London and other cities; but they were soon reduced to great distress. After the Revolution had broken out in Paris, they tried to make money by publishing libels on the queen, in which they are believed to have obtained the aid of some who in former times had been under great personal obligations to Marie Antoinette. But the scheme failed: they were overwhelmed with debt; writs were issued against them, and in trying to escape from the sheriff's officers, the countess fell from a window at the top of a house, and received injuries which proved fatal.

A most accomplished writer of the present day, who has devoted much care and ability to the examination of the case, has pronounced an opinion that the cardinal was innocent of dishonesty,[10] and limits his offense to that of insulting the queen by the mere suspicion that she could place her confidence in such an unworthy agent as Madame La Mothe, or that he himself could be allowed to recover her favor by such means as he had employed. But his absolute ignorance of the countess's schemes is not entirely consistent with the admitted fact that, when he was arrested, his first act was to send orders to his secretary to burn all the letters which he had received from her on the subject; and unquestionably neither Louis nor Marie Antoinette doubted his full complicity in the conspiracy. Louis at once deprived him of his office of grand almoner, and banished him from the court, declaring that "he knew too well the usages of the court to have believed that Madame La Mothe had really been admitted to the queen's presence and intrusted with such a commission.[11]" And Marie Antoinette gave open expression to her indignation at the acquittal "of an intriguer who had sought to ruin her, or to procure money for himself, by abusing her name and forging her signature," adding, with undeniable truth, that still more to be pitied than herself was a "nation which had for its supreme tribunal a body of men who consulted nothing but their passions; and of whom some were full of corruption, and others were inspired with a boldness which always vented itself in opposition to those who were clothed with lawful authority.[12]"

But her magnanimity and her sincere affection for the whole people were never more manifest than now even in her first moments of indignation. Even while writing to Madame de Polignac that she is "bathed in tears of grief and despair," and that she can "hope for nothing good when perverseness is so busy in seeking means to chill her very soul," she yet adds that "she shall triumph over her enemies by doing more good than ever, and that it will be easier for them to afflict her than to drive her to avenging herself on them.[13]" And she uses the same language to her sister Christine, even while expressing still more strongly her indignation at being "sacrificed to a perjured priest and a shameless intriguer." She demands her sister's "pity, as one who had never deserved such injurious treatment;[14] but who had only recollected that she was the daughter of Maria Teresa--to fulfill her mother's exhortations, always to show herself French to the very bottom of her heart;" but she concludes by repeating the declaration that "nothing shall tempt her to any conduct unworthy of herself, and that the only revenge that she will take shall he to redouble her acts of kindness."

It is pleasing to be able to close so odious a subject by the statement that the disgrace which the cardinal had thus brought upon himself may be supposed in some respects to have served as a lesson to him, and that his conduct in the latter days of his life was such as to do no discredit to the noble race from which he sprung.

A great part of his diocese as Bishop of Strasburg lay on the German side of the Rhine; and thither,[15] when the French Revolution began to assume the bloodthirsty character which has made it a warning to all future ages, he was fortunate to escape in safety from the fury of the assassins who ruled France. And though he was no longer rich, his less fortunate countrymen, and especially his clerical brethren, found in him a liberal protector and supporter.[16] He even levied a body of troops to re-enforce the royalist army. But, when the First Consul wrung from the Pope a concordat of which he disapproved, he resigned his bishopric, and shortly afterward died at Ettenheim,[17] where, had he remained but a short time longer, he, like the Duke d'Enghien, might have found that a residence in a foreign land was no protection against the ever-suspicious enmity of Bonaparte.

CHAPTER XXI.

It was owing to Marie Antoinette's influence that Louis himself in the following year began to enter on a line of conduct which, if circumstances had not prevented him from persevering in it, might have tended, more perhaps than any thing else that he could have done, to make him also popular with the main body of the people. The emperor, while at Versailles, had strongly pressed upon him that it was his duty, as king of the nation, to make himself personally acquainted with every part of his kingdom, to visit the agricultural districts, the manufacturing towns, the fortresses, arsenals, and harbors of the country. Joseph himself had practiced what he preached. No corner of his dominions was unknown to him; and it is plain that there can be no nation which must not be benefited by its sovereign thus obtaining a personal knowledge of all the various interests and resources of his subjects. But such personal investigations were not yet understood to be a part of a monarch's duties. Louis's contemporary, our own sovereign, George

III., than whom, if rectitude of intention and benevolence of heart be the principal standards by which princes should be judged, no one ever better deserved to be called the father of his country, scarcely ever went a hundred miles from Windsor, and never once visited even those Midland Counties which before the end of his reign had begun to give undeniable tokens of the contribution which their industry was to furnish to the growing greatness of his empire; and the last two kings of France, though in the course of their long reigns they had once or twice visited their armies while waging war on the Flemish or German frontier, had never seen their western or southern provinces.

But now Marie Antoinette suggested to her husband that it was time that he should extend his travels, which, except when he had gone to Rheims for his coronation, had never yet carried him beyond Compiegne in one direction and Fontainebleau in another; and, as of all the departments of Government, that which was concerned with the marine of the nation interested her most (we fear that she was secretly looking forward to a renewal of war with England), she persuaded him to select for the object of his first visit the fort of Cherbourg in Normandy, where those great works had been recently begun which have since been constantly augmented and improved, till they have made it a worthy rival to our own harbors on the opposite side of the Channel. He was received in all the towns through which he passed with real joy. The Normans had never seen their king since Henry IV. had made their province his battle-field; and the queen, who would gladly have accompanied him, had it not been that such a journey undertaken by both would have resembled a state procession, and therefore have been tedious and comparatively useless, exulted in the reception which he had met with, and began to plan other expeditions of the same kind for him, feeling assured that his presence would be equally welcomed in other provinces--at Bourdeaux, at Lyons, or at Toulon. And a series of such visits would undoubtedly have been calculated to strengthen the attachment of the people everywhere to the royal authority; which, already, to some far-seeing judges, seemed likely soon to need all the re-enforcement which it could obtain in any quarter.

In the summer of 1786 she had a visit from her sister Christine, the Princess of Teschen, who, with her husband, had been joint governor of Hungary, and since the death of her uncle, Charles of Lorraine, had been removed to the Netherlands.

She had never seen her sister since her own marriage, and the month which they spent together at Versailles may be almost described as the last month of perfect enjoyment that Marie Antoinette ever knew; for troubles were thickening fast around the Government, and were being taken wicked advantage of by her enemies, at the head of whom the Duc d'Orleans now began openly to range himself. He was a man notorious, as has been already seen, for every kind of infamy; and though he well knew the disapproval with which Marie Antoinette regarded his way of life and his character, it is believed that he had had the insolence to approach her with the language of gallantry; that he had been rejected with merited indignation; and that he ever afterward regarded her noble disdain as a provocation which it should be the chief object of his life to revenge. In fact, on one occasion he did not scruple to avow his resentment at the way in which, as he said, she had treated him; though he did not mention the reason.[1]

Calumny was the only weapon which could be employed against her; but in that he and his partisans had long been adept. Every old libel and pretext for detraction was diligently revived. The old nickname of "The Austrian" was repeated with pertinacity as spiteful as causeless; even the king's aunts lending their aid to swell the clamor on that ground, and often saying, with all the malice of their inveterate jealousy, that it was not to be expected that she should have the same feelings as their father or Louis XIV., since she was not of their blood, though it was plain that the same remark would have applied to every Queen of France since Anne of Brittany. Even the embarrassments of the revenue were imputed to her; and she, who had curtailed her private expenses, even those which seemed almost necessary to her position, that she might minister more largely to the necessities of the poor--who had declined to buy jewels that the money might be applied to the service of the State--was now held up to the populace as being by her extravagance the prime cause of the national distress. Pamphlets and caricatures gave her a new nickname of "Madame Deficit;" and such an impression to her disfavor was thus made on the minds of the lower classes, that a painter, who had just finished an engaging portrait of her surrounded by her children, feared to send it to the exhibition, lest it should be made a pretext for insult and violence. Her unpopularity did not, indeed, last long at this time, but was superseded, as we shall presently see, by fresh feelings of gratitude for fresh labors of charity; nevertheless, the outcry now raised left its seed behind it, to grow hereafter into a more enduring harvest of distrust and hatred.

She had troubles, too, of another kind which touched her more nearly. A second daughter, Sophie[2], had been born to her in the summer of 1786; but she was a sickly child, and died, before she was a year old, of one of the illnesses to which children are subject, and for some months the mother mourned bitterly over her "little angel," as she called her. Her eldest boy, too, was getting rapidly and visibly weaker in health: his spine seemed to diseased, Marie Antoinette's only hope of saving him rested on the fact that his father had also been delicate at the same age. Luckily his brother gave her no cause for uneasiness; as she wrote to the emperor[3]--"he had all that his elder wanted; he was a thorough peasant's child, tall, stout, and ruddy.[4]" She had also another comfort, which, as her troubles thickened, became more and more precious to her, in the warm affection that had sprung up between her and her sister-in-law, the Princess Elizabeth. A letter[5] has been preserved in which the princess describes the death of the little Sophie to one of her friends, which it is impossible to read without being struck by the sincerity of the sympathy with which she enters into the grief of the bereaved mother. In these moments of anguish she showed herself indeed a true sister, and, the two clinging to one another the more the greater their dangers and distresses became, a true sister she continued to the end.

Meanwhile the embarrassments of the Government were daily assuming a more formidable appearance. Calonne had for some time endeavored to meet the deficiency of the revenue by raising fresh loans, till he had completely exhausted the national credit; and at last had been forced to admit that the scheme originally propounded by Turgot, and subsequently in a more modified degree by Necker, of abolishing the exemptions from taxation which were enjoyed by the nobles--the privileged classes, as they were often called--was the only expedient to save the nation from the disgrace and ruin of total bankruptcy. But, as it seemed probable that the nobles would resist such a measure, and that their resistance would prove too strong for him, as it had already been found to be for his predecessors, he proposed to the king to revive an old assembly which had been known by the title of the Notables; trusting that, if he succeeded in obtaining the sanction of that body to his plans, the nobles would hardly venture to insist on maintaining their privileges in defiance of the recorded judgment of so respectable a council. His hopes were disappointed. He might fairly have reckoned on obtaining their concurrence, since it was the unquestioned prerogative of the king to nominate all the members; but, even when he was most deliberate and resolute, his rashness and carelessness were incurable. He took no pains whatever to select members favorable to his views; and the consequence was that, in March, 1787, in the very first month of the session of the Notables, the whole body protested against one of the taxes which he desired to impose; and his enemies at once urged the king to dismiss him, basing their recommendation on the practice of England, where, as they affirmed, a minister who found himself in a minority on an important question immediately retired from office.

Marie Antoinette, who, as we have seen, had been a diligent reader of Hume, had also been led to compare the proceedings of the refractory Notables with the conduct of our English parliamentary parties, and to an English reader some of her comments can not fail to be as interesting as they are curious. The Duchess de Polignac was drinking the waters at Bath, which at that time was a favorite resort of French valetudinarians, and, while she was still in that most beautiful of English cities, the queen kept up an occasional correspondence with her. We have two letters which Marie Antoinette wrote to her in April; one on the 9th, the very day on which Calonne was dismissed; the second, two days latter; and even the passages which do not relate to politics have their interest as specimens of the writer's character, and of the sincere frankness with which she laid aside her rank and believed in the possibility of a friendship of complete equality.

"April 9th, 1787.

"I thank you, my dear heart, for your letter, which has done me good. I was anxious about you. It is true, then, that you have not suffered much from your journey. Take care of yourself, I insist on it, I beg of you; and be sure and derive benefit from the waters, else I should repent of the privation I have inflicted on myself without your health being benefited. When you are near I feel how much I love you; and I feel it much more when you are far away. I am greatly taken up with you and yours, and you would be very ungrateful if you did not love me, for I can not change toward you.

"Where you are you can at least enjoy the comfort of never hearing of business. Although you are in the country of an Upper and a Lower House, you can stop your ears and let people talk. But here it is a noise that deafens one in spite of all I can do. The words 'opposition' and 'motions' are established here as in the English Parliament, with this difference, that in London, when people go into opposition, they begin by denuding themselves of the favors of the king; instead of which, here numbers oppose all the wise and beneficent views of the most virtuous of masters, and still keep all he has given them. It may be a cleverer way of managing, but it is not so gentleman-like. The time of illusion is past, and we are tasting cruel experience. We are paying dearly to-day for our zeal and enthusiasm for the American war. The voice of honest men is stifled by members and cabals. Men disregard principles to bind themselves to words, and to multiply attacks on individuals. The seditious will drag the State to its ruin rather than renounce their intrigues."

And in her second letter she specifies some of the Opposition by name; one of whom, as will be seen hereafter, contributed greatly to her subsequent miseries.... "The repugnance which you know that I have always had to interfering in business is today put cruelly to the proof; and you would be as tired as I am of all that goes on. I have already spoken to you of our Upper and Lower House,[6] and of all the absurdities which take place there, and of the nonsense which is talked. To be loaded with benefits by the king, like M. de Beauvau, to join the Opposition, and to surrender none of them, is what is called having spirit and courage. It is, in truth, the courage of infamy. I am wholly surrounded with folks who have revolted from him. A duke,[7] a great maker of motions, a man who has always a tear in his eye when he speaks, is one of the number. M. de La Fayette always founds the opinions he expresses on what is done at Philadelphia.... Even bishops and archbishops belong to the Opposition, and a great many of the clergy are the very soul of the cabal. You may judge, after this, of all the resources which they employ to overturn the plans of the king and his ministers."

Calonne, however, as has already been intimated, had been dismissed from office before this last letter was written. There had been a trial of strength between him and his enemies; which he, believing that he had won the confidence of Louis himself, reckoned on turning to his own advantage, by inducing the king to dismiss those of his opponents who were in office. To his astonishment, he found that Louis preferred dispensing with his own services, and the general voice was probably correct when it, affirmed that it was the queen who had induced him to come to that decision.

Lomenie de Brienne, Archbishop of Toulouse, was again a candidate for the vacant post, and De Vermond was as diligent as on the previous occasion[8] in laboring to return the obligations under which that prelate had formerly laid him, by extolling his abilities and virtues to the queen, and recommending him as a worthy successor to Calonne, whom she had never trusted or liked. In reality, the archbishop was wholly destitute of either abilities or virtues. He was notorious both for open profligacy and for avowed infidelity, so much so that Louis had refused to transfer him to the diocese of Paris, on the ground that "at least the archbishop of the metropolis ought to believe in God.[9]" But Marie Antoinette was ignorant of his character, and believed De Vermond's assurance that the appointment of so high an ecclesiastic would propitiate the clergy, whose opposition, as many of her letters prove, she thought specially formidable, and for whose support she knew her husband to be nervously anxious. Some of Calonne's colleagues strongly urged the king to re-appoint Necker, whose recall would have been highly popular with the nation. But Necker had recently given Louis personal offense by publishing a reply to some of Calonne's statements, in defiance of the king's express prohibition, and had been banished from Paris for the act; and the queen, recollecting how he had formerly refused to withdraw his resignation at her entreaty, felt that she had no reason to expect any great consideration for the opinions or wishes of either herself or the king from one so conceited and self-willed, who would be likely to attribute his re-appointment, not to the king's voluntary choice, but to his necessities: she therefore strongly pressed that the archbishop should be preferred. In an unhappy moment she prevailed;[10] and on the 1st of May, 1787, Lomenie de Brienne was installed in office with the title of Chief of the Council of Finance.

A more unhappy choice could not possibly have been made. The new minister was soon seen to be as devoid of information and ability as he was known to be of honesty. He had a certain gravity of outward demeanor which imposed upon many, and he had also the address to lead the conversation to points which, his hearers understood still less than himself; dilating on finance and the money market even to the ladies of the court, who had had some share in persuading the queen of his fitness for office.[11] But his disposition was in reality as rash as that of Calonne; and it was a curious proof of his temerity, as well as of his ignorance of the feeling of parties in Paris, that though he knew the Notables to be friendly to him, as indeed they would have been to any one who might have superseded Calonne, he dismissed them before the end of the month. And the language held on their dissolution both by the ministers and by the President of the Notables, and which was cheerfully accepted by the people, is remarkable from the contrast which it affords to the feelings which swayed the national council exactly two years afterward. Some measures of retrenchment which the Notables had recommended had been adopted; some reductions had been made in the royal households; some costly ceremonies had been abolished; and one or two imposts, which had pressed with great severity on the poorer classes, had been extinguished or modified. And not only did M. Lamoignon, the Keeper of the Seals, in the speech in which he dismissed them, venture to affirm that these reductions would be found to have effected all that was needed to restore universal prosperity to the kingdom; but the President of the Assembly, in his reply, thanked God "for having caused him to be born in such an age, under such a government, and for having made him the subject of a king whom he was constrained to love," and the thanksgiving was re-echoed by the whole Assembly. But this contentment did not last long. The embarrassments of the Treasury were too serious to be dissipated by soft speeches. The Notables were hardly dissolved before the archbishop proposed a new loan of an enormous amount; and, as he might have foreseen, their dissolution revived the pretensions of the Parliament. The queen's description of the rise of a French opposition at once received a practical commentary. The debates in the Parliament became warmer than they had ever been since the days of the Fronde: the citizens, sharing in the excitement, thronged the palace of the Parliament, expressing their approval or disapproval of the different speakers by disorderly and unprecedented clamor; the great majority hooting down the minister and his supporters, and cheering those who spoke against him. The Duc d'Orleans, by open bribes, gained over many of the councilors to oppose the court in every thing. The registration of several of the edicts which the minister had sent down was refused; and one member of the Orleanist party even demanded the convocation of the States- general, formerly and constitutionally the great council of the nation, but which had never been assembled since the time of Richelieu.

The archbishop was sometimes angry, and sometimes terrified, and as weak in his anger as in his terror. He persuaded the king to hold a bed of justice to compel the registration of the edicts. When the Parliament protested, he banished it to Troyes. In less than a month he became alarmed at his own vigor, and recalled it. Encouraged by his pusillanimity, and more secure than ever of the support of the citizens who had been thrown into consternation by his demand of a second loan, nearly[12] six times as large as the first, it became more audacious and defiant than ever, D'Orleans openly placing himself at the head of the malcontents. Lomenie persuaded the king to banish the duke, and to arrest one or two of his most vehement partisans; and again in a few weeks repented of this act of decision also, released the prisoners, and recalled the duke.

As a matter of course, the Parliament grew bolder still. Every measure which the minister proposed was rejected; and under the guidance of one of their members, Duval d'Espremesnil, the councilors at last proceeded so far as to take the initiative in new legislation into their own hands. In the first week in May, 1788, they passed a series of resolutions affirming that to be the law which indeed ought to have been so, but which had certainly never been regarded as such at any period of French history. One declared that magistrates were irremovable, except in cases of misconduct; another, that the individual liberty and property of every citizen were inviolable; others insisted on the necessity of convoking the States- general as the only assembly entitled to impose taxes; and the councilors hoped to secure the royal acceptance of these resolutions by some previous votes which asserted that, of those laws which were the very foundation of the Constitution, the first was that which assured the "crown to the reigning house and to its descendants in the male line, in the order of primogeniture.[13]"

But Louis, or rather his rash minister, was not to be so conciliated; and a scene ensued which is the first of the striking parallels which this period in France affords to the events which had taken place in England a century and a half before. As in 1642 Charles I. had attempted to arrest members of the English Parliament in the very House of Commons, so the archbishop now persuaded Louis to send down the captain of the guard, the Marquis d'Agoust, to the palace of the Parliament, to seize D'Espremesnil, and another councilor named Montsabert, who had been one of his foremost supporters in the recent discussions. They behaved with admirable dignity. Marie Antoinette was not one to betray her husband's counsels, as Henrietta Maria had betrayed those of Charles. D'Espremesnil and his friend, wholly taken by surprise, had had no warning of what was designed, no time to withdraw, nor in all probability would they have done so in any case. When M. d'Agoust entered the council hall and demanded his prisoners, there was a great uproar. The whole Assembly made common cause with their two brethren who were thus threatened. "We are all d'Espremesnils and Montsaberts," was their unanimous cry; while the tumult at the doors, where a vast multitude was collected, many of whom had arms in their hands and seemed prepared to use them, was more formidable still. But D'Agoust, though courteous in the discharge of his duty, was intrepid and firm; and the two members voluntarily surrendered themselves and retired in custody, while the archbishop was so elated with his triumph that a few days afterwards he induced the king to venture on another imitation of the history of England, though now it was not Charles, but the more tyrannical Cromwell, whose conduct was copied. Before the end of the month the Governor of Paris entered the palace of the Parliament, seized all the registers and documents of every kind, locked the doors, and closed them with the king's seal; and a royal edict was issued suspending all the parliaments both in the capital and the provinces.

CHAPTER XXII.

Formidable Riots take place in some Provinces.--The Archbishop invites Necker to join his Ministry.--Letter of Marie Antoinette describing her Interview with the Archbishop, and her Views.--Necker refuses.--The Queen sends Messages to Necker.--The Archbishop resigns, and Necker becomes Minister.--The Queen's View of his Character.--General Rejoicing.--Defects in Necker's Character.--He recalls the Parliament.--Riots in Paris.-- Severe Winter.--General Distress.--Charities of the King and Queen.-- Gratitude of the Citizens.--The Princes are concerned in the Libels published against the Queen.--Preparations for the Meeting of the States- general.--Long Disuse of that Assembly.--Need of Reform.--Vices Of the Old Feudal System.--Necker's Blunders in the Arrangements for the Meeting of the States.--An Edict of the King concedes the Chief Demands of the Commons.--Views of the Queen.

The whole kingdom was thrown into great and dangerous excitement by these transactions. Little as were the benefits which the people had ever derived from the conduct of the Parliament, their opposition to the archbishop, who had already had time to make himself generally hated and despised, caused the councilors to be very generally regarded as champions of liberty; and in the most distant provinces, in Bearn, in Isere, and in Brittany, public meetings (a thing hitherto unknown in the history of the nation) were held, remonstrances were drawn up, confederacies were formed, and oaths were administered by which those who took them bound themselves never to surrender what they affirmed to be the ancient privileges of the nation.

The archbishop became alarmed; a little, perhaps, for the nation and the king, but far more for his own place, which he had already contrived to render profitable to himself by the preferments which it had enabled him to engross. And, in the hope of saving it, he now entreated Necker to join the Government, proposing to yield up the management of the finances to him, and to retain only the post of prime minister.

A letter from the queen to Mercy shows that she acquiesced in the scheme. Her disapproval of Necker's past conduct was outweighed by her sense of the need which the State had of his financial talents; though, for reasons which she explains, she was unwilling wholly to sacrifice the archbishop; and the letter has a further interest as displaying some of the difficulties which arose from the peculiar disposition of the king, while every one was daily more and more learning to look upon her as the more important person in the Government. On the 19th of August, 1783, she writes to Mercy,[1] whom the archbishop had employed as his agent to conciliate the stubborn Swiss Banker:

"The archbishop came to me this morning, immediately after he had seen you, to report to me the conversation which he had had with you. I spoke to him very frankly, and was touched by what he said. He is at this moment with the king, to try and get him to decide; but I very much fear that M. Necker will not accept while the archbishop remains. The animosity of the public against him is pushed so far that M. Necker will be afraid of being compromised, and, indeed, perhaps it might injure his credit; but, at the same time, what is to be done? In truth and conscience we can not sacrifice a man who has made for as all these sacrifices of his reputation, of his position in the world, perhaps even of his life; for I fear they would kill him. There is yet M. Foulon, if M. Necker refuses absolutely.[2] But I suspect him of being a very dishonest man; and confidence would not be established with him for comptroller. I fear, too, that the public is pressing us to take a part much more humiliating for the ministers, and much more vexatious for ourselves, inasmuch as we shall have done nothing of our own will. I am very unhappy. I will close my letter after I know the result of this evening's conference. I greatly fear the archbishop will be forced to retire altogether, and then what man are we to take to place at the head of the whole? For we must have one, especially with M. Necker. He must have a bridle; and the person who is above me[3] is not able to be such; and I, whatever people may say, and whatever happens, am never any thing but second; and, in spite of the confidence which the first has in me, he often makes me feel it.... The archbishop has just gone. The king is very unwilling; and could only be brought to make up his mind by a promise that the person[4] should only be sounded; and that no positive engagement should be made."

Necker refused. The next day Mercy reported to the queen that, though the excitement was great, it confined itself to denunciations of the archbishop and of the keeper of the seals; and that "the name of the queen had never once been mentioned;" and on the 22d, Marie Antoinette,[5] from a conviction of the greatness of the emergency, determined to see Necker herself; and employed the embassador and De Vermond to let him know that her own wish for his restoration to the direction of the finances was sincere and earnest, and to promise him that the archbishop should not interfere in that department in any way whatever. Two days later,[6] she wrote again to mention that the king had vanquished his repugnance to Necker, and had come wholly over to her opinion. "Time pressed, and it was more essential than ever that Necker should accept;" and on the 25th she writes a final letter to report to Mercy that the archbishop has resigned, and that she has just summoned Necker to come to her the next morning. Though she felt that she had done what was both right and indispensable, she was not without misgivings. "If," she writes, in a strain of anxious despondency very foreign to her usual tone, and which shows how deeply she felt the importance of the crisis, and of every step that might be taken-- "if he will but undertake the task, it is the best thing that can be done; but I tremble (excuse my weakness) at the fact that it is I who have brought him back. It is my fate to bring misfortune, and, if infernal machinations should cause him once more to fail, or if he should lower the authority of the king, they will hate me still more."

In one point of view she need not have trembled at being known to have caused Necker's re-appointment, since it is plain that no other nomination was possible. Vergennes had died a few months before, and the whole kingdom did not supply a single statesman of reputation except Necker. Nor could any choice have for the moment been more universally popular. The citizens illuminated Paris; the mob burned the archbishop in effigy; and the leading merchants and bankers showed their approval in a far more practical way. The funds rose; loans to any amount were freely offered to the Treasury; the national credit revived; as if the solvency or insolvency of the nation depended on a single man, and him a foreigner.

Yet, if regarded in any point of view except that of a financier, he was extremely unfit to be the minister at such a crisis; and the queen's acuteness had, in the extract from her letter which has been, quoted above, correctly pointed out the danger to be apprehended, namely, that he might lower the authority of the king.[7] It was, in fact, to his uniform and persistent degradation of the king's authority that the greater part, if not the whole, of the evils which ensued may be clearly traced, and the cause that led him to adopt this fatal system was thoroughly visible to one gifted with such intuitive penetration into character as Marie Antoinette. For he had two great defects or weaknesses; an overweening vanity, which, as it is valued applause above every thing, led him to regard the popularity which they might win for him as the natural motive and the surest test of his actions; and an abstract belief in human perfection and in the submission of all classes to strict reason, which could only proceed from a total ignorance of mankind.[8] Yet, greatly as financial skill was needed, if the kingdom was to be saved from the bankruptcy which seemed to be imminent, it was plain that a faculty for organization and legislation was no less indispensable if the vessel of the State was to be steered safely along the course on which it was entering; for the archbishop's last act had been to induce the king to promise to convoke the States-general. The 1st of May of the ensuing year was fixed for their meeting; and the arrangements for and the management of an assembly, which, as not having met for nearly two hundred years, could not fail to present many of the features of an entire novelty, were a task which would have severely tested the most statesman-like capacity.

But, unhappily, Necker's very first acts showed him equally void of resolution and of sagacity. He was not only unable to estimate the probable conduct of the people in future, but he showed himself incapable of profiting by the experience of the past; and, in spite of the insubordinate spirit which the Parliament had at all times displayed, he at once recalled them in deference to the clamor of the Parisian citizens, and allowed them to enter Paris in a triumphal procession, as if his very object had been to parade their victory over the king's authority. Their return was the signal for a renewal of riots, which assumed a more formidable character than ever. The police, and even the guardhouses, were attacked in open day, and the Government had reason to suspect that the money which was employed in fomenting the tumults was supplied by the Duc d'Orleans. A fierce mob traversed the streets at night, terrifying the peaceable inhabitants with shouts of triumph over the king as having been compelled to recall the Parliament against his will; while those who were supposed to be adverse to the pretensions of the councilors were insulted in the streets, and branded as Royalists, the first time in the history of the nation that ever that name had been used as a term of reproach.

Yet, presently the whole body of citizens, with their habitual impulsive facility of temper, again, for a while, became Royalists. The winter was one of unprecedented severity. By the beginning of December the Seine was frozen over, and the whole adjacent country was buried in deep snow. Wolves from the neighboring forests, desperate with hunger, were said to have made their way into the suburbs, and to have attacked people in the streets. Food of every kind became scarce, and of the poorer classes many were believed to have died of actual starvation. Necker, as head of the Government, made energetic and judicious efforts to relieve the universal distress, forming magazines in different districts, facilitating the means of transport, finding employment for vast numbers of laborers and artisans, and purchasing large quantities of grain in foreign countries; and, not only were Louis and Marie Antoinette conspicuous for the unstinting liberality with which they devoted their own funds to the supply of the necessities of the destitute, but the queen, in many cases of unusual or pressing suffering that were reported to her in Versailles and the neighboring villages, sent trustworthy persons to investigate them, and in numerous instances went herself to the cottages, making personal inquiries into the condition of the occupants, and showing not only a feeling heart, but a considerate and active kindness, which doubled the value of her benefactions by the gracious, thoughtful manner in which they were bestowed.

She would willingly have done the good she did in secret, partly from her constant feeling that charity was not charity if it were boasted of, partly from a fear that those ready to misconstrue all her acts would find pretexts for evil and calumny even in her bounty. One of her good deeds struck Necker as of so remarkable a character that he pressed her to allow him to make it known. "Be sure, on the contrary," she replied, "that you never mention it. What good could it do? they would not believe you;[9]" but in this she was mistaken. Her charities were too widely spread to escape the knowledge even of those who did not profit by them; and they had their reward, though it was but a short-lived one. Though the majority of her acts of personal kindness were performed in Versailles rather than in Paris, the Parisians were as vehement in their gratitude as the Versaillese; and it found a somewhat fantastic vent in the erection of pyramids and obelisks of snow in different quarters of the city, all bearing inscriptions testifying the citizens' sense of her benevolence. One, which far exceeded all its fellows in size--the chief beauty of works of that sort--since it was fifteen feet high, and each of the four faces was twelve feet wide at the base, was decorated with a medallion of the royal pair, and bore a poetical inscription commemorating the cause of its erection:

> "Reine, dont la beaute surpasse les appas
> Pres d'un roi bienfaisant occupe ici la place.
> Si ce monument frele est de neige et de glace,
> Nos coeurs pour toi ne le sont pas.
> De ce monument sans exemple,
> Couple auguste, l'aspect bien doux pur votre coeur
> Sans doute vous plaira plus qu'un palais, qu'un temple
> Que vous eleverait un peuple adulateur.[10]"

Neither the queen's feelings nor her conduct had been in any way altered; but six months later the same populace who raised this monument and applauded these verses were, with ferocious and obscene threats, clamoring for her blood. And there is hardly any thing more strange or more grievous in the history of the nation, hardly any greater proof of that incurable levity which was one great cause of the long series of miseries which soon fell upon it, than that the impressions of gratitude which were so vivid at the moment, and so constantly revived by the queen's untiring benevolence, could yet be so easily effaced by the acts of demagogues and libelers, whom the people thoroughly despised even while suffering themselves to be led by them. How great a part in these libels was borne by those who were bound by every tie of blood to the king to be his warmest supporters, we have a remarkable proof in an Edict of Council which was issued during the ministry of the archbishop, and which deprived the palaces of the Count de Provence, the Count d'Artois, and the Duc d'Orleans of their usual exemption from the investigation of the syndics of the library, as those officers were called whose duty it was to search all suspected places for libelous or seditious pamphlets; the reason publicly given for this edict being that the dwellings of these three princes were a perfect arsenal for the issue of publications contrary to the laws, to morality, and to religion.[11]

With the return of spring, the severity of the distress began to pass away. But, even while it lasted, it scarcely diverted the attention of the middle classes from the preparations for the approaching meeting of the States-general, from which the whole people, with few exceptions, promised themselves great advantages, though comparatively few had formed any precise notion of the benefits which they expected, or of the mode in which they were to be attained. The States-general had been originally established in the same age which saw the organization of our own Parliament, with very nearly the same powers, though the members had more of the narrower character of delegates of their constituents than was the case in England, where they were more wisely regarded as representatives of the entire nation. [12] And it was an acknowledged principle of their constitution that they could neither propose any measure nor ask for the redress of any grievance which was not expressly mentioned in the instructions with which their constituents furnished them at the time of their election.

In England, the two Houses of Parliament, by a vigilant and systematic perseverance, had gradually extorted from the sovereign a great and progressive enlargement of their original powers, till they had almost engrossed the entire legislative authority in the kingdom. But in France, a variety of circumstances had prevented the States-general from arriving at a similar development. And, consequently, as in human affairs very little is stationary, their authority had steadily diminished, instead of increasing, till they had become so powerless and utterly insignificant that, since the year 1615, they had never once been convened. Not only had they been wholly disused, but they seemed to have been wholly forgotten. During the last two reigns no one had ever mentioned their name; much less had any wish been expressed for their resuscitation, till the financial difficulties of the Government, and the general and growing discontent of the great majority of the nation, with which, since the death of Turgot, every successive minister had been manifestly incompetent to deal, had, as we have seen, led some ardent reformers to demand their restoration, as the one expedient which had not been tried, and which, therefore, had this in its favor, that it was not condemned by previous failure.

That great reforms were indispensable was admitted in every quarter. There was no country in Europe where the feudal system had received so little modification.[13] Every law seemed to have been made, and every custom to have been established for the exclusive benefit of the nobles. They were even exempted from many of the taxes, an exemption which was the more intolerable from the vast number of persons who were included in the list. Practically it may be said that there were two classes of nobles--the old historic houses, as they were sometimes called, such as the Grammonts or Montmorencies, which were not numerous, and many of which had greatly decayed in wealth and influence; and an inferior class whose nobility was derived from their possession of office under the crown in any part of the kingdom. Even tax-gatherers and surveyors, if appointed by royal warrant, could claim the rank; and new offices were continually being created and sold which conferred the same title. Those so ennobled were not reckoned the equals of the higher class. They could not even be received at court until their patents were four hundred years old, but they had a right to vote as nobles at elections to any representative body. Those whose patents were twenty-four years old could be elected as representatives; and from the moment of their creation they all enjoyed great exemptions; so that, as the lowest estimate reckoned their numbers at a hundred thousand, it is a matter for some wonder how the taxes to which they did not contribute produced any thing worth collecting. It was, of course, manifest that the exemptions enormously increased the burden to be borne by the classes which did not enjoy such privileges.

But, heavy as the grievance of these exemptions was, it was as nothing when compared with the feudal rights claimed by the greater nobles. The peasants on their estates were forced to grind their corn at the lord's mill, to press their grapes at his wine-press, paying for such act whatever price he might think fit to exact, and often having their crops wholly wasted or spoiled by the delays which such a system engendered. The game-laws forbade them to weed their fields lest they should disturb the young partridges or leverets; to manure the soil with any thing which might injure their flavor; or even to mow or reap till the grass or corn was no longer required as shelter for the young coveys. Some of the rights of seigniory, as it was called, were such as can hardly be mentioned in this more decorous age; some were so ridiculous that it is inconceivable how their very absurdity had not led to their abolition. In the marshy districts of Brittany, one right enjoyed by the great nobles was "the silence of the frogs,[14]" which, whenever the lady was confined, bound the peasants to spend their days and nights in beating the swamps with long poles to save her from being disturbed by their inharmonious croaking. And if this or any other feudal right was dispensed with, it was only commuted for a money payment, which was little less burdensome.

The powers exercised by the crown were more intolerable still. The sovereign was absolute master of the liberties of his subjects. Without alleging the commission of any crime, he could issue warrants--letters under seal, as they were called--which consigned the person named in them to imprisonment, which was often perpetual. The unhappy prisoner had no power of appeal. No judge could inquire into his case, much less release him. The arrests were often made with such secrecy and rapidity that his nearest relations knew not what had become of him, but he was cut off from the outer world, for the rest of his life, as completely as if he had at once been handed over to the executioner.[15]

It was impossible but that such customs should produce general discontent, and a resolute demand for a complete reformation of the system. And one of the problems which the minister had to determine was, how to organize the States-general so that they should be disposed to promote such measures as reform as should be adequate without being excessive; as should give due protection to the middle and lower classes without depriving the nobles of that dignity and authority which were not only desirable for themselves, but useful to their dependents; and, lastly, such as should carefully preserve the rightful prerogatives of the crown, while putting an end to those arbitrary powers, the existence of which was incompatible with the very name of freedom.

In making the necessary arrangements, the long disuse of the Assembly was a circumstance greatly in favor of the Government, if Necker had had skill to avail himself of it, since it wholly freed him from the obligation of being guided by former precedents. Those arrangements were long and warmly debated in the king's council. Though the records of former sessions had been so carelessly preserved that little was known of their proceedings, it seemed to be established that the representatives of the Commons had usually amounted to about four-tenths of the whole body, those of the clergy and of the nobles being each about three-tenths; and that they had almost invariably deliberated and voted in separate chambers; and the princes and the chief nobles presented memorials to the king, in which they almost unanimously recommended an adherence to these ancient forms; while, with patriotic prudence, they sought to obviate all jealousy of their own pretensions or views which might be entertained or feigned in any quarter, by announcing their willingness to abandon all the exclusive privileges and exemptions which they had hitherto possessed, and which were notoriously one chief cause of the generally prevailing discontent.

But the party which had originated the clamor for the States-general, now, encouraged by their success, put forward two fresh demands; the first, that the number of the representatives of the Commons should equal that of both the other orders put together, which they called "the duplication of the Third Estate;" the second, that the three orders should meet and vote as one united body in one chamber; the two proposition taken together being manifestly calculated and designed to throw the whole power into the hands of the Commons.

Necker had great doubts about the propriety and safety of the first proposal, and no doubt at all of the danger of the second. His own judgment was that the wisest plan would be to order the clergy and nobles to unite in an Upper Chamber, so as in some degree to resemble the British House of Lords; while the Third Estate, in a Lower Chamber, would be a tolerably faithful copy of our House of Commons. But he could never bring himself to risk his popularity by opposing what he regarded as the opinion of the masses. He was alarmed by the political clubs which were springing up in Paris; one, whose president was the Duc d'Orleans, assuming the significant and menacing title of Les Enrages;[16] and by the vast number of pamphlets which were circulated both in the capital and the chief towns of the provinces by thousands,[17] every writer of which put himself forward as a legislator,[18] and of which the vast majority advocated what they called the rights of the Third Estate, in most violent language; and, finally, he adopted the course which is a great favorite with vain and weak men, and which he probably represented to himself as a compromise between unqualified concession and unyielding resistance, though, every one possessed of the slightest penetration could see that it practically surrendered both points: he advised the king to issue his edict that the number of representatives to be returned to the States-general should be twelve hundred, half of whom were to be returned by the Commons, a quarter by the clergy, and a quarter by the nobles;[19] and to postpone the decision as to the number of the chambers till the Assembly should meet, when he proposed to allow the States themselves to determine it; trusting, against all probability, that, after having thus given the Commons the power to enforce their own views, he should be able to persuade them to abandon the same in deference to his judgment.

Louis, as a matter of course, adopted his advice; and, after several different towns--Blois, Tours, Cambrai, and Compiegne among them--had been proposed as the place of meeting, he himself decided in favor of Versailles,[20] as that which would afford him the best hunting while the session lasted. The queen in her heart disapproved of every one of these resolutions. She saw that Necker had, as she had foreboded, sacrificed the king's authority by his advice on the two first questions; and she perceived more clearly than any one the danger of fixing the States- general so near to Paris that the turbulent population of the city should be able to overawe the members. She pressed these considerations earnestly on the king,[21] but it was characteristic of the course which she prescribed to herself from, the beginning, and from which she never swerved, that when her advice was overruled she invariably defended the course which had been taken. Her language, when any one spoke to her either of her own opinions and wishes, or of the feelings with which the different classes of the nation regarded her, was invariably the same. "You are not to think of me for a moment. All that I desire of you is to take care that the respect which is due to the king shall not be weakened;[22]" and it was only her most intimate friends who knew how unwise she thought the different decisions that had been adopted, or how deep were her forebodings of evil.

CHAPTER XXIII.

The Reveillon Riot.--Opening of the States-general.--The Queen is insulted by the Partisans of the Duc d'Orleans.--Discussions as to the Number of Chambers.--Career and Character of Mirabeau.--Necker rejects his Support. --He determines to revenge himself.--Death of the Dauphin.

The meeting of the States-general, as has been already seen, was fixed for the 4th of May, 1789; and, as if it were fated that the bloody character of the period now to be inaugurated should be displayed from the very outset, the elections for the city of Paris, which were only held in the preceding week, were stained with a riot so formidable as to be commonly spoken of in the records of the time as an insurrection.[1]

One of the candidates for the representation of the Third Estate was a paper-maker of the name of Reveillon, a man eminent for his charity and general liberality, but one who was believed to regard the views of the extreme reformers with disfavor. He was so popular with his own workmen, who were very numerous, and with their friends, who knew his character from them, that he was generally expected to succeed. The opposite party, who had candidates of their own, and had the support of the purse of the Duc d'Orleans, were determined that he should not; and no way seemed so sure as to murder him. Bands of ferocious-looking ruffians were brought in from the country districts, armed with heavy bludgeons, and, as was afterward learned, well supplied with money; and on the morning of the 28th of April news was brought to the Baron de Besenval, the commander of the Royal Guards, that a mob of several thousand men had collected in the streets, who had read a mock sentence, professing to have been passed by the Third Estate, which condemned Reveillon to be hanged, after which they had burned him in effigy, and then attacked his house, which they were sacking and destroying. They even ventured to attack the first company of soldiers whom De Besenval sent to the rescue; and it was not till he dispatched a battalion with a couple of field-pieces to the spot that the plunderers were expelled from the house and the riot was quelled. Nearly five hundred of the mob were killed, but when the Parliament proceeded to set on foot a judicial inquiry into the cause of the tumult, Necker prevailed on the secretary of state to suppress the investigation, as he feared to exasperate D'Orleans further by giving publicity to his machinations, which he did not yet suspect either the extent or the object.[2]

A momentary tranquility was, however, restored at Paris; and all eyes were turned from the capital to Versailles, where the first few days of May were devoted to the receptions of the States-general by the king and queen, ceremonies which might have had a good effect, since the bitterest adversaries of the court were favorably impressed by the grace and affability of the queen; but which many shrewd judges afterward believed to have had a contrary influence, from the offense taken by the representatives of the Commons at some of the details of the ancient etiquette, which on so solemn an occasion was revived in all its stately strictness. The dignitaries of the Church wore their most sumptuous robes. The Nobles glittered with silk and gold lace; jeweled clasps fastened plumes of feathers in their hats; orders glittered on their breasts; and many a precious stone sparkled in the hilts of their swords. The representatives of the Commons were allowed neither feathers, nor embroidery, nor swords; but were forced to content themselves with plain black cloaks, and an unadorned homeliness of attire, which seemed as if intended to exclude all idea of their being the equals of those other orders of which they had for a moment become the colleagues. And, in a similar spirit it was arranged that, after the folding-doors of the saloon in which the sovereigns were awaiting them were thrown wide open to admit the representatives of the higher orders, the Commons were let in through a side door. And though in the eyes of persons habituated to the ceremonious niceties of court life these distinctions seemed matters of course, and, as such, unworthy of notice, it can hardly be wondered at if they were galling to men accustomed only to the simpler manners of a provincial town; and who, proud of their new position and deeply impressed with its importance, fancied they saw in them a settled intention to degrade both them and their constituents by thus stamping them with a badge of inferiority before all the spectators.

The opening of the States-general was fixed for the 5th of May, and on the day before, which was Sunday, a solemn mass was performed at the principal church in Versailles, that of Notre Dame; after which the congregation proceeded to another church, that of St. Louis, to hear a sermon from the Bishop of Nancy. It was a stately procession that moved from one church to the other, and it was afterward remembered as the very last in which the royal pair appeared before their subjects with the undiminished magnificence of ancient ceremony. First, after a splendid escort of troops, came the members of the States in their several orders; then the king marched by himself; the queen followed; and behind her came the princes and princesses of the royal family of the blood, the officers of state and of the household, and companies of the Body-guard brought up the rear. The acclamations of the spectators were loud as the deputies of the States, and especially as the representatives of the Commons, passed on; loud, too, as the king; moved forward, bearing himself with unusual dignity; but, when the queen advanced, though still the main body of the people cheered with sincere respect, a gang of ruffians, among whom were several women,[3] shouted out "Long live the Duke of Orleans!" in her ear, with so menacing an accent that, she nearly fainted with terror. By a strong mastery over herself she shook off the agitation, which was only perceived by her immediate attendants; but the disloyal feeling thus shown toward her at the outset was a sad omen of the spirit in which one party at least was prepared to view the measures of the Government; and, so far as she was concerned, of the degree in which her enemies had succeeded in poisoning the minds of the people against her, as the person whose resistance to their meditated encroachments on the royal authority was likely to prove the most formidable.

It was a significant hint, too, of the projects already formed by the worthless prince whose adherents these ruffians proclaimed themselves. The Duc d'Orleans conceived himself to have lately received a fresh provocation, and an additional motive for revenge. His eldest son, the Duc de Chartres,[4] was now a boy of sixteen, and he had proposed to the king to give him Madame Royale in marriage; an idea which the queen, who held his character in deserved abhorrence, had rejected with very decided marks of displeasure. He was also stimulated by views of personal ambition. The history of England had been recently studied by many persons in France besides the king and queen; and there were not wanting advisers to point out to the duke that the revolution which had taken place in England exactly a century before had owed its success to the dethronement of the reigning sovereign and the substitution of another member of the royal family in his place. As William of Orange was, after the king's own children, the next heir to James II., so was the Duc d'Orleans now the next heir, after the king's children and brothers, to Louis XVI.; and for the next five months there can be no doubt that he and his partisans, who numbered in their body some of the most influential members of the States-general, kept constantly in view the hope of placing him on the throne from which they were to depose his cousin.

The next day the States were formally opened by Louis in person. The place of meeting was a spacious hall which, two years before, had been used for the meeting of the Notables. It had been the scene of many a splendid spectacle in times past, but had never before witnessed so imposing or momentous a ceremony. The town itself had not risen into notice till the memory of the preceding States-general had almost passed away. And now, after all the deputies had ranged themselves to receive their sovereign, the representatives of the clergy on the right of the throne, the Nobles on the left, the Commons in denser masses at the bottom of the hall;[5] as the king, accompanied by the queen, leading two of her children[6] by the hand, and attended by all the princes of the royal family and of the blood, by the dukes and peers of the kingdom, the ministers and great officers of state, entered and took his seat on the throne, the most unimpassioned spectator must have felt that he was beholding a scene at once magnificent and solemn; and one, from long desuetude, as novel as if it had been wholly unprecedented, such as might well inaugurate a new policy or a new constitution.

Could those who beheld it as spectators, could those who bore a part in the solemnity, have looked into futurity; could they have divined that no other hall would ever again see that virtuous and beneficent king surrounded with that pomp, or received with that reverential homage which was now paid to him as as unquestioned right; nay, that the end, of which this day was the beginning, scarcely one single person of all those now present, whether men in the flower of their strength, women in the pride of their beauty, or even children in their infantine innocence and grace, would live to behold; but that sovereigns and subjects were destined, almost without exception, to perish with circumstances of unutterable, unimaginable horror and misery, as the direct consequence of this day's pageant; we may well believe that the most sanguine of those who now greeted it with eager hope and exultation would rather have averted his eyes from the ill-omened spectacle, and would have preferred to bear the worst evils of which he was anticipating the abolition, to bringing on his country the calamities which were about to fall upon it.

A large state arm-chair, a little lower than the throne, had been set beside it for the queen; the princes and princesses were ranged on each side on a row of chairs without arms; and, when all had taken their places, the king opened the session with a short speech, leaving the real business to be unfolded at greater length by his ministers. In order to feel assured of the proper emphasis and expression, he had rehearsed his speech frequently to the queen; and, as he now delivered it with unusual dignity and gracefulness, it was received with frequent acclamations, though some of those who were watching all that passed with the greatest anxiety fancied that one or two compliments to the queen which it contained met with a colder response; while, at its close, the representatives of the Third Estate gave an indication of their feeling toward the other orders, and provoked a display on their part which promised little cordiality to their deliberations. The king, who had uncovered himself while speaking, on resuming his seat replaced his hat. The Nobles, according to the ancient etiquette, replaced theirs; and many of the Commons at once asserted their equality with them by also covering themselves. Such an assumption was a breach of all established custom. The Nobles were indignant, and with angry shouts demanded the removal of the Commons' hats. They were met with louder clamor by the Commons, and in a moment the whole hall was in an uproar, which was only allayed by the presence of mind of Louis himself, who, as if oppressed by the heat, laid aside his own hat, when, as a matter of course, the Nobles followed his example. The deputies of the Commons did the same, and peace was restored.

The king's speech was followed by another short one from the keeper of the seals, which received but little attention; and by one of prodigious length from Necker, which was equally injudicious and unacceptable to his hearers, both in what it said and in what it omitted. He never mentioned the question of constitutional reform. He said nothing of what the Commons, at least, thought still more important--the number of chambers in which the members were to meet; and, though he dilated at the most profuse length on the condition of the finances, and on his own success in re-establishing public credit, they were by no means pleased to hear him assert that success had removed any absolute necessity for their meeting at all, and that they had only been called together in fulfillment of the king's promise, that so the sovereign might establish a better harmony between the different parts of the Constitution.

Before any business could be proceeded with, it was necessary for the members to have the writs of their elections properly certified and registered, for which they were to meet on the following day. We need not here detail the artifices and assumptions by which the members of the Third Estate put forward pretensions which were designed to make them masters of the whole Assembly; nor is it necessary to unfold at length the combination of audacity and craft, aided by the culpable weakness of Necker, by which they ultimately carried the point they contended for, providing that the three orders should deliberate and vote together as one united body in one chamber. Emboldened by their success, they even proceeded to a step which probably not one among them had originally contemplated; and, as if one of their principal objects had been to disown the authority of the king by which they had been called together, they repudiated the title of States-general, and invented for themselves a new name, that of "The National Assembly," which, as it had never been heard of before, seemed to mark that they owed their existence to the nation, and not to the sovereign.

But the discussions that took place before all these points were settled, presented, besides the importance of the conclusion which was adopted, another feature of powerful interest, since it was in them that the members first heard the voice of the Count de Mirabeau, who, more than any other deputy, was supposed during the ensuing year to be able to sway the whole Assembly, and to hold the destinies of the nation in his hands.

Necker's daughter, the celebrated Baroness de Stael, wife of the Swedish embassador, who was present at the opening of the States, which, as her father's daughter, she regarded with exulting confidence as the body of legislators who were to regenerate the nation, remarked, as the long procession passed before her eyes, that of the six hundred deputies of the Commons[7], the Count de Mirabeau alone bore a name which was previously known; and he was manifestly out of his place as a representative of the Commons. His history was a strange one. He was the eldest son of a Provencal noble, of Italian origin, great wealth, and a ferocious eccentricity of character, which made him one of the worst possible instructors for a youth of brilliant talents, unbridled passions, and a disposition equally impetuous in its pursuit of good and of evil. Even before he arrived at manhood he had become notorious for every kind of profligacy; while his father, in an almost equal degree, provoked the censure of those who interested themselves in the career of a youth of undeniable ability, by punishments of such severity as wore the appearance of vengeance rather than of fatherly correction. In six or seven years he obtained no fewer than fifteen warrants, or letters under seal, for the imprisonment of his son in different jails or fortresses, while the young man seemed to take a wanton pleasure in showing how completely all efforts for his reformation were thrown away. Though unusually ugly (he himself compared his face to that of a tiger who had had the small-pox), he was irresistible among women. While one of the youngest subalterns in the army, he made love, rarely without success, to the mistresses or wives of his superior officers, and fought duel after duel with those who took offense at his gallantries, From one castle in which he was imprisoned he was aided to escape by the wife of an officer of the garrison, who accompanied his flight. From another he was delivered by the love of a lady of the highest rank, the Marchioness de Monnier, whom he had met at the governor's table.

When, after some years of misery, the marchioness terminated them by suicide, he seduced a nun of exquisite beauty to leave her convent for his sake; and as France was no longer a safe residence for them, he fled to Frederick of Prussia, who, equally glad to welcome him as a Frenchman, a genius, and a profligate, received him for a while into high favor. But he was penniless; and Frederick was never liberal of his money. Debt soon drove him from Prussia, and he retired to England, where he made acquaintance with Fox, Fitzpatrick, and other men of mark in the political circles of the day. He was at all times and amidst all his excesses both observant and studious; and while witnessing in person the strife of parties in this country, he learned to appreciate the excellencies of our Constitution, both in its theory and in its practical working. But presently debt drove him from London as it had driven him from Berlin; and, after taking refuge for a short time in Holland and Switzerland, he was hesitating whither next to betake himself, when, hearing of the elections for the States-general, he resolved to offer himself as a candidate;

and returned to Provence to seek the suffrages of the Nobles of his own county.

Unluckily, his character was too well known in his native district; and the Nobles, unwilling to countenance the ambition of one who had obtained so evil a notoriety, rejected him. Full of indignation, he turned to the Third Estate, offering himself as a representative of the Commons. In his speeches to the citizens of Aix and Marseilles--for he canvassed both towns--he inveighed against Necker and the Government with an eloquence which electrified his audience, who had never before been addressed in the language of independence. He was returned for both towns, and hastened to Versailles, eager to avenge on the Nobles, the body which, as he felt, he had a right to have represented, the affront which had driven him, against his will, to seek the votes of a class with which he had scarcely a feeling in common; for in the whole Assembly there was no man less of a democrat in his heart, or prouder of his ancestry and aristocratic privileges.

He differed from most of his colleagues, inasmuch as he, from the first, had distinct views of the policy desirable for the nation, which he conceived to be the establishment of a limited constitutional monarchy, such as he had seen in England.[8] But no man in the whole Assembly was more inconsistent, as he was ever changing his views, or at least his conduct and language, at the dictates of interest or wounded pride; sometimes, as it might seem, in the mere wantonness of genius, as if he wished to show that he could lead the Assembly with equal ease to take a course, or to retrace its steps--that it rested with him alone alike to do or to undo. The only object from which he never departed was that of making all parties feel and bow to his influence. And it is this very inconsistency which so especially connects his career for the rest of his life with the fortunes of the queen, since, while he misunderstood her character, and feared her power with the king and ministers as likely to be exerted in opposition to his own views, he was the most ferocious and most foul of her enemies: when he saw that she was willing to accept his aid, and when he therefore began to conceive a hope of making her useful to himself in the prosecution of his designs, no man was louder in her praise, nor, it must be admitted, more energetic or more judicious in the advice which he gave her.

His language on the first occasion on which he made his voice heard in the Assembly was eminently characteristic of him, so manifestly was it directed to the attainment of his own object--that of making himself necessary to the court, and obtaining either office or some pension which might enable him to live, since his own resources had long been exhausted by his extravagance. D'Espresmenil had strongly advocated the doctrine that the meeting of the three orders in separate chambers was a fundamental principle of the monarchy; and Mirabeau, in opposition to him, moved an address to the king, which represented the Third Estate as desirous to ally itself with the throne, so as to enable it to resist the pretensions of the clergy and the nobles; and, as this speech of his produced no overture from the minister, in the middle of June he made a direct offer to Necker to support the Government, if Necker had any plan at all which was in the least reasonable;[9] and he gave proof of his sincerity by vigorously opposing some proposals of the extreme reformers. But, with incredible folly, Necker rejected his support, treating his arguments to his face as insignificant, and affirming that their views were irreconcilable, since Mirabeau wished to govern by policy, while he himself preferred morality.

He at once resolved to revenge himself on the minister who had thus slighted him,[10] and he was not long in finding an opportunity. On the 23d of June, after the States had assumed their new form, and Louis at a royal sitting had announced the reforms he had resolved to grant, and which were so complete that the most extreme reformers admitted that they could have wished for nothing more, except that they should themselves have taken them, and that the king should not have given them, Mirabeau took the lead in throwing down a defiance to his sovereign; refusing to consent to the adjournment of the Assembly, as was natural on the withdrawal of the king, and declaring that they, the members of the Commons, would not quit the hall unless they were expelled by bayonets.

But, violently as Versailles and Paris were agitated throughout May and June, Marie Antoinette took no part in the discussion which these questions excited. She had a still graver trouble at home. Her eldest son, the dauphin, whose birth had been greeted so enthusiastically by all classes, had, as we have seen, long been sickly. Since the beginning of the year his health had been growing worse, and on the 4th of June he died; and, though his bereaved mother bore up bravely under his loss, she felt it deeply, and for a time was almost incapacitated from turning her attention to any other subject.

CHAPTER XXIV.

Troops are brought up from the Frontier.--The Assembly petitions the King to withdraw them.--He refuses.--He dismisses Necker.---The Baron de Breteuil is appointed Prime Minister.--Terrible Riots in Paris.--The Tri-color Flag is adopted.--Storming of the Bastile and Murder of the Governor.--The Count d'Artois and other Princes fly from the Kingdom.--The King recalls Necker.--Withdraws the Soldiers and visits Paris.--Formation of the National Guard.-Insolence of La Fayette and Bailly.--Madame de Tourzel becomes Governess of the Royal Children--Letters of Marie Antoinette on their Character, and on her own Views of Education.

But even so solemn, a grief as that for a dead child she was not suffered to indulge long. Even for such a purpose royalty is not always allowed the respite which would be conceded to those in a more moderate station; and affairs in Paris began to assume so menacing a character that she was forced to rouse herself to support her husband. Demagogues in Paris excited the lower classes of the citizens to formidable tumults. The troops were tampered with; they mutinied; and when the Assembly so violated its duty as to take the mutineers under its protection, and to intercede with the king for their pardon, Louis, or, as we should probably say, Necker, did not venture to refuse, though it was plain that the condign punishment of such an offense was indispensable to the maintenance of discipline for the future. And Louis felt the humiliation so deeply that some of those about him, the Count d'Artois taking the lead in that party, were able to induce him to bring up from the frontier some German and Swiss regiments, which, as not having been exposed to the contagion of the capital, were free from the prevailing taint of disloyalty. But Louis was incapable of carrying out any plan resolutely. He selected the commander with judgment, placing the troops under the orders of a veteran of the Seven Years' War, the old Marshal de Broglie, who, though more than seventy years of age, gladly brought once more his tried skill and valor to the service of his sovereign. But the king, even while intrusting him with this command, disarmed him at the same moment by a strict order to avoid all bloodshed and violence; though nothing could be more obvious than that such outbreaks as the marshal was likely to be called on to suppress could not be quelled by gentle means.

The Orleanists and Mirabeau probably knew nothing of this humane or rather pusillanimous order, though most of the secrets of the court were betrayed to them; but Mirabeau saw in the arrival of the soldiers a fresh opportunity of making the king feel the folly of the minister in rejecting his advances; and in a speech of unusual power he thundered against those who had advised the bringing-up of troops, as he declared, to overawe the Assembly; though, in fact, nothing but their presence and active exertions could prevent the Assembly from being overawed by the mob. But, undoubtedly, at this time his own first object was to use the populace of Paris to terrify the members into obedience to himself. In one of his ends he succeeded; he drove Necker from office. He carried the address which he proposed, to entreat the king to withdraw the troops; but Louis had for the moment resolved on adopting bolder counsels than those of Necker. He declined to comply with the petition, declaring that it was his duty to keep in Paris a force sufficient to preserve the public tranquillity, though, if the Assembly were disquieted by their neighborhood, he expressed his unwillingness to remove their session to some more distant town. And at the same time he dismissed Necker from office, banishing him from France, but ordering him to keep his departure secret.

The queen had evidently had great influence in bringing him to this decision; but how cordially she approved of all the concessions which the king had already made, and how clearly she saw that more still remained to be done before the necessary reformation could be pronounced complete, the letter which on the evening of Necker's dismissal she wrote to Madame de Polignac convincingly proves. She had high ideas of the authority which a king was legitimately entitled to exercise; and to what she regarded as undue restrictions on it, injurious to his dignity, she would never consent. She probably regarded them as abstract questions which had but little bearing on the substantial welfare of the people in general; but of all measures to increase the happiness of all classes, even of the very lowest, she was throughout the warmest advocate.

"July 11th, 1789.

"I can not sleep, my dear heart, without letting you know that M. Necker is gone. MM. de Breteuil and de la Vauguyon will be summoned to the council to-morrow. God grant that we may at last be able to do all the good with which we are wholly occupied. The moment will be terrible; but I have courage, and, provided that the honest folks support us without exposing themselves needlessly, I think that I have vigor enough in myself to impart some to others. But it is more than ever necessary to bear in mind that all classes of men, so long as they are honest, are equally our subjects, and to know how to distinguish those who are right-thinking in every district and in every rank. My God! if people could only believe that these are my real thoughts, perhaps they would love me a little. But I must not think of myself. The glory of the king, that of his son, and the happiness of this ungrateful nation, are all that I can, all that I ought to, wish for; for as for your friendship, my dear heart, I reckon on that always..."

Such language and sentiments were worthy of a sovereign. That the feelings here expressed were genuine and sincere, the whole life of the writer is a standing proof; and yet already fierce, wicked spirits, even of women (for never was it more clearly seen than in France at this time how far, when women are cruel, they exceed the worst of men in ferocity), were thirsting for her blood. Already a woman in education and ability far above the lowest class, one whose energy afterward raised her to be, if not the avowed head, at least the moving spirit, of a numerous party (Madame Roland), was urging the public prosecution, or, if the nation were not ripe for such a formal outrage, the secret assassination, of both king and queen. [1] But, however benevolent and patriotic were the queen's intentions, it became instantly evident that those who had counseled the dismissal of Necker had given their advice in entire ignorance of the hold which he had established on the affections of the Parisians; while the new prime minister, the Baron de Breteuil, whose previous office had connected him with the police, was, on that account, very unpopular with a class which is very numerous in all large cities. The populace of Paris broke out at once in riots which amounted to insurrection. Thousands of citizens, not all of the lowest class, decorated with green cockades, the color of Necker's livery, and armed with every variety of weapon, paraded the streets, bearing aloft busts of Necker and the Duc d'Orleans, without stopping, in their madness, to consider how incongruous a combination they were presenting. The most ridiculous stories were circulated about the queen: it was affirmed that she had caused the Hall of the Assembly to be undermined, that she might blow it up with gunpowder;[2] and, by way of averting or avenging so atrocious an act, the mob began to set fire to houses in different quarters of the city. Growing bolder at the sight of their own violence, they broke open the prisons, and thus obtained a re-enforcement of hundreds of desperadoes, ripe for any wickedness. The troops were paralyzed by Louis's imbecile order to avoid bloodshed, and in the same proportion the rioters were encouraged by their inaction and evident helplessness. They attacked the great armory, and equipped themselves with its contents, applying to the basest uses time-honored weapons, monuments of ancient valor and patriotism. The spear with which Dunois had cleared his country of the British invaders; the sword with which the first Bourbon king had routed Egmont's cavalry at Ivry, were torn down from the walls to arm the vilest of mankind for rapine and slaughter. They stormed the Hotel de Ville, and got possession of the municipal chest, containing three millions of francs; and now, more and more intoxicated with their triumph, and with the evidence which all these exploits afforded that the whole city was at their mercy, they proceeded to give their riot a regular organization, by establishing a committee to sit in the Guildhall and direct their future proceedings. Lawless and ferocious as was the main body of the rioters, there were shrewd heads to guide their fury; and the very first order issued by this committee was marked by such acute foresight, and such a skillful adaptation to the requirements of the moment and the humor of the people, that it remains in force to this day. It was hardly strange that men in open insurrection against the king's authority should turn their wrath against one of its conspicuous emblems, consecrated though it was by usage of immemorial antiquity and by many a heroic achievement--the snow-white banner bearing the golden lilies. But that glorious ensign could not be laid aside till another was substituted for it; and the colors of the city, red and blue, and white, the color of the army, were now blended together to form the tricolor flag which has since won for itself a wider renown than even the deeds of Bayard or Turenne had shed upon the lilies, and with which, under every form of government, the nation has permanently identified itself.

They demanded more men, and a committee with three millions of francs could easily command recruits. They stormed the Hotel des Invalides, where thousands of muskets were kept fit for instant use; one division of regular troops, whose commander, the Baron de Besenval, was a resolute man, determined to do his duty, mutinying against his orders, and refusing to fire on the mob. They took possession of the city gates, and, thinking themselves now strong enough for any exploit, on the third day of the insurrection, the 14th of July, they marched in overpowering force to attack the Bastile.

In former times the Bastile had been the great fortress of the city; and, as such, it had been fortified with all the resources of the engineer's art. Massive well-armed towers rose at numerous points above walls of great height and solidity. A deep fosse surrounded it, and, when well supplied and garrisoned, it had been regarded with pride by the citizens, as a bulwark capable of defying the utmost efforts of a foreign enemy, and not the less to be admired because they never expected it to be exposed to such a test; but as a warlike fortress it had long been disused. In recent times it had only been known as the State-prison, identified more than any other with the worst acts of despotism and barbarity. As such it was now as much detested as it had formerly been respected; and it had nothing but the outward appearance of strength to resist an attack. Evidently the military authorities had never anticipated the possibility that the mob would rise to such a height of audacity. But the rioters were now encouraged by two days of unbroken success, and those who spurred them on were well-informed as well as fearless. They knew that the castle was in such a state that its apparent strength was its real weakness; that its entire garrison consisted of little more than a hundred soldiers, most of whom were superannuated veterans, a force inadequate to man one-tenth of the defenses; and that the governor, De Launay, though personally brave, was a man devoid of presence of mind, and nervous under responsibility.

Led by a brewer, named Santerre, who for the next three years bore a conspicuous part in all the worst deeds of ferocity and horror, they assailed the gates in vast numbers. While the attention of the scanty garrison was fully occupied by this assault, another party scaled the walls at a point where there was not even a sentinel to give the alarm, and let down one draw-bridge across the fosse, while another was loosened, as is believed, by traitors in the garrison itself. Swarming across the passage thus opened to them, thousands of the assailants rushed in; murdered the governor, officers, and almost every one of the garrison; and with a savage ferocity, as yet unexampled, though but a faint omen of their future crimes, they cut off the head and hands of De Launay and several of their chief victims, and, sticking them on pikes, bore them as trophies of their victory through the streets of the city.

The news of what had been done came swiftly to Versailles, where it excited feelings in the Assembly which, had the king or his advisers been capable of avail-ing themselves of it with skill and firmness, might have led to a salutary change in the policy of that body; for the greater part of the deputies were thoroughly alarmed at the violence of Santerre and his companions, and would in all probability have supported the king in taking strong measures for the restoration of order. But Louis could not be roused, even by the murder of his own faithful servant, to employ force to save those who might be similarly menaced. The only expedient which oc-curred to his mind was to concede all that the rioters required; and at midday on the 15th he repaired to the Assembly, and announced that he had ordered the removal of the troops from Paris and from Versailles; declaring that he trusted himself to the Assembly, and wished to identify himself with the nation. The Assembly could hardly have avoided feeling that it was a strange time to select for withdrawing the troops, when an armed mob was in possession of the capital; but, as they had for-merly requested that measure, they thought themselves bound   now to applaud it, and, being for the moment touched by the compliment paid to themselves, when he quit the Hall they unanimously rose and followed him, escorting him back to the palace with vehement cheers. A vast crowd filled the outer courts, who caught the contagion, and shouted out a demand for a sight of the whole royal family; and presently, when the queen brought out on the balcony her only remaining boy, whom the death of his brother had raised to the rank of dauphin, and saluted them, with a graceful bow, the whole mass burst out in one vociferous acclamation.

Yet even in that moment of congratulation there were base and malignant spirits in the crowd, full of bitterness against the royal family, and especially against the queen, whom they had evidently been taught to regard as the chief obstacle to the reforms which they desired. Her faithful waiting-woman, Madame de Campan, had gone down into the court-yard and mingled with the crowd, to be the better able to judge of their real feelings. She could see that many were disguised; and one woman, whose veil of black lace, with which she concealed her features, showed that she did not belong to the lowest class, seized her violently by the arm, calling her by her name, and bid her "go and tell her queen not to interfere any more in the Government, but to leave her husband and the good States-general to work out the happiness of the people." Others she heard uttering threats of vengeance against Madame de Polignac. And one, while pouring forth "a thousand invectives" against both king and queen, declared that it should soon be impossible to find even a fragment of the throne on which they were now seated.

Marie Antoinette was greatly alarmed, not for herself, but for her husband; and, now that he had determined on withdrawing the soldiers from the capital, she earnestly entreated him to accompany them, taking the not unreasonable view that the violence of the Parisian mob would be to some extent quelled, and the well-intentioned portion of the Assembly would have greater boldness to support their opinions, if the king were thus placed out of the reach of danger from any fresh outbreak; and it was generally understood that an attack on Versailles itself was anticipated.[3] She felt so certain of the wisdom of such a course, and so sanguine of prevailing, that she packed up her diamonds, burned many of her papers, and drew up a set of orders for the arrangement of the details of the journey. But on the morning of the 16th she was compelled to inform Madame Campan that the plan was given up. Large portions of the Parisian mob, and among them one deputation of the fish-women, who in this, as well as on more festive occasions, claimed equally to take the lead, had come out to demand that the king should visit Paris; and the Ministerial Council thought it safer for him to comply with that petition than to throw himself into the arms of the soldiers, a step which might not improbably lead to a civil war.

To the queen this seemed the most dangerous course of all. She knew that both at Versailles and at Paris the agents of the Duke of Orleans had been scattering money with a lavish hand; and she scarcely doubted that either on his road, or in the city, her husband would be assassinated, or at the least detained by the mob as a prisoner and a hostage.

Had she not feared to increase his danger, she would have accompanied him; but at such a crisis it required more courage and fortitude to separate herself from him; and the most courageous part was ever that which was most natural to her. But, though she took no precautions for herself, she was as thoughtful as ever for her friends; and, knowing how obnoxious the Duchess de Polignac was to the multitude, she insisted on her departing with her family. The duchess fled, not unwillingly; and at the same time others also quit Versailles who had not the same plea of delicacy of sex to excuse their terrors, and who were bound by every principle of duty to remain by the king's side the more steadily the greater might be the danger. The Prince de Conde, who certainly at one time had been a brave man, and had won an honorable name, worthy of his intrepid ancestor, in the Seven Years' War; his brother, the Prince de Conti; the Count d'Artois, who, having always been the advocate of the most violent measures, was doubly bound to stand forward in defense of his king and brother, all fled, setting the first example of that base emigration which eventually left the king defenseless in the midst of his enemies. The Baron de Breteuil and some of the ministers made similar provision for their own safety; though it may be said, as some extenuation of their ignoble flight, that they had no longer any official duties to detain them, since the king had already dismissed them, and on the evening of the 16th had written to Necker to beg him to return without delay and resume his office, claiming his instant obedience as a proof of the attachment and fidelity which he had promised when departing five days before.

On the morning of the 17th, Louis set out for Paris in a single carriage, escorted by a very slender guard and accompanied by a party of the deputies. He was fully alive to the danger he was incurring. He knew that threats had been openly uttered that he should not reach Paris alive;[4] and he had prepared for his journey as for death, burning his papers, taking the sacrament, and making arrangements for a regency. Marie Antoinette was almost hopeless of his safety. She sat with her children in her private room, shedding no tears, lest the knowledge of her grief should increase the alarm of her attendants; but her carriages were kept harnessed, and she had prepared and learned by heart a short speech, with which, if the worst news which she apprehended should arrive, she intended to repair to the Assembly, and claim its protection for the wife and children of their sovereign.[5] But often, as she rehearsed it, her voice, in spite of all her efforts, was broken by sobs, and her reiterated exclamation, "They will never let him return!" but too truly expressed the deep forebodings of her heart.

They were not yet fated to be realized; the Insurrection Committee had already organized a force which they had entitled the National Guard, and of which they had conferred the command on the Marquis de La Fayette, And at the gates of the city the king was met by him and the mayor, a man named Bailly, who had achieved a considerable reputation as a mathematician and an astronomer, but who was thoroughly imbued with the leveling and irreligious doctrines of the school of the Encyclopedists. No men in Paris were less likely to treat their sovereign with due respect.

Since his return from America, La Fayette had been living in retirement on his estate, till at the recent election he had been returned to the States-general as one of the representatives of the nobles for his native province of Auvergne. He had taken no part in the debates, being entirely destitute of political abilities;[6] and he had apparently no very distinct political views, but wavered between a desire for a republic, such, as that of which he had witnessed the establishment in America, and a feeling in favor of a limited monarchy such as he understood to exist in Great Britain, though he had no accurate comprehension of its most essential principles. But his ruling passion was a desire for popularity; and as he had always been vain of his unbending ill-manners as a proof of his liberal sentiments,[7] and as his vanity made him regard kings and queens with a general dislike, as being of a rank superior to his own, he looked on the present occurrence as a favorable opportunity for gaining the good-will of the mob, by showing marked disrespect to Louis. He would not even pay him the ordinary compliment of appearing in uniform, but headed his new troops in plain clothes; and even those were not such as belonged to his rank, but were the ordinary dress of a plain citizen; while Bailly's address, as Louis entered the gates, was marked with the most studied and gratuitous insolence. "Sire," said he, "I present to your majesty the keys of your good city of Paris. They are the same which were presented to Henri IV. He had conquered his people: to-day the people have conquered their king."

Louis proceeded onward to the Hotel de Ville, in a strange procession, headed by a numerous band of fish-women, always prominent, and recruited at every step by a crowd of rough peasant-looking men, armed with bludgeons, scythes, and every variety of rustic weapons, evidently on the watch for some opportunity to create a tumult, and seeking to provoke one by raising from time to time vociferous shouts of "Vive la nation!" and uttering ferocious threats against any one who might chance to exclaim, "Vive le roi!" But they were disconcerted by the perfect calmness of the king, on whom danger to himself seemed the only thing incapable of making an impression. On Bailly's insolent speech he had made no comment, remarking, in a whisper to his principal attendant, that he had better appear not to have heard it. And now at the Hotel de Ville his demeanor was as unruffled as if every thing that had happened had been in perfect accordance with his wishes. He made a short speech, in which he confirmed all the concessions and promises which he had previously made. He even placed in his hat a tricolor cockade, which the mayor had the effrontery to present to him, though it was the emblem of the revolt of his subjects and of the defeat of his troops. And at last such an effect had his fearless dignity on even the fiercest of his enemies, that when he afterward came out on the balcony to show himself to the crowd beneath, the whole mass raised the shout of "Vive le roi!" with as much enthusiasm as had ever greeted the most feared or the most beloved of his predecessors.

His return to the barrier resembled a triumphal procession. Yet, happy as it seemed that outrage had thus been averted and unanimity restored, the result of the day can not, perhaps, be deemed entirely fortunate, since it probably contributed to fix more deeply in the king's mind the belief that concession to clamor was the course most likely to be successful. Nor did the queen, though for the moment her despondency was changed to thankful exultation, at all conceal from herself that the perils which had been escaped were certain to recur; and that vigilance and firmness would surely again be called for to repel them--qualities which she could find in herself, but which she might well doubt her ability to impart to others.[8]

Her own attention was for a moment occupied by the necessary work of se-lecting a new governess for her children in the place of Madame de Polignac; and after some deliberation her choice fell on the Marchioness de Tourzel, a lady of the most spotless character, who seems to have been in every respect well fitted for so important an office. As Marie Antoinette had scarcely any previous acquaintance with her, it was by her character alone that she had been recommended to her; as was gracefully expressed in the brief speech with which Marie Antoinette deliv-ered her little charges into her hands. "Madame," said she, "I formerly intrusted my children to friendship; to-day I intrust them to virtue;[9]" and, a day or two afterward, to make easier the task which the marchioness had not undertaken without some unwillingness, she addressed her a letter in which she describes the character of her son, and her own principles and method of education, with an impartiality and soundness of judgment which could not have been surpassed by one who had devoted her whole attention to the subject:

"July 25th, 1789.

"My son is four years and four months old, all but two days. I say nothing of his size nor of his general appearance; it is only necessary to see him. His health has always been good, but even in his cradle we perceived that his nerves were very delicate.... This delicacy of his nerves is such that any noise to which he is not accustomed frightens him. For instance, he is afraid of dogs because he once heard one bark close to him; and I have never obliged him to see one, because I believe that, as his reason grows stronger, his fears will pass away. Like all children who are strong and healthy, he is very giddy, very volatile, and violent in his passions; but he is a good child, tender, and even caressing, when his giddiness does not run away with him. He has a great sense of what is due to himself, which, if he be well managed, one may some day turn to his good. Till he is entirely at his ease with any one, he can restrain himself, and even stifle his impatience and his inclination to anger, in order to appear gentle and amiable. He is admirably faithful when once he has promised any thing, but he is very indiscreet; he is thoughtless in repeating any thing that he has heard; and often, without in the least intending to tell stories, he adds circumstances which his own imagination has put into his head. This is his greatest fault, and it is one for which he must be corrected. However, taken altogether, I say again, he is a good child; and by treating him with allowance, and at the same time with firmness, which must be kept clear of severity, we shall always be able to do all that we can wish with him. But severity would revolt him, for he has a great deal of resolution for his age. To give you an instance: from his very earliest childhood the word ***pardon*** has always offended him. He will say and do all that you can wish when he is wrong, but as for the word ***pardon***, he never pronounces it without tears and infinite difficulty.

"I have always accustomed my children to have great confidence in me, and, when they have done wrong, to tell me themselves; and then, when I scold them, this enables me to appear pained and afflicted at what they have done rather than angry. I have accustomed them all to regard 'yes' or 'no,' once uttered by me, as irrevocable; but I always give them reasons for my decision, suitable to their ages, to prevent their thinking that my decision comes from ill-humor. My son can not read, and he is very slow at learning; but he is too giddy to apply. He has no pride in his heart, and I am very anxious that he should continue to feel so. Our children always learn soon enough what they are. He is very fond of his sister, and has a good heart. Whenever any thing gives him pleasure, whether it be the going anywhere, or that any one gives him any thing, his first movement always is to ask that his sister may have the same. He is light-hearted by nature. It is necessary for his health that he should be a great deal in the open air; and I think it is better to let him play and work in the garden on the terrace, than to take him longer walks. The exercise which children take in running about and playing in the open air is much more healthy than forcing them to walk, which often makes their backs ache.[10]"

Some of these last recommendations may seem to show that the governess was, to some extent, regarded as a nurse as well as a teacher; and when we find Marie Antoinette complaining of want of discretion in a child of four years old, it may perhaps be thought that she is expecting rather more of such tender years than is often found in them; that she is inclined to be overexacting rather than overindulgent; an error the more venial, since it is probable that the educators of princes are more likely to go astray in the opposite direction. But it is impossible to avoid being struck with the candor with which she judges her boy's character, and with the judiciousness of her system of education; and equally impossible to resist the conviction that a boy of good disposition, trained by such a mother, had every chance of becoming a blessing to his subjects, if fate had only allowed him to succeed to the throne which she had still a right to look forward to for him as his assured inheritance.

CHAPTER XXV.

Necker resumes Office.--Outrages in the Provinces.--Pusillanimity of the Body of the Nation.--Parties in the Assembly.--Views of the Constitution-alists or "Plain."--Barnave makes Overtures to the Court.--The Queen re-jects them.--The Assembly abolishes all Privileges, August 4th.-- Debates on the Veto.--An Attack on Versailles is threatened.--Great Scarcity in Paris.--The King sends his Plate to be melted down.--The Regiment of Flanders is brought up to Versailles.--A Military Banquet is held in the Opera-house.--October 5th, a Mob from Paris marches on Versailles.--Blunders of La Fayette--Ferocity of the Mob on the 5th.-- Attack on the Palace on the 6th.--Danger and Heroism of the Queen.--The Royal Family remove to Paris.--Their Reception at the Barrier and at the Hotel de Ville.--Shabbiness of the Tuileries.--The King fixes his Residence there.

Necker had obeyed the king's summons the moment that he received it, and before the end of the month he returned to Versailles and resumed his office. But, even before the king's dispatch reached him, Paris had witnessed terrible proofs that the tranquillity which the king's visit to the capital was supposed to have re-established was but temporary. The populace had broken out into fresh tumults, murdering some of Breteuil's colleagues with circumstances of frightful barbarity; while intelligence of similar disturbances in the provinces was constantly arriving. In Normandy, in Alsace, and in Provence, in the towns, and in the rural districts, the towns-people and the peasants rose against their wealthier neighbors or their landlords, burning their houses, and common-ly murdering the owners with the most revolting barbarity. Some were torn into pieces; some were roasted alive; some had actually portions of their flesh cut off and eaten by their murderers in their own sight, before the blow was given which terminated their agonies. Their sex did not save ladies from being victims of the same cruelties, nor did it prevent women from being actors in them.

Yet the horror of these scenes was scarcely stranger than the pusillanimity of those who endured them unresistingly; for there were not wanting instances of magistrates honest enough to detest, and courageous enough to chastise, such outrages; and wherever the effort was made it succeeded so completely as to fix no slight criminality on those who submitted to them. In Dauphiny, the States of the province raised a small guard, which quelled the first attempts to cause riots there, and hanged the ringleaders. In Macon, a similar force, though not three hundred strong, encountered a band of brigands, six thousand in number, and brought back two hundred prisoners, the chiefs of whom were instantly executed, and by their prompt punishment tranquillity was restored. Similar firmness would have saved other districts, which now allowed themselves to be the victims of ravage and murder; as afterward it would have preserved the whole country, even when the madness and wickedness of subsequent years were at their height; for in no part of the kingdom did those who perpetrated or sympathized with the crimes which have made the Revolution a by-word, approach the number of those who loathed them, but who had not the courage or foresight to withstand them. It seemed as if a long course of misgovernment, and the example of the profligacy and impiety set by the higher classes for many generations, had demoralized the entire people, some in their excesses discarding the ordinary instincts of human beings; while the bulk of the nation had lost even that courage which had once been among its most shining qualities, and had no longer the manliness to resist outrages which they abhorred, even when their own safety was staked upon their repression.

And similar weakness was exhibited in the Assembly itself; for, unquestionably, the party which at last prevailed was not that which was originally the strongest. Like most assemblies of the kind, it was divided into three parties--the extreme Royalists, or "the Right;" the extreme Reformers (who were subdivided into several sections), or "the Left;" and between them the moderate Constitutionalists, or "the Plain," as they were called, from occupying seats in the middle of the hall, between the raised benches on either side. And to the last party belonged all the men most distinguished either for statesman-like perceptions or for eloquence, Mirabeau himself agreeing with them in all their leading principles, though he never formally enrolled himself in the ranks of any party.

The majority of the Constitutionalists were as loyal to the king's person and dignity as the extreme Royalists; their most eloquent speaker, a young lawyer named Barnave, at the first opening of the States had even sought to open a direct communication with the court, begging Madame de Lamballe[1] to assure the queen of the wish of himself and all his friends to maintain the king in the full enjoyment and exercise of what he called a Constitutional authority, borrowing the idea and expression from the English Government. But though Marie Antoinette had no objection to the king of his own accord renouncing portions of the power which had been claimed and exerted by his predecessors, she would not hear of the States taking upon themselves to impose such sacrifices on him, or to curtail his authority by any exercise of their own; and she rejected with something like disdain the support of those whose alliance was only to be purchased on such conditions. Barnave, like Mirabeau, felt insulted; determined to revenge himself, and for a while united himself to the fiercest of the Republicans; while the Right, with incredible folly, often played into his hand, joining the Left, of which many members avowedly aimed at the abolition of royalty, and with none of whom they had one opinion or sentiment in common to defeat the Constitutionalists, with whom they practically had but very slight differences. And thus, as with a base pusillanimity, many, both of the Right and of the Plain, fled from the country after the tumults of October, the mastery of the Assembly gradually fell into the hands of that party which contained by far fewer men of ability or honesty than either of the others, but which surpassed them both in distinctness of object, and in unscrupulous resolution to carry out its views.

But the events of July, the mutiny of the troops, the successful insurrection of the mob, the destruction of the Bastile, and the visit of Louis to Paris, had been a series of damaging blows to the Government; and as each successive exploit gave encouragement to the movement party, events proceeded with extreme rapidity. Necker, who returned to Versailles on the 27th of July, showed more clearly than ever his unfitness for the chief post in the administration at such a crisis, by devoting himself solely to financial arrangements, and omitting to take, on the part of the crown, the initiative in any one of the reforms which the king had promised. Those he permitted to be intrusted to a committee of the Assembly; and the committee had scarcely met when the Assembly took the matter into its own hands; and in a strange panic, and at a single sitting, swept away the privileges of both Nobles and clergy, those who seemed personally most concerned in their maintenance being the foremost in urging their suppression. A member of the oldest nobility proposed the abolition of the privileges of the Nobles. A bishop moved the extinction of tithes; Bretons, Burgundians, Provencals, renounced for their fellow- citizens the old distinctions and immunities to which each province had hitherto clung with an unyielding if somewhat unreasoning attachment; and the whole was crowned by the Archbishop of Paris proposing a celebration of the *Te Deum*, as an expression of gratitude to God for having inspired a series of actions calculated to confer so much happiness on the nation.

Though he could not avoid seeing the mischievous character of many of the resolutions thus tumultuously passed, and though his royal assent to them was asked in language unceremonious and almost peremptory in its curtness, Louis could not bring himself, or perhaps did not venture, to refuse his sanction to them. He had laid down a rule for himself to refuse no concession except such as on religious grounds his conscience might revolt from; and on the 18th he signified his formal acceptance of the resolutions, and of the title of "Restorer of French Liberty." It was an act of great weakness, and was rewarded, as such acts generally are, by further encroachments on his authority. The progress of the Left was not even arrested by a quarrel between some of its members (who, being clergymen, were not inclined to be reduced to beggary by the extinction of their incomes), and Mirabeau, who, not unnaturally, bore the priests especial ill-will. Before the end of the month, the Assembly even deprived the king of the power of withholding his assent from measures which it might pass, enacting that he should no longer possess an absolute "veto," as it was called, and Necker, exhibiting on this question an incapacity more glaring than even his former conduct had displayed, induced the king to yield this point also; and to express his own preference for what its contrivers called a sus-pensive veto--a power, that is, of withholding his assent to any measure till it had been passed by two successive Assemblies. The discussions on this most momentous point had been very vehement in the Assembly itself; and, besides the greatness of the principle involved in the decision, they have a peculiar importance as showing that Mirabeau had not the absolute power over the minds of the members which he believed himself to possess; since he contended with all the energy of his temper, and with irresistible force of argument, against a vote which, as he declared, could only take the power from the king to vest it in the Assembly, and yet was wholly unable to carry more than a small minority with him in his opposition.

And this defeat may have had some share in prompting him to countenance and aid, if indeed he was not the original contriver of, a plot which was undoubtedly intended to produce a change in the whole frame-work of the Government. The harvest had been bad, and at the beginning of September Paris was suffering under a scarcity almost as severe as had ever been felt in the depth of winter. The emergency was so great that the king sent all his plate to the Mint to be melted down, to procure money to purchase food for the starving citizens; and many patriotic individuals, Necker himself being among the most munificent, gave their plate and jewels for the same benevolent object. But relief procured from such sources was unavoidably of too limited a character to last long. Though Necker proposed and the Assembly voted taxes of prodigious amount, they could not at once be made available, and some of the lower classes were said to have died of actual famine. In their distress the citizens looked to the king, and attributed their misery in a great degree to his ignorance of their situation, which was caused by his living at Versailles. They nicknamed him the "Baker," as if he could supply them with bread, and began to clamor for him at least to take up an occasional residence among them in in his capital. From raising a cry, the step was easy to organize a riot to compel him to do so. And to this object the partisans of the Duke of Orleans, assisted, if not prompted, by Mirabeau, now began to apply themselves, hoping that the result would be the deposition of Louis and the enthronement of the duke, who might be glad to take the great orator for his prime minister.

So certain did the conspirators feel of success, that they took no pains to keep their machinations secret. As early as the middle of September intelligence was received at Versailles that the Parisians would march upon that town in force, on the 5th of October; and the Assembly was greatly alarmed, believing, not without reason, that the object of the intended attack was to overawe and overbear them. The magistrates of the town were even more terrified, and besought the king to bring up at least one regiment for their protection. And, prudent and reasonable as the request was, the compliance with it furnished the agents of sedition with pretexts for further violence.

A regiment, known as that of Flanders, was sent for from the frontiers, and speedily arrived at Versailles, when, according to their old and hospitable fashion, the Body-guard,[2] who regarded Versailles as their home, invited the officers, and with them the officers of the Swiss Guard, and those of the town militia also, to a banquet on the 1st of October. The opera-house, as had often been done in similar instances, was lent for the occasion; and the boxes were filled with the chief ladies of the court and of the town, and also with many members of the Assembly, as spectators. So enthusiastic were the acclamations that greeted the toast of the king's health, that, though Marie Antoinette had previously desired that the royal family should not appear to have any connection with the entertainment, the captain of the guard, the Count de Luxembourg, had no difficulty in persuading her that it would but be a graceful recognition of such spontaneous and sincere loyalty at such a time if she were to honor the banquet with her presence, though but by the briefest visit. Louis, too, accepted the proposal with greater warmth than usual, and when the royal pair with their children--the queen, as was her custom, leading one in each hand--descended from their apartments and walked through the banquet-hall, the enthusiasm was redoubled. The spectators, among whom were many members of the Assembly, caught the contagion. Loyal cheers resounded from every part of the theatre, and the feelings excited became so fervid that some officers of the National Guard, who were among the guests, reversed their new tricolor cockade, and, displaying the white side outermost, seemed to have resumed the time-honored badge under which the army had reaped all its old glories. The band struck up a favorite air from one of the new operas, "Peut-on affliger ce qu'on aime?" which those who saw the anxiety which recent events had already stamped upon the queen's majestic brow could hardly avoid applying to their royal mistress; and when it followed it up by Blondel's lamentation for Richard, "O Richard, O mon roi, l'univers t'abandonne," the first notes of the well-known song touched a chord in every heart, and the whole company, courtiers, ladies, soldiers, and deputies, were all carried away in a perfect delirium of loyal rapture. The whole company escorted the royal family back to their apartments; though it was remarked afterward that some of the soldiers, who on this occasion were the most vociferous in their exultation, were, before the end of the same week, among the most furious threateners and assailants of the palace.

But a demonstration such as this, in which the whole number of the soldiers concerned did not exceed fifteen hundred men, could not deter the organizers of the impending riot from carrying out their plan: if it did not even aid them by the opportunities which it afforded for spreading abroad exaggerated accounts of what had taken place, as an additional proof of the settled hatred and contempt which the court entertained for the people. Mirabeau had suggested that the best chance of success for an insurrection in Paris lay in placing women at its head; and, in compliance with his hint, at day-break on the appointed morning a woman of notorious infamy of character moved toward the chief market-place of Paris, beating a drum, and calling on all who heard her to follow her.[3] She soon gathered round her a troop of followers worthy of such a leader, market- women, fish-women, and men in women's clothes, whose deep voices, and the power with which they brandished their weapons, betrayed their sex through their disguise.

One man, Maillard, who had been conspicuous as one of the fiercest of the stormers of the Bastile, disdained any concealment or dress but his own; they chose him for their leader, mingling with their cries for bread horrid threats against the queen and the aristocrats. Their numbers increased till they felt themselves strong enough to attack the Hotel de Ville. A detachment of the National Guard who were on duty offered them no resistance, pleading that they had received no orders from La Fayette; and the rioters, now amounting to many thousands, having armed themselves from the store of muskets and swords which they found in the armory, passed on to the barrier and took the road to Versailles.

The riot had lasted four hours, and the very last of the rioters had already passed through the gates before La Fayette reached the Hotel de Ville, though his office of Commander of the National Guard made the preservation of tranquillity one of his most especial duties. He had evidently feared to risk his popularity by resisting the mob, and even now he refused to act at all till be had received a written order from the Municipal Council; and, when he had obtained that, he did not obey it; but preferred complying with the demands of his own soldiers, who insisted on following the rioters to Versailles, where they would exterminate the regiment of Flanders; bring the king back to Paris; and perhaps depose him and appoint a Regent. Yet even this open avowal of their treasonable views did not deter their unworthy general from submitting to their dictates. He had indeed no desire for the success of their designs; for he had no connection with the Duc d'Orleans, and no inclination to co-operate with Mirabeau, who he knew was in the habit of speaking of him with contempt; but he had not firmness to resist their demand. His vanity, too, always his most predominant feeling, was flattered by the desire they expressed to retain him as their commander, and at last he procured from the magistrates a fresh order, authorizing him to comply with the soldiers' clamor, and to lead them to Versailles.

When before the magistrates he had professed an expectation that he should be able to induce the king to comply with the wishes of the Assembly, and a determination to restrain the excesses of the mob; but the whole day had been so wasted by his irresolution that when he at last put his regiment in motion it was seven o'clock in the evening--full four hours after Maillard and his fish-women had reached Versailles. The news of their approach and of their designs had been brought to the palace by Monsieur de Chinon, the eldest son of the Duc de Richelieu, who, at great personal risk, had disguised himself as an artisan, and had marched some way with the crowd to learn their object. He reported that even the women and children were armed, that the great majority were drunk; that they were beguiling the way with the most ferocious threats, and that they had been joined by a gang of men who gave themselves the name of "Coupe-tetes," and boasted that they should have ample opportunity of proving their title to it.

In addition to the warnings previously received, a rumor had reached the palace on the preceding evening that the Duc d'Orleans had come down to Versailles in disguise,[4] a movement which could hardly have an innocent object; but so little heed had been given to the intelligence, or, it may perhaps be said, so little was it supposed that, if such an attack was really meditated, any warning would have been given, that Monsieur de Chinon found the palace empty. Louis had gone to hunt in the Bois de Meudon; Marie Antoinette was at the Little Trianon. But messengers easily found them. The queen came in with speed from her garden, which she was destined never to behold again; the king hastened hack from his coverts; and by the time that they returned, the Count de St. Priest, the Minister of the Household, had their carriages ready for them to retire to Rambouillet, and he earnestly pressed the adoption of such a course. Louis, as usual, could not make up his mind. He sat in his chair, repeating that it was a moment to think seriously. "Rather," said Marie Antoinette, "say that it is a time to act promptly." He would gladly have had her depart with her children, but she refused to leave him, declaring that her place was by his side; that, as the daughter of Maria Teresa, she did not fear death; and after a time he changed his mind and ceased to wish even her to retire, clinging to his old conviction that conciliation was always possible. He believed that he had won over even the worst of the mob, and that all danger was past.

Versailles witnessed a strange scene that morning. The moment that the mob reached the town, they forced their way into the Assembly Hall, where Maillard, as their spokesman, after terrifying the members with ferocious threats against the whole body of the Nobles, demanded that the Assembly should send a deputation to the king to represent to him the distress of the people, and that a party of the women should accompany it. Louis consented to receive them, and when they reached the palace, the women, disorderly and ferocious as they were, were so awed by the magnificence and pomp which they beheld, and by the actual presence of the king and queen, that they could only summon up a few modest and humble words of petition, and one, a young and pretty girl of seventeen, fainted with the excitement. One of the princesses brought her a glass of water: she recovered, and, as she knelt to kiss the king's hand, Louis kissed her himself, and, transported by his affability, she and her companions quit the apartment, uttering loud cheers for the king and queen. But this had not been the impression which their leaders had intended them to receive; and, when they reached the streets, their new-born loyalty so exasperated their comrades that the soldiers had some difficulty in saving them from their fury.

Meanwhile, the mob increased every hour. They occupied the court-yard of the palace, roaring out ferocious threats, the most sanguinary of which were directed against the queen. The President of the Assembly moved that the members should adjourn and repair to the palace for the protection of the royal family, but Mirabeau resisted the proposal, and procured its rejection; and when a large party of the members went, as individuals, to place their services at the king's disposal, he mingled with the rioters, tampering with the soldiers, and urging them to espouse what he called the cause of the people. As it grew dark, the crowd grew more and more tumultuous and violent. The Body-guard, who were all gentlemen, were faithful and fearless; but it began to be seen that none of the other troops, not even the regiment of Flanders, could be trusted. Some of them even fired on the Body-guard, and mortally wounded its commander, the Marquis de Savonieres; while Louis, adhering to his unhappy policy of conciliation even at such a moment, sent down orders to the officer who succeeded to the command that the men were not to use their weapons, and that all bloodshed was to be avoided. "Tell the king," replied M. d'Huillier, "that his orders shall be obeyed; but that we shall all be assassinated."

The mob grew fiercer when it became known that La Fayette and his regiment were approaching. No one knew what course he might take, but the ringleaders of the rioters resolved on a strenuous effort to render his arrival useless by their previous success. Guns were fired, heavy blows were dealt on the railings of the inner court-yard and on the gates; and the danger seemed so imminent that the mob might force its way into the palace, that the deputies themselves besought the king to delay no longer, but to retire to Rambouillet. He was still irresolute, and still trusting to his plan of conciliating by non-resistance. The queen, though more earnest than ever that he should depart, still nobly adhered to her own view of duty, and refused to leave him; but, hoping that he might change his mind, she gave a written order to keep the carriages harnessed, and to prepare to force a passage for them if the life of the king should appear to be in danger; but, she added, they were not to be used if she alone were threatened.

At last, when it was nearly midnight, La Fayette arrived. With a singular perverseness of folly, at a time when every moment was of consequence, he had halted his men a mile out of the town to make them a speech in praise of himself and his own loyalty, and to administer to them an oath to be faithful to the nation, to the law, and to the king; an oath needless if they were inclined to keep it; useless, if they were not; and in the state of feeling then common, mischievous in the order in which he ranged the powers to which he required them to profess allegiance. At last he reached the palace. Leaving his men below, he ascended to the king's apartments, and, laying his hand on his heart, assured the king that he had no more loyal servant than himself. Louis was not given to sarcasm: yet some of the bystanders fancied that there was a tone of irony in his voice when in reply he expressed his conviction of the marquis's sincerity; and perhaps La Fayette thought so too, for he proceeded to harangue his majesty on his favorite subject of his own courage;

describing the dangers which, as he affirmed, he had incurred in the course of the day. After which he descended into the court-yard to assure the soldiers that the king had promised to accede to their wishes; and then returned to the royal apartments to inform the king that contentment was restored, and that he himself would be responsible for the tranquillity of the night.

The royal family, exhausted with the fatigues of so terrible a day, retired to rest, the queen expressly enjoining her ladies to follow her example. Fortunately they were too anxious for her safety to obey her, and, with their own attendants, kept watch in the room outside her bed-chamber. But La Fayette, in spite of the responsibility which he had taken upon himself, felt no such anxiety. He declared himself tired and sleepy; and, leaving the palace, went to a friend's house to ask for a bed. [5] Yet he well knew that the crowd was still assembled around the palace, and was increasing in violence. Though the night was stormy and wet, the rioters sought no shelter except such as was afforded by a hurried resort to the wine-shops in the neighborhood, where they inflamed their intoxication, and from which they soon returned to renew their savage clamor and threats, increasing the disorder by keeping up a frequent fire of their muskets. Throughout the night the Duc d'Orleans was briskly going to and fro, his emissaries scattering money among the rioters, who seemed to have no definite purpose or plan, till, as day began to break, one of the gates leading into the Princes' Court was seen to be open. It had been intrusted to some of La Fayette's soldiers, and could not have been opened without treachery. The crowd poured in, uttering fiercer threats than ever, from the belief that their prey was within their reach. There was, in truth, nothing between them and the staircase which led to the royal apartments except two gallant gentlemen, M. des Huttes and M. Moreau, the sentries of the detachment of the Body- guard on duty, whose quarters were at the head of the staircase in a saloon opposite to the queen's chamber. But these brave men were worthy of the best days of the French army. The more formidable the mob, and the greater the danger, the more imperative to their loyal hearts was the duty to defend those whose safety was intrusted to their vigilance; and with so dauntless a front did they stand to their posts that for a moment the ruffians recoiled and shrunk from attacking them, till D'Orleans himself came forward, waving to them with his hand a signal to force the way in, and pointing out to them which way to take.

What, then, could two men effect against such a multitude? Des Huttes perished, pierced by a hundred pikes, and torn into pieces by his blood- thirsty assailants. Moreau, with equal valor, but with better fortune, backed up the stairs, fighting so desperately as he retreated that he gave his comrades time to barricade the doors leading to the queen's apartments, and to come to his assistance. As they drew him back, terribly wounded, into the guardroom, De Varicourt and Durepaire took his place. De Varicourt was soon slain, but Durepaire, a man of prodigious strength and prowess, held the assassins at bay for some time, till he too fell, reduced to helplessness by a score of deep wounds; when he, in his turn, was replaced by Miomandre. His devotion and intrepidity equaled that of his comrades; he was eminently skillful also in the use of his weapons, and with his own hand he struck down many of his assailants, till he was gradually forced back by numbers, when he placed his musket as a barrier across the door-way, and thus still kept his enemies at bay, while he shouted to the queen's ladies, now separated from him by but a single partition, to save the queen, for "the tigers with whom he was struggling were aiming at her life."

In the annals of the ancient chivalry of the nation it had been recorded as the most brilliant feat of Bayard, that, on a bridge of the Garigliano, he had for a while, with his single arm, stemmed the onset of two hundred Spaniards; and that glorious exploit of the model hero of the nation had never been more faithfully copied and more nobly rivaled than it was on this morning of shame and danger by Miomandre and his intrepid comrades, as they successively stepped into the breach to fight against those whom he truly called, not men, but tigers. It was but a brief moment before he too was struck down; but he had gained for the ladies a respite sufficient to enable them to secure the safety of their royal mistress. They roused her from her bed, for her fatigue had been so great that she had hitherto slept soundly through the uproar, and hurried her off to the apartments of the king, who, having in been just similarly awakened, was coming to seek her; and in a few minutes the whole family was collected in his antechamber; while the Body-guard occupied the queen's bedroom, and the rioters, balked of their intended victim, were pillaging the different rooms into which they had been able to make their way. Luckily, La Fayette was still absent: he was having his hair dressed with great composure, while the mob, for whose contentment and orderly behavior he had vouched, was plundering the royal palace and seeking its owners to murder them; and in his absence the Marquis de Vaudreuil and a body of nobles took upon themselves the office of defenders of the crown, and, going down to the court-yard, reproached the National Guard with their inaction at such a moment of danger, and with their manifest sympathy with the rioters. At first, out of mere shame, the National Guard attempted to justify themselves: "they had been told," they said, "that the Body-guard were the aggressors; that they had attacked the people." "Do you pretend to believe," said the gallant marquis, "that two hundred men have been mad enough to attack thirty thousand?" The argument was irresistible; they declared that if the Body-guard would assume the tricolor, they would stand by them as brothers. And, by a reaction not uncommon at such times of excitement, the two regiments became reconciled in a moment. As no tricolor cockades could be procured, they exchanged shakos, and, in many cases, arms. And presently, when the Coup-tetes, after mutilating the bodies of two of the Body-guard who had been killed on the previous evening, were preparing to murder two or three more who had fallen into their hands, the National Guard dashed to their rescue, shouting out, with a curious identification of their force with the old French army, that "they would save the Body-guard who saved them at Fontenoy," and brought them off unhurt.

Balked of their expected prey, the rioters grew more furious than ever; in useless wrath they kept firing against the walls of the palace, and shouting out a demand for the queen to show herself. She, with her children, was still in the king's apartment, where the princesses, the ministers, and a few courtiers were also assembled. Necker, in an agony of terror and distress, sat with his face buried in his hands, unable to offer any advice; La Fayette, who had just arrived, dwelt upon the dangers which he had run, though no one else knew what they were, and assured the king of the power which he still possessed to allay the tumult, if the reasonable demands of the people (as he called them) were granted. Marie Antoinette alone was undaunted and calm; or, at least, if in the depths of her woman's heart she felt terror at the sanguinary and obscene threats of her ruffianly enemies, she scorned to show it. When the firing began, M. de Luzerne, one of the ministers, had quietly placed himself between her and the window; but, while she thanked him for his devotion, she begged him to retire, saying, with her habitually gracious courtesy, that it was her place to be there,[6] not his, since the king could not afford to have so faithful a servant endangered. And now, holding her little son and daughter, one in each hand, she stepped out on the balcony, to confront those who were shouting for her blood. "No children!" was their cry. She led the dauphin and his sister back into the room, and, returning to the balcony, stood before them alone, with her hands crossed and her eyes looking up to heaven, as one who expected instant death, with a firmness as far removed from defiance as from supplication. Even those ruthless miscreants were awed by her magnanimous fearlessness; not a shot was fired; for a moment it seemed as if her enemies had become her partisans. Loud shouts of "Bravo!" and "Long live the queen!" were heard on all sides; and one ruffian, who raised his gun to take aim at her, had his weapon beaten down by those who stood near him, and ran some risk of being himself sacrificed to their indignation. But this impulse of respect, like other impulses of such a people, was short-lived, and presently the multitude began to raise a shout, which expressed the original purpose which had led the majority to march upon Versailles. "To Paris!" was the cry, and again La Fayette volunteered his advice, urging the king to comply with the request. By this time Louis had learned the value of the marquis's loyalty. But he had no alternative. It was evident that the rioters had the power of compelling compliance with their demand. And accordingly he authorized the marquis to promise that he would remove his family to Paris, and a few minutes afterward he himself went out on the balcony with the queen, and himself announced his intention, with the view of giving his act a greater appearance of being voluntarily resolved upon.

Soon after midday he set out, accompanied by the queen, his brother the Count de Provence, his sister the Princess Elizabeth, and his children. It was a strange and shameful retinue that escorted the King of France to his capital. One party of the rioters, with Maillard and another ruffian named Jourdan, the chief of the Coupe-tetes, at their head, had started two hours before, bearing aloft in triumph the heads of the mangled Body-guards, and combining such hideous mockery with their barbarity that they halted at Sevres to compel a barber to dress the hair on the lifeless skulls. And now the royal carriage was surrounded by a vast and confused medley; market-women and the rest of the female rabble, with drunken gangs of the ruffians who had stormed the palace in the morning, still brandishing their weapons, or bearing loaves of bread on their pike-heads, and singing out that they should all have enough of bread now, since they were bringing the baker, the bakeress, and the baker's boy to Paris.[7] The only part of the procession that bore even a decent appearance was a small escort of 'different regiments--the Guards, the National Guards, and the Body-guards; many of the latter still bleeding from the wounds which they had received in the conflict and tumult of the morning. A train of carriages containing a deputation of the members of the Assembly also followed; Mirabeau himself having just earned a motion that the Assembly was inseparable from the king, and that wherever he was there must be the place of meeting for the great council of the nation. Yet, in spite of the confidence which their presence might have been expected to diffuse among the mob, and in spite of the hopes of coming plenty which the rioters themselves announced, the royal party was not even yet safe from further attacks. Some ruffians stabbed at the royal carriage as it passed with their pikes, and several shots were fired at it, though fortunately they missed their aim and no one was injured.[8]

To the queen the journey was more painful than to any one else. A few weeks before she had congratulated Mademoiselle de Lamballe on not being a mother--perhaps the bitterest exclamation that grief and anxiety ever wrung from her lips; and now the keenest anxieties of a mother were indeed added to those of a queen. The procession moved with painful slowness. No provisions had been taken in the carriage, and the little dauphin was suffering from hunger and begging for some food. Tears, which her own danger could not bring to her eyes, flowed plentifully as she witnessed the suffering of her child. She could only beg him to bear his privations with patience; and she had the reward of the pains she had always taken to inspire him with confident in her, in the fortitude with which, for the rest of the day, he bore what to children of his age is probably the severest hardship to which they can be exposed.[9]

So vast and disorderly was the procession that it was nine o'clock at night before it reached Paris. Bailly again met the royal carriage at the barrier, and, re-assuming the tone of coarse insult which he had adopted on the king's previous visit, had the effrontery to describe the day so full of horror to every one, and of humiliation and agony to those whom he was addressing, as a glorious day. It was at such moments as these that Louis's impassibility assumed the character of dignity. He disdained to notice the mayor's insolence, and briefly answered that it was always with pleasure and with confidence that he found himself among the inhabitants of his good city of Paris. He proceeded to the Hotel de Ville, where the council of civic magistrates was sitting; and where the president addressed him in language which afforded a marked contrast to that of the mayor, calling him "an adored father who had come to visit the place where he could meet with the greatest number of his children." And it seemed as if Bailly himself had become in some degree ashamed of his insolence; for now, when Louis desired him, in reply to the president's address, to repeat the answer which he had made to him at the barrier, he merely said that the king had come with pleasure among the Parisians. "The king, sir," interrupted the queen, "added, 'and with confidence.'" "Gentlemen," said Bailly, "you hear her majesty's words. You are happier in doing so than if I myself had uttered them." The whole company burst into one rapturous cheer, and at their request the king and queen showed themselves for a few minutes at the windows, beneath which, late as the hour was, a vast multitude was still collected, which received them with vociferous cheers. And then the royal family, quitting the Hotel, drove to the Tuileries, where their attendants had been hastily making such preparations as a few hours allowed for their reception.

Since the completion of the Palace at Versailles the Tuileries had been almost deserted.[10] The paint and gilding were tarnished, the curtains were faded, many most necessary articles of furniture were altogether wanting; and the whole was so shabby that it attracted the notice of even the little dauphin. "How bad, mamma," said he, "every thing looks here." "My boy," she replied, "Louis XIV. lived here comfortably enough." But they had not yet decided on making it their permanent residence. La Fayette, who had tried to induce the king to promise to do so, had been distinctly refused; and for some days Louis did not make up his mind. But, after a time, the fear, if he should propose to return, to Versailles, of being met by an opposition on the part of the Assembly or the civic magistrates, which he might be unable to surmount, or, if he should again settle there, of his absence from the city furnishing a pretext for fresh tumults, caused him to announce his intention of making Paris his principal abode for the future. He gave orders for the removal of some furniture and of the queen's library to the Tuileries; and, with something of the apathy of despair, began to reconcile himself to his new abode and his changed position.

CHAPTER XXVI.

Feelings of Marie Antoinette on coming to the Tuileries.--Her Tact in winning the Hearts of the Common People.--Mirabeau changes his Views.--Quarrel between La Fayette and the Duc d'Orleans.--Mirabeau desires to offer his Services to the Queen.--Riots in Paris.--Murder of Francois.-- The Assembly pass a Vote prohibiting any Member from taking Office.--The Emigration.--Death of the Emperor Joseph II.--Investigation into the Riots of October.--The Queen refuses to give Evidence.--Violent Proceedings in the Assembly.--Execution of the Marquis de Favras.

The comment made by Marie Antoinette on quitting Versailles was that "they were undone; they were being dragged off, perhaps to death, which was never far removed from captive sovereigns;[1]" and such henceforward was her prevailing feeling. She may occasionally, prompted by her own innate courage and sanguineness of disposition, have cherished a short-lived hope, founded on a consciousness of the king's and her own purity of intention, or on a belief, which she never wholly discarded, in the natural goodness of heart of the French people when not led astray by demagogues; and of their impulsive levity of disposition, which seemed to make no change of temper on their part impossible; but her general feeling was one of humiliation for the past and despair for the future. Not only did the example of Charles I., whose fate was ever before her eyes, fill her with dread for her husband's life (to her own danger she never gave a thought), but she felt also that the cause and principle of royalty had been degraded by the shameful scenes through which she had lately passed; and we shall fail to do justice to the patience, fortitude, and energy of her conduct during the remainder of her life, if we allow ourselves to forget that these high qualities were maintained and exerted in spite of the most depressing circumstances and the most discouraging convictions; that she was struggling because it was her duty to struggle for her husband's honor and her child's inheritance; but that she was never long sustained by that incentive which, with so many, is absolutely indispensable to steady and useful exertion--the anticipation of eventual success.

A letter which the very next morning she wrote to Mercy, who fortunately still retained his old post as embassador, shows the courage with which she still caught at every circumstance which seemed in the least hopeful; and with what unfaltering tact she sought every opportunity of acting on the impulsiveness which she regarded as one chief characteristic of the French people.

"October 7th, 1789.

"I am quite well. You may be easy about me. If we could only forget where we are and how we came here, we ought to be satisfied with the feelings of the people, especially this morning. I hope, if bread does not fall short, that many things will return to their proper order. I speak to the people, militia, fish-women, and all: all offer me their hands; I give them mine. In the Hotel de Ville I was personally well received. The people this morning begged us to remain here. I answered them, speaking for the king, who was by my side, that it depended on themselves whether we remained; that we desired nothing better; that all animosities must be laid aside; that the slightest renewal of bloodshed would make us flee, with horror. Those who were nearest to me swore that all that was over. I told the fish-women to go and tell others all that we had just said to one another.[2]"

And a day or two later, on the 10th, even while giving fuller expression to her feelings of unhappiness, and of disgust at the events of the past week, as to which she assures Mercy that "no description could be exaggerated; on the contrary, that any account must fall far short of what the king and she had seen and experienced," she yet repeats that "she hopes to bring back to a right feeling the honest and sound portion of the citizens and people. Unhappily, however," as she adds, "they are not the most numerous body. Still, with gentleness and unwearied patience, she may hope that at least she shall succeed in doing away with the horrible distrust which occupies every mind, and which has dragged the king and herself into the gulf in which they are at present." So keen at this time was her feeling that one principal cause of their miseries was the unjust distrust which the citizens in general conceived of the views and designs of the court, that she desires Mercy not to try to see

her; and, while she describes the scantiness of the accommodation which her attendants had as yet been able to provide for her, so that Madame Royale had a bed in
her dressing-room, and the little dauphin was in her own room, she finds advantage
in these arrangements, inconvenient as they were, since they prevented any suspicion from arising that she was giving audiences which she desired to keep secret.

She did not overrate the impression which she had made on the people; and
her faithful attendant, Madame Campan, has preserved more minute details of the
events of the 7th than she herself reported to the embassador. She was hardly dressed
when a huge crowd collected on the terrace under her window, shouting for her to
show herself; and, when she came forward, they began to accost her in a mingled
tone of expostulation and menace. "She must drive away the courtiers who were
the ruin of kings. She must love the inhabitants of her good city." She replied "that
she had always felt so toward them; she had loved them while at Versailles; she
should continue to love them at Paris." "Ah," interrupted a virago, hardier than her
companions, "but on the 14th of July you would have besieged and bombarded the
city; and on the 6th of October you wanted to flee to the frontier." She answered,
in the gentlest tone, that "these were idle stories, which they were wrong to believe; tales like these were what caused at once the misery of the people and that
of the best of kings." Another woman addressed her in German. Marie Antoinette
declared that "she did not understand what she said; that she had become so completely French that she had forgotten her native language;" and the compliment to
their country fairly vanquished them. They received it with shouts of "Bravo," and
with loud clapping of their hands. They begged the ribbons and flowers of her bon-
net. She took them off with her own hand and distributed them among them; and
they divided the spoils with thankful exultation, smiling, waving their hands, and
crying out, "Long live Marie Antoinette! Long live our good queen![3]"

For a time it seemed as if the fortunes of the king and country were being
weighed in an uncertain balance. One day some circumstances seemed to hold out
a prospect of the re-establishment of tranquillity, and of the return of the masses to
a better feeling. The next day these favorable appearances were more than counterbalanced by fresh evidences of the increasing power of the factious and unscrupulous demagogues. It was greatly in favor of the crown that the triumph of the mob
on the 6th of October had led to violent quarrels between the Duc d'Orleans, La

Fayette, and Mirabeau. La Fayette had charged the duke with having entered into a plot to assassinate him, and threatened to impeach him formally if he did not at once quit the kingdom.[4] The duke trembled and consented, easily procuring from the ministers, who were glad to get rid of him, a diplomatic mission to England as a pretext for his departure; and Mirabeau, who despised both the duke and the marquis, full of contempt for the pusillanimity which the former had shown in the quarrel, abandoned all idea of placing him on his cousin's throne. "Make him my king!" he exclaimed; "I would not have him for my valet."

Emboldened by his success with the duke, La Fayette, who had great confidence in his own address, next tried to win over or to get rid of Mirabeau himself. He proposed to obtain an embassy for him also. The suggestion of what was clearly an honorable exile in disguise was at once declined.[5] He then offered him a large sum of money, for at that moment he had the entire disposal of the civil list; but he found that the great orator was disinclined to connect himself with him in any way, much more to lay himself under any obligation to him. In fact, Mirabeau was at this moment hoping to obtain a post in the home administration, where, if he could once succeed in procuring a footing, he had no doubt of soon obtaining the entire mastery; and the royal family was hardly settled at the Tuileries before he applied to his friend, the Count de la Marck, whom he rightly believed to enjoy the queen's good opinion, begging him to express to her his ardent wish to serve her. He even drew up a long memorial on the existing state of affairs, indicating the line of conduct which, in his opinion, the king ought to pursue; the leading feature of which was an early departure from Paris to some city at no great distance, that he might be safe and free; while in the capital it was evident that he was neither. And the step which he thus recommended at the outset deserves attention as being also that on which a year later he still insisted as the indispensable preliminary to whatever line of conduct might be decided on.

But at this moment his advice never reached those for whom it was intended. La Marck, with all his good-will both to his friend and to the court, could not venture to bring before the queen's notice the name of one who, only a few days before, had denounced her in the foulest manner in the Assembly for having appeared at the soldiers' banquet, and whom she with her own eyes had beheld uniting with the assailants of the palace. He thought it more politic, even for the eventual attainment of his friend's objects, to content himself for the time with giving the memorial and stating the views of the writer to the Count de Provence; and that prince declared that it would be useless to bring it to the knowledge of either king or queen: "that the queen had not sufficient influence over her husband to induce him to adopt such a plan;" and he even hinted that at times Louis was disposed to be jealous of her appearing to influence him.

But if these circumstances--the quarrel between the enemies of the court, and the conversion of one more able and formidable than either--were in the king's favor, other events which took place in the same few weeks were full of mischief and danger. Before the end of the month fresh riots broke out in Paris. Bread, the supply of which Marie Antoinette, as we have seen, rightly regarded as a matter of the first importance to the tranquillity of the city, continued scarce and dear; and the mob broke open the bakers' shops, and murdered one baker, a man named Francois, with a ferocity more terrible than they had even shown toward De Launay, or the guards at Versailles. They tore his body to pieces, and, having cut off his head, compelled his wife to kiss the scarcely cold lips, and then left her fainting on the pavement still covered with his blood. Even La Fayette was horror-stricken at such brutality. It was the only occasion on which he did his duty during the whole progress of the Revolution. He came down with a company of the National Guard, dispersed the rioters, seized the ruffian who was bearing aloft, the head of the murdered man on a pole, and caused him to be hanged the next day. And during the next few weeks he more than once brought his soldiers to the support of the civil power, and inflicted summary punishment on gangs of miscreants, whose idea of reform was a state of things which should afford impunity to crime.

But in the next month the Assembly dealt a heavier blow on the king's authority than could be inflicted by the worst excesses of an informal mob--they passed a resolution prohibiting any of its members from accepting any office in the administration: it was an imitation of the self-denying ordinance into which Cromwell had tricked the English Parliament; and, though bearing an appearance of disinterestedness in closing the access to official emoluments and honors against themselves, was in reality an injury to the king, as depriving him of his right to select his ministers from the entire body of the nation; and to the nation itself, as preventing it from obtaining the services of those who might be presumed to be its ablest citizens, as having been already selected as its representatives.

But a far more irreparable injury than any that could be inflicted on the court by either populace or Assembly came from its friends. We have seen that the Count d'Artois, with some nobles who had especial reason to fear the enmity of the Parisians, had fled from the country in July; and now their example was followed by a vast number of the higher classes, several of them having hitherto been prominent as the leaders of the Moderate or Constitutional section of the Assembly--men who had no grounds for complaining that, except in one or two instances, at moments of extraordinary excitement, their influence had been overborne, but who now yielded to an infectious panic. Before the end of the year more than three hundred deputies had resigned their seats and quit the country; salving over to themselves the dereliction of the duties which a few months before they had voluntarily sought, and their performance of which was now a more imperative duty than ever, by denunciations of the crimes which had been committed, and which they had found themselves unable to prevent. They did not see that their pusillanimous flight must lead to a continuance of such atrocities, leaving, as it did, the undisputed sway in the Assembly to those very men who had been the authors of the outrages of which they complained. They were, in fact, insuring the ruin of all that they most wished to preserve; for, in the progress of the debates in the Assembly during the winter, many questions of the most vital importance were decided by very small majorities, which their presence would have turned into minorities. The greater the danger was, the more irresistible they ought to have felt the obligation to stand to the last by the cause of which they were the legitimate champions; and the final triumph of the Jacobin party owed hardly more to the energy of its leaders than to the cowardly and inglorious flight of the princes and nobles who left the field open without resistance to their wickedness and audacity.

It was a melancholy winter that the queen now passed. So far as she was able, she diverted her mind from political anxieties by devoting much of her time to the education of her children. A little plot of ground was railed off in the garden of the Tuileries for the dauphin's[6] amusement; and one of her favorite relaxations was to watch him working at the flower-beds himself with his little hoe and rake; though, as if to mark that they were in fact prisoners, both she and he were followed wherever they went by grenadiers of the city-guard, and were not allowed to dispense with their attendance for a single moment. Marie Antoinette had reason to complain that she was watched as a criminal[7]. Sad as she was at heart, she was not allowed the comfort of privacy and retirement. She was forced to hold receptions for the nobles and chief citizens, and as the court was now formally established at the Tuileries, she dined every week in public with the king; but she steadily resisted the entreaties of some of the ministers and courtiers to visit the theatres, thinking, with great justice, that an attendance at public spectacles of that character would have had an appearance of gayety, as unbecoming at such a period of anxiety, as it was inconsistent with her feelings; and before the end of the winter she sustained a fresh affliction in the loss of her brother the emperor[8]; whose death bore with it the additional aggravation of depriving her of a counselor whose advice she valued, and of an ally on whose active aid she believed that she could rely far more than she could on that of their brother Leopold, who now succeeded to the imperial throne.

Not that Leopold can be charged with indifference to his sister's welfare. In the very week of his accession to the throne he wrote to her with great affection, assuring her of his devotion to her interests, and expressing his desire to correspond with her in the most unreserved confidence. But the same letter shows that as yet he knew but very little of her;[9] and that he regarded the difficulties in which some of Joseph's recent measures had involved the Imperial Government as sufficiently serious to engross his attention. A few extracts from her reply are worth preserving, as proving how steadily in her conduct and language to every one she adhered to her rule of concealing her husband's defects, and putting him forward as the first person on whose wishes and directions her own conduct most depend. It also shows what advances she was herself making in the perception of the true character of the crisis, so far as the objects of the few honest members who still remained in the Assembly were concerned, and the extent to which she was trying to reconcile herself to some curtailment of her husband's former authority.

Thanking him for the assurance of his friendship, she says: "Believe me, my dear brother, we shall always be worthy of it. I say we, because I do not separate the king from myself. He was touched by your letter, as I was myself, and bids me assure you of this. His heart is loyalty and honesty itself; and if ever again we become, I do not say what we have been, but at least what we ought to be, you may then depend on the entire fidelity of a good ally.

"I do not say any thing to you of our actual position: it is too heart- rending. It ought to afflict every sovereign in the universe, and still more an affectionate relation like you. It is only time and patience that can bring back men's minds to a healthy state. It is a war of opinions, and one which is still far from being terminated. It is only the justice of our cause and the feeling of a good conscience that can support us ... My most sincere wish is that you may never meet with ingratitude. My own melancholy experience proves to me that, of all evils, that is the most terrible."

Yet no indignation at the thanklessness of the Parisians could chill her constant benevolence toward them; and amidst all the anxieties which filled her mind for herself, her husband, and her child, she founded an asylum for the education of a number of orphan daughters of old soldiers, and found time to give her careful attention to a code of regulations for its management.[10]

Meanwhile circumstances were gradually paving the way for her accepting the help of him who, during the earliest discussions of the Assembly, had been, not so much through his own malice as through Necker's folly, her worst enemy. We have seen how, immediately after the attack on Versailles, Mirabeau had once more endeavored to find an opening through which to place himself at her service. He alone, perhaps, of all men in the kingdom, perceived the reality and greatness of the danger which threatened even the lives of the sovereigns;[11] and, as amidst all the errors into which his regard for his own interests, his vindictiveness, or his caprice impelled him, he always preserved the perceptions and instincts of a genuine statesman, many of the transactions of the winter increased his conviction of the peril in which every interest in the whole kingdom was placed, if the headlong folly of the Assembly could not be restrained, and if even, proverbially difficult as such a course is, some of its acts could not be rescinded; while one transaction, which, more than any other that had yet taken place, showed the greatness of the queen's heart, much sharpened his eagerness to prove himself a worthy servant of so noble-minded a mistress.

Some of the magistrates who still desired to discharge their duty had instituted an investigation into the conspiracy which had originated the attack on Versailles, and all its multiplied horrors. They had examined a great body of witnesses, whose evidence left no doubt of the active part taken in it by the Duc d'Orleans and his partisans, and by Mirabeau, whether he were to be included among that prince's adherents or not; but they conceived it specially important to procure the testimony of the queen herself. However, it was in vain that they applied to her for the slightest information. Appeals to her indignation, to her pride, and to her danger, were equally disregarded by her. No denunciation of those who, whatever had been their crimes, were still the subjects of her husband, could, in her eyes, be becoming to her as queen; and when those who hoped to make a tool of her to crush their political rivals urged that no evidence would be accepted as equally conclusive with hers, since no one had seen so much of what had taken place, or had in so great a degree preserved that coolness which was indispensable to a clear account of it, and to the identification of the guilty, her reply was a dignified and magnanimous pardon of the outrages beneath which she had so nearly perished. "I have seen every thing; I have known every thing; I have forgotten every thing;" and Mirabeau, not unthankful for the protection which her magnanimity thus throw around him, was eager to make atonement for his past insults and injuries.

And many of the recent events had convinced him that there was no time to lose. The vote of November, debarring him, in common with all other members of the Assembly, from office, was a severe blow to the most important of his projects, so far as his own interests were concerned. Within a month it had been followed by another, proposed by the Abbe Sieyes, a busy priest who boasted that he had made himself master of the whole science of politics, but who was in fact a mere slave of abstract theories, the safety or even the practicability of which he was utterly unable to estimate. On his motion, the Assembly, in a single evening, abolished all the ancient territorial divisions of the kingdom, and the very names of the provinces; dividing the country anew into eighty-three departments, and coupling with this new arrangement a number of details which were evidently calculated to wrest the whole executive authority of the kingdom from the crown and to vest it in the populace. At another sitting, the whole property of the Church was confiscated. On another night, the Parliaments were abolished; and on a fourth, the party which had carried these measures made a still more direct and audacious attack on the royal prerogative, by passing a resolution which deprived the crown of all power of revising the sentences of the judicial tribunals, and of pardoning or mitigating the punishment of those who might have been condemned. And, if to bring home to the tender-hearted monarch the full effect of this last inroad upon his legitimate power, they at the same time created a new crime to which they gave the name of treason against the nation,[12] without either defining it, or specifying the kind of evidence which should he required to prove it; and they proceeded at once to put it in force to procure the condemnation of a nobleman of decayed fortune, but of the highest character, the Marquis de Favras, in a manner which showed that their real object was to strike terror into the whole Royalist party. The charges on which he was brought to trial were not merely unfounded, but ridiculous. He was charged with designing to raise an army of thirty thousand men, with the object of carrying off the king from Paris, of dissolving the Assembly by force, and putting La Fayette and Bailly to death. The evidence with which it was pretended to support these charges broke down on every point, and its failure of itself established the prisoner's innocence, even without the aid of his own defense, which was lucid and eloquent. But the marquis was known to be a Royalist in feeling, and, though very poor, to stand high in the confidence of the princes. The demagogues collected mobs round the courthouse to intimidate the judges, and the judges proved as base as the accusers themselves. They professed, indeed, to fear not so much for their own lives as for the public tranquillity, but they pronounced him guilty. One of them had even the effrontery to acknowledge his innocence to Favras himself, and to affirm that his life was a necessary sacrifice to the public peace.

No event since the attack on Versailles had caused Marie Antoinette equal anguish. It showed that attachment to the king and herself was in itself regarded as an inexpiable crime, and her distress was greatly augmented when, on the Sunday following the execution of the marquis, some of his friends brought to the table where, as usual, she was dining in public with the king, the widowed marchioness and her orphaned son in deep mourning, and presented them to their majesties. Their introducers evidently expected that the king, or at least the queen, by the distinguished reception which she would accord to them, would mark their sense of the merits of their late husband and father, and of the indignity of the sentence under which he had suffered.

Marie Antoinette was sadly embarrassed and distressed: she was taken wholly by surprise; and it happened by a cruel perverseness of fortune that Santerre, the brewer, whose ruffianly and ferocious enmity to the whole royal family, and especially to herself, had been conspicuous throughout the worst outrages of the past summer and autumn, was on the same day on duty at the palace as commander of one of the battalions of the Parisian Guard, and was standing behind her chair when the marchioness and her son were introduced. Her embarrassment and all her feelings on the occasion were described by herself in the course of the afternoon to Madame Campan.

After the dinner was over, she went up to her attendant's room, saying that it was a relief to find herself where she could weep at her ease; for weep she must at the folly of the ultra-Royalists. "We can not but be destroyed," she continued, "when we are attacked by people who unite every kind of talent to every kind of wickedness; and when we are defended by folks who are indeed very estimable, but who have no just notion of our position. They have now compromised me with both parties, in their presenting to me the widow and son of Favras. If I had been free to do as I would, I should have taken the child of a man who had just been sacrificed for us, and have placed him at table between the king and myself; but surrounded as I was by the very murderers who had caused his father's death, I could not venture even to bestow a glance upon him. Yet the Royalists will blame me for not having seemed to be interested in the poor child; while the Revolutionists will be furious, thinking that those who presented him to me knew that it would please me." And all that she could venture to do she did. She knew that the marchioness was very poor, and she sent her by a trusty agent a few hundred louis, and with it a kind message, assuring the unhappy widow that she would always watch over her and her son's interests.

CHAPTER XXVII.

The King accepts the Constitution so far as it has been settled.--The Queen makes a Speech to the Deputies.--She is well received at the Theatre.--Negotiations with Mirabeau.--The Queen's Views of the Position of Affairs.--The Jacobin Club denounces Mirabeau.--Deputation of Anacharsis Clootz.--Demolition of the Statue of Louis XIV.--Abolition of Titles of Honor.--The Queen admits Mirabeau to an Audience.--His Admiration of her Courage and Talents.--Anniversary of the Capture of the Bastile.--Fete of the Champ de Mars.--Presence of Mind of the Queen.

What was probably as painful to Marie Antoinette as these occurrences themselves was the apathy with which the king regarded them. The English traveler to whose journal we have more than once referred, and who, in the first week of the year, saw the royal pair waiting in the gardens of the Tuileries, remarked that though the queen did not appear in good health, but showed melancholy and anxiety in her face, the king, on the other hand, "was as plump as ease could render him.[1]" And in the course of February, in spite of all her remonstrances, Necker succeeded in persuading him to go down to the Assembly, and to address the members in a long speech, in which, though some of his expressions were clearly intended as a reproof of the Assembly itself for the precipitation and violence of some of its measures, he nevertheless declared his cordial assent to the new Constitution, so far as they had yet settled it, and promised to co-operate in a spirit of affection and confidence in the labors which still remained to be achieved.

The greater part of the speech is believed to have been his own composition; and it is characteristic of the fidelity with which, on every occasion, Marie Antoinette adhered to her rule of strengthening her husband's position by her own cordial and conspicuous support, that, strongly as she had objected to the step before it was taken, now that it was decided on, she professed a decided approval of it; and when a deputation of the Assembly, which had been appointed to escort the king with honor back to the palace, solicited an audience of herself to pay their respects, she assured the deputies that "she partook of all the sentiments of the king; that she united with all her heart and mind in the measure which his love for his people had just dictated to him." And then, bringing the dauphin forward, she added: "Behold my son. I shall unceasingly speak to him of the virtues of his most excellent father. I shall teach him from the earliest age to cherish public liberty, and I hope that he will be its firmest bulwark."

For a moment the step seemed to have succeeded, though the proofs of its success were still more strongly proofs of the utter want of sense that marked all the proceedings of the Assembly. As Louis had expressed his assent to the Constitution so far as it was settled, it was proposed, as a fitting compliment to him, that the Assembly and the whole body of the citizens of Paris should take an oath of fidelity to the Constitution without any such reservation. But in the course of the next few weeks the Assembly showed how little his reproof of its former precipitation and violence had been heeded, since, among the first measures with which it proceeded to the completion of the Constitution, one deprived him of the right of deciding on peace and war, a power which all wise statesmen regard as inseparable from the executive government; another extinguished the right of primogeniture; and a third confiscated all the property of the monastic establishments.

However, those who took the lead in the management of affairs (for Necker and the ministers had long ceased to exert the slightest authority) were blinded by their own fury to the absurdity and inconsistency of their conduct. Their exultation was unbounded, and, adhering to the line of conduct which she had marked out for herself, Marie Antoinette now yielded to their entreaties that she would show herself to the citizens at the theatre. Even in the days of her earliest popularity she had never met a more enthusiastic reception. The greater part of the house rose at her entrance, clapping their hands and cheering, and the disloyalty of a few malcontents only made her triumph more conspicuous, so roughly were they treated by the rest of the audience. Marie Antoinette was herself touched at the cordiality with which she was greeted, and saw in it another proof that "the people and citizens were good at heart if left to themselves; but," she added to the Princess de Lamballe, to whom she described the scene, "all this enthusiasm is but a gleam of light, a cry of conscience which weakness will soon stifle.[2]"

It is probably doing no injustice to Mirabeau to believe that the crimes which had made the greatest impression on the queen were not the events which affected him the most strongly. But he was not only a statesman in intellect, but an aristocrat in every feeling of his heart. No man was fonder of referring to his illustrious ancestors; or of claiming kindred with men of old renown, such as the Admiral de Coligny, of whom he more than once boasted in the Assembly as his cousin; and each blow dealt at the consideration of the Nobles was an additional incentive to him to seek to arrest the progress of a revolution which had already gone far beyond his wishes or his expectations. And as he was always energetic in the pursuit of his plans, he had, by some means or other, in spite of the discouragement derived from the language and conduct of the Count de Provence, contrived to get information of his willingness to enlist in the Royalist party conveyed to the queen. The Count de la Marck, who was still his chief confidant, was at Brussels at the beginning of the spring, when he received a letter from Mercy, begging him to return without delay to Paris. He lost no time in obeying the summons, when he learned, to his great delight, though his pleasure was alloyed by some misgiving, that the king and queen had resolved to avail themselves of Mirabeau's services, and that he himself was selected as the intermediate agent in the negotiation. La Marck's misgiving,[3] as he frankly told the embassador at the outset, was caused by the fear that Mirabeau had done more harm than he could repair; but he gladly undertook the commission, though its difficulty was increased by a stipulation which showed at once the weakness of the king, and the extraordinary difficulties which it placed in the way of his friends. The count was especially warned to keep all that was passing a secret from Necker. He was startled, as he well might be, at such an injunction. But he did not think it became his position to start a difficulty; and, as he was fully impressed with the importance of not losing time, the negotiation proceeded rapidly. He introduced Mirabeau to Mercy, and he himself was admitted to an interview with the queen, when he learned that her greatest objections to accepting Mirabeau's services were of a personal nature, founded partly on the general badness of his character, partly on the share he had borne in the events of the 5th and 6th of October. By the count's own account, he went rather beyond the truth in his endeavors to exculpate his friend on this point; and he probably deceived himself when he believed that he had convinced the queen of his innocence. But both she and Louis, who was present at a part of the interview, had evidently made up their minds to forget the past, if they could trust his promises for the future. And the interview ended in the further conduct of the necessary arrangements being left by Louis to the queen.

In a subsequent conversation with the count, she explained her own views of the existing situation of affairs, describing them, indeed, according to her custom, as the ideas of the king, in a manner which shows how much she was willing that the king should abate of his old prerogatives, provided only that the concessions were made voluntarily by himself, and not imposed by violent and illegal resolutions of the Assembly. Mirabeau had drawn up an elaborate memorial for the consideration of the king, in which he pointed out in general terms his sense of the state of "utter anarchy" into which France had fallen, his shame and indignation at feeling "that he himself had contributed to bring affairs into such a bad state." and his "profound conviction of the necessity, in the interests of the whole nation, of re-establishing the legitimate authority of the king.[4]" And Marie Antoinette, commenting on this expression, assured La Marck that "the king had no desire to recover the full extent of the authority which he had formerly possessed; and that he was far from thinking it necessary for his own personal happiness any more than for the welfare of his people.[5]" And it seemed to the count that she placed unlimited confidence in Mirabeau's ability to re-establish her husband's power on a sufficient and satisfactory basis; so full was her conversation, during the latter part of the interview, of the good which she expected to be again able to do, and of the warm affection with which she regarded the people.

The benefits of this new alliance were not to be all on one side. Mirabeau was overwhelmed with debt; and though his father had died in the preceding summer, he had not yet entered into his inheritance, but was in a state little short of absolute destitution. From this condition he was to be relieved, and the arrangements for the discharge of his debts, and the securing to him the enjoyment of a sufficient though by no means excessive income, were intrusted to Marie Antoinette by the king, and by her to her almoner, M. de Fontanges, who, when Lomenie de Brienne was promoted to the archbishopric of Sens, had succeeded him at Toulouse. The archbishop, who was sincerely devoted to his royal mistress, carried out the necessary arrangements with great skill, but they could not be managed with such secrecy as entirely to escape notice. Among the clubs which had been set on foot at the beginning of the previous year the most violent had been that known as the Breton Club, from being founded by some of the deputies from the great province of Brittany; but, when the court removed to Paris, and the Assembly was established in a large building close to the garden of the Tuileries, the Bretons obtained the use of an apartment in an old convent of Dominican or Jacobin friars (as they were called), the same which two centuries before had been the council-room of the League, and they changed their own designation also, and called themselves the Jacobins; and, canceling the rule which limited the right of membership to deputies, they now admitted every one who, by application for election, avowed his adherence to their principles. Their leaders at this time were Barnave; a young noble named Alexander Lameth, whose mother, having been left in necessitous circumstances, owed to the bounty of the king and queen the means of educating her children, a benefit which they repaid with the most unremitting hostility to the whole royal family; and a lawyer named Duport. Mirabeau was in the habit of ridiculing them as the triumvirate; but they were crafty and unscrupulous men, skillful in procuring information; and, having obtained intelligence of his negotiations with the court, they retaliated on him by hiring pamphleteers and journalists to attack him, and narratives of the treason of the Count de Mirabeau were hawked about the streets.

To apply such language to the adherence of a French noble to the crown was the most open avowal of disloyalty on which the revolutionary party had yet ventured; and in the next four weeks it received a practical development in a series of measures, some of which were so ridiculous as only to deserve notice from the additional evidence which they furnished of the extreme folly of those who now had the lead in the Assembly, and of the strange excitement in which the whole nation, or at least the whole population of Paris, must have been wrought up before they could mistake their acts for those of sagacity or patriotism; but others of which, though not less unwise, were of greater importance as being irrevocable steps in the downward course of destruction along which the whole country was being dragged.

The leaders of the revolutionary party had already selected two days in the past year as especially memorable for the triumphs won over the crown: one was the 20th of June, on which, in the Tennis Court at Versailles, the members of the Assembly had bound themselves to effect the regeneration of the kingdom; the other the 14th of July, on which, as they boasted, they had forever established freedom by the destruction of the Bastile; and they determined this year to celebrate both these anniversaries in a becoming manner. Accordingly, on the 20th of June, a crack-brained member of the Jacobin Club, a Prussian of noble birth, named Clootz, who, to show his affinity with the philosophers of old, had assumed the name of Anacharsis, hired a band of vagrants and idlers, and, dressing them up in a variety of costumes to represent Arabs, red Indians, Turks, Chinese, Laplanders, and other tribes, savage and civilized, led them into the Assembly as a deputation from all the nations of the earth to announce the resurrection of the whole world from slavery; and demanded permission for them to attend the festival of the ensuing month, that each, on behalf of his country, might give in his adhesion to the principles of liberty as expounded by the Assembly. The president of the day replied with an oration thanking M. Clootz for the honor done to France by such an embassy; and Alexander Lameth followed up the president's harangue by fresh praises of the deputation as holy pilgrims who had thrown off the shackles of superstition. Nor was he content with a barren panegyric. He had devised an appropriate sacrifice with which to commemorate such exalted virtue. In the finest square of the city, the Place des Victoires, the Duke de la Feuillade had erected a statue of Louis XIV. to celebrate his royal master's triumphs, the pedestal of which was decorated with allegorical representations of the nations which had been conquered by the French marshals. It was generally regarded as the finest work of art in the city, and as such it had long been an object of admiration and pride to the citizens. But M. Lameth, in his new-born enthusiasm, regarded it with other eyes, and closed his speech by proposing that, as monuments of despotism and flattery could not fail to be shocking to so enlightened a body, the Assembly should order its instant demolition. His proposal was received with enthusiastic cheers, and the noble monument was instantly overthrown in a fit of blind fury more resembling the orgies of drunken Bacchanals, or the thirst for desolation which had animated the Goths and Huns, than the conduct of the chosen legislators of a polite and accomplished people.

But even this was not all. The insult to the memory of a king who, little as he deserved it, had a century before been the object of the unanimous admiration of his subjects, was but a prelude to other resolutions of far greater moment, as giving an indelible character to the future of the nation. A deputy, M. Lambel, whose very name was previously unknown to the majority of his colleagues, rose and made a speech of three lines, as if the proposal which it contained only required to be mentioned to command instant and universal assent "This day," said he, "is the tomb of vanity. I demand the suppression of the titles of duke, count, marquis, viscount, baron, and knight." La Fayette and Alexander Lameth's brother, Charles, supported the demand with almost equal brevity; a representative of one of the most ancient families in the kingdom, the Viscount Matthieu de Montmorency moved a prohibition of the use of armorial bearings; another noble, M. de St. Targeau, proposed that the use of names derived from the estates of the owners should be abolished. Every proposal was carried by acclamation. Louder and louder cheers followed each suggestion of a new abolition; a member who ventured to propose an amendment to one proposal was hooted down; and in little more than an hour the whole series of resolutions, which struck at once at the recollections and glories of the past and at the dignity of the future, was made the law of the land.

Every one of these attacks on the nobles was a fresh provocation to Mirabeau, and increased his eagerness to complete his reconciliation with the crown. He pronounced the abolition of titles a torch to kindle civil war, and pressed more earnestly than ever for an interview with the queen, in which he might both learn her views and explain his own. Marie Antoinette had foreseen that she should be forced to admit him to her presence, but there was nothing to which she felt a stronger repugnance. His profligate character excited a feeling of perfect disgust in her mind; but for the public good she overcame it, and, having in the course of June removed to St. Cloud for change of air, on the 3d of July she, accompanied by the king, received him in the garden of that palace. The account which she sent her brother of the interview shows with what a mixture of feelings she had been agitated. She speaks of herself as "shivering with horror" as the moment drew near, and can not bring herself to describe him except as a "monster," though, she admits that his language speedily removed her agitation, which, when he was first presented to her, had nearly made her ill. "He seemed to be actuated by entire good faith, and to be altogether devoted to the king; and Louis was highly pleased with him, so that they now thought every thing was safe.[6]"

She, on her part, had made an equally favorable impression on him. She had adroitly flattered his high opinion of himself by saying that "if she had been speaking to persons of a different class and character she should have felt the necessity of being guarded in her language, but that in dealing with a Mirabeau there could be no need of such caution;" and he told his confidant, La Marck, that till he knew "the soul and thoughts of the daughter of Maria Teresa, and learned how fully he could reckon on that august ally, he had seen nothing of the court but its weakness; but now confidence had raised his courage, and gratitude had made the prosecution of his principles a duty;[7]" and in some subsequent letters he speaks of every thing as depending on the queen, and describes in brief but forcible language his appreciation of the dangers which surrounded her, and of the magnanimous courage with which he sees that she is prepared to confront them. "The king," he says, "has but one man about him, and that is his wife. There is no safety for her but in the reestablishment of the royal authority. I love to believe that she would not desire to preserve life without the crown. What I am quite certain of is, that she will not preserve her life unless she preserves her crown."

In his interview with her, as she reported it to the emperor, he had recommended, as the first step to be adopted by the king and herself, a departure from Paris; and, in reference to that plan, which he at all times regarded as the foundation of every other, he tells La Marck: "The moment will soon come when it will be necessary to try what can be done by a woman and a child on horseback. For her it is but the adoption of an hereditary mode of action.[8] But she must be prepared for it, and must not suppose that one can extricate one's self from an extraordinary crisis by mere chance or by the combinations of an ordinary man."

The hopes with which the acquisition of such an ally inspired the queen at this time nerved her to bear her part in the festival with which the Assembly had decided on celebrating the demolition of the Bastile. The arrangements for it were of a gigantic character. Round the sides of the Champ de Mars a vast embankment was raised, so as to give the plain the appearance of an amphitheatre, and to afford accommodation to three hundred thousand spectators. At the entrance a magnificent arch of triumph was erected. The centre was occupied by a grand altar; and on one side a gorgeous pavilion was appropriated to the king, his family, and retinue, the members of the Assembly, and the municipal magistrates. They were all to be performers in the grand ceremony which was to be the distinguishing feature of the day. The Constitution was scarcely more complete than it had been when Louis signified his acceptance of it five months before; but now, not only were he, the deputies, and municipal authorities of Paris to swear to its maintenance, but the same oath was to be taken by the National Guard, and by a deputation from every regiment in the army; and it was to bind the soldiers throughout the kingdom to the new order of things that the ceremony was originally designed.[9]

As a spectacle few have been more successful, and perhaps none has ever been so imposing. Before midnight on the 13th of July, the whole of the vast amphitheatre was filled with a dense crowd, in its gayest holiday attire--a marvelous and magnificent sight from its mere numbers; and early the next morning the heads of the procession began to defile under the arch at the entrance of the plain--La Fayette, at the head of the National Guard, leading the way. It was a curious proof of the king's weakness, and of the tenacity with which he clung to his policy of conciliation, that, in spite of his knowledge of the general's bitter animosity to his authority and to himself, and of his recent vote for the suppression of all titles of honor, Louis had offered him the sword of the Constable of France, a dignity which had been disused for many years; and it was an equally striking evidence of La Fayette's inveterate disloyalty that, gratifying as the succession to Duguesclin and Montmorency would have been to his vanity, he nevertheless refused the honor, and contented himself with the dignity which the enrollment of the detachments from the different departments under his banner conferred on him, by giving him the appearance of being the commander-in-chief of the National Guard throughout the kingdom. The National Guard was followed by regiment after regiment, and deputation after deputation, of the regular army; and, to show the subordination to the law which they were expected to acknowledge for the future, their swords were all sheathed, while the deputies, the municipal magistrates, and other peaceful citizens who bore a part in the procession had their swords drawn. Sailors from the fleet, magistrates and deputations from every department, and from every city or town of importance in the kingdom, followed; and after them came two hundred priests, with Talleyrand, Bishop of Autun, in his episcopal vestments at their head, their white robes somewhat uncanonically decorated with tricolor ribbons, who passed on into the centre of the plain and ranged themselves on the steps of the altar. So vast was the procession that it was half-past three in the afternoon before the detachment of Royal Guards which closed it took up their position.

When at last all were in their places, Louis, accompanied by the queen and other members of his family, entered the royal pavilion. He was known by sight to the deputations from the most distant provinces, for he had reviewed them in a body the day before, when several of them had been separately presented to him, toward whom he had for once laid aside his habitual reserve, assuring them of his fatherly regard for all his subjects with warmth and manifest sincerity. The queen, too, as she always did, had made a most favorable impression on those members whom she had seen by her judicious and cordial affability. Louis wore no robes, but only the ordinary dress of a French noble. Marie Antoinette was in full evening costume, and her hair was dressed with a plume of tricolor feathers. Yet even on this day, which was intended to be one of universal joy and friendliness, evil signs were not wanting to show how powerful were the enemies of both king and queen; for no seat whatever had been provided for her, while by the aide of that constructed for the king another on very nearly the same level had been placed for the President of the Assembly.

But these refinements of discourtesy were lost on the spectators. They cheered the royal pair joyously the moment that they appeared. Before the shouts had died away, Bishop Talleyrand began the service of the mass; and, on its termination, administered the oath "of fidelity to the nation, the law, the king, and the Constitution as decreed by the Assembly and accepted by the king." La Fayette took the oath first in the name of the army. Talleyrand followed on behalf of the clergy. Bailly came next, as the representative of the citizens of Paris. It was a stormy day; and when the moment arrived for the king to set the seal to the universal acceptance of the constitution by swearing to exert all his own power for its maintenance, the rain came down so heavily as to render it impossible for him to leave the shelter of his own pavilion. As it happened, the momentary disappointment gave a greater effect to his act. With more than usual presence of mind, he advanced to the front of the pavilion, so as to be seen by the whole of the assembled multitude, and took the oath with a loud voice and perfect dignity of manner. As he resumed his seat, the rain cleared away, the sun burst through the clouds; and the queen, as if by a sudden inspiration, brought forward the little dauphin, and, lifting him up in her arms, showed him to the people. Those whom the king's voice could not reach saw the graceful action; and from every side of the plain one universal acclamation burst forth, which seemed to bear out Marie Antoinette's favorite assertion that the people were good at heart, and that it was not without great perseverance in artifice and malignity that they could be excited to disloyalty and treason.

CHAPTER XXVIII.

Great Tumults in the Provinces.--Mutiny in the Marquis de Bouille's Army.
--Disorder of the Assembly.--Difficulty of managing Mirabeau.--Mercy is
removed to The Hague.--Marie Antoinette sees constant Changes in the Aspect of Affairs.--Marat denounces Her.--Attempts are made to assassinate
Her.--Resignation of Mirabeau.--Misconduct of the Emigrant Princes.

But men less blinded by the feverish excitement of revolutionary enthusiasm would have seen but little in the state of France at this time to regard
as matter for exultation. Many of the recent measures of the Assembly,
and especially the extinction of the old provinces, had created great discontent in the rural districts. Formidable riots had broken out in many quarters,
especially in the great southern cities, in some of which the mob had rivaled the
worst excesses of its Parisian brethren; massacring the magistrates, tearing their
bodies into pieces, and terrifying the peaceable inhabitants by processions, in which
the mangled remains of their victims formed the most conspicuous feature. At Brest
and at Toulon the sailors showed that they fully shared the general dissatisfaction;
while in the army a formidable mutiny broke out among the troops which were
under the command of the Marquis de Bouille, in Lorraine. That, indeed, had a different object, since it had been excited by Jacobin emissaries, who were aware that
the marquis, the soldier who, of the whole French army at that time, enjoyed the
highest reputation, was firmly attached to the king; though he was not one of the
nobles who had opposed all reform, nor had he hesitated to follow his royal master's
example and to declare his acceptance of the new Constitution. Fortunately he had
subalterns worthy of him, and faithful to their oaths; and as he was a man of great
promptitude and decision, he, with their aid, quelled the mutiny, though not without a sanguinary conflict, in which he himself lost above four hundred men, while

the loss which he inflicted on the mutineers was far heavier. But he had set a noble example, and had given an undeniable proof of the possibility of quelling the most formidable tumults; and it may be said that his quarters were the only spot in all France which was not wholly given up to anarchy and disorder.

For even the Assembly itself was a prey to tumult and violence. From the time of its assuming that title admission had been given to every one who could force his way into the chamber, whether he was a member or not; nor was any order preserved among those who thus obtained admission; but they were allowed to express their opinion of every speaker and of every speech by friendly or unfriendly clamor: a practice which, as may well be supposed, materially influenced many votes. And presently attendance for that purpose became a trade; some of the most violent deputies hiring a regularly appointed troop to take their station in the galleries, and paying them daily wages to applaud or hiss in accordance with the signs which they themselves made from the body of the hall.[1] And if the populace was thus the master of the Assembly while at Versailles, this was far more the case after its removal to Paris, where the number of the idle portion of the population furnished the Jacobins with far greater means of intimidating their adversaries.

It was remarkable that La Marck himself, as has been already intimated, did not fully share the hopes which the king and queen founded on the adhesion of Mirabeau. It was not only that on one point he had sounder views than Mirabeau himself--doubting, as he did, whether the mischief which his vehement friend had formerly done could now be undone by the same person, merely because he had changed his mind--but he also felt doubts of Mirabeau's steadiness in his new path, and feared lest eagerness for popularity, or an innate levity of disposition, might still lead him astray. As he described him in a letter to Mercy, "he was sometimes very great and sometimes very little; he could be very useful, and he could be very mischievous: in a word, he was often above, and sometimes greatly below, any other man." At another time he speaks of him as "by turns imprudent through excess of confidence, and lukewarm from distrust;" and this estimate of the great demagogue, which was not very incorrect, shows, too, how high an opinion La Marck had formed of the queen's ability and force of character, for he looks to her "to put a curb on his inconstancy,[2]" trusting for that result not so much to her power of fascination as to her clearness of view and resolution.

And she herself was never so misled by her high estimate of Mirabeau's abilities and influence as to think his judgment unerring. On the contrary, her comment to Mercy on one of the earliest letters which he addressed to the king was that it was "full of madness from one end to the other," and she asked "how he, or any one else, could expect that at such a moment the king and she could be induced to provoke a civil war?" alluding, apparently, to his urgent advice that the royal family should leave Paris, a step of the necessity for which she was not yet convinced. Her hope evidently was that he would bring forward some motions in the Assembly which might at least arrest the progress of mischief, and perhaps even pave the way for the repair of some of the evil already done.

On one point she partly agreed with him, but not wholly. He insisted on the necessity of dismissing the ministers; but she, though thinking them, both as a body and individually, unequal to the crisis, saw great difficulty in replacing them, since the vote of the preceding winter forbade the king to select their successors from the members of the Assembly;[3] and she feared also lest, if he should dismiss them, the Assembly would carry out a plan which, as it seemed to her, it already showed great inclination to adopt, of managing every thing by means of committees, and preventing the appointment of any new administration. Her view of the situation, and of the king's and her position, varied from time to time, as indeed their circumstances and the views of the Assembly appeared to alter. In August she is in great distress, caused by a decision of the emperor to remove Mercy to the Hague. "I am," she writes to the embassador, "in despair at your departure, especially at a moment when affairs are becoming every day more embarrassing and more painful, and when I have therefore the greater need of an attachment as sincere and enlightened as yours. But I feel that all the powers, under different pretexts, will withdraw their ministers one after another. It is impossible to leave them incessantly exposed to this disorder and license; but such is my destiny, and I am forced to endure the horror of it to the very end.[4]" But a fortnight later she tells Madame de Polignac that "for some days things have been wearing a better complexion. She can not feel very sanguine, the mischievous folks having such an interest in perverting every thing, and in hindering every thing which, is reasonable, and such means of doing so; but at the moment the number of ill-intentioned people is diminished, or at least the right-thinking of all classes and of all ranks are more united ... You may depend upon it," she adds, "that misfortunes have not diminished my resolution or my courage: I shall not lose any of that; they will only give me more prudence.[5]" Indeed, her own strength of mind, fortitude, and benevolence were the only things in France which were not constantly changing at this time; and she derived one lesson from the continued vicissitudes to which she was exposed, which, if partly grievous, was also in part full of comfort and encouragement to so warm a heart. "It is in moments such as these that one learns to know men, and to see who are truly attached to one, and who are not. I gain every day fresh experiences in this point; sometimes cruel, sometimes pleasant; for I am continually finding that some people are truly and sincerely attached to us, to whom I never gave a thought."

Another of her old vexations was revived in the renewed jealousy of Austrian influence with which the Jacobin leaders at this time inspired the mob, and which was so great that, when in the autumn Leopold sent the young Prince de Lichtenstein as his envoy to notify his accession, Marie Antoinette could only venture to give him a single audience; and, greatly as she enjoyed the opportunity of gathering from him news of Vienna and of the old friends of the childhood of whom she still cherished an affectionate recollection, she was yet forced to dismiss him after a few minutes' conversation, and to beg him to accelerate his departure from Paris, lest even that short interview should be made a pretext for fresh calumnies. "The kindest thing that any Austrian of mark could do for her," she told her brother, "was to keep away from Paris at present.[6]" She would gladly have seen the Assembly interest itself a little in the politics of the empire, where Leopold's own situation was full of difficulties; but the French had not yet come to consider themselves as justified in interfering in the internal government of other countries. As she describes their feelings to the emperor, "They feel their own individual troubles, but those of their neighbors do not yet affect them; and the names of Liberty and Despotism are so deeply engraved in their heads, even though they do not clearly define them, that they are everlastingly passing from the love of the former to the dread of the latter;" and then she adds a sketch of her own ideas and expectations, and of the objects which she conceives it her duty to keep in view, in which it is affecting to see that her utter despair of any future happiness for the king and herself in no degree weakens her desire to promote the happiness of the very people who have caused her suffering. "Our task is to watch skillfully for the moment when men's heads have returned to proper ideas sufficiently to make them enjoy a reasonable and honest freedom, such as the king has himself always desired for the happiness of his people; but far from that license and anarchy which have precipitated the fairest of kingdoms into all possible miseries. Our health continues good, but it would be better if we could only perceive the least gleam of happiness around us; as for ourselves, that is at an end forever, happen what will. I know that it is the duty of a king to suffer for others; and it is one which we are discharging thoroughly."

She had indeed at this time sufferings to which it is characteristic of her undaunted courage that she never makes the slightest allusion in her letters. Of all the Jacobin party, one of the most blood-thirsty was a wretch named Marat.[7] At the very outset of the Revolution he had established a newspaper to which he gave the name of *The People's Friend*, and the staple topic of which was the desirableness of bloodshed and massacre. He had been exasperated at the receptions given to the royal family at the festival of July; and for some weeks afterward his efforts were directed to inflame the populace to a new riot, in which the king and queen should be dragged into Paris from St. Cloud, as in 1789 they had been dragged in from Versailles, and which should end in the murder of the queen, the ministers, and several hundreds of other innocent persons; and his denunciations very nearly bore a part of their intended fruit. The royal family had hardly returned to St. Cloud, when a man named Rotondo was apprehended in the inner garden, who confessed that he had made his way into it with the express design of assassinating Marie Antoinette, a design which was only balked by the fortunate accident of a heavy shower which prevented her from leaving the house; and a week or two afterward a second plot was discovered, the contrivers of which designed to poison her. Her attendants were greatly alarmed; and her physician furnished Madame Campan with an antidote for such poisons as seemed most likely to be employed. But Marie Antoinette herself cared little for such precautions. Assassination was not the end which she anticipated. On one occasion, when she found Madame Campan changing some powdered sugar which, it was suspected, might have been tampered with, she thanked her, and praised M. Vicq-d'Azyr, the physician by whose instructions Madame Campan was acting, but told her that she was giving herself needless trouble. "Depend upon it," she added, "they will not employ a grain of poison against me. The Brinvilliers[8] do not belong to this age; people now use calumny, which is much more effectual for killing people; and it is by calumny that they will work my destruction.[9] But even thus, if my death only secures the throne to my son, I shall willingly die."

One of the measures which Mirabeau strongly urged, and as to which Marie Antoinette hesitated, balancing the difficulties to which it was not unlikely to give rise against the advantages which were more obvious, was arranged without her intervention. Necker had but one panacea for all the ills of a defective constitution or an ill-regulated government--the re-establishment of the finances of the country; and, as public confidence is indispensable to national credit, the troubles of the last year had largely increased the embarrassments of the Treasury. He was also but scantily endowed with personal courage. In the denunciations of Marat he had not been spared, and by the beginning of September fear had so predominated over every other feeling in his mind that he resolved to quit a country which, as he was not one of her sons, seemed to him to have no such claim on his allegiance that he should imperil his life for her sake. But in carrying out his determination, he exhibited a strange forgetfulness, not only of the respect due to his royal master as king, but also of all the ordinary rules of propriety; for he did not resign his office into the hands of the sovereign from whom he had received it, but he announced his retirement to the Assembly, sending the president of the week a letter in which he attributed his reasons for the step partly to his health, which he described as weak, and partly to the "mortal anxieties of his wife, as virtuous as she was dear to his heart." It was hardly to be wondered at that the members present were moved rather to laughter than to sympathy by this sentimental effusion. They took no notice of the letter, and passed to the order of the day; and certainly, if it afforded evidence of his amiable disposition, it supplied proof at least equally strong of the weakness of his character, and of his consequent unfitness for any post of responsibility at such a time.

It was more to his credit that he at the same time placed in the treasury a sum of two millions of francs to cover any incorrectness which might be discovered or suspected in his accounts, and any loss which might be sustained from the depreciation of the paper money lately issued under his administration, though not with his approbation. All the rest of his colleagues retired at the same time, except the foreign secretary, M. Montmorin. They had recently been attacked with great violence in the Assembly by a combination of the most extreme democrats and the most extreme Royalists, the latter of whom accused them of having betrayed the royal authority by unworthy accessions. But, though, in the division which had taken place they had been supported by a considerable majority, they feared a repetition of the attack, and resigned their offices; in some degree undoubtedly weakening their royal master by their retirement, since those by whom he found himself compelled to replace them had still less of his confidence. Two--Duport de Tertre, Keeper of the Seals, and Duportail, Minister of War--were creatures of La Fayette, and the first mentioned was notoriously unfriendly to the queen. Two others--Lambert, the successor of Necker, and Fleurieu, the Minister of Marine--were under the influence of Barnave and the Jacobins. The only member of the new ministry who was in the least degree acceptable to Louis was M. de Lessart, the Minister of the Interior; but he, though loyal in purpose, was of too moderate talents for his appointment to add any real strength to the royal cause.

Marie Antoinette, however, paid but little attention to these ministerial changes; she disregarded them--and her view was not unsound--as but the displacement of one set of weak men by another set equally weak; and she saw, too, that the Assembly had established so complete a mastery over the Government, that even men of far greater ability and force of character would have been impotent for good. Her whole dependence was on Mirabeau; and his course at this time was so capricious and erratic that it often caused her more perplexity and alarm than pleasure or confidence. He regarded himself as having a very difficult part to play. He could not conceal from himself that he was no longer able to lead the Assembly as he had done at first, except when he was urging it along a road which it desired to take. In spite of one of his most brilliant efforts of eloquence, he had recently been defeated in an endeavor to preserve to the king the right of peace and war; and, to regain his ascendency, he more than once in the course of the autumn supported measures to which the king and queen had the greatest repugnance, and made speeches so inflammatory that even his own friend, La Marck, was indignant at his language, and expostulated with him with great earnestness. He justified himself by explaining his view[10] that no man in the country could at present bring the people back to reasonable notions; that they could only at this moment be governed by flattering their prejudices; that the king must trust to time alone; and that his own sole prospect of being of use to the crown lay in his preservation of his popularity till the favorable moment should arrive, even if, to preserve that popularity, it were necessary for him at times still to appear a supporter of revolutionary principles. It is not impossible that the motives which he thus described did really influence him; but it was not strange that Marie Antoinette should fail to appreciate such refined subtlety. She had looked forward to his taking a bold, straightforward course in defense of Royalist principles; and she could hardly believe in the honesty of a man who for any object whatever could seem to disregard or to despise them. Her feelings may be shown by some extracts from one of her letters to the emperor written just after one of Mirabeau's most violent outbursts, apparently his speech in support of a motion that the fleet should be ordered to hoist the tricolor flag.

"October 22d, 1790.

"We are again fallen back into chaos and all our old distrust. Mirabeau had sent the king some notes, a little violent in language, but well argued, on the necessity of preventing the usurpations of the Assembly ... when, on a question concerning the fleet, he delivered a speech suited only to a violent demagogue, enough to frighten all honest men. Here, again, all our hopes from that quarter are overthrown. The king is indignant, and I am in despair. He has written to one of his friends, in whom I have great confidence, a man of courage and devoted to us, an explanatory letter, which seems to me neither an explanation nor an excuse. The man is a volcano which would set an empire on fire; and we are to trust to him to put out the conflagration which is devouring us. He will have a great deal to do before we can feel confidence in him again. La Marck defends Mirabeau, and maintains that if at times he breaks away, he is still in reality faithful to the monarchy ... The king will not believe this. He was greatly irritated yesterday. La Marck says that he has no doubt that Mirabeau thought that he was acting well in speaking as he did, to throw dust in the eyes of the Assembly, and so to obtain greater credit when circumstances still more grave should arise. O my God! if we have committed faults, we have sadly expiated them.[11]"

And before the end of the year, the royal cause had fresh difficulties thrown in its way by the perverse and selfish wrongheadedness of the emigrant princes, who were already evincing an inclination to pursue objects of their own, and to disown all obedience to the king, on the plea that he was no longer master of his policy or of his actions. They showed such open disregard of his remonstrances that, in December, as Marie Antoinette told the emperor, Louis had written both to the Count d'Artois and to the King of Sardinia (in whose dominions the count was at the time), that, if his brothers persisted in their designs, "he should be compelled to disavow them peremptorily, and summon all his subjects who were still faithful to him to return to their obedience. She hoped," she said, "that that would make them pause. It seemed certain to her that no one but those on the spot, no one but themselves, could judge what moments and what circumstances were favorable for action, so as to put an end to their own miseries and to those of France. And it will be then," she concludes, "my dear brother, that I shall reckon on your friendship, and that I shall address myself to you with the confidence with which I am inspired by the feelings of your heart, which are well known to me, and by the good-will which you have shown us on all occasions.[12]"

CHAPTER XXIX.

Louis and Marie Antoinette contemplate Foreign Intervention.--The Assembly passes Laws to subordinate the Church to the Civil Power.--Insolence of La Fayette.--Marie Antoinette refuses to quit France by Herself.--The Jacobins and La Fayette try to revive the Story of the Necklace.--Marie Antoinette with her Family.--Flight from Paris is decided on.--The Queen's Preparations and Views.--An Oath to observe the new Ecclesiastical Constitution is imposed on the Clergy.--The King's Aunts leave France.

The last sentence of the letter just quoted points to a new hope which the king and she had begun to entertain of obtaining aid from foreign princes. As it can hardly have been suggested to them by any other advisers, we may probably attribute the origination of the idea to the queen, who was naturally inclined to rate the influence of the empire highly, and to rely on her brother's zeal to assist her confidently. And Louis caught at it, as the only means of extricating him from a religious difficulty which was causing him great distress, and which appeared to him insurmountable by any means which he could command in his own country. As has been already seen, he had had no hesitation in yielding up his own prerogatives, and in making any concessions or surrenders which the Assembly required, so long as they touched nothing but his own authority. He had even (which was a far greater sacrifice in his eyes) sanctioned the votes which had deprived the Church of its property; but, in the course of the autumn the Assembly passed other measures also, which appeared to him absolutely inconsistent with religion. They framed a new ecclesiastical constitution which not only reduced the number of bishops (which, indeed, in France, as in all other Roman Catholic countries, had been unreasonably excessive), but which also vested the whole patronage of the Church in the municipal authorities, and generally subordinated the Church to the civil law. And having completed these arrangements, which to a conscientious Roman Catholic bore the character of sacrilege, they required the whole body of the clergy to accept them, and to take an oath to observe them faithfully.

Louis was in a great strait. Many of the chief prelates appealed to him for protection, which he thought his duty as a Christian man bound him to afford them. But the protection which they implored could only be given by refusal of the royal assent to the bill. And he could not disguise from himself that such an exercise of his veto would furnish a pretext to his enemies for more violent denunciations of himself and the queen than had yet been heard. He had also, though his personal safety was at all times very slightly regarded by him, begun to feel himself a prisoner, at the mercy of his enemies. La Fayette, as Commander-in-chief of the National Guard of Paris, had the protection of the royal palace intrusted to him; and he availed himself of this charge, not as the guardian of the royal family, but rather as their jailer,[1] placing his sentries so as to be spies and a restraint upon all their movements, and seeking every opportunity to gain an ignoble popularity by an ostentatious disregard of all their wishes, and of all courtesy, not to say decency, in his behavior to them.[2] And these considerations led the king, not only to authorize the Baron de Breteuil, who, as we have seen, had fled from the country in the previous year, to treat with any foreign princes who might he willing to exert themselves in his cause, but even to write, with his own hand, to the principal sovereigns, informing them that "in spite of his acceptance of the Constitution, the factious portion of his subjects openly manifested their intention of destroying the monarchy," and suggesting the idea of "an armed congress of the principal powers of Europe, supported by an armed force, as the best measure to arrest the progress of factions, to re-establish order in France, and to prevent the evils which were devouring his country from seizing on the other states of Europe.[3]"

The historians of the democratic party have denounced with great severity the conduct of Louis in thus appealing to foreign aid, as a proof that, in spite of his acceptance of the Constitution, he was meditating a counter- revolution. The whole tenor of his and the queen's correspondence proves that this charge is groundless; but it is equally certain that it was an impolitic step, one wholly opposed to every idea of Constitutional principles, of which the very foundation must always be perfect freedom from foreign influence, and from foreign connection in the internal government of the country.

Fortunately, his secret was well kept, so that no knowledge of this step reached the leaders of the popular party; and, however great may have been the queen's secret anxieties and fears, she kept them bravely to herself, displaying outwardly a serenity and a patience which won the admiration of all those who, in foreign countries, were watching the course of events in France with interest.[4] When she wept, she wept by herself. Her one comfort was that her children were always with her; and though the dauphin could only witness without understanding her grief, "remarking on one occasion, when in one of his childish books he met the expression 'as happy as a queen,' that all queens are not happy, for his mamma wept from morning till night." Her daughter was old enough to enter into her sorrows; and, as she writes to Madame de Polignac, mingles her own tears with hers. She had also the society of her sister-in-law Elizabeth, whom she had learned to love with an affection which could not be exceeded even by that which she bore her own sister, and which was cordially returned. She tells Madame de Polignac that Elizabeth's calmness is one great relief and support to them all; and Elizabeth can not find adequate words to express to one of her correspondents her admiration for the queen's "piety and resignation, which alone enable her to bear up against troubles such as no one before has ever known."

But amidst all her grief she cherishes hope--hope that the people (the "good people," as she invariably terms them) will return to their senses; and her other habitual feeling of benevolence, though she can now only exert it in forming projects for conferring further benefits on them when tranquillity should be restored. The feeling shows itself even in letters which have no reference to her own position. There had been discontent and signs of insurrection in the Netherlands which Mercy's recent letters led her to believe were passing away; and her congratulations to her brother on this peaceful result dwell on the happiness "which it is to be able to pardon one's subjects without shedding one drop of blood, of which sovereigns are bound to be always careful.[5]"

Her brother, and many of her friends in France, were at this time pressing her to quit the country, professing to believe that if her enemies knew that she was out of their reach, they would be less vehement in their hostility to the king; but she felt that such a course would be both unworthy of her, as timid and selfish, and in every way injurious rather than beneficial to her husband. It could not save his authority, which was what the Jacobins made it their first object to destroy; and it would deprive him of the support of her affection and advice, which he constantly needed.

"Pardon me, I beg of you," she replied to Leopold, "if I continue to reject your advice to leave Paris. Consider that I do not belong to myself. My duty is to remain where Providence has placed me, and to oppose my body, if the necessity should arise, to the knives of the assassins who would fain reach the king. I should be unworthy of the name of our mother, which is as dear to you as to me, if danger could make me desert the king and my children.[6]"

We have seen that Marie Antoinette dreaded calumny more than the knife or poison of the assassin; and there could hardly have been a greater proof how well founded her apprehensions were, and how unscrupulous her enemies, than is afforded by the fact that, in the latter part of this year, they actually brought back Madame La Mothe to Paris with the purpose of making a demand for a re-investigation of the whole story of the fraud on the jeweler--a pretense for reviving the libelous stories to the disparagement of the queen, the utter falsehood and absurdity of which had been demonstrated to the satisfaction of the whole world four years before. Nor was it wholly a Jacobin plot. La Fayette himself was, to a certain extent, an accomplice in it. As commander of the National Guard of the city, it was his duty to apprehend one who was an escaped convict; but instead of doing so he preferred identifying himself with her, and on one occasion had what Mirabeau rightly called the inconceivable insolence to threaten the queen with a divorce on the ground of unfaithfulness to her husband. She treated his insinuations with the dignity which became herself, and the scorn which they and their utterers deserved; and he found that his conduct had created such general disgust among all people who made the slightest pretense to decency, that he feared to lose his popularity if he did not disconnect himself from the plotters. Accordingly, he separated himself from the lady, though he still forbore to arrest her, and for some time confined himself to his old course of heaping on the royal family these petty annoyances and insults, which he could inflict with impunity because they were unobserved except by his victims. It is remarkable, however, that Mirabeau, who held him in a contempt which, however deserved, had in it some touch of rivalry and envy, believed that the queen was not really so much the object of his animosity as the king. In his eyes "all the manoeuvres of La Fayette were so many attacks on the queen; and his attacks on the queen were so many steps to bring him within reach of the king. It was the king whom he really wanted to strike; and he saw that the individual safety of one of the royal pair was as inseparable from that of the other as the king was from his crown.[7]" And this opinion of Mirabeau is strongly corroborated by the Count de la Marck, who, a few weeks later, had occasion to go to Alsace, and who took great pains to ascertain the general state of public feeling in the districts through which he passed. During his absence he was in constant correspondence with those whom he had left behind, and he reports with great satisfaction that in no part of the country had he found the very slightest ill-feeling toward the queen. It was in Paris alone that the different libels against her were forged, and there alone that they found acceptance; and, manifestly referring to the projected departure from Paris, he expresses his firm conviction that the moment that she is at liberty, and able to show herself in the provinces, she will win the confidence of all classes.[8]

However greatly Mirabeau would, on other grounds, have preferred personal intercourse with the court, he thought that his power of usefulness depended so entirely on his connection with it being unsuspected, that he did not think it prudent to solicit interviews with the queen. But he kept up a constant communication with the court, sometimes by notes and elaborate memorials, addressed indeed to Louis, but intended for Marie Antoinette's perusal and consideration; and sometimes by conversations with La Marck, which the count was expected to repeat to her. But, in all the counsels thus given, the thing most to be remarked is the high opinion which they invariably display of the queen's resolution and ability. Every thing depends on her; it is from her alone that he wishes to receive instructions; it is her resolution that must supply the deficiencies of all around her. When he urges that a line of conduct should be adopted calculated to render their majesties more popular; that they should show themselves more in public; that they should walk in the most frequented places; that they should visit the hospitals, the artisans' workshops, and make themselves friends by acts of charity and generosity, it is to her that he looks to carry out his suggestions, and to her affability and presence of mind that he trusts for the success which is to result from them;[9] and La Marck is equally convinced that "her ability and resolution are equal to the conduct of affairs of the first importance."

Meantime her health continued good. It showed her strength of mind that she never intermitted the recreations which contributed to her strength, about which she was especially anxious, that she might at all times be ready to act on any emergency; but rode with Elizabeth with great regularity in the Bois de Boulogne, even in the depth of the winter; and, while watching with her habitual vigilance of affection over the education of her children, she found a pleasant relaxation for herself in providing them with amusement also; often arranging parties, to which other children of the same age were invited, and finding amusement herself from watching their gambols in the long corridor of the Tuileries, their blindman's-buff and hide-and-seek.[10]

The new year opened with grave plans for their extrication from their troubles--plans requiring the utmost forethought, ingenuity, and secrecy to bring them to a successful issue; and also with fresh injuries and insults from the Assembly and the municipal authorities, which every week made the necessity of promptitude in carrying such plans out more manifest. Mirabeau, as we have seen, had from the very first recommended that the king and his family should withdraw from Paris. In his eyes such a step was the indispensable preliminary to all other measures; and some of the earliest of the queen's letters in 1791 show that the resolution to leave the turbulent city had at last been taken. But though what he recommended was to be done, it was not to be done as he recommended; yet there was a manliness about the course of action which he proposed which would of itself have won the queen's preference, if she had not been forced to consider not what was best and fittest, but what it was most easy to induce him on whom the final choice must impend, the king, to adopt. Mirabeau advised that the king should depart publicly, in open day, "like a king," as he expressed himself,[11] and he affirmed his conviction that it would in all probability be quite unnecessary to remove farther than Compiegne; but that the moment that it should be known that the king was out of Paris, petitions demanding the re-establishment of order would flock in from every quarter of the kingdom, and public opinion, which was for the most part royalist, would compel the Assembly to modify the Constitution which it had framed, or, if it should prove refractory, would support the king in dissolving it and convoking another.

But this was too bold a step for Louis to decide on. He anticipated that the Assembly or the mob might endeavor to prevent such a movement by force, which could only be repelled by force; and force he was resolved never to employ. The only alternative was to flee secretly; and in the course of January, Mercy learns that that plan has been adopted, and that Compiegne is not considered sufficiently distant from Paris, but that some fortified place will be selected; Valenciennes being the most likely, as he himself imagined, since, if farther flight should become necessary, it would be easy from thence to cross the frontier into the Belgian dominions of the queen's brother. But if Valenciennes had ever been thought of, it was rejected on that very account; for Louis had learned from English history that the withdrawal of James II. from his kingdom had been alleged as one reason for declaring the throne vacant; and he was resolved not to give his enemies any plea for passing a similar resolution with respect to himself. Valenciennes was so celebrated as a frontier town, that the mere fact of his fixing himself there might easily be represented as an evidence of his intention to quit the kingdom. But there was a small town of considerable strength named Montmedy, in the district under the command of the Marquis de Bouille, which afforded all the advantages of Valenciennes, and did not appear equally liable to the same objections. Montmedy, therefore, was fixed upon; and, in the very first week of February, Marie Antoinette announced the decision to Mercy; and began her own preparations by sending him a jewel-case full of those diamonds which were her private property. She explained to him at considerable length the reasons which had dictated the choice. The very smallness of Montmedy was in itself a recommendation, since it would prevent any one from thinking it likely to be selected as a refuge. It was also so near Luxembourg that, in the present temper of the nation, which regarded the Austrian power with "a panic fear," any addition which M. de Bouille might make to either the garrison or to his supplies would seem only a wise precaution against the much-dreaded foreigner. Moreover, the troops in that district were among the most loyal and well-disposed in the whole army; and if the king should find it unsafe to remain long at Montmedy, he would have a trustworthy escort to retreat to Alsace.

She also explained the reasons which had led them to decide on quitting Paris secretly by night. If they started in the daytime, it would be necessary to have detachments of troops planted at different spots on their road to protect them. But M. de Bouille could not rely on all his own regiments for such a service, and still less on the National Guards in the different towns; while to bring up fresh forces from distant quarters would attract attention, and awaken suspicions beforehand which might be fatal to the enterprise. Montmedy, therefore, had been decided on, and the plans were already so far settled that she could tell Mercy that they should take Madame de Tourzel with them, and travel in one single carriage, which they had never been seen to use before.

Their preparations had even gone beyond these details, minute as they were. The king was already collecting materials for a manifesto which he designed to publish the moment that he found himself safely out of Paris. It would explain the reasons for his flight; it would declare an amnesty to the people in general, to whom it would impute no worse fault than that of being misled (none being excepted but the chief leaders of the disloyal factions; the city of Paris, unless it should at once return to its ancient tranquillity; and any persons or bodies who might persist in remaining in arms). To the nation in general the manifesto would breathe nothing but affection. The Parliaments would be re-established, but only as judicial tribunals, which should have no pretense to meddle with the affairs of administration or finance. In short, the king and she had determined to take his declaration of the 23d of June[12] as the basis of the Constitution, with such modifications as subsequent circumstances might have suggested. Religion would be one of the matters placed in the foreground.

So sanguine were they, or rather was she, of success, that she had even taken into consideration the principles on which future ministries should be constituted; and here for the first time she speaks of herself as chiefly concerned in planning the future arrangements. "In private we occupy ourselves with discussing the very difficult choice which we shall have to make of the persons whom we shall desire to call around us when we are at liberty. I think that it will be best to place a single man at the head of affairs, as M. Maurepas was formerly; and if it be settled in this way, the king would thus escape having to transact business with each individual minister separately, and affairs would proceed more uniformly and more steadily. Tell me what you think of this idea. The fit man is not easy to find, and the more I look for him, the greater inconveniences do I see in all that occur to me."

She proceeds to discuss foreign affairs, the probable views and future conduct of almost every power in Europe--of Holland, Prussia, Spain, Sweden, England; still showing the lingering jealousy which she entertained of the British Government, which she suspected of wishing to detach the chivalrous Gustavus from the alliance of France by the offer of a subsidy. But she is sanguine that, "though some may he glad to see the influence of France diminished, no wise statesman in any country can desire her ruin or dismemberment. What is going on in France would be an example too dangerous to other countries, if it were left unpunished. Their cause is the cause of all kings, and not a simple political difficulty.[13]"

The whole letter is a most remarkable one, and fully bears out the eulogies which all who had an opportunity of judging pronounced on her ability. But the most striking reflection which it suggests is with what admirable sagacity the whole of the arrangements for the flight of the royal family had been concerted, and with what judgment the agents had been chosen, since, though the enterprise was not attempted till more than four months after this letter was written, the secret was kept through the whole of that time without the slightest hint of it having been given, or the slightest suspicion of it having been conceived, by the most watchful or the most malignant of the king's enemies.

Yet during the winter and early spring the conduct of the Jacobin party in the Assembly, and of the Parisian mob whom they were keeping in a constant state of excitement, increased in violence; while one occurrence which took place was, in Mirabeau's opinion, especially calculated to prompt a suspicion of the king's intentions. Louis had at, last, and with extreme reluctance, sanctioned, the bill which required the clergy to take an oath to comply with the new ecclesiastical arrangements, in the vain hope that the framers of it would be content with their triumph, and would forbear to enforce it by fixing any precise date for administering the oath. But, at the end of January, Barnave obtained from the Assembly a decree that it should be taken within twenty-four hours, under the penalty of deprivation of all their preferments to all who should refuse it; the clerical members of the Assembly were even threatened by the mob in the galleries with instant death if they declined or even delayed to swear. And as very few of any rank complied, the main body of the clergy was instantly stripped of all their appointments and reduced to beggary, and a large proportion of them fled at once from the kingdom. Those who took the oath, and who in consequence were appointed to the offices thus vacated, were immediately condemned and denounced by the pope; and the consequence was that a great number of their flocks fled with their old priests, not being able to reconcile to their consciences to stay and receive the sacrament and rites of the Church from ministers under the ban of its head.

Among those who thus fled were the king's two aunts, the Princesses Adelaide and Victoire. Bigotry was their only virtue; and they determined to seek shelter in Rome. Louis highly disapproved of the step, which, as Mirabeau,[14] in a very elaborate and forcible memorial which he drew up and submitted to him, pointed out, might be very dangerous for the king and queen as well as for themselves, since it could be easily represented by the evil-minded as a certain proof that they also were designing to flee. And he even recommended that Louis should formally notify to the Assembly that he disapproved of his aunts' journey, and should make it a pretext for demanding a law which should give him the power of regulating the movements of the members of his family.

The flight of the princesses, however, did not, as it turned out, cause any in-convenience to the king or queen, though it did endanger themselves; for, though they were furnished with passports, the municipal authorities tried to stop them at Moret; and at Arnay-le-Duc the mob unharnessed their horses and detained them by force They appealed to the Assembly by letter; Alexander Lameth, on this occa-sion uniting with the most violent Jacobins, was not ashamed to move that orders should be dispatched to send them back to Paris: but the body of the Assembly had not yet descended to the baseness of warring with women; and Mirabeau, who treated the proposal as ridiculous, and overwhelmed the mover with his wit, had no difficulty in procuring an order that the fugitives, "two princesses of advanced age and timorous consciences," as he called them, should be allowed to proceed on their journey.

CHAPTER XXX.

The Mob attacks the Castle at Vincennes.--La Fayette saves it.--He insults the Nobles who come to protect the King.--Perverseness of the Count d'Artois and the Emigrants.--Mirabeau dies.--General Sorrow for his death.--He would probably not have been able to arrest the Revolution.-- The Mob prevent the King from visiting St. Cloud.--The Assembly passes a Vote to forbid him to go more than twenty Leagues from Paris.

The mob, however, was more completely under Jacobin influence; and, at the end of February, Santerre collected his ruffians for a fresh tumult; the object now being the destruction of the old castle of Vincennes, which for some time had been almost unoccupied. La Fayette, whose object at this time was apparently regulated by a desire to make all parties acknowledge his influence, in a momentary fit of resolution marched a body of his National Guard down to save the old fortress, in which he succeeded, though not without much difficulty, and even some danger. He found he had greatly miscalculated his influence, not only over the populace, but over his own soldiers. The rioters fired on him, wounding some of his staff; and at first many of the soldiers refused to act against the people. His officers, however, full of indignation, easily quelled the spirit of mutiny; and, when subordination was restored, proposed to the general to follow up his success by marching at once back into the city and seizing the Jacobin demagogues who had caused the riot. There was little doubt that the great majority of the citizens, in their fear of Santerre and his gang, would joyfully have supported him in such a measure; but La Fayette's resolution was never very consistent nor very durable. He became terrified, not, indeed, so much at the risk to his life which he had incurred, as at the symptom that to resist the mob might cost him his popularity; and to appease those whom he might have offended, he proceeded to insult the king. A report had got abroad, which was not improbably well founded, that Louis's life had been in danger, and that an assassin had been detected while endeavoring to make his way into the Tuileries; and the report had reached a number of nobles, among whom D'Espremesnil, once so vehement a leader of the Opposition in Parliament, was conspicuous, who at once hastened to the palace to defend their sovereign. It was not strange that he and Marie Antoinette should receive them graciously; they had not of late been used to such warm-hearted and prompt displays of attachment. But the National Guards who were on duty were jealous of the cordial and honorable reception which those Nobles met with; they declared that to them alone belonged the task of defending the king; though they took so little care to perform it that they had allowed a gang of drunken desperadoes to get possession of the outer court of the palace, where they were menacing all aristocrats with death. Louis became alarmed for the safety of his friends, and begged them to lay aside their arms; and they had hardly done so when La Fayette arrived. He knew that the mob was exasperated with him for his repression of their outrages in the morning, and that some of his soldiers had not been well pleased at being compelled to act against the rioters. So now, to recover their good-will, he handed over the weapons of the Nobles, which were only pistols, rapiers, and daggers, to the National Guard; and after reproaching D'Espremesnil and his companions for interfering with the duties of his troops, he drove them down the stairs, unarmed and defenseless as they were, among the drunken and infuriated mob. They were hooted and ill-treated; but not only did he make no attempt to protect them, but the next day he offered them a gratuitous insult by the publication of a general order, addressed to his own National Guard, in which he stigmatized their conduct as indecent, their professed zeal as suspicious, and enjoined all the officials of the palace to take care that such persons were not admitted in future. "The king of the Constitution," he said, "ought to be surrounded by no defenders but the soldiers of liberty."

Marie Antoinette had good reason to speak as she did the next week to Mercy; though we can hardly fail to remark, as a singular proof of the strength of her political prejudices, and of the degree in which she allowed them to blind her to the objects and the worth of the few honest or able men whom the Assembly contained, that she still regards the Constitutionalists as only one degree less unfavorable to the king's legitimate authority than the Jacobins. And we shall hereafter see that to this mistaken estimate she adhered almost to the end. "Mischief," she says, "is making progress so rapid that there is reason to fear a speedy explosion, which can not fail to be dangerous to us, if we ourselves do not guide it There is no middle way; either we must remain under the sword of the factions, and consequently be reduced to nothing, if they get the upper hand, or we must submit to be fettered under the despotism of men who profess to be well-intentioned, but who always have done, and always will do us harm. This is what is before us, and perhaps the moment is nearer than we think, if we can not ourselves take a decided line, or lead men's opinions by our own vigor and energetic action. What I here say is not dictated by any exaggerated notions, nor by any disgust at our position, nor by any restless desire to be doing something. I perfectly feel all the dangers and risks to which we are exposed at this moment. But I see that all around us affairs are so full of terror that it is better to perish in trying to save ourselves than to allow ourselves to be utterly crushed in a state of absolute inaction.[1]"

And she held the same language to her brother, the emperor, assuring him that "the king and herself were both convinced of the necessity of acting with prudence, but there were cases in which dilatoriness might ruin every thing; and that the factious and disloyal were prosecuting their objects with such celerity, aiming at nothing less than the utter subversion of the kingly power, that it would be extremely dangerous not to offer a resistance to their plans.[2]" And referring to her project of foreign aid, she reported to him that she had promises of assistance from both Spain and Switzerland, if they could depend on the co-operation of the empire.

And still the emigrant princes were adding to her perplexity by their perverseness. She wrote herself to the Count d'Artois to expostulate with him, and to entreat him "not to abandon himself to projects of which the success, to say the least, was doubtful, and which would expose himself to danger without the possibility of serving the king.[3]" No description of the relative influence of the king and queen at this time can be so forcible as the fact that it was she who conducted all the correspondence of the court, even with the king's brothers. But her remonstrances had no influence. We may not impute to the king's brothers any intention to injure him; but unhappily they had both not only a mean idea of his capacity, but a very high one, much worse founded, of their own; and full of self-confidence and self-conceit, they took their own line, perfectly regardless of the suspicions to which their perverse and untractable conduct exposed the king, carrying their obstinacy so far that it was not without difficulty, that the emperor himself, though they were in his dominions, was able to restrain their machinations.

Meanwhile, the queen was steadily carrying on the necessary arrangements for flight. Money had to be provided, for which trustworthy agents were negotiating in Switzerland and Holland, while some the emperor might be expected to furnish. Mirabeau marked out for himself what he regarded as a most important share in the enterprise, undertaking to defend and justify their departure to the Assembly, and nothing doubting that he should be able to bring over the majority of the members to his view of that subject, as he had before prevailed upon them to sanction the journey of the princesses. But in the first days of April all the hopes of success which had been founded on his cooperation and support were suddenly extinguished by his death. Though he had hardly entered upon middle age, a constant course of excess had made him an old man before his time. In the latter part of March he was attacked by an illness which his physicians soon pronounced mortal, and on the 2d of April he died. He had borne the approach of death with firmness, professing to regret it more for the sake of his country than for his own. He was leaving behind him no one, as he affirmed, who would he able to arrest the Revolution as he could have done; and there can be no doubt that the great bulk of the nation did place confidence in his power to offer effectual resistance to the designs of the Jacobins. The various parties in the State showed this feeling equally by the different manner in which they received the intelligence. The court and the Royalists openly lamented him. The Jacobins, the followers of Lameth, and the partisans of the Duke of Orleans, exhibited the most indecent exultation.[4] But the citizens of Paris mourned for him, apparently, without reference to party views. They took no heed of the opposition with which he had of late often defeated the plots of the leaders whom they had followed to riot and treason. They cast aside all recollection of the denunciations of him as a friend to the court with which the streets had lately rung. In their eyes he was the personification of the Revolution as a whole; to him, as they viewed his career for the last two years, they owed the independence of the Assembly, the destruction of the Bastile, and of all other abuses; and through him they doubted not still to obtain every thing that was necessary for the completion of their freedom.

His remains were treated with honors never before paid to a subject. He lay in state; he had a public funeral. His body was laid in the great Church of St. Genevieve, which, the very day before, had been renamed the Pantheon, and appropriated as a cemetery for such of her illustrious sons as France might hereafter think worthy of the national gratitude. Yet, though his great confidant and panegyrist, M. Dumont,[5] has devoted an elaborate argument to prove that he had not overestimated his power to influence the future; and though the Russian embassador, M. Simolin, a diplomatist of extreme acuteness, seems to imply the same opinion by his pithy saying that "he ought to have lived two years longer, or died two years earlier," we can hardly agree with them. La Marck, as has been seen, even when first opening the negotiation for his connection with the court, doubted whether he would be able to undo the mischief which he had acquiesced in, measures not of reform nor of reconstruction, but of total abolition and destruction, are in their very nature irrevocable and irremediable. The nobility was gone; he had not resisted its suppression. The Church was gone; he had himself been among the foremost of its assailants. How, even if he had wished it, could he have undone these acts? and if he could not, how, without those indispensable pillars and supports, could any monarchy endure? That he was now fully alive to the magnitude of the dangers which encompassed both throne and people, and that he would have labored vigorously to avert them, we may do him the justice to believe. But it seems not so probable that he would have succeeded, as that he would have added one more to the list of these politicians who, having allowed their own selfish aims to carry them beyond the limits of prudence and justice, have afterward found it impossible to retrace their steps, but have learned to their shame and sorrow that their rashness has but led to the disappointment of their hopes, the permanent downfall of their own reputations, and the ruin of what they would gladly have defended and preserved. And, on the whole, it is well that from time to time such lessons should be impressed upon the world. It is well that men of lofty genius and pure patriotism should learn, equally with the most shallow empiric or the most self-seeking demagogue, that false steps in politics can rarely be retraced; that concessions once made can seldom, if ever, be recalled, but are usually the stepping-stones to others still more extensive; that what it would have been easy to preserve, it is commonly impossible to repair or to restore.

He had been laid in the grave only a fortnight, when, as if on purpose to show how utterly defenseless the king now was, the Jacobins excited the mob and the assembly to inflict greater insults on him than had been offered even by the attack on Versailles, or by any previous vote. As Easter, which was unusually late this year, approached, Louis became anxious to spend a short time in tranquillity and holy meditation; and, since the tumultuousness of the city was not very favorable for such a purpose, he resolved to pass a fortnight at St. Cloud. But when he was preparing to set out, a furious mob seized the horses and unharnessed them; the National Guards united with the rioters, refusing to obey La Fayette's orders to clear the way for the royal carriage, and the king and queen were compelled to dismount and to return to their apartments; while, a day or two afterward, the Assembly came to a vote which seemed as if designed for an express sanction of this outrage, and which ordained that the king should not be permitted ever to move more than twenty leagues from Paris.

Of all the decrees which it had yet enacted, this, in some sense, may be regarded as the most monstrous. It was not only passing a penal sentence on the royal family such as in no country or age any but convicted criminals had even been subjected to, but it was an insult and an injury to every part of the kingdom except the capital, which, by an intolerable assumption, it treated as if it were the whole of France. Joseph, as has been seen, had wisely pointed out to his brother-in-law that it was one, and no unimportant part, of a sovereign's duty to visit the different provinces and chief cities of his kingdom, and Louis had in one instance acted on his advice. We have seen how gladly he was received by the citizens of Cherbourg, and what advantages they promised themselves from his having thus made himself personally acquainted with their situation and wants and prospects; and we can not doubt that other towns and cities shared this feeling, nor that it was well founded, and that the acquisition by a king of a personal knowledge of the resources and capabilities and interests of the great cities, of agriculture, manufactures, and commerce, is a benefit to the whole community; but of this every province and every city but Paris was now to be deprived. It was to be an offense to visit Rouen, or Lyons, or Bordeaux; to examine Riquet's canal or Vauban's fortifications. The king was the only person in the kingdom to whom liberty of movement was to be denied; and the peasants of every province, and the citizens of every other town, were to be refused for a single day the presence of their sovereign, whom the Parisians thus claimed a right to keep as a prisoner in their own district.

It is hardly strange that such open attacks on their liberty made a deeper impression on the queen, and even on the phlegmatic disposition of the king, than any previous act of violence, or that it increased their eagerness to escape with as little delay as possible. Indeed, the queen regarded the public welfare as equally concerned with their own in their safe establishment in some town to which they should also be able to remove the Assembly, so that that body as well as themselves should be protected from the fatal influence of the clubs of Paris, and of the populace which was under the dominion of the clubs.[6] Accordingly, on the 20th of April, she writes to the emperor[7] that "the occurrence which has just taken place has confirmed them more than ever in their plans. The very guards who surrounded them are the persons who threaten them most. Their very lives are not safe; but they must appear to submit to every thing till the moment comes when they can act; and in the mean time their captivity proves that none of their actions are done by their own accord." And she urges her brother at once to move a strong body of troops toward some of his fortresses on the Belgian frontier--Arlon, Vitron, or Mons--in order to give M. de Bouille a pretext for collecting troops and munitions of war at Montmedy. "Send me an immediate answer on this point; let me know, too, about the money; our position is frightful, and we must absolutely put an end to it next month. The king desires it even more than I do."

As May proceeds she presses on her preparations, and urges the emperor to accelerate his, especially the movements of his troops; but the Count d'Artois and his followers are a terrible addition to her anxieties. Leopold had told her that the ancient minister, Calonne, always restless and always unscrupulous, was now with the count, and was busily stirring him up to undertake some enterprise or other;[8] and her reply shows how justly she dreads the results of such an alliance. "The prince, the Count d'Artois, and all those whom they have about them, seem determined to be doing something. They have no proper means of action, and they will ruin us, without our having the slightest connection with their plans. Their indiscretion, and the men who are guiding them, will prevent our communicating our secret to them till the very last moment."

To Mercy she is even more explicit in her description of the imminence of the danger to which the king and she are now exposed than she had been to her brother. As the time for attempting to escape grew nearer, the embassador became the more painfully impressed with the danger of the attempt. Failure, as it seems to him, will be absolutely fatal. He asks her anxiously whether the necessity is such that it has become indispensable to risk such a result;[9] and she, in an answer of considerable length and admirable clearness of expression and argument, explains her reasons for deciding that it is absolutely unavoidable: "The only alternative for us, especially since the 18th of April,[10] is either blindly to submit to all that the factions require, or to perish by the sword which is forever suspended over our heads. Believe me, I am not exaggerating the danger; you know that my notion used to be, as long as I could cherish it, to trust to gentleness, to time, and to public opinion. But now all is changed, and we must either perish or take the only line which remains to us. We are far from shutting our eyes to the fact that this line also has its perils; but, if we must die, it will be at least with glory, and in having done all that we could for our duty, for honor, and for religion.... I believe that the provinces are less corrupted than the capital; but it is always Paris which gives the tone to the whole kingdom. We should greatly deceive ourselves if we fancied that the events of the 18th of April, horrible as they were, produced any excitement in the provinces. The clubs and the affiliations lead France where they please; the right-thinking people, and those who are dissatisfied with what is taking place, either flee from the country or hide themselves, because they are not the stronger party, and because they have no rallying-point. But when the king can show himself freely in a fortified place, people will be astonished to see the number of dissatisfied people who will then come forward, who, till that time, are groaning in silence; but the longer we delay, the less support we shall have....

"Let us resume. You ask two questions: 1st. Is it possible or useful to wait? No; by the explanation of our position which I gave at the beginning of this letter, I have sufficiently proved the impossibility.... As to the usefulness, it could only be useful on the supposition that we could count on a new legislative body.... 2d. Admitting the necessity of acting promptly, are we sure of means to escape; of a place to retreat to, and of having a party strong enough to maintain itself for two months by its own resources? I have answered this question several times. It is more than probable that the king, once escaped from here, and in a place of safety, will have, and will very soon find, a very strong party. The means of escape depend on a flight the most immediate and the most secret. There are only four persons who are acquainted with our secret; and those whom we mean to take with us will not know it till the very moment. None of our own people will attend us; and at a distance of only thirty or thirty-five leagues we shall find some troops to protect our march, but not enough to cause us to be recognized till we reach the place of our destination.

"....I can easily conceive the repugnance which, on political grounds, the emperor would feel to allowing his troops to enter France.... But if their movement is solicited by his brother-in-law, his ally, whose life, existence, and honor are in danger, I conceive the case is very different; and as to Brabant, that province will never be quiet till this country is brought back to a different state. It is, then, for himself also that my brother will be working in giving us this assistance, which is so much the more valuable to us, that his troops will serve as an example to ours, and will even be able to restrain them.

"And it is with this view that the person[11] of whom I spoke to you in my letter in cipher demands their employment for a time ... We can not delay longer than the end of this month. By that time I hope we shall have a decisive answer from Spain. But till the very instant of our departure we must do everything that is required of us, and even appear to go to meet them. It is one way, perhaps the only one, to lull the mob to sleep and to save our lives."

CHAPTER XXXI.

Plans for the Escape of the Royal Family.--Dangers of Discovery.-- Resolution of the Queen.--The Royal Family leave the Palace.--They are recognized at Ste. Menehould.--Are arrested at Varennes.--Tumult in the City, and in the Assembly.--The King and Queen are brought back to Paris.

Marie Antoinette, as we have seen, had been anxious that their departure from Paris should not be delayed beyond the end of May, and De Bouille had agreed with her; but enterprises of so complicated a character can rarely be executed with the rapidity or punctuality that is desired, and it was not till the 20th of June that this movement, on which so much depended, was able to be put in execution. Often during the preceding weeks the queen's heart sunk within her when she reflected on the danger of discovery, whether from the acuteness of her enemies or the treachery of pretended friends; and even more when she pondered on the character of the king himself, so singularly unfitted for an undertaking in which it was not the passive courage with which he was amply endowed, but daring resolution, promptitude, and presence of mind, which were requisite. She was cheered, however, by repeated letters from the emperor, showing the warm and affectionate interest which he took in the result of the enterprise, and promising with evident sincerity "his own most cordial co-operation in all that could tend to her and her husband's success, when the time should come for him to show himself."

But her main reliance was on herself; and all who were privy to the enterprise knew well that it was on her forethought and courage that its success wholly depended. Those who were privy to it were very few; and it is a singular proof how few Frenchmen, even of the highest rank, could be trusted at this time, that of these few two were foreigners--a Swede, the Count de Fersen, whose name has been mentioned in earlier chapters of this narrative, and (an English writer may be proud to add) an Englishman, Mr. Craufurd. In such undertakings the simplest arrangements are the safest; and those devised by the queen and her advisers, the chief of whom were De Fersen and De Bouille, were as simple as possible. The royal fugitives were to pass for a traveling party of foreigners. A passport signed by M. Montmorin, who still held the seals of the Foreign Department, was provided for Madame de Tourzel, who, assuming the name of Madame de Korff, a Russian baroness, professed to be returning to her own country with her family and her ordinary equipage. The dauphin and his sister were described as her children, the queen as their governess; while the king himself, under the name of Durand, was to pass as their servant. Three of the old disbanded Body-guard, MM. De Valory, De Malden, and De Moustier, were to attend the party in the disguise of couriers; and, under the pretense of providing for the safe conveyance of a large sum of money which was required for the payment of the troops, De Bouille undertook to post a detachment of soldiers at each town between Chalons and Montmedy, through which the travelers were to pass.

Some of the other arrangements were more difficult, as more likely to lead to a betrayal of the design. It was, of course, impossible to use any royal carriage, and no ordinary vehicle was large enough to hold such a party. But in the preceding year De Fersen had had a carriage of unusual dimensions built for some friends in the South of Europe, so that he had no difficulty now in procuring another of similar pattern from the same maker; and Mr. Craufurd agreed to receive it into his stables, and at the proper hour to convey it outside the barrier.

Yet in spite of the care displayed in these arrangements, and of the absolute fidelity observed by all to whom the secret was intrusted, some of the inferior attendants about the court suspected what was in agitation. The queen herself, with some degree of imprudence, sent away a large package to Brussels; one of her waiting-women discovered that she and Madame Campan had spent an evening in packing up jewels, and sent warning to Gouvion, an aid-de-camp of La Fayette, and to Bailly, the mayor, that the queen at last was preparing to flee. Luckily Bailly had received so many similar notices that he paid but little attention to this; or perhaps he was already beginning to feel the repentance, which he afterward exhibited, at his former insolence to his sovereign, and was not unwilling to contribute to their safety by his inaction; while Gouvion was not anxious to reveal the source from which he had obtained his intelligence. Still, though nothing precise was known, the attention of more than one person was awakened to the movements of the royal family, and especially that of La Fayette, who, alarmed lest his prisoners should escape him, redoubled his vigilance, driving down to the palace every night, and often visiting them in their apartments to make himself certain of their presence. Six hundred of the National Guard were on duty at the Tuileries, and sentinels were placed at the end of every passage and at the foot of every staircase; but fortunately a small room, with a secret door which led into the queen's chamber, as it had been for some time unoccupied, had escaped the observation of the officers on guard, and that passage therefore offered a prospect of their being able to reach the courtyard without being perceived.[1]

On the morning of the day appointed for the great enterprise, all in the secret were vividly excited except the queen. She alone preserved her coolness. No one could have guessed from her demeanor that she was on the point of embarking in an undertaking on which, in her belief, her own life and the lives of all those dearest to her depended. The children, who knew nothing of what was going on, went to their usual occupations--the dauphin to his garden on the terrace, Madame Royale to her lessons; and Marie Antoinette herself, after giving some orders which were to be executed in the course of the next day or two, went out riding with her sister-in-law in the Bois de Boulogne. Her conversation throughout the day was light and cheerful. She jested with the officer on guard about the reports which she understood to be in circulation about some intended flight of the king, and was re-lieved to find that he totally disbelieved them. She even ventured on the same jest with La Fayette himself, who replied, in his usual surly fashion, that such a project was constantly talked of; but even his rudeness could not discompose her.

As the hour drew near she began to prepare her children. The princess was old enough to be talked to reasonably, and she contented herself, therefore, with warn-ing her to show no surprise at any thing that she might see or hear. The dauphin was to be disguised as a girl, and it was with great glee that he let the attendants dress him, saying that he saw that they were going to act a play. The royal sup-per usually took place soon after nine; at half-past ten the family separated for the night, and by eleven their attendants were all dismissed; and Marie Antoinette had fixed that hour for departing, because, even if the sentinels should get a glimpse of them, they would be apt to confound them with the crowd which usually quit the palace at that time.

Accordingly, at eleven o'clock the Count de Fersen, dressed as a coachman, drove an ordinary job-carriage into the court-yard; and Marie Antoinette, who trusted nothing to others which she could do herself, conducted Madame de Tourzel and the children down-stairs, and seated them safely in the carriage. But even her nerves nearly gave way when La Fayette's coach, brilliantly lighted, drove by, passing close to her as he proceeded to the inner court to ascertain from the guard that every thing was in its usual condition. In an agony of fright she sheltered herself behind some pillars, and in a few minutes the marquis drove back, and she rejoined the king, who was awaiting her summons in his own apartment, while one of the disguised Body-guards went for the Princess Elizabeth. Even the children were inspired with their mother's courage. As the princess got into the carriage she trod on the dauphin, who was lying in concealment at the bottom, and the brave boy spoke not a word; while Louis himself gave a remarkable proof how, in spite of the want of moral and political resolution which had brought such miseries on himself and his country, he could yet preserve in the most critical moments his presence of mind and kind consideration for others. He was half way down-stairs when he returned to his room. M. Valory, who was escorting him, was dismayed when he saw him turn back, and ventured to remind him how precious was every instant. "I know that," replied the kind-hearted monarch; "but they will murder my servant to-morrow for having aided my escape;" and, sitting down at his table, he wrote a few lines declaring that the man had acted under his peremptory orders, and gave the note to him as a certificate to protect him from accusation. When all the rest were seated, the queen took her place. De Fersen drove them to the Porte St. Martin, where the great traveling-carriage was waiting, and, having transferred them to it, and taken a respectful leave of them, he fled at once to Brussels, which, more fortunate than those for whom he had risked his life, he reached in safety.

For a hundred miles the royal fugitives proceeded rapidly and without interruption. One of the supposed couriers was on the box, another rode by the side of the carriage, and the third went on in advance to see that the relays were in readiness. Before midday they reached Chalons, the place where they were to be met by the first detachment of De Bouille's troops; and, when the well-known uniforms met her eye, Marie Antoinette for the first time gave full expression to her feelings. "Thank God, we are saved!" she exclaimed, clasping her hands; the fervor of her exclamation bearing undesigned testimony to the greatness of the fears which, out of consideration for others, she had hitherto kept to herself; but in truth out of this employment of the troops arose all their subsequent disasters.

De Bouille had been unwilling to send his detachments so far forward, pointing out that the notice which their arrival in the different towns was sure to attract would do more harm than their presence as a protection could do good. But his argument had been overruled by the king himself, who apprehended the greatest danger from the chance of being overtaken, and expected it, therefore, to increase with every hour of the journey. De Bouille's fears, however, were found to be the best justified by the event. In more than one town, even in the few hours that had elapsed since the arrival of the soldiers, there had been quarrels between them and the towns-people; in others, which was still worse, the populace had made friends with them and seduced them from their loyalty, so that the officers in command had found it necessary to withdraw them altogether; and anxiety at their unexpected absence caused Louis more than once to show himself at the carriage window. More than once he was recognized by people who knew him and kept his counsel; but Drouet, the postmaster at Ste. Menehould, a town about one hundred and seventy miles from Paris, was of a less loyal disposition. He had lately been in the capital, where he had become infected with the Jacobin doctrines. He too saw the king's face, and on comparing his somewhat striking features with the stamp on some public documents which he chanced to have in his pocket, became convinced of his identity. He at once reported to the magistrates what he had seen, and with their sanction rode forward to the next town, Clermont, hoping to be able to collect a force sufficient to stop the royal carriage on its arrival there. But the king traveled so fast that he had quit Clermont before Drouet reached it, and he even arrived at Varennes before his pursuer. Had he quit that place also he would have been in safety, for just beyond it De Bouille had posted a strong division which would have been able to defy all resistance. But Varennes, a town on the Oise, was so small as to have no post-house, and by some mismanagement the royal party had not been informed at which end of the town they were to find the relay. The carriage halted while M. Valory was making the necessary inquiries; and, while it was standing still, Drouet rode up and forbade the postilions to proceed. He himself hastened on through the town, collected a few of the towns-people, and with their aid upset a cart or two on the bridge to block up the way; and, having thus made the road impassable, he roused the municipal authorities, for it was nearly midnight, and then, returning to the royal carriage, he compelled the royal family to dismount and follow him to the house of the mayor, a petty grocer, whose name was Strausse. The magistrates sounded the tocsin: the National Guard beat to arms: the king and queen were prisoners.

How they were allowed to remain so is still, after all the explanations that have been given, incomprehensible. Two officers with sixty hussars, all well disposed and loyal, were in a side street of the town waiting for their arrival, of which they were not aware. Six of the troopers actually passed the travelers in the street as they were proceeding to the mayor's house, but no one, not even the queen, appealed to them for succor; or they could have released them without an effort, for Drouet's whole party consisted of no more than eight unarmed men. And when, an hour afterward, the officers in command learned that the king was in the town in the hands of his enemies, instead of at once delivering him, they were seized with a panic: they would not take on themselves the responsibility of acting without express orders, but galloped back to De Bouillé to report the state of affairs. In less than an hour three more detachments, amounting in all to above one hundred men, also reached the town; and their commanders did make their way to the king, and asked his orders. He could only reply that he was a prisoner, and had no orders to give; and not one of the officers had the sense to perceive that the fact of his announcing himself a prisoner was in itself an order to deliver him.

One word of command from Louis to clear the way for him at the sword's point would yet have been sufficient; but he had still the same invincible repugnance as ever to allow blood to be shed in his quarrel. He preferred peaceful means, which could not but fail. With a dignity arising from his entire personal fearlessness, he announced his name and rank, his reasons for quitting Paris and proceeding to Montmedy; declaring that he had no thought of quitting the kingdom, and demanded to be allowed to proceed on his journey. While the queen, her fears for her children overpowering all other feelings, addressed herself with the most earnest entreaties to the mayor's wife, declaring that their very lives would be in danger if they should be taken back to Paris, and imploring her to use her influence with her husband to allow them to proceed. Neither Strausse nor his wife was ill-disposed toward the king, but had not the courage to comply with the request of the royal couple whom, after a little time, the mayor and his wife could not have allowed to proceed, however much they might have wished it; for the tocsin had brought up numbers of the National Guard, who were all disloyal; while some of the soldiers began to show a disinclination to act against them. And so matters stood for some hours; a crowd of towns-people, peasants, National Guards, and dragoons thronging the room; the king at times speaking quietly to his captors; the queen weeping, for the fatigue of the journey, and the fearful disappointment at being thus baffled at the last moment, after she had thought that all danger was passed, had broken down even her nerves. At first she had tried to persuade Louis to act with resolution; but when, as usual, she failed, she gave way to despair, and sat silent, with touching, helpless sorrow, gazing on her children, who had fallen asleep.

At seven o'clock on the morning of the 22d a single horseman rode into the town. He was an aid-de-camp of La Fayette. On the morning of the 21st the excitement had been great in Paris when it became known that the king had fled. The mob rose in furious tumult. They forced their way into the Tuileries, plundering the palace and destroying the furniture. A fruit-woman took possession of the queen's bed, as a stall to range her cherries on, saying that to-day it was the turn of the nation; and a picture of the king was torn down from the walls, and, after being stuck up in derision outside the gates for some time, was offered for sale to the highest bidder.[2] In the Assembly the most violent language was used. An officer whose name has been preserved through the eminence which after his death was attained by his widow and his children, General Beauharnais, was the president; and as such, he announced that M. Bailly had reported to him that the enemies of the nation had carried off the king. The whole Assembly was roused to fury at the idea of his having escaped from their power. A decree was at once drawn up in form, commanding that Louis should be seized wherever he could be found, and brought back to Paris. No one could pretend that the Assembly had the slightest right to issue such an order; but La Fayette, with the alacrity which he always displayed when any insult was to be offered to the king or queen, at once sent it off by his own aid-de-camp,

M. Romeuf, with instructions to see that it was carried out The order was now delivered to Strausse; the king, with scarcely an attempt at resistance, declared his willingness to obey it; and before eight o'clock he and his family, with their faithful Body-guard, now in undisguised captivity, were traveling back to Paris.

When was there ever a journey so miserable as that which now brought its sovereigns back to that disloyal and hostile city! The National Guard of Varennes, and of other towns through which they passed, claimed a right to accompany them; and as they were all infantry, the speed of the carriage was limited to their walking pace. So slowly did the procession advance, that it was not till the fourth day that it reached the barrier; and, in many places on the road, a mob had collected in expectation of their arrival, and aggravated the misery of their situation by ferocious threats addressed to the queen, and even to the little dauphin. But at Chalons they were received with respect by the municipal authorities; the Hotel de Ville had been prepared for their reception: a supper had been provided. The queen was even entreated to allow some of the principal ladies of the city to be presented to her; and, as the next day was the great Roman Catholic festival of the Fete Dieu, they were escorted with all honor to hear mass in the cathedral, before they resumed their journey. Even the National Guard were not all hostile or insolent. At Epernay, though a menacing crowd surrounded the carriage as they dismounted, the commanding officer took up the dauphin in his arms to carry him in safety to the door of the hotel; comforting the queen at the same time with a loyal whisper well suited to her feelings, "Despise this clamor, madame; there is a God above all."

But, miserable as their journey was, soon after leaving Chalons it became more wretched still. They were no longer to be allowed the privilege of suffering and grieving by themselves. The Assembly had sent three of its members to take charge of them, selecting, as might have been expected, two who were known as among their bitterest enemies--Barnave, and a man named Petion; the third, M. Latour Maubourg, was a plain soldier, who might be depended on for carrying out his orders with resolution. In one respect those who made the choice were disappointed. Barnave, whose hostility to the king and queen had been chiefly dictated by personal feelings, was entirely converted by the dignified resignation of the queen, and from this day renounced his republicanism; and, though he adhered to what were known as Constitutionalist views, was ever afterward a zealous advocate of both the monarch and the monarchy. But Petion took every opportunity of insulting Louis, haranguing him on the future abolition of royalty, and reproaching him for many of his actions, and for what he believed to be his feelings and views for the future.

It was the afternoon of the 25th when they came in sight of Paris. So great had been Marie Antoinette's mental sufferings that in those few days her hair had turned white; and fresh and studied humiliations were yet in store for her. The carriage was not allowed to take the shortest road, but was conducted some miles round, that it might be led in triumph down the Champs Elysees, where a vast mob was waiting to feast their eyes on the spectacle, whose display of sullen ill-will had been bespoken by a notice prohibiting any one from taking off his hat to the king, or uttering a cheer. The National Guard were forbidden to present arms to him; and it seemed as if they interpreted this order as a prohibition also against using them in his defense; for, as the carriage approached the palace, a gang of desperate ruffians, some of whom were recognized as among the most ferocious of the former assailants of Versailles, forced their way through their ranks, pressed up against the carriage, and even mounted on the steps. Barnave and Latour Maubourg, fearing that they intended to break open the doors, placed themselves against them; but they contented themselves with looking in at the window, and uttering sanguinary threats. Marie Antoinette became alarmed--not for herself, but for her children. They had so closed up every avenue of air that those within were nearly stifled, and the youngest, of course, suffered most. She let down a glass, and appealed to those who were crowding round: "For the love of God," she exclaimed, "retire; my children are choking!" "We will soon choke you," was the only reply they vouchsafed to her. At last, however, La Fayette came up with an armed escort, and they were driven off; but they still followed the carriage up to the very gate of the palace with yells of insult. And it had a stranger follower still: behind the royal carriage came an open cabriolet, in which sat Drouet, with a laurel crown on his head,[3] as if the chief object of the procession wore to celebrate his triumph over his king.

The mob was even hoping to add to its impressiveness by the slaughter of some immediate victims--not of the king and queen, for they believed them to be destined to public execution; but they were eager to massacre the faithful Body-guards, who had been brought back, bound, on the box of the carriage; and they would undoubtedly have carried out their bloody purpose had not the queen remembered them, and, as she was dismounting, entreated Barnave and La Fayette to protect them. Though during the last three days many things had had their names altered,[4] the Tuileries had been spared. It was still in name a royal palace, but those who now entered it knew it for their prison. The sun was setting, the emblem of the extinction of their royalty, as they ascended the stairs to find such rest as they might, and to ponder in privacy for this one night over their fatal disappointment, and their still more fatal future.

Yet, though their return was full of ignominy and wretchedness, though their home had become a prison, the only exit from which was to be the scaffold, still, if posthumous renown can compensate for miseries endured in this life; if it be worth while to purchase, even by the most terrible and protracted sufferings, an undying, unfading memory of the most admirable virtues--of fidelity, of truth, of patience, of resignation, of disinterestedness, of fortitude, of all the qualities which most ennoble and sanctify the heart--it may be said, now that her agonies have long been terminated, and that she has been long at rest, that it was well for Marie Antoinette that she had failed to reach Montmedy, and that she had thus fallen again, without having to reproach herself in any single particular, into the hands of her enemies. As a prisoner to the basest of mankind, as victim to the most ferocious monsters that have ever disgraced humanity, she has ever commanded, and she will never cease to command, the sympathy and admiration of every generous mind. But the case would have been widely different had Louis and she found the refuge which they sought with the loyal and brave De Bouille. Their arrival in his camp could not have failed to be a signal for civil war; and civil war, under such circumstances as those of France at that time, could have had but one termination--their defeat, dethronement, and expulsion from the country. In a foreign land they might, indeed, have found security, but they would have enjoyed but little happiness. Wherever he may be, the life of a deposed and exiled sovereign must be one of ceaseless mortification. The greatest of the Italian poets has well said that the recollection of former happiness is the bitterest aggravation of present misery; and not only to the fugitive monarch himself, but to those who still preserve their fidelity to him, and to the foreign people to whom he is indebted for his asylum, the recollection of his former greatness will ever be at hand to add still further bitterness to his present humiliation. The most friendly feeling his misfortunes can ever excite is a contemptuous pity, such as noble and proud minds must find it harder to endure than the utmost virulence of hatred and enmity.

From such a fate, at least, Marie Antoinette was saved. During the remainder of her life her failure did indeed condemn her to a protraction of trial and agony such as no other woman has ever endured; but she always prized honor far above life, and it also opened to her an immortality of glory such as no other woman has ever achieved.

CHAPTER XXXII.

Marie Antoinette's Feelings on her Return.--She sees Hopes of Improvement.--The 17th of July.--The Assembly inquire into the King's Conduct on leaving Paris.--They resolve that there is no Reason for taking Proceedings.--Excitement in Foreign Countries.--The Assembly proceeds to complete the Constitution.--It declares all the Members Incapable of Election to the New Assembly.--Letters of Marie Antoinette to the Emperor and to Mercy.--The Declaration of Pilnitz.--The King accepts the Constitution.--Insults offered to him at the Festival of the Champ de Mars.--And to the Queen at the Theatre.--The First or Constituent Assembly is dissolved.

It was eminently characteristic of Marie Antoinette that her very first act, the morning after her return, was to write to De Fersen, to inform him that she was safe and well in health; but though she had roused herself for that effort of gratitude and courteous kindness, for some days she seemed stupefied by grief and disappointment, and unable to speak or think for a single moment of any thing but the narrow chance which had crushed her hopes, and changed success, when it had seemed to be secured, into ruin; and, if ever she could for a moment drive the feeling from her mind, her enemies took care to force it back upon her every hour. Before they reached the Tuileries, La Fayette had obtained from the Assembly authority to place guards wherever he might think fit; and no jailer ever took more rigorous precautions for the safe-keeping of the most desperate criminals than this man of noble birth, but most ignoble heart[1], now practiced toward his king and queen. Sentinels were placed along every passage of the palace, and, that they might have their prisoners constantly in sight, the door of every room was kept open day and night. The queen was not allowed even to close her bed-chamber, and a soldier was placed so as at all times to command a sight of the whole room; the only moment that the door was permitted to be shut being a short period each morning while she was dressing.

But after a time she rallied, and even began again to think the future not wholly desperate. She always looked at the most promising side of affairs, and the first shock of the anguish felt at Varennes had scarcely passed away, when, with irrepressible sanguineness, she began to look around her and search for some foundation on which to build fresh hopes. She even thought that she had found it in the divisions which were becoming daily more conspicuous in the Assembly itself. She had yet to learn that at such times violence always overpowers moderation, and that the worse men are, the more certain are they to obtain the upper hand.

The divisions among her enemies were indeed so furious as to justify at one time the expectation that one party would destroy the other. The Jacobins summoned a vast meeting, whose members they fixed beforehand at a hundred thousand citizens, to meet on Sunday, the 17th of July, to petition the Assembly to dethrone the king. On the appointed day, long before the hour fixed for the meeting, a fierce riot took place, the causes and even the circumstances of which have never been clearly ascertained, but which soon became marked with scenes of extraordinary violence. La Fayette, who tried to crush it in the bud, was pelted and fired at. Bailly hung out the red flag, the token of martial law being proclaimed, at the Hotel de Ville, The mob pelted the National Guard. The National Guard, too much exasperated and alarmed to obey La Fayette's order to fire over the people's heads, at one volley shot down a hundred of the rioters. The Jacobin leaders fled in alarm. Robespierre, who had been one of the chief organizers of the tumult, being also one of the basest of cowards, was the most terrified of all, and fled for shelter to his admirer, of congenial spirit, Madame Roland, whose protection he afterward repaid by sending her to the scaffold. The riot was quelled, and the officers of the National Guard urged La Fayette to take advantage of the opportunity, and lead them on to close by force the club of the Jacobins, and another of equal ferocity, known as the Cordeliers[2], lately founded by the fiercest of the Jacobins, Danton, and a butcher named Legendre, who boasted of his ferocity as his only title to interfere in the Government. If he had been honest in his professions of a desire to save the monarchy, La Fayette would have adopted their advice, for it had already become plain to every one that the existence of these clubs was incompatible with the preservation of the kingly authority; but his imbecile love of popularity made him fear to offend even such a body of miscreants as the followers of Danton and Robespierre, and he professed to believe that he had given them a sufficient lesson, and had so convinced them of his power to crush them that they would be grateful to him for sparing them, and learn to act with more moderation in future.

The decision of the Assembly also on the question, of the king's conduct in leaving Paris was not without its encouragement to one of the queen's disposition. She herself had been interrogated by commissioners appointed by the Assembly to inquire into the circumstances connected with the transaction, and her statement has been preserved. With her habitual anxiety to conceal from others the king's incapacity and want of resolution, she represented herself as acting wholly under his orders. "I declare," said she, "that as the king desired to quit Paris with his children, it would have been unnatural for me to allow any thing to prevent me from accompanying him. During the last two years, I have sufficiently proved, on several occasions, that I should never leave him; and what in this instance determined me most was the assurance which I felt that he would never wish to quit the kingdom. If he had had such a desire, all my influence would have been exerted to dissuade him from such a purpose[3]." And she proceeded further to exculpate all their attendants. She declared that Madame de Tourzel, who had been ill for some weeks, had never received her orders till the very day of the departure. She knew not whither she was going, and had taken no luggage, so that the queen herself had been forced to lend her some clothes. The three Body-guards were equally ignorant, and the waiting-women. Though it was true, she said, that the Count and Countess de Provence had gone to Flanders, they had only taken that course to avoid interfering with the relays which were required by the king, and had intended to rejoin him at Montmedy. The king's own statement tallied with hers in every respect, though it was naturally more explicit as to his motives and intentions; and his innocence of purpose was so irresistibly demonstrated, that, though Robespierre, in the most sanguinary speech which, he had ever yet uttered, demanded that he should be brought to trial, not concealing his desire that it should end in his condemnation; and though Petion, and a wretch named Buzot, a warm admirer and intimate friend of Madame Roland, demanded his deposition and the proclamation of a republic, Barnave had no difficulty in carrying the Assembly with him in opposition to their violence; and it was finally resolved that nothing which had happened furnished grounds for taking proceedings against any member of the royal family. It was ordered at the same time that De Bouille should be arrested and impeached; but when he found that nothing could be effected for the deliverance of the king, he had fled across the frontiers, and was safe from their malice.

Meanwhile, the unconstitutional and unprecedented violence which had been offered to the king naturally created the greatest excitement and indignation in all foreign countries. A month before the late expedition, the emperor had addressed a formal note to M. Montmorin, as Secretary of State, declaring that he would regard any ill-treatment of his sister as an injury done to himself;[4] and now[5] the chivalrous Gustavus of Sweden proposed to address to the Assembly a joint letter of warning from all the sovereigns of Europe, to declare that they would all make common cause with the King of France if any attempt were made to offer him further violence. But even the Austrian ministers regarded such a declaration as more likely to aggravate than to diminish the dangers of those whom it was designed to serve; and the queen herself preferred waiting for a time, to see the result of the strife between the rival parties in the Assembly.

The Assembly was at this time fully occupied with the completion of the Constitution, a work for which it had but little time left, since its own duration had been fixed at two years, which would expire in September; and also with the consideration of a question concerning the composition of the next Assembly which had been lately brought forward, and on which the queen was unfortunately misled into using her influence to procure a decision which was undoubtedly, in its eventual consequences, as disastrous to the king's fortunes as it was irreconcilable with common sense. Robespierre brought forward a resolution that no members of the existing Assembly should be eligible for a seat in that by which it was to be replaced. It was in reality a resolution to exclude from the new Assembly not only every one who had any parliamentary or legislative experience, but also all the adherents or friends of the throne, and to place the coming elections wholly in the power of the Jacobins. Robespierre was willing to be excluded himself from a conviction, that, with such an Assembly as would surely be returned, the Jacobin Club would practically exercise all the power of the State. But the Constitutional party, who saw that it was aimed at them, opposed it with great vigor; and would probably have been able to defeat it if the Royalist members who still retained their seats would have consented to join them. Unhappily the queen took the opposite view. With far more acuteness, penetration, and fertility of imagination than are usually given to women, or to men either, she had still in some degree the defect common to her sex, of being prone to confine her views to one side of a question; and to overrule her reason by her feelings and prejudices. Though she acknowledged the service which Barnave had rendered by defeating those who had wished to bring the king and herself to trial, she, nevertheless, still regarded the Constitutionalists in general with deep distrust as the party which desired to lower, and had lowered, the authority and dignity of the throne; and, viewing the whole Assembly with not unnatural antipathy, she fancied that one composed wholly of new members could not possibly be, more unfriendly to the king's person and government, and might probably be far better disposed toward them. She easily brought the king to adopt her views, and exerted the whole of her influence to secure the passing of the decree, sending agents to canvass those deputies who were opposed to it. With the Royalist members, the Extreme Right, her voice was law, and, by the unnatural union of them and the Jacobins, the resolution was carried.

It is the more singular that she should have been willing thus, as it were, to proscribe the members of the present Assembly, because, in a very remarkable letter which she wrote to her brother the emperor at the end of July, she founds the hopes for the future, which she expresses with a degree of sanguineness which can hardly fail to be thought strange when the events of June are remembered, on the conduct of the Assembly itself. The letter is too long to quote at full length, but a few extracts from it will help us in our task of forming a proper estimate of her character, from the unreserved exposition which it contains of her feelings, both past and present, with her views and hopes for the future, even while she keenly appreciates the difficulties of the king's position; and from the unabated eagerness for the welfare of France which it displays in every reflection and suggestion. That she still considers the imperial alliance of great importance to the welfare of both nations will surprise no one. The suspension of the royal authority which the Assembly had decreed on the 26th of June had been removed on the decision that the king was not to be proceeded against. Yet her first sentence shows that she was still subjected to cruel and lawless tyranny, which even hindered her correspondence with her own relations. A queen might have expected to be able to write in security to another sovereign; a sister to a brother; but La Fayette and those in authority regarded the rights of neither royalty nor kindred.

"A friend, my dear brother, has undertaken to convey this letter to you, for I myself have no means of giving you news of my health. I will not enter into details of what preceded our departure. You have already known all the reasons for it. During the events which befell us on our journey, and in the situation in which we were immediately after our return to Paris, I was profoundly distressed. After I recovered from the first shock of the agitation which they produced, I set myself to work to reflect on what I had seen; and I have endeavored to form a clear idea of what, in the actual state of affairs, the king's interests are, and what the conduct is which they prescribe to me. My ideas have been formed by a combination of motives which I will proceed to explain to you.

"...The situation of affairs here has greatly changed since our journey. The National Assembly was divided into a multitude of parties. Far from order being re-established, every day seemed to diminish the power of the law. The king, deprived of all authority, did not even see any possibility of recovering it on the completion of the Constitution through the influence of the Assembly, since that body itself was every day losing more the respect of the people. In short, it was impossible to see any end to disorder.

"To-day, circumstances present much more hope. The men who have the greatest influence in affairs are united together, and have openly declared for the preservation of the monarchy and the king, and for the re-establishment of order. Since their union, the efforts of the seditious have been defeated by a great superiority of strength. The Assembly has acquired a consistency and an authority in every part of the kingdom, which it seems disposed to use to establish the observance of the laws and to put an end to the Revolution. At this moment the most moderate men, who have never ceased to be opposed to revolutionary acts, are uniting, because they see in union the only prospect of enjoying in safety what the Revolution has left them, and of putting an end to the troubles of which they dread the continuance. In short, every thing seems at this moment to contribute to put an end to the agitations and commotions to which France has been given over for the last two years. This termination of them, however, natural and possible as it is, will not give the Government the degree of force and authority which I regard as necessary; but it will preserve us from greater misfortunes; it will place us in a situation of greater tranquillity, and, when men's minds have recovered from their present intoxication, perhaps they will see the usefulness of giving the royal authority a greater range.

"This, in the course which matters are now taking, is what one can foresee for the future, and I compare this result with what we could promise ourselves from a line of conduct opposed to the wishes which the nation displays. In that ease I see an absolute impossibility of obtaining any thing except by the employment of a superior force; and on this last supposition I will say nothing of the personal dangers which the king, my son, and I myself may have to encounter. But what could be the consequences but some enterprise, the issue of which is uncertain, and the ultimate result of which, whatever it might be, presents disasters such as one can not endure to contemplate? The army is in a bad state from want of leaders and of subordination; but the kingdom is full of armed men, and their imagination is so inflamed that it is impossible to foresee what they might do, and the number of victims who might be sacrificed.... It is impossible, when one sees what is going on here, to calculate what might be the effects of their despair. I only see, in the events which might arise out of such an attempt, but very doubtful prospects of success, and the certainty of great miseries for every one....

"If the Revolution should be terminated in the manner of which I have spoken, then it will be important that the king shall acquire, in a solid manner, the confidence and consideration which alone can give a real strength to the royal authority. No means are so well calculated to procure them for him as the influence which we might have over one of your resolutions[6] which would contribute to insure peace to France, and to dispel disquietude, which are so much the more grievous for the whole world, that they are among the principal obstacles to the re-establishment of public tranquillity. The share which in that way we should have in the termination of these troubles would win over to us all men of moderate temper, while the others, especially the chiefs of the Revolution, would attach themselves to us because of the sincere and efficacious inclination which we should have shown to conduct matters to the end, which they all wish for. Your own interests seem to me also to have a place in this system of conduct. The National Assembly, before separating, will desire, in concert with the king, to determine the alliances to which France is to continue attached; and the power of Europe which shall be the first to recognize the Constitution, after it has been accepted by the king, will undoubtedly be the one with which the Assembly will be inclined to form the closest alliance; and to these general views I might add the means which I myself have to dispose men's minds to maintain this alliance-- means which will be extremely strengthened, if you share my view of the present circumstances.

"I can not doubt that the chiefs of the Revolution, who have supported the king in the last crisis, will be desirous to assure to him the consideration and respect necessary to the exercise of his authority, and that they will see in a close alliance of France with that power with which he is connected by ties of blood, a means of combining his dignity with the interests of the nation, and in that way of consolidating and strengthening a Constitution of which they all agree that the majesty of the king is one essential foundation.

"I do not know if, independently of all other reasons, the king will not find in that feeling and in the inclinations of the nation, when it has recovered its calmness, more deference, and a temper more favorable to him, than he could expect from the majority of those Frenchmen who are at present out of the kingdom.[7]"

And a letter which she wrote to Mercy a fortnight later is perhaps even more worthy of attention, as supplying abundant proof, if proof were needed, of the good-will and good faith which were the leading principles of herself and the king in all their dealings with the Assembly. Since her letter to her brother, matters had been proceeding rapidly. She had found some means of treating more directly than on any previous occasion, not only with Barnave, but with the far more unscrupulous A. Lameth; and the Assembly had made such progress in completing the Constitution that it was on the point of submitting it to the king for his acceptance. We have seen in Marie Antoinette's letter to the emperor that she was convinced of the necessity of Louis signifying that acceptance, and she adhered to that view of the policy to be pursued, though the last touches given to the Constitution had rendered many of its articles far more unreasonable than she had anticipated, and though the great English statesman, Burke, whose "Reflections" of the preceding year had naturally caused him to be regarded as one of the ablest advisers on whom she could rely, forwarded to her an earnest exhortation to induce her husband to reject it. He implored her "to have nothing to do with traitors." Using the argument which, to one so sensitive for her honor as Marie Antoinette, was well calculated to exert an almost irresistible influence over her mind, he declared that "her resolution at this most critical moment was to decide whether her glory was to be maintained, and her distresses to cease, or whether" (and he begged pardon for ever mentioning such an alternative) "shame and affliction were to be her portion for the rest of her life;" and he declared that "if the king should accept the Constitution, both king and queen were ruined forever."

The great writer was, as in more than one other instance of his career, too earnest in his conviction that principles were at stake in the course which he recommended, to consider whether that course were safe for those on whom he urged it, or even practicable. But Marie Antoinette, as one on whose decision the very lives of her husband and her child might depend, felt bound to consider, in the first place, how far her adoption of the advice thus tendered might endanger both; and, accordingly, while expressing to Mercy the full extent of her repugnance to the system of government, if indeed it deserved the name of a system, which the new Constitution had framed, she shows that her disapproval of it has in no degree led her to change her mind on the practical question of the course which the king should pursue. She justifies her decision to Mercy in a most elaborate letter, in which the whole position is surveyed with admirable good sense.[8]

"Our position is this: We are now on the point of having the Constitution brought to us for acceptance. It is in itself so monstrous that it is impossible that it should be long maintained. But, in the position in which we are, can we risk refusing it? No; and I will prove it to you. I am not speaking of the personal dangers which we should run. We have fully shown by the journey which we undertook two months ago that we do not take our own safety into account when the public welfare is at stake. But this Constitution is so intrinsically bad that it can only acquire consistence from any resistance which we might oppose to it. Our business, therefore, is to take a middle course, which may save our honor, and may put us in such a position that the people may come back to us when once their eyes are opened, and they have become weary of the existing state of affairs. I think also that it is necessary that, when they have presented the act to the king, he should keep it by him a few days; for he is not supposed to know what it is till it has been presented to him in all legal form; and that then he should summon the Commissioners before him, not to make any comments, not to demand any alterations, which perhaps might not be admitted, and which would be interpreted as an admission that he approved of the basis, but to declare that his opinions are not changed; that, in his declaration of the 20th of June,[9] he proved the absolute impossibility of governing under the new system, and that he is still of the same mind; but that, for the sake of the tranquillity of his country, he sacrifices himself; and that, as his people and the nation stake their happiness on his accepting it, he does not hesitate to signify that acceptance; and that the sight of their happiness will speedily make him forget the cruel and bitter griefs which they have inflicted on him and on his family.

"But if we take this line we must adhere to it; and, above all things, we must avoid any step which can create distrust, and we must move on, so to say, always with the law in our hand. I promise you that this is the best way to give them an early disgust at the Constitution. The mischief is, that for this we shall want an able and a trustworthy ministry.... Several people urge us to reject the act, and the king's brothers press upon him every day that it is indispensable to do so, and affirm that we shall be supported. By whom?" And she proceeds to examine the situation and policy of Spain, of the empire of England, and of Prussia, to prove that from none of them is there any hope of active aid, while to trust to the emigrants would be the worst expedient of all, because "we should then fall into a new slavery worse than the first, since, while we should appear to be in some degree indebted to them, we should not be able to extricate ourselves from their toils. They already prove this when they refuse to listen to the persons who are in our confidence, on the pretext that they do not trust them, while they seek to force us to give ourselves up to M. de Calonne, who, I fear, in all that he does is guided by nothing but his own ambition, his private enmities, and his habitual levity, thinking every thing he wishes not only possible, but already done.

"... One circumstance worthy of remark is that in all these discussions on the Constitution the people take no interest, and concern themselves solely about their own affairs, limiting their wishes to having a Constitution and getting rid of the aristocrats... As to our acceptance of the Constitution, it is impossible for any thinking being to avoid seeing that we are not free. But it is essential that we should not awaken a suspicion of our feelings in the monsters who surround us. Let me know where the emperor's forces are and what is their present position. In every case the foreign powers can alone save us. The army is lost. There is no money. There is no bond, no curb which can restrain the populace, which is everywhere armed. Even the chiefs of the Revolution, when they wish to speak of order, are not listened to. This is the deplorable condition in which we are placed. Add that we have not a single friend-- that every one betrays us, some out of hatred, others out of weakness or ambition. In short, I actually am reduced to dread the day when they will have the appearance of giving us a kind of freedom. At least, in the state of nullity in which we are at present, no one can reproach us.... You know the character of the person with whom I have to do.[10] At the last moment, when one seems to have convinced him, an argument, a word, will make him change his mind before any one suspects it. This is the reason why many expedients can not be even attempted."

On the 21st she hears that the Charter will be presented at the end of the week, and she repeats her fears that the conduct of the emigrants may involve them in fresh troubles. "It is essential that the French, and most especially the brothers of the king, should keep in the background, and allow the foreign princes to act by themselves. But no entreaty, no argument from us will induce them to do so. The emperor must insist upon it. It is the only way in which he can serve us. You know yourself the mischievous wrong-headedness and evil designs of the emigrants. The cowards! after having abandoned us, they seek to make us expose ourselves alone to danger, and serve nothing but their interests. I do not accuse the king's brothers; I believe their hearts and their intentions to be pure, but they are surrounded and guided by ambitious men who will ruin them after having first ruined us." ... On the 26th she hears that it will still be a week before the Constitution is brought to the king. "It is impossible, considering our position, that the king should refuse to accept it. You may depend upon this being true, since I say it. You know my character sufficiently to be sure that it would incline me rather to a noble and bold course. We have no resource but in the foreign powers. They must come to our assistance; but it is the emperor who must put himself at the head of every thing, and manage every thing.... I declare to you that matters are now come to such a state that it would be better to be king of a single province than of a kingdom so abandoned and disordered as this. I shall endeavor, if I can, to send the emperor information on all these matters. But, in the mean time, do you tell him all that you consider necessary to prove to him that we have no longer any resource except in him, and that our happiness, our existence, and that of my child depend on him alone, and on his prudence and promptitude in action.[11]"

And, however she from time to time caught at momentary hopes arising from other sources, the only one on which she placed any permanent reliance were the affection and power of her brother; and that hope, in the course of the winter, was cut from under her by his death.[12] Yet so correct was her judgment and appreciation of sound political principles, or, perhaps we might say, so keen was her sense of what was due to the independence and dignity of France, in spite of its present disloyalty, that a report that the emperor and Prussia had, by implication, claimed a right to dictate to France in matters of her internal government drew from her a warm remonstrance. As sovereign and brother she conceived that Leopold had a right to interfere to insure the safety of his own sister and of a brother sovereign; but she never desired him to interpose for any other object. From her childhood, as we have seen more than once, she had learned to regard the Prussian character and Prussian designs with abhorrence. And in a letter to Mercy of the 12th of September, after expressing an earnest hope that the emperor will not allow himself to be guided by "the cunning of Calonne, and the detestable policy of Prussia," she adds, "It is said here that in the agreement signed at Pilnitz,[13] the two powers engage never to permit the new French Constitution to be established. There certainly are things which foreign powers have a right to oppose, but, as to what concerns the internal laws of a country, every nation has a right to adopt those which suit it. They would be wrong, therefore, to intervene in such a matter; and all the world would see in such an act a proof of the intrigues of the emigrants.[14]"

She proceeds to tell him that all is settled. The king had adopted the line which she had marked out for him in her former letter. The Constitution had been presented to him on the 3d of September. He had taken a few days to consider it, not with the idea of proposing the slightest alteration, but in order to avoid the appearance of acting under compulsion; and, on the same day on which she wrote to Mercy, he was drawing up a letter to the Assembly, to announce his intention of visiting the Assembly to give it his royal assent in due form. But, though she would not have had him act otherwise, she can not announce this apparent termination of the contest without some natural expressions of grief and indignation.

"At last the die is cast. All that we have now to do is to regulate the future progress and conduct of affairs as circumstances may permit. I only wish that others would regulate their conduct by mine. But even in our own inner circle we have great difficulties and great conflicts. Pity me: I assure you that it requires more courage to support the condition in which I am placed than to encounter a pitched battle. And the more so that I do not deceive myself, and that I see nothing but misery in the want of energy shown by some, and the evil designs of others. My God! is it possible that, endowed as I am with force of character, and feeling as I do so thoroughly the blood which runs in my veins, I should yet be destined to pass my days in such an age and with such men! But, for all this, never believe that my courage is deserting me. Not for my own sake, but for the sake of my child, I will support myself, and I will fulfill to the end my long and painful career, I can no longer see what I am writing. Farewell.[15]"

Tears, we may suppose, were blinding her eyes, in spite of all her fortitude. There was no exaggeration in her declaration to the Empress Catherine of Russia, with whom at this time she was in frequent communication, that the "distrust which was shown by all around them was a moral and continual death, a thousand times worse than that physical death which was a release from all miseries.[16]" And in the same letter she explains that to remove this distrust was one principal object which the king and she had in view in all their measures. Yet, in spite of all his concessions, the week was not to pass without fresh insults being offered to the king, which shocked even his phlegmatic apathy. The letter which he sent to the Assembly to announce his compliance with its wishes was indeed received with acclamations which, if not sincere, were at least loud, and apparently unanimous; and, as if in reply to it, La Fayette proposed and carried a motion that the Assembly should pass an act of amnesty for all political offenses; and a magnificent festival was appointed to be held in the Champ de Mars on the following Sunday, in celebration of the joyful event. But, after the first brief excitement had passed away, the Jacobin faction recovered its ascendency, and contrived to make that very festival, which was designed to express the gratitude of the nation, an occasion of further humiliation to the unhappy Louis. Every arrangement for the day was discussed in a spirit of the bitterest disloyalty. When the question was raised, which in any other Assembly that ever met in the world would have been thought needless, what attitude the members were to preserve while the king was taking the prescribed oath to observe the Constitution, a hundred voices shouted out that they should all keep their seats, and that the king should swear, standing and bare-headed; and when one deputy of high reputation, M. Malouet, remonstrated against such a vote, arguing that so to treat the chief of the State would be a greater insult to the nation than even to himself, a deputy from Brittany cried out that M. Malouet and those who thought with him might receive Louis on their knees, if they liked, but that the rest of the Assembly should be seated.

And, in accordance with the feeling thus shown, every mark of respect was studiously withheld from the unhappy monarch, and every care was taken to show him that every deputy considered himself his equal. Two chairs exactly similar were provided for him and for the president; and when, after taking the oath and affixing his signature to the act, the king resumed his seat, the president, who, having to reply to him in a short address, had at first risen for that purpose, on seeing that Louis retained his seat, sat down beside him, and finished his speech in that position. Louis felt the affront. He contained himself while in the hall, and while the members were conducting him back to the palace, which they presently did amidst the music of military bands and the salutes of artillery. But when his escort had left him, and he reached his own apartments, his pride gave way. The queen with the dauphin had been present in a box hastily fitted up for her, and had followed him back. He felt for her more than for himself. Bursting into tears, he said, "It is all over. You have seen my humiliation. Why did I ever bring you into France for such degradation?" And the queen, while endeavoring to console him, turned to Madame de Campan, who has recorded the scene, and dismissed her from her attendance.[17] "Leave us," she said, "leave us to ourselves." She could not bear that even that faithful servant should remain to be a witness to the despair and prostration of her sovereign.

The very rejoicings were turned by the agents of the Jacobins into occasions for further outrages. The whole city was illuminated, and the sovereigns yielded to the entreaties of the popular leaders, to drive through the streets and the Champs Elysees to see the illumination. The populace, who believed the Revolution at an end and their freedom secured, cheered them heartily as they passed; but at every cry of "Vive le roi," a stentorian voice, close to the royal carriage, shouted out, "Not so: Vive la nation!" and the queen, though it was plain that the ruffian had been hired thus to outrage them, almost fainted with terror at his ferocity. A few days afterward, the insults were renewed even more pointedly. The royal family went in state to the opera, where, before their arrival, the Jacobins had packed the pit with a gang of their own hirelings, whose unpowdered hair made them conspicuous objects.[18] The opera was one of Gretry's, "Les Evenements Imprevus," in which one of the duets contains the line "Ah, comme j'aime ma maitresse." Madame Dugazon, a popular singer of the day, as she uttered the words, bowed toward the royal box, and instantly the whole pit was in a fury. "No mistress for us! no master! Liberty!" The whole house was in an uproar. The king's partisans and adherents replied with loyal cheers, "Vive le roi! Vive la reine!" The pit roared out, "No master! no queen!" and the Jacobins even proceeded to acts of violence toward all who refused to join in their cry. Blows were struck, and it became necessary to send for a company of the Guard to restore order.

Yet when, on the last day of the month, the king visited the Assembly[19] to declare its dissolution, the president addressed him in terms of the most loyal gratitude, affirming that by his acceptance of the Constitution, he had earned the blessings of all future generations; and when he quitted the hall, the populace escorted the royal carriage back to the palace with vociferous cheers. Though, in the eyes of impartial observers, this display of returning good-will was more than counterbalanced when, as the members of the Assembly came out, some of the Royalists and Constitutionalists were hooted, and some of the fiercest Jacobins were greeted with still more enthusiastic acclamations.

CHAPTER XXXIII.

Composition of the New Assembly.--Rise of the Girondins,--Their Corruption and Eventual Fate.--Vergniaud's Motions against the King.--Favorable Reception of the King at the Assembly, and at the Opera.--Changes in the Ministry.--The King's and Queen's Language to M. Bertrand de Moleville.-- The Count de Narbonne.--Petion is elected Mayor of Paris.--Scarcity of Money, and Great Hardships of the Royal Family.--Presents arrive from Tippoo Sahib.--The Dauphin.--The Assembly passes Decrees against the Priests and the Emigrants.--Misconduct of the Emigrants.--Louis refuses his Assent to the Decrees.--He issues a Circular condemning Emigration.

The new Assembly met on the 1st of October, and its composition afforded the Royalists, or even the Constitutionalists, the party that desired to stand by the Constitution which had just been ratified, very little prospect of a re-establishment of tranquillity. The mischievous effect of the vote which excluded members of the last Assembly from election was seen in the very lists of those who had been returned. In the whole number there were scarcely a dozen members of noble or gentle birth; the number of ecclesiastics was equally small; while property was as little represented as the nobility or the Church. It was reckoned that of the whole body scarcely fifty possessed two thousand francs a year. The general youth of the members was as conspicuous as their poverty; half of them had hardly attained middle age; a great many were little more than boys. The Jacobins themselves, who, before the elections, had reckoned on swaying their decisions by terror, could hardly have anticipated a result which would place the entire body so wholly at their mercy.

But what was still move ominous of evil was the rise of a new party, known as that of the Girondins, from the circumstance of some of its most influential members coming from the Gironde, one of the departments which the late Assembly had carved out of the old province of Gascony. It was not absolutely a new party, since the foundations of it had been laid, during the last two months of the old Assembly, by Petion and a low-born pamphleteer named Brissot, who, as editor of a newspaper to which he gave the name of *Le Patriote Francais*, rivaled the most blood-thirsty of the Jacobins in exciting the worst passions of the populace. But Petion and Brissot had only sown the seeds. The opening of the new Assembly at once gave it growth and vigor, when the deputies from the Gironde plunged into the arena of debate, and showed an undeniable superiority in eloquence to every other party. The chiefs, Vergniaud, Gensonne, and Gaudet, were lawyers who had never obtained any practice. Isnard, the first man to make an open profession of atheism in the Assembly, was the son of a perfumer in Provence. They were adventurers as utterly without principle as without resources. And their first thought appears to have been to make money of the king's difficulties, and to sell themselves to him. They applied to the Minister of the Interior, M. de Lessart, proposing to place the whole of their influence at the service of the Government, on condition of his securing each of them a pension of six thousand francs a month.[1] M. de Lessart would not have objected to buy them, but he thought the price which they set upon themselves too high; and as they adhered to their demand, the negotiation went off, and they resolved to revenge themselves on his royal master with all the malice of disappointed rapacity.

As none of them had any force of character, they fell under the influence of the wife of one of their number, a small manufacturer, named Roland, the same who, as we have already seen, was the first to raise the cry of blood in France, and to recommend the assassination of the king and queen while they were still in fancied security at Versailles. Under the direction of this fierce woman, whose ferocity was rendered more formidable by her undoubted talents, the Girondins began an internecine war with the king, who had refused them the wages which they had asked. They planned and carried out the sanguinary attacks on the palace in the summer of the next year. They brought Louis to the scaffold by the unanimity of their votes. Yet it would have been more fortunate for themselves as well as for him had they been less exorbitant in their demands, and had they connected themselves with the Government as they desired. For though they succeeded in their treason, though

Madame Roland saw the accomplishment of her wish in the murder of the king and queen, their success was equally fatal to themselves. Almost all of them perished on the same scaffold to which they had consigned their virtuous sovereigns, meeting a fate in one respect worse even than theirs, from the infamy of the names which they have left behind them.

Yet for a few days it seemed as if their malignity would miss its aim. They did not wait a single day before displaying it; but, at the preliminary meeting of the Assembly, before it was opened for the dispatch of business, Vergniaud proposed to declare it illegal to speak of the king as his majesty, or to address him as "sire;" while another deputy, named Couthon, who at first belonged to the same party, though he afterward joined the Jacobins, carried a motion that, when Louis came to open the Assembly, the president should occupy the place of honor, and the second seat should be allotted to the sovereign.

Still, for a moment it seemed as if they had overshot their mark, and as if the more loyal party would be able to withstand and defeat them. The Assembly itself was compelled to repeal its recent votes, since Louis, whom indignation for once inspired with greater firmness than he usually displayed, refused to open the new Assembly in person unless he were to be received with the honors to which his rank entitled him. The offensive resolutions were canceled; and, when he had therefore opened the session in a dignified and conciliatory speech which was chiefly of his own composition, the president, M. Pastoret, a member of the Constitutional party, replied in a language which was not only respectful, but affectionate. The Constitution, he said, had given the king friends in those who were formerly only styled his subjects. The Assembly and the nation felt the need of his love. As the Constitution had rendered him the greatest monarch in the world, so his attachment to it would place him among the kings most beloved by their people.

And it seemed as if the Parisians in general shared to the full the loyal sentiments uttered by M. Pastoret. Writing the same week to her brother, Marie Antoinette, with a confidence which could only spring from a sincere attachment to the whole nation, reiterated her old opinion that "the good citizens and good people had always in their hearts been friendly to the king and herself;[2]" and expressed her belief that since the acceptance of the Constitution the people "had again learned to trust them." She was "far from giving herself up to a blind confidence. She knew that the disaffected had not abandoned their treasonable purposes; but, as the king and she herself were resolved to unite themselves in sincere good faith to the people, it was impossible but that, when their real feelings were known, the bulk of the people should return to them. The mischief was that the well-meaning knew not how to act in concert."

It did seem as if she were correct in her estimate of the feelings of the citizens, when, in the evening of the day on which Louis had opened the Assembly, the whole royal family, including the two children, went to the opera; and, as if with express design to ratify the loyal language of the president of the Assembly, the whole audience greeted them with a most enthusiastic reception. More than once they interrupted the performance with loud cheers for both king and queen; and as the pleasure of children is always an attractive sight, they sympathized especially with the delight of the little dauphin, their future king, as they all then thought him, who, being new to such a spectacle, only took his eyes off the stage to imitate the gestures of the actors to his mother, and draw her attention to them.

In more than one of her letters the queen had vehemently deplored the want of a stronger ministry than of late had been in the king's service. It was a natural complaint, though in fact the ability or want of ability displayed by the ministers was a matter of but slight practical importance, so completely had the Assembly engrossed the whole power of the State; but in the course of the autumn some changes were made, one of which for a time certainly added to the comfort of the sovereigns. M. Montmorin retired; M. de Lessart was transferred to his office; and M. Bertrand de Moleville, who was entirely new to official life, became the minister of marine. The whole kingdom did not contain a man more attached to the king and queen. But he combined statesman-like prudence with his loyalty; and his conduct before he took office elicited a very remarkable proof of the singleness of mind and purpose with which the king and queen had accepted the Constitution. M. Bertrand had previously refused office, and was very unwilling to take it now; and he frankly told Louis that he could not hope to be of any real service to him unless he knew the plans which the king might have formed with respect to the Constitution, and the line of conduct which he desired his ministers to observe on the subject; and Louis told him distinctly that though "he was far from regarding the Constitution as a masterpiece, and though he thought it easy to reform it advantageously in many particulars, yet he had sworn to observe it as it was, and that he was bound to be, and resolved to be, strictly faithful to his oath; the more so because it seemed to him that the most exact observance of the Constitution was the surest method to lead the nation to understand it in all its bearings; when the people themselves would perceive the character of the changes in it which it was desirable to make."

M. Bertrand expressed his warm approval of the wisdom of such a policy, but thought it so important to know how far the queen coincided in her husband's sentiments that he ventured to put the question to his majesty. The king assured him that he had been speaking her sentiments as well as his own, and that he should hear them from her own lips; and accordingly the queen immediately granted the new minister an audience, in which, after expressing, with her habitual grace and kindness, her feeling that, by accepting office at such a time, he was laying both the king and herself under a personal obligation, she added, "The king has explained to you his intentions with respect to the Constitution; do not you think that the only plan for him to follow is to be faithful to his oath?" "Undoubtedly, madame." "Well, you may depend upon it that nothing will make us change. Have courage, M. Bertrand; I hope that, with patience, firmness, and consistency, all is not yet lost.[3]"

Nor was M. Bertrand the only one of the ministers who received proofs of the resolution of the queen to adhere steadily to the Constitution. There was also a new minister of war, the Count de Narbonne, as firmly attached to the persons of the sovereigns as M. Bertrand himself, though in political principle more inclined to the views of the Constitutionalists than to those of the extreme Royalists. He was likewise a man of considerable capacity, eloquent and fertile in resources; but he was ambitious and somewhat vain; and he was so elated at the approval expressed by the Assembly of a report on the military resources of the kingdom which he laid before it soon after his appointment, that he obtained an audience of the queen, the object of which was to convince her that the only means of saving the State was to confer on a man of talent, energy, sagacity, and activity, who enjoyed the confidence of the Assembly and of the nation, the post of prime minister; and he admitted that he intended to designate himself by this description. Marie Antoinette, though fully aware of the desirableness of having a single man of ability and firmness at the head of the administration, was for a moment surprised out of her habitual courtesy. She could not forbear a smile, and in plain terms asked him "if he were crazy.[4]" But she proceeded with her usual kindness to explain to him the impracticability of the scheme which he had suggested, and the foundation of her argument was an explanation that such an appointment would be a violation of the Constitution, which forbade the king to create any new ministerial office. And the count deserves to have it mentioned to his honor that the rebuff which he had received in no degree cooled his attachment to the king and queen, or the zeal with which he labored for their service.

We have no information how far the new minister coincided in a step which the queen took in the course of November, and which is commonly ascribed to her judgment alone. Before its dissolution, the late Assembly had broken up the National Guard of Paris into separate legions, and had suppressed the appointment of commander-in-chief of the forces; and La Fayette, whom this measure had left without employment, feeling keenly the diminution of his importance, and instigated by the restlessness common to men of moderate capacity, conceived the hope of succeeding Bailly in the mayoralty of Paris, which that magistrate was on the point of resigning.

It had become a post of great consequence, since the extent to which the authority of the crown had been pared away tended to make the mayor the absolute dictator of the capital; and consequently the Jacobins were anxious to secure the office for one of the extreme Revolutionary party, and set up Petion as a rival candidate. The election belonged to the citizens, and, as in the city the two parties possessed almost equal strength, it was soon seen that the court, which had by no means lost its influence among the tradesmen and shop-keepers, had the power of deciding the contest in favor of the candidate for whom it should pronounce, Marie Antoinette declared for Petion. She knew him to be a Jacobin,[5] but he was so devoid of any reputation for ability that she did not fear him. Nor, except that he had behaved with boorish disrespect and ill-manners during their melancholy return from Varennes, had she any reason for suspecting him of any special enmity to the king.

But La Fayette, though always loud in his professions of loyalty, had never lost an opportunity of offering personal insults to both the king and herself. It was to his shameful neglect (to put his conduct in the most favorable light) that she justly attributed the danger to which she had been exposed at Versailles, and the compulsion which had been put upon the king to take up his residence in Paris; and, not to mention a constant series of petty insults which he had heaped on both Louis and herself, and on the Royalists as a body, he had given unmistakable proofs of his personal animosity toward the king by his conduct on the 21st of June, and by the indecent rigor with which he treated them both after their return from Varennes. Even when he was loudest in the profession of his desire and power to influence the Assembly in the king's favor, one of his own friends had told him to his face that he was insincere,[6] and that Louis could not and ought not to trust his promises; and every part of his conduct toward the royal pair was stamped with duplicity as well as with ill-will. It was not strange, therefore, indeed it was fully consistent with the honest openness of Marie Antoinette's own character, that she should prefer an open enemy to a pretended friend. She even believed what, from the very commencement of the Revolution, many had suspected, that La Fayette cherished views of personal ambition, and aimed at reviving the old authority of a Maire du Palais over a Roi Faineant[7]. She therefore directed her friends to throw their weight into the scale in favor of Petion, who was accordingly elected by a great majority, while the marquis, greatly chagrined, retired for a time to his estate in Auvergne.

The victory, however, was an unfortunate one for the court. It contributed to increase the confidence of its enemies; and, as their instinct showed them that it was from the resolution of the queen that they had the most formidable opposition to dread, it was against her that, from their first entrance into the Assembly, Vergniaud and his friends specially exerted themselves; Vergniaud openly contending that the inviolability of the sovereign, which was an article of the new Constitution, applied only to the king himself, and in no degree to his consort; while in the Jacobin and Cordelier Clubs the coarsest libels were poured forth against her with unremitting perseverance to stimulate and justify the most obscene and ferocious threats. The coarsest ruffians in a street quarrel never used fouler language of one another than these men of education applied to the pure-minded and magnanimous lady whose sole offense was that she was the wife of their kind-hearted king.

And, in addition to this daily increase of their danger which such denunciations could not fail to augment, the royal family were now suffering inconveniences which even those whose measures had caused them had never designed. They were in the most painful want of money. The agitation of the last two years had rendered the treasury bankrupt. The paper money, which now composed almost the whole circulation of the country, was valueless. While, as it was in this paper money (assignats, as the notes were called, as being professedly secured by assignments on the royal domains and on the ecclesiastical property which had been confiscated), that the king's civil list was paid, at the latter end of each month it was not uncommon for him and the queen to be absolutely destitute. It was with great reluctance that they accepted loans from their loyal adherents, because they saw no prospect of being able to repay them; but had they not availed themselves of this resource, they would at times have wanted absolute necessaries.[8]

The royal couple still kept their health, the king's apathy being in this respect as beneficial as the queen's courage: they still rode a great deal when the weather was favorable; and on one occasion, at the beginning of 1792, the queen, with her sister-in-law and her daughter, went again to the theatre. The opera was the same which had been performed at the visit in October; but this time the Jacobins had not been forewarned so as to pack the house, and Madame du Gazon's duet was received with enthusiasm. Again, as she sung "Ah, que j'aime ma maitresse!" she bowed to the royal box, and the audience cheered. As if in reply to one verse, "Il faut les rendre heureux," "Oui, oui!" with lively unanimity, came from all parts of the house, and the singers were compelled to repeat the duet four times. "It is a queer nation this of ours," says the Princess Elizabeth, in relating the scene to one of her correspondents, "but we must allow that it has very charming moments.[9]"

A somewhat curious episode to divert their minds from these domestic anxieties was presented by an embassy from the brave and intriguing Sultan of Mysore, the celebrated Tippoo Sahib, who sought to engage Louis to lend him six thousand French troops, with whose aid he trusted to break down the ascendency which England was rapidly establishing in India. Tippoo backed his request, in the Oriental fashion, by presents, though not such as, in the opinion of M. Bertrand, were quite worthy of the giver or of the receiver. To the king he sent some diamonds, but they were yellow, ill-cut, and ill-set; and the rest of the offering was composed of a few pieces of embroidered silk, striped cloth, and cambric: while the queen's present consisted of nothing more valuable than a few bottles of perfume of no very exquisite quality, and a few boxes of powdered scents, pastils, and matches. The king and queen gave nearly the whole present to M. Bertrand for his grandchildren, the queen only reserving a bottle of attar of rose and a couple of pieces of cambric; and that chiefly to afford a pretext for seeing M. Bertrand once or twice, without his reception being imputed to a desire to promote some Austrian intrigue; for the Jacobins had lately revived the clamor against Austrian influence with greater vehemence than ever.

As M. Bertrand had grandchildren, he could well appreciate the pleasure of the queen at an incident which closed one of his audiences. While he was thus receiving her commands, the little dauphin, "beautiful as an angel," as the minister describes him, was capering about the room in high delight, brandishing a wooden sword, a new toy which had just been given him. An attendant called him to go to supper; and he bounded toward the door. "How is this, my boy?" said Marie Antoinette, calling him back; "are you going off without making M. Bertrand a bow?" "Oh, mamma," said the little prince, still skipping about, and smiling, "that is because I know well that M. Bertrand is one of our friends.... Good-evening, M. Bertrand." "Is not he a nice child?[10]" said the queen, after he had left the room. "He is very happy to be so young. He does not feel what we suffer, and his gayety does us good." Alas! that which was now perhaps her only pleasure--the contemplation of her child's opening grace and amiability--before long became even an addition to her affliction, as the probabilities increased that the madness of the people and the wickedness of their leaders would deprive him of the inheritance, to preserve which to him was the principal object of all her cares and exertions.

But these moments of gratification were becoming fewer as time went on. Each month, each week brought fresh and increasing anxieties to engross all her thoughts. As the Girondin leaders began to feel their strength, the votes of the Assembly became more violent. One day it passed a fresh decree against the priests, depriving all who refused to take the oath to the new ecclesiastical constitution of the stipends for which their former preferments had been commuted, placing them under strict supervision, and declaring them liable to instant banishment if they should venture to exercise their functions in private. Another day it vented its wrath upon the emigrants, summoning the Count de Provence by name to return at once to France; and, with respect to the rest of the body, now very numerous, declaring their conduct in being assembled on the frontier of the kingdom in a state of readiness for war in itself an act of treason; and condemning to death and confiscation of their estates all who should fail to return to their native land before a stated day.

But in these decrees the advocates of violence had for the moment gone too far--they had outrun the feelings of the nation. The emigrants, indeed, neither deserved nor found sympathy in any quarter. The main body of them was at this time settled at Coblentz, where their conduct was such that it is hard to say whether it were more offensive to their country, more injurious to their king, or more discreditable to themselves. They could not even act in harmony. The king's two brothers established rival courts, with a mistress at the head of each. Madame de Balbi still ruled the Count de Provence; Madame de Polastron was the presiding genius of the coterie of the Count d'Artois. The two ladies, regarding each other with bitter jealousy, agitated the whole town with their rivalries and wranglings, and agreed in nothing but in their endeavors to excite some foreign sovereign or other to make war upon their native land. It was in vain that Louis himself first entreated them, and, when he found his entreaties were disregarded, commanded his brothers to return. They positively refused obedience to his order, telling him, in language which can only be characterized as that of studied insult, that he was writing under coercion; that his letter did not express his real views, and that "their honor, their duty, even their affection for him, alike forbade them to obey him.[11]" The queen could not command, but she wrote to them more than one letter of most earnest entreaty, and, as the princes founded part of their hopes on the co-operation of the Northern sovereigns, she wrote also to the empress and to Gustavus, pressing both, and especially the King of Sweden,[12] to restrain them; but they were too headstrong and full of their own projects to listen to her entreaties any more than to the king's commands, and did not even take the trouble to conceal their negotiations with foreign powers, nor their object, which could be nothing but war.

It was impossible that such conduct steadily pursued by the king's own brothers could be any thing but most pernicious to his cause. It could not fail to excite suspicions of his own good faith. It supplied the Jacobins with pretexts for putting fresh restraints on his authority; and it frightened even the Constitutionalists, since it was plain that civil war must ensue, with, very probably, the addition of foreign war also, if these machinations of the emigrants were not suppressed.

Still, these sweeping proscriptions of entire classes were not yet to the taste of the nation. Petitions from the country, and even one from the department of the Seine, were presented to Louis, begging him to refuse his assent to the decree against the priests; and the feeling which they represented was so strong, and the reputation of some of the petitioners stood so high for ability and influence, that the ministers believed that he could safely refuse his sanction to both the votes. Even without their advice he would have rejected the decree against the priests, as one absolutely incompatible with his reverence for religion and its ministers; and his conduct on this subject supplies one more striking parallel to the history of the great English rebellion; since there can hardly be a more precise resemblance between events occurring in different ages and different countries than is afforded by the resistance made by Charles to the last vote of the London Parliament against the bishops, and this resistance of Louis to the will of the Assembly on behalf of the priests, and by the fatal effect which, in each case, their conscientious and courageous determination had upon the fortunes of the two sovereigns.

Louis therefore put his veto on both the decrees, with the exception of that clause in the act against the emigrants which summoned his brothers to return to the kingdom. But, that no one might pretend to fancy that he either approved of the conduct of the emigrants or sympathized with their principles or designs, he issued a circular letter to the governors of the different sea-ports, in which he remonstrated most earnestly with the sailors, numbers of whom, as it was reported in Paris, were preparing to follow their example. He pointed out in it that those who thus deserted their country mistook their duty to that country, to him as their king, and to themselves; that the present aspect of the nation, desirous to return to order and to submission to the law, removed every pretext for such conduct. He set before them his own example, and bid them remain at their posts, as he was remaining at his; and, in language more impressive than that of command, he exhorted them not to turn a deaf ear to his prayers; and at the same time he addressed letters to the electors of Treves and Mayence, and to the other petty German princes whose territories, bordering on the Rhine, were the principal resort of the emigrants, requiring them to cease to give them shelter, and announcing that if they should refuse to remove them from their dominions he should consider their refusal a sufficient ground for war; while, to show that he did not intend this menace to be a dead letter, he soon afterward announced to the Assembly that he had ordered a powerful army of a hundred and fifty thousand men to be moved toward the frontier, under the command of Marshal Luckner, Marshal Rochambeau, and General La Fayette, and he invited the members to vote a levy of fifty thousand more men to raise the force of the nation to its full complement.

CHAPTER XXXIV.

Death of Leopold.--Murder of Gustavus of Sweden.--Violence of Vergniaud.
--The Ministers resign.--A Girondin Ministry is appointed.--Character of
Dumouriez.--Origin of the Name Sans-culottes.--Union of Different Parties
against the Queen.--War is declared against the Empire.--Operations in the
Netherlands.--Unskillfulness of La Fayette.--The King falls into a State of
Torpor.--Fresh Libels on the Queen.--Barnave's Advice.--Dumouriez has
an Audience of the Queen.--Dissolution of the Constitutional Guard.-- for-
mation of a Camp near Paris.--Louis adheres to his Refusal to assent to the
Decree against the Priests.--Dumouriez resigns his Office, and takes command of the Army.

War of some kind--foreign war, civil war, or both combined--had apparently become inevitable; and Marie Antoinette deceived herself
if she thought that the armed congress of sovereigns, for which she
was above all things anxious, could lead to any other result. In any
ease, a congress must have produced one consequence which she deprecated as
much as any other, a waste of time, while, as she truly said, her enemies never wasted a moment. Nor, with the very different views of the policy to be pursued, which
the emperor and the King of Prussia entertained (Frederick being an advocate of
an armed intervention in the affairs of France, which Leopold opposed as impracticable, and, if practicable, impolitic), was it easy to see how a congress could have
brought those monarchs to agree on any united system of action. But all projects of
that kind necessarily fell to the ground in consequence of the death of the emperor,
which took place, after a very short illness, on the 1st of March, 1792; and before
the end of the same month the royal family lost another warm friend in Gustavus
of Sweden, who was assassinated in the very midst of preparations which he confi-

dently hoped might contribute to deliver his brother sovereign from his troubles.

Marie Antoinette spoke truly when she said that the enemies of the crown never lost time. The very prospect of war increased the divisions of the Assembly, since the Jacobins were undisguisedly averse to it. Not one of their body had any reputation for skill in arms, so that in the event of war it was evident that the chief commands, both in army and navy, must be conferred on persons unconnected with them; while the Girondins, though, as far as was yet known, equally destitute of members possessed of any military ability, looked on war as favorable to their designs, whatever might be the issue of a campaign. They were above all things eager for the destruction of the monarchy, and they reckoned that if the French army were victorious, its success would disable those who were most willing and might be most able to support the throne; while, if the enemy should prevail, it would be easy to represent their triumph as the fruit of the mismanagement, if not of the treachery, of the king's generals and ministers; and the opposition of these two parties was at this time so notorious that the queen thought it favorable to the king, since each would be eager to preserve him as a possible ally against its adversaries. It is for her husband's and her child's safety that she expresses anxiety, never for her own. With respect to herself her uniform language is that of fearlessness. She does not for a moment conceal from her correspondents her sense of the dangers which surround her. She has not only open hostility to fear, but treachery, which is far worse; and she declares that "a perpetual imprisonment in a solitary tower on the sea-shore would be a less cruel fate than that which she daily endures from the wickedness of her enemies and the weakness of her friends. Every thing menaces an inevitable catastrophe; but she is prepared for every thing. She has learned from her mother not to fear death. That may as well come to-day as to-morrow. She only fears for her dear children, and for those she loves; and high among those whom she loves she places her sister-in-law Elizabeth, who is always an angel aiding her to support her sorrows, and who, with her poor, dear children, never quits her.[1]"

A long continuance of sorrows and fears, such as had now for nearly three years pressed upon the writer of this letter, would so wear away and break down ordinary souls that, when a crisis came, they would be found wholly unequal to grapple with it; and we may therefore the better form some idea of the strength of mind and almost superhuman fortitude of this admirable queen, if, from time to time, we fix our attention on these not exaggerated complaints, for indeed the misfortunes that elicited them admit of no exaggeration; and then remember that, after so long a period of such uninterrupted suffering, her spirit was so far from being broken, that, as increasing dangers and horrors thickened around her, her courage seemed to increase also. Her faithful attendant, Madame de Campan, has remarked that her troubles had not even affected her temper; that no one ever saw her out of humor. In every respect, to the very last, she showed herself superior to the utmost malice of her enemies.

The news of the death of Leopold, whose son and successor, Francis, was but three-and-twenty years of age, gave fresh encouragement to his sister's enemies. The intelligence had hardly reached Paris when Vergniaud began to prepare the way for a fresh assault on the crown by a denunciation of the ministers, while the Jacobins and Cordeliers made an open attack upon another club which the Constitutionalists had lately formed under the name of Les Feuillants, holding its meetings in a convent of the Monks of St. Bernard,[2] and closed it by main force. Though several soldiers, and La Fayette among them, were members of the Feuillants, they made no resistance; they only applied to Petion, as mayor of the city, for protection; and that worthy magistrate refused them aid, telling them that though the law forbade them to be attacked, the voice of the people was against them, and to that voice he was bound to listen.

The ministers fell before Vergniaud, and the unhappy king had no resource but to choose their successors from the party which had triumphed over them. The absurd law by which the last Assembly had excluded its members from office was still in force, so that the orator himself and his colleagues could obtain no personal promotion; but they were able to nominate the new ministers, who, with but one exception, were all men equally devoid of ability and reputation, and therefore were the better fitted to be the tools of those to whom they owed their preferment. The names of three were Lacoste, Degraves, and Duranton, of whom nothing beyond their names is known. A fourth was Roland, who was indeed known, though not for any abilities of his own, but as the husband of the woman who, as has been already mentioned, was the first person in the whole nation to raise the cry for the murder of the king and queen, and whose fierce thirst for blood so predominated over every other feeling that a few weeks afterward she even began to urge the assassination of the only one among her husband's colleagues who was possessed of the slightest ability because his views did not altogether coincide with her own.

General Dumouriez, whom she thus honored by singling him out for her especial hatred, was an exception to his colleagues in several points. He was a man of middle age, who enjoyed a good reputation, not only for military skill, but also for diplomatic sagacity and address, earned as far back as the latter years of the preceding reign; and he was so far from being originally imbued with revolutionary principles that, when, in the summer of 1789, a mutinous spirit first appeared among the troops in Paris, he volunteered to place his services at the king's disposal, recommending measures of vigor and resolution, which, if they had been adopted, might have quelled the spirit of rebellion, and have changed the whole subsequent history of the nation. But as Necker had rejected Mirabeau a few weeks before, so he also rejected Dumouriez; and discontent at the treatment which he received from the minister, and which seemed to prove that active employment, of which he was desirous, could only be obtained through some other influence, drove the general into the ranks of the Revolutionary party. He now accepted the post of foreign secretary in the new ministry; but the connection with the enemies of the monarchy was uncongenial to his taste; and, after a short time, the frequent intercourse with Louis, which was the necessary consequence of his appointment, and the conviction of the king's perfect honesty and patriotism which this intercourse forced upon him, revived his old feelings of loyalty, and, so long as he remained in office, he honestly endeavored to avert the evils which he foresaw, and to give the advice and to support the policy by which, in his honest belief, it was alone possible for Louis to preserve his authority.

Dumouriez was a gentleman in birth and manners; but his colleagues had so little of either the habits or appearance of decent society that the attendants on the royal family gave them the name of the Sans-culottes; and this name, meant originally to describe the absence of the ordinary court dress, without which no previous ministers had ever ventured to appear in the presence of royalty, was presently adopted as a distinctive title by the whole body of the extreme revolutionists, who knew the value of a name under which to bind their followers together.[3]

The attacks on the ministry were accompanied with more direct attacks on the king and queen themselves than had ever been ventured on in the former Assembly.

By this time the system of espial and treachery by which they were surrounded had become so systematic that they could not even send a messenger to their nephew, the emperor, except under a feigned name;[4] and the Baron de Breteuil, who announced his mission to Francis, reported to him at the same time that the chiefs of the Assembly were proposing to pass votes suspending the "king from his functions, and to separate the queen from him on the ground that an impeachment was to be presented against both, as having solicited the late emperor to form a confederacy among the great powers of Europe in favor of the royal prerogative." The queen was, in fact, now, as always, more the object of their hatred than her husband, and toward the end of March a reconciliation of all her enemies took place, that the attack upon her might be combined with a strength that should insure its success. The Marquis de Condorcet, a man of some eminence in philosophy, as the word had been understood since the reign of the Encyclopedists, and closely connected with the Girondins, though not formally enrolled in their party, gave a supper, at which the Duc d'Orleans formally reconciled himself to La Fayette; and both, in company with Brissot and the Abbe Sieyes, who of late had scarcely been heard of, drew up an indictment against the queen.[5] Their malignity even went the length of resolving to separate the dauphin from his mother, on the plea of providing for his education; but the means which the Girondins took to secure their triumph for the moment defeated them. La Fayette did not keep the secret. One of his friends gave information to the king of the plot that was in contemplation, and the next day the Constitutionalists mustered in the Assembly in such strength that neither Girondins nor Jacobins dared bring forward the infamous proposal.

But Louis and Marie Antoinette reasonably regarded the attack on them as only postponed, not as defeated or abandoned. They began to prepare for the worst. They burned most of their papers, and removed into the custody of friends whom they could trust those which they regarded as too valuable to destroy; and at the same time they sent notice to their partisans to cease writing to them. They could neither venture to send nor to receive letters. They believed that at this time the plan of their enemies was to terrify them into repeating their attempt to escape; an attempt of which the espial and treachery with which they were surrounded would have insured the failure, but which would have given the Jacobins a pretext for their trial and condemnation. But this scheme they could themselves defeat by remaining at their posts. Patience and courage was their only possible defense, and with those qualities they were richly endowed.

A vital difference of principle distinguished the old from the new ministry: the former had wished to preserve, the majority of the latter were resolved to destroy, the throne; and the means by which each sought to attain its end were as diametrically opposite as the ends themselves. Bertrand and De Lessart, the ministers who, in the late administration, had enjoyed most of the king and queen's confidence, had been studious to preserve peace, believing that policy to be absolutely essential for the safety of Louis himself. Because they entertained the same opinion, the new ministers were eager for war; and, unhappily Dumouriez, in spite of his desire to uphold the throne, was animated by the same feeling. His own talents and tastes were warlike, and his office enabled him to gratify them in this instance. For the conciliatory tone which De Lessart had employed toward the Imperial Government, he now substituted a language not only imperious, but menacing. Prince Kaunitz, who still presided over the administration at Vienna, attached though he was to the system of policy which he had inaugurated under Maria Teresa, could not avoid replying in a similar strain, until at last, on the 20th of April, Louis, sorely against his will, was compelled to announce to the Assembly that all his efforts for the preservation of peace had failed, and to propose an instant declaration of war.

The declaration was voted with enthusiasm; but for some time it brought nothing but disaster. The campaign was opened in the Netherlands, where the Austrians, taken by surprise, were so weak in numbers that it seemed certain that they would be driven from the country without difficulty or delay. Marshal Beaulieu, their commander-in-chief, had scarcely twenty thousand men, while the Count de Narbonne had left the French army in so good a condition that Degraves, his successor, was able to send a hundred and thirty thousand men against him; and Dumouriez furnished him with a plan for an invasion of the Netherlands, which, if properly carried out, would have made the French masters of the whole country in a few days. But the largest division of the army, to which the execution of the most important portions of the intended operations was intrusted, had been placed under the command of La Fayette, who proved equally devoid of resolution and of skill. Some of his regiments showed a disorderly and insubordinate temper. One battalion first mutinied and murdered some of its officers, and then disgraced itself by cowardice in the field. Another displayed an almost equal want of courage; and La Fayette, disheartened and perplexed, though the number of his troops still more than doubled those opposed to him, retreated into France, and remained there in a state of complete inactivity.

But, as has been said before, disaster was almost as favorable to the political views of the Girondins as success, while it added to the dangers of the sovereigns by encouraging the Jacobins, who were elated at the failure of a general so hateful to them as La Fayette. They now adopted a party emblem, a red cap; and the Duc d'Orleans and his son, the Duc de Chartres,[6] assumed it, and with studied insult paraded in it up and down the gardens of the palace, under the queen's windows; and if the two factions did not formally coalesce, they both proceeded with greater boldness than ever toward their desired object, not greatly differing as to the means by which it was to be attained.

The palace was now indeed a scene of misery. The king's apathy was degenerating into despair. At one time he was so utterly prostrated that he remained for ten days absolutely silent, never uttering a word except to name his throws when playing at backgammon with Elizabeth. At last the queen roused him from his torpor, throwing herself at his feet, and mingling caresses with her expostulations; entreating him to remember what he owed to his family, and reminding him that, if they must perish, it was better at least to perish with honor, and be king to the last, than to wait passively till assassins should come and murder them in their own rooms. She herself was in a condition in which nothing but her indomitable courage prevented her from utterly breaking down. Sleep had deserted her. By day she rarely ventured out-of-doors. Riding she had given up, and she feared to walk in the garden of the Tuileries, even in the little portion marked off for the dauphin's playground, lest she should expose herself to the coarse insults which, the basest of hirelings were ever on the watch to offer her.[7] She could not even venture to go openly to mass at Easter, but was forced to arrange for one of her chaplains to perform the service for her before daylight. Balked of their wish to offer her personal insults, her enemies redoubled their diligence in inventing and spreading libels. The demagogues of the Palais Royal revived the stories of her subservience to the interests of Austria, and even sent letters forged in her name to different members of the Assembly, inviting them to private conferences with her in the apartments of Madame de Lamballe. But she treated all such attacks with lofty disdain, and was even greatly annoyed when she learned that the chief of the police, with the king's sanction, had bought up a life of Madame La Mothe, in which that infamous woman pretended to give a true account of the affair of her necklace, and had had it burned in the manufactory of Sevres. She thought, with some reason, that to take a step which seemed to show a dread of such attacks was the surest way to encourage more of them, and that apparent indifference to them was the only line of action consistent with her innocence or with her dignity.

The increasing dangers of her position moved the pity of some who had once been her enemies, and sharpened their desire to serve her. Barnave, who probably overrated his present influence[8] in many letters pressed his advice upon her; of which the substance was that she should lay aside her distrust of the Constitutional-ist party, and, with the king, throw herself wholly on the Constitution, to which the nation was profoundly attached. He even admitted that it was not without defects; but held out a hope that, with the aid of the Royalists, he and his friends might be able to amend them, and in time to re-invest the throne with all necessary splendor. And the queen was so touched by his evident earnestness that she granted him an audience, and assured him of her esteem and confidence. Barnave was partly cor-rect in his judgment, but he overlooked one all-essential circumstance. There is no doubt that he spoke truly when he declared that the nation in general was attached to the Constitution; but he failed to give sufficient weight to the consideration that the Jacobins and Girondins were agreed in seeking to overthrow it, and that for that object they were acting with a concert and an energy to which he and his party were strangers.

Dumouriez too was equally earnest in his desire to serve the king and her, with far greater power to be useful than Barnave. He too was admitted to an audience, of which he has left us an account which, while it shows both his notions of the state of the country and of the rival parties, and also his own sincerity, is no less characteristic of the queen herself. Admitted to her presence, he found her, as he describes the interview, looking very red, walking up and down the room with im-petuous strides, in an agitation which presaged a stormy discussion. The different events which had taken place since the king in the preceding autumn had ratified the Constitution, the furious language held in, and the violent measures carried by, the Assembly, had evidently changed her belief in the possibility of attempting, even for a short time, to carry on the Government under the conditions imposed by that act. She came toward him with an air which was at once majestic and yet showed irritation, and said:

"You, sir, are all-powerful at this moment; but it is only by the favor of the people, which soon breaks its idols to pieces. Your existence depends on your conduct. You are said to have great talents. You must see that neither the king nor I can endure all these novelties nor the Constitution. I tell you this frankly. Now choose your side."

To this fervid apostrophe Dumouriez replied in a tone which he intended to combine a sorrowful tenderness with loyal respect:

"Madame," said he, "I am overwhelmed with the painful confidence which your majesty has reposed in me. I will not betray it; but I am placed between the king and the nation, and I belong to my country. Permit me to represent to you that the safety of the king, of yourself, and of your august children is bound up with the Constitution, as well as is the re-establishment of the king's legitimate authority. You are both surrounded with enemies who are sacrificing you to their own interests." The unfortunate queen, shocked as well as surprised at this opposition to her views, replied, raising her voice, "That will not last; take care of yourself." "Madame," replied he, in his turn, "I am more than fifty years old. My life has been passed in countless dangers, and when I took office I reflected deeply that its responsibility was not the greatest of its perils." "This was alone wanting," cried out the queen, with an accent of indignant grief, and as if astonished herself at her own vehemence.

"This alone was wanting to calumniate me! You seem to suppose that I am capable of causing you to be assassinated!" and she burst into tears. Dumouriez was as agitated as she was. "God forbid," he replied, "that I should do you such an injustice!" And he added some flattering expressions of attachment, such as he thought calculated to soothe a mind so proud, yet so crushed. And presently she calmed herself, and came up to him, putting her hand on his arm; and he resumed: "Believe me, madame, I have no object in deceiving you; I abhor anarchy and crime as much as you do. Believe me, I have experience; I am better placed than your majesty for judging of events. This is not a short-lived popular movement, as you seem to think. It is the almost unanimous insurrection of a great nation against inveterate abuses. There are great factions which fan this flame. In all factions there are many scoundrels and many madmen. In the Revolution I see nothing but the king and the entire nation. Every thing which tends to separate them tends to their mutual ruin: I am laboring as much as I can to reunite them. It is for you to help me. If I am an obstacle to your designs, and if you persist in thinking so, tell me so. and I will at once send in my resignation to the king, and will retire into a corner to grieve over the fate of my country and of you." And he concludes his narrative by expressing his belief that he had regained the queen's confidence by his frank explanation of his views, while he himself in his turn was evidently fascinated by the affability with which, after a brief further conversation, she dismissed him.[9] Though, if we may trust Madame de Campan, Marie Antoinette was not as satisfied as she had seemed to be, but declared that it was not possible for her to place confidence in his protestations when she recollected his former language and acts, and the party with which he was even now acting.

Madame de Campan probably gives a more correct report of the queen's feelings than the general himself, whom the consciousness of his own integrity of purpose very probably misled into believing that he had convinced her of it. But, though, if Marie Antoinette did listen to his professions and advice with some degree of mistrust, she undoubtedly did him less than justice: she can hardly be blamed for indulging such a feeling, when it is remembered in what an atmosphere of treachery she had lived for the last three years. Undoubtedly Dumouriez, though not a thorough-going Royalist like M. Bertrand, was not only in intention an honest and friendly counselor, but was by far the ablest adviser who had had access to her since the death of Mirabeau, and in one respect was a more judicious and trustworthy adviser than even that brilliant and fertile statesman; since he did not fall into the error of miscalculating what was practical, or of overrating his own influence with the Assembly or the nation.

Yet, had the king and queen adopted his views ever so unreservedly, it may well be doubted whether they would have averted or even deferred the fate which awaited them. The leaders of the two parties, before whose union they fell, had as little attachment to the new Constitution as the queen. The moment that they obtained the undisputed ascendency, they trampled it underfoot in every one of its provisions. Constitution or no Constitution, they were determined to overthrow the throne and to destroy those to whom it belonged; and to men animated with such a resolution it signified little what pretext might be afforded them by any actions of their destined victims. The wolf never yet wanted a plea for devouring the lamb.

One of the first fruits of the union between the Jacobins and the Girondins was the preparation of an insurrection. The Assembly did not move fast enough for them. It might be still useful as an auxiliary, but the lead in the movement the clubs assumed to themselves. Their first care was to deprive the king of all means of resistance, and with this view to get rid of the Constitutional Guard, the commander of which was still the gallant Duke de Brissac, a noble-minded and faithful adherent of Louis amidst all his distresses. But it was not easy to find any ground for disbanding a force which was too small to be formidable to any but traitors; and the pretext which was put forward was so preposterous that it could excite no feeling but that of amusement, if the object aimed at were not too serious and shocking for laughter. At Easter the dauphin had presented the mess of the regiment with a cake, one of the ornaments of which was a small white flag taken from among his own toys. Petion now issued orders to search the officers' quarters for this child's flag, and, when it was found, one of the Jacobin members was not ashamed to produce it to the Assembly as a proof that the court was meditating a counter- revolution and a massacre of the patriots, and to propose the instant dissolution of the Guard. The motion was carried, though some of the Constitutionalist party had the honesty to oppose it, as one which could have only regicide for its object; and Louis did not dare refuse it his assent.

He was now wholly disarmed. To render his defeat in the impending struggle more certain, one of the ministers, Servan, himself proposed a levy of twenty thousand fresh soldiers, to be stationed permanently at Paris, and this motion also was passed. Again Louis could not venture to withhold his sanction from the bill, though he comforted himself by dismissing the mover, with two of his colleagues, Roland and Claviere. Roland's dismissal had indeed become indispensable, since, on the preceding day, he had had the audacity to write him an insolent letter, composed by his ferocious wife, which in express terms threatened him with death "if he did not give satisfaction to the Revolution.[10]" Nor was Madame Roland inclined to be satisfied with the murder of the king and queen. As has been already mentioned, she at the same time urged upon her submissive husband the assassination of Dumouriez, who, having intelligence of her enmity, began in self-defense to connect himself with the Jacobins. On the dismissal of Roland and the others, he had exchanged the foreign port-folio for that of war, and was practically the prime minister, being in fact the only one whom Louis admitted to any degree of confidence; but this arrangement lasted less than a single week. Louis had yielded to and adopted his advice on every point but one. He had sanctioned the dismissal of the Constitutional Guard, and the formation of the new body of troops, which, no one doubted, was intended to be used against himself; but he was as firmly convinced as ever that his religious duty bound him to refuse his assent to the decree against the priests, and he refused to do a violence to his conscience, and to commit what he regarded as a sin. But this very decree was the one which Dumouriez regarded as the most dangerous one for him to reject, as being that which the Assembly was most firmly resolved to make law; and, as his most vigorous remonstrances failed to shake the king's resolution on this point, he resigned his post as a minister, and repaired to the Flemish frontier to take the command of the army, which greatly needed an able leader.

CHAPTER XXXV.

The Insurrection of June 20th.

Both Jacobins and Girondins felt that the departure of Dumouriez from Paris had removed a formidable obstacle from their path, and they at once began to hurry forward the preparations for their meditated insurrection. The general gave in his resignation on the 15th of June, and the 20th was fixed for an attack on the palace, by which its contrivers designed to effect the overthrow of the throne, if not the destruction of the entire royal family. It was organized with unusual deliberation. The meetings of conspirators were attended not only by the Girondin leaders, to whom Madame Roland had recently added a new recruit, a young barrister from the South, named Barbaroux, remarkable for his personal beauty, and, as was soon seen, for a pitiless hardness of heart, and energetic delight in deeds of cruelty that, even in that blood-thirsty company, was equaled by few; with them met all those as yet most notorious for ferocity--Danton and Legendre, the founders of the Cordeliers; Marat, daily, in his obscene and blasphemous newspaper, clamoring for wholesale bloodshed; Santerre, odious as the sanguinary leader of the very first outbreaks of the Revolution; Rotondo, already, as we have seen, detected in attempting to assassinate the queen; and Petion, who thus repaid her preference of him to La Fayette, which had placed him in the mayoralty, whose duties he was now betraying. Some, too, bore a part in the foul conspiracy as partisans of the Duc d'Orleans, who were generally understood to have instructions to be lavish of their master's gold, the vile prince hoping that the result of the outbreak would be the assassination of his cousin, and his own elevation to the vacant throne. In their speeches they gave Louis the name of Monsieur Veto, in allusion to the still legal exercise of his prerogative, by which he had sought to protect the priests;

while the queen was called Madame Veto, though in fact she had finally joined Dumouriez in urging her husband to give his royal assent to the decree against them, not, as thinking it on any pretense justifiable, but as believing, with the general, in the impossibility of maintaining its rejection. Yet nothing could more completely prove the absolute innocence and unimpeachable good faith of both king and queen than the act of his enemies in giving them this nickname; so clear an evidence was it that they could allege nothing more odious against them than the possession by Louis, in a most modified degree, of a prerogative which, without any modification at all, has in every country been at all times regarded as indispensable to, and inseparable from, royalty; and the exercise of it for the defense of a body of men of whom none could deny the entire harmlessness.

On the night of the 19th the appointed leaders of the different bands into which the insurgents were to be divided separated; the watch-word, "Destruction to the palace," was given out; and all Paris waited in anxious terror for the events of the morrow. Louis was as well aware as any of the citizens of the intended attack, and prepared for it as for death. On the afternoon of the 19th he wrote to his confessor to desire him to come to him at once. "He had never," he said, "had such need of his consolations. He had done with this world, and his thoughts were now fixed on Heaven alone. Great calamities were announced for the morrow; but he felt that he had courage to meet them." And after the holy man had left him, as he gazed on the setting sun he once more gave utterance to his forebodings. "Who can tell," said he, "whether it be not the last that I shall ever see?" The Royalists felt his danger almost as keenly as himself, but were powerless to prevent it by any means of their own. The Duke de Liancourt, who had some title to be listened to by the Revolutionary party, since no one had been more zealous in promoting the most violent measures of the first Assembly, pressed earnestly on Petion that his duty as mayor bound him to call out the National Guards, and so prevent the intended outbreak, but was answered by sarcasms and insults; while Vergniaud, from the tribune of the Assembly itself, dared to deride all who apprehended danger.

On the morning of the 20th, daylight had scarcely dawned when twenty thousand men, the greater part of whom were armed with some weapon or other--muskets, pikes, hatchets, crowbars, and even spits from the cook-shops forming part of their equipment--assembled on the place where the Bastile had stood. Santerre was already there on horseback as their appointed leader; and, when all were collected and marshaled in three divisions, they began their march. One division had for its chief the Marquis de St. Huruge, an intimate friend and adherent of the Duc d'Orleans; at the head of another, a woman of notorious infamy, known as La Belle Liegeoise, clad in male attire, rode astride upon a cannon; while, as it advanced, the crowd was every moment swelled by vast bodies of recruits, among whom were numbers of women, whose imprecations in ferocity and foulness surpassed even the foulest threats of the men.

The ostensible object of the procession was to present petitions to the king and the Assembly on the dismissal of Roland and his colleagues from the administration, and on the refusal of the royal assent to the decree against the priests. The real design of those who had organized it was more truthfully shown by the banners and emblems borne aloft in the ranks. "Beware the Lamp,[1]" was the inscription on one. "Death to Veto and his wife," was read upon another. A gang of butchers carried a calf's heart on the point of a pike, with "The Heart of an Aristocrat" for a motto. A band of crossing-sweepers, or of men who professed to be such, though the fineness of their linen was inconsistent with the rags which were their outward garments, had for their standard a pair of ragged breeches, with the inscription, "Tremble, tyrants; here are the Sans-culottes." One gang of ruffians carried a model of a guillotine. Another bore aloft a miniature gallows with an effigy of the queen herself hanging from it. So great was the crowd that it was nearly three in the afternoon before the head of it reached the Assembly, where its approach had raised a debate on the propriety of receiving any petition at all which was to be presented in so menacing a guise; M. Roederer, the procurator-syndic, or chief legal officer of the department of Paris, recommending its rejection, on the ground that such a procession was illegal, not only because of its avowed object of forcing its way to the king, but also because it was likely to lead into acts of violence even if it had not premeditated them.

His arguments were earnestly supported by the constitutionalists, and opposed and ridiculed by Vergniaud. But before the discussion was over, the rioters, who had now reached the hall, took the decision into their own hands, forced open the door, and put forward a spokesman to read what they called a petition, but which was in truth a sanguinary denunciation of those whom it proclaimed the enemies of the nation, and of whom it demanded that "the land should be purged." Insolent and ferocious as it was, it, however, coincided with the feelings of the Girondins, who were now the masters of the Assembly. One orator carried a motion that the petitioners should receive what were called the honors of the Assembly; or, in other words, should be allowed to enter the hall with their arms and defile before them. They poured in with exulting uproar. Songs, half blood-thirsty and half obscene, gestures indicative some of murder, some of debauchery, cries of "Vive la nation!" interspersed with inarticulate yells, were the sounds, the guillotine and the queen upon the gallows were the sights, which were thought in character with the legislature of a people which still claimed to be regarded as the pattern of civilization by all Europe. Evening approached before the last of the rabble had passed through the hall; and by that time the leading ranks were in front of the Tuileries.

There were but scanty means of resisting them. A few companies of the National Guard formed the whole protection of the palace; and with them the agents of Orleans and the Girondins had been briskly tampering all the morning. Many had been seduced. A few remained firm in their loyalty; but those on whom the royal family had the best reason to rely were a band of gentlemen, with the veteran Marshal de Noailles at their head, who had repaired to the Tuileries in the morning to furnish to their sovereign such defense as could be found in their loyal and devoted gallantry. Some of them besides the old marshal, the Count d'Hervilly, who had commanded the cavalry of the Constitutional Guard, and M. d'Acloque, an officer of the National Guard, brought military experience to aid their valor, and made such arrangements as the time and character of the building rendered practicable to keep the rioters at bay. But the utmost bravery of such a handful of men, for they were no more, and even the more solid resistance of iron gates and barriers, were unavailing against the thousands that assailed them. Exasperated at finding the gates closed against them, the rioters began to beat upon them with sledge-hammers. Presently they were joined by Sergent and Panis, two of the municipal magistrates, who ordered the sentinels to open the gates to the sovereign people. The sentinels fled; the gates were opened or broken down; the mob seized one of the cannons which stood in the Place du Carrousel, carried it up the stairs of the palace, and planted it against the door of the royal apartments; and, while they shouted out a demand that the king should show himself, they began to batter the door as before they had battered the gates, and threatened, if it should not yield to their hatchets, to blow it down with cannon-shot.

Fear of personal danger was not one of the king's weaknesses. The hatchets beat down the outer door, and, as it fell, he came forth from the room behind, and with unruffled countenance accosted the ruffians who were pouring through it. His sister, the Princess Elizabeth, was at his side. He had charged those around him to keep the queen back; and she, knowing how special an object of the popular hatred and fury she was, with a fortitude beyond that which defies death, remained out of sight lest she should add to his danger. For a moment the mob, respecting, in spite of themselves, the calm heroism with which they were confronted, paused in their onset; but those in front were pushed on by those behind, and pikes were leveled and blows were aimed at both the king and the princess, whom they mistook for the queen. At first there were but one or two attendants at the king's side, but they were faithful and brave men. One struck down a ruffian who was lifting his weapon to aim a blow at Louis himself. A pike was even leveled at his sister, when her equerry, M. Bousquet, too far off to bring her the aid of his right hand, called out, "Spare the princess." Delicate as were her frame and features, Elizabeth was worthy of her blood, and as dauntless as the rest. She turned to her preserver almost reproachfully: "Why did you undeceive him? it might have saved the queen." But after a few seconds, Acloque with some grenadiers of the National Guard on whom he could still rely, hastened up by a back staircase to defend his sovereign; and, with the aid of some of the gentlemen who had come with the Marshal de Noailles, drew the king back into a recess formed by a window; and raised a rampart of benches in front of him, and one still more trustworthy of their own bodies. They would gladly have attacked the rioters and driven them back, but were restrained by Louis himself. "Put up your swords," said he; "this crowd is excited rather than wicked." And he addressed those who had forced their way into the room with words of condescending conciliation. They replied with threats and imprecations; and sought to force their way onward, pressing back by their mere numbers and weight the small group of loyal champions who by this time had gathered in front of him.

So great was the uproar that presently a report reached the main body of the insurgents, who were still in the garden beneath, that Louis had been killed; and they mingled shouts of triumph with cheers for Orleans as their new king, and demanded that the heads of the king and queen should be thrown down to them from the windows; but no actual injury was inflicted on Louis, though he owed his safety more to his own calmness than even to the devotion of his guards. One ruffian threatened him with instant death if he did not at once grant every prayer contained in their petition. He replied, as composedly as if he had been on his throne at Versailles, that the present was not the time for making such a demand, nor was this the way in which to make it. The dignity of the answer seemed to imply a contempt for the threateners, and the mob grew more uproarious. "Fear not, sire," said one of Acloque's grenadiers, "we are around you." The king took the man's hand and placed it on his heart, which was beating more calmly than that of the soldier himself. "Judge yourself," said he, "if I fear." Legendre, the butcher, raised his pike as if to strike him, while he reproached him as a traitor and the enemy of his country. "I am not, and never have been aught but the sincerest friend of my people," was the gentle but fearless answer. "If it be so, put on this red cap," and the butcher thrust one into his hand on the end of his pike, prepared, as Louis believed, to plunge the weapon itself into his breast if he refused. The king put it on, and so little regarded it that he forgot to remove it again, as he afterward repented that he had not done, thinking that his conduct in allowing it to remain on his head bore too strong a resemblance to fear or to an unworthy compromise of his dignity.

But still the uproar increased, and above it rose loud cries for the queen, till at last she also came forward. As yet, from the motives that have already been mentioned, she had consented to remain out of sight; but each explosion of the mob increased her unwillingness to keep back. It was, she felt, her duty to be always at the king's side; if need be, to die with him; to stand aloof was infamy; and at last, as the demands for her appearance increased, even those around her confessed that it might be safer for her to show herself. The door was thrown open, and, leading forth her children, from whom she refused to part, and accompanied by Madame de Tourzel, Madame de Lamballe, and others of her ladies, the most timid of whom seemed as if inspired by her example, Marie Antoinette advanced and took her place by the side of her husband, and, with head erect and color heightened by the sight of her enemies, faced them disdainfully. As lions in their utmost rage have recoiled before a man who has looked them steadily in the face, so did even those miscreants quail before their pure and high-minded queen. At first it seemed as if her bitterest enemies were to be found among her own sex. The men were for a moment silenced; but a young girl, whose appearance was not that of the lowest class, came forward and abused her in coarse and furious language, especially reviling her as "the Austrian." The queen, astonished at finding such animosity in one apparently tender and gentle, condescended to expostulate with her. "Why do you hate me? I have never injured you." "You have not injured me, but it is you who cause the misery of the nation." "Poor child," replied Marie Antoinette, "they have deceived you. I am the wife of your king, the mother of your dauphin, who will be your king. I am a Frenchwoman in every feeling of my heart. I shall never again see Austria. I can only be happy or unhappy in France, and I was happy when you loved me." The girl was melted by her patience and gentleness. She burst into tears of shame, and begged pardon for her previous conduct. "I did not know you," she said; "I see now that you are good.[2]" Another asked her, "How old is your girl?" "She is old enough," replied the queen, "to feel acutely such scenes as these." But, while these brief conversations were going on, the crowd kept pressing forward. One officer had drawn a table in front of the queen as she advanced, so as to screen her from actual contact with any of the rioters, but more than one of them stretched across it as if to reach her. One fellow demanded that she should put a red cap, which he threw to her, on the head of the dauphin, and, as she saw the king wearing one, she consented; but it was too large and fell down the child's face, almost stifling him with its thickness. Santerre himself reached across and removed it, and, leaning with his hands on the table, which shook beneath his vehemence, addressed her with what he meant for courtesy. "Princess," said he, "do not fear. The French people do not wish to slay you. I promise this in their name." Marie Antoinette had long ago declared that her heart had become French; it was too much so for her to allow such a man's claim to be the spokesman of the nation. "It is not by such as you," she replied, with lofty scorn; "it is not by such as you that I judge of the French people, but by brave men like these;" and she pointed to the gentlemen who were standing round her as her champions, and to the faithful grenadiers. The well-timed and well-deserved compliment roused them to still greater enthusiasm, but already the danger was passing away.

The Assembly had seen with indifference the departure of the mob to attack the Tuileries, and had proceeded with its ordinary business as if nothing were likely to happen which could call for its interference. But when the uproar within the palace became audible in the hall, the Count de Dumas, one of the very few men of noble birth who had been returned to this second Assembly, with a few other deputies of the better class, hastened to see what was taking place, and, quickly returning, reported the king's imminent danger to their colleagues. Dumas gave such offense by the boldness of his language that some of the Jacobins threatened him with violence, but he refused to be silenced; and his firmness prevailed, as firmness nearly always did prevail in an Assembly where, though there were many fierce and vehement blusterers, there were very few men of real courage. In compliance with his vehement demand for instant action, a deputation of members was sent to take measures for the king's safety; and then, at last, Petion, who had carefully kept aloof while there seemed to be a chance of the king being murdered, now that he could no longer hope for such a consummation, repaired to the palace and presented himself before him. To him he had the effrontery to declare that he had only just become apprised of his situation. From the Assembly, at a later hour in the evening, he claimed the credit of having organized the riot. But Louis would not condescend to pretend to believe him. "It was extraordinary," he replied, "that Petion should not have earlier known what had lasted so long." Even he could not but be for a moment abashed at the king's unwonted expression of indignation. But he soon recovered himself, and with unequaled impudence turned and thanked the crowd for the moderation and dignity with which they had exercised the right of petition, and bid them "finish the day in similar conformity with the law, and retire to their homes." They obeyed. The interference of the deputies had convinced their leaders that they could not succeed in their purpose now. Santerre, whose softer mood, such as it had been, had soon passed away, muttered with a deep oath that they had missed their blow, but must try it again hereafter. For the present he led off his brigands; the palace and gardens were restored to quiet, though the traces of the assault to which they had been exposed could not easily be effaced; and Louis and his family were left in tranquillity to thank God for their escape, but to forebode also that similar trials were in store for them, all of which, it was not likely, would have so innocent a termination.[3]

CHAPTER XXXVI.

Feelings of Marie Antoinette.--Different Plans are formed for her Escape.
--She hopes for Aid from Austria and Prussia.--La Fayette comes to Paris.
--His Mismanagement.--An Attempt is made to assassinate the Queen.--
The Motion of Bishop Lamourette.--The Feast of the Federation.--La Fay-
ette proposes a Plan for the King's Escape.--Bertrand proposes Another.--
Both are rejected by the Queen.

We can do little more than guess at the feelings of Marie Antoinette after such a day of horrors. She could scarcely venture to write a letter, lest it should fall into hands for which it was not intended, and be misinterpreted so as to be mischievous to herself and to her correspondents. And two brief notes--one on the 4th of July to Mercy, and one written a day or two later to the Landgravine of Hesse-Darmstadt--are all that, so far as we know, proceeded from her pen in the sad period between the two attacks on the palace. Brief as they are, they are characteristic as showing her unshaken resolution to perform her duty to her family, and proving at the same time how absolutely free she was from any delusion as to the certain event of the struggle in which she was engaged. No courage was ever more entirely founded on high and virtuous principle, for no one was ever less sustained by hope. To Mercy she says:

"July 4th, 1792.

"You know the occurrences of the 20th of June. Our position becomes every day more critical. There is nothing but violence and rage on one side, weakness and inactivity on the other. We can reckon neither on the National Guard nor on the army. We do not know whether to remain in Paris, or to throw ourselves into some other place. It is more than time for the powers to speak out boldly. The 14th of July and the days which will follow it may become days of general mourning for France, and of regret to the powers who will have been too slow in explaining themselves. All is lost if the factions are not arrested in their wickedness by fear of impending chastisement. They are resolved on a republic at all risks. To arrive at that, they have determined to assassinate the king. It would be necessary that any manifesto[1] should make the National Assembly and Paris responsible for his life and the lives of his family.

"In spite of all these dangers, we will not change our resolution. You may depend on this as much as I depend on your attachment. It is a pleasure to me to believe that you allow me a share of the attachment which bound you to my mother. And this is a moment to give me a great proof of it, in saving me and mine, if there be still time.[2]"

The letter to the landgravine was one of reply to a proposal which that princess, who had long been one of her most attached friends, had lately made to her, that she should allow her brother, Prince George of Darmstadt, to carry out a plan by which, as he conceived, he could convey the queen and her children safely out of Paris; the enterprise being, as both he and his sister flattered themselves, greatly facilitated by the circumstance that the prince's person was wholly unknown in the French capital.

"July, 1792.[3]

"Your friendship and your anxiety for me have touched my very inmost soul. The person[4] who is about to return to you will explain the reasons which have detained him so long. He will also tell you that at present I do not dare to receive him in my own apartment. Yet it would have been very pleasant to talk to him about you, to whom I am so tenderly attached. No, my princess, while I feel all the kindness of your offers, I can not accept them. I am vowed for life to my duties, and to those beloved persons whose misfortunes I share, and who, whatever people may say of them, deserve to be regarded with interest by all the world for the courage with which they support their position. The bearer of this letter will be able to give you a detailed account of what is going on at present, and of the spirit of this place where we are living. I hear that he has seen much, and has formed very correct ideas. May all that we are now doing and suffering one day make our children happy! This is the only wish that I allow myself. Farewell, my princess; they have taken from me every thing except my heart, which will always remain constant in its love for you. Be sure of this; the loss of your love would be an evil which I could not endure. I embrace you tenderly. A thousand compliments to all yours. I am prouder than ever of having been born a German."

In her mention of the 14th of July as likely to bring fresh dangers, she is alluding to the announcement of an intention of the Jacobins to hold a fresh festival to commemorate the destruction of the Bastile on the anniversary of that exploit; a celebration which she had ample reason to expect would furnish occasion for some fresh tumult and outrage. And we may remark that in one of these letters she rests her whole hope on foreign assistance; while in the other, she rejects foreign aid to escape from her almost hopeless position. But the key to her feeling in both cases is one and the same. Above all things she was a devoted, faithful wife and mother. To herself and her own safety she never gave a thought. Her first duty, she rightly judged, was to the king, and she looked to such a manifesto as she desired Austria and Prussia to issue, backed by the movements of a powerful army, as the measure which afforded the best prospect of saving her husband, who could hardly be trusted to save himself; while, for the very same reason, she refused to fly without him, even though flight might have saved her children, her son and heir, as well as herself, because it would have increased her husband's danger. In each case her decision was that of a brave and devoted wife, not perhaps in both instances judicious; for when Prussia did mingle in the contest, as it did in the first week in July, it evidently increased the perils of Louis, if indeed they were capable of aggravation, by giving the Jacobins a plea for raising the cry "that the country was in danger." But in the second case, in her refusal to flee, and to leave her husband by himself to confront the existing and impending dangers, she judged rightly and worthily of herself; and the only circumstance that has prevented her from receiving the credit due for her refusal to avail herself of Prince George's offer is that throughout the whole period of the Revolution her acts of disinterestedness and heroism are so incessant that single deeds of the kind are lost in the contemplation of her entire career during this long period of trial.

It was the peculiar ill-fortune of Louis that more than once the very efforts made by people who desired to assist him increased his perils. The events of the 20th of June had shocked and alarmed even La Fayette. From the beginning of the Revolution he had vacillated between a desire for a republic and for a limited monarchy on something like the English pattern, without being able to decide which to prefer. He had shown himself willing to court a base popularity with the mob by heaping uncalled-for insults on the king and queen. But though he had coquetted with the ultra- revolutionists, and allowed them to make a tool of him, he had not nerve for the villainies which it was now clear that they meditated. He had no taste for bloodshed; and, though gifted with but little acuteness, he saw that the success of the Jacobins and Girondins would lead neither to a republic nor to a limited monarchy, but to anarchy; and he had discernment enough to dread that. He therefore now sincerely desired to save the king's life, and even what remained of his authority, especially if he could so order matters that their preservation should be seen to be his own work. He was conscious also that he could reckon on many allies in any effort which he might make for the prevention of further outrages. The more respectable portion of the Parisians viewed the recent outrages with disgust, sharpened by personal alarm. The dominion of Santerre and his gangs of destitute desperadoes was manifestly fraught with destruction to themselves as well as to the king. The greater part of the army under his command shared these feelings, and would gladly have followed him to Paris to crush the revolutionary clubs, and to inflict condign punishment on the authors and chief agents in the late insurrection. If he had but had the skill to avail himself of this favorable state of feeling, there can be little doubt that it was in his power at this moment to have established the king in the full exercise of all the authority vested in him by the Constitution, or even to have induced the Assembly to enlarge that authority. He so mismanaged matters that he only increased the king's danger, and brought general contempt and imminent danger on himself likewise. His enemies had more than once accused him of wishing to copy Cromwell. His friends had boasted that he would emulate Monk. But if he was too scrupulous for the audacious wickedness of the one, he proved himself equally devoid of the well-calculating shrewdness of the other. If, subsequently, he had any reason to congratulate himself on the result of his conduct, it was that, like the stork in the fable, after be had thrust his head into the mouth of the wolf, he was allowed to draw it out again in safety.

Louis's enemies had abundantly shown that they did not lack boldness. If they were to be defeated, it could only be by action as bold as their own. Unhappily, La Fayette's courage had usually found vent rather in blustering words than in stout deeds; and those were the only weapons he could bring himself to employ now. He resolved to remonstrate with the Assembly; but instead of bringing up his army, or even a detachment, to back his remonstrance, he came to Paris with a single aid-de-camp, and, on the 28th of June, presented himself at the bar of the Assembly and demanded an audience. A fortnight before he had written a letter to the president, in which he had denounced alike the Jacobin leaders of the clubs and the Girondin ministers, and had called on the Assembly to suppress the clubs; a letter which had produced no effect except to unite the two parties against whom it was aimed more closely together, and also to give them a warning of his hostility to them, which, till he was in a position to show it by deeds, it would have been wiser to have avoided.

He now repeated by word of mouth the statements and arguments which he had previously advanced in writing, with the addition of a denunciation of the recent insurrection and its authors, whom, he insisted, the Assembly was bound instantly to prosecute. His speech was not ill received; for the Constitutionalists, who knew what he designed to say, had mustered in full force, and had packed the galleries beforehand with hired clappers; and many even of the Deputies who did not belong to that party cheered him, so obvious to all but the most desperate was the danger to the whole State, if Santerre and his brigands should be allowed to become its masters. But they cared little for a barren indignation which had no more effectual weapon than reproaches. He had said enough to exasperate, but had not done enough to intimidate; while those whom he denounced had greater boldness and presence of mind than he, and had the forces on which they relied for support at hand and available. They instantly turned the latter on himself, and in their turn denounced him for having left his army without leave. He was frightened, or at least perplexed, by such a charge. He made no reply, but seemed like one stupefied; and it was only through the eloquence of one of his friends, M. Ramond, that he was saved from the impeachment with which Guadet and Vergniaud openly threatened him for quitting the army without leave.

Ramond's oratory succeeded in carrying through the Assembly a motion in his favor, and several companies of the National Guard and a vast multitude of the citizens showed their sympathy with his views by escorting him with acclamations to his hotel. But neither their evident inclination to support him, nor even the danger with which he himself had been threatened, could give him resolution and firmness in action. For a moment he made a demonstration as if he were prepared to secure the success of his designs by force. He proposed that the king should the next morning review Acloque's companies of the National Guard, after which he himself would harangue them on their duty to the king and Constitution. But the Girondins persuaded Petion to exert his authority, as mayor, to prohibit the review. La Fayette was weak enough to submit to the prohibition; and, quickened, it is said, by intelligence that Petion was preparing to arrest him, the next day retired in haste from Paris and rejoined the army.

He had done the king nothing but harm. He had shown to all the world that though the Royalists and Constitutionalists might still be numerically the stronger party, for all purposes of action they were by far the weaker. He had encouraged those whom he had intended to daunt, and strengthened those whom he had hoped to crush; and they, in consequence, proceeded in their treasons with greater boldness and openness than ever. Marie Antoinette, as we have seen, had expressed her belief that they designed to assassinate Louis, and she now employed herself, as she had done once before, in quilting him a waistcoat of thickness sufficient to resist a dagger or a bullet; though so incessant was the watch which was set on all their movements that it was with the greatest difficulty that she could find an opportunity of trying it on him. But it was not the king, but she herself, who was the victim whom the traitors proposed to take off in such a manner; and in the second week of July a man was detected at the foot of the staircase leading to her apartments, disguised as a grenadier, and sufficiently equipped with murderous weapons. He was seized by the guard, who had previous warning of his design; but was instantly rescued by a gang of ruffians like himself, who were on the watch to take advantage of the confusion which might be expected to arise from the accomplishment of his crime.

Meanwhile the Assembly wavered, hesitated, and did nothing; the Girondins and Jacobins were fertile in devising plots, and active in carrying them out. One day, as if seized with a panic at some report of the strength of the Austrian and Prussian armies, the Assembly again passed a vote declaring the country in danger; on another, roused by a letter which a Madame Gouges, a daughter of a fashionable dress-maker, a lady of more notoriety than reputation, but who cultivated a character for philosophy, took upon herself to write to them, and still more by a curiously sentimental speech of the Bishop of Lyons, with the appropriate name of Lamourette,[5] the members bound themselves to have for the future but one heart and one sentiment; and for some minutes Jacobins, Girondins, Constitutionalists, and Royalists were rushing to and fro across the floor of the hall in a frenzy of mutual benevolence, embracing and kissing one another, and swearing an eternal friendship. They even sent a message to Louis to beg him to come and witness this new harmony. He came at once. With his disposition, it was not strange that he yielded to the illusion of the strange spectacle which he beheld. He shed tears of joy, declared the complete agreement of his sentiments with theirs, and predicted that their union would save France. They escorted him back to the Tuileries with cheers, and the very same evening, after a stormy debate, which was a remarkable commentary on the affection which they had just vowed to one another, they set him at defiance, insulting him by annulling some decrees to which he had given his assent, and passing a vote of confidence in Petion as mayor.

The Feast of the Federation, as it was called, passed off quietly. The king again recognized the Constitution before the altar erected in the Champ de Mars, and, as he drove back to the palace, the populace accompanied him the whole way, never ceasing their acclamations of "Vivent le roi et la reine![6]" till they had dismounted and returned to their apartments. Such a close of the day had been expected by no one. La Fayette, who seems at last to have become really anxious to save the lives of the king and queen, and to have been seriously convinced that they were in danger, had now formally opened a communication with the court. He concerted his plans with Marshal Luckner, and had learned so much wisdom from his recent failure that he now placed no reliance on any thing but a display of superior force. He accordingly proposed to Louis to bring up a battalion of picked men from his and the marshal's armies to escort him to the Champ de Mars; and, judging that, even if the feast should pass off without any fresh danger, the king could never be considered permanently safe while he remained in Paris, he recommended that on the next day, Louis, still under the protection of the same troops, should announce to the Assembly his departure for Compiegne, and should at once quit the capital for that town, to which trusty officers would in the mean time have brought up other divisions of the army in sufficient strength to set all disaffected and seditious spirits at defiance.

The plan was at all events well conceived, but it was declined. Louis did not apparently distrust the marquis's good faith, but he doubted his ability to carry out an enterprise requiring an energy and decision of which no part of La Fayette's career had given any indication; while the queen distrusted his loyalty even more than his capacity. One of those with whom she took counsel expressed his opinion of the marquis's real object by saying that he might save the monarch, but not the monarchy; and she replied that his head was still full of republican notions which he had brought from America, and refused to place the slightest confidence in him. We may suspect that she did not do him entire justice, and may rather believe, with Louis, that he was now acting in good faith; but, with a recollection of all that she had suffered at his hands, we can not wonder at her continued distrust of him. [A7]

But his was not the only plan proposed for the escape of the royal family. Bertrand de Moleville, though no longer Louis's minister, retained his undiminished confidence, and he had found a place which he regarded as admirably suited for a temporary retreat--the Castle of Gaillon, near the left bank of the Seine, in Normandy, the people of which province were almost universally loyal. It was within the twenty leagues from Paris which the Assembly had fixed for the limit of the royal journeys; while yet, in case of the worst, it was likewise within easy distance of the coast. An able engineer officer had pronounced it to be thoroughly defensible; and the Count d'Hervilly, with other officers of proved courage and presence of mind, undertook the arrangement of all the military measures necessary for the safe escort of the entire royal family, which they themselves were willing to conduct, with the aid of some detachments of the Swiss Guards; while the necessary funds were provided by the loyal devotion of the Duke de Liancourt, who placed a million of francs at his sovereign's disposal, and of one or two other nobles who came forward with almost equally lavish offerings. Louis certainly at first regarded the plan with favor, and, in the opinion of M. Bertrand, it would not have been difficult to induce him to adopt it, if the queen could have been brought over to a similar view.

Unhappily several motives combined to disincline her to it. The insurrection which the Girondins[8] were preparing had originally been fixed for the 29th of July; but, a few days before, M. Bertrand learned that it had been postponed till the

10th of August. This gave him time to mature his arrangements, all of which, as he reckoned, could be completed in time for the king to leave Paris on the evening of the 8th. But before that day arrived news had reached the court that the Duke of Brunswick, the Prussian commander-in-chief, had put his army in motion, and that he was not likely to meet any obstacle sufficient to prevent him from marching at once on Paris; a measure which, to quote the language of M. Bertrand, "the queen was too anxious to see accomplished to hesitate at believing in its execution.[9]" And at the same time some of the Jacobin leaders--Danton, Petion, and Santerre-- had opened communications with the Government, and had undertaken for a large bribe to prevent the threatened outbreak. The money had been paid to them, and Marie Antoinette more than once boasted to her attendants that they were now safe, as having gained over Danton; placing the firmer reliance on this mode of extrication because it coincided with her belief that the mutual jealousy of the two parties would dispose one of them at least eventually to embrace the cause of the king, as their beat ally against the other. The result seems to show that the Jacobins only took the bribe the more effectually to lull their destined victims into a false security.

A third consideration, and that apparently not the weakest, was Marie Antoinette's rooted dislike of the Constitutionalist party. In their rants the Duc de Liancourt had taken his seat in the first Assembly; though, as he assured M. Bertrand, the king himself was aware that his object in so doing had been to serve his majesty in the most effectual manner; and he was also the statesman whose advice had mainly contributed to induce the king to visit Paris after the destruction of the Bastile, a step which she had always regarded as the forerunner and cause of some of the most irremediable encroachments of the Revolutionists. Even the duke's present devotion to the king's cause could not entirely efface from her mind the impression that he was not in his heart friendly to the royal authority. She urged these arguments on the king. The last probably weighed with him but little: the two former he felt as strongly as the queen herself; and he delayed his decision, sending word to M. Bertrand that he had resolved to defer his departure "till the last extremity. [10]" His faithful servant was in amazement. "When," he exclaimed, "was the last extremity to be looked for, if it had not already come?" But his astonishment was turned to absolute despair when the next day M. Montmorin informed him that the project had been entirely given up, the queen herself remarking "that M. Bertrand overlooked the circumstance that he was throwing them altogether into the hands of the Constitutionalists."

She has been commonly blamed for this decision, as that which was the chief cause of all the subsequent calamities which overwhelmed her and the whole family. Yet it is not difficult to understand the motives which influenced her, and it is impossible to refrain from regarding them with sympathy. She was now at the decisive moment of a crisis which might well perplex the clearest head. There could be no doubt that the coming insurrection would be the turning-point of the long conflict which had now lasted three years; and it was a conflict in which her husband's throne was certainly at stake, perhaps even his and her own life. They had indeed been so for three years; and throughout the whole contest her view had constantly been that honor was still dearer than life; and honor she identified with the preservation of her husband's crown, her children's inheritance. Mirabeau had said that she would not care to save her life if she could not save the crown also; and, though she can not have decided without a terrible conflict of feeling, her decision was now in conformity with Mirabeau's judgment of her. In the preceding year the journey to Varennes had been treated by the Republicans as a plea for pronouncing the deposition of the king; and, though they were defeated then, they were undoubtedly stronger in the new Assembly. On the other hand, she suspected that they themselves had some misgivings as to the chance of a second attack on the palace being more successful than the former one had proved; and that the openness with which the preparations for it were announced was intended to terrify Louis and herself into a second flight; and she might not unreasonably infer that what their enemies desired was not the wisest course for them to adopt. To fly would evidently be to leave the whole field in both the Assembly and the city open to their enemies. It might save their lives, but it would almost to a certainty forfeit the crown. To stay and face the coming danger might indeed lose both, but it might also save both; and she determined rather to risk all, both crown and life, in the endeavor to save all, rather than to save the one by the deliberate sacrifice of the other. It was a gallant and unselfish determination: if in one point of view it was unwise, it was at least becoming her lofty lineage, and consistent with her heroic character.

CHAPTER XXXVII.

Preparation for a New Insurrection.--Barbaroux brings up a Gang from Marseilles.--The King's last Levee.--The Assembly rejects a Motion for the Impeachment of La Fayette.--It removes some Regiments from Paris.--Preparations of the Court for Defense.--The 10th of August.--The City is in Insurrection.--Murder of Mandat.--Louis reviews the Guards.--He takes Refuge with the Assembly.--Massacre of the Swiss Guards.--Sack of the Tuileries.--Discussions in the Assembly.--The Royal Authority is suspended.

The die was cast. Nothing was left but to wait, with such patience as might be, for the coming explosion, which was sure not to be long deferred. Madame de Stael has said that there never can be a conspiracy, in the proper sense of the word, in Paris; and that if there could be one, it would be superfluous, since every one at all times follows the majority, and no one ever keeps a secret. But on this occasion the chief movers of sedition studiously discarded all appearance of concealment. Vergniaud, Guadet, and Gensonne wrote the king a letter couched in terms of the most insolent defiance, and signed with all their names, in which they openly announced to him that an insurrection was organized which should be abandoned if he replaced Roland and his colleagues in the ministry, but which should surely break on the palace and overwhelm it if he refused. And Barbaroux, who had promised Madame Roland to bring up from Marseilles and other towns in the south a band of men capable of any atrocity, had collected a gang of five hundred miscreants, the refuse of the galleys and the jails, and paraded them in triumph through the streets, which their arrival was destined and intended to deluge with blood.

And yet Louis, or, to speak more correctly, Marie Antoinette, for it was with her that every decision rested, preferred to face the impending struggle in Paris. She still believed that the king had many friends in whose devotion and gallantry he could confide to the very death. On Sunday, the 5th of August, the very last Sunday which he was ever to behold as the acknowledged sovereign of the land, his levee was attended by a more than usually numerous and brilliant company; though the gayety appropriate to such a scene was on this occasion clouded over by the anxiety for their royal master and mistress which sobered every one's demeanor, and spread a gloom over every countenance. And three days later both the Assembly and the National Guard displayed feelings which, to so sanguine a temper as hers, seemed to show a disposition to make a stout resistance to the further progress of disorder. The Assembly, by a majority of more than two to one, rejected a motion made by Vergniaud for the impeachment of La Fayette for his conduct in June; and when the mob fell upon those who had voted against it, as they came out of the hall, the National Guard came promptly to their rescue, and inflicted severe chastisement on the foremost of the rioters.

The vote of the Assembly may be said to have been the last it ever gave for any object but the promotion of anarchy. It more than neutralized its effect the very next day, when it passed a decree for the immediate removal of three regiments of the line which were quartered in Paris. It even at first included in its resolution the Swiss Guards also; but was subsequently compelled to withdraw that clause, since an old treaty with Switzerland expressly secured to the republic the right of always furnishing a regiment for the honorable service of guarding the palace. And at the same time, as if to punish the National Guard for its conduct on the previous day, another vote broke up the staff of that force; cashiered its finest companies, the grenadiers and the mounted troopers, on the plea that such distinctions were inconsistent with equality; and filled up the vacancies with men who were the very dregs of the city, many of whom were, in fact, secret agents of the Jacobins, by whose aid they hoped to spread disaffection through the entire force.

The afternoon of the 9th was passed in anxious preparation by both the conspirators and those whom they were about to attack. The king and queen were not destitute of faithful adherents, whom their very danger only rendered the more zealous to place all their strength, their valor, and, as they truly foreboded, their lives, at the disposal of their honored and threatened sovereigns. The veteran Marshal de Mailly, one of those gallant nobles whose devoted loyalty had been so scandalously insulted by La Fayette[1] in the spring of the preceding year, though now eighty years of age, hastened to the defense of his royal master and mistress, and brought with him a chivalrous phalanx of above a hundred gentlemen, all animated with the same self-sacrificing heroism, as his own, to fight, or, if need should be, to die for their king and queen, though they had no arms but their swords. It seemed fortunate, too, that the command of the National Guard for the day fell by rotation to an officer named Mandat, a man of high professional skill, intrepid courage, and unshaken in his zeal for the royal cause, though in former days the constitutionalists had reckoned him among their adherents. His brigade numbered about two thousand four hundred men, on most of whom he could thoroughly rely. And it was no slight proof of his force of character and energy, as well as of his address, that, as the National Guard could not be employed out of the routine of their regular duty without a special authorisation from the civil power, he contrived to extort from Petion, as mayor of the city, a formal authority to augment his brigade for the special occasion, and, if force should be used against him, to repel it by force.

The Swiss Guard of about a thousand men were all trustworthy; and there was also a small body of heavy cavalry of the gendarmery who had proved true enough to resist all the seductions of the conspirators. There were likewise a few cannon. In all, nearly four thousand men could be mustered for the defense of the palace; a force, if well equipped and well led, not inadequate to the task of holding it out for some time against any number of undisciplined assailants. But they were not well armed. They were nearly destitute of ammunition, and Mandat's most vehement entreaties and remonstrances could not wring out from Petion an order for a supply of cartridges, though, as he told him, several companies had not four rounds left, some had only one; and though it was notorious that the police had served out ammunition to the Marseillese, who had no claim to a single bullet. Still less were they well led; for at such a crisis every thing depended on the king's example, and Louis was utterly wanting to himself.

As night approached, the agitation in the palace, and still more in the city, grew more and more intense. It was a brilliant and a warm night. By ten o'clock the mob began to cluster in the streets, many only curious and anxious from uncertain fear; those in the secret hastening toward the point of rendezvous. The rioters also had cannon, and by eleven their artillery-men had taken charge of their guns. The conspirators had got possession of all the churches; and as the hour of midnight struck, a single cannon-shot gave the signal, and from every steeple and tower in the city the fatal tocsin began to peal. The insurrection was begun.

Petion, who, from some motive which is not very intelligible, wished to save appearances, and who, though in fact he had been eager in promoting the insurrection, pretended innocence of all complicity in it even to the Assembly, whom he was aware that he was not deceiving, on the first sound of the bells repaired to the Hotel de Ville. He found, as indeed he was aware that he should find, a strange addition to the Municipal Council. The majority of the sections of the city had declared themselves in insurrection; had passed resolutions that they would no longer obey the existing magistrates; and had appointed a body of commissioners to overbear them, trusting in the cowardice of the majority, and in the willing acquiescence and co-operation of Danton and the other members of the party of violence. The commissioners seized on a room in the Hotel by the side of the regular council-room, and their first measures were marked with a cunning and unscrupulousness which largely contributed to the success of their more active comrades in the streets. Even Petion himself was not wicked enough or resolute enough for them. The authority which Mandat had wrung from him on the previous morning was, in their eyes, a proof of unpardonable weakness. He might be terrified into issuing some other order which might disconcert or at least impede their plans; and accordingly they put him under a kind of honorable arrest, and sent him to his own house under the guard of an armed force, which was instructed to allow no one access to him; and at the same time they sent an order in his name to Mandat to repair to the Hotel de Ville, to concert with them the measures necessary for the safety of the city.

Had he acted on his own judgment, Mandat would have disregarded the summons; but M. Roederer urged upon him that he was bound to comply with an order brought in the name of the mayor. Accordingly he repaired to the Hotel de Ville, and gave to the Municipal Council so distinct an account of his measures, and of his reason for taking them, that, though Danton and some of his more factious colleagues reproached him for exhibiting what they called a needless distrust of the people, the majority of the Council approved of his conduct, and dismissed him to return to his duties. But as he quit their chamber, he was dragged before the other body, the Commissioners of the Sections,[2] and subjected to another examination, which, as a matter of course, they conducted with every kind of insult and violence. The Municipal Council sent down a deputation to remonstrate with them; they rose on the Council and expelled them from their own council-chamber by main force, and then sent off Mandat to prison, whither, a few minutes later, they dispatched a gang of assassins to murder him.

The news of his death soon reached the Tuileries, where it struck a chill even into the firm heart of the queen,[3] who had deservedly placed great reliance on his fidelity and resolution. She had now to trust to the valor and loyalty of the troops themselves, though thus deprived of their commander; and, as a last hope, she persuaded the king to go down and review them, hoping that his presence might animate the faithful, and perhaps fix the waverers. Louis consented, as he would have consented to any course that was recommended to him; but on such occasions more depends on the grace and spirit with which a thing is done than on the act itself, and grace and spirit were now less than ever to be looked for in the unhappy Louis. He visited first the courts of the palace, and the Carrousel, and then the gardens, at whose different entrances strong detachments of troops were stationed. When he first appeared he was greeted by one general cheer of "Vive le roi!" But as he passed along the ranks the unanimity and loyalty began to disappear. Even of those regiments which were still true to him the cheers were faint, as if half suppressed by alarm; while many companies mingled shouts for "the nation" with those for himself, and individual soldiers murmured audibly, "Down with the Veto!" or, "Long live the Sans-culottes!" secure that their officers would not venture to reprove, much less to chastise them. The Swiss Guard alone showed enthusiasm in their loyalty and resolution in their demeanor.

But when he reached the artillery, on whom perhaps most depended, many of the gunners made no secret of their disaffection. Some even quit their ranks to offer him personal insults, doubling their fists in his face, and shouting out the coarsest threats which the Revolution had yet taught them. Both cheers and insults the hapless king received with almost equal apathy. The despair which was in his heart was shown in his dress, which had no military character or decoration, but was a suit of plain violet such as was never worn by kings of France but on occasions of mourning. It was to no purpose that the queen put a sword into his hand, and exhorted him to take the command of the troops himself, and to show himself ready to fight in person for his crown. It was only once or twice that he could even be brought to utter a few words of acknowledgment to those who treated him with respect, of expostulation to those who insulted and threatened him; and presently, pale, and, as it seemed, exhausted with that slight effort, he returned to his apartments.

The queen was almost in despair. She told Madame de Campan that all was lost; that the king had shown no energy; that such a review as that had done harm rather than good. All that could now be done was for her to show herself not wanting to the occasion, nor to him. Her courage rose with the imminence of the danger. Those who beheld her, as with dilating eyes and heightened color she listened to the unceasing tumult, and, repressing every appearance of alarm, strove with unabated energy to rouse her husband, and to fortify the good disposition of the loyal friends around her, have described in terms of enthusiastic admiration the majestic dignity of her demeanor at this trying moment. She had need of all her presence of mind; for even among those who were most faithful to her dissensions were springing up. At the first alarm Marshal de Mailly and his company of gallant nobles and gentlemen had hastened to her side; but the National Guards were jealous of them. It seemed as if they expected to be allowed to remain nearest to the royal person; and the soldiers disdained to yield the post of honor to men who were not in uniform, and whom, as they were mostly in court dress, they even disliked as aristocrats. They besought the queen to dismiss them. "Never!" she replied; and, trusting rather that the example of their self-sacrificing devotion might stimulate those who thus complained, and full of that royal magnanimity which feels that it confers honor on those whom it trusts, and that it has a right to look for the loyalty of its servants even to the death, she added, "They will serve with you, and share your dangers. They will fight with you in the van, in the rear, where you will. They will show you how men can die for their king."

But meanwhile the insurgents were rapidly approaching the palace, and already the tramp of the leading column might be heard. The tocsin had continued its ominous sound throughout the night, and at six in the morning the main body of the insurgents, twenty thousand strong, and well armed--for the new council had opened to them the stores of the arsenal-- began their march under the command of Santerre. As they advanced they were joined by the Marseillese, who had been quartered in a barrack near the Hall of the Cordeliers, and their numbers were further swelled by thousands of the populace. Soon after eight they reached the Carrousel, forced the gates, and pressed on to the royal court, the National Guard and Swiss falling back before them to the entrance to the royal apartments, where the more confined space seemed to afford a better prospect of making an effectual resistance.

But already the palace was deserted by those who were the intended objects of the attack. Roederer, and one or two of the municipal magistrates, in whom the indignity with which the new commissioners of the sections had treated them had excited a feeling of personal indignation, had been actively endeavoring to rouse the National Guards to an energetic resistance; but they had wholly failed. Those who listened to them most favorably would only promise to defend themselves if attacked, while some of the artillery-men drew the charges from their guns and extinguished their matches. Roederer, whom the strange vicissitudes of the crisis had for the moment rendered the king's chief adviser, though there seems no reason to doubt his good faith, was not a man of that fiery courage which hopes against hope, and can stimulate waverers by its example. He saw that if the rioters should succeed in storming the palace, and should find the king and his family there, the moment that made them masters of their persons would be the last of their lives and of the monarchy. He returned into the palace to represent to Louis the utter hopelessness of making any defense, and to recommend him, as his sole resource, to claim the protection of the Assembly. The queen, who, to use her own words, would have preferred being nailed to the walls of the palace to seeking a refuge which she deemed degrading, pointed to the soldiers, and showed by her gestures that they were the only protectors whom it became them to look to. Roederer assured her that they could not he relied on. She seemed unconvinced. He almost forgot his respect in his earnestness. "If you refuse, madame, you will be guilty of the blood of the king, of your two children; you will destroy yourself, and every soul within the palace." While she was still hesitating between her feeling of shame and her anxiety for those dearest to her, the king gave the word. "Let us go," said he. "Let us give this last proof of our devotion to the Constitution." The princess spoke. "Could Roederer answer for the king's life?" He affirmed that he would answer for it with his own. The queen repeated the question. "Madame," he replied, "we will answer for dying at your side--that is all that we can promise." "Let us go," said Louis, and moved toward the door. Even at the last moment, one officer, M. Boscari, commander of a battalion of the National Guard, known as that of Les Filles St. Thomas, whose loyalty no disaster had ever been able to shake, implored him to change his mind. His men, united to the Swiss, would be able, he said, to cut a way for the royal family to the Rouen road; the insurgents were all on the other side of the city, and nothing could resist him. But again, as on all previous occasions, Louis rejected the brave advice. He pleaded the risk to which he should expose those dearest to him, and led them to almost certain death in committing them to the Assembly. Some of De Mailly's gentlemen gathered round him to accompany him; but such an escort seemed to Roederer likely to provoke additional animosity, and at his entreaty Louis trusted himself to a company of his faithful Swiss and to a detachment of the National Guard, who formed themselves into an escort to conduct him to the Assembly, whose hall looked into one side of the palace garden.

The minister for foreign affairs walked at his side. The queen leaned on the arm of M. Dubouchage, the minister of marine, and with the other hand led the dauphin. The Princess Elizabeth and the princess royal followed with another minister. And thus, with the Princess de Lamballe, Madame de Tourzel, and one or two other ministers and attendants, the royal family left the palace of their ancestors, which only one of them was ever to behold again. As they quit the saloon, moved down the stairs, and crossed the garden, their every step was one toward a downfall and a destruction which could never be retraced. Marie Antoinette felt it to be so, and, as she reached the foot of the staircase, cast restless and anxious glances around, looking perhaps even then for any prospect of succor or of effectual resistance which might present itself. One of the Swiss misunderstood her, and with rude fidelity endeavored to encourage her. "Fear nothing, madame," said he, "your majesty is surrounded by honest citizens." She laid her hand on her heart. "I do fear nothing," and passed on without another word.

As they crossed the garden the king broke the silence. "How unusually early," he remarked, "the leaves fall this year!" To those who heard him, the bareness which he remarked seemed an omen of the fate which awaited himself, about to be stripped of his royal dignity; perhaps even, like some superfluous crowder of the grove, to fall beneath the axe. The Assembly had already been deliberating whether it should invite him to take refuge with them when they heard that he was approaching. It was instantly voted that a deputation should be sent to meet him, which, after a few words of respectful salutation, fell in behind. A vast crowd was collected outside the doors of the hall. They hooted the king, and, still more bitterly, the queen, as they advanced. "Down with Veto!" was the chief cry; but mingled with it were still more unmanly insults, invoking more especially death on all the women. But the Guards kept the mob at a distance, though when they reached the hall the Jacobins made an effort to deprive them of that protection. They declared that it was illegal for soldiers to enter the hall, as indeed it was; yet without them the princes must at the last moment have been exposed to all the fury of the mob. At this critical moment Roederer showed both fidelity and presence of mind. He implored the deputies to suspend the law which forbade the entrance of the troops, and, while the Jacobins were reviling him and his proposal, he pretended to suppose that it had been agreed to, and led forward a detachment of soldiers who cleared the way. One grenadier look up the dauphin in his arms and carried him in; and, although the pressure of the crowd was extreme, at last the whole family were placed within the hall in such safety as the Assembly was able or disposed to afford them.

Louis bore himself not without dignity. His words were few but calm. "I am come here to prevent a great crime. I think I can not be better placed, nor more safely, gentlemen, than among you." The president, who happened to be Vergniaud, while appearing to desire to give him confidence, yet avoided uttering a single word, except the simple address of "sire," which should be a recognition of the royal dignity, if indeed his speech was not a studied disavowal of it. Louis might reckon, he said, on the firmness of the National Assembly: its members had sworn to die in support of the rights of the people and of the constituted authorities: and then, on the plea that the Assembly must continue its deliberations, and that the law forbade them to be conducted in the presence of the sovereign, he assigned him and his family a little box behind the president's chair, which was usually set apart for the reporters of the debates. A Jacobin deputy proposed their removal into one of the committee-rooms, with the idea, as he afterward boasted, that it would be easy there to admit a band of assassins to murder them all; but Vergniaud and his party divined his object and overruled him. It might seem that the Girondins, though they had been the original promoters and chief organizers of the insurrection, were as yet disposed to be content with the overthrow of the throne, and had not arrived at the hardihood which can not be sated without murder; and it is a remarkable instance of the rapidity with which unprincipled men sink deeper and deeper into iniquity, that they who now exerted themselves successfully to save the life of Louis, five months afterward were as unanimous as the most ferocious Jacobins in destroying him.

One object of Louis in abandoning his palace had been to save the lives of the National Guards and of the Swiss, by withdrawing them from what he regarded as an unequal combat with the infuriated multitude; and of the National Guard the greater part did escape, drawing off silently in small detachments, when the sovereign whom it had been their duty to defend, seemed no longer to require their service. But the Swiss remained bravely at their posts around the royal staircase, though, as they abstained from provoking the rioters by any active opposition, which now seemed to have no object, they hoped that they might escape attack. But the mob and Santerre were bent on their destruction. Some of the insurgents tried to provoke them by threats. Some endeavored to tamper with them to desert their allegiance. But an accidental interruption suddenly terminated their brief period of inaction. In the confusion a pistol went off, and the Swiss fancied it was meant as a signal for an assault upon them. Thinking that the time was come to defend their own lives, they leveled their muskets and fired: they charged down the steps, driving the insurgents before them like sheep; they cleared the inner or royal court, forced their way into the Carrousel, recovered the cannon which were posted in the large square, and were so completely victorious that, had there been any superior officer at hand to direct their movements, they might even now have checked the insurrection.

There might even have been some hope had not Louis himself actually interfered to check their exertions. Hearing what they had accomplished, the gallant D'Hervilly made his way to them, and called on them to follow him to the rescue of the king. They hesitated, unwilling to leave their wounded comrades to the mercy of their enemies; but their hesitation was brief, for it was put an end to by the wounded men themselves, who bid them hasten forward; their duty, they told them, was to save the king; for themselves, they could but die where they lay.[4] There were still plenty of gallant spirits to do their duty to the king, if he could but have been persuaded to take a right view of his duty to himself and to them.

The Swiss gladly obeyed D'Hervilly's summons. Forming in close order, and as steady as on parade, they marched through the garden, one battalion moving toward the end opposite to the palace, where there was a draw-bridge which it was essential to secure; the other following D'Hervilly to the Assembly hall. Nothing could resist their advance: they forced their way up the stairs; and in a few moments a young officer, M. de Salis, at the head of a small detachment, sword in hand, entered the chamber. Some of the deputies shrieked and fled, while others, more calm, reminded him that armed men were forbidden to enter the hall, and ordered him to retire. He refused, and sent his subaltern to the king for orders. But Louis still held to his strange policy of non-resistance. Even the terrible scenes of the morning, and the deliberate attack of an armed mob upon his palace, had failed to eradicate his unwillingness to authorize his own Guards to fight in his behalf, or to convince him that when his throne (perhaps even his life and the lives of all his family) was at stake, it was nobler to struggle for victory, and, if defeated, to die with arms in his hands, than tamely to sit still and be stripped of his kingly dignity by brigands and traitors. Could he but have summoned energy to put himself at the head of his faithful Guards, as we may be sure that his brave wife urged him to do; could he have even sent them one encouraging order, one cheering word, there still might have been hope; for they had already proved that no number of Santerre's ruffians could stand before them.[5] But Louis could not even now bring himself to act; he could only suffer. His command to the officer, the last he ever issued, was for the whole battalion to lay down their arms, to evacuate the palace, and to retire to their barracks. He would not, he said, that such brave men should die. They knew that in fact he was consigning them to death without honor; but they were loyal to the last. They obeyed, though their obedience to the first part of the order rendered the last part impracticable. They laid down their arms, and were at once made prisoners; and the fate of prisoners in such hands as those of their captors was certain. A small handful, consisting, it is said, of fourteen men, escaped through the courage of one or two friends, who presently brought them plain clothes to exchange for their uniforms, but before night all the rest were massacred.

Not more fortunate were their comrades of the other battalion, except in falling by a more soldier-like death. Though no longer supported by the detachment under D'Hervilly, they succeeded in forcing their way to the draw-bridge. It was held by a strong detachment of the National Guard, who ought to have received them as comrades, but who had now caught the contagion of successful treason, and fired on them as they advanced. But the gallant Swiss, in spite of their diminished numbers still invincible, charged through them, forced their way across the bridge into the Place Louis XV., and there formed themselves into square, resolved to sell their lives dearly. It was all that was left to them to do. The mounted gendarmery, too, came up and turned against them. Hemmed in on all sides, they fell one after another; Louis, who had refused to let them die for him, having only given their death the additional pang that it had been of no service to him.

The retreat of the king had left the Tuileries at the mercy of the rioters. Furious to find that he had escaped them, they wreaked their rage on the lifeless furniture, breaking, hewing, and destroying in every way that wantonness or malice could devise. Different articles which had belonged to the queen were the especial objects of their wrath. Crowds of the vilest women arrayed themselves in her dresses, or defiled her bed. Her looking-glasses were broken, with imprecations, because they had reflected her features. Her footmen were pursued and slaughtered because they had been wont to obey her. Nor were the monsters who slew them contented with murder. They tore the dead bodies into pieces; devoured the still bleeding fragments, or deliberately lighted fire and cooked them; or, hoisting the severed limbs on pikes, carried them in fiendish triumph through the streets.

And while these horrors were going on in the palace, the tumult in the Assembly was scarcely less furious. The majority of the members--all, indeed, except the Girondins and Jacobins, who were secure in their alliance with the ringleaders--were panic-stricken. Many fled, but the rest sat still, and in terrified helplessness voted whatever resolutions the fiercest of the king's enemies chose to propose. It was an ominous preliminary to their deliberations that they admitted a deputation from the commissioners of the sections into the hall, where Guadet, to whom Vergniaud had surrendered the president's chair, thanked them for their zeal, and assured them that the Assembly regarded them as virtuous citizens only anxious for the restoration of peace and order. They were even formally recognized as the Municipal Council; and then, on the motion of Vergniaud, the Assembly passed a series of resolutions, ordering the suspension of Louis from all authority; his confinement in the Luxembourg Palace; the dismissal and impeachment of his ministers; the re-appointment of Roland and those of his colleagues whom he had dismissed, and the immediate election of a National Convention. A large pecuniary reward was even voted for the Marseillese, and for similar gangs from one or two other departments which had been brought up to Paris to take a part in the insurrection.

Yet so deeply seated were hope and confidence in the queen's heart, so sanguine was her trust that out of the mutual enmity of the populace and the Assembly safety would still be wrought for the king and the monarchy, that even while the din of battle was raging outside the hall, and inside deputy after deputy was rising to heap insults on the king and on herself, or to second Vergniaud's resolutions for his formal degradation, she could still believe that the tide was about to turn in her favor. While the uproar was at its height she turned to D'Hervilly, who still kept his post, faithful and fearless, at his master's side. "Well, M. d'Hervilly," said she, with an air, as M. Bertrand, who tells the story, describes it, of the most perfect security, "did we not do well not to leave Paris?" "I pray God," said the brave noble, "that your majesty may be able to ask me the same question in six months' time.[6]" His foreboding was truer than her hopes. In less than six months she was a desolate, imprisoned widow, helplessly awaiting her own fate from her husband's murderers.

All these resolutions of Vergniaud, all the ribald abuse with which different members supported them, the unhappy sovereigns were condemned to hear in the narrow box to which they had been removed. They bore the insults, the queen with her habitual dignity, the king with his inveterate apathy; Louis even speaking occasionally with apparent cheerfulness to some of the deputies. The constant interruptions protracted the discussions through the entire day. It was half-past three in the morning before the Assembly adjourned, when the king and his family were removed to the adjacent Convent of the Feuillants, where four wretched cells had been hastily furnished with camp-beds, and a few other necessaries of the coarsest description. So little was any attempt made to disguise the fact that they were prisoners, that their own domestic servants were not allowed the next day to attend them till they had received a formal ticket of admittance from the president. Yet even in this extremity of distress Marie Antoinette thought of others rather than of herself; and when at last her faithful attendant, Madame de Campan, obtained access to her, her first words expressed how greatly her own sorrows were aggravated by the thought that she had involved in them those loyal friends whose attachment merited a very different recompense.[7]

CHAPTER XXXVIII.

Indignities to which the Royal Family are subjected.--They are removed to the Temple.--Divisions in the Assembly.--Flight of La Fayette.--Advance of the Prussians.--Lady Sutherland supplies the Dauphin with Clothes.--Mode of Life in the Temple.--The Massacres of September.--The Death of the Princess de Lamballe.--Insults are heaped on the King and Queen.--The Trial of the King.--His Last Interview with his Family.--His Death.

From the 11th of August the life of Marie Antoinette is almost a blank to us. We may be even thankful that it is so, and that we are spared the details, in all their accumulated miseries, of a series of events which are a disgrace to human nature. For month after month the gentle, benevolent king, whom no sovereign ever exceeded in love for his people, or in the exercise of every private virtue; the equally pure-minded, charitable, and patriotic queen, who, to the somewhat passive excellences of her husband added fascinating graces and lofty energies of which he was unhappily destitute, were subjected to the most disgusting indignities, to the tyranny of the vilest monsters who ever usurped authority over a nation, and to the daily insults of the meanest of their former subjects, who thought to make a merit with their new masters of their brutality to those whose birthright had been the submission and reverence of all around them.

Vergniaud's motion had only extended to the suspension of the king from his functions till the meeting of the Convention; but no one could doubt that that suspension would never be taken off, and that Louis was in fact dethroned. Marie Antoinette never deceived herself on the point, and, retaining the opinion as to the fate of deposed monarchs which she had expressed three years before, pronounced that all was over with them. "My poor children," said she, apostrophizing the little dauphin and his sister, "it is cruel to give up the hope of transmitting to you so noble an inheritance, and to have to say that all is at an end with ourselves;" and, lest any one else should have any doubt on the subject, the Assembly no longer headed its decrees with any royal title, but published them in the name of the nation. In one point the resolutions of the 10th were slightly departed from. The municipal authorities reported that the Luxembourg had so many outlets and subterranean passages, that it would be difficult to prevent the escape of a prisoner from that palace; and accordingly the destination of the royal family was changed to the Temple. Thither, after having been compelled to spend two more days in the Assembly, listening to the denunciations and threats of their enemies, whom even the knowledge that they were wholly in their power failed to pacify, they were conveyed on the 13th; and they never quit it till they were dragged forth to die.

The Temple had been, as its name imported, the fortress and palace of the Knights Templars, and, having been erected by them in the palmy days of their wealth and magnificence, contained spacious apartments, and extensive gardens protected from intrusion by a lofty wall, which surrounded the whole. It was not, unfit for, nor unaccustomed to, the reception of princes; for the Count d'Artois had fitted up a portion of it for himself whenever he visited the capital. And to his apartments those who had the custody of the king and queen at first conducted them. But the new Municipal Council, whom the recent events had made the real masters of Paris, considered those rooms too comfortable or too honorable a lodging for any prisoners, however royal; and the same night, before they could retire to rest, and while Louis was still occupying himself in distributing the different apartments among the members of his family and the few attendants who were allowed to share his captivity, an order was sent down to remove them all into a small dilapidated tower which had been used as a lodging for some of the count's footmen, but whose bad walls and broken windows rendered it unfit for even the servants of a prince. Besides their meanness and ruinous condition, the number of the rooms it contained was so scanty, that for the first few days the only room that could be found for the Princess Elizabeth was an old, disused kitchen; and even after that was remedied, she was forced to share her new chamber, though it was both small and dark, with her niece, Madame Royale; while the dauphin's bed was placed by the side of the queen's, in one which was but little large.[1] And the dungeon-like appearance of the entire place impressed the whole family with the idea that it was not intended that they should remain there long, but that an early death was preparing for them.

Even this distress was speedily aggravated by a fresh severity. Four days afterward an order was sent down which commanded the removal of all their attendants, with the exception of one or two menial servants. Madame de Tourzel, the governess of the royal children, was driven away with the coarsest insults. The Princess de Lamballe, that most faithful and affectionate friend of the queen, was rudely torn from her embrace by the municipal officers; and, though no offense was even imputed to her, was dragged off to a prison, where she was soon to pay the forfeit of her loyalty with her blood.

From this time forth the king and queen were completely cut off from the outer world. They were treated with a rigor which in happier countries is not even experienced by convicted criminals. They were forbidden to receive letters or newspapers; and presently they were deprived of pens, ink, and paper; though they would neither have desired to write nor receive letters which would have been read by their jailers, and could only have exposed their correspondents to danger. After a few days they were even deprived of the attendance of all their servants but two[2]--a faithful valet named Clery (fidelity such as his may well immortalize his name), to whom we are indebted for the greater part of the scanty knowledge which we possess of the fate of the captive princes as long as Louis himself was permitted to live; and Turgy, a cook, who, by an act of faithful boldness, had obtained a surreptitious entrance into the Temple, and whose services seemed to have escaped notice, though at a later period they proved of no trivial importance.

Had they but known what was passing in the Assembly, Marie Antoinette would in all probability have still found matter for some comfort and hope in the fierce mutual strife of the Jacobins and Girondins, which for some weeks kept the Assembly in a constant state of agitation; and she would have found even greater encouragement in the dissatisfaction which in many departments the people expressed at the late events; and in the conduct of La Fayette's army, which at first cordially approved of and supported the town-council and magistrates of Sedan, who arrested and threw into prison the commissioners whom the Assembly had sent to announce the suspension of the royal authority. But the intelligence of that demonstration in their favor never reached them, nor that of its suppression a few days later; when La Fayette, who, as on a former occasion, had committed himself to measures beyond his strength to carry out, was forced to fly from the country, and by a strange violation of military law was thrown into an Austrian prison. Nor again, when for a moment the Duke of Brunswick appeared likely to realize the hopes on which Marie Antoinette had built so confidently, and by the capture of Longwy seemed to have opened to himself the road to Paris, did any tidings of his achievement come to the ears of those who had felt such deep interest in his operations. After a time the ingenuity of Clery found a mode of obtaining for them some little knowledge of what was passing outside, by contriving that some of his friends should send criers to cry an abstract of the news contained in the daily journals under his windows, which he in his turn faithfully reported to them while employed in such menial offices about their persons as took off the attention of their guards, who day and night maintained an unceasing espial on all their actions and even words.

From the very first they had to endure strange privations for princes. They had not a sufficient supply of clothes; the little dauphin, in particular, would have been wholly unprovided, had not the English embassadress, Lady Sutherland, whose son was of a similar age and size, sent in a stock of such as she thought might be wanted. But as the garments thus received wore out, and as all means of replacing them were refused, the queen and princess were reduced to ply their own needles diligently to mend the clothes of the whole family, that they might not appear to their jailers, or to the occupants of the surrounding houses, who from their windows could command a view of the garden in which they took their daily walks, absolutely ragged.

Such enforced occupation must indeed in some degree have been welcome as a relief from thought, which their unbroken solitude left them but too much leisure to indulge. Clery has given us an account of the manner in which their day was parceled out.[3] The king rose at six, and Clery, after dressing his hair, descended to the queen's chamber, which was on the story below, to perform the same service for her and for the rest of the family. And the hour so spent brought with it some slight comfort, as he could avail himself of that opportunity to mention any thing that he might have learned of what was passing out-of-doors, or to receive any instructions which they might desire to give him. At nine they breakfasted in the king's room. At ten they came down-stairs again to the queen's apartments, where Louis occupied himself in giving the dauphin lessons in geography, while Marie Antoinette busied herself in a corresponding manner with Madame Royale. But, in whatever room they were, their guards were always present; and when, at one o'clock, they went down-stairs to walk in the garden, they were still accompanied by soldiers: the only member of the family who was not exposed to their ceaseless vigilance being the little dauphin, who was allowed to run up and down and play at ball with Clery, without a soldier thinking it necessary to watch all his movements or listen to all his childish exclamations. At two dinner was served, and regularly at that hour the odious Santerre, with two other ruffians of the same stamp, whom he called his aids-de-camp, visited them to make sure of their presence and to inspect their rooms; and Clery remarked that the queen never broke her disdainful silence to him, though Louis often spoke to him, generally to receive some answer of brutal insult. After dinner, Louis and Marie Antoinette would play piquet or backgammon; as, while they were thus engaged, the vigilance of their keepers relaxed, and the noise of shuffling the cards or rattling the dice afforded them opportunities of saying a few words in whispers to one another, which at other times would have been overheard. In the evening the queen and the Princess Elizabeth read aloud, the books chosen being chiefly works of history, or the masterpieces of Corneille and Racine, as being most suitable to form the minds and tastes of the children; and sometimes Louis himself would seek to divert them from their sorrows by asking the children riddles, and finding some amusement in their attempts to solve them. At bed-time the queen herself made the dauphin say his prayers, teaching him especially the duty of praying for others, for the Princess de Lamballe, and for Madame de Tourzel, his governess; though even those petitions the poor boy was compelled to utter in whispers, lest, if they were repeated to the Municipal Council, he should bring ruin on those whom he regarded as friends. At ten the family separated for the night, a sentinel making his bed across the door of each of their chambers, to prevent the possibility of any escape.

In this way they passed a fortnight, when the monotony of their lives was fearfully disturbed. The Jacobins had established their ascendency. They had created a Revolutionary Tribunal, which at once began its course of wholesale condemnation, sending almost every one who was brought before it to the scaffold with merely a form of trial; the guillotine being erected, as it was said, ***en permanence***, that the deaths of the victims might never be delayed for want of means to execute them; while, that a succession of victims might never be wanting, Danton, in his new character of Minister of Justice, instituted a search of every house for arms or papers, or any thing which might afford evidence or even suggest a suspicion that the owners disliked or feared the new authorities.

But it was not enough to strike terror into all the peaceful citizens. The Girondins had always been objects of jealous rivalry to the Jacobins. Fanatical and relentless as they were in their cruelty, they had recently given proofs that they disapproved of the furious blood-thirstiness that was beginning to decimate the city, and they had carried the Assembly with them in a vote for the dissolution of the new Municipal Council. At the same time, intelligence of the Prussian successes readied the capital, intelligence which, it seemed possible, might animate the Royalists to some fresh effort; and, lest they should find means of reconciling themselves to Vergniaud and his party, the Jacobins and Cordeliers resolved to give both a lesson by a deed of blood which should strike terror into them. We may spare ourselves the pain of relating the horrors of the September massacre, when, for more than four days, gangs of men worse than devils, and of women unsexed by profligacy and cruelty till they had become worse even than the men, gave themselves up to the work of indiscriminate slaughter, deluging the streets with blood, and where they could spare time, aggravating the pangs of death by superfluous tortures. It will be sufficient for our purpose to record the fate of one of the most innocent of all the victims, who owed her death to the fact that she had long been the queen's most chosen friend, and whose murder was gloated over with special ferocity by the monsters who perpetrated it, as enabling them to inflict an additional pang on her wretched friend and mistress.

Madame de Lamballe, as we have seen, had accompanied the queen to the Temple on the first day of her captivity, and had subsequently been removed to one of the city prisons known as La Force. It was on the prisoners in the different places of confinement that the work of death was to be done: and she had been specially marked out for slaughter, not solely because she was beloved by Marie Antoinette, but also, it was understood, because, as she was very rich, and sister-in-law to the Duc d'Orleans, that detestable prince desired to add her inheritance to his OWD already vast riches. She was dragged before Hebert, one of the foulest of the Jacobin crew, who had taken his seat at the gate of the prison to preside over the trials, as they were called, of the prisoners in La Force. "Swear," said he, "devotion to liberty and to the nation, and hatred to the king and queen, and you shall live." "I will take the first oath," she replied, "but the second never; it is not in my heart. The king and queen I have ever loved and honored." Almost before she had finished speaking she was pushed into the gate-way. One ruffian struck her from behind with his sabre. She fell. They tore her into pieces. A letter of the queen's fell from her hair, in which she had hidden it. The sight of it redoubled the assassins' fury. They stuck her head on a pike, and carried it in triumph to the Palais Royal to display it to D'Orleans, who was feasting with some of the companions of his daily orgies, and then proceeded to the Temple to brandish it before the eyes of the queen.

It was about three o'clock.[4] Dinner had just been removed, and the king and queen were sitting down to play backgammon, when horrid shouts were heard in the street. One of the soldiers on guard in the room, who had not yet laid aside every feeling of humanity, closed the window and even drew the curtain. Another of different temper insisted that Louis should come to the window and show himself. As the uproar increased, the queen rose from her seat, and the king asked what was the matter. "Well," said the man, "since you wish to know, they want to show you the head of Madame de Lamballe." No event that had yet occurred had struck the queen with such anguish. The uproar increased. Those who bore the head had wished even to force the doors, and bring their trophy, still bleeding, into the very room where the royal family were, and were only prevented by a compromise which permitted them to parade it round their tower in triumph. As the shouts died away, Petion's secretary arrived with a small sum of money which had been issued for the king's use. He noticed that the queen stood all the time that he was in the room, and fancied she assumed that attitude out of respect to the mayor. She had never stirred since she had heard of the princess's death, but had stood rooted, as it were, to the ground, stupefied and speechless with horror and anguish. It was long before she could be restored; and all through the night the rest of the princesses, if at least they could have slept, was broken by her sobs, which never ceased.

As time passed on, the prospects of the unhappy prisoners became still more gloomy. On the 21st of September the Convention met, and its first act was to abolish royalty and declare the government a republic, and an officer was instantly sent to make proclamation of the event under the Temple walls; and, as if the establishment of a republic authorized an increase of insolence on the part of the guards of the prisoners, the insults to which they were subjected grew more frequent and more gross. Sentences both menacing and indecent were written on the walls where they must catch their eye: the soldiers puffed their tobacco-smoke in the queen's face as she passed, or placed their seats in the passages so much in her way that she could hardly avoid stumbling over their legs as she went down to the garden. Sometimes they even assailed her with direct abuse, calling her the assassin of the people, who in their turn would assassinate her. More than once the whole family had to submit to a personal search, and to empty their pockets, when the officers who made the search carried off whatever they chose to term suspicious, especially their knives and scissors, so that, when at work, the queen and princess were forced to bite off the threads with their teeth. And amidst all this misery no one ever heard Marie Antoinette utter a word to lament her own fate, or to ask pity for herself. She mourned over her husband's fall; she pitied Elizabeth, to whom malice itself could not impute a share in the wrongs of which Danton and Vergniaud had taught the people to complain. Most of all did she bewail the ruined prospects of her son; and more than once she brought tears into Clery's eyes by the earnest tenderness with which she implored him to provide for the safety of the noble child after his parents should have been destroyed.

The insults increased, each being an additional omen of the future. The most painful injuries were reserved for the queen. Toward the end of October the dauphin was removed from her apartment to that of the king, that she might thus be deprived of the comfort of ministering to his daily wants. But Louis himself was not spared. One day an order came down to deprive him of his sword; on another he was stripped of his different decorations and orders of knighthood. The system of espial, too, was carried out with increased severity. Their linen, when it came hack from the washer-woman, and even their washing-bills, were held to the fire to see if any invisible ink had been employed to communicate with them. Their loaves and biscuits were cut asunder lest they should contain notes. The end was approaching. A week or two later the king was removed to another tower, and was only permitted to see his family during a certain portion of the day. At last it was determined to bring him to trial. On the 11th of December he was suddenly informed that he was to be brought before the Convention; and from that day forth he was cut off from all intercourse with his family, even his wife being forbidden to see or hear from him. The barbarous restriction afforded him one more opportunity of showing his amiable unselfishness and fortitude. The regulation had been made by the Municipal Council, not by the Assembly; and its inhuman and unprecedented severity, coupled with a jealousy of the Council, as seeking to usurp the whole authority of the State, induced the Assembly to rescind it, and to grant permission, for Louis to have the dauphin and his sister with him. Yet, lest these innocent children should prove messengers of conspiracy between him and the queen and Elizabeth, it was ordered at the same time that, so long as they were allowed to visit him, they should be separated from their mother and their aunt; and Louis, though never in greater need of comfort, thought it so much better for the children themselves that they should be with the queen, that for their sakes he renounced their society, and allowed the decree of the Council to be carried out in all its pitiless cruelty.

And, again, we may spare ourselves from dwelling on the details of what, in hideous mockery, was called the king's trial, though it was in fact a mere ceremonious prelude to his murder, which had been determined on before it began. Deep as is the disgrace with which it has forever covered the nation which tolerated such an abomination, it was relieved by some incidents which did honor to the country and to human nature. The murderers of Louis, in their ignoble pedantry, wearied the ear with appeals to the examples of the ancient Romans, of Decius[5] and of Brutus. But no Roman ever gave a nobler proof of contempt of danger, and devotion to duty, than was afforded by the intrepid lawyers, Malesherbes, De Seze, and Tronchet, who voluntarily undertook the king's defense, though Louis himself warned them that their utmost efforts would be fruitless, and would only bring destruction on themselves without saving him. One member, too, of the Convention, Lanjuinais, though originally he had been a member of the Breton Club, and had latterly been generally regarded as connected with the Girondins, made more than one eloquent effort in the king's behalf, provoking the Jacobins and Girondins to their very wildest fury by his contemptuous defiance of their menaces. And even when the verdict was being given; when Jacobins, Girondins, and Cordeliers, Robespierre, Vergniaud, Danton, and the infamous Duc d'Orleans were vying with one another in the eagerness with which they pushed forward to record their votes of condemnation; and when a mob of hired ruffians, who thronged the hall, were cheering every vote for death, and holding daggers to the throat of every one from whom they apprehended a contrary judgment; one noble of frail body, but of a spirit worthy of his birth and rank, the Marquis de Villette, laughed in the faces of his threateners, looked the assassins in the face, and told them that he would not obey their orders, and that they dared not kill him; and with a loud voice pronounced a vote of acquittal.

But no courage or devotion of a few honest men could save Louis. One vote by an immense majority pronounced him guilty; a second refused all appeal to the people; a third, by a majority of fifty voices, condemned him to death. And on the morning of the 20th of January, 1793, Louis was roused from his bed to hear his sentence, and to learn that it was to be carried out the next day.

While the trial lasted, the queen and those with her had been kept in almost absolute ignorance of what was taking place. They never, however, doubted what the result would be,[6] so that it was scarcely a shock to them when they heard the news-men crying the sentence under their windows --the only mercy that was shown to either the prisoner who was to die, or to those who were to survive him, being that they were allowed once more to meet on earth. At eight in the evening the queen, his children, and his sister were to be allowed to visit him. He prepared for the interview with astonishing calmness, making the arrangements so deliberately that, when he noticed that Clery had placed a bottle of iced water on the table, he bid him change it, lest, if the queen should require any, the chill should prove injurious to her health. Even that last interview was not allowed to pass wholly without witnesses, since the Municipal Council refused, even on such an occasion, to relax their regulation that their guards were never to lose sight-of the king; and all that was permitted was that he might retire with his family into an inner room which had a glass door, so that, though what passed must be seen, their last words might not be overheard. His daughter, Madame Royale, now a girl of fourteen, and old enough, as her mother had said a few months before, to realize the misery of the scenes which she daily saw around her, has left us an account of the interview, necessarily a brief one, for the queen and princess were too wretched to say much. Louis wept when he announced to them how short was the time which he had to live, but his tears were those of pity for the desolation of those he loved, and not of fear for himself. He was even, in some sense, a willing victim, for, as he told them, it had been proposed to save him by appealing to the primary Assemblies of the nation; but he had refused his consent to a step which must throw the whole country into confusion, and might be the cause of civil war. He would rather die than risk the bringing of such calamities on his people. He even sought to comfort the queen by making some excuses for the monsters who had condemned him; and his last words to his family were an entreaty to forgive them; to his son, an injunction never to seek to revenge his death, even, if some change of fortune should enable him to do so.

The queen said nothing, but sat clinging to him in speechless agony. At last he begged them to retire, that he might seek rest to prepare himself for the morrow; and then she spoke, to beg that at least they might meet again the next morning. "Yes," said he, "at eight o'clock." "Why not at seven?" asked she. "Well, then, at seven." But, after she had left him he determined to avoid this second meeting, not so much because he feared its unnerving himself, but because he felt that the second parting must be too terrible for her.

When she returned to her own chamber she had scarcely strength left to place the dauphin in his bed. She threw herself, dressed as she was, on her own bed, where her sister-in-law and daughter heard her, as the little princess describes her state, "shivering with cold and grief the whole night long.[7]"

Even if she could have slept, her rest would soon have been disturbed by the movement of troops, the beating of the drums, and the heavy roll of the cannon passing through the street. For the miscreants who bore sway in the city knew well that the crime which they were about to commit was viewed with horror by the great majority of the nation, and even of the Parisians, and to the last moment were afraid of a rescue. But no one could interpose between Louis and his doom; and the next intelligence of him that reached his wife, who was waiting the whole morning in painful anxiety for the summons to see him once more, was that he had perished beneath the fatal guillotine, and that she was a widow.

CHAPTER XXXIX.

The Queen is refused Leave to see Clery.--Madame Royale is taken Ill.--Plans are formed for the Queen's Escape by MM. Jarjayes, Toulan, and by the Baron de Batz.--Marie Antoinette refuses to leave her Son.--Illness of the young King.--Overthrow of the Girondins.--Insanity of the Woman Tison.--Kindness of the Queen to her.--Her Son is taken from her, and intrusted to Simon.--His Ill-treatment.--The Queen is removed to the Conciergerie.--She is tried before the Revolutionary Tribunal.--She is condemned.--Her last Letter to the Princess Elizabeth.--Her Death and Character.

S houts in the streets announced to her and those around her that all was over. All the morning she had alarmed the princesses by the speechless, tearless stupor into which she seemed plunged; but at last she roused herself, and begged to see Clery, who had been with Louis till he left the Temple, and who, therefore, she hoped, might have some last message for her, some last words of affection, some parting gift. And so indeed he had;[1] for the last act of Louis had been to give that faithful servant his seal for the dauphin, and his ring for the queen, with a little packet containing portions of her hair and those of his children which he had been in the habit of wearing. And he had bid him tell them all--"the queen, his dear children, and his sister--that he had promised to see them that morning, but that he had desired to save them the pain of so cruel a separation. How much," he continued, "does it cost me to go without receiving their last embraces! You must bear to them my last farewell."

But even the poor consolation of receiving these sad tokens of unchanged affection was refused to her. The Council refused Clery admittance to her, and seized the little trinkets and the packet of hair. The king's last words never reached her. But a few days afterward, Toulan, one of the commissioners of the Council, who sympathized with her bereavement, found means to send her the ring and seal.[2] Her sister and her daughter were the more anxious that she should see Clery, from the hope that conversation with him might bring on a flood of tears, which would have given her some relief. But her own fortitude was her best support. Miserable as she was, hopeless as she was, it was characteristic of her magnanimous courage that she did not long give way to womanly lamentations. She recollected that she had still duties to perform to the living, to her daughter and sister, and, above all, to her son, now her king, whom, if some happier change of fortune, when the nation should have recovered from its present madness, should replace him on his father's throne, it must be her care to render worthy of such a restoration. She began to apply herself diligently to the work of giving him lessons such as his father had given him, mingling them with the constant references to that father's example, which she never ceased to hold up to him, dwelling with the emphatic exaggeration of lasting affection on his gentleness, his benevolence, his love for his subjects; qualities which, in truth, he had possessed in sufficient abundance, had he but been gifted with the courage and firmness indispensable to secure to his people the benefits he wished them to enjoy.

She had too, for a time, another occupation. The princess royal was, as she had said not long before, of an age to feel keenly the miseries of her parents, and the agitation into which she had been thrown had its natural effect upon her health. Her own language on the subject affords a striking proof how well Marie Antoinette had succeeded in imbuing her with her own forgetfulness of self. As she has recorded the occurrence in her journal, "Fortunately her affliction increased her illness to so serious a degree as to cause a favorable diversion to her mother's despair.[3]"

Youth, however, and a strong constitution prevailed, and the little princess recovered; while other matters also for a time claimed a large share of her mother's attention. For herself, Marie Antoinette felt, as she well might feel, that, come what would, happiness and she were forever parted; and the death to which she never doubted that her enemies destined her could hardly have been anticipated by her as any thing but a relief, if she had thought only of her own feelings. But, again, she had others to think of besides herself--of her children. And she presently learned that others were thinking of her, and were willing (it should rather be said were eager and proud) to encounter any danger, if they might only have the happiness and honor of securing and saving her whom they still regarded as their queen. Two had long been attached to the royal household: the wife of M. de Jarjayes, a gentleman of ancient family in Dauphine, had been one of Marie Antoinette's waiting-women, and he himself, since the fatal expedition to Varennes, had been employed by Louis on several secret missions. From the moment that his royal master was brought before the Convention he had despaired of his life, and had, therefore, bent all his thoughts on the preservation of the queen. M. Turgy, the second, was in a humbler rank of life. He was, as we have seen, one of the officers of the kitchen; but in the household of a king of France even the cooks had pretensions to gentle blood. A third was a man named Toulan, who had originally been a music-seller in Paris, but had subsequently obtained employment under the Municipal Council, and was now a commissioner, with duties which brought him into constant contact with the imprisoned queen. Either he had never in his heart been her enemy, or he had been converted by the dignified fortitude with which she bore her miseries, and by the irresistible fascination which even in prison she still exercised over all whose hearts had not been hardened by fanatical wickedness against every manly or honest feeling; he won the queen's confidence by the most welcome service, which has been already mentioned, of conveying to her her husband's seal and ring. She gave him a letter to recommend him to the confidence of Jarjayes; and their combined ingenuity devised a plan for the escape of the whole family. It was in their favor that a man, who came daily to look to the lamps, usually brought with him his two sons, who nearly matched the size of the royal children. And Jarjayes and Toulan, aided by another of the municipal commissioners, named Lepitre, who had also learned to abhor the indignities practiced on fallen royalty, had prepared full suits of male attire for the queen and princess, with red scarfs and sashes as were worn by the different commissioners, of whom there were too many for all of them to be known to the sentinels; and also clothes for the two children, ill-fitting and shabby, to resemble the dress of the lamp-lighter's boys. Passports, too, by the aid of Lepitre, whose duties lay in the department which issued them, were provided for the whole family; and after careful discussion of the arrangements to be adopted when once the prisoners were clear of the Temple, it was settled that they should take the road to Normandy in three cabriolets, which would be less likely to attract notice than any larger and less ordinary carriage.

The end of February or the beginning of March was fixed for the attempt; but before that time the Government and the people had become greatly disquieted by the operations of the German armies, which were about to receive the powerful assistance of England. Prussia had gained decided advantages on the Rhine. An Austrian army, under the Archduke Charles, was making formidable progress in the Netherlands. Rumors, also, which soon proved to be well founded, of an approaching insurrection in the western departments of France, reached the capital. The vigilance with which the royal prisoners were watched was increased. Information, too, though of no precise character, that they had obtained means of communicating with their partisans who were at liberty, was conveyed to the magistrates. And at last Jarjayes and Toulan were forced to abandon the idea of effecting the escape of the whole family, though they were still confident that they could accomplish that of the queen, which they regarded as the most important, since it was plain that it was she who was in the most immediate danger. Elizabeth, as disinterested as herself, besought her to embrace their offers, and to let her and the children, as being less obnoxious to the Jacobins, take their chance of some subsequent means of escape, or perhaps even mercy.

But such a flight was forbidden alike by Marie Antoinette's sense of duty and by her sense of honor, if indeed the two were ever separated in her mind. Honor forbade her to desert her companions in misery, whose danger might even be increased by the rage of her jailers, exasperated at her escape. Duty to her boy forbade it still more emphatically. As his guardian, she ought not to leave him; as his mother, she could not. And her renunciation of the whole design was conveyed to M. Jarjayes in a letter which did honor alike to both by the noble gratitude which it expressed, and which was long cherished by his heirs as one of their most precious possessions, till it was destroyed, with many another valuable record, when Paris a second time fell under the rule of wretches scarcely less detestable than the Jacobins whom they imitated.[4] It was written by stealth, with a pencil; but no difficulties or hurry, as no acuteness of disappointment or depth of distress, could rob Marie Antoinette of her desire to confer pleasure on others, or of her inimitable gracefulness of expression. Thus she wrote:

"We have had a pleasant dream, that is all. I have gained much by still finding, on this occasion, a new proof of your entire devotion to me. My confidence in you is boundless. And on all occasions you will always find strength of mind and courage in me. But the interest of my son is my sole guide; and, whatever happiness I might find in being out of this place, I can not consent to separate myself from him. In what remains, I thoroughly recognize your attachment to me in all that you said to me yesterday. Rely upon it that I feel the kindness and the force of your arguments as far as my own interest is concerned, and that I feel that the opportunity can not recur. But I could enjoy nothing if I were to leave my children; and this idea prevents me from even regretting my decision.[5]"

And to Toulan she said that "her sole desire was to be reunited to her husband whenever Heaven should decide that her life was no longer necessary to her children." He was greatly afflicted, but he could no longer be of use to her. Her last commission to him was to convey to her eldest brother-in-law, the Count de Provence, her husband's ring and seal, that they might be in safer custody than her own, and that she or her son might reclaim them, if either should ever be at liberty. She gave Toulan also, as a memorial of her gratitude, a small gold box, one of the few trinkets which she still possessed, and which, unhappily, proved a fatal present. In the summer of the next year it was found in his possession, its history was ascertained, and he was sent to the scaffold for the sole offense of having and valuing a relic of his murdered sovereign.

Nor was this the only plan formed for the queen's rescue. The Baron de Batz was a noble of the purest blood in France, seneschal of the Duchy of Albret, and bound by ancient ties of hereditary friendship to the king, as the heir of Henry IV., whose most intimate confidence had been enjoyed by his ancestor. He was still animated by all the antique feelings of chivalrous loyalty, and from the first breaking-out of the troubles of the Revolution he had brought to the service of his sovereign the most absolute devotion, which was rendered doubly useful by an inexhaustible fertility of resource, and a presence of mind that nothing could daunt or perplex. On the fatal 21st of January, he had even formed a project of rescuing Louis on his way to the scaffold, which failed, partly from the timidity of some on whose co-operation he had reckoned, and partly, it is said, from the reluctance of Louis himself to countenance an enterprise which, whatever might be its result, must tend to fierce conflict and bloodshed. Since his sovereign's death he had bent all the energies of his mind to contrive the escape of the queen, and he had so far succeeded that he had enlisted in her cause two men whose posts enabled them to give must effectual resistance: Michonis, who, like Toulan, was one of the commissioners of the Council; and Cortey, a captain of the National Guard, whose company was one of those most frequently on duty at the Temple. It seemed as if all that was necessary to be done was to select a night for the escape when the chief outlets of the Temple should be guarded by Cortey's men; and De Batz, who was at home in every thing that required manoeuvre or contrivance, had provided dresses to disguise the persons of the whole family while in the Temple, and passports and conveyances to secure their escape the moment they were outside the gates. Every thing seemed to promise success, when at the last moment secret intelligence that some plan or other was in agitation was conveyed to the Council. It was not sufficient to enable them to know whom they were to guard against or to arrest, but it was enough to lead them to send down to the Temple another commissioner whose turn of duty did not require his presence there, but whose ferocious surliness of temper pointed him out as one not easily to be either tricked or overborne. He was a cobbler, named Simon, the very same to whose cruel superintendence the little king was presently intrusted.

He came down the very evening that every thing was arranged for the escape of the hapless family. De Batz saw that all was over if he staid, and hesitated for a moment whether he should blow out his brains, and try to accomplish the queen's deliverance by force; but a little reflection showed him that the noise of fire-arms would bring up a crowd of enemies beyond his ability to overpower, and it soon appeared that it would tax all his resources to secure his own escape. He achieved that, hoping still to find some other opportunity of being useful to his royal mistress; but none offered. The Assembly did him the honor to set a price on his head; and at last he thought himself fortunate in being able to save himself. Those who had cooperated with him had worse fortune. Those in authority had no proofs on which to condemn them; but in those days suspicion was a sufficient death-warrant. Michonis and Cortey were suspected, and in the course of the next year a belief that they had at least sympathized with the queen's sorrows sent them both to the scaffold.

With the failure of De Batz every project of escape was abandoned; and a few weeks later the queen congratulated herself that she had refused to flee without her boy, since in the course of May he was seized with illness which for some days threatened to assume a dangerous character. With a brutality which, even in such monsters as the Jacobin rulers of the city, seems almost inconceivable, they refused to allow him the attendance of M. Brunier, the physician who had had the charge of his infancy. It would be a breach of the principles of equality, they said, if any prisoner were permitted to consult any but the prison doctor. But the prison doctor was a man of sense and humanity, as well as of professional skill. He of his own accord sought the advice of Brunier; and the poor child recovered, to be reserved for a fate which, even in the next few weeks, was so foreshadowed, that his own mother must almost have begun to doubt whether his restoration to health had been a blessing to her or to himself.

The spring was marked by important events. Had one so high-minded been capable of exulting in the misfortunes of even her worst enemies, Marie Antoinette might have triumphed in the knowledge that the murderers of her husband were already beginning that work of mutual destruction which in little more than a year sent almost every one of them to the same scaffold on which he had perished. The jealousies which from the first had set the Jacobins and Girondins at variance had reached a height at which they could only be extinguished by the annihilation of one party or the other. They had been partners in crime, and so far were equal in infamy; but the Jacobins were the fiercer and the readier ruffians; and, after nearly two months of vehement debates in the Convention, in which Robespierre denounced the whole body of the Girondin leaders as plotters of treason against the State, and Vergniaud in reply reviled Robespierre as a coward, the Jacobins worked up the mob to rise in their support. The Convention, which hitherto had been divided in something like equality between the two factions, yielded to the terror of a new insurrection, and on the 2d of June ordered the arrest of the Girondin leaders. A very few escaped the search made for them by the officers--Roland, to commit suicide; Barbaroux, to attempt it; Petion and Buzot reached the forests to be devoured by congenial wolves. Lanjuinais,[6] whom the decree of the Convention had identified with them, but who, even in the moments of the greatest excitement, had kept himself clear of their wickedness and crimes, was the only one of the whole body who completely eluded the rage of his enemies. The rest, with Madame Roland, the first prompter of deeds of blood, languished in their well-deserved prisons till the close of autumn, when they all perished on the same scaffold to which they had sent their innocent sovereign.[7]

But it may be that Marie Antoinette never learned their fall; though that if she had, pity would at least have mingled with, if it had not predominated over, her natural exultation, she gave a striking proof in her conduct toward one from whom she had suffered great and constant indignities. From the time that her own attendants were dismissed, the only person appointed to assist Clery in his duties were a man and woman named Tison, chosen for that task on account of their surly and brutal tempers, in which the wife exceeded her husband. Both, and especially the woman, had taken a fiendish pleasure in heaping gratuitous insults on the whole family; but at last the dignity and resignation of the queen awakened remorse in the woman's heart, which presently worked upon her to such a degree that she became mad. In the first days of her frenzy she raved up and down the courtyard declaring herself guilty of the queen's murder. She threw herself at Marie Antoinette's feet, imploring her pardon; and Marie Antoinette not only raised her up with her own hand, and spoke gentle words of forgiveness and consolation to her, but, after she had been removed to a hospital, showed a kind interest in her condition, and amidst all her own troubles found time to write a note to express her anxiety that the invalid should have proper attention.[8]

But very soon a fresh blow was struck at the hapless queen which made her indifferent to all else that could happen, and even to her own fate, of which it may be regarded as the precursor. At ten o'clock on the 3d of July, when the little king was sleeping calmly, his mother having hung a shawl in front of his bed to screen his eyes from the light of the candle by which she and Elizabeth were mending their clothes, the door of their chamber was violently thrown open, and six commissioners entered to announce to the queen that the Convention had ordered the removal of her boy, that he might he committed to the care of a tutor--the tutor named being the cobbler, Simon, whose savageness of disposition was sufficiently attested by the fact of his having been chosen on the recommendation of Marat. At this unexpected blow, Marie Antoinette's fortitude and resignation at last gave way. She wept, she remonstrated, she humbled herself to entreat mercy. She threw her arms around her child, and declared that force itself should not tear him from her. The commissioners were not men likely to feel or show pity. They abused her; they threatened her. She begged them rather to kill her than take her son. They would not kill her, but they swore that they would murder both him and her daughter before her eyes if he were not at once surrendered. There was no more resistance. His aunt and sister took him from the bed and dressed him. His mother, with a voice choked by her sobs, addressed him the last words he was ever to hear from her. "My child, they are taking you from me; never forget the mother who loves you tenderly, and never forget God! Be good, gentle, and honest, and your father will look down on you from heaven and bless you!" "Have you done with this preaching?" said the chief commissioner. "You have abused our patience finely," another added; "the nation is generous, and will take care of his education." But she had fainted, and heard not these words of mocking cruelty. Nothing could touch her further.

If it be not also a mockery to speak of happiness in connection with this most afflicted queen, she was happy in at least not knowing the details of the education which was in store for the noble boy whose birth had apparently secured for him the most splendid of positions, and whose opening virtues seemed to give every promise that he would be worthy of his rank and of his mother. A few days afterward Simon received his instructions from a committee of the Convention, of which Drouet, the postmaster of Ste. Menehould, was the chief. "How was he to treat the wolf cub?" he asked (it was one of the mildest names he ever gave him). "Was he to kill him?" "No." "To poison him?" "No." "What then?" "He was to get rid of him,[9]" and Simon carried out this instruction by the most unremitting illtreatment of his pupil. He imposed upon him the most menial offices; he made him clean his shoes; he reviled him; he beat him; he compelled him to wear the red cap and jacket which had been adopted as the Revolutionary dress; and one day, when his mother obtained a glimpse of him as he was walking on the leads of the tower to which he had been transferred, it caused her an additional pang to see that he had been stripped of the suit of mourning for his father, and had been clothed in the garments which, in her eyes, were the symbol, of all that was most impious and most loathsome.

All these outrages were but the prelude of the final blow which was to fall on herself; and it shows how great was the fear with which her lofty resolution had always had inspired the Jacobins--fear with such natures being always the greatest exasperation of hatred and the keenest incentive to cruelty--that, when they had resolved to consummate her injuries by her murder, they did not leave her in the

Temple as they had left her husband, but removed her to the Conciergerie, which in those days, fitly denominated the Reign of Terror, rarely led but to the scaffold. On the night of the 1st of August (the darkest hours were appropriately chosen for deeds of such darkness) another body of commissioners entered her room, and woke her up to announce that they had come to conduct her to the common prison. Her sister and her daughter begged in vain to be allowed to accompany her. She herself scarcely spoke a word, but dressed herself in silence, made up a small bundle of clothes, and, after a few words of farewell and comfort to those dear ones who had hitherto been her companions, followed her jailers unresistingly, knowing, and for her own sake certainly not grieving, that she was going to meet her doom. As she passed through the outer door it was so low that she struck her head. One of the commissioners had so much decency left as to ask if she was hurt. "No," she replied, "nothing now can hurt me.[10]" Six weeks later, an English gentleman saw her in her dungeon. She was freely exhibited to any one who desired to behold her, on the sole condition--a condition worthy of the monsters who exacted it, and of them alone--that he should show no sign of sympathy or sorrow.[11] "She was sitting on an old worn-out chair made of straw which scarcely supported her weight. Dressed in a gown which had once been white, her attitude bespoke the immensity of her grief, which appeared to have created a kind of stupor, that fortunately rendered her less sensible to the injuries and reproaches which a number of inhuman wretches were continually vomiting forth against her."

Even after all the atrocities and horrors of the last twelve months, the news of the resolution to bring her to a trial, which, it was impossible to doubt, it was intended to follow up by her execution, was received as a shook by the great bulk of the nation, as indeed by all Europe. And Necker's daughter, Madame de Stael, who, as we have seen, had been formerly desirous to aid in her escape, now addressed an energetic and eloquent appeal to the entire people, calling on all persons of all parties, "Republicans, Constitutionalists, and Aristocrats alike, to unite for her preservation." She left unemployed no fervor of entreaty, no depth of argument. She reminded them of the universal admiration which the queen's beauty and grace had formerly excited, when "all France thought itself laid under an obligation by her charms;[12]" of the affection that she had won by her ceaseless acts of beneficence and generosity. She showed the absurdity of denouncing her as "the Austrian"--her who had left Vienna while still little more than a child, and had ever since fixed her heart as well as her home in France. She argued truly that the vagueness, the ridiculousness, the notorious falsehood of the accusations brought against her were in themselves her all-sufficient defense. She showed how useless to every party and in every point of view must be her condemnation. What danger could any one apprehend from restoring to liberty a princess whose every thought was tenderness and pity? She reproached those who now held sway in France with the barbarity of their proscriptions, with governing by terror and by death, with having overthrown a throne only to erect a scaffold in its place; and she declared that the execution of the queen would exceed in foulness all the other crimes that they had yet committed. She was a foreigner, she was a woman; to put her to death would be a violation of all the laws of hospitality as well as of all the laws of nature. The whole universe was interesting itself in the queen's fate. Woe to the nation which knew neither justice nor generosity! Freedom would never be the destiny of such a people.[13]

It had not been from any feeling of compunction or hesitation that those who had her fate in their hands left her so long in her dungeon, but from the absolute impossibility of inventing an accusation against her that should not be utterly absurd and palpably groundless. So difficult did they find their task, that the jailer, a man named Richard, who, when alone, ventured to show sympathy for her miseries, sought to encourage her by the assurance that she would be replaced in the Temple. But Marie Antoinette indulged in no such illusion. She never doubted that her death was resolved on. "No," she replied to his well-meant words of hope, "they have murdered the king; they will kill me in the same way. Never again shall I see my unfortunate children, my tender and virtuous sister." And the tears which her own sufferings could not wring from her flowed freely when she thought of what they were still enduring.

But at last the eagerness for her destruction overcame all difficulties or scruples. The principal articles of the indictment charged her with helping to overthrow the republic and to effect the reestablishment of the throne; with having exerted her influence over her husband to mislead his judgment, to render him unjust to his people, and to induce him to put his veto on laws of which they desired the enactment; with having caused scarcity and famine; with having favored aristocrats; and with having kept up a constant correspondence with her brother, the emperor; and the preamble and the peroration compared her to Messalina, Agrippina, Brunehaut, and Catherine de' Medici--to all the wickedest women of whom ancient or modern history had preserved a record. Had she been guided by her own feelings alone, she would have probably disdained to defend herself against charges whose very absurdity proved that they were only put forward as a pretense for a judgment that had been previously decided on. But still, as ever, she thought of her child, her fair and good son, her "gentle infant," her king. While life lasted she could never wholly relinquish the hope that she might see him once again, perhaps even that some unlooked-for chance (none could be so unexpected as almost every occurrence of the last four years) might restore him and her to freedom, and him to his throne; and for his sake she resolved to exert herself to refute the charges, and at least to establish her right to acquittal and deliverance.

Louis had been tried before the Convention. Marie Antoinette was to be condemned by the, if possible, still more infamous court that had been established in the spring under the name of the Revolutionary Tribunal; and on the 13th of October she was at last conducted before a small sub-committee, and subjected to a private examination. To every question she gave firm and clear answers.[14] She declared that the French people had indeed been deceived, but not by her or by her husband. She affirmed "that the happiness of France always had been, and still was, the first wish of her heart;" and that "she should not even regret the loss of her son's throne, if it led to the real happiness of the country." She was taken back to her cell. The next day the four judges of the tribunal took their seats in the court. Fouquier-Tinville, the public prosecutor, a man whose greed of blood stamped him with an especial hideousness, even in those days of universal barbarity, took his seat before them; and eleven men, the greater part of whom had been carefully picked from the very dregs of the people--journeymen carpenters, tailors, blacksmiths, and discharged policemen--were constituted the jury.

Before this tribunal--we will not dignify it with the name of a court of justice--Marie Antoinette, the widow Capet, as she was called in the indictment, was now brought. Clad in deep mourning for her murdered husband, and aged beyond her years by her long series of sorrows, she still preserved the fearless dignity which became her race and rank and character. As she took her place at the bar and cast her eyes around the hall, even the women who thronged the court, debased as they were, were struck by her lofty demeanor. "How proud she is!" was the exclamation, the only sign of nervousness that she gave being that, as those who watched her closely remarked, she moved her fingers up and down on the arm of her chair, as if she had been playing on the harpsichord. The prosecutor brought up witness after witness; some whom it was believed that some ancient hatred, others whom it was expected that some hope of pardon for themselves, might induce to give evidence such as was required. The Count d'Estaing had always been connected with her enemies. Bailly, once Mayor of Paris, as has been seen, had sought a base popularity by the wantonness of the unprovoked insults which he had offered to the king. Michonis knew that his head was imperiled by suspicions of his recent desire to assist her. But one and all testified to her entire innocence of the different charges which they had been brought forward to support, and to the falsehood of the statements contained in the indictment. Her own replies, when any question was addressed to herself, were equally in her favor. When accused of having been the prompter of the political mesures of the king's government, her answer could not be denied to be in accordance with the law: "That she was the wife and subject of the king, and could not be made responsible for his resolutions and actions." When charged with general indifference or hostility to the happiness of the people, she affirmed with equal calmness, as she had previously declared at her private examination, that the welfare of the nation had been, and always was, the first of her wishes.

Once only did a question provoke an answer in any other tone than that of a lofty imperturbable equanimity. She had not known till that moment the depth of her enemies' wickedness, or the cruelty with which her son's mind had been dealt with, worse ten thousand times than the foulest tortures that could be applied to the body. Both her children had been subjected to an examination, in the hope that something might be found to incriminate her in the words of those who might hardly be able to estimate the exact value of their expressions. The princess had been old enough to baffle the utmost malice of her questioners; and the boy had given short and plain replies from which nothing to suit their purpose could be extracted, till they forced him to drink brandy, and, when he was stupefied with drink, compelled him to sign depositions in which he accused both the queen and Elizabeth of having trained him in lessons of vice. At first, horror at so monstrous a charge had sealed the queen's lips; but when she gave no denial, a juryman questioned her on the subject, and insisted on an answer. Then at last Marie Antoinette spoke in sublime indignation. "If I have not answered, it was because nature itself rejects such an accusation made against a mother. I appeal from it to every mother who hears me."

Marie Antoinette had been allowed two counsel, who, perilous as was the duty imposed upon them, cheerfully accepted it as an honor; but it was not intended that their assistance should be more than nominal. She had only known their names on the evening preceding the trial; but when she addressed a letter to the President of the Convention, demanding a postponement of the trial for three days, as indispensable to enable them to master the case, since as yet they had not had time even to read the whole of the indictment, adding that "her duty to her children bound her to leave nothing undone which was requisite for the entire justification of their mother," the request was rudely refused; and all that the lawyers could do was to address eloquent appeals to the judges and jurymen, being utterly unable, on so short notice, to analyze as they deserved the arguments of the prosecutor or the testimony by which he had professed to support them. But before such a tribunal it signified little what was proved or disproved, or what was the strength or weakness of the arguments employed on either side. It was long after midnight of the second day that the trial concluded. The jury at once pronounced the prisoner guilty. The judges as instantly passed sentence of death, and ordered it to be executed the next morning.

It was nearly five in the morning of the 16th of October when the favorite daughter of the great Empress-queen, herself Queen of France, was led from the court, not even to the wretched room which she had occupied for the last ten weeks, but to the condemned cell, never tenanted before by any but the vilest felons. Though greatly exhausted by the length of the proceedings, she had heard the sentence without betraying the slightest emotion by any change of countenance or gesture. On reaching her cell she at once asked for writing materials. They had been withheld from her for more than a year, but they were now brought to her; and with them she wrote her last letter to that princess whom she had long learned to love as a sister of her own, who had shared her sorrows hitherto, and who, at no distant period, was to share the fate which was now awaiting herself.

"16th October, 4.30 A.M.

"It is to you, my sister, that I write for the last time. I have just been condemned, not to a shameful death, for such is only for criminals, but to go and rejoin your brother. Innocent like him, I hope to show the same firmness in my last moments. I am calm, as one is when one's conscience reproaches one with nothing. I feel profound sorrow in leaving my poor children: you know that I only lived for them and for you, my good and tender sister. You who out of love have sacrificed everything to be with us, in what a position do I leave you! I have learned from the proceedings at my trial that my daughter was separated from you. Alas! poor child; I do not venture to write to her; she would not receive my letter. I do not even know whether this will reach you. Do you receive my blessing for both of them. I hope that one day when they are older they may be able to rejoin you, and to enjoy to the full your tender care. Let them both think of the lesson which I have never ceased to impress upon them, that the principles and the exact performance of their duties are the chief foundation of life; and then mutual affection and confidence in one another will constitute its happiness. Let my daughter feel that at her age she ought always to aid her brother by the advice which her greater experience and her affection may inspire her to give him. And let my son in his turn render to his sister all the care and all the services which affection can inspire. Let them, in short, both feel that, in whatever positions they may be placed, they will never be truly happy but through their union. Let them follow our example. In our own misfortunes how much comfort has our affection for one another afforded us! And, in times of happiness, we have enjoyed that doubly from being able to share it with a friend; and where can one find friends more tender and more united than in one's own family? Let my son never forget the last words of his father, which I repeat emphatically; let him never seek to avenge our deaths. I have to speak to you of one thing which is very painful to my heart, I know how much pain the child must have caused you. Forgive him, my dear sister; think of his age, and how easy it is to make a child say whatever one wishes, especially when he does not understand it.[15] It will come to pass one day, I hope, that he will better feel the value of your kindness and of your tender affection for both of them. It remains to confide to you my last thoughts. I should have wished to write them at the beginning of my trial; but, besides that they did not leave me any means of writing, events have passed so rapidly that I really have not had time.

"I die in the Catholic Apostolic and Roman religion, that of my fathers, that in which I was brought up, and which I have always professed. Having no spiritual consolation to look for, not even knowing whether there are still in this place any priests of that religion[16] (and indeed the place where I am would expose them to too much danger if they were to enter it but once), I sincerely implore pardon of God for all the faults which I may have committed during my life. I trust that, in his goodness, he will mercifully accept my last prayers, as well as those which I have for a long time addressed to him, to receive my soul into his mercy. I beg pardon of all whom I know, and especially of you, my sister, for all the vexations which, without intending it, I may have caused you. I pardon all my enemies the evils that they have done me. I bid farewell to my aunts and to all my brothers and sisters. I had friends. The idea of being forever separated from them and from all their troubles is one of the greatest sorrows that I suffer in dying. Let them at least know that to my latest moment I thought of them.

"Farewell, my good and tender sister. May this letter reach you. Think always of me; I embrace you with all my heart, as I do my poor dear children. My God, how heart-rending it is to leave them forever! Farewell! farewell! I must now occupy myself with my spiritual duties, as I am not free in my actions. Perhaps they will bring me a priest; but I here protest that I will not say a word to him, but that I will treat him as a person absolutely unknown."

Her forebodings were realized; her letter never reached Elizabeth, but was carried to Fouquier, who placed it among his special records. Yet, if in those who had thus wrought the writer's destruction there had been one human feeling, it might have been awakened by the simple dignity and unaffected pathos of this sad farewell. No line that she ever wrote was more thoroughly characteristic of her. The innocence, purity, and benevolence of her soul shine through every sentence. Even in that awful moment she never lost her calm, resigned fortitude, nor her consideration for others. She speaks of and feels for her children, for her friends, but never for herself. And it is equally characteristic of her that, even in her own hopeless situation, she still can cherish hope for others, and can look forward to the prospect of those whom she loves being hereafter united in freedom and happiness. She thought, it may be, that her own death would be the last sacrifice that her enemies would require. And for even her enemies and murderers she had a word of pardon, and could address a message of mercy for them to her son, who, she trusted, might yet some day have power to show that mercy she enjoined, or to execute the vengeance which with her last breath she deprecated.

She threw herself on her bed and fell asleep. At seven she was roused by the executioner. The streets were already thronged with a fierce and sanguinary mob, whose shouts of triumph were so vociferous that she asked one of her jailers whether they would tear her to pieces. She was assured that, as he expressed it, they would do her no harm. And indeed the Jacobins themselves would have protected her from the populace, so anxious were they to heap on her every indignity that would render death more terrible. Louis had been allowed to quit the Temple in his carriage. Marie Antoinette was to be drawn from the prison to the scaffold in a common cart, seated on a bare plank; the executioner by her side, holding the cords with which her hands were already bound. With a refinement of barbarity, those who conducted the procession made it halt more than once, that the people might gaze upon her, pointing her out to the mob with words and gestures of the vilest insult. She heard them not; her thoughts were with God: her lips were uttering nothing but prayers. Once for a moment, as she passed in sight of the Tuileries, she was observed to cast an agonized look toward its towers, remembering, perhaps, how reluctantly she had quit it fourteen months before. It was midday before the cart reached the scaffold. As she descended, she trod on the executioner's foot. It might seem to have been ordained that her very last words might be words of courtesy. "Excuse me, sir," she said, "I did not do it on purpose;" and she added, "make haste." In a few moments all was over.

Her body was thrown into a pit in the common cemetery, and covered with quicklime to insure its entire destruction. When, more than twenty years afterward, her brother-in-law was restored to the throne, and with pious affection desired to remove her remains and those of her husband to the time-honored resting-place of their royal ancestors at St. Denis, no remains of her who had once been the admiration of all beholders could be found beyond some fragments of clothing, and one or two bones, among which the faithful memory of Chateaubriand believed that he recognized the mouth whose sweet smile had been impressed on his memory since the day on which it acknowledged his loyalty on his first presentation, while still a boy, at Versailles.

Thus miserably perished, by a death fit only for the vilest of criminals, Marie Antoinette, the daughter of one sovereign, the wife of another, who had never wronged or injured one human being. No one was ever more richly endowed with all the charms which render woman attractive, or with all the virtues that make her admirable. Even in her earliest years, her careless and occasionally undignified levity was but the joyous outpouring of a pure innocence of heart that, as it meant no evil, suspected none; while it was ever blended with a kindness and courtesy which sprung from a genuine benevolence. As queen, though still hardly beyond girlhood when she ascended the throne, she set herself resolutely to work by her admonitions, and still more effectually by her example, to purify a court of which for centuries the most shameless profligacy had been the rule and boast; discountenancing vice and impiety by her marked reprobation, and reserving all her favor and protection for genius and patriotism, and honor and virtue. Surrounded at a later period by unexampled dangers and calamities, she showed herself equal to every vicissitude of fortune, and superior to its worst frowns. If her judgment occasionally erred, it was in cases where alternatives of evil were alone offered to her choice, and in which it is even now scarcely possible to decide what course would have been wiser or safer than that which she adopted. And when at last the long conflict was terminated by the complete victory of her combined enemies-- when she, with her husband and her children, was bereft not only of power, but even of freedom, and was a prisoner in the hands of those whose unalterable object was her destruction--she bore her accumulated miseries with a serene resignation, an intrepid fortitude, a true heroism of soul, of which the history of the world does not afford a brighter example.

NOTES

PREFACE

[1] One entitled "Marie-Antoinette, correspondance secrete entre Marie-Therese et le Comte Mercy d'Argenteau, avec des lettres de Marie-Therese et de Marie-Antoinette." (The edition referred to in this work is the greatly enlarged second edition in three volumes, published at Paris,

1875.) The second is entitled "Marie-Antoinette, Joseph II., and Leopold II," published at Leipsic, 1866.

[2] Entitled "Louis XVI, Marie-Antoinette, et Madame Elizabeth," in six volumes, published at intervals from 1864 to 1873.

[3] In his "Nouveau Lundi," March 5th, 1866, M. Sainte-Beuve challenged M. Feuillet de Conches to a more explicit defense of the authenticity of his collection than he had yet vouchsafed; complaining, with some reason, that his delay in answering the charges brought against it "was the more vexatious because his collection was only attacked in part, and in many points remained solid and valuable." And this challenge elicited from M.F. de Conches a very elaborate explanation of the sources from which he procured his documents, which he published in the _Revue des Deux Mondes_,

July 15th, 1866, and afterward in the Preface to his fourth volume. That in a collection of nearly a thousand documents he may have occasionally been too credulous in accepting cleverly executed forgeries as genuine letters is possible, and even probable; in fact, the present writer regards it as certain. But the vast majority, including all those of the greatest value, can not be questioned without imputing to him a guilty knowledge that they were forgeries--a deliberate bad faith, of which no one, it is believed, has ever accused him.

It may be added that it is only from the letters of this later period that any quotations are made in the following work; and the greater part of the letters so cited exists in the archives at Vienna, while the others, such as those, addressed by the Queen, to Madame de Polignac, etc., are just such as were sure to be preserved as relics by the families of those to whom they were addressed, and can therefore hardly be considered as liable to the slightest suspicion.

CHAPTER I.

[1] Sainte-Beuve, "Nouveaux Lundis," August 8th, 1864.

CHAPTER II.

[1] "Histoire de Marie Antoinette," par E. and J. de Goncourt, p. 11.

[2] How popular masked halls were in London at this time may be learned from Walpole's "Letters," and especially from a passage in which he gives an account of one given by "sixteen or eighteen young Lords" just two months before this ball at Vienna.--_Walpole to Mann_, dated February 27th, 1770. Some one a few years later described the French nation as half tiger and half monkey; and it is a singular coincidence that Walpole's comment on this masquerading fashion should be, "It is very lucky, seeing how much of the tiger enters into the human composition, that there should be a good dose of the monkey too."

[3] "Memoires concernant Marie Antoinette," par Joseph Weber (her foster-brother), i., p. 6.

[4] "Goethe's Biography," p. 287.

[5] "Memoires de Bachaumont," January 30th, 1770.

[6] La maison du roi.

[7] Chevalier d'honneur. We have no corresponding office at the English court.

[8] The king said, "Vous etiez deja de la famille, car votre mere a l'ame de Louis le Grand."--SAINTE-BEUVE, _Nouveaux Lundis_, viii., p. 322.

[9] In the language of the French heralds, the title princes of the royal family was confined to the children or grandchildren of the reigning sovereign. His nephews and cousins were only princes of the blood.

CHAPTER III.

[1] The word is Maria Teresa's own; "anti-francais" occurring in more than one of her letters.

[2] Quoted by Mme. du Deffand in a letter to Walpole, dated May 19th, 1770 ("Correspondance complete de Mme. du Deffand," ii., p.59).

[3] Mercy to Marie-Therese, August 4th, 1770; "Correspondance secrete entre Marie-Therese et la Comte de Mercy Argenteau, avec des Lettres de Marie-Therese et Marie Antoinette," par M. le Chevalier Alfred d'Arneth, i., p. 29. For the sake of brevity, this Collection will be hereafter referred to as "Arneth."

[4] "The King of France is both hated and despised, which seldom happens to the same man."--LORD CHESTERFIELD, _Letter to Mr. Dayrolles_, dated May
19th, 1752.

[5] Maria Teresa died in December, 1780.

[6] Mme. du Deffand, letter of May 19th, 1770.

[7] Chambier, i., p. 60.

[8] Mme. de Campan, i., p. 3.

[9] He told Mercy she was "'vive et un peu enfant, mais," ajouta-t-il, "cela est bien de son age.'"--ARNETH, i., p. 11.

[10] Arneth, i., p.9-16

CHAPTER IV.

[1] Dates 9th and 12th., Arneth, i., pp. 16, 18.

[2] Marly was a palace belonging to the king, but little inferior in splendor to Versailles itself, and a favorite residence of Louis XV., because a less strict etiquette had been established there. Choisy and Bellevue, which will often be mentioned in the course of this narrative, were two others of the royal palaces on a somewhat smaller scale. They have both been destroyed. Marly, Choisy, and Bellevue were all between Versailles and Paris.

[3] Mem. de Goncourt, quoting a MS. diary of Hardy, p. 35.

[4] De Vermond, who had accompanied her from Vienna as her reader.

[5] See St. Simon's account of Dangeau, i., p. 392.

[6] The Duc de Noailles, brother-in-law of the countess, "l'homme de France qui a peut-etre le plus d'esprit et qui connait le mieux son souverain et la cour," told Mercy in August that "jugeant d'apres son experience et d'apres les qualites qu'il voyait dans cette princesse, il etait persuade qu'elle gouvernerait un jour l'esprit du roi."--ARNETH, i., p. 34.

[7] La petite rousse.

[8] "De monter a cheval gate le teint, et votre taille a la longue s'en ressentira."--_Marie-Therese a Marie-Antoinette_, Arneth, i., p. 104.

[9] "On fit chercher partout des anes fort doux et tranquilles. Le 21 on repeta la promenade sur les anes. Mesdames voulurent etre de la partie ainsi que le Comte de Provence et le Comte d'Artois."--_Mercy a Marie-Therese_, September 19, 1770, Arneth, i., p. 49.

[10] "Madame la Dauphine, a laquelle le tresor royal doit remettre 6000 frs. par mois, n'a reellement pas un ecu dont elle peut disposer elle-meme et sans le concours de personne" (Octobre 20).--ARNETH, i. p. 69.

[11] "Ses garcons de chambre recoivent cent louis [a louis was twenty-four francs, so that the hundred made 2100 francs out of her 6000] par mois pour la depense du jeu de S.A.R.; et soit qu'elle perde ou qu'elle gagne, on ne revoit rien de cette somme."--ARNETH, i.

[12] "Mme. Adelaide ajouta, 'On voit bien que vous n'etes pas de notre sang.'"--ARNETH, i., p. 94.

[13] Arneth, i., p. 95.

[14] "Finalement, Mme. la Dauphine se fait adorer de ses entours et du public; il n'est pas encore survenu un seul inconvenient grave dans sa conduite."--_Mercy a Marie-Therese_, Novembre 16, Arneth, i., p. 98.

[15] Prince de Ligne, "Mem." ii., p. 79.

[16] Mercy to Maria Teresa, dated November 17th, 1770, Arneth, i., p. 94.

[17] Mercy to Maria Teresa, dated February 25th, 1771, Arneth, i, p. 134.

CHAPTER V

[1] See the "Citizen of the World," Letter 55. Reference has often been made to Lord Chesterfield's prediction of the French Revolution. But I am not aware that any one has remarked on the equally acute foresight of Goldsmith.

[2] Letter of April 16th, 1771, Arneth, i., p. 148.

[3] Arneth, i., p. 186.

[4] Maria Teresa to Marie Antoinette, July 9th, and August 17th, Arneth, i., p. 196.

[5] "Ne soyez pas honteuse d'etre allemande jusqu'aux gaucheries.... Le Francais vous estimera plus et fera plus de compte sur vous s'il vous trouve la solidite et la franchise allemande."--_Maria Teresa to Marie Antoinette._ May 8th, 1771, Arneth, i., p. 159.

[6] Walpole's letter to Sir H. Mann, June 8th, 1771, v., p. 301.

[7] Mercy to Maria Teresa, January 23d, 1772, Arneth, i., p. 265.

[8] The Duc de la Vauguyon, who, after the dauphin's marriage, still retained his post with his younger brother.

CHAPTER VI

[1] Mercy's letter to the empress, August 14th, 1772, Arneth, i., p. 335.

[2] Mercy to Maria Teresa, November 14th, 1772, Arneth, i., p. 307.

[3] Marie Antoinette to Maria Teresa, December 15th, 1772, Arneth, i., p. 382.

[4] Her sister Caroline, Queen of Naples.

[5] Her brother Leopold, at present Grand Duke of Tuscany, afterward emperor. His wife, Marie Louise, was a daughter of Charles III. of Spain.

[6] They, with several of the princes of the blood and some of the peers, as already mentioned, had been banished for their opposition to the abolition of the Parliaments; but now, in the hopes of obtaining the king's consent to his marriage with Madame de Montessan, a widow of enormous wealth, the Due d'Orleans made overtures for forgiveness, accompanying them, however, with a letter so insolent that it might we be regarded as an aggravation of his original offense. According to Madame du Deffand (letter to Walpole, December 18th, 1772, vol. ii., p. 283), he was only prevented from reconciling himself to the king some months before by his son, the Due de Chartres (afterward the infamous Egalite), whom she describes as "a young man, very obstinate, and who hopes to play a great part by putting himself at the head of a faction." The princes, however, in the view of the shrewd old lady, had made the mistake of greatly overrating their own importance. "These great princes, since their protest, have been just citizens of the Rue St. Denis. No one at court ever perceived their absence, and no one in the city ever noticed their presence."

[7] Lord Stormont, the English Embassador at Vienna, from which city he was removed to Paris. In the preceding September Maria Teresa had complained to him of being "animated against her cabinet, from indignation at the partition of Poland."

[8] That is, sisters-in-law--the Princesses Clotilde and Elizabeth.

[9] The Hotel-Dieu was the most ancient hospital in Paris. It had already existed several hundred years when Philip Augustus enlarged it, and gave it the name of Maison de Dieu. Henry IV. and his successors had further enlarged it, and enriched it with monuments; and even the revolutionists respected it, though when they had disowned the existence of God they changed its name to that of L'Hospice de l'Humanite. It had been almost destroyed by fire a fortnight before the date of this letter, on the night of the 29th of December.

[10] St. Anthony's Day was June 14th, and her name of Antoinette was regarded as placing her under his especial protection.

CHAPTER VII

[1] They have not, however, been preserved.

[2] Mercy to Maria Teresa, June 16th, 1773, Arneth, i., p. 467.

[3] "Marie Antoinette, Louis XVI., et la Famille Royale", p. 23.

[4] Marie Antoinette to Maria Theresa, July 17th, Arneth, ii., p. 8.

[5] "Histoire de Marie Antoinette," par M. de Goncourt, p. 50. Quoting an unpublished journal by M.M. Hardy, in the Royal Library.

[6] It is the name by which she is more than once described in Madame du Deffand's letters. See her "Correspondence," ii., p. 357.

[7] Mercy to Maria Teresa, December 11th, 1773, Arneth, ii., p. 81.

[8] "Memoires de Besenval," i., p. 304.

CHAPTER VIII

[1] Mercy to Maria Teresa, August 14th, 1773, Arneth, ii., p. 31.

[2] The money was a joint gift from herself as well as from him. Great distress, arising from the extraordinarily high price of bread, was at this time prevailing in Paris.

[3] The term most commonly used by Marie Antoinette in her letters to her mother to describe Madame du Barri. She was ordered to retire to the Abbey of Pont-aux-Dames, near Meaux. Subsequently she was allowed to return to Luciennes, a villa which her royal lover had given her.

[4] Madame de Mazarin was the lady who, by the fulsomeness of her servility to Madame du Barri, provoked Madame du Deffand (herself a lady not altogether _sans reproche_) to say that it was not easy to carry "the heroism of baseness and absurdity farther."

[5] Lorraine had become a French province a few years before, on the death of Stanislaus Leczinsky, father of the queen of Louis XV.

[6] Maria Teresa to Marie Antoinette, May 18th, and to Mercy on the same day, Arneth, ii., p. 149.

[7] See his letter of 8th May to Maria Teresa. "Il faut que pour la suite de son bonheur, elle commence a s'emparer de l'autorite que M. le Dauphin n'exercera jamais que d'une facon convenable, et ... ce serait du dernier danger et pour l'etat et pour le systeme general que qui ce soit s'emparat de M. le Dauphin et qu'il fut conduit par autre que par Madame la Dauphine."--ARNETH, ii., p. 137.

[8] "Je parle a l'amie, a la confidente du roi."--_Maria Teresa to Marie

Antoinette_, May 30th, 1770, Arneth, ii., p. 155.

[9] "Jusqu'a present l'etiquette de cette cour a toujours interdit aux reines et princesses royales de manger avec des hommes."--_Mercy to Maria Teresa_, June 7th, 1774, Arneth, ii, p. 164

[10] "Elle me traite, a mon arrivee, comme tous les jeunes gens qui composaient ses pages, qu'elle comblait de bontes, en leur montrant une bienveillance pleine de dignite, mais qu'on pouvait aussi appeler maternelle."--_Marie Therese, Memoires de Tilly_, i., p. 25.

[11] Le don, ou le droit, de joyeux avenement.

[12] La ceinture de la reine. It consisted of three pence (deniers) on each hogs-head of wine imported into the city, and was levied every three years in the capital.--ARNETH, ii, p. 179.

[13] The title "ceinture de la reine" had been given to it because in the old times queens and all other ladies had carried their purses at their girdles.

CHAPTER IX

[1] The title by which the count was usually known: that of the countess was madame.

[2] St. Simon, 1709, ch. v., and 1715, ch. i, vols. vii. and xiii., ed. 1829.

[3] Ibid., 1700, ch xxx., vol. ii., p. 469.

[4] Arneth, ii, p. 206.

[5] Madame de Campan, ch. iv.

[6] Madame de Campan, ch. v., p. 106.

[7] _Id._, p. 101.

[8] "_Sir Peter_. Ah, madam, true wit is more neatly allied to good--nature than your ladyship is aware of."--_School for Scandal_, act ii., sc. 2.

CHAPTER X

[1] "Elle avait entierement le defaut contraire [a la prodigalite], et je pouvais prouver qu'elle portait souvent l'economie jusqu'a des details d'une mesquinerie blamable, surtout dans une souveraine."--MADAME DE CAMPAN, ch. v., p. 106, ed. 1858.

[2] Arneth, ii., p. 307.

[3] See the author's "History of France under the Bourbons," iii., p. 418. Lacretelle, iv., p. 368, affirms that this outbreak, for which in his eyes "une pretendue disette" was only a pretext, was "evidemment fomente par des hommes puissans," and that "un salaire qui etait paye par des hommes qu'on ne pouvait nommer aujourd'hui avec assez de certitude, excitait leurs fureurs factices."

[4] La Guerre des Farines.

[5] Arneth, ii., p. 342.

[6] "Souvenirs de Vaublanc," i., p. 231.

[7] August 23d, 1775, No. 1524, in Cunningham's edition, vol. vi., p. 245.

[8] The Prince of Wales and the Duke of York, who were just at this time astonishing London with their riotous living.

CHAPTER XI

[1] "Gustave III. et la Cour de France," i. p. 279.

[2] The Duc d'Angouleme, afterward dauphin, when the Count d'Artois succeeded to the throne as Charles X.

[3] Marie Antoinette to Maria Teresa, August 12th, 1775, Arneth, ii., p. 366.

[4] "Le projet de la reine etait d'exiger du roi que le Sieur Turgot fut chasse, meme envoye a la Bastille ... et il a fallu les representations les plus fortes et les plus instantes pour arreter les effets de la colere de la Reine."--_Mercy to Maria Teresa_, May 16th, 1776, Arneth, ii., p. 446.

[5] The compiler of "Marie Antoinette, Louis XVI., et La Famille Royale" (date April 24th, 1776) has a story of a conversation between the king and queen which illustrates her feeling toward the minister. She had just come in from the opera. He asked her "how she had been received by the Parisians; if she had had the usual cheers." She made no reply; the king understood her silence. "Apparently, madame, you had not feathers enough." "I should have liked to have seen you there, sir, with your St. Germain and your Turgot; you would have been rudely hissed." St. Germain was the minister of war.

[6] Mercy to Maria Teresa, May 16th, 1776, Arneth, ii., p. 446.

[7] January 14th, 1776, Arneth, ii., p. 414.

[8] The ground-floor of the palace was occupied by the shops of jewelers and milliners, some of whom were great sufferers by the fire.

[9] In a letter written at the end of 1775, Mercy reports to the empress that some of Turgot's economical reforms had produced real discontent among those "qui trouvent leur interet dans le desordre," which they had vented in scandalous and seditious writings. Many songs of that character had come out, some of which were attributed to Beaumarchais, "le roi et la reine n'y ont point ete respectes."--_December 17th_, 1775. Arneth, ii, p. 410.

[10] Mercy to Maria Teresa, November 15th, 1776, Arneth, ii., p. 524.

CHAPTER XII.

[1] "Le petit nombre de ceux que la Reine appelle 'sa societe'"--_Mercy to Marie Teresa_, February 15th, 1777, Arneth, iii., p. 18.

[2] "Il faut cependant convenir que dans ces circonstances si rapprochees de la familiarite, la Reine, par un maintien qui tient a son ame, a toujours su imprimer a ceux qui l'entouraient une contenance de respect qui contrebalancait un peu la liberte des propos."--_Mercy to Maria Teresa_, Arneth, ii, p.520.

[3] Brunoy is about fifteen miles from Paris.

[4] "Au reste il est temps pour la sante de la Reine que le carnaval finisse. On remarque qu'elle s'en altere, et que sa Majeste maigrit

beaucoup."--_Marie Therese a Louis XVI._, la date Fevrier 1, 1777, p 101.

[5] Once when he had spoken to her with a severity which alarmed Mercy, who feared it might irritate the queen, "Il me dit en riant qu'il en avait agi ainsi pour sonder l'ame de la reine, et voir si par la force il n'y aurait pas moyen d'obtenir plus que par la douceur."--_Mercy to Maria Teresa_, Arneth, iii., p. 79.

[6] Arneth, iii., p. 73.

CHAPTER XIII.

[1] When Mercy remonstrated with her on her relapse into some of her old habits from which at first she seemed to have weaned herself, "La seule reponse que j'aie obtenu a ete la crainte de s'ennuyer."--_Mercy to Maria Teresa_, November 19th, 1777, Arneth, iii., p. 13.

[2] See Marie Antoinette's account to her mother of his quarrel with the Duchess de Bourbon at a _bal de l'opera_, Arneth, iii., p. 174.

[3] "Il y a apparence que notre marine dont on s'occupe depuis longtemps va bientot etre en activite. Dieu veuille que tous ces mouvements n'amenent pas la guerre de terre."--_Marie Antoinette to Maria Teresa_, March 18th, 1777, Arneth, iii., p. 174.

[4] "Jamais les Anglais n'ont eu tant de superiorite sur mer; mais ils en eurent sur les Francais dans tous les temps."--_Siecle de Louis_, ch xxxv.

[5] The Comte de la Marck, who knew him well, says of him, "Il etait gauche dans toutes ses manieres; sa taille etait tres elevee, ses cheveux tres roux, il dansait sans grace, montait mal a cheval, et les jeunes gens avec lesquels il vivait se montraient plus adroits que lui dans les

diverses exercices d'alors a la mode." He describes his income as "une fortune de 120,000 livres de rente," a little under L5000 a year.-- _Correspondance entre le Comte de Mirabeau et le Comte de la Marck_, i. p. 47.

[6] "On a parle de moi dans tous les cercles, meme apres que la bonte de la reine m'eut valu le regiment du roi dragons."--_Memoires de ma Main, Memoires de La Fayette_, i., p 86.

[7] "La lettre ou Votre Majeste, parlant du Roi de Prusse, s'exprime ainsi .... 'cela ferait un changement dans notre alliance, ce qui me donnerait la mort,' j'ai vu la reine palir en me lisant cet article."--_Mercy to Maria Teresa_, February 18th, 1778, Arneth, iii., p. 170.

[8] See Coxe's "House of Austria," ch. cxxi. The war, which was marked by no action or event of importance, was terminated by the treaty of Teschen, May 10th, 1779.

[9] "Il n'a pas voulu y consentir, et a toujours ete attentif a exciter lui-meme la reine aux choses qu'il jugeait pouvoir lui etre agreables."-- _Mercy to Maria Teresa_, March 29th, 1778, Arneth, iii., p. 177.

[10] Marie Antoinette to Joseph II, and Leopold II., p. 21, date January 16th, 1778.

[11] Louis.

[12] Marie Antoinette to Maria Teresa, May 16th, Arneth, iii., p. 200.

[13] Weber, i., p.40.

[14] One of his admirers, seeing his mortification, said to him: "You are very simple to have wished to go to court. Do you know what would have

happened to you? I will tell you. The king, with his usual affability, would have laughed in your face, and talked to you of your converts at Ferney. The queen would have spoken of your plays. Monsieur would have asked you what your income was. Madame would have quoted some of your verses. The Countess of Artois would have said nothing at all; and the count would have conversed with you about 'the Maid of Orleans.'"--_Marie Antoinette, Louis XVI. et la Famille Royale_, p. 125, March 3d.

CHAPTER XIV.

[1] "La cour se precipite pele-mele avec la foule, car l'etiquette de France veut que tous entrent a ce moment, que nul ne soit refuse, et que le spectacle soit public d'une reine qui va donner un heritier a la couronne, ou seulement un enfant au roi."--_Mem. de Goncourt_, p. 105.

[2] Arneth, iii., p. 270.

[3] Madame de Campan, ch. ix.

[4] _Ibid_., ch. ix.

[5] Chambrier, i., p. 394.

[6] "Marie Antoinette, Louis XVI., et la Famille Royale," p. 147, December 24th, 1778.

[7] _Garde-malades_ was the name given to them.

[8] "Du moment qu'ils [les enfants] peuvent etre a l'air on les y accoutume petit a petit, et ils finissent par y etre presque toujours; je crois que c'est la maniere la plus saine et la meilleure des les elever."

[9] Letter of Marie Antoinette to Maria Teresa, May 15th, 1779, Arneth, iii., p. 311.

[10] Maria Teresa had offered the mediation of the empire to restore peace between England and France.

[11] Spain had recently entered into the alliance against England in the hope of recovering Gibraltar. And just at the date of this letter the combined fleet of sixty-six sail of the line sailed into the Channel, while a French army of 50,000 men was waiting at St. Malo to invade England so soon as the British Channel fleet should have been defeated; but, though Sir Charles Hardy had only forty sail under his orders, D'Orvilliers and his Spanish colleague retreated before him, and at the beginning of September, from fear of the equinoctial gales, of which the queen here speaks with such alarm, retired to their own harbors, without even venturing to come to action with a foe of scarcely two-thirds of their own strength. See the author's "History of the British Navy," ch. xiv.

[12] Letter of September 15th.

[13] Letter of October 14th.

[14] Letter of November 16th.

[15] Letter of November 17th.

[16] Kaunitz had been the prime minister of the empress, who negotiated the alliances with France and Russia, which were the preparations for the Seven Years' War.

CHAPTER XV.

[1] "On assure que sa majeste ne joue pas bien; ce que personne, excepte le roi, n'a ose lui dire. Au contraire, on l'applaudit a tout rompre."--_Marie Antoinette, Louis XVI. et la Famille Royale_ p. 203, date September 28th, 1780.

[2] In May, 1780, Sir Henry Clinton took Charleston, with a great number of prisoners, a great quantity of stores and four hundred guns.--LORD STANHOPE'S _History of England_, ch. lxii.

[3] "Cette disposition a ete faite deux ans plutot que ne le comporte l'usage etabli pour les enfants de France."--_Mercy to Maria Teresa_, October 14th, Arneth, iii. p. 476.

[4] Madame de Campan, ch. ix.

[5] "Gustave III. et la Cour de France," i., p. 349.

[6] An order known as that "du Merite" had been recently distributed for foreign Protestant officers, whose religion prevented them from taking the oath required of the Knights of the Grand Order of St. Louis.

[7] "Sa figure et son air convenaient parfaitement a un heros de roman, mais non pas d'un roman francais; il n'en avait ni le brillant ni legerete."--_Souvenirs et Portraits_, par M. de Levis, p. 130.

[8] "La Marck et Mirabeau," p. 32.

[9] See his letter to Lord North proposing peace, date December 1st, 1780. Lord Stanhope's "History of England," vol. vii., Appendix, p. 13.

CHAPTER XVI.

[1] "Gustave III. et la Cour de France," i., p. 357.

[2] Chambrier, i., p. 430; "Gustave III.," etc., i., p. 353.

[3] "Gustave III.," etc., i., p. 353.

[4] "Memoires de Weber," i., p. 50.

[5] "On s'arretait dans les rues, on se parlait sans se connaitre."-- Madame de Campan, ch. ix.

[6] L'Oeil de Boeuf.

[7] Madame de Campan, ch. ix.; "Marie Antoinette, Louis XII., et la Famille Royale," p. 238.

[8] "Un soleil d'ete"--Weber, i., p. 53.

[9] La Muette derived its name from _les mues_ of the deer who were reared there. It had been enlarged by the Regent d'Orleans, who gave it to his daughter, the Duchess de Berri; and it, was the frequent scene of the orgies of that infamous father and daughter, while more recently it had been known as the Parc aux Cerfs, under which title it had acquired a still more infamous reputation.

[10] "Apres le diner il y eut appartement jeu, et la fete fut terminee par un feu d'artifice."--Weber, i., p. 57, from whom the greater part of those details are taken. For the etiquette of the "jeu," see Madame de Campan, ch. ix., p. 17, and 2 ed. 1858.

CHAPTER XVII.

[1] Mercy to Maria Teresa, June 18th, 1780, Arneth iii., p. 440.

[2] Le tabouret. See St. Simon.

[3] See _infra_, the queen's letter to Madame de Tourzel, date July 25th, 1789.

[4] "Souvenirs de Quarante Ans," by Mademoiselle de Tourzel, p. 20.

[5] "Filia dolorosa."--Chateaubriand.

[6] Napoleon, in 1814, called her the only man of her family.

[7] Madame de Campan, ch. x.

[8] Memoires de Madame d'Oberkirch, i., p. 279

[9] The Marshal Prince de Soubise, whose incapacity and cowardice caused the disgraceful rout of Rosbach, was the head of this family; his sister, Madame Marsan, as governess of the "children of France", had brought up Louis XVI.

[10] "Il [Rohan] a meme menace, si on ne veut pas prendre le bon chemin qui lui indique, que ma fille s'en ressentira."--_Marie-Therese a Mercy_, August 28th, 1774, Arneth, ii., p. 226.

[11] "Ils paraissent si excedes du grand monde et des fetes, qu'avec d'autres petites difficultes qui se sont elevees, nous avons decide qu'il n'y aurait rien a Marly."--_Marie Antoinette to Mercy; Marie Antoinette, Joseph II., and Leopold II_., p. 27.

[12] "No fewer than five actions were fought in 1782, and the spring of

1783, by those unwearied foes. De Suffrein's force was materially the stronger of the two; it consisted of ten sail of the line, one fifty-gun ship, and four frigates; while Sir E. Hughes had but eight sail of the line, a fifty-gun ship, and one frigate," See the author's "History of the British Navy," i., p. 400.

[13] Weber, i., p. 77. For the importance at this time attached to a reception at court, see Chateaubriand, "Memoires d'Outre-tombe," i., p. 221.

CHAPTER XVIII.

[1] Joseph to Marie Antoinette, date September 9th, 1783.--_Marie Antoinette, Joseph II., and Leopold II._, p.30, which, to save such a lengthened reference, will hereafter be referred to as "Arneth."

[2] She was again expecting a confinement; but, as had happened between the birth of Madame Royale and that of the dauphin, an accident disappointed her hope, and her third child was not born till 1785.

[3] Date September 29th, 1783, Arneth, p. 35.

[4] Ministre de la maison du roi.

[5] Arneth, p. 38.

CHAPTER XIX.

[1] "Le roi signa une lettre de cachet qui defendait cette representation."--Madame de Campan, ch. xi.; see the whole chapter. Madame

de Campan's account of the queen's inclinations on the subject differs from that given by M. de Lomenie, in his "Beaumarchais et son Temps," but seems more to be relied on, as she had certainly better means of information.

[2] See M. Gaillard's report to the lieutenant of police.--_Beaumarchais et son Temps_, ii., p. 313.

[3] "Il n'y a que les petits hommes qui redoutent les petits ecrits."--_Act v., scene_ 3.

[4] "Avec _Goddam_ en, Angleterre on ne manque de rien nulle part. Voulez-vous tater un bon poulet gras ... _Goddam_ ... Aimez-vous a boire un coup d'excellent Bourgogne ou de clairet? rien que celui-ci _Goddam_. Les Anglais a la verite ajoutent par-ci par-la autres mots en conversant, mais il est bien aise de voir que _Goddam_ est le fond de la langue."--_Act_ iii., _scene_ 5.

[5] "Gustave III. et la Cour de France," ii., p.22

[6] _Ibid_., p. 35.

CHAPTER XX.

[1] "De par la reine."

[2] Madame de Campan, ch. xi.

[3] "'La legerete a tout croire et a tout dire des souverains,' ecrit tres justement M. Nisard (_Moniteur_ du 22 Janvier, 1886), 'est un des travers de notre pays, et comme le defaut de notre qualite de nation monarchique. C'est ce travers qui a tue Marie Antoinette par la main des furieux qui

eurent peut-etre des honnetes gens pour complices. Sa mort devait rendre a jamais impossible en France la calomnie politique.'"--Chambrier, i., p. 494.

[4] "Memoires de la Reine de France," par M. Lafont d'Aussonne, p. 42.

[5] See her letters to Mercy, December 26th, 1784, and to the emperor, December 31st, 1784, and February 4th, 1785, Arneth, p. 64, _et seq._

[6] "J'ai ete reellement touchee, de la raison et de la fermete que le roi a mises dans cette rude seance."--_Marie Antoinette to Joseph II._, August 22d, 1785, Arneth, p. 93.

[7] "La calomnie s'est attachee a poursuivre la reine, meme avant cette epoque ou l'esprit de parti a fait disparaitre la verite de la terre."--Madame de Stael, _Proces de la Reine_, p. 2

[8] Madame de Campan, "Eclaircissements Historiques," p. 461; "Marie Antoinette et le Proces du Collier," par M. Emile Campardon, p. 144, _seq._

[9] "Permet au Cardinal de Rohan et au dit de Cagliostro de faire imprimer et afficher le present arret partout ou bon leur semblera."--Campardon, p. 152.

[10] "Sans doute le cardinal avait les mains pures de toute fraude; sans doute il n'etait pour rien dans l'escroquerie commise par les epoux de La Mothe."--Campardon, p. 155.

[11] Campardon, p. 153, quoting Madame de Campan.

[12] The most recent French historian, M.H. Martin, sees in this trial a proof of the general demoralization of the whole French nation.

"L'impression qui en resulte pour nous est l'impossibilite que la reine ait ete coupable. Mais plus les imputations dirigees contre elle etaient vraisemblables, plus la creance accordee a ces imputations etait caracteristique, et attestait la ruine morale de la monarchie. C'etait l'ombre du Parc aux Cerfs qui couvrait toujours Versailles."--_Histoire de France_, xvi., p. 559, ed. 1860.

[13] Feuillet de Conches, i., p. 161.

[14] Feuillet de Conches, i., p. 162. Some of the critics of M.F. de Conches's collection have questioned without sufficient reason the probability of there having been any correspondence between the queen and her elder sister. But the genuineness of this letter is strongly corroborated by a mistake into which no forger would have fallen. The queen speaks as if the cardinal had alleged that he had given her a rose; while his statement really was that Oliva, personating the queen, had dropped a rose at his feet. A forger would have made the letter Correspond with the evidence and the fact. The queen, in her agitation, might easily make a mistake.

[15] "Il se retira dans son eveche de l'autre cote du Rhin. La sa noble conduite fit oublier les torts de sa vie passee," etc.--Campardon, p. 156.

[16] Campardon, p. 156.

[17] It was from Ettenheim that the Duke d'Enghien was carried off in March, 1804. The cardinal died in February, 1803.

CHAPTER XXI.

[1] "Le duc declarait de son cote a Mr. Elliott que ... si la reine l'eut mieux traite il eut peut-etre mieux fait."--Chambrier, i., p.519

[2] Sophie Helene Beatrix, born July 9th, 1786, died June 9th, 1787, F. de Conches, i. p. 195.

[3] See her letter to her brother, February, 1788, Arneth, p. 112.

[4] "C'est un vrai enfant de paysan, grand frais et gros."--Arneth, pp. 113.

[5] Feuillet de Conches, i, p. 195.

[6] Apparently she means the Notables and the Parliament.

[7] The Duc de Guines.

[8] See _ante_, ch. xviii.

[9] "'Il faut,' dit-il, avec un mouvement d'impatience qui lui fit honneur, 'que, du moins, l'archeveque de Paris croie en Dieu.'"-- _Souvenirs par le Duc de Levis_, p. 102.

[10] The continuer of Sismondi's history, A. Renee, however, attributes the archbishop's appointment to the influence of the Baron de Breteuil.

[11] "Son grand art consistait a parler a chacun des choses qu'il croyait qu'on ignorait."--De Levis, p. 100.

[12] The loan he proposed in June was eighty millions (of francs); in October, that which he demanded was four hundred and forty millions.

[13] It is worth noticing that the French people in general did not regard the power of arbitrary imprisonment exercised by their kings as a grievance. In their eyes it was one of his most natural prerogatives. A

year or two before the time of which we are speaking, Dr. Moore, the author of "Zeluco," and father of Sir John Moore, who fell at Corunna, was traveling in France, and was present at a party of French merchants and others of the same rank, who asked him many questions about the English Constitution, When he said that the King of England could not impose a tax by his own authority, "they said, with some degree of satisfaction, 'Cependant c'est assez beau cela.'"... But when he informed them "that the king himself had not the power to encroach upon the liberty of the meanest of his subjects, and that if he or the minister did so, damages were recoverable in a court of law, a loud and prolonged 'Diable!' issued from every mouth. They forgot their own situation, and turned to their natural bias of sympathy with the king, who, they all seemed to think, must be the most oppressed and injured of manhood. One of them at last, addressing himself to the English politician, said, 'Tout ce que je puis vous dire, monsieur, c'est que votre pauvre roi est bien a plaindre.'"--_A View of the Society and Manners in France_, etc., by Dr. John Moore, vol. i., p. 47, ed. 1788.

CHAPTER XXII.

[1] Feuillet de Conches, i., p. 205.

[2] M. Foulon was about this time made paymaster of the army and navy, and was generally credited with ability as a financier; but he was unpopular, as a man of ardent and cruel temper, and was brutally murdered by the mob in one of the first riots of the Revolution.

[3] The king.

[4] Necker.

[5] Feuillet de Conches, i., p. 214.

[6] _Ibid_., p. 217.

[7] On one occasion when the Marquis de Bouille pointed out to him the danger of some of his plans as placing the higher class at the mercy of the mob, "dirige par les deux passions les plus actives du coeur humain, l'interet et l'amour propre, ... il me repondit froidement, en levant les yeux au ciel, qu'il fallait bien compter sur les vertus morales des hommes."--_Memoires de M. de Bouille_, p. 70; and Madame de Stael admits of her father that he was "se fiant trop, il faut l'avouer, a l'empire de la raison," and adds that he "etudia constamment l'esprit public, comme la boussole a laquelle les decisions du roi devaient se conformer."--_Considerations sur la Revolution Francaise_, i., pp. 171, 172.

[8] Her exact words are "si ... il fasse reculer l'autorite du roi" (if he causes the king's authority to retreat before the populace or the Parliament).

[9] "Histoire de Marie Antoinette," par M. Montjoye, p. 202.

[10] Madame de Campan, p. 412.

[11] This edict was registered in the "Chambre Syndicate," September 13th, 1787.--_La Reine Marie Antoinette et la Rev. Francaise, Recherches Historiques_, par le Comte de Bel-Castel, p. 246.

[12] There is at the present moment so strong a pretension set up in many constituencies to dictate to the members whom they send to Parliament as if they were delegates, and not representatives, that it is worth while to refer to the opinion which the greatest of philosophical statesman, Edmund Burke, expressed on the subject a hundred years ago, in opposition to that at a rival candidate who admitted and supported the claim of constituents to furnish the member whom they returned to Parliament with "instructions"

of "coercive authority." He tells the citizens of Bristol plainly that such a claim he ought not to admit, and never will. The "opinion" of constituents is "a weighty and respectable opinion, which a representative ought always to rejoice to hear, and which he ought most seriously to consider; but _authoritative instruction_, mandates issued which the member is bound blindly and implicitly to obey, to vote, and to argue for, though contrary to the clearest conviction of his judgment and his conscience; these are things utterly unknown to the laws of this land, and which arise from a fundamental mistake of the whole order and tenor of our constitution. Parliament is not a _congress_ of embassadors from different and hostile interests...but Parliament is a _deliberative_ assembly of _one_ nation, with _one_ interest, that of the whole, where not local purposes, not local prejudices ought to guide, but the general good resulting from the general reason of the whole. You choose a member indeed; but when you have chosen him, he is not member of Bristol, but he is a member of Parliament."--_General Election Speech at the Conclusion of the Poll at Bristol_, November 3d, 1774, Burke's Works, vol. iii., pp. 19, 20, ed. 1803.

[13] De Tocqueville considers the feudal system in France in many points more oppressive than that of Germany.--_Ancien Regime_, p. 43.

[14] Silence des grenouilles. Arthur Young, "Travels in France during 1787, '88, '89," p. 537. It is singular proof how entirely research into the condition of the country and the people of France had been neglected both by its philosophers and its statesmen, that there does not seem to have been any publication in the language which gave information on these subjects. And this work of Mr. Young's is the one to which modern French writers, such as M. Alexis de Tocqueville, chiefly refer.

[15] "The _lettres de cachet_ were carried to an excess hardly credible; to the length of being sold, with blanks, to be filled up with names at the pleasure of the purchaser, who was thus able, in the gratification of

private revenge, to tear a man from the bosom of his family, and bury him in a dungeon, where he would exist forgotten and die unknown."--A. Young, p. 532. And in a note he gives an instance of an Englishman, named Gordon, who was imprisoned in the Bastile for thirty years without even knowing the reason of his arrest.

[16] Arthur Young, writing January 10th, 1790, identifies Les Enrages with the club afterward so infamous as the Jacobins. "The ardent democrats who have the reputation of being so much republican in principle that they do not admit any political necessity for having even the name of the king, are called the Enrages. They have a meeting at the Jacobins', the Revolution Club which assembles every night in the very room in which the famous League was formed in the reign of Henry III." (p. 267).

[17] M. Droz asserts that a collector of such publications bought two thousand five hundred in the last three months of 1788, and that his collection was far from complete.--_Histoire de Louis XVI_., ii., p. 180.

[18] "Tout auteur s'erige en legislateur."--_Memorial of the Princes to the King_, quoted in a note to the last chapter of Sismondi's History, p. 551, Brussels ed., 1849.

[19] In reality the numbers were even more in favor of the Commons: the representatives of the clergy were three hundred and eight, and those of the nobles two hundred and eighty-five, making only five hundred and ninety-three of the two superior orders, while the deputies of the Tiers-Etat were six hundred and twenty-one.--_Souvenirs de la Marquise de Crequy_, vii., p. 58.

[20] "Se levant alors, 'Non,' dit le roi, 'ce ne peut etre qu'a Versailles, a cause des chasses.'"--LOUIS BLANC, ii., p. 212, quoting Barante.

[21] "La reine adopta ce dernier avis [that the States should meet forty or sixty leagues from the capital], et elle insista aupres du roi que l'on s'eloignat de l'immense population de Paris. Elle craignait des lors que le peuple n'influencat les deliberations des deputes."--MADAME DE CAM-PAN,
ch 83.

[22] Chambrier, i., p. 562.

CHAPTER XXIII.

[1] It was called "L'insurrection du Faubourg St. Antoine."

[2] The best account of this riot is to be found in Dr. Moore's "Views of the Causes and Progress of the French Revolution," i., p. 189.

[3] Madame de Campan specially remarks that the disloyal cry of "Vive le Duc d'Orleans" came from "les femmes du peuple" (ch. xiii.).

[4] Afterward Louis Philippe, King of the French.

[5] "View of the Causes and Progress of the French Revolution," by Dr. Moore, i., p. 144.

[6] The dauphin was too ill to be present. The children were Madame Royale and the Duc de Normandie, who became dauphin the next month by the death
of his elder brother.

[7] "Aucun nom propre, excepte le sien, n'etait encore celebre dans les six cents deputes du Tiers."--_Considerations sur la Revolution Francaise_, pp. 186, 187

[8] In the first weeks of the session he told the Count de la Marck, "On ne sortira plus de la sans un gouvernement plus ou moins semblable a celui d'Angleterre."--_Correspondance entre le comte de la Marck_, i., p. 67.

[9] He employed M. Malouet, a very influential member of the Assembly, as his agent to open his views to Necker, saying to him, "Je m'adresse donc a votre probite. Vous etes lie avec MM. Necker et de Montmorin, vous devez savoir ce qu'ils veulent, et s'ils ont un plan; si ce plan est raisonnable je le defendrai."--_Correspondance de Mirabeau et La Marck_, i., p. 219.

[10] There is some uncertainty about Mirabeau's motives and connections at this time. M. de Bacourt, the very diligent and judicious editor of that correspondence with De la Marck which has been already quoted, denies that Mirabeau ever received money from the Duc d'Orleans, or that he had any connection with his party or his views. The evidence on the other side seems much stronger, and some of the statements of the Comte de la Marck contained in that volume go to exculpate Mirabeau from all complicity in the attack on Versailles on the 9th of October, which seems established by abundant testimony.

CHAPTER XXIV.

[1] A letter of Madame Roland dated the 26th of this very month, July, 1789, declares that the people "are undone if the National Assembly does not proceed seriously and regularly to the trial of the illustrious heads [the king and queen], or if some generous Decius does not risk his life to take theirs."

[2] This story reached even distant province. On the 24th of July Arthur Young, being at Colmar, was assured at the _table-d'hote_ "That the queen had a plot, nearly on the point of execution, to blow up the National

Assembly by a mine, and to march the army instantly to massacre all
Paris." A French officer presumed but to doubt of the truth of it, and was
immediately overpowered with numbers of tongues. A deputy had written it;
they had seen the letter. And at Dijon, a week later, he tells us that
"the current report at present, to which all possible credit is given, is
that the queen has been convicted of a plot to poison the king and
monsieur, and give the regency to the Count d'Artois, to set fire to
Paris, and blow up the Palais Royal by a mine."--ARTHUR YOUNG'S _Trav-
els,
etc., in France_, pp. 143, 151.

[3] "Car des ce moment on menacait Versailles d'une incursion de gens
armes de Paris."--MADAME DE CAMPAN, ch. xiv.

[4] Lacretelle, vol. vii., p. 105.

[5] She meant to say, "Messieurs, je viens remettre entre vos mains
l'epouse et la famille de votre souverain. Ne souffrez pas que l'on
desunisse sur la terre ce qui a ete uni dans le ciel."--MADAME DE CAMPAN,
ch. xiv.

[6] Napoleon seems to have formed this opinion of his political views:
"Selon M. Gourgaud, Buonaparte, causant a Ste. Helene le traitait avec
plus de mepris [que Madame de Stael]. 'La Fayette etait encore un autre
niais. Il etait nullement taille pour le role qu'il avait a jouer....
C'etait un homme sans talents, ni civils, ni militaires; esprit borne,
caractere dissimule, domine par des idees vagues de liberte mal digerees
chez lui; mal concues.'"--_Biographie Universelle_.

[7] In his Memoirs he boasts of the "gaucherie de ses manieres qui ne se
plierent jamais aux graces de la Cour," p. 7.

[8] See her letter to Mercy, without date, but, apparently written a day

or two after the king's journey to Paris, Feuillet de Conches, i., p. 238.

[9] "Souvenirs de Quarante Ans" (by Madame de Tourzel's daughter), p. 30.

[10] Feuillet de Conches, i., p. 240.

CHAPTER XXV.

[1] "Memoires de la Princesse de Lamballe," i., p. 342.

[2] Les Gardes du Corps.

[3] Louis Blanc, iii., p. 156, quoting the Procedure du Chatelet.

[4] "Souvenirs de la Marquise de Crequy," vol. vii, p. 119.

[5] There is some uncertainty where La Fayette slept that night. Lacretelle says it was at the "Maison du Prince de Foix, fort eloignee du chateau." Count Dumas, meaning to be as favorable to him as possible, places him at the Hotel de Noailles, which is "not one hundred paces from the iron gates of the chapel" ("Memoirs of the Count Dumas," p. 159). However, the nearer he was to the palace, the more incomprehensible it is that he should not have reached the palace the next morning till nearly eight o'clock, two hours after the mob had forced their entrance into the Cour des Princes.

[6] Weber, i., p. 218.

[7] Le Boulanger (the king), la Boulangere (the queen), et le petit mitron (the dauphin).

[8] "Souvenirs de la Marquise de Crequy," vii., p. 123.

[9] Weber, ii, p. 226.

[10] "Souvenirs de Quarante Ans," p. 47.

CHAPTER XXVI.

[1] Madame de Campan, ch. xv.

[2] F. de Conches, p. 264.

[3] Madam de Campan, ch. xv.

[4] See a letter from M. Huber to Lord Auckland, "Journal and Correspondence of Lord Auckland," ii, p. 365.

[5] La Marck et Mirabeau, ii., pp. 90-93, 254.

[6] "Arthur Young's Travels," etc., p. 264; date, Paris, January 4th, 1790.

[7] Feuillet de Conches, iii., p. 229.

[8] Joseph died February 20th.

[9] "Je me flatte que je la meriterai [l'amitie et confiance] de votre part lorsque ma facon de penser et mon tendre attachement pour vous, votre epoux, vos enfants, et tout ce qui peut vous interesser vous seront mieux connus."--ARNETH, p. 120. Leopold had been for many years absent from Germany, being at Florence as Grand Duke of Tuscany.

[10] Feuillet de Conches, iii., p. 260.

[11] As early as the second week in October (La Marck, p. 81, seems to place the conversation even before the outrages of October 5th and 6th; but this seems impossible, and may arise from his manifest desire to represent Mirabeau as unconnected with those horrors), Mirabeau said to La Marck, "Tout est perdu, le roi et la reine y periront et vous le verrez, la populace battra leurs cadavres."

[12] Lese-nation.

CHAPTER XXVII.

[1] Arthur Young's "Journal," January 4th, 1790, p. 251.

[2] Feuillet de Conches, i., p. 315.

[3] "Le mal deja fait est bien grave, et je doute que Mirabeau lui-meme puisse reparer celui qu'on lui a laisse faire."--_Mirabeau et La Marck_, i., p. 100.

[4] La Marck et Mirabeau, i., p. 315.

[5] _Ibid._, p. 111.

[6] Feuillet de Conches, i., p. 345.

[7] Mirabeau et La Marck, i., p. 125.

[8] He alludes to Maria Teresa's appearance at Presburg at the beginning of the Silesian war.

[9] "Il lui [a l'Assemblee] importait de faire une epreuve sur toutes les

Gardes Nationales de France, d'animer ce grand corps dont tous les membres etaient encore epars et incoherents, de leur donner une meme impulsion.... Enfin, de faire sous les yeux de l'Europe une imposante revue des force qu'elle pourrait un jour opposer a des rois inquiets ou courrouces."-- LACRETELLE, vii., p. 359.

CHAPTER XXVIII.

[1] We learn from Dr. Moore that there was a leader with five subaltern officers and one hundred and fifty rank and file in each gallery of the chamber; that the wages of the latter were from two to three francs a day; the subaltern had ten francs, the leaders fifty. The entire expense was about a thousand francs a day, a sum which strengthens the suspicion that the pay-master (originally, at least) was the Duc d'Orleans.--DR. MOORE'S _View of the Causes, etc., of the French Revolution_, i., p. 425.

[2] Mirabeau et La Marck, ii., p. 47.

[3] Feuillet de Conches, i., p. 352.

[4] Marie Antoinette to Mercy, Feuillet de Conches, i., p. 355.

[5] _Ibid_., i., p. 365.

[6] Arneth, p. 140.

[7] It is remarkable that he, like one or two of the Girondin party, belonged by birth to the Huguenot persuasion, and Marat had studied medicine at Edinburgh.

[8] The Marquise de Brinvilliers had been executed for poisoning several of her own relations in the reign of Louis XIV.

[9] Madame de Campan, ch. xvii.; Chambrier, ii., p. 12.

[10] He said to La Marck, "Aucun homme seul ne sera capable de ramener les Francais an bon sens, le temps seul peut retablir l'ordre dans les esprits," etc., etc.--_ Mirabeau et La Marck_, i., p. 147.

[11] Feuillet de Conches, i., p, 376.

[12] Marie Antoinette to Leopold, date December 11th, 1790, Arneth, p. 143.

CHAPTER XXIX.

[1] The Marshal de Bouille, who was La Fayette's cousin, says, in October of this year, "L'eveque de Pamiers me fit le tableau de la situation malheureux de ce prince et de la famille royale ... que la rigueur et durete de La Fayette, devenu leur geolier, rendent de jour en jour plus insupportable."--_Memories de De Bouille_, pp. 175, 181. And in June he had remarked, "Que sa popularite (de La Fayette) dependait plutot de la captivite du roi, qu'il tenait prisonnier, et qui etait sous sa garde, que de sa force personnelle, qui n'avait plus d'autre appui que la milice Parisienne."

[2] _Ibid_., p. 130.

[3] The letter to the King of Prussia is given by Lamartine; its date is December 3d, 1790.--_Histoire des Girondins_, book v., § 12.

[4] Mercy to Marie Antoinette, from The Hague, December 17th, 1790, Feuillet de Conches, i., p. 398.

[5] Feuillet de Conches, i., p. 401.

[6] _Ibid., p. 403, date December 27th, 1790.

[7] "Mirabeau et La Marck," ii., pp. 57--61.

[8] Letter to the queen, date February 19th, 1791; "Correspondance de Mirabeau et La Marck," ii., p. 229.

[9] "Mirabeau et La Marck," ii., pp. 153, 194, _et passim._

[10] "Souvenirs de Quarante Ans," p. 54.

[11] "Mirabeau aurait prefere que Louis XVI. sortit publiquement, et en roi, M. de Bouille pensait de meme."--_Mirabeau et La Marck_, i., p. 172.

[12] 1789, see _ante_, p. 256.

[13] Date February 18th, 1791, Feuillet de Conches, i., p. 465.

[14] "Mirabeau et La Marck," ii., p., 216 date February 3d, 1791.

CHAPTER XXX.

[1] Feuillet de Conches, ii., p. 14, date March 7th.

[2] Arneth, p. 146, letter of the queen to Leopold, February 27th, 1791.

[3] Feuillet de Conches, ii., p. 20, date March 20th, 1791.

[4] Letter of M. Simolin, the Russian embassador, April 4th, 1791, Feuillet de Conches, ii., p. 31.

[5] "Souvenirs sur Mirabeau," par Etienne Dumont, p. 201.

[6] In her letter to Mercy of August 16th, of which extracts are given in ch. xi., she takes credit for having encountered the dangers of the journey to Montmedy for the sake of "the public welfare."

[7] Arneth, p. 155.

[8] Letter of Leopold to Marie Antoinette, date May 2d, 1791, Arneth, p. 162.

[9] "Cette demarche est le terme extreme de reussir ou perir. Les choses en sont-elles au point de rendre ce risque indispensable?"--_Mercy to Marie Antoinette_, May 11th, 1791, Arneth, p. 163.

[10] The day on which the king and she had been prevented from going to St. Cloud.

[11] The king.

CHAPTER XXXI.

[1] Chambrier, ii., p. 86-88.

[2] Lamartine's "Histoire des Girondins," ii., p. 15.

[3] Moore's "View," ii., p. 367.

[4] The Palais Royal had been named the Palais National. All signs with the portraits of the king or queen, all emblems of royalty, had been torn down. A shop-keeper was even obliged to erase his name from his shop

because it was Louis.--MOORE'S _View_, etc., ii., p. 356.

CHAPTER XXXII.

[1] A certain set of writers in this country at one time made La Fayette a subject for almost unmixed eulogy, with such earnestness that it may be worth while to reproduce the opinion expressed of him by the greatest of his contemporaries--a man as acute in his penetration into character as he was stainless in honor--the late Duke of Wellington. In the summer of 1815, he told Sir John Malcolm that "he had used La Fayette like a dog, as he merited. The old rascal," said he, "had made a false report of his mission to the Emperor of Russia, and I possessed complete evidence of his having done so. I told him, the moment he entered, of this fact; I did not even state it in the most delicate manner. I told him he must be sensible he had made a false report. He made no answer." And the duke bowed him out of the room with unconcealed scorn.--Kaye's _Life of Sir J. Malcolm_, ii., p. 109.

[2] Lamartine calls the Cordeliers the Club of Coups-de-main, as he calls the Jacobins the Club of Radical Theories.--_Histoire des Girondins_, xvi., p. 4.

[3] Dr. Moore, ii., p. 372; Chambrier, ii., p. 142.

[4] Mercy to Marie Antoinette, May 16th, Feuillet de Conches, ii., p. 60.

[5] _Ibid._, p. 140.

[6] A resolution, that is, to recognize the Constitution.

[7] Arneth, p. 188; Feuillet de Conches, ii, p. 186.

[8] The letter took several days to write, and was so interrupted that portions of it have three different dates affixed, August 16th, 21st, 26th. Mercy's letter, which incloses Burke's memorial, is dated the 20th, from London, so that the first portion of the queen's letter can not be regarded as an intentional answer to Burke's arguments, though it is so, as embodying all the reasons which influenced the queen.

[9] The manifesto which he left behind him when starting for Montmedy.

[10] The king.

[11] Feuillet de Conches, ii., p. 228; Arneth, p. 203.

[12] The Emperor Leopold died March 1st, 1792.

[13] The declaration of Pilnitz, drawn up by the emperor and the King of Prussia at a personal interview, August 21st, 1791, did not in express words denounce the new Constitution (which, in fact, they had not seen), but, after declaring "the situation of the King of France to be a matter of common interest to all European sovereigns," and expressing a hope that "the reality of that interest will be duly appreciated by the other powers whose assistance they invoke," they propose that those other powers "shall employ, in conjunction with their majesties, the most efficacious means, in order to enable the King of France to consolidate in the most perfect liberty the foundation of a monarchical government, conformable alike to the rights of sovereigns and the well-being of the French nation."-- Alison, ch. ix., Section 90.

[14] Arneth, p. 208.

[15] _Ibid_, p. 210; Feuillet de Conches, ii., p. 325.

[16] Letter, date December 3d, 1791. Feuillet de Conches, iv., p. 278.

[17] Madame de Campan, ch xix.

[18] "Leurs touffes de cheveux noirs volaient dans la salle, eux seuls a cette epoque avaient quitte l'usage de poudrer les cheveux."--_Note on the Passage by Madame de Campan_, ch xix.

[19] This first Assembly, as having framed the Constitution, is often called the Constituent Assembly; the second, that which was about to meet, being distinguished as the Legislative Assembly.

CHAPTER XXXIII.

[1] "Memoires Particuliers," etc., par A.F. Bertrand de Moleville, i., p. 355. Brissot, Isnard, Vergniaud, Gaudet, and an infamous ecclesiastic, the Abbe Fauchet, are those whom he particularly mentions, adding: "Mais M. de Lessart trouva que c'etait les payer trop cher, et comme ils ne voulurent rien rabattre de leur demande, cette negociation n'eut aucune suite, et ne produisit d'autre effet que d'aigrir davantage ces cinq deputes contre ce ministre."

[2] Feuillet de Conches, ii., p.414, date October 4th: "Je pense qu'au fond le bon bourgeois et le bon peuple ont toujours ete bien pour nous."

[3] "Memoires Particuliers," etc., par A.F. Bertrand de Moleville, i., p. 10-12. It furnishes a striking proof of the general accuracy of Dr. Moore's information, that he, in his "View" (ii., p. 439), gives the name account of this conversation, his work being published above twenty years before that of M. Bertrand de Moleville.

[4] "La reine lui repondit par un sourire de pitie, et lui demanda s'il

etait fou.... C'est par la reine elle-meme que, le lendemain de cette etrange scene, je fus instruit de tous les details que je viens de rapporter."--BERTRAND DE MOLEVILLE, i., p. 126.

[5] She herself called him so on this occasion, and he belonged to the Jacobin Club; but he was also one of the Girondin party, of which, indeed, he was one of the founders, and it was as a Girondin that he was afterward pursued to death by Robespierre.

[6] Narrative of the Comte Valentin Esterhazy, Feuillet de Conches, iv., p. 40.

[7] The queen spoke plainly to her confidants: "M. de La Fayette will only be the Mayor of Paris that he may the sooner become Mayor of the Palace. Petion is a Jacobin, a republican; but he is a fool, incapable of ever becoming the leader of a party. He would be a nullity as mayor, and, besides, the very interest which he knows we take in his nomination may bind him to the king."--Lamartine's _Histoire des Girondins_ vi., p.22.

[8] "Elle [Madame d'Ossun, dame d'atours de la reine] m'a dit, il y a trois semaines, que le roi et la reine avaiet ete neuf jours sans un sou." _Letter of the Prince de Nassau-Siegen to the Russian Empress Catherine_, Feuillet de Conches, iv., p. 316; of also Madame de Campan, ch. xxi.

[9] Letter of the Princess to Madame de Bombelles, Feuillet de Conches, v., p.267.

[10] "N'est-il pas bien gentil, mon enfant?"--_Memoires Particuliers_, p. 235.

[11] See two most insolent letters from the Count de Provence and Count d'Artois to Louis XVI, Feuillet de Conches, v., pp. 260, 261.

[12] Feuillet de Conches, iv., p. 291

CHAPTER XXXIV.

[1] Letter to Madame de Polignac, March 17th, Feuillet de Conches, v., p. 337.

[2] The Monks of St. Bernard were known as Feuillants, from Feuillans, a village in Languedoc where their principal convent was situated.

[3] Lamartine, "Histoire des Girondins," xiii., p.18.

[4] The messenger was M. Goguelat: he took the name of M. Daumartin, and adhered to the cause of his sovereigns to the last moment of their lives.

[5] Letter of the Count de Fersen, who was at Brussels, to Gustavus (who, however, was dead before it could reach him), dated March 24th, 1792. In many respects the information De Fersen sends to his king tallies precisely with that sent by Breteuil to the emperor; he only adds a few circumstances which had not reached the baron.

[6] Afterward Louis Philippe, King of the French, who was himself driven from the throne by insurrection above half a century afterward.

[7] Madame de Campan, ch. xx.

[8] _Ibid._, ch. XIX.

[9] "Vie de Dumouriez," ii, p. 163, quoted by Marquis de Ferrieres, Feuillet de Conches, and several other writers.

[10] Even Lamartine condemns the letter, the greater part of which he

inserts in his history as one in which "the threat is no less evident than the treachery."--_Histoire des Girondins,_ xiii., p. 16.

CHAPTER XXXV.

[1] "Gare la Lanterne," alluding to the use of the chains to which the street-lamps were suspended as gibbets.

[2] Madame de Campan, ch. xxi.

[3] Dumas, "Memoirs of his Own Time," i., p. 353.

CHAPTER XXXVI.

[1] To be issued by the foreign powers.

[2] Feuillet de Conches, vi., p. 192, and Arneth, p. 265.

[3] The day is not mentioned. "Lettres de la Reine Marie Antoinette a la Landgravine Louise," etc. p. 47.

[4] The bearer was Prince George himself, but she does not venture to name him more explicitly.

[5] Lamourette might correspond to the English name Lovekin.

[6] Letter of the Princess Elizabeth, date July 16th, 1792, Feuillet de Conches, vi., p. 215.

[7] It is remarkable, however, that, if we are to take Lamartine as a guide in any respect, and he certainly was not in intention unfavorable to

La Fayette, the marquis was even now playing a double game. Speaking of this very proposal, he says: "La Fayette himself did not disguise his ambition for a protectorate under Louis XVI. At the very moment when he seemed devoted to the preservation of the king he wrote thus to his confidante, La Colombe: 'In the matter of liberty I do not trust myself either to the king or any other person, and if he were to assume the sovereign, I would fight against him as I did in 1789.'"--_Histoire des Girondins_, xvii., p.7 (English translation). It deserves remark, too, if his words are accurately reported, that the only occasion 1789 on which he "fought against" Louis must have been October 5th and 6th, when he professed to be using every exertion for his safety.

[8] M. Bertrand expressly affirms the insurrection of August 10th to have been almost exclusively the work of the Girondin faction.--_Memoires Particuliers,_ ii., p. 122.

[9] _Memoires Particuliers,_ ii., p. 132.

[10] "Memoires Particuliers," p. 111.

CHAPTER XXXVII.

[1] See _ante_.

[2] "Histoire de la Terreur," par Mortimer Ternaux, ii., p. 269. For the transactions of this day, and of the following months, he is by far the most trustworthy guide, as having had access to official documents of which earlier writers were ignorant. But he admits the extreme difficulty of ascertaining the precise details and time of each event. And it is not easy in every instance to reconcile his account with that of Madame de Campan, on whom for many particulars he greatly relies. He differs from her especially as to the hour at which the different occurrences of this

day took place. For instance, he says (p. 268, note 2) that Mandat left the Tuileries a little after five, while Madame de Campan says it was four o'clock when the queen told her he had been murdered. Both, however, agree that it was soon after eight o'clock when the king left the palace.

[3] "A quatre heures la reine sortit de la chambre du roi, et vint nous dire qu'elle n'esperait plus rien; que M. Mandat venait d'etre assassine."--MADAME DE CAMPAN, ch. xxi.

[4] "La Terreur," viii., p. 4.

[5] It is clear that this is the opinion formed by M Mortimer Ternaux. He sums up the fourth chapter of his eighth book with the conclusion that "le palais de la royaute ne fut pas enleve de vive force, mais abandonne par ordre de Louis XVI." And in a note he affirms that the entire number of killed and wounded on the part of the rioters did not exceed one hundred and sixty "en chiffres ronds."

[6] Bertrand de Moleville, ch. xxvii.

[7] Madame de Campan, ch. xxi.

CHAPTER XXXVIII.

[1] "Dernieres Annees du Regne et de la Vie de Louis XVI.," par Francois Hue, p. 336.

[2] For about a fortnight they had two, both men--Hue, the valet to the dauphin, as well as Clery; but Hue was removed on the 2d of September. He, as well as Clery, has left an account of the imprisonment till the day of his dismissal.

[3] "Journal de ce qui s'est passe a la tour du Temple," etc. p.28, _seq._

[4] "Memoires Particuliers," par Madame la Duchesse d'Angouleme, p. 21.

[5] Decius was the hero whose example was especially invoked by Madame Roland. The historians of his own country had never accused him of murdering any one; but she, in the very first month of the Revolution, had called, with a very curious reading of history, for "some generous Decius to risk his life to take theirs" (the lives of the king and queen).

[6] The princess told Clery, "La reine et moi nous nous attendons a tout, et nous ne nous faisons aucune illusion sur le sort qu'on prepare au roi," etc.--CLERY, p. 106.

[7] "Memoires" de la Duchesse d'Angouleme, p. 53.

CHAPTER XXXIX.

[1] Clery's "Journal," p. 169.

[2] In March, having an opportunity of communicating with the Count de Provence, she sent these precious memorials to him for safer custody, with a joint letter from herself and her three fellow-prisoners: "Having a faithful person on whom we can depend, I profit by the opportunity to send to my brother and friend this deposit, which may not be intrusted to any other hands. The bearer will tell you by what a miracle we were able to obtain these precious pledges. I reserve the name of him who is so useful to us, to tell it you some day myself. The impossibility which has hitherto existed of sending you any intelligence of us, and the excess of our misfortunes, make us feel more vividly our cruel separation. May it not lie long. Meanwhile I embrace you as I love you, and you know that that is with all my heart.--M.A." A line is added by the princess royal,

and signed by her brother, as king, as well as by herself: "I am charged for my brother and myself to embrace you with all my heart.--M.T. [MARIA TERESA], LOUIS." And another by the Princess Elizabeth: "I enjoy beforehand the pleasure which you will feel in receiving this pledge of love and confidence. To be reunited to you and to see you happy is all that I desire. You know if I love you. I embrace you with all my heart.--E." The letters were shown by the Count de Provence to Clery, whom he allowed to take a copy of them.--CLERY'S _Journal_, p. 174.

[3] "Memoires" de la Duchesse d'Angouleme, p. 56.

[4] It was burned in 1871, in the time of the Commune.

[5] Feuillet de Conches, vi., p. 499. The letter is neither dated nor signed.

[6] Lanjuinais had subsequently the singular fortune of gaining the confidence of both Napoleon and Lounis XVIII. The decree against him was reversed in 1795, and he became a professor at Rennes. Though he had opposed the making of Napoleon consul for life, Napoleon gave him a place in his Senate; and at the first restoration, in 1814, Louis XVIII named him a peer of France. He died in 1827.

[7] Some of the apologists of the Girondins--nearly all the oldest criminals of the Revolution have found defenders, except perhaps Marat and Robespierre--have affirmed that the Girondins, though they had not courage to give their votes to save the life of Louis, yet hoped to save him by voting for an appeal to the people; but the order in which the different questions were put to the Convention is a complete disproof of this plea. The first question put was, Was Louis guilty? They all voted "Oui" (Lacretelle, x., p. 403). But though on the second question, whether this verdict should be submitted to the people for ratification, many of them did vote for such an appeal being made, yet after the appeal had been

rejected by a majority of one hundred and forty-two, and the third question, "What penalty shall be inflicted on Louis?" (Lacretelle, x., p. 441) was put to the Convention, they all except Lanjuinais voted for "death." The majorities were, on their question, 683 to 66; on the second, 423 to 281; on the third, 387 to 334; so that on this last, the fatal question, it would have been easy for the Girondins to have turned the scale. And Lamartine himself expressly affirms (xxxv., p.5) that the king's life depended on the Girondin vote, and that his death was chiefly owing to Vergniaud.

[8] Goncourt, p. 370, quoting "Fragments de Turgy."

[9] "S'en defaire."--_Louis XVII., sa Vie, son Agonie, sa Mort_, par M. de Beauchesne, quoting Senart. See Croker's "Essays on the Revolution," p. 266.

[10] Duchesse d'Angouleme, p. 78.

[11] See a letter from Miss Chowne to Lord Aukland, September 23d, 1793, Journal, etc., of Lord Aukland, ii., p. 517.

[12] "Le peuple la recut non seulement comme une reine adoree, mais il semblait aussi qu'il lui savait gre d'etre charmante," p.5, ed. 1820.

[13] Great interest was felt for her in England. In October Horace Walpole writes: "While assemblies of friends calling themselves _men_ are from day to day meditating torment and torture for his [Louis XVI.'s] heroic widow, on whom, with all their power and malice, and with every page, footman, and chamber-maid of hers in their reach, and with the rack in their hands, they have not been able to fix a speck. Nay, do they not talk of the inutility of evidence? What other virtue ever sustained such an ordeal?" Walpole's testimony in such a matter is particularly valuable, because he had not only been intimately acquainted with all the gossip of the French

capital for many years, but also because his principal friends in France did not belong to the party which might have been expected to be most favorable to the queen. Had there been the very slightest foundation for the calumnies which had been propagated against her, we may be sure that such a person as Madame du Deffand would not only have heard them, but would have been but too willing to believe them. His denunciation of them is a proof that she knew their falsehood.

[14] Goncourt, p. 388, quoting _La Quotidienne_ of October 17th, 18th.

[15] The depositions which the little king had been compelled to sign contained accusations of his aunt as well as of his mother.

[16] As we shall see in the close of the letter, she did not regard those priests who had taken the oath imposed by the Assembly, but which the Pope had condemned, as any longer priests.

The Codes Of Hammurabi And Moses
W. W. Davies

The discovery of the Hammurabi Code is one of the greatest achievements of archaeology, and is of paramount interest, not only to the student of the Bible, but also to all those interested in ancient history...

Religion   ISBN: *1-59462-338-4*

QTY

Pages:132
MSRP $12.95

The Theory of Moral Sentiments
Adam Smith

This work from 1749. contains original theories of conscience amd moral judgment and it is the foundation for systemof morals.

Philosophy   ISBN: *1-59462-777-0*

QTY

Pages:536
MSRP $19.95

Jessica's First Prayer
Hesba Stretton

In a screened and secluded corner of one of the many railway-bridges which span the streets of London there could be seen a few years ago, from five o'clock every morning until half past eight, a tidily set-out coffee-stall, consisting of a trestle and board, upon which stood two large tin cans, with a small fire of charcoal burning under each so as to keep the coffee boiling during the early hours of the morning when the work-people were thronging into the city on their way to their daily toil...

Childrens   ISBN: *1-59462-373-2*

QTY

Pages:84
MSRP $9.95

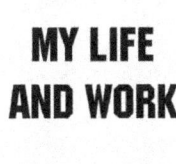

My Life and Work
Henry Ford

Henry Ford revolutionized the world with his implementation of mass production for the Model T automobile. Gain valuable business insight into his life and work with his own auto-biography... "We have only started on our development of our country we have not as yet, with all our talk of wonderful progress, done more than scratch the surface. The progress has been wonderful enough but..."

Biographies/   ISBN: *1-59462-198-5*

QTY

Pages:300
MSRP $21.95

www.bookjungle.com *email: sales@bookjungle.com fax: 630-214-0564 mail: Book Jungle PO Box 2226 Champaign, IL 61825*

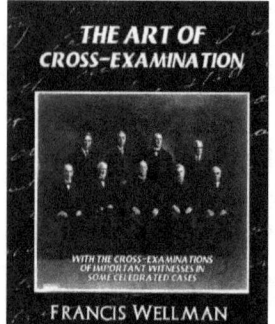

The Art of Cross-Examination
Francis Wellman

QTY

I presume it is the experience of every author, after his first book is published upon an important subject, to be almost overwhelmed with a wealth of ideas and illustrations which could readily have been included in his book, and which to his own mind, at least, seem to make a second edition inevitable. Such certainly was the case with me; and when the first edition had reached its sixth impression in five months, I rejoiced to learn that it seemed to my publishers that the book had met with a sufficiently favorable reception to justify a second and considerably enlarged edition. ..

Reference   ISBN: *1-59462-647-2*

Pages:412

MSRP $19.95

On the Duty of Civil Disobedience
Henry David Thoreau

QTY

Thoreau wrote his famous essay, On the Duty of Civil Disobedience, as a protest against an unjust but popular war and the immoral but popular institution of slave-owning. He did more than write—he declined to pay his taxes, and was hauled off to gaol in consequence. Who can say how much this refusal of his hastened the end of the war and of slavery ?

Law   ISBN: *1-59462-747-9*

Pages:48

MSRP $7.45

Dream Psychology Psychoanalysis for Beginners
Sigmund Freud

QTY

Sigmund Freud, born Sigismund Schlomo Freud (May 6, 1856 - September 23, 1939), was a Jewish-Austrian neurologist and psychiatrist who co-founded the psychoanalytic school of psychology. Freud is best known for his theories of the unconscious mind, especially involving the mechanism of repression; his redefinition of sexual desire as mobile and directed towards a wide variety of objects; and his therapeutic techniques, especially his understanding of transference in the therapeutic relationship and the presumed value of dreams as sources of insight into unconscious desires.

Pages:196

Psychology   ISBN: *1-59462-905-6*

MSRP $15.45

The Miracle of Right Thought
Orison Swett Marden

QTY

Believe with all of your heart that you will do what you were made to do. When the mind has once formed the habit of holding cheerful, happy, prosperous pictures, it will not be easy to form the opposite habit. It does not matter how improbable or how far away this realization may see, or how dark the prospects may be, if we visualize them as best we can, as vividly as possible, hold tenaciously to them and vigorously struggle to attain them, they will gradually become actualized, realized in the life. But a desire, a longing without endeavor, a yearning abandoned or held indifferently will vanish without realization.

Pages:360

Self Help   ISBN: *1-59462-644-8*

MSRP $25.45

QTY

The Rosicrucian Cosmo-Conception Mystic Christianity *by Max Heindel*   ISBN: *1-59462-188-8*   **$38.95**
The Rosicrucian Cosmo-conception is not dogmatic, neither does it appeal to any other authority than the reason of the student. It is: not controversial, but is: sent forth in the, hope that it may help to clear..   *New Age/Religion Pages 646*

Abandonment To Divine Providence *by Jean-Pierre de Caussade*   ISBN: *1-59462-228-0*   **$25.95**
"The Rev. Jean Pierre de Caussade was one of the most remarkable spiritual writers of the Society of Jesus in France in the 18th Century. His death took place at Toulouse in 1751. His works have gone through many editions and have been republished...   *Inspirational/Religion Pages 400*

Mental Chemistry *by Charles Haanel*   ISBN: *1-59462-192-6*   **$23.95**
Mental Chemistry allows the change of material conditions by combining and appropriately utilizing the power of the mind. Much like applied chemistry creates something new and unique out of careful combinations of chemicals the mastery of mental chemistry...   *New Age Pages 354*

The Letters of Robert Browning and Elizabeth Barret Barrett 1845-1846 vol II   ISBN: *1-59462-193-4*   **$35.95**
by Robert Browning and Elizabeth Barrett   *Biographies Pages 596*

Gleanings In Genesis (volume I) *by Arthur W. Pink*   ISBN: *1-59462-130-6*   **$27.45**
Appropriately has Genesis been termed "the seed plot of the Bible" for in it we have, in germ form, almost all of the great doctrines which are afterwards fully developed in the books of Scripture which follow...   *Religion/Inspirational Pages 420*

The Master Key *by L. W. de Laurence*   ISBN: *1-59462-001-6*   **$30.95**
In no branch of human knowledge has there been a more lively increase of the spirit of research during the past few years than in the study of Psychology, Concentration and Mental Discipline. The requests for authentic lessons in Thought Control, Mental Discipline and...   *New Age/Business Pages 422*

The Lesser Key Of Solomon Goetia *by L. W. de Laurence*   ISBN: *1-59462-092-X*   **$9.95**
This translation of the first book of the "Lernegton" which is now for the first time made accessible to students of Talismanic Magic was done, after careful collation and edition, from numerous Ancient Manuscripts in Hebrew, Latin, and French...   *New Age/Occult Pages 92*

Rubaiyat Of Omar Khayyam *by Edward Fitzgerald*   ISBN: *1-59462-332-5*   **$13.95**
Edward Fitzgerald, whom the world has already learned, in spite of his own efforts to remain within the shadow of anonymity, to look upon as one of the rarest poets of the century, was born at Bredfield, in Suffolk, on the 31st of March, 1809. He was the third son of John Purcell...   *Music Pages 172*

Ancient Law *by Henry Maine*   ISBN: *1-59462-128-4*   **$29.95**
The chief object of the following pages is to indicate some of the earliest ideas of mankind, as they are reflected in Ancient Law, and to point out the relation of those ideas to modern thought.   *Religion/History Pages 452*

Far-Away Stories *by William J. Locke*   ISBN: *1-59462-129-2*   **$19.45**
"Good wine needs no bush, but a collection of mixed vintages does. And this book is just such a collection. Some of the stories I do not want to remain buried for ever in the museum files of dead magazine-numbers an author's not unpardonable vanity..."   *Fiction Pages 272*

Life of David Crockett *by David Crockett*   ISBN: *1-59462-250-7*   **$27.45**
"Colonel David Crockett was one of the most remarkable men of the times in which he lived. Born in humble life, but gifted with a strong will, an indomitable courage, and unremitting perseverance...   *Biographies/New Age Pages 424*

Lip-Reading *by Edward Nitchie*   ISBN: *1-59462-206-X*   **$25.95**
Edward B. Nitchie, founder of the New York School for the Hard of Hearing, now the Nitchie School of Lip-Reading, Inc, wrote "LIP-READING Principles and Practice". The development and perfecting of this meritorious work on lip-reading was an undertaking...   *How-to Pages 400*

A Handbook of Suggestive Therapeutics, Applied Hypnotism, Psychic Science   ISBN: *1-59462-214-0*   **$24.95**
by Henry Munro   *Health/New Age/Health/Self-help Pages 376*

A Doll's House: and Two Other Plays *by Henrik Ibsen*   ISBN: *1-59462-112-8*   **$19.95**
Henrik Ibsen created this classic when in revolutionary 1848 Rome. Introducing some striking concepts in playwriting for the realist genre, this play has been studied the world over.   *Fiction/Classics/Plays 308*

The Light of Asia *by sir Edwin Arnold*   ISBN: *1-59462-204-3*   **$13.95**
In this poetic masterpiece, Edwin Arnold describes the life and teachings of Buddha. The man who was to become known as Buddha to the world was born as Prince Gautama of India but he rejected the worldly riches and abandoned the reigns of power when...   *Religion/History/Biographies Pages 170*

The Complete Works of Guy de Maupassant *by Guy de Maupassant*   ISBN: *1-59462-157-8*   **$16.95**
"For days and days, nights and nights, I had dreamed of that first kiss which was to consecrate our engagement, and I knew not on what spot I should put my lips..."   *Fiction/Classics Pages 240*

The Art of Cross-Examination *by Francis L. Wellman*   ISBN: *1-59462-309-0*   **$26.95**
Written by a renowned trial lawyer, Wellman imparts his experience and uses case studies to explain how to use psychology to extract desired information through questioning.   *How-to/Science/Reference Pages 408*

Answered or Unanswered? *by Louisa Vaughan*   ISBN: *1-59462-248-5*   **$10.95**
Miracles of Faith in China   *Religion Pages 112*

The Edinburgh Lectures on Mental Science (1909) *by Thomas*   ISBN: *1-59462-008-3*   **$11.95**
This book contains the substance of a course of lectures recently given by the writer in the Queen Street Hail, Edinburgh. Its purpose is to indicate the Natural Principles governing the relation between Mental Action and Material Conditions...   *New Age/Psychology Pages 148*

Ayesha *by H. Rider Haggard*   ISBN: *1-59462-301-5*   **$24.95**
Verily and indeed it is the unexpected that happens! Probably if there was one person upon the earth from whom the Editor of this, and of a certain previous history, did not expect to hear again...   *Classics Pages 380*

Ayala's Angel *by Anthony Trollope*   ISBN: *1-59462-352-X*   **$29.95**
The two girls were both pretty, but Lucy who was twenty-one who supposed to be simple and comparatively unattractive, whereas Ayala was credited, as her Bombwhat romantic name might show, with poetic charm and a taste for romance. Ayala when her father died was nineteen...   *Fiction Pages 484*

The American Commonwealth *by James Bryce*   ISBN: *1-59462-286-8*   **$34.45**
An interpretation of American democratic political theory. It examines political mechanics and society from the perspective of Scotsman James Bryce   *Politics Pages 572*

Stories of the Pilgrims *by Margaret P. Pumphrey*   ISBN: *1-59462-116-0*   **$17.95**
This book explores pilgrims religious oppression in England as well as their escape to Holland and eventual crossing to America on the Mayflower, and their early days in New England...   *History Pages 268*

www.bookjungle.com *email: sales@bookjungle.com fax: 630-214-0564 mail: Book Jungle PO Box 2226 Champaign, IL 61825*

QTY

The Fasting Cure *by Sinclair Upton* **ISBN:** *1-59462-222-1* **$13.95**

In the Cosmopolitan Magazine for May, 1910, and in the Contemporary Review (London) for April, 1910, I published an article dealing with my experiences in fasting. I have written a great many magazine articles, but never one which attracted so much attention... New Age/Self Help/Health Pages 164

Hebrew Astrology *by Sepharial* **ISBN:** *1-59462-308-2* **$13.45**

In these days of advanced thinking it is a matter of common observation that we have left many of the old landmarks behind and that we are now pressing forward to greater heights and to a wider horizon than that which represented the mind-content of our progenitors... Astrology Pages 144

Thought Vibration or The Law of Attraction in the Thought World **ISBN:** *1-59462-127-6* **$12.95**

by William Walker Atkinson *Psychology/Religion Pages 144*

Optimism *by Helen Keller* **ISBN:** *1-59462-108-X* **$15.95**

Helen Keller was blind, deaf, and mute since 19 months old, yet famously learned how to overcome these handicaps, communicate with the world, and spread her lectures promoting optimism. An inspiring read for everyone... Biographies/Inspirational Pages 84

Sara Crewe *by Frances Burnett* **ISBN:** *1-59462-360-0* **$9.45**

In the first place, Miss Minchin lived in London. Her home was a large, dull, tall one, in a large, dull square, where all the houses were alike, and all the sparrows were alike, and where all the door-knockers made the same heavy sound... Childrens/Classic Pages 88

The Autobiography of Benjamin Franklin *by Benjamin Franklin* **ISBN:** *1-59462-135-7* **$24.95**

The Autobiography of Benjamin Franklin has probably been more extensively read than any other American historical work, and no other book of its kind has had such ups and downs of fortune. Franklin lived for many years in England, where he was agent... Biographies/History Pages 332

Name	
Email	
Telephone	
Address	
City, State ZIP	

☐ **Credit Card**   ☐ **Check / Money Order**

Credit Card Number	
Expiration Date	
Signature	

Please Mail to: Book Jungle
                    PO Box 2226
                    Champaign, IL 61825
or Fax to: 630-214-0564

ORDERING INFORMATION

web: *www.bookjungle.com*
email: *sales@bookjungle.com*
fax: *630-214-0564*
mail: *Book Jungle PO Box 2226 Champaign, IL 61825*
or PayPal *to sales@bookjungle.com*

Please contact us for bulk discounts

DIRECT-ORDER TERMS

**20% Discount if You Order
Two or More Books**
Free Domestic Shipping!
Accepted: Master Card, Visa,
Discover, American Express

www.ingramcontent.com/pod-product-compliance
Lightning Source LLC
Chambersburg PA
CBHW080722020726
47503CB00010B/2752